W9-AZM-840

"I WANT TO BE FREE OF YOU!" SHE SPAT.

"I don't want you! You hurt me . . . and hurt me," screamed Cameron, his proximity, the heat of him, the male scent of him, the strength of him plunging her into wrenching conflict.

"And you hurt me," Alex growled in a low, menacing voice. "I've tried to be free of you. There's no way. You're in my head, my heart, my blood . . . and there we both are joined irreversibly. I will have you, Cameron!"

Throwing caution to the wind, he picked her up in his arms. She fought as he stalked purposefully to the bedroom, kicked the door shut behind him, and deposited her roughly on the bed. Before she could scramble away, he covered her struggling body with his own. . . .

By the author of

THE TAMING

RIDE OUT THE STORM

ALEEN MALCOLM

A DELL BOOK

Published by
Dell Publishing Co., Inc.
1 Dag Hammarskjold Plaza
New York, New York 10017

Copyright © 1981 by Aleen Malcolm

All rights reserved. No part of this book
may be reproduced or transmitted in any form
or by any means, electronic or mechanical, including
photocopying, recording or by any information storage
and retrieval system, without the written permission
of the Publisher, except where permitted by law.

Dell ® TM 681510, Dell Publishing Co., Inc.

ISBN: 0-440-17399-X

Printed in the United States of America
First printing—July 1981

RIDE OUT
THE STORM

BOOK ONE
THE HOMECOMING

April 1762

(The war-note of Lochiel, which Albyn's hills have heard,
and heard, too, have her Saxon foes.)

How in the noon of night that pibroch thrills
Savage and shrill! But with breath which fills
Their mountain-pipes, so fill the mountaineers
With the fierce native daring which instills
The stirring memory of a thousand years.

LORD BYRON, *Childe Harold's Pilgrimage*

CHAPTER ONE

Sir Alexander Sinclair stared at the small, ragged rider who cantered beside him perched on the bare back of a large black stallion. To the other travelers traversing the busy Stirling Road the raven-haired urchin would appear to be nothing more than a stableboy mounted on remarkably good horseflesh, and yet this was his wife, the Lady Sinclair, he mused. As if sensing his eyes, Cameron turned and smiled inquiringly at him, her breath misting the crisp spring air, and Alex caught his own breath at her exquisite beauty.

" 'Tis rude to stare, my lord," she teased, impishly reminding Alex of another journey the summer before when he, as her guardian, had been driven to despair by her sensuous and defiant nature.

"Aye, my lady," he returned roguishly, and Cameron tossed her thick mane of ebony hair, hiding her brilliant green eyes as she dug her heels into her horse's firm sides, urging him to gallop.

My lady . . . my lady . . . my lady . . . my lady, echoed her horse's hooves and the panic that pounded her heart. How could she possibly be a lady? By midnight they would reach Glen Aucht, Alex's estate on the Firth of Forth, where she would be expected to act with propriety in a manner befitting her new station in life. But how? There was so much about social behavior she didn't know. Customs and manners that seemed to have no rhyme or reason, so her common sense and intelligence could in no way help her. If only etiquette, decorum, and the seeming multitude of social graces were logical, she would have somewhat of a chance, she raged inwardly. The life she and Alex were riding toward loomed like a terrifying nightmare. Most people were born into it, so all that was expected of them was obvious and familiar, like their own fingers and toes; but being reared as she had been away from civilization on the isolated coast of Cape Wrath and by an embittered Highland outlaw, had in no way prepared her for what now lay ahead. How far had she really traveled from the untamed child of barely nine months before? A wave of homesickness swept through her as her pulses roared like the sea against the purple-gray rocks of her childhood home, and small, lonely whimpers burst from her lips, reminding her of the haunting cries of the seals and kittiwake gulls.

"Cameron!"

Alex's voice cut through her thoughts and she stared in bewilderment at him galloping alongside, surprised that she had been racing so recklessly. Alex reined to a halt and turned to look behind him. Following his gaze, Cameron saw her old hound, Torquil, out of breath, unable to keep up with the grueling pace she had set. She wheeled her horse and sped back to him, furious with herself.

"When am I going to grow up?" she muttered angrily. "I'm fifteen years old . . . possibly sixteen. I'm a married woman. This isn't even a question of social behavior! I'm just thoughtless and selfish," she berated herself.

Reaching her dog, she dismounted and wrapped her arms about him. Torquil was her oldest, most loyal friend. Perhaps her only friend. There had never been a time that she could not remember his loving and protecting her, but now he was old and nearing the end of his life. Cameron thrust the thought from her; life without Torquil did not bear thinking about.

"I'm sorry . . . so sorry," she crooned as the great beast sat panting, his long, freckled tongue dangling. Cameron sat hugging her pet, heedless of the busy traffic that sped by in both directions. Alex swore as he saw a coach and four narrowly miss hitting them, the coachman releasing a long stream of crude epithets at Cameron, who swung around and answered in kind. Alex closed his ears to the earthy abuse that poured from his wife's mouth as he cantered back to them.

"Could we stop and rest awhile?" asked Cameron.

"Aye, but not in the middle of the road," he answered tersely. She heard the censure in his tone, which fanned her already ignited anger, but she checked the impulse to fly at him as they rode up the high bank and dismounted under some trees.

Alex chewed on a stalk of grass, watching Cameron, who lay with her face averted, pillowed on her shaggy dog. He frowned as he realized that she purposefully avoided his eyes. Why was she withdrawing from him? He knew their descent from their mountain retreat into the teeming social world was frightening to her, but she had left that very morning with such optimism and courage. It was barely afternoon, and already he sensed the thunderclouds gathering in his stormy bride.

"Cameron?"

"What?" she grunted, still keeping her face hidden.

"Hungry?" he asked, not willing to open a flood tide of emotions until they were safely home in the privacy of their chambers. Her ebony head shook vigorously.

"Then we should be on our way, unless you've changed your mind and prefer to stay the night at an inn and explain your strange mode of dress?" he cajoled, knowing she preferred to return to Glen Aucht hidden by darkness, with the servants sleeping, so that she could start a new day and a new life dressed as Lady Sinclair. Aside from sensible flannel nightshirts and lurid peignoirs, there had been no other suitable female apparel in the isolated mountain lodge where they had spent the winter.

Without a word, Cameron remounted her horse, Torquod, and urged him carefully down the bank. She stared straight ahead down the long road, not really seeing as her mind raced. She smiled as she thought of Mackie and Fergus, Alex's old retainers, who had become like parents to her when Alex had dragged her, kicking and spitting, from Cape Wrath. She frowned as she realized she'd have to curb her desire to throw herself into their arms. Such a display would be unseemly for Lady Sinclair. Childhood had been so short, scarcely two months to make up for fifteen years devoid of loving parental arms. She longed to see them and yet was afraid, knowing that for some inexplicable reason their different stations in life caused an insurmountable obstacle, a chasm—mistress and servant. What would the other servants think of her? Especially the way she had behaved before with her rebellious tantrums?

How could she be the Lady Sinclair telling them what to do? They were older than she. Taller than she. Knew more about civilized life than she. She would have to pretend, she determined. Aye, really pretend to be a lady. It would be hard, but it seemed the only way if she was to stay with Alex. The thought of the rest of her life being spent in such a charade made her head ache as if encircled by a tight iron band. Was it worth it?

She stared across at Alex, who rode lost in his own thoughts of the future. He was her husband. That tall, handsome man was her husband, Sir Alexander, Lord Sinclair. It seemed ludicrous to Cameron as she appraised his tanned, chiseled cheekbones and thick, tawny hair that glinted like gold in the sun. He looked stern and unapproachable, and she was afraid. Maybe he was also realizing he had made a mistake. He was so dignified and educated, while she was ignorant and awkward. How could he possibly love her as much as she loved him? It wasn't as though he had wanted to marry her, she remembered painfully. She had unknowingly entrapped him, not realizing public declaration of marriage in front of witnesses was binding by Scottish law. No, he had definitely not wanted to marry her. He had been in love with Lady Fiona Hurst at the time. At the thought of the voluptuous, worldly woman Cameron felt sick and longed to kick her horse into a furious gallop back to the wilderness. Why couldn't she be knowledgeable and worldly?

Alex noted Cameron's set little profile, her forehead creased with anxious lines. He too was remembering the night of their marriage. She had stood on the bed at the inn in all her naked glory, her green eyes flashing, as she had informed the audience of nightgowned people that she and Alex were married. He had been caught. He had registered at the inn with a small stableboy who was discovered to be a passionate female . . . and sooner than be jailed for molesting a child, he had not denied her declaration. He laughed aloud at seeing the image of her with one hand on her naked hip, her ebony head flung proudly back, and her small breasts quivering with indignation as she proclaimed to the shocked assemblage that she was his wife. At the time it had been no laughing matter, but now he remembered the scene with joy. How else could he envision marrying the turbulent Cameron?

Cameron, hearing his chuckle, turned, looking deeply into his warm amber eyes, and some of her fear melted away.

"Look at me like that, my lady, and we'll not be reaching home tonight," he murmured huskily. Cameron felt a delicious shiver streak through at the implication, even as a cold pang at "my lady" cut into her. Maybe delaying their arrival was the answer, she thought. She moved her horse closer so that her leg brushed Alex's as she smiled provocatively. Oh, to be in his strong arms, her seething worrying mind stilled by his caresses. She lithely swung her legs up and crouched on her horse's broad back before agilely launching herself onto the front of Alex's saddle. His horse reared in fright at the sudden added weight, and Cameron laughed as Alex swore and tried to calm the excited animal.

"For God's sake, Cameron, where's your sense?" he cursed, all too aware of the shocked expressions of his fellow travelers. Cameron giggled and nuzzled his neck.

"Have you no propriety? You're making a spectacle!" he hissed, pushing her away. Cameron froze at the harshness of his voice and then glanced around at the curious onlookers.

"I'm sorry, I didna think—" she stammered.

"Obviously," he snapped as Cameron transferred herself back to her own mount with the expertise of a circus performer.

"Well, I hope there's none who know my identity, or there'll be some sordid rumors about Lord Sinclair and a stableboy," laughed Alex, trying to lighten the situation as he saw the flash of humiliation and fear in Cameron's eyes. She didin't answer but stared steadily straight ahead, and they rode silently, each lost again in his own thoughts.

Cameron was miserable. So this was how it was going to be from now on. No more just the two of them able to run, laugh, play, and make love how, when, and where they wanted, away from the rest of the world. From now on every action and word would have to be watched and weighed carefully. Nothing would be the same anymore.

Even Alex seemed to have already changed, seemed more interested in what strangers thought than what she did. What did it matter what a stranger thought if it were not true, she puzzled, but she didn't ask Alex the question for fear it was improper and would show her to be even more ignorant. She wished fervently that they could turn back to the hunting lodge high in the mountains where there were no other people to be compared unfavorably to.

Alex's mind was also back at the hunting lodge where in late autumn he'd finally caught up with the runaway Cameron. He had welcomed the snows that had cut them off from the outside world, and he had devoted the winter to trying to heal and gentle the wild, frightened woman-child. He stared at her straight, proud back, knowing that her rebellious posture masked her apprehensions, and he wondered how well he had succeeded. He smiled to himself, ruefully remembering her incredible prowess with a knife and gun. She was his diminutive warrior of the moors, more fearsome than many a soldier with her flashing green eyes and deadly accuracy. He longed to take her in his arms and to comfort her, but the lack of privacy made it impossible, so he contented himself by pointing out various places of interest.

Each landmark Alex drew her attention to heightened Cameron's fear as less and less green was seen where towns ate into the verdancy. Sprawling, smoky-gray masses clumped closer and closer together until she felt her chest constrict, making breathing difficult. She steeled herself against the urge to turn tail and run. Twice before she had run from Alex and nearly lost her life in her frantic bids for freedom. Now she knew she could never really be free from him, as her love tied her more securely than any rope or chain.

"I am Lady Sinclair," she chanted over and over again under her breath as the bustle of civilization grew louder and louder.

"Would you like to be free of the road for a while?" offered Alex, sensing the pressure that was building and knowing that as they traveled deeper into the central lowlands there'd be no more opportunity to cut across quiet countryside.

"Free of the road?" echoed Cameron.

"Aye," returned Alex, pointing to the thickly treed slopes that rose to the east of them. "Do you want to?"

"Aye," she laughed as her horse pranced up the steep bank.

They rode quietly and slowly in and out of the trees, each savoring the sweet serenity after the dusty bustle of the road. The buds had burst, and the fresh new leaves were a vibrant, tender green. The first delicate spring flowers bloomed pastel between the brown root-forks of tall trees, and birds and squirrels chattered excitedly at their intrusion. Cameron breathed deeply, feeling her tension ebb.

" 'Tis spring," she stated.

"Aye," smiled Alex.

" 'Tis different."

"From what?"

"From home . . . I mean Cape Wrath," amended Cameron.

"How is it different?"

"Here 'tis softer somehow . . . and quieter," she struggled to explain. "There the joyous splashings and choruses of the gray seal, struttings of the grouse, terns, and kittiwakes, well, 'tis like a loud, happy waking cry after the long sleep of winter."

Cameron felt a fierce aching at the nostalgic remembrances. Her nose almost quivered as she imagined smelling the salt spray of the sea. She couldn't go backward, she must go forward into the future—no matter how hard it was.

" 'Tis like even the spring is more civilized in the south," she said bitterly. "Even the animals are polite."

"In what way?" asked Alex after waiting a moment for her to continue. Cameron stared at him a moment, her eyes narrowed as though speculating.

"There are no rutting sounds. Do animals in the south hide their lust for new life away like the upper class of Edinburgh?" she challenged rebelliously.

"Would you be trying to provoke me, wife?" laughed Alex, lifting an eyebrow quizzically.

"Maybe," retorted Cameron. "But I'll not be like that!"

"Like what?" he asked, totally bewildered.

"Scared and hiding. I won't be like that. I'll ride into Glen Aucht in broad daylight . . . astride, dressed as I am. I'll not sneak!"

"Whoa now! Isna there something in the middle? You're talking of two extremes," cautioned Alex, who certainly preferred her high spirits to her docility but drew the line at the public flaunting of convention. Living in a country occupied by the English when one's own father had been outlawed for fighting for the Stuart cause made discretion the better part of valor. He had chosen co-existence with his enemy, feeling that enough Scots had died, including his own parents and two sisters. Cameron, on the other hand, was ready to fight the English single-handed, and any compromise to her was tantamount to treachery.

"Tell me what's in the middle?" she challenged.

"We've been through it before, Cameron," he sighed.

"Then go through it again!"

"To buy you a suitable riding habit and a sidesaddle—"

"No!" she interrupted vehemently. "I'll not ride that silly way anymore. 'Tis unnatural . . . I've just made up my mind to that . . . this very minute!"

Alex didn't answer. He gave her a long, searching look before turning to survey the scenery as he whistled non-chalantly. He felt he knew her game. She was covering her fear with her usual defiance, trying to initiate a quarrel so she could explode and release the pressure. He'd not be used that way again. They had come too far in their relationship to revert to old, hurtful patterns.

"And I'll not be all bound up so I canna breathe in cor-sets and layer upon layer of stupid clothes . . . nor shoes that cripple and break my ankles neither," she con-tinued after a pause, but Alex still didn't answer as his mind wrestled for a way to change the subject and hope-fully avert the storm that was definitely brewing.

"I'll not be hobbled so I canna run . . . nor breath. 'Tis against nature," she ranted. "And I'll not—oh, look!" she exclaimed, pointing through the trees to where a small mountain tarn sparkled through the leaves, reflecting the clear blue of the sky.

"Oh, no!" exclaimed Alex as Cameron dug in her heels and galloped toward the small lake. He had wanted a diversion from the previous subject, but this choice seemed even more troublesome. "Oh, no," he repeated, cantering after her, all too aware of his young bride's immodest habit of tearing off all her clothes at the sight of water to swim in. They were too near farms and towns for her to indulge in that sort of natural behavior. Which was worse, a spitting, fighting Cameron or a nude one, he wondered as he chased after her.

Cameron reached the edge of the water and stared across the shimmering expanse that was broken by scudding ducklings and paddling moorhens.

"Cameron?" warned Alex, stopping beside her. She turned furiously at him. How dare he not trust her! She knew what that warning sound in his voice was all about. It made her want to rip all her clothes off and plunge in just to spite him. She had wanted to but had remembered it was not the proper thing for a lady to do. She was very confused as to the reason, as it was obvious that everyone was made either male or female, and each hopefully knew the difference. Goaded, she started undoing the buttons of her shirt. She stared as if daring him to stop her when a burst of raucous laughter caused her to look around. Camped to the right of them at the far end of the tarn was a group of soldiers. English soldiers in their hated red coats. Alex reached out and firmly pulled the reins from Cameron's hands and quickly led them back into the shelter of the trees.

"I'm not a baby," spat Cameron, retrieving control of her own horse. "I am supposed to be your wife . . . so why are you being so overbearing?"

"I wasna sure—with your long list of what you'll not do. It seems you were spoiling for a fight one way or the other . . . and I prefer it to be with me instead of with twenty soldiers," replied Alex tersely. "And as for overbearing, Cameron . . . I will be so when you act without prudence."

"I wasna going to swim until you—"

"Until I didna trust you," interrupted Alex. "I'm sorry."

"You knew what I was feeling?" she questioned, won-deringly.

"Aye. There's many mistakes we'll be making with each other, so we'll both have to be patient," informed Alex, gently reaching across and kissing her softly on the lips. Cameron reached out to cling to him, but he had with-drawn. "Could we not rest awhile? Lie together?" she ventured.

"There is nothing I would rather do, but—"

" 'Twould not be prudent," finished Cameron as another burst of laughter shattered the tranquility. "I wish them all dead," she added with a venomous look in the di-rection of the soldiers.

"They are not just English, Cameron. They are the Union Army of Great Britain—probably mostly Scottish," informed Alex.

"Traitors!" she spat.

"I wore the red coat . . . am I a traitor?" he asked as they wended their way through the woods that skirted the tarn. Cameron didn't answer. Although she loved Alex, there were some aspects of him she did not even want to think about because they seemed unjustifiable to her.

"Do you think me a traitor?" repeated Alex. Cameron shrugged uncomfortably.

"I don't think about it," she muttered defensively.

"I had no choice but death, transportation, or being a fugitive for the rest of my life if I didna obey orders."

"Each would've been better!" spat Cameron irrationally.

Alex gritted his teeth and cursed himself for allowing the subject to develop, as it was a topic of contention between them. He understood her position only too well, as the destruction of his own family and the confiscation of most of his lands had caused a deep, bitter wound with-in him. But he also realized the abject futility of revenge, as the clans were dispersed and Scotland was drained physi-cally and economically.

"You mean, if ordered, you'd leave me to fight for the English again?" asked Cameron in a small voice, breaking the silence that built between them.

"Nay, hopefully those days are behind me."

"But what if they're not?" persisted Cameron.

"Let's worry about it when it happens. I'm hungry. My belly's growling so loud 'tis frightening the birds." Alex was striving to change the subject. "We'll stop for a while atop that next rise."

"If you have to go, you'll not leave me behind," promised Cameron in such a tone that Alex decided it was best not to answer.

"Look down there," he directed, pointing through a gap in the trees to the Stirling Road, which now snaked far below them, the many travelers appearing like tiny ants, but Cameron's eyes rested apprehensively on the smoky sight of the towns beyond.

"Where did you fight?" asked Cameron as Alex unpacked the meat and bread they'd brought for their journey.

"Was it against our own?" she challenged at no answer.

"Nay, 'twas the other side of the world," replied Alex, filling his mouth and chewing as he remembered the grueling, terrifying march along the Potomac River under the command of General Braddock. It had been July of 1755, and he was barely nineteen years old. Every shrub and tree they'd passed caused him terror, each movement of wind or bird had caused his heart to stop in panic for a second. From a seemingly serene countryside would fly silent arrows, and more than once a soldier in front or by the side of him would drop with a barely audible grunt, but still they trudged on and on toward the Monongahela. It had been a nightmare, a strange, alien land with death stalking silently, picking them off one by one. Each time they turned, no one was there except for another dead man at their feet.

"Tell me," insisted Cameron, peeved at his long silence, "what is it like on the other side of the world?"

"Vast, very vast," sighed Alex, finishing his food and stretching out flat on his back, closing his eyes. Cameron watched him resentfully. She felt lonely and afraid, so she sat hugging her knees and looking around, unable to relax and rest. The horses cropped the sweet spring grass, and Torquil noisily gnawed on the shank of a deer, not heeding the small bird that saucily hopped forward to steal a morsel.

"Why won't you tell me of it?" she repeated, staring at Alex's long lean body. He didn't answer, just lay as though sleeping, his thoughts far away in place and time. At the end of the torturous march where death had stalked silently there had been loud, raucous slaughter. The screams and explosions, the vivid, bloodcurdling clamor of violent death. General Braddock had been killed along with the majority of the company, leaving a handful of men lost and in shock in the alien world.

Cameron crept forward and quietly knelt between Alex's outstretched legs. He didn't stir, and her excitement grew. She would seduce him so that they could lie together one last time on the earth beneath the trees before she had to play her role with propriety, on a bed with the ceiling hiding the sky, as mistress of Glen Aucht. She gently ran her hands up his legs, barely skimming the tight leather trousers yet feeling the warmth of his flesh beneath. Increasing the pressure, her fingers massaged the firm thigh muscles, circling higher and higher until she cupped the object of her desire.

"Cameron?" growled Alex, but she ignored him as quicksilver flickers of anticipation shivered through her. Leaning forward, she stretched her body above his and slowly and carefully lowered her hips to meet his groin. Alex stiffened beneath her but made no other movement. Cameron thrust forward, straining against his hardness as her desire mounted and his immobility just fanned the flames that roared inside her. She moved rhythmically against him, increasing her speed.

Alex's own desire built, although he wrestled with himself, not willing to be caught by a passing stranger in so compromising a position. Cameron's urgent mouth encompassed his, yet he kept his lips firmly closed from the onslaught of her determined little tongue. Oh, God, the little witch, he moaned as his frustration grew, knowing she would pound against him until she got her release, leaving him aching and unfulfilled. Making a quick decision, he grasped her shoulders and quickly stood as she still clung to him. Looking both ways and seeing no sign of other people, he strode, still carrying her, to a large tree. Leaning her against the broad trunk, he shimmied down her trews, released himself, and, lifting her, fitted himself into her. Cameron moaned with pleasure and curled her legs around him as he thrust. A warning growl from Torquil caused them both to freeze, and Alex blessed his foresight that kept them hidden behind the broad trunk of the tree as a company of noisy soldiers tramped into view. Alex quickly uncoupled himself and with difficulty thrust his unruly member out of sight as Cameron tried to get into her trews.

"Stay hidden," he hissed as he untucked his shirt to hide his arousal and sauntered into the clearing, where the soldiers examined his horses.

"Alexander, is that you?" hailed a disbelieving voice. Alex turned, puzzled.

"'Pon my soul, it is!" declared a ruddy-faced older soldier, smiling fondly at Alex's furrowed brow. "Och, lad, you mean after all we went through together, you're not remembering me?"

"Douggie Cathcart!" he exclaimed, and the two men embraced, laughing.

"Step back a pace and let me look at you, lad. Och, aye, you've become a braw man these last four years . . . there's no callow stripling there now," growled Cathcart, nodding his appreciation.

"'Tis good to see you, Douggie. 'Tis fey I'm getting. I was thinking of those days a few moments ago. I thought you still over in the New World."

"Still fighting, or buried?" chortled Cathcart.

"Either," laughed Alex. "But what are you doing in these parts?"

"Should be me asking you that question, seeing as how there's a warrant out for your arrest," whispered the older man.

"My arrest?" exclaimed Alex. "For what?"

"Failing to report to duty."

"I've had no notice . . . but I've not been home for six months," explained Alex. "You mean they're recalling? That makes no sense. From the last news I had, the French were routed, and peace was just a formality."

"Aye, but Pitt has this bee in his bonnet about keeping us Highlanders occupied . . . putting our wondrous martial talents to better uses than fighting them," laughed the burly soldier. "Sssh! What's that?" he stiffened, drawing his sword as sounds of a skirmish issued from behind some trees.

"Take your stinking Sassanach paws off me, you bastard!" screamed Cameron.

"You young puppy . . . I'll teach you to mind your elder," roared an enraged voice.

"Get back from me or I'll pin your ears back!"

"What in hell!" shouted Cathcart as Alex ran toward the sounds.

Cameron, a dirk in each hand, kept two soldiers at bay.

"Move any closer and I'll kill you," she threatened, brandishing the twin daggers that she had always possessed.

"Call your men off, Cathcart. The boy's my concern," ordered Alex.

"Irving? Jardin? What the hell is going on here?" roared Cathcart.

"Found the young lad spying on you from behind the trees, and the rest you see," offered one of the men, trying to keep one eye on Cameron and the other on Torquil, who bared his teeth, growling menacingly.

"Put the knives away, Cameron," said Alex, relieved that she had managed to get her trews on. "I said put the knives away," he repeated as she hesitated.

"Call yourselves soldiers, scared of a wee bairn who probably couldn't hit the side of a barn four paces away," laughed Cathcart.

"Put them away," insisted Alex, seeing her stiffen at the old soldier's mockery.

" 'Twas the dog, not the lad," answered one of the soldiers sullenly.

"This old beastie?" chuckled Cathcart, scratching behind Torquil's floppy ears. "Why he's so old his teeth'd crumble on your tough hide."

"Put them away, Cameron!" commanded Alex as she still hesitated.

"Back off from the bairn," ordered Cathcart to the two soldiers. "Join the rest down the rise."

Cameron stood poised, holding the daggers by each blade as the soldiers ambled away, grumbling, and Alex seethed at her disobedience. Cathcart surveyed her, his brow furrowed.

"If you weren't so scrawny, I'd swear you were some-one else," he puzzled.

"Put them away or I'll wrest them from you," hissed Alex, striding determinedly toward her. Cameron felt caught. If she put them away like a docile child, she'd lose pride in front of the mocking old soldier.

"Not hit the side of a barn?" she challenged as she flung one with deadly accuracy, pinning Alex's sleeve to a tree.

"Goddamnit, Cameron, I've taken all I can from you!" he roared, savagely pulling his arm free and ripping his coat in the process. "Gie it to me!"

" 'Tis away," she spat rebelliously, thrusting the weapon down her boot. Cathcart strode slowly between the seeth-ing Alex and the defiant Cameron. He grasped her chin in his hard, rough hand and stared into the flashing green eyes.

"The lad is your concern, you say, Sinclair?" he asked, turning suddenly and glaring at Alex.

"Aye, and I apologize for the brat."

" 'Tis strange the same combination of the green eyes and the coal-black hair . . . the same deftness with a knife . . . and yet this one is smaller and obviously a Scot from the brogue," pondered Cathcart. Both Alex and Cameron froze.

"This one?" ventured Alex.

"Aye, the other was a Frenchie . . . though looked more like a savage. I'd give my eye teeth for his scalp on my belt!" he said, rubbing his thigh.

"What other one?"

"Green like new grass . . . just like this lad's eyes. I've never seen the like before. But they say we've all got a double walking the earth somewhere. I've yet to meet mine," chuckled Cathcart.

" 'Tis a strange combination, the eyes and hair. Where did you see it before?" asked Alex casually. "French, you say?"

"Aye. Goes by the name of Méron. Looks as though it's a lethal combination. You've certainly got your hands full, Sinclair."

"Aye," agreed Alex vehemently.

"Well, I'm due at the barracks by nightfall and I have a ways to go. Best take care of that other business, or they'll be a price for deserting on your head, if there isn't already. I hear they're already occupying those lands you fought so hard to regain."

"What?"

"Aye, your man Fergus MacDonald has been hightailing it around the country trying to find you. Och, 'tis a relief to see you back in one piece . . . but chances are you'll soon be awishing you weren't," rambled Cathcart.

"Weren't what?" asked Alex, his brain in an uproar from the information being given so casually. "Here, have a drink and tell me slowly. Maybe my head is still not put together right," he added, pulling a flask from his saddlebag.

" 'Tis a wonder your head is still between your shoulders, the knocking it took at Fort Duquesne, but it seems to have healed all right . . . whereas I'll be limping around like the only whore for the regiment the rest of my born days. Four of those heathen arrows," he stated proudly, rubbing his right thigh. "A little further to the left and I'd be singing like a lass."

"Douggie, I didna ken," muttered Alex frustratedly.

"Thanks to those arrows I don't have to go back to that heathen hell. Och, you missed some bonny battles. I was with Wolf in '59 when we took the whole of New France. Aye, the Plains of Abraham saw what fighting Highlanders can do. But can't say I'm not glad to see the last of them red savages, but that, young-fellow-me-lad, is where Mr. Pitt will be sending you. Aye, and you'll thank your lucky stars it is there and not the West Indies, where 'tis said men die like flies from pagan curses and rotting diseases."

"Wait a minute! My lands are forfeited again, you say?"

"Nay, just occupied, so to speak . . . more like a welcoming committee. Ha, and aspeaking of welcoming committees, you should have seen what greeted us when we were carried off the ship after spilling our blood and guts in that heathen land! More dead than alive we were, and all for them bloody English muckers . . . for their glory, not ours. At first we thought it was our well-earned hero's welcome, so great was the crowd that choked the London docks . . . and not understanding their strange way of speaking nor the deafening roar, we waved back. Aye, but then the rotten eggs and apples started to smash our faces . . . aye and stinking fish. 'NO SCOTS! NO SCOTS! NO SCOTS!' they was yelling." Cathcart's face diffused with angry color at the memory, and he took a long swallow from the flask. "Aye, makes my blood boil, but I'm just abiding my time. Just a few more months and I'll be out of this uniform and off," he added vehemently.

"Off where?"

"Anywhere where there's no English," he vowed.

"Is there such a place?" returned Alex cynically.

"I'll find one," promised Cathcart. "Well, thanks for the wee drop," he sighed, tucking the flask in his own hip pocket. "It was good seeing you again, young Sinclair. Have a good life, and I'd keep that wee savage on a tight rein if I were you."

Alex and Cameron stood silently watching the old soldier until he disappeared among the trees.

"What does it all mean?" whispered Cameron.

"Trouble . . . a lot of trouble," sighed Alex. "We'd best be on our way."

"Méron?" pronounced Cameron, giving the name a French accent. "Méron . . . Cam . . . Méron," she repeated wonderingly. Could it be her twin, the brother she had been separated from eight years before? she puzzled. It had to be, she decided.

" 'Tis Jumeau! 'tis Jumeau!" she cried excitedly, using the only name she had ever had for her brother, the French masculine word for twin. "Alex, 'tis Jumeau! Where is he? Alex, go after the soldier and ask him!" she implored, tugging at Alex's sleeve.

"Aren't you jumping to conclusions? Right now your brother is the least of our worries," snapped Alex, who immediately softened at seeing the hurt flare in her eyes.

"Cameron, 'tis first things first. We have to find out what is happening at Glen Aucht. Thank God we ran into Cathcart, or we could have walked unprepared into an impossible situation."

"But you promised me we would go to Rona, off the Isle of Skye, to find my brother . . . and if you're going to fight for the English, we won't be able to," protested Cameron. Alex bit down on his tongue, knowing that the chance that her twin was still in Scotland was very remote, from what Cathcart had said. It seemed the young man was in North America from the reference to scalps and savages, but luckily Cameron did not have much frame of knowledge outside Scotland, so she was unable to put two and two together. He kept his suspicions to himself, all too aware of Cameron's headstrong nature. She'd probably get it into her head to stow away on the first vessel leaving for the New World.

"I'm not sure whether to go straight home to Glen Aucht or stop in at the Drummonds and hope Ian is home," he said thoughtfully, referring to his lifetime friend, whose estate joined his on the northern boundary. Ian Drummond had lost his father and two older brothers on Culloden Moor and had also fought for the Union Army in the New World to prove his loyalty so that he could retain his lands. The only male left of his family, Ian supported his vitriolic English grandmother and ebullient middle-aged Aunt Morag. In many ways Alex and Ian's lives ran parallel. Alex had lost his father and mother and two younger sisters, not quickly in the bloody battle of Culloden in 1746, but slowly and more painfully. His mother and two sisters had died of cholera on a boat on their way from France toward the promise of the New World, and this had started the decay that brought his proud Highland warrior father to his knees. At twelve Alex had become protector to his own crumbling father and at fifteen brought him back to Scotland so he could die and be buried on his native soil. Alex grinned ruefully, remembering his boyhood vow never to be vulnerable to a female. Not the English, not the Scottish defeat, nor the taking of his lands had broken his father, but the death of his wife had robbed him of everything . . . pride, manhood, and the desire to live. Just nine short months ago Alex had been true to that vow, but now his heart was hopelessly captured by the elfin ragamuffin at his side.

Cameron, watching the expressions flit across Alex's tanned face, was loath to break the silence. She stared up apprehensively, recognizing the pain in his amber eyes before he grinned ruefully and regarded her. She frowned as she wondered what he was brooding on so intensely.

"I thought you were very angry with Ian Drummond?" she said hesitantly, remembering how she had cajoled Ian into teaching her how to be a lady.

"Not anymore. He helped open my eyes as to how much I love you, little witch. I owe him much."

"You're not angry with me anymore for the knives and the . . . er . . . um—?"

"Imprudence?" laughed Alex.

"Aye," gurgled Cameron, staring into the warm depths of his whiskey eyes.

"Not angry but frustrated," he growled roguishly, sending a delicious shiver of anticipation through her body.

"Then couldna we finish?" she asked hopefully.

"No, we couldna," he stated firmly, as much to chastise himself. "At least not now. We've lost enough time and nearly enough dignity," he added, giving her a chaste kiss.

CHAPTER TWO

It was near midnight when Alex and Cameron finally rode through the wrought-iron gates and up the sweeping driveway of Glen Aucht. The scent of hyacinths and jasmine seeped through the thick velvet darkness, suffocating Cameron's senses with a sickly sweet premonition. It was as though everything held its breath . . . was in suspension. Her watchful eyes saw the silhouettes of trees poised, waiting to pounce, the branches like frozen fingers clawed to clutch. The sharp crunch of the horses' hooves on the gravel jarred the cloying stillness and crackled like thunder in her ears. Unable to bear the conspicuous clatter, she guided her mount onto the rolling manicured lawn, frosted with silver in the moonlight. But even the muffled tread on the soft, springy turf became ominous, as though danger stalked without a sound. She abruptly reined to a halt.

"What's the matter?"

"Sssh!" she hissed, finding even Alex's softly spoken question too loud and rasping like the gravel . . . grating her nerve endings so that each pore prickled. "Alex, are you sure?" she whispered.

"Aye, we've nothing to hide except the impropriety of your dress. So I'll ride straight to the front door, and you'll skirt around to the stables and in through the servants' way. Mackie'll take care of you while I deal with whatever has to be dealt with," he answered, urging his horse into a slow walk across the soft lawn. Cameron felt her own horse move beneath her as she stared in the direction of the Firth of Forth, hearing the muted sound of the water against the shore. Seeing the curve of the coastline against the sky, she yearned to kick her mount into a furious gallop and race out the panic that was inexorably building as they seemed to move so slowly toward the large house. The muffled, measured rhythm of the horse joined with the relentless ticking of her fear, and she longed to scream out and shatter the smothering anticipation. Her hands gripped the leather reins so tightly that her knuckles gleamed white against the glossy blackness as she desperately tried to curb her terror.

"You'll have me sneak in the back way like a coward!" she spat as they neared the house that loomed, the dark windows seeming to mock their painfully slow approach.

" 'Tis not cowardly but sensible. There's no point in asking for more trouble until we see how much we've already got," returned Alex evenly, purposefully keeping the leisurely pace, hoping to calm Cameron.

" 'Tis sneaking!" hissed Cameron, her body rocking forward and back against the unbearable suspense.

"Cameron, you'll obey me without question," he ordered tensely and immediately regretted his impatient words as Cameron snapped.

"I won't! I canna!" she screamed, digging her heels and whipping her horse into a frenzied gallop up the driveway so that the gravel sprayed like sparks from the ironclad hooves. Alex continued his slow pace, watching her wild race, and some of his own unbearable tension ebbed. He suddenly realized he'd been waiting all day for Cameron to explode . . . had been watching and weighing his every word and movement, trying to avoid the impossible feat of getting home without serious incident or fanfare. He had to laugh. Of course it was impossible for Cameron to sneak, to be anything but the wild, free spirit that she was. He reined to a stop and watched the small flying figure race around and around the sloping front lawn as Duncan Fraser's dying words came back to him.

" 'Tis the spirit of true Scotland . . . wild and free but, alas, undisciplined and with no direction," Alex mouthed out loud as he remembered. The old Highland outlaw's voice echoed as if it had been a lifetime ago, and yet the words had been uttered just the autumn before. "I give my bairn into your keeping." And he, Alex, had at twenty-five become guardian to the tempestuous fifteen-year-old Cameron.

"Wake up! Wake up! Fergus? Mackie? We're back! We're back!" yelled Cameron at the top of her voice. One by one windows were warmed, and the large front door was flung open so that light streamed down the broad stone steps, illuminating the large lions who had patiently guarded the entrance for two hundred years. Alex looked lovingly at the sculpted beasts, remembering when he, as a little boy, had sat astride them lost in fanciful dreams of the adventure of being grown up.

"Oh, for a little peace," he sighed resignedly, reining his horse and nodding briefly at the sleepy assortment of amazed people who clustered on the steps. He followed their stunned gazes back to his wife, who still raced frantically around now screaming out Gaelic war cries. Luckily her emotions and belabored breathing jumbled her tongue, rendering most of the words unintelligible, although Alex had a very clear idea of the insults she was proclaiming to the English. After one particular guttural utterance Cameron's eye caught her audience. There was a still moment as she reined her horse sharply, causing him to rear backward, but as soon as his hooves retouched the ground, Cameron hunched over his neck and urged him to leap over a low hedge, and they were swallowed by the darkness, followed by the not so fleet Torquil.

"She'll ride it out," growled a deep voice, and Alex looked down into Fergus's lined face.

"Aye," he replied ruefully. "Been building all day," he added wearily, dismounting in one lithe movement and wrapping his arms around the lean old man who had known him since birth.

"We've visitors," informed Fergus, inclining his head slightly to indicate a group of nightshirted men huddled just inside the great oak door.

"So I've heard. We met Douggie Cathcart. Where's Mackie?"

"My wife's making herself decent, no doubt. MacNab, settle the master's horse in," ordered Fergus, and a sleepy young groom took the bridle of Alex's stallion and led him to the stables.

"Sinclair?"

"Aye?" answered Alex, turning in the direction of the voice and slowly mounting the stone steps.

"I am Colonel Randall Beddington from London, lately assigned to your regiment, the Black Watch," announced a portly, middle-aged man with an enormous handlebar moustache who strove to appear dignified in his night attire. Alex clicked his heels and saluted.

"At ease," barked Beddington.

"I heard that you were here and came posthaste. I was on my . . . er . . . um . . . honeymoon, sir," explained Alex, eager to get any false notion of his flagrantly disobeying orders out of the way as they walked through the spacious hall.

"Who was that causing a dickens of a commotion?"

"My wife, sir," confessed Alex after a pause, hoping the Englishman had no understanding of the Gaelic tongue. Beddington eyed Alex without a word as he twirled one side of his extravagant moustache.

"If you'll excuse me, sir, I should like to remove some of this grime . . . unless of course you'd prefer to wait until morning, as it appears that my late arrival has inconvenienced your sleep," offered Alex, uncomfortable under the older man's silent scrutiny and wanting to find out as much as he could from Fergus before an interview with the superior officer.

"Your wife, you say?"

"Yes, sir."

"Bears looking into. I think it preferable to get right down to the issues at hand, Sinclair . . . but confess to feeling at a decided disadvantage attired as I am. I shall expect you in the library in one hour. I trust that will give us both sufficient time," he stated crisply as he started up the staircase. "Oh, and incidently, I am housed in what I understand to be your suite of rooms. I hope that in no way inconveniences you," he added.

"I hope you find my bed to your comfort," replied Alex, dryly.

"I hope I find no sarcasm in your tone?"

"It was not intended, sir."

"I hope not."

The two men locked eyes almost in a battle of wills before Beddington broke the gaze and resumed his way up the carved stairway. Alex seethed with fury as he watched the portly man's back. He noted viciously the fat that swayed from side to side and the grunts of exertion. Damn the pompous English ass! How dare he rest his lard in my bed! Was there nowhere sacred to the presumptuous English, he fumed. As though feeling Alex's gaze, Beddington turned before reaching the second-floor landing. He leaned against the bannister, catching his breath.

"Harris? Drummond? Introduce yourselves," he panted.

"Yessir," chorused two voices, and heels clicked behind, causing Alex to turn.

"Ian!" he exclaimed warmly.

"Alex," muttered the young man guardedly.

" 'Tis good to see you, old friend."

"I must confess I've been regarding this meeting with some trepidation . . . after our parting of ways in Edinburgh last year."

"Ian . . . I canna apologize enough nor thank you enough. You are the truest friend a man could have . . . helped me open my stubborn eyes. I owe you much," stated Alex with sincerity.

"Dinna overdo it," laughed Ian, grasping Alex's outstretched hand. "How is Cameron?" he added softly.

"Cameron is . . . Cameron," replied Alex ruefully after a pause, not knowing how to respond because he knew Ian also loved her. Ian Drummond was like a brother to him. They had played together from infancy and shared many tragedies, but jealousy over Cameron had caused a rift that Alex instinctively knew could never really be wholly mended.

"Major Drummond, sir?" ventured a timid voice.

"Yes, Harris?" replied Ian, not taking his eyes from Alex's face.

"Will you be needing me further tonight?"

"I won't, will you, Major Sinclair?" answered Ian mischievously, breaking the tension. Alex surveyed the pale, thin, embarrassed young man who hopped barefooted up and down on the cold marble floor.

"Attention!" barked Ian, his eyes brimming with forced merriment.

"Sorry, sir," stammered Harris as he snapped to attention and saluted his two superior officers.

"That's better. Now at ease. We won't be needing you, but I daresay the colonel might, so you'd better prepare yourself for anything."

"Beg pardon, sir?"

"Not too bright, this one," whispered Ian with a rueful shake of his head. "Get your clothes on, Harris."

"Oh, yessir. Of course, sir," babbled the nervous young man, saluting quickly and tripping over his nightshirt in his haste to get up the stairs. Alex stared at Ian, who kept his eyes glued on the young soldier's retreat. It was sad, the awkwardness between them.

"Ian?" he ventured, wanting desperately to break through and find the easy camaraderie they had had before.

"Aye?" murmured Ian, forcing himself to look at Alex. Alex fought for the words but couldn't find any.

"Master Alex," breathed a warm, loving voice that released the uneasy tension between the two men.

"Mackie, my love!" exclaimed Alex joyfully, enveloping a small, round woman in his arms.

" 'Tis not seemly," fussed the old lady, struggling half-heartedly in his strong embrace.

"Still trying to teach me to mind my manners, are you?"

"Glad I am that you're home at last. It'll take some of the weight off me," joined in Ian. "Mackie has to have someone to fuss over, so I've been your proxy, so to speak."

"Get along wie you, you young rapscallion . . . and tuck your shirt in."

"See what I mean?" laughed Ian.

"I've put you in the red rooms on the third floor, and there's hot water being carried up right now. Your uniform's clean and pressed and waiting for you . . . and Fergus is at the stables waiting for the wee-un . . . I mean Lady Cameron . . . to return," chattered Mackie as she herded Alex up the stairs as though he were still a small boy and she his nurse.

"I'll see you in a bit, Ian," laughed Alex as he was borne away by the energetic little housekeeper.

Ian looked after them thoughtfully as he tucked his nightshirt into his breeches. So Fergus was at the stables waiting for Cameron. Cameron, his love. Cameron, his best friend's wife. Cameron, who loved and trusted him like a brother, he thought cynically. She haunted his dreams and his waking hours. He smiled to himself, remembering the stream of Gaelic curses that poured from her sweet mouth. Thank God she wasn't as he had feared she'd be. She was still Cameron, and from Alex's answer, he allowed her to be. All winter he'd worried about the fate of the two people he most cared about, wondering who would kill whom or whether Alex's rigid stubbornness would bow Cameron's wild pride. Seeing her in all her untamed glory had comforted him and yet reopened another wound. How painful would it be to live in such close proximity? Maybe he should request another assignment, but from the little he knew of the colonel's prejudice against Scots, he doubted the request would be granted. Deep in thought, Ian left the house and strode, without conscious design, to the stables.

Cameron was only conscious of the thunder in her ears that joined with the thundering of her heart. All her fears and thoughts were successfully blocked by her horse's galloping hooves, that pounded throughout her body uniting with the rhythm of her pulse and the roar of the air as they raced through the night.

Gradually the horse tired, slowing his pace . . . gentling the rhythm. The rage diminished . . . ebbed until each sound separated and regained its rightful place. Cameron reined her sweating mount and looked over the waters of the Firth of Forth. The moonlight tipped the edges of the waves, foreshortening them to the horizon where they joined the sky in a shimmering bar of light. She felt soothed and at peace in the night's serenity. Everything now felt as it should. No fears lurked. Nothing was smothered and muffled, nor shrouded with evil expectancy. The night was crisp and clean. She sat on her horse, delighting in the completeness of all she felt, smelled, heard, and saw . . . in harmony with herself and all around. She smiled, hearing the mischievous scramblings and furtive scufflings of the tiny nocturnal animals as they foraged for food. An owl hooted loudly, answered by the haunting cry of its mate. A few sharp bursts of frantic rustling and then a terrible stillness . . . a fearful suspension as the night once more seemed to hold its breath. Cameron sat frozen upon her horse, her teeth clenched, her muscles tensed . . . waiting. She imagined herself as the wee, cowering

animal trapped in the pounding of its own heart, unable
to see danger but nonetheless feeling its presence in every
pore. The large, dark shadows of the predator's wings
played across the flimsy grasses that hid the furry scraps
of life. She closed her eyes and felt the oppressive weight of
the looming shadow as though she were the hunted. A
shrill shriek tore the night, and the languid, almost bored
flapping of heavy wings relaxed the cruel suspension, and
once again the mischievous scramblings resumed with even
more fervor as the living rejoiced in the kindness of fate.

Cameron whistled for Torquil and wheeled her horse
around in the direction of Glen Aucht. She had thought to
stay out longer, shrouded by the night, but now such solitude was not comforting, and she yearned to curl up in the
warmth of Alex's strong body, safe in their own bed. Why
had she been so disturbed by the fate of one small mouse
or mole, she wondered. She had been reared with nature,
and such a small incident was really insignificant and mundane in the whole circle of life. She threw her head back
and stared fearfully at the sky. Its heavy darkness hung,
weighing her down like the shadow of the owl's wings. She
stared frantically behind her, feeling an unseen, intangible
presence. An inexplicable foreboding filled her, and she
urged her horse faster toward the warm, inviting windows
of the house.

Alex's temper simmered just below the surface as he
lowered himself into the steaming water. The long, tense
day had drained him of any reserves. The anger at the
English colonel's intrusion into his home was fanned
further on hearing that Fergus was unavailable to him and
that Ian Drummond was last seen making his way also to
the stables. Even Mackie had seemed in a great hurry to
be free of him as she professed to seeing to the Lady Cameron's needs. Instead of relaxing him, the scalding heat of
the too-hot water burned his flesh, seeming to add to the
fury that threatened to boil over. He reasoned with himself as he closed his eyes, willing his tension to ebb. A
sharp rap at the door caused him to sit up suddenly, slop-
ping the water over the rim of the copper bath so that it
beaded in puddles on the thick red carpet.

"Major Sinclair?" whined a nasally voice.

"What is it, Harris?" he answered testily.

"Colonel Beddington is waiting in the library, sir."

"It has not been one hour yet!"

"He sent me to inform you, sir."

Alex muttered angrily as he stood, abruptly drenching the carpet with even more water.

"Beg pardon, sir?"

"That'll be all, Harris," roared Alex, soaping himself furiously.

"Shall I tell the colonel that you'll be right down, sir?"

"No! You shall tell the colonel that you have delivered his message!"

"But sir, he wants you immediately," whined the young captain. With an oath, Alex stepped out of the tub and strode to the door, which he flung open savagely. The pale-faced soldier tottered backward in alarm at the sight of the furious, naked man.

"Immediately, you say?" he bellowed. "Let me just get my hat!"

Captain Harris turned and fled, and Alex had the slight satisfaction of hearing the flustered soldier trip and go crashing down the stairs. He slammed the door and proceeded to dry himself and dress, purposefully taking his time as he tried to calm his temper.

Cameron reached the stable yard and flung herself off her heaving mount, to be grasped by strong hands. She screamed and fought.

"Lassie, lassie . . . dinna fash yourself," soothed a deep voice.

"Fergus!" rejoiced Cameron, turning and burrowing her face into his heather-smelling tweeds.

"Aye," smiled the old man, holding her close with his lean, sinewy arms and rocking her gently. "MacNab, settle Lady Cameron's horse," he ordered.

"Torquil!" she remembered, pushing herself away from the safety of Fergus.

"Dinna fash . . . dinna fash. Be calm. He's inspecting his new family."

"New family?" she inquired, looking up at Fergus's lined brown face that crinkled with merriment.

"Aye," he returned, with his blue eyes twinkling. "Four dogs and four bitches. Dinna ken the old beastie had it in him." He laughed as he led Cameron into the stables.

Torquil stood stunned, his great legs planted firmly apart as though to balance him against the shock, as a muddle of eight large, lively pups attacked him with ferocious fervor, licking, lapping, nipping, and yapping . . . with round, milky potbellies they clumsily leaped, losing balance and falling backward upon each other, squealing and squirming like little pigs.

"Whelped in the Daft Days after Christmastide," informed Fergus as Cameron knelt and was immediately assaulted and toppled backward by the boisterous bunch. She lay back laughing in the hay as her face was thoroughly cleansed by wet, warm tongues and her clothes were fought over and worried by sharp little teeth. Torquil shook his massive, shaggy head and gave a parental growl. His exuberant offspring paid not the least attention but continued pummeling and playing with their new toy, Cameron, who vainly struggled to sit up. Each pup, though scarcely four months old, was already as big as a full-grown medium-size dog.

"Down . . . down," gurgled Cameron ineffectively as she tried to push them away, only to have her sleeves captured and fought over so that her arms were pulled in two directions. Torquil sprang forward and barked authoritatively. The pups looked up in surprise as their sire bared his teeth and menacingly approached them. They backed away, wagging their tails so furiously their whole bodies moved and their back legs skipped from side to side as they fought to maintain their balance and placate the enormous grown-up who snarled down on them. Fergus helped the giggling Cameron to her feet.

"Look what a good father Torquil is. He's never been one before that I know of . . . and how well he does," she laughed, watching the enormous hound standing so dictatorially in front of his cowed but still wiggling offspring. "Where's their mother?"

Fergus stared down at her, wishing she'd asked any

question but that as he noted her sparkling green eyes and her glossy ebony hair that radiated like a halo around her flushed, happy face.

"Cameron?" hailed a voice from the shadows, rescuing Fergus from the unhappy task of informing her that the pups' dam had been shot by Colonel Beddington, who had ignorantly tried to pick up a pup in the protective mother's presence.

"Ian!" Cameron exclaimed happily as he emerged from behind a stall from which he'd witnessed the joyful scene. She impulsively rushed toward him, and the pups, thinking her sudden movement meant the end of recess, hurtled themselves forward, tripping her. Ian reached out to help and found himself knocked backward into a pile of hay with Cameron in his arms and eight tongues and tails and thirty-two paws pummeling his body with ecstatic exuberance. Unable to stand up, Cameron and Ian collapsed back, roaring with laughter.

At this precise moment Alex, who had furtively tiptoed down the servants' stairs hoping for news of his errant wife before his uncomfortable interview with Colonel Beddington, strode into the stables. At hearing Cameron's free, untrammeled laughter, he had quickened his pace, eager to see her, but had stopped short at the sight that met his eyes. The warm browns, golds, and yellows of the stable, lit by lamps, seemed as intimate and seductive as a bedchamber to his jealous eye. His wife, her face flushed, alive, and more radiant than he'd seen it for some time, was cradled in the arms of Ian Drummond as they lay on a thick pallet of hay. His jealous eye saw not the eight boisterous pups or Fergus, who stood hands on hips, wheezing out his own merriment, his weather-beaten face creased into myriads of laughter lines. Alex stood in the shadows as the rage burned, throbbing his senses and joining with the rest of the day's irritations, and intrusions. His nails dug sharply into the palms of his hands, drawing blood before he coldly and mechanically turned on his heels away from the warmth into the cold, biting darkness. He strode back to the house, his boots ringing sharply on the hard cobblestones, his face set in uncompromising lines, his tall, lean body stiff and unyielding.

CHAPTER THREE

Cameron entered the warmth of the kitchen and was enfolded into Mackie's maternal softness. She felt choked by the tenderness she felt for the plump old woman as she buried herself into the amble bosom, smelling the sweetness of lavender and freshly baked bread.

"Oh, Mackie . . . Mackie, how I have missed you."

Mackie sniffed and bobbed her neatly bunned head up and down, unable to answer as she held Cameron close. Her twinkling currant eyes brimmed with tears of joy at her "wee black lamb" being safely home. Recollecting her place, she sniffed again and patted the dark, shining hair with a small dimpled hand, removing a few bristles of straw from the tangled curls.

"There's hot water upstairs," she clucked, smoothing her apron and tucking a few loose strands of hair behind her ears, then, dropping her voice to a conspiratorial whisper, added, "That fat Sassanach of an English soldier helped hisself to yours and the laird's own chambers. Can you believe that for brass? Those English think they own the world, they do. Och, fair turns my innards to have to serve the likes of him . . . fouling a good home wie his lechery and lusty fornications!"

"Wie his what?" giggled Cameron.

"Forgetting myself and my place, I am. I dinna ken what I'm adoing. 'Tis that Curr-nell Beddington . . . well named he is, he has me fretting and fashing so I dinna ken what's up nor down . . . and my aggravation makes my tongue runaway wie me. Now, I've my strict orders to see you tucked into a nice cuddly bed," she flustered.

"But Alex . . ." protested Cameron as she was bustled out of the kitchen.

"That curr of a Sassanach will be akeeping the poor lad up until past dawn, I don't doubt," grumbled Mackie, shaking her head with disapproval as she herded her charge up the back stairs.

Alex stood stiffly at attention, staring at Colonel Beddington, who posed with his back to the fire and one polished boot on the gleaming copper fender. He noted that the portraits of his mother and father had been removed and an abominable, lurid likness of the colonel in leaner days now hung above the mantelpiece in their stead.

"I'm sorry if I kept you waiting, sir," said Alex without a trace of apology in his tone.

"Harris, more cognac," ordered the officer testily without glancing at Alex, who saw that the superior contents of his wine cellar had also been appropriated in the same manner as had his bed. He entertained the thought of languidly strolling to his own sideboard and pouring himself a generous portion of his own brandy and then sitting in his own chair in his own library in his own house. But he resisted the temptation, knowing that he didn't trust himself not to lose his temper and that standing at attention was the only way to control his emotions. He did not want his position weakened in front of the fat, arrogant Englishman, who now noisily slurped the old French brandy as though it were country cider. Beddington stared back at him with distaste.

"Well, Sinclair?" he belched, rivulets of brandy dripping from his clownish moustache and coursing down the greedy furrows of his fat face. Alex looked at him with studied boredom and deigned not to answer.

"Well, Sinclair? . . . By Jove, man, answer me!" sputtered Beddington, unable to bear the ticking silence or the hard, unwavering look of the taller, younger, thinner man. "I'll have no insubordination . . . answer me!"

"I thought your 'Well, Sinclair?' a rhetorical question, sir," replied Alex evenly.

"Rhetorical! Rhetorical! Confound your impudence! What have you to say for yourself?"

My impudence, seethed Alex, but he restrained himself and answered cordially as though at a social gathering.

"On what subject, sir?"

Colonel Beddington choked, his already alarmingly

florid complexion turned to even more violent shades of violet, purple, and red.

"May I help, sir?" offered Harris, eagerly rushing forward. Alex watched the sycophantic administrations of the pale, runtish captain to the brutish, livid colonel with cynical amusement. Harris was like a brittle, bald sparrow fussing, twitting, flitting, and flapping around the large choking man.

"Damnation! Get away from me, you prissy sissy!" bellowed Beddington with such ferocity that it seemed the slight, wan man was blown backward like a straw in the wind. Alex clenched his teeth at the thought of straw as Cameron held in Ian's arms flashed into his mind.

"On what subject?! On what subject?!" continued the colonel, consumed by impotent rage.

"Yes, sir."

"Why, on the subject of your absence, Sinclair. On the subject of your disobeying orders, Sinclair. On the subject of your not reporting to your regiment for duty, Sinclair! The subject under discussion is utterly obvious, Sinclair!"

"I explained to you previously, sir, that I did not receive orders . . . that I was on my honeymoon, sir," informed Alex with patient boredom.

"That is neither here nor there. There are only the facts, Sinclair. FACTS! Fact one . . . you grossly disobeyed orders in not reporting to your regiment . . . so, fact two . . . you were absent without leave, which is desertion, which is punishable by death!" spat the colonel, looking extremely apoplectic but fixing Alex with a triumphant and malicious leer. To his added fury the composed young Scot before him just nodded contemplatively, as though he had heard his maiden aunt's cat had passed away.

"Your conduct, Major Sinclair, is atrocious . . . audacious . . . outrageous . . . insolent . . . insubordinate . . . impertinent . . . impudent . . . disrespectful . . . disgusting . . . dishonorable. . . ." He sputtered to a halt, at a loss for adjectives, thought Alex savagely, receiving a macabre pleasure at the whole proceedings. "You have the infernal cheek . . . the gall . . . the nerve . . . the temerity . . . the conceit . . . the boldness . . . shamelessness . . . to . . . to to . . . to . . . ." Again he spluttered to a stop, this time at a loss for nouns, whimsically mused Alex, himself delightfully detached as though watching a comic operetta. "To stand before me guilty of such . . . such . . . pernicious . . . er . . . guilt with such self-assured effrontery!" Unconsciously Alex let out a long sigh of relief at the obvious lame conclusion of the first paragraph, or sentence, of the superior officer's tirade, which enraged the colonel even further. To Alex's surprise, instead of the resumption of the diatribe or another fit of choking, the fat man started to laugh. Not a deep ha-ha of jovial enjoyment but rather a high-pitched, unpleasant sneering whine, as he waved his empty glass toward the cowering Harris for a refill.

"What else did I expect?" he chortled when there was a pause in his acid hilarity, but another fit shuddered him, and he flung himself down into Alex's favorite chair, squealing and drumming his feet in his mirth.

"What else did I expect? Oh, Randall Beddington, what else? What else? A gloomy, barbarous, backward country . . . this Northern England," he cried bitterly, his laughter changing almost to hysterical weeping. He sat up composing himself and stared at Alex with abhorrence. " 'Tis an insult to England's fair name to call pagan Scotland so. This savage, uncivilized land of no comforts. This abominable, depraved, base, corrupt country where Scot feeds upon Scot. You're an animalistic, noxious, subhuman race!" he taunted.

Alex detached himself even further as he stared into the bloated, spitting face. He contented himself with analyzing the officer's visage feature by feature. The hair, non-existent on the shiny pate, resided in a limp patch (the moustache wax having been melted by the brandy, ascertained Alex) beneath a red, bulbous nose with lots of little black hairs that resembled an overripe strawberry. The large, loose mouth with spittled, flapping lips contorted up and down, up and down, giving ghastly glimpses of yellow, broken teeth as the violent invective against Scotland continued. Faster and faster moved the mouth . . . the words having little meaning to Alex, who was just mesmerized by the irritating sound that became more and more frantic, like a bluebottle caught in the marmalade. He turned his gaze to the petrified Harris, who shifted his weight from leg to leg as a small boy with a full bladder, his tight little mouth in a tense circle as he wrung thin, nervous fingers.

Hopping Harris, mused Alex humorously. Colonel Beddington, catching the fleet smile of amusement cross the young major's countenance, stopped his diatribe in mid-sentence. A heavy silence ensued, measured painfully by the steady beat of a large grandfather clock. Beddington sat wearily. A look of pure incredulity sagged his face, his skin hanging like a wet, heavy cloth. Alex observed with interest the color gathering again, ballooning the collapsed folds until the red-flecked eyes like two agates seemed to pop out of the turgid bags. Was he watching a man about to explode, he wondered, as the colonel continued to swell. Colonel Beddington rose to his feet, and although Alex expected him to keep rising until he floated to the ornate ceiling, he didn't.

"By Gad, I'll break you, Sinclair! Hoist your severed head on a pike above Temple Bar to join the moldering skulls of your fellow barbarians!" he roared, indicating to Harris to refill his glass again. Alex thought on the grizzly remains of two of his father's friends, Jacobite officers, who had been killed in 1745 when Prince Charles Edward had led his army almost to the English capital. Highlanders were certainly hardy even in death, he mused sadly, if their heads were still recognizable as such, nearly seventeen years later.

"That went through your tough animal hide, I see," gloated Beddington, swaying as the brandy took effect. "Made some . . . sort of im . . . im . . . presshun, I shee," he slurringly added. A puzzled, frightened look crossed his bloated face as he fought a wave of dizziness. He staggered and then fell heavily into a chair, the brandy glass smashing against the carved arm, and the amber liquid beading on his uniform and the upholstery. Alex was filled with irritation and disgust, and yet no expression showed on his stony face. His back and legs ached unbearably, and yet he made no movement to shift his weight or stand more comfortably. He watched dispassionately as Beddington rocked backward and forward.

"Damn! Damn that Scottish bashtard! Damn! Damn!

Damn! May he rot in hell!" He yelled, his impotent rage giving way to maudlin self-pity. "Damn John Stuart!"

"John Stuart? Earl of Bute?" Alex questioned, surprised that he was not the Scottish bastard that Beddington was cursing.

"And damn that lowbred pig. Pitt, for his sh . . . shtupidity! I tried to tell him, Harrish . . . didn't I?" he wept.

"Yes, sir. You certainly did, sir," agreed the skinny captain comfortingly.

"I warned him . . . did my duty, and this is my reward. . . . Sh . . . sh . . . not fair, ish it, Harrish?"

"No, sir. It certainly isn't, sir."

"Itsh a plot, Harrish . . . a Sh . . . Sh . . . Shottish plot. Shuart shleeping with the princess of Wales . . . the king's very mother . . . and playing falsh friend to King George hishelf . . . itsh a plot!"

"Yes, sir," responded Harris obediently.

"What'sh that?" barked Beddington.

"I . . . I . . . I . . . was agreeing with you, sir. It is definitely a plot."

"What ish?"

"Well . . . er . . . um . . . about John Stuart, Earl of Bute, sir."

"You are right, Harrish . . . smart man. Never thought you had much intelligence . . . but you are right. I warned Pitt and the Cabinet, you know, and am now exshiled to thish barren barbaric land . . . leaving Bute to hish treachery in London," sobbed Randall Beddington, burying his face into a pillow that he cuddled much like a stuffed toy. Alex, whose interest had finally been sparked, was disappointed as he waited for a resumption of the news from London. Instead a loud, hiccoughing snore broke the silence followed by another and another in slobbering succession. After a few moments, Alex relaxed his stance and leisurely crossed to the sideboard, where he poured himself a generous portion of brandy.

"I say, what the hell do you think you're doing?" protested Harris. Alex turned and silenced him with a withering look before quitting the room.

"I should neither wake him nor leave your post, Harris. That is an order," he commanded as he closed the door.

Cameron couldn't sleep. She lay cold and uncomfortable in the large, strange bed. For a while it had been warm and wonderful as she and Mackie had chatted away excitedly. The room had been cheerful and inviting—the firelight merrily reflecting off the furniture and the deep burgundy-red of the velvet hangings—the steam from the scented bath softening each hard line. She had been cozily tucked into the enormous bed and propped by fluffy pillows, and Mackie had fed her savory soup. Cameron had felt happy and secure, but when Mackie had fussed out, all the warmth and cheer had left with her. The fire, although still burning healthily, seemed bright and brittle, accentuating forbidden shadows and hard cutting edges—the burgundy-red velvet appeared black and shroudlike, and the furniture took on alien, coffinlike shapes in Cameron's eyes as she lay motionless waiting for Alex. The minutes ticked by, measured painfully by the seconds as she tried to bring her seething brain to order, but the lateness of the hour and her mental and physical fatigue just heightened each thought to nightmare intensity.

Who was she? She was Cameron Sinclair by marriage, but who was she before that? Just Cameron. Cameron who? or Who Cameron? There had been a mother, Dolores MacLeod, of whom she had no recollection, and a father . . . or rather a sire, whose name she'd probably never know. In short she was a bastard. The bastard Lady Sinclair, she thought bitterly. How simple life had been once. Alone on the moors at Cape Wrath with her hound, Torquil, and horse, Torquod. What was she doing between the fancy, cold bed linens of this unwelcoming chamber? Alex was the answer. Only with Alex did she feel complete and sure of herself and her future.

Cameron sat up, determined to find him, when there was a scratching and low growl at the door. She sprang out of bed to let her hound in and buried her face in his shaggy warmth. With the door open she listened, but there was nothing to hear but the heavy, dark silence of the sleeping house. She tiptoed to the staircase, keeping her hand on her dog's broad head. Not a sound. She looked back to the open door of her bedchamber, but the ominous, dancing shadows did not invite her back. Carefully she descended the stairs to the ground floor. A thin strip of light bled from beneath Alex's study door. Pressing her ear against the wood, she listened. There was the crackle and hiss of a fire and a low, rhythmic snoring. Had Alex fallen asleep beside the hearth? she wondered. Quietly she turned the handle and peered into the room. By the light of the burning logs she saw a figure crumpled carelessly in a chair by the hearth. She smiled impishly and, motioning her dog to be silent, stole into the room. As she neared the sleeping form, a thin, pale soldier stepped groggily out of the shadows. Torquil growled deep in his throat. Captain Harris's sleepy eyes widened as the firelight glinted off the enormous dog's large teeth, and he uttered a high-pitched squeal. Cameron screamed, and Colonel Beddington awoke with a curse.

"Goddamnit! What is this infernal noise?" he roared. Cameron stepped back with horror.

"Oh, I say, it's an apparition . . . a maidenly apparition at that," murmured Beddington, greedily eyeing Cameron's lithe figure, which was silhouetted through her nightgown. "Oh, delicious honey bun," he drooled, twirling his rather limp moustache as Cameron backed toward the door.

"Catch the nymph!" he bellowed as she darted out, followed by the hound.

"But the dog, sir," whined Harris, hanging back.

"You've got a sword, you sissy," roared Beddington, withdrawing his own and charging after the girl. Fortunately an ornate hassock obstructed him, and he fell flat on his face.

"Are you hurt, sir?" asked Harris solicitously, trying to help the heavy colonel to his feet.

"After them, Harris . . . after them. I'll not be cheated of that tempting morsel. Come back here, girl, that is an order!" he panted, struggling to his feet and pushing the young captain's helping hands away with irritation.

"I'm coming to get you, little girlie," he cajoled, staggering to the door and popping his head around.

"May I help you, Colonel?" asked Ian, blocking his view.

"Ah, Drummond, where the dickens did you spring from?"

"I've just come in from a turn outside, sir. 'Tis a nice spring night . . . though nearly morning," answered Ian cordially.

"I'm not interested in the weather. Did you see a girl?"

"A girl, sir?"

"Yes, a girl . . . dressed or rather undressed to please. The little sylph's playing teasing games with me. Where are you, my pretty little nymphette? Where are you? I'm coming to get you," sang out Beddington coaxingly.

"I did see a female running into the garden, sir," offered Ian, waving toward the front door.

With a cry of triumph and holding his sword aloft, the portly officer charged, followed by Harris.

"Come along, Harris, come along. Tally Ho . . . Tally Ho! The hunt is on, my pretty. Randall's coming to get you!" And with that the two disappeared into the night.

"Has he gone?" inquired Cameron, peeking out from the shadows.

"Aye, and you'd better stay as far away from him as possible. Strange thing to say it, being your own house, but I'd keep to your chambers. You shouldna be wandering around at night dressed as, such. . . . But knowing him, it wouldna matter how you were clad. How did you come to be there with him? Where's Alex?" ranted Ian, unnerved by her close proximity and furious at the fat colonel's lechery.

"I was looking for him."

"I trust I'm not intruding."

"Alex!" exclaimed Cameron as he strode out of the door from the kitchens. She was about to run to him, but his obvious fury froze her.

"What is the meaning of this?" he asked coldly of Ian.

"I thought it was you, but it was that fat soldier . . . and he came after me . . . and . . ." stammered Cameron.

"Listen," she added, pointing to the open front door. Faint tally ho's echoed. "Ian saved me," she giggled nervously.

"I see I am once more in your debt, Drummond," returned Alex stiffly. Ian nodded coldly and turned on his heel. Cameron watched him leave with a puzzled look on her face.

"You should be in bed, not prowling around the house in that attire," hissed Alex, firmly leading her to the stairs.

"I waited and waited, but you didna come, and I had so much to tell you."

"Nothing that canna wait 'til morning, I trust, because I've heard more than enough words for one night. 'Tis nearly sunrise, and I need some sleep," he responded coldly, opening their bedroom door.

CHAPTER FOUR

Cameron lay between the cold sheets where Alex had roughly deposited her, watching him disrobe. She noted apprehensively his stern expression and short, abrupt movements as he almost threw the uniform from him. Tension crackled the air. Her body was stiff with tension, her fists clenched beneath the covers, her feet crossed and her knees tightly pressed together. Who was this strange man? What was she doing in this strange bed? In this strange chamber? In this strange house?

The firelight glinted on Alex's lean, strong body, accentuating his true beauty but at the same time making him seem unyielding and incapable of giving warmth and comfort. Cameron shut her eyes, hoping to block out the traitorous thought of needing to feel safe and taken care of in his strong arms. She chided herself for such weakness and fought the pangs of loneliness.

Alex stood naked, staring into the fire, trying to calm his icy rage. He felt his body relax and turned to the bed. Cameron lay stiffly with her eyes tightly closed. His stern features softened at the sight of her raven hair fanned across the pillow and her rebellious, stubborn expression. He strode lithely to the bed and looked down at her, silently willing her to open her brilliant green eyes.

Cameron felt his presence above her. She tried to still her breathing and feign sleep, but the weight of Alex's shadow seemed as oppressive and foreboding as the owl's wings.

"Cameron?" whispered Alex, knowing full well she was pretending. Cameron gave a sleepy grunt and turned over, away from him, curling her body into a tight ball beneath the covers. Alex's temper flared. He had no patience left for games. He strode to the other side of the bed, got in, turned his back on her, and closed his eyes.

Once again Cameron lay unable to sleep. She opened her

eyes and stared at the broad, brown back, and was filled with desolation. Where was the warm, golden, fun-loving Alex of the hunting lodge? She yearned to clamber mischievously over him and burrow into the safety of his belly, but the expanse and set of his back seemed unsurmountable. Her pride warred with her needs as she debated with herself. She hadn't done anything to warrant his attitude toward her, she seethed, even as she ruefully remembered her unladylike arrival at Glen Aucht. Even so, she'd had a narrow escape from the English colonel, and yet instead of being grateful to Ian for saving her, he'd seemed almost angry.

Alex was also unable to sleep. He was too conscious of Cameron's presence. He opened his eyes and stared at the fire as the picture of Ian and Cameron rolling in the hay caused his anger to build. What a sorry start to their married life this was, he thought. All the promises of sharing joys, sorrows, anxieties, and fears, broken on their very first day in civilization. Filled with fury, Alex suddenly turned over. Cameron gasped and backed away from the sudden movement. Her green eyes widened at the sight of his angry amber ones. Alex leaned on one elbow and stared down at her silently. Cameron stared back, rebelliously hiding her apprehension. Her own quick temper flared, but she closed her mouth in a firm line, refusing to speak the first word. Almost a minute of unbearable tension passed with neither of them blinking or looking away, each almost daring the other in a battle of wills.

What on earth am I doing? wondered Alex, and suddenly the ridiculousness of the situation caused him to laugh. Cameron's fury was fanned, and her eyes flashed warningly. "Now, now, there'll be no hitting unless you're asking to be skelped," chuckled Alex with a touch of steel beneath his warm, deep voice. Cameron clenched and unclenched her fists and, taking a deep breath, stared at him with contempt, and slowly and deliberately turned her back on him. Two strong hands picked her up and sat her facing him as though she were a doll. Cameron quelled the urge to fight and forced herself to sit stiffly. She avoided his eyes and stared over his shoulder.

"Stop behaving like a spoiled brat," chided Alex softly.

Cameron quashed the need to lash out, giving no indication that she'd heard.

"It has been a very long, strange day with many changes, and we're both a bit put out," struggled Alex, trying to choose his words carefully in the knowledge that Cameron, in the mood she was in, would jump on and misinterpret any careless word. "But I'll not sleep our first night home with this cold silence between us," he stated firmly.

" 'Tis not home," said Cameron.

"Aye, doesna feel so," agreed Alex. "I'm sorry, my love." Cameron felt the tears rush to her eyes, prickling her nose. She breathed deeply, flaring her nostrils to stop the torrent that threatened to sweep her away. She turned her head away sharply, but Alex had seen the sudden welling and snatched her up, holding her closely to him like a small child. Cameron struggled, feeling shame, wanting to creep away to some dark corner and hide her tears. She might have been a small mouse for all that her struggling attained. Alex held her tightly to his chest and rocked.

"Cry them out, love. Cry them out," he crooned, and to Cameron's horror, she did. She let go, and a storm of weeping consumed her. Tears of loneliness, fear, apprehension, anger, plus many feelings she knew no names for poured down Alex's chest. Spent, she sat hiccoughing on his lap as he stroked her hair back from her hot, wet face. She sat feeling shy and ashamed, trying to control herself, unable to look at him, her eyes glued to the brown, strong arm that encircled her.

"Look at me, Cameron," ordered Alex gently. Cameron tossed her mane of hair and shook her head, but his large hand cupped her small chin, and he relentlessly turned her face. She closed her eyes, feeling very vulnerable. Alex smiled softly, knowing her shame at having cried. Tears still hung on her long, dark lashes, and he bent his head and gently kissed them off. His lips traveled to the soft, flushed cheeks and to the velvety hollows below her ears. Cameron felt an aching rush of hunger, and she writhed impatiently against him, trying to quicken his leisurely pace. She didn't want to think. She wanted to submerge the whole of herself, be carried along by the flood of longing that could hammer her pulses, drowning out everything but her urgent need. She pushed him back against the pillows, trying to dislodge his nuzzling mouth as it traveled sensuously toward her breasts so she could capture it with her own lips and press herself closer to him. Her body was frenzied. Every part of her tingled. Alex laughed with delight. This was his Cameron, his mercurial maiden, with her lightning changes of mood. Cameron felt the shaking and deep chuckle reverberating through her as she lay full length upon his prone body. She pushed herself back, and with both small hands firmly planted on his broad chest, stared at him with a mixture of anger and puzzlement. Why wouldn't he let her lose herself for a while? His face, full of mischievous merriment and love, glowed back at her, but she fought against the choking tenderness she saw and felt and ground her lithe, young hips challengingly. Alex grinned roguishly and idly stretched his golden arms wide in mock surrender, inviting her to have her way.

"I'm all yours, my lady," he murmured wickedly, putting aside his need for a savoring of their love until she had fulfilled her urgency. He noted her grim, set little face and flashing emerald eyes above him as she regarded him with determination. He chuckled again as a look of cunning crossed her features and she shimmied her satiny body down until he felt her soft breath against his lower abdomen. His own passion flared in anticipation as she lay between his parted legs with her ebony head pillowed on one of his thighs. Her nimble fingers and softly blowing mouth circled and circled, never touching his throbbing firmness, which reared, trying to connect.

Cameron teased and teased, her own excitement billowing as Alex writhed, his own labored breathing fanning the flames of her desire. It was now her turn to giggle as she squeezed her thighs together and rolled away from him, curling into a tight little ball. She held her breath with delicious anticipation, hoping he would roughly turn her over and master her. She lay in ecstasy waiting, the suspense thrilling every nerve. Alex grinned as he willed his body to be calm, knowing his climax was near and wanting to prolong the sensuous joy. He traced the curve of her spine from the soft, warm nape of her neck to the triangle above her firm buttocks, delighting in the shiver that rippled through her as she opened and stretched, allowing him access to her breasts. She arched her body toward him, her nipples straining, demanding to be encompassed, but now Alex teased, circling the erect pink buds with his mouth while his hands tantalizingly caressed until Cameron bucked trying to connect her hungry body to his. Alex stopped her moans with his mouth, probing her open, inviting lips with his tongue, delighting in the small hands that played along the length of his firm, muscled body. They lost all sense of time and place as they matched each other, their passions soaring . . . both now unwilling to let go and race toward that final release . . . both holding back as long as they could to prolong the excruciatingly glorious suspension until all became a vortex of climactic sensations encompassing them both. Their labored breathing and frantic heartbeats calmed in accord until they slept, still coupled together, without the outside stresses and worries disturbing them.

Cameron slept dreamlessly, enclosed in strong, safe arms. Alex stared down, marveling at her beauty and childlike appearance. So small and yet all woman, fierce and loving. He hated to wake her, but the sun was almost up and he had put off an unpleasant task as long as he could. To hamper, to restrict her in any way would cause sparks to fly, but for her own protection he had to. His assessment of Colonel Randall Beddington was of a weak, bullying man, infinitely more dangerous than a strong man who knew his worth. The Englishman's feelings of inferiority made him suspicious and cruel, and that combined with Cameron's rebellious, fiery nature could cause untold damage. There would be no equality in their marriage today, thought Alex ruefully, caressing his wife's velvet cheek. He had to give orders, and she must obey or it could mean her very life. The very thing he loved in her could mean her downfall. Her uniqueness came from being reared away from so-called society. She was as natural and free, as uninhibited as the wild birds and animals, her only preconceptions being her hatred of the English and an abhorrence of corseted, simpering females.

"Cameron, love?" he whispered, kissing her gently. He

kept his lips on her warm, sleepy ones, delighting in the awakening awareness that he felt as her soft pliancy tightened to abandoned desire. He reveled in the way she gave herself without thought or pretense, following the instincts of her emotions and body. It had caused him much anxiety at the beginning of their relationship, as other women he'd slept with were like himself, products of a society where only men could appear to show the pleasure of coupling and the women were expected to submit with a little reluctance and distaste.

"Cameron?" he repeated with difficulty as her lips sweetly melted into his and her firm, lithe body seductively aroused him.

"Um?" she breathed, more as an expression of appreciation than an inquiry. Alex didn't answer. He postponed his task and gave himself up to the delights of his wife.

"I like waking up this way," informed Cameron later as she lay nestled against his chest, playing with the golden hairs that curled against his tanned skin. "What'll we do today?" she added idly.

"That is what we must talk about," replied Alex, his muscles tightening involuntarily. He fell silent, not knowing quite how to inform her without raising her hackles. He felt so close and at one with her, he hated to break the bond.

"What is it?" demanded Cameron, raising herself and staring down at him.

"You must be unobtrusive and circumspect," replied Alex slowly, tensed for a violent reaction in spite of himself.

"What?" giggled Cameron.

"Unfortunately, I am very serious. That fat fool is dangerous, and you had a wee taste of him last night. You must stay here in the chamber . . . keep out of his and the other soldiers' way. You mustna draw attention to yourself. You'll not go out alone but stay here, locked in our chambers. Is that clear?"

Cameron stared at him with undisguised horror. Unable to bear her accusing look, Alex tried to draw her to him to hide her face in his chest, but she pulled away from him.

"Stay locked up in here? I can take care of myself. I did before and I can again!" she stated.

"Cameron, you dinna understand. You must do as I say or I'll have to lock you in and take the key myself. Help me, love. You dinna ken what we're up against," appealed Alex.

"Explain it to me, then, unless you think me as stupid as that fat Sassanach," demanded Cameron.

"I dinna ken all the ins and outs myself, Cameron, and until I do, you must abide by what I say. Will you trust me? I know 'tis hard to be confined, and I would not demand it unless the danger was real. Trust me?"

Cameron nodded silently.

"As long as I know you're wie me, we'll survive," urged Alex, apprehensive of her silent assent. Cameron looked at him, her green eyes probing his searching amber ones and then threw both arms around his neck and held him tightly. Alex enfolded her in his, and they stayed thus for several minutes, each feeling the beat of the others heart, neither wanting to be the first to end the embrace. Reluctantly Cameron pushed back from Alex, hoping that by so doing he'd see she was strong and self-reliant.

"So I'm to stay in all day?" she ventured as she watched him dress in his uniform.

"I'll send Mackie to you so you'll not starve and see that she brings you some books so you'll not be too bored."

"What'll you be doing?"

"Riding around the estate to ascertain what is going on," answered Alex, pulling on his boots.

"It wouldna hurt, surely, for me to ride wie you?" questioned Cameron hopefully.

"There's nothing I'd rather do than ride wie you, my love, but not until I see how the land lies," responded Alex gently.

"Why are you wearing the red?"

"'Tis on duty I am now," smiled Alex, ignoring the disdain in her voice. "Your husband is back a soldier, whether you like it or not."

"For the wrong side, it seems," spat Cameron, somehow, without really realizing it, wanting to push him away so his parting would be less painful.

"Oh, so you're determined to push me out the door?" parried Alex, knowing all too well her emotions.

"How do you know what I'm doing before I know myself?" laughed Cameron in spite of herself.

"Because I'd do the same," confessed Alex, hugging her to him.

"Well, I'll just rid you of the hated clothes," giggled Cameron, undoing the gleaming buttons.

"Witch," chuckled Alex, gently and firmly putting her from him and tickling until she let go and lay staring at him from the bed. "Watch your willful mistress," he said to the large hound on the hearthrug as he opened the door.

"When will I see you?" asked Cameron.

"Whenever I have a moment, I'll take you by surprise. So you'd better behave yourself," growled Alex before leaving and shutting the door after himself. "Lock it!" he ordered through the door, and Cameron skipped off the bed and shot the large bolt. She jumped back under the covers and listened to his heavy footsteps fade, feeling very bereft. She sat, feeling the rage pound her pulses. She was meant to be Lady Sinclair, mistress of Glen Aucht, and yet she was locked in her bedchamber like a recalcitrant child. She lay back, seething, against the pillows, and then the thought of Alex's warm whiskey eyes melted her rage and she closed her eyes and within minutes fell asleep with a contented smile on her face.

"Just look at my kitchen. 'Tis like a wake," whispered Mackie to Fergus as they sat eating breakfast. The normally warm, cheerful room seemed gray and sorrowing. The old gillies and fresh young maids ate silently, their eyes dull and listless. The only sound besides the clinking of spoons in bowls was the sniffing and stifled sobs of a young girl.

"There's evil about to happen, I feel it in my bones."

"There's no doubt about it. 'Tis happening," stated Fergus baldly.

"Three churns of milk were curdled this morn," hissed his wife.

" 'Tis time for work," said Fergus, eager to change the subject as he pushed back his chair. "The chicks'll be hatching. Nothing stops nature. 'Twill be a fine spring wie new life."

"Hah, if the eggs aren't curst and addled," added Mackie darkly.

" 'Twill do no good stirring up superstition, Mrs. Mac-Donald," Fergus warned his wife as he shrugged into his jacket and the old gillies took their guns from the rack.

" 'Tis not superstition but the way of life, as well you know it," retorted Mackie to her husband's back as he strode purposefully out of the kitchen door. "All right, lassies, stir yourselves. You know your places, so up and at them, and keep yer silly clatter down; 'tis best to let sleeping English dogs lie." A loud wail from the small red-headed girl caused the women to hush her quickly.

"Now, now, now, Ailsa-Lass, there's nothing to be afeared of," fussed Mackie, bustling to her and encompassing her in plump, rocking arms. "We'll keep you well hid with Young-MacNab at the stables, where you can play wie the other puir motherless pups."

"That Sassanach should burn in hell, trying to rape a wee innocent lass. Thank the Lord the liquor made him wilt!" growled an old man with a pipe between gritted teeth.

"Hush yer tongue, Daft-Dougal," hissed Mackie indignantly. "Young-MacNab, take the wee-un wie you," she ordered of a slight youth with a pronounced limp. After seeing the two out she turned on the old man.

"And what are you doing taking your ease wie the rest out working, and saying such things so the puir wee-un can hear and keep remembering!" she ranted.

"You needed to vent some steam, Mackie," chuckled the cross-eyed old man. "Thought 'twere better vented myself than at that guid mon of yours. See you at the noon meal, and it better be better than the lumpy porridge you just poisoned us wie."

"Out before I whack you wie the sticky spurtle," laughed Mackie, brandishing the porridge spoon.

"I'll be wie yer mon Fergus on upper braeside if you need me to rile yer spirits more," chortled Daft-Dougal, slamming the door behind him.

Mackie sat heavily at the kitchen table, staring into space.

Ian Drummond popped his head around the door and watched her for a few seconds.

"Penny for your darkest thoughts, Mistress MacDonald," he said.

"They're worth more than that, you young rapscallion!" retorted Mackie, smoothing her hair. "They'd burn the hairs off yer chest if the truth be known. Well, you're up wie the sun, lad."

"Have na been to bed. Is there breakfast to be had?"

"It'll be served in the dining room wie the rest of you gentry," returned Mackie shortly, Ian's red Union uniform raising her hackles.

"Take pity on a puir Scottish lad, having to wear this is enow to turn one's stomach wie out sitting across from that English pig," replied Ian mischievously.

"That Curr-nell would turn the gut off a sin-eater, that's the truth," relented Mackie. "Well, sit you down. You weigh my shoulders towering over me like that. Och, I remember when you only come to a bee's knees. 'Tis sorrowful, the lad has to die for the mon to be born."

Ian sat at the well-scrubbed table watching the small round woman he'd known all his life.

"Fashed, you are this morning, Mackie mine," he said softly. "Just a bit of bread and cheese will suffice." Mackie cocked her head to one side, much like a small bird.

"There'll be a death. I feel the shadow of its wings," she prophesied.

"Whose?" asked Ian after a pause, her words shivering his spine.

"I dinna ken . . . but 'tis near . . . drawing closer."

"Well, I hope 'tis the English whoreson's," cursed Ian savagely. "Well, I warrant he'll sleep until the supper hour. He was rushing around blind drunk being John Peel wie his coat of gray all night. Tallyhoing," added Ian, trying to lighten the oppressive foreboding.

"Tallyhoing? Who?" puzzled Mackie.

"Colonel Beddington."

"Who was he hunting?"

"What do you think? The fox from his lair in the morning," sang Ian, not wishing to worry the old woman further by bringing Cameron into it. "Oh, you know these English, they're all a wee bit tetched," he added, tapping his head.

"A wee bit tetched! That's treading lightly!" exploded Mackie, banging down a plate of food in front of Ian. "A wee bit tetched, is it! He's the De'il's pa hisself, is that one. A wee bit tetched, indeed! He tried to rape the wee MacFarlane lass wie that puny English captain aholding the puir bairn down!"

Alex entered the kitchen, and the sight of Ian Drummond calmly eating breakfast did nothing to dissipate the anger that molded his features into stern, uncompromising lines. The few hours of forgetful respite with Cameron in his arms had abruptly been shattered as he'd tiptoed past his own suite of rooms, where the sonorous snoring of Colonel Beddington had shuddered through him. The fury at the man's intrusion into his domain, coupled with barely two hours sleep and having to keep his wife locked up, burned in him.

"Good morning, Master Alex," clucked Mackie fondly, smiling tenderly up at his lean, handsome face that she'd first seen red and crumpled from his mother's womb.

"Where's Fergus?" asked Alex without acknowledging Ian's nod.

"On upper braeside wie the other old gillies making the rounds of the nests and vermin traps," informed Mackie.

Alex made a snort of annoyance.

"They'll be back for the noon meal or Young-MacNab can lead you to him if 'tis urgent. The grouse, pheasant, and partridge will be hatching soon, and what with all the fuss and being short-staffed, one man has to do the work of ten or there'll be no harvest come autumn," explained Mackie.

"Short-staffed?" questioned Alex.

"Aye, and if you'll be sitting down instead of pacing and snarling like a pent-up wildcat, I'll be feeding you and telling you all."

Alex sat with ill grace at the opposite end of the table from Ian, who stared at him sadly for a few moments and then quietly left the room.

"And where might you be running off to? You have na

finished," fussed Mackie to the closed door. "Is there still ill will between you two lads?" she asked, placing a plate of food in front of Alex.

"We're not lads," answered Alex curtly.

"Then stop pouting like one," she retorted sharply.

"Short-staffed, you say?"

"Aye. Five farms left wie just old men, women, and bairns. Fathers and sons sent off to fight the Spanish in the New World."

"Makes no sense. The war was almost done last year with the taking of New France."

"When have the English ever made sense? They're happiest taking the freedom of others. 'Tis that mucker Pitt, I hear. Scared to death of us Scots is he, and well he should be. He'll drain all of Scotland of breeding fighting blood and send his misbegotten debauchers to rape our lassies, tainting and weakening our lines," ranted Mackie.

"How long has Beddington been here?"

" 'Twas scarce a month after you left after your lass. November early, I recollect," answered the old woman, running from the range to the pantry and back to the table again. "He come wie nigh on thirty of the lechers. Turned the place upside-down, they did, and what they got up to would've turned your hair white."

"Sit down, Mackie, you're making me dizzy. PLEASE SIT DOWN!" he repeated as the small, determined housekeeper bristled at his tone, smoothed her apron, and took her own sweet time at obeying him. Alex stared at her disapproving expression, waiting for her to resume, but she sat obediently with her hands neatly folded and her mouth pursed shut.

"I apologize for raising my voice to my old nurse, but I should like to be informed as to what has been happening and is happening in my own house and on my own lands."

"Nothing much. Rape, a few murders, good honest men and boys deported, families that God put together pulled asunder. . . . Oh, and a few of our bonnier lassies sent to English pleasure houses."

"Rape? Murder? Deportation? Surely you exaggerate?" exclaimed Alex.

"You know me better than that, Sir Alex," returned Mackie coldly.

"Who?"

"Who was or who did?"

"Goddamnit, no more riddles, Mackie! I'm sorry if I've ruffled your feathers, but 'tis all too much. 'Tis a sad homecoming."

Mackie softened.

"Aye, lad, it is. Remember Jeannie, the upstairs maid whose tongue never stopped awagging?"

"Aye."

"Like a midge she was, irritating keek, but no real harm in her. Just a wee bit small in the brains, that's all. She sort of asked for what she got but didna really ken what she was asking for wie her preening and wiggling. Fell for the uniform, she did. Och, she liked to be noticed by the lads, did that one, but a good lass at heart," chattered Mackie.

"So Jeannie was a flirt?" answered Alex impatiently.

"Aye, but she didna deserve such desserts."

"She was raped?"

"Aye, the animals near tore her in half."

"Did she die?"

"It might have been more merciful if she had. We got a skilly to her, the doctor having been shipped off wie the rest of our able-bodied men. Her mind has gone, and she's wie bairn. We have her hid in the attic in the south wing. Old Gran MacNab tends her. Grandson Young-MacNab has took it bad. He wants to wed Jeannie, but the lass screams at the sight of any man, and I canna say I blame her."

"And the dead?" probed Alex and at Mackie's quizzical look, added, "You mentioned a few murders?"

"There lads wie scarce hair on their chins who didna want to fight for the English king. They tried to flee wie their families. Robert, Donald, and Wee-John."

"Donald MacCauley?"

"Aye," answered Mackie. "Robert MacFarlane, too."

Lost for words, Alex punched the table.

"And there's a problem wie the wee MacFarlane lass,

Ailsa. Remember her, always skipping after you she was wie her red hair flying. She saw her pa killed and her brothers shipped off, and if that weren't enow to addle the wee bairn's brains, that fat, sotted English curr-nell tried to rape her . . . and her not even to her woman's ripening yet. We have to keep her hid wie Young-MacNab at the stables."

"Where's her mother?"

"You're forgetting Robert MacFarlane's woman died in childbirth two years back. All the farms are occupied, so to speak, by English soldiers, och, not to tend the land or the cattle but to . . . well, billet it they calls it, but I've other words for it. 'Tis a sin to take a man's wife and daughters! It fair boils my blood!"

Alex pushed his uneaten food from him. He was filled with disgust and nausea.

"How many men are there at the farms?"

"Theirs or ours?" asked Mackie.

"Both."

"About thirty at the farms, and then there's the fat curr-nell here wie his puny Captain Harris. There's more of them over at Drummonds, but I dinna ken just how many. Of ours there's none but our gillies, Old-Petey and Daft-Dougal. Then there's my own Fergus, Young-Mac-Nab, and a few toothless old men who were set to rock the little of their lives left in idleness after all their years at labor. I'm telling you they took all except the ancient and the tetched, and they dinna care for Young-MacNab's lameness."

Alex and Mackie sat in silence at the table. There were no words to comfort or reassure. Mackie blew her nose loudly, trying to shake Alex from his frozen immobility as he sat lost in bleak thoughts. His lands and home were robbed of strong, eager arms that had toiled alongside of him from the first spring planting through the golden harvest until the long, fallow winter's rest. On regaining some of his lands, he had chosen to get rid of the feudal system of strip farming, where those under his protection would have scratched out a meager hand-to-mouth existence for themselves and increased his wealth, and instead he had leased his farms in return for honest labor and a sharing of the profits. None had gone hungry under his system, and all the children had been required to go to school, only working by happily helping with the harvest.

"And the school?" he asked savagely, breaking the silence.

"The young curate had all his faculties, so was sent off wie the other men."

"So there's wee-uns in the fields?"

"Aye," answered Mackie softly, knowing his abhorrence of child labor, having seen bairns no more than five crawling out of the Ayrshire mines, bent and choking like old men, and just as young at the Falkirk Iron Foundry with their spindly, rickety legs scarred by burns that would never heal for the rest of their mercifully short lives. She stared at Alex's sculpted features, sadly recognizing the hard, bitter look she'd first seen close his young face ten years before, when he'd returned from the New World carrying the brittle, wasted body of his father. A fifteen-year-old boy drained of youth, compassion, and joy had returned in place of the gentle, mischievous, golden-haired lad of before.

"Dinna let it taint your humanity. Dinna let it feed on you, closing your eyes, Master Alex. Dinna let it make you cruel and unfeeling again," she pleaded. " 'Tis times like this we need the warmth of each other."

But Alex seemed unaware of her presence as he sat as though encased in cold steel, his face hard and unyielding. Mackie wiped her eyes and stood.

" 'Tain't no use crying in our porridge. There's plenty to be done. How's our Lady Cameron?"

"Hopefully sleeping."

" 'Twill do her good."

"She's locked herself in wie her hound. After last night and all you've been telling me I'll take no chances with that Beddington."

"Why? What happened last night?"

"Nothin, 'twas a miracle . . . and Ian Drummond again," he added savagely.

" 'Tis no time to be feuding wie loyal friends. Seems you and Master Ian best mend your bridges and put your heads together, no matter how much pride is to be swallowed. He canna help loving her no more than the rest of us. But that wee lass chooses you, remember that," chattered the round housekeeper, but Alex was gone. She stared around at her empty kitchen, and her shoulders sagged despondently.

"And I thought the bad times were over. Seems they are beginning all over again."

CHAPTER FIVE

For five days Cameron paced the floor of the red bed-chamber. She was ready to explode. The long, gray boredom had been intermittently broken by Mackie bustling in, out of breath, with trays of food. From the window she'd watch Alex riding across the fields in the bright spring sunlight. He had informed her of the situation at Glen Aucht, but even her most eloquent pleading had not moved him when it came to her request to be allowed out of the room. Each minute of her confinement stretched interminably, and she found herself longing for Mackie's visits, but irritation gnawed, and she found she could be barely civil to the loving, round woman. Mackie herself was adamant about Cameron staying where she was put, and no amount of wheedling, cajoling, or temper tantrums would budge her.

Cameron stared out the window, her untouched lunch beside her. "I'll not be a prisoner any longer," she resolved suddenly to her hound, Torquil, who opened one lazy eye for a second and thumped his heavy tail. " 'Tis spring. 'Tis a beautiful day. We'll race across the land and shake off the cobwebs!" she sang, staring over the shimmering expanse of the Firth of Forth that winked, reflecting the sun. The old dog slumped lower and looked at her balefully, showing no enthusiasm for the proposed excursion.

" 'Twill do no good to look at me like that, you silly beastie. 'Tis time you shook the cold, long winter out of your creaky old bones," she declared merrily, flinging open the doors of the wardrobe in the dressing room. The row upon row of maidenly, sedate gowns were like a splash of cold water dampening her sunny mood. She sat on the floor, numbly staring at the pastel, frilly dresses as the realization dawned. How could she have forgotten? She was supposed to be the Lady Sinclair! Visions of herself simpering as she poured tea and indulged in polite, empty chitchat, dressed in the minty green, flashed through her head. Sewing old adages on samplers gowned in the gauzy pink. Arranging cut flowers to die in vases in the rosebud-sprigged muslin. Tinkling away at the spinet in the cloud of white frothy lace. She savagely kicked the door shut, hiding the confining, hated clothes from view. She sat cross-legged on the bed as an idea germinated.

"I am the Lady Sinclair," she stated resolutely. "I will not be kept locked up in my own house!"

Twenty minutes later Cameron surveyed herself in the looking glass. Something didn't look quite right. Forsaking the abhorrent, strangling undergarments, she had managed to somehow hook herself into a dress of pale green. She had no idea whether it was a morning, afternoon, or evening dress, being only concerned that it was the right way around. She studied herself more closely. What was wrong? She looked like a child, she decided. She was not sophisticated or haughty enough. Rummaging through the dressing-table drawer, she found hair combs and set about trying to pile her thick, raven hair on top of her head. Half an hour later Cameron was in tears. No matter how hard she tried, all she could create was a monstrous, messy bird's nest. Hearing Mackie's laborious tread approaching, Cameron stuffed the discarded garments into the wardrobe and shut the door. She then dived into bed, pulled the covers up to her neck and closed her eyes. Mackie tapped softly at the door.

"Miss Cameron? Miss Cameron?" The doorknob rattled.

"What is it, Mackie? I'm sleeping," called Cameron, realizing she would have to get out of the bed to slide back the bolt.

"Sorry, my pet, I'll be back later," puffed Mackie out of breath.

Cameron lay still, feeling guilty for the old woman's long, fruitless climb up the stairs. She listened to her footsteps receding. What was the use? She could never look like a real lady. Her plan of regally walking down the stairs as though she owned the place would not work. She stood once again before the glass eyeing herself critically. She looked absurdly young and messy, she decided. Maybe she could pass for a maid if she tore the lace flounces off the dress, and tied something around her waist for an apron.

A few minutes later Cameron carefully slid back the heavy bolt and peered down the long corridor. There was not a sound. She smoothed the makeshift apron that she'd fashioned out of a pillowcase, took a deep breath, and ran fleetly on bare feet to the back stairs. After listening intently, she tiptoed down the wide, shiny steps, carefully keeping one hand on the precarious turban she had fashioned to hide her luxurious raven hair. Soot from the fireplace was smeared up her arms, across the dress, and all over her face, but for all her ingenuity she displayed two very pink feet.

On the first-floor landing she quietly opened the door and looked along the corridor to where the English colonel was housed in the master suite of rooms. Not hearing a sound and assuming the soldiers would be lunching at such an hour, she stole along the quiet corridor, not willing to be seen in the kitchen where the back stairs ended. Her heart thudded as she neared the central staircase. From below she could hear gruff men's voices. She crouched down and looked through the carved bannisters and, not seeing any sign of life in the spacious central hall, lithely flew down the stairs. The rumble of voices came from the library, and her curiosity got the better of her. After looking both ways she pressed her ear against the solid-oak door.

"I have yet to see a sign of this elusive wife of yours," bellowed Beddington.

"I have informed you on countless occasions that she is indisposed and we fear it may be catching. Several lesions have erupted that might be the pox," returned Alex's voice evenly. "Unfortunately it seems our doctor was transported, and so there is nothing we can do."

"Transported? He enlisted willingly," barked Beddington.

"With your permission, sir, I should again like to inquire as to your plans for my estate, myself, my wife, and those under my protection?" demanded Alex civilly.

"You do not have my permission!" returned Beddington sneeringly. "Is there news yet of the *Edna Rae*, Drummond?"

"No, sir," answered Ian's voice tonelessly.

"Drat! That ship should have arrived at Crail by now," cursed the fat colonel. Cameron was so intent on listening, she realized too late that the Englishman's voice had neared the door. Just in time she leaped back and turned around as the door was opened abruptly. Her mad dash across the marble floor was halted.

"You, girl, stop!" ordered Harris's nasally whine. Cameron debated running for it, but not knowing what lay behind each of the doors in front of her she skidded to a halt, her head bent staring at her feet and wringing her hands in her skirts.

"I think she was listening at the door, sir," volunteered the puny man.

"Come here, wench!" barked Beddington.

Cameron didn't move, just stood hanging her head, wishing she knew where Alex and Ian stood but afraid to look up, knowing how conspicuous were her bright green eyes.

Alex stared at his wife, recognizing her lithe, young body despite the soot and the strange assortment of clothes. Cameron didn't move. She kept her eyes on the floor as Beddington pompously walked around and around her.

"A tasty young morsel this. Let's see what she looks like," salivated the fat colonel, his pink, plump hand reaching to pull up her skirts. Cameron started twitching and jerking as though she was palsied, emitting a high-pitched insane laugh. Colonel Beddington backed off in horror, and Ian Drummond stifled a laugh at Cameron's quick ingenuity. Alex's face was stony with rage. Taking advantage, Cameron fleetly ran down the corridor to the kitchens.

"Who was that insane child?" spluttered Beddington. "I've not seen her before."

" 'Twas Tetched-Tilly, sad case," volunteered Ian when Alex didn't answer. "She's usually locked up, isn't that right, Major Sinclair?"

"Aye," managed Alex, his hands itching to get on his errant wife.

"She can be dangerous wie a knife at the full moon," Ian elaborated. "I think it best one of us who know her contain her, sir."

Beddington stared suspiciously from Ian's face to Alex's, but neither young man showed any emotion.

"Harris, go find her," he ordered. "You two will keep me company at luncheon, which I hope is ready."

"But, sir . . ." stammered Harris.

Cameron flew across the kitchen, not heeding Mackie's startled gasp, and outside to the cobbled yard, intent on the stables where she hoped to find her black stallion, Torquod. All thought of her near-escape and Alex's intense anger were forgotten in her desire for an exhilarating gallop along the coastline of the firth to sweep away the mustiness of the five days without a breath of freedom.

Young-MacNab was at that very moment trying to lead the proud stallion to a nearby meadow. Also unused to confinement, he pranced and skittered on the slippery cobblestones. Without a change in pace, Cameron leaped upon his high, glossy back in one lithe movement, loosing the makeshift turban from her head and releasing the cloud of shining jet-black hair. The horse reared, throwing the slight youth backward, and Torquod and Cameron were off. Young-MacNab sat bewildered, staring in amazement at the wild sight of the small figure who sat with skirts pulled to her waist, exhibiting bare legs upon the tall, broad back of the racing stallion. Mackie, Fergus, and Daft-Dougal clustered at the kitchen door, silently staring after them.

" 'Tis Tetched-Tilly, you must catch her. 'Tis the colonel's orders!" shrilled a high-pitched voice. The three old people blocking the door turned as one and looked in amazement at Captain Harris jumping up and down impotently.

Cameron was at one with her horse, which flew like the wind, racing out the pent-up frustrations of the past days. She was blind to the full, blossoming glory of the spring and the small children and bent old people that toiled laboriously along the long, brown furrows of the fields that should have been showing green. She was oblivious to the small troupe of redcoats who halted and watched, lecherously admiring her naked limbs and flowing hair. They sat on their horses, stunned at such an apparition, before raising a whoop of delight and kicking their mounts into giving chase. Their raucous voices and the thundering hooves penetrated Cameron's senses. She stared behind her and, at seeing the band of soldiers pursuing, leaned over Torquod's neck, giving him his head.

There was a small, secluded cove where Cameron used to hide away, swimming naked in the waters of the Forth as she had done as a child in the cold waters off the coast of Cape Wrath. It was a tranquil, hidden inlet, unfortunately without the seals of her childhood home but with the same nostalgic, plaintive cries of the gulls. To this haven Cameron headed, leaving the redcoats far behind. She purposefully passed the hidden entrance, keeping on the well-worn path before doubling back and carefully guiding her horse through the thick underbrush of prickly gorse. Horse and rider stood silently as the noisy group of whooping soldiers galloped past, and then she quietly walked him down to the peace of the little cove.

"Well, Harris?" burped Beddington with his mouth full, leaning back from the table and fixing the thin, nervous captain with apoplectic eye.

"She got away, sir," stammered Harris.

"Can't you do anything?" roared the irate fat man, letting fly particles of food and saliva into the captain's face. "You can't even manage to catch a half-wit child! That's the second time, Harris! The second time! What are you good for?"

"I don't know, sir. But she did have a horse . . ."

"Enough of your excuses! Get out of my sight, your cowardly yellow face is putting me off my luncheon!" bellowed Beddington, stuffing his mouth with more food. "Get out!" At another barrage of half-chewed victuals Harris fled the room. Ian and Alex exchanged a noncommittal look.

"Who is this lunatic child?" demanded the fat man of Alex.

"Just a willful, lunatic child, sir," answered Alex evenly. "There are many caused by rape, hunger, poverty, and maltreatment," he added cryptically.

"And interbreeding," interjected the colonel pointedly. "What can be expected from such a barbaric country?"

"Quite, sir," agreed Ian, not wishing to rile the man when Alex remained silent.

"But this particular insane brat, Milly—"

"Tilly," corrected Ian. "Tetched-Tilly."

"I want to see her. I have a suspicious nature, and I smell a rat."

"Aye, so do I," agreed Ian ironically. "But I dinna think we'll see her for a while, sir. She seems to have run away. She has before, and sometimes 'tis months before she's seen again. She's a will-o'-the-whisp, sir. Bairn of the wee folk."

"Wee folk!" expostulated Beddington. "That pagan drivel! You believe all that claptrap, Drummond?"

"Of course not, but the simple people do, and they fear Tetched-Tilly. They feed her and gie her clothes so as not to anger the wee folk. 'Tis said she has the power, sir," improvised Ian.

"What power?"

"The power, sir," parried Ian at a loss to come up with a sufficiently frightening thing to deter Beddington.

"The power to bring painful death," volunteered Alex with relish. "The power to bring about a living death," he added maliciously.

"Living death?"

"Aye, to a man the loss of his manhood is such, is it not?" drawled Alex cryptically.

Beddington attempted to cross his obese thighs and avoided Alex's eyes.

"Would you like me to try to fetch her back, sir?" offered Ian helpfully. "I can't promise I can find her, for 'tis said she flies with the wind and none can catch her."

Beddington pushed his large belly back from the table and stared from one young Scot to the other as he noisily chewed. Both men stared impassively back.

"I have the distinct, the decided, the absolute impression . . . idea . . . notion that you, Major Sinclair, and you, Major Drummond, are playing with me . . . toying with me . . . trying to make an idiot of me."

Alex stood dispassionately, inwardly cursing Ian's over-active imagination and his small part in embellishing the myth of Tetched-Tilly. If Beddington started asking the staff about such a person, the fat would surely be in the fire as neither he nor Ian had had an opportunity to spread the fable. He would have been much reassured to know that Mackie's keen ear was pressed to the door. The silence ticked on as the colonel stared from one to the other. The tension was broken by Mackie bustling in without the briefest of knocks.

"What is it?" snapped Beddington with irritation at the little round woman's agitation as she tried to clear the table, emitting loud sobs and gasps.

"Oh, sir!" cried Mackie, collapsing in a chair and crossing herself hurriedly. " 'Tis Tetched-Tilly, she's been seen again. She just flew through the house and over the firth like a bat." Alex avoided Ian's eyes. "It means a death, sir. Each time there's a death," she added, hauling herself to her feet and stacking the platters noisily.

"Enough of this pagan superstition!" howled Beddington, unnerved. He stood with difficulty and waddled from the room. "Harris? Harris?" he roared.

Mackie, Alex, and Ian eyed each other. Ian opened his mouth to speak, but Alex stopped him by silently shaking his head and putting a finger to his mouth. Mackie noisily cleared the table, the clatter of platters covering her whispered words.

"I knew it would happen. You canna lock such a wild and free spirit up. She were good, Master Alex . . . tried so hard, she did. Fergus dinna think she'd last two days cooped up so," she hissed pleadingly, trying to soften Alex's stern expression, but he curtly turned on his heels and quit the room.

"Will she return, you think?" whispered Ian, also clattering plates in case someone eavesdropped.

"I hope so," returned Mackie quietly. " 'Tis no use sending any to find her. And if she returns, she can move in the shadows so none can see."

Alex paced the red carpet of their bedchamber, also knowing there was no point in following Cameron. He suspected Beddington would have him followed, and such an action would endanger her more. He paced, cursing her

RIDE OUT THE STORM 73

recklessness. He knew how hard it was for her to remain hidden in the house, and each night, however late or riled from Beddington's sadistic baitings, he'd attempted to come to her with love, joy, and hope, their two hungry young bodies making up for the day's long separation. Now his anger at her disobedience melded with the furious impotence of his situation at having his domain ruled and abused by the English colonel and his men. He had a very good notion as to where Cameron was, and yet he had to bide his time, hoping she'd return. He flung himself on their bed and pictured her floating in the choppy waters of the firth, her long black hair streaming behind her. He relaxed and indulged himself in the sensuous picture, but then sat up angrily as he thought of the countryside teeming with lecherous redcoats. There was nothing he could do, and he prayed that she would use her common sense and natural instincts in returning unobtrusively to the house. Would she return? He was worried.

Cameron lay in the water, feeling the gentle lapping cleansing and relaxing her. She stared at the sky, feeling herself floating and soaring with the swooping gulls in the clouds. She delighted in the gentle rocking of the waves that calmed her naked body, easing it of the gray tightness that had encased her. Her horse cropped the young spring grass under the shade of a tree. She floated her mind away from all the problems, soothed to a peaceful nothingness, lulled by the water, clouds, and gulls. When the iciness seeped into her senses, goose-bumping her skin, she turned on her belly and swam like an otter to the shore, where she lay on a sunbaked rock, closing her eyes and submerging herself in the warm, golden haze that filtered through her eyelids. No thought of Glen Aucht or the consequences of her disobedience penetrated her mind. She was absorbed in her own precious freedom, in harmony with the natural elements.

The day wore on, and the dinner table was being set in the dining hall. Ian and Alex stood stiffly and tensely in the library as Beddington plied himself with whiskey and talked endlessly and insultingly, trying to cause Alex to lose his temper. In the kitchen Mackie was sharp-tongued to all around, so that soon a heavy silence fell, punctuated only by the clatter and banging of pots and pans.

A loud, noisy shouting was heard, and fifteen soldiers stamped into the central hall.

"Here are our dinner guests now," pronounced Beddington, waving a hand to Harris, who opened the door of the library to the redcoats, who suddenly became silent and shy. They filed into the room, stood at attention, and saluted Beddington, who lolled obscenely, his tunic buttons bursting across his opulence.

"At ease, men. Relax," he proclaimed. " 'Tis a social evening we'll be having. All you can eat or drink. Help yourself." The men shuffled uneasily. " 'Tis a tavern we're in. Undo your buttons and doff your hats and let's make merry," he urged, undoing the buttons of his own uniform. Still the men hesitated. " 'Tis an order!" barked Beddington, and there was an immediate rush to the sideboard, where generous portions of whiskey were thrown back.

Ian and Alex stood watching as the handsome room was turned upside down. Within an hour every soldier was jacketless and glassy-eyed as filthy jokes were bandied about.

"Harris, go and see what is taking so long. We'll starve to death at this rate," slurred Beddington to the thin captain, who staggered from the room. "And we need all our energy for the after-dinner entertainment, don't we, men?" he added, and a chorus of filthy epithets agreed with him.

Alex frowned at Ian inquiringly, wondering what was planned, but Ian just shrugged.

The evening wore into night at an unbearably slow pace for Alex, who stood stoically, forced to endure the abuse of his home and servants. At the dinner table Beddington and the fifteen junior officers ate like pigs, spilling and swilling, throwing food at and insulting Mackie, Fergus, and Young-MacNab, who served them impassively.

"Ain't there no females beside that old fatty?" yelled one drunk soldier, throwing a chicken bone at Mackie.

"The old fatty hides them all away," answered Beddington jovially. "They're all old and toothless and need to be hid. Not a decent piece of meat anywhere in this house. That's why you've orders to have some brought along for dessert."

Alex stiffened. So that was the plan. The nearest large town was too far, so prostitutes were not the company Beddington was expecting. It had to be the girls and women at the farms.

"We saw a rare piece today atop a great black stallion, riding like the wind . . . naked under a whispy dress of green that flew out showing all she had," volunteered one soldier, freezing Alex's blood and pushing out all thoughts of how to stop the rape of innocent women and children.

"Aye, we took after her, but she disappeared into thin air," joined in another.

"Tetched-Tilly!" cried Harris excitedly. "Sir? Sir? It was Tetched-Tilly."

"Wouldn't mind being tetched by her," laughed another lecherously.

Alex clenched his fists to his sides, relieved that Cameron managed to elude them but furious at the implications and salacious suggestions that were being thrown back and forth across the messy table.

Terrified screams penetrated the raucous feast and the thick carved door.

"Dessert has arrived," shouted Beddington, banging his spoon against a silver tankard. "Major Sinclair, throw open the doors!"

Alex stood motionless.

"That is an order, Sinclair, which, if you choose to disobey in front of so many witnesses, would mean your court-martial. Which in turn would mean the confiscation of your lands, if in fact they are your lands, a highly debatable point. Which in turn would mean your deportation or death in front of a firing squad," the English colonel crowed with great relish.

Ian, seeing his lifetime friend's dilemma, made a motion toward the door, breaking the inertia that held Alex, who put out a strong arm to stop him. Alex strode evenly to the door, opened it, and stared out with horror at the throng of frightened women and girls. Some cowed, weeping, and others stood with their eyes empty of all expression. Bile flooded his throat as he saw and recognized lassies of no more than ten or eleven. Children he had played with when they were small babies, was godfather to. His people, who had put their trust in him. He stood, his body barring them from the soldiers in the dining room. What good were his lands or his life? He could not allow these gentle, vulnerable people to be used so. His decision made, he turned back into the dining hall, determined to confront the colonel, but was knocked against the heavy paneled wall by the rush of greedy, drunken soldiers, who swarmed over the fragile, shivering women and children. He reached for his saber and was withdrawing it from the scabbard when he was hit across the temple. He fought the waves of blackness, bracing himself against the wall, but slowly slid down until he lay slumped. Ian stood over Alex, looking down at his unconscious friend as Beddington waddled up.

"I'm afraid he's had a wee drop too much," improvised Ian, hastily hiding the wine bottle he'd hit Alex with. "Hit his head on that jutting piece of molding by the look of it," he added as a thin trickle of blood ran down the brown, chiseled cheek.

Beddington laughed nastily and staggered by into the marble hall. Ian watched him go, fighting the temptation to unsheath his own sword and plunge it into the fat back. The door shut, closing out the sight of the soldiers hungrily and brutally slaking their drunken lust, muffling the hoarse rutting grunts and pitiful cries, Ian's stomach heaved, and he was filled with impotent rage, knowing well Beddington's penchant for children and voyeurism.

"I'll help you get him to his room," offered a gruff voice, and Ian shook his head to clear the mist of red rage and looked into Fergus's weather-beaten face.

"Is there nothing we can do?" cried young Drummond in pain.

"You saved his life," answered the old man gruffly, his eyes mirroring Ian's own agony. "There's naught to do but bide our time. 'Tis getting worse, the *Edna Rae* has been sighted."

"What is the *Edna Rae?*"

Ian and Fergus stared down at Alex, who groggily tried

to focus his eyes. Fergus gave an apprehensive glance at
the door to the hall through which the muffled cries could
be heard. Ian, understanding his concern, bent to help Alex
to his feet, not wanting his dazed friend to risk his life
again trying to interfere. Together Fergus and Ian helped
Alex to the kitchen, where the heavy door closed, cutting
off all sounds from the rest of the house. Mackie bustled
around, clucking her concern at the blood on Alex's face.

Sitting at the kitchen table, submitting to the housekeeper's ministrations, Alex tried to concentrate, although
his head pounded painfully.

"It seems Beddington has an investment in a vessel
called the *Edna Rae,* deals in flesh," explained Ian savagely.

"Healthy young virgins sold to the houses in London, not
so pretty and slightly used sold as bonded servants to the
Colonies using some trumped-up charge . . . and some
young lads to pander to the tastes of some filthy Cata-
mites," ranted Mackie.

"Here, drink this, lad," growled Fergus, handing Alex a
glass of brandy. Alex drained the burning liquid and sat
trying to marshal his senses. As the memory of the frightened women and children tore into his brain, he stood
with an oath.

"Whoa, lad, sit a wee time until you've your color back.
That's a nasty knock you took," cautioned Mackie. Alex
swayed, pointing in the direction of the hall. He tried to
talk but he seemed to have no control over his tongue, and
the room span at a dizzying rate. With a quick jerk of his
head, Fergus motioned Ian to grab Alex's waving arm, and
taking the other one, they caught him as he lost consciousness again.

"My God, how hard did I hit him?" exclaimed Ian, his
face as white as Alex's with the thought he'd seriously injured his friend.

" 'Twas not you, lad, so dinna fash. I put a wee drop of
one of Daft-Dougal's potions into the brandy. He'll sleep
it off by dawn and not get himself killed trying to take on
twenty men. There's more than a wee drop in them rutting animals, though, of a different nature entirely. There'll
not be any getting it up unless they abstained from the

spirits . . . and we kept our eyes peeled, did we not, Mrs. MacDonald?" said Fergus.

"What was it?" asked Ian incredulously.

"Wilting mixture, Daft-Douglas calls it."

"From the noises I heard I dinna think it worked too well," replied Ian bitterly.

"Aye, but I'm hoping 'tis just the exertion of trying we were hearing. Hopefully soon they'll be sleeping and we can clean up the hall of the rubbish and tend the lassies and hide them in the caves, where they'll not be found," planned Fergus. "But first to get the young master into his bed and out of harm's reach."

With Alex tucked peacefully in bed in the red chamber, Fergus, Ian, Mackie, Daft-Dougal, and Old-Petey quietly listened at the door. All they could hear was whimpers, stifled sobs, and snores. Opening the door quietly, they stared in amazement at the sprawled, unconscious soldiers, some asleep with terrified, wide-eyed women still pinned under them, afraid to move for fear of waking the drunken men.

Gently and efficiently Mackie herded the women and girls into the kitchen, clucking her disapproval over the torn dresses that they clutched around them, trying pitifully to hide their nakedness.

Cameron sat on a rock staring up at the crescent of the moon. She shivered as a sharp breeze cut through the thin material of her tattered green gown and hugged her knees. She knew she would have to return and face Alex's wrath but procrastinated, not wanting to give up one little bit of her unfettered time. Her horse whinnied a warning, and she froze, straining her ears to hear through the thick blanket of night. All seemed still, too still, she realized. There was no sound of the scramblings of the nocturnal animals. She noiselessly climbed the steep bank to the cliff road and put her ear to the ground and felt the vibration of many feet. She shrank back into the shadows as bobbing blurrs of light-colored clothes appeared through the darkness and the shuffling of feet could be heard. A child cried and was hushed quickly. Cameron stared in amazement as the assortment of old men, women, and children came abreast of her hiding place.

"Fergus?" she called as she recognized his long, lean stride. At her appearance coming suddenly from the shadows some of the women and children shrank back and whimpered in alarm.

" 'Tis all right, 'tis the mistress," comforted Old-Petey.

"What's happening?" asked Cameron.

" 'Tis a long story, and you're needed at the house," answered Fergus shortly."

"But I want to help," she protested.

"Then hightail it back to your man while the English muckers sleep off their excesses. Mackie's waiting for you wie young Drummond."

"But—"

"No room for your buts, your man is hurt and needs you," returned Fergus, striding from her carrying a small child. Cameron stood bewildered, watching the sorry band disappear along the coast road until they were swallowed up by the night. Her pulses hammered painfully. Alex was hurt? How badly? She shook her head trying to get her racing thoughts in order, and then her piercing whistle penetrated the night. The black stallion whinnied and trotted up the steep bank to her. Entwining her hand in his thick mane, she leaped onto his bare back and, kicking with her small bare feet, urged him into a frantic gallop toward the lighted windows of Glen Aucht.

CHAPTER SIX

Alex awoke the following morning with a blinding headache. He lay orienting himself for a few moments, and the events of the previous day flooded into his bruised brain. He sat up with a curse and the sight of Cameron sleeping peacefully beside him fanned his fury further. How could she lie there, seeming so guileless and innocent? He longed to shake her awake violently but didn't trust his self-control. He would either strangle her or mount her, pounding out his helpless rage. He tore his eyes away and got out of the bed. He kept his eyes averted as he hurriedly threw on his clothes. He quit the room purposefully, avoiding looking at her as though just the sight of her might make him soften, make him vulnerable.

Cameron watched him sadly, knowing she had caused the rift between them. As the door shut after him, she sat up to call him back, but the words died in her throat as she heard the door firmly locked from the outside, the key extracted, and his strong, purposeful tread echoing down the hall.

She sat shaking with rage, all thought of apology gone. How could he lock her up like an animal? It had been bad enough having been ordered to lock herself in, but this was inexcusable. He didn't trust her! She pushed away the knowledge that she had abused his trust as she pummeled the bed with her small fists.

Cameron had ruefully crept into their chamber from the kitchen the night before. Mackie had made her eat, reassuring her that Alex was not badly hurt. Young-MacNab had sat silently with a small, red-haired child curled sleeping in his arms. Cameron grew angrier at the memory. She had entered the kitchen as they were talking, but they had clammed up at her appearance, and no amount of questioning had got her any acceptable answers.

"Where were Old-Petey and Fergus talking the people?" she had demanded.

"To safety," had been the laconic answer.

"How did Alex get hurt?" she had probed.

"Bumped his head." Finally she had walked out of the kitchen door to the central hallway against Mackie's protestations, and there a sight had met her eyes. Men lay in various stages of undress all over the marble-slabbed floor. Some flat on their backs with their limp members exposed, others on their stomachs with bare buttocks and trews pulled to their knees. At first she had gaped in horror, but curiosity overcame her when she realized that they all lay in a drunken stupor. She had walked around, staring with undisguised interest. Mackie hissed at her from the kitchen door, shaking her head with disapproval, but Cameron ignored her. She knew something was being kept from her, so she'd find out for herself. She slowly and methodically went from one soldier to the next, staring at all the exposed male parts, marveling at the assortment. Mackie could not contain herself longer, she scurried over to Cameron and grabbed her arm.

" 'Tis not decent!" she scolded.

"Why are they so?" demanded Cameron, pulling her arm free.

" 'Tis not for your ears or eyes," hissed Mackie.

"Look at the fat colonel," insisted Cameron wickedly. "His belly is so fat, he couldna find his tail." She giggled at the sight of Beddington slumped asleep on an ottoman, his hand hidden beneath his monstrous stomach.

Mackie's hand itched to slap Cameron's mischievous face as she told herself that she had best tell Cameron the truth. "Come along up to your man and I'll wipe the smile off your face with the goings-on of tonight," she whispered.

Cameron sat in bed pondering all Mackie's furtive whisperings of rape, a word she knew but could not envision. To her, mating meant excitement and great joy. No man but Alex had ever taken her, and so there was no horror or fear of sex. What woman would not want it? she wondered, never having witnessed or been threatened by enforced mating. She let her mind think back on entering the bedroom and watching Alex sleep, lit by the light of the fire. She had gently kissed his bruised temple, and had lain beside him, pressing her smooth body against his hard, muscled one, but he hadn't stirred. She had played with him, and there had been no reaction. She had lain awake long into the night puzzling over the phenomenon. It had been the first time she had failed to get a response from him, waking or asleep.

"Why will they not share the troubles wie me?" she cried bitterly. "They keep me locked up like a useless bairn," she railed, causing her old hound to raise his head and stare at her woefully. "Well, I'll not be locked up. I'll find something to do about it all," she promised, jumping out of bed and flinging open the wardrobe. A row of empty hangers greeted her. She frantically searched the room and the adjoining dressing room to find not one stitch of her clothes. None of Alex's were there, either. When her flood of fury subsided so that she could think rationally, her eyes lit once more on the pillowcases. She'd fashion a tunic. Finding a manicure set in the bureau drawer, she set about unpicking the stitching to make head- and armholes. She stood before the glass surveying herself. The garment barely covered her bottom, but she shrugged, showing even more of herself.

"I dinna care if you don't, old beastie," she laughed. Cameron opened the window and looked down to the ground from her third-story prison. The distance was too great to jump without risking serious injury, but a narrow parapet ran just below the sill to the corner of the building, where an enormous chestnut tree spread its candle-flowered branches. She carefully stepped off the sill to the narrow ledge. Torquil growled his concern.

"Hush yourself, you timorous beastie, you'll make me fall," she hissed, finding the weather-beaten stone cold and too smooth to find a secure handhold. Carefully Cameron inched her way to the corner, passing several windows with some trepidation, but to her good fortune the rooms had been uninhabited. Reaching the corner, she stood poised, planning her leap into space.

From her bedchamber window the tree's branches had seemed to brush the very house, but now she realized it had been an illusion. They, in fact, fell short by several feet, and the nearest limb tips were too fragile to bear her weight safely. As she stood wondering as to the sanity of launching herself into the air to either smack into the tree or the distant ground, she remembered the empty rooms she'd passed. For a moment she was in awe of her own stupidity. It took her breath away. Blindly she inched her way back to the nearest casement. Balancing herself against the arched stonework, she pressed the latch, and to her relief the window opened. She agilely jumped into the room, closing the window quickly behind her. She turned and surveyed her surroundings. She was in a children's playroom. All sorts of dusty dolls sat neatly, patiently waiting. Cameron looked in wonder at the delicately, daintily dressed china dolls, not daring to touch. A whole shelf of soldiers stood at attention like a miniature army. Each figure intricately painted and holding microscopic swords. Some mounted on horseback, some pulling cannons, but each perfectly in proportion. This had to be where Alex had played as a little boy with his sisters. Two much-used tattered dolls sat at a table in front of tiny dishes, their faces worn and devoid of paint from too much washing and loving, their hair sparse from too much fashioning and brushing. One sported a bandage where the stuffing from the soft, cuddled body had leaked through from too much loving play. Cameron felt a wave of sadness for the two little girls who had died from cholera along with their mother before casting their toys aside. She herself had never had such playthings in the cold castle of her childhood, and with the fascination and puzzlement at the contents of the room, she forgot her reason for being there as she explored each shelf and cupboard. A gaily painted dappled rocking horse stared at her from a corner, as if to dare her to ride it. She gently patted the cold, shiny head before climbing on its back, but it moved with such a protesting, creaking scream that she quickly leaped off and stilled its movement.

"One day I'll have children to bring you all back to life," she whispered before opening a closet in the adjoining room. It was filled with children's clothes. Tiny dresses and little boy's trews and jackets. Excitedly she searched the row of boy's clothes from Alex's first baby dresses through to the rugged clothes of when she estimated he was eleven or twelve, and selected trews, shirt, and jerkin.

Cameron once again surveyed herself critically in the dusty, tarnished mirror. Except for the mane of hair, she looked like a passable boy. The trews fit snugly, molding to her lithe body. The shirt was a little snug across the chest, but with the leather jerkin she looked as flat as a youth. A pair of knee boots completed the ensemble.

" 'Tis just a lend," she explained to one of the dolls as she gently untied a faded ribbon from the much-abused hair. "Besides, you have plenty more," she added, patting the elaborate, overdone hairstyle.

With her hair tied back and her body swathed in a black riding cape, Cameron peered furtively down the expanse of shiny corridor and, seeing the coast was clear, quietly made her way to the back stairs.

Just outside the kitchen she stopped and listened to the clatter of pots. She peered around the corner and watched Mackie sitting wtih Old Gran MacNab, who dunked bread in her tea and slurped it into her toothless mouth.

"There's no change, then, Granny?" asked the house-keeper.

"Nay," responded the old lady.

"Who's wie her? You've surely not left her to wander around out of her puir empty head?" fussed Mackie, setting up a breakfast tray.

"Nay, Old-Petey's wie her. The lass is sleeping, so she'll no ken 'tis a man . . . and the door's barred."

Were they talking about her? wondered Cameron. Sleeping with the door barred sounded so, but there'd been no old man in her room.

"Best get back to her afore she wakes and screams blue murder at seeing Old-Petey. I'll carry the tray for you," offered Mackie.

"You're not much younger than I, Mrs. MacDonald. Get a young lass," carped the old crone.

"Would, but they're all gone. Besides, I want to see how the chit is," answered Mackie, picking up the tray and advancing toward Cameron's hiding place. Cameron quickly raced up to the second floor, pushed open the landing door, and hid behind it. She crouched, looking fearfully toward the suite of rooms that housed Colonel Beddington, hoping he still lay in the central hall on the ottoman.

"Hurry up . . . hurry up," raced her heart at the painfully slow progress of the two old women. It seemed an eternity as they labored up the stairs to the second floor, and when they reached the landing, Cameron stifled a cry of vexation to hear them say, "I need a breather, I do."

"Aye, my puir old bones!" Whereupon both Mackie and Old Gran MacNab leaned against the wall of the stairs and gasped for breath. Cameron felt trapped and was certain that any moment the colonel's door would fly open and she'd be caught. After what seemed to be an extravagantly long "breather" the two women resumed their panting ascent. Cameron waited, listened a moment, and then opened the door and fleetly dashed down the stairs. The kitchen was empty, so she hurriedly helped herself to a wedge of bread and cheese and let herself furtively out the back door. Walking in the shade of the wall of the house, she made her way to the stables.

Young-MacNab whistled tunelessly as he mucked out the stalls and kept an eye on Ailsa-Lass, who'd refused to go to the caves with the other women and girls as she'd clung hysterically to the lean, lame youth. The red-haired child sat cuddling a pup while the other seven protested noisily, scratching against the confining slatted wall of the stall where they were housed. Cameron stepped into the stables, and the small girl screamed and let go of the dog.

"Dinna fear," comforted Cameron, scooping up the liberated puppy.

"Never you fear, Ailsa-Lass," shouted Young-MacNab, limping in, holding his rake like a spear. "Why, Miss Cameron . . . I mean, my lady, mum," he amended hurriedly.

" 'Tis just Cameron, MacNab," she laughed. "As you can see, I have na changed much," she added, spinning around to show off her boy's attire.

" 'Tis good to see you, mum," stammered the young man as the red-haired girl buried her face in his stomach and wrapped her skinny, freckled arms around him. "Ailsa-Lass, 'tis all right. 'Tis the laird's own wife, and she'll not harm you. 'Tis Robert MacFarlane's bairn, she is, mum.

Go play wie the puppy dogs, lass. They need you, remember, having lost their own ma, too," he coaxed, unwrapping her clinging arms and nudging her toward the hay. "Up you go and sit upon that bale and I'll hand you up another wee orphan to love. That's a guid lass, I dinna ken what those poor wee-uns would do without you."

"The dam is dead?" asked Cameron once the child was settled.

"Aye," returned Young-MacNab. "That English Colonel Beddington shot her for showing her teeth when he tried to touch the wee-uns. He's the De'il hisself . . . tried to ravish wee Ailsa-Lass there," he whispered.

"Ravish? . . . Rut?" inquired Cameron.

"Aye," answered MacNab, blushing to the roots of his hair and busily raking nonexistent hay.

"But she's a wee bairn. Has na even sprouted titties! 'Tis unnatural!" she exclaimed. "Och, she canna even have bled yet, 'tis agin all nature!"

Young-MacNab, unused to a woman talking so frankly about unmentionable things, could neither reply nor remove his eyes from the tips of his boots.

"I'd like to kill the man!" spat Cameron picking up one of Torquil's pups and rubbing her nose against the furry softness. She stared up at the wide-eyed, frightened girl and then climbed onto the bale and sat beside her.

"I'll sing you a song?" she comforted as the child backed away, clutching at the puppy that squealed at the painfully tight hold. "See the wee Sandy-Lass sittin' on a stane . . . Cryin' and akeenin' all the day alane. Rise up, wee Sandy-Lass, wipe your tears awa' . . . and choose the one you love the best and tak' them awa'," sang Cameron.

"I have none to love na mair," sniffled the child.

"What about the wee pups?"

"They're not of my own."

"Would you like one for your own?" asked Cameron gently.

"My very own?"

Cameron nodded. The child stared at her in amazement. "Och, aye."

"Then rise up, wee Sandy-Lass, and wipe those tears

awa', and choose the one you love the best," laughed Cameron.

"I choose the wee-un," pronounced Ailsa-Lass without hesitation.

"The wee-un! They all look big to me."

"She means the runt, mum. She ain't much smaller, but she's not as feisty as the rest. 'Tis this one, mum," offered MacNab, holding a rusty-red pup aloft.

"Her coat is the color of your hair, Ailsa-Lass," said Cameron, taking the pup from the youth's outstretched hands and placing her in the girl's lap. "Well, here she is, and what'll you call her by?"

"Maggie, mum," lisped the child.

" 'Twas their dam's name," informed the young ostler.

"Well, Maggie, meet your new mistress," said Cameron softly before springing lithely down to the stable floor. "I'd like my horse, MacNab."

"They're all out to pasture. I'll go catch him if'n he'll let me . . . if you'll keep an eye on the lass. I'm not to let her from my sight on account of the colonel, mum," explained MacNab, taking down a bridle and sidesaddle.

"I'll not need those and I'll fetch him myself," replied Cameron, disdaining the bridle and saddle. She stalked from the stable filled with rage at all she'd heard of Colonel Beddington. All that Mackie had told her of the night before she now understood by the fear in the small girl's eyes. She stared into the home pasture but only cows lazily grazed. A low whistle from the hayloft caused her to turn and see Young-MacNab waving for her attention. He pointed toward the hill that rolled away from the firth to the north. Cameron nodded her understanding and, keeping to the shadow of the fruit trees, made her way to the top meadow near the upper braeside woods. She watched Torquod gracefully cropping grass, the sun reflecting on his glossy blue-black coat. She whistled, and he whinnied in welcome, prancing and showing off to her. He butted her gently, and she laughed.

"Hey, there. What d'ye think you're up to?" shouted an angry voice. Cameron didn't turn to see, but sprang upon the great horse's back and urged Torquod to a gallop. He easily jumped the stone wall that encircled the pasture, and they took off toward the firth as two shots whistled past their ears.

"Stop, yer great lummock!" growled Fergus, knocking aside the gun aimed to take another potshot. "What's wie yer eyes, Old-Petey? 'Tis the mistress herself."

Three weather-beaten old men watched the black horse and rider until they were out of sight.

" 'Tis a fine sight," breathed Fergus, turning away.

"Dinna seem proper for the laird's wife to be gallivantin' dressed and riding astride like a man," grumbled Old-Petey.

"Och, yer just jealous," teased Daft-Dougal.

"Jealous am I? Of what?"

"Youth, that's what," cackled the old cross-eyed gillie.

"That's enow of the jabber, there's work to be done," chided Fergus as he tied the limp body of a weasel above a grouse nest. "There you are, ma grouse. Soon this futret will fester and the plump maggots drop off to feed your wee chicks. Och, there's other vermin I'd like to string up for the maggots to breed on, but I doubt the rotting carcass of a Sassanach could better another or enrich the earth."

"He should be libbed fer his unnatural lechery!" hissed Old-Petey.

"Libbed? How?" cackled Daft-Dougal. "By trying to rape bairns just proves he hasna bollox . . . or maybe just teeny weeny tit's eggs. So what's to lib?"

Ferbus shaded his eyes, looking toward the gleaming waters of the firth for sight of Cameron.

"I hope the lass'll be all right wie all them redcoats nosing around," worried Petey.

"I see'd the laird ride in that direction an hour since, ain't seen him ride back neither," comforted Dougal.

"I dinna ken if that's a blessing or not," sighed Fergus as the three old men methodically tramped the long undergrowth that bordered the woods.

As things stood, Alex did not meet up with Cameron. He returned to Glen Aucht as Mackie worriedly cleaned away the remains of the noon meal. She had been fretting for hours after taking up Cameron's breakfast and finding the room empty but for the dog. He strode into the kitchen in a foul temper. The sight of his fields lying fallow, full of tares and thistles instead of the orderly rows of thrusting green sprouts, had fanned his fury. Even the wondrous sight of the blossom-laden boughs in the orchards hadn't lightened his black mood, just weighed it down further as the festive profusion seemed jeering and mocking among the oppressive misery. He sat heavily at the kitchen table without a word of welcome as Mackie wrang her hands in her apron. Torquil, snoozing in front of the fire, raised his heavy head and thumped his great tail in welcome.

"Why's the hound here?" he demanded sharply of Mackie's back as she busily ladled a plate of stew for him. "Well?" he insisted of her as she placed the steaming bowl before him.

"Fergus was hoping you'd meet up wie her, seeing as she rode the same direction as yourself. He was just the now saying it as he ate his noon meal," chattered Mackie awkwardly.

"Meet up wie her? I locked her in and gie you the key wie strict orders to see she stayed there!" exploded Alex, crashing his fist onto the table and deriving some satisfaction from the release of a small part of the pounding fury that consumed him.

"Aye, you locked her in and gie me the key, and when I went wie her food, she wasna there . . . just her big beastie," returned the old woman feistily as she banged down a board of bread and cheese. "So I brought the beastie down and locked the door again, so if she were hiding 'twould do her no good! But she is nay there, and she were seen riding that great brute of an ungelded horse!" Mackie stood with her dimpled knuckles placed stolidly on her solid hips and glared at him, her black eyes twinkling and flashing.

"Where is she?" roared Alex.

"Up in Annie's room behind the clock!" spat Mackie sarcastically, also pleased to release some of her steaming pressure. The two glowered at each other, neither finding the right words to respond as Ailsa-Lass, dressed in trews and a jerkin, ran in tugging the pup Maggie, who objected to the leash and slid across the floor with all four paws splayed, trying to dig into the red clay tiles.

"Och, Mrs. Mackie, I need some rags. Maggie forgie her manners agin. Oooh, beg pardon, Yer Lairdship, I didna ken you was visiting the kitchen," panted the child, bobbing a difficult curtsy.

"You maun bow, Jemmy-Lad. Bow, nay curtsy. Yer a lad now, remember," laughed Mackie, collapsing into the nearest chair and giggling rather hysterically. Alex reluctantly turned his gaze from his usually sedate housekeeper and surveyed the small, red-haired child. His eyes narrowed, trying to place the boy.

"Who are you?" he barked sharply, causing the child to back away.

"There's no need to take your temper out on a wee-un," snapped Mrs. MacDonald. " 'Tis wee Ailsa MacFarlane, Robert's lass I was atellin' you of. Fergus and Young-MacNab come up wie the idea of dressing her as a lad to keep the English colonel away. She's to be called Jemmy-Lad now."

" 'Twas my own idea, if you dinna mind me saying so," returned the child. "On account of Lady Cameron, sir. She looks right fine dressed as she is, and I wanna look like her, and she gie me Maggie, sir," added the child, excitedly pulling on the rope and pulling the reluctant pup closer.

"And where is my wife?" asked Alex, trying to gentle his tone.

"I dinna ken, sir. 'Twas hours ago. She acome to the stable and gie me Maggie and sang a song to me and then went to fetch her black horse from the upper meadow, sir."

"Here's yer rags, child, now scoot," said Mackie, handing a wad of cloths to the child and pushing her out the door.

"You'd nay recognize her as the same. 'Twas Miss Cameron wrought the change in the wee-un. For months that child has been pining away, wouldna say boo to a goose. Shrinking and screaming from all but Young-MacNab, but now the sun's coming up in her eyes and her childhood's returning."

"Beddington and Harris about?"

"Nary a peek. They pulled themselves decent from the central hall and crawled to their beds, and I've not heard a sound since."

"Well, 'twere best I find my wife before the mucker rises. What direction did she take?"

"Same as yourself, so said Fergus. That's why he expected you to meet."

"And Drummond?" asked Alex savagely.

"Far as I know still abed hisself, though 'tis unusual," frowned Mackie.

"If I know him, he's up and about, and that's who Cameron has met up with." Alex stood up and whistled for Torquil.

"Come along, yer lazy beastie, let's find your mistress before she gets herself in a spot."

"Och, no, I knew it were too good to be true!" exclaimed Mackie as a bell persistently rang.

"Well, the colonel's all yours," stated Alex callously, leaving with the large dog.

"Thank you, I'm sure," muttered Mackie.

Alex strode through the yard to his horse and mounted slowly, ignoring Captain Harris, who hailed him from a second-story window.

"Sinclair! Hey there, Sinclair, the colonel wants you! Sinclair?"

Alex made no motion of hearing as he trotted his horse through the apple orchard to the firth. He rode oblivious to the beauty of the day and the activity of spring as the bees buzzed busily and the birds sang and puffed their chests, strutting to impress their would-be mates. Torquil, pulled out of his lethargy, ambled this way and that, sniffing and exploring with his great tail wagging. Keeping an even gait, Alex rode, trying to find a solution to the trouble his home and all under his protection were in from Beddington and his troops. Obviously the pompous blowhard couldn't be abided in London and so had been shipped to Scotland, but why Glen Aucht? Of all Scotland to choose from, he raged, why his lands? Was it not enough that Glen Aucht, a rather modest holding, was all that was left of the

Sinclairs' once vast estates, the northern lands from John O'Groats to the castle at Dunbeath having been confiscated after the Battle of Culloden?

Alex rode east along the coastline, keeping a leisurely pace that belied the furious pounding of his anger. About two miles from the house he reined and watched a mounted figure racing toward him. Despite his fury he could not help but appreciate the fine horsemanship and the exhilarating picture of the rider on the jet-black stallion. Cameron slowed her horse and smiled at him, her rosy, flushed cheeks causing her eyes to appear an even more brilliant green. Alex noted that her hair was wet, and her clothes seemed almost nostalgically familiar. He stared at her without speaking. Cameron covered her apprehensions at recognizing his harsh mood by smiling even more brightly.

"Good day, my lord. 'Tis fine weather we're having, is it not?"

Alex didn't trust himself to answer. He sat perfectly still, breathing deeply, trying to control his murderous rage, and glowered at her. How dare she look so beautiful? How dare she behave in such a carefree manner? Didn't she have the sensitivity to see what was happening all around? He raged inwardly. He felt like taking her slight shoulders between his large hands and shaking some sense and awareness into her, but he curbed the desire, knowing he'd also like to tumble her in the long grass and pound out some of his frustrated anger in lovemaking. It would be a sweet, savage release.

Cameron stared at his stern face, searching for some softening, some glimmer of her warm, loving Alex, but nothing changed the hard, chiseled lines. Her own fury mounted, and she angrily turned her horse away. Alex reached out and grasped her arm. Frantically she pulled Torquod's mane, trying to make him rear and shake free the iron hold, and found herself plucked easily from her mount. She lay across Alex's firmly muscled thighs, looking up rebelliously into his hard amber eyes. Neither spoke for a moment as he fought the temptation to crush her soft, pouting mouth to his, and she remembered all that he withheld and the locking of the door.

"You think me a child . . . locked me in and took all

my clothes . . . will na tell me—" she protested as he bent his head slowly and took possession of her lips. Cameron's resistance melted, and she flung her arms around his neck, curling her hungry young body around his.

"You're a willful brat, Cameron," growled Alex gruffly. "I should be tanning your hide, not making love to you."

She laughed wickedly.

"Och, here comes trouble," groaned Alex, spying another horseman approaching from the direction of Glen Aucht. "Get on your own horse," he ordered tersely. Cameron obeyed silently. " 'Tis Captain Harris, and you'll not open your mouth. You ken?"

Cameron refused to acknowledge. She fumed.

"You'll do as I say without question, Cameron! You ken?" Captain Harris bumped up, sliding all around in his saddle, and saved her from answering.

"Major Sinclair," puffed the captain. "The colonel wants to see you and Major Drummond immediately."

"I canna speak for Major Drummond, but I will return at once," responded Alex tersely, kicking his horse to a canter.

"You, boy," barked Harris to Cameron as she prepared to follow. "Find Major Drummond."

"Find him yourself, you English mucker!" she spat.

"How dare you speak to me in that manner, you insolent savage!" screamed the captain hysterically, raising his riding whip.

"Cameron!" roared Alex, hearing the exchange and turning just in time to see Harris fly out of the saddle as Cameron deftly caught the end of the whip and kicked her horse into a gallop. The man hit the ground with a sickening thud and lay winded in a soggy mud puddle. His horse, glad to be rid of such a poor, bullying rider, ambled out of reach to graze.

"Never raise a hand to me again, you English bastard, or I'll jobe yer scrapple wie this!" threatened Cameron, demonstrating as she passed her dagger across her throat. Alex took a long breath and exhaled.

"There's trouble enough wie out asking for more."

"I didna ask for it, he did!" she retorted hotly.

"I'll have him whipped!" screeched Harris, standing

shakily and trying ineffectually to brush the mud from his uniform.

"You'll do no such thing, *Captain*. You'll remember your rank and not give orders in my presence to *my* men, is that clear? Fetch the captain's horse, lad!"

"I'll do no such thing!" she protested sullenly.

"You'll not have that rank for long! You'll not be able to put on your superior airs for long!" screamed Harris. Alex stared coldly at the childish young man, who shrank from the piercing gaze.

"Fetch his horse!" he roared in a tone that brooked no argument, without moving his eyes from the thin, cowering man.

"No!" responded Cameron, kicking her horse into a gallop. Once again with lightning speed, Alex's arm shot out and stopped Cameron's mad dash as he grabbed the clothes at the back of her neck and hauled her unceremoniously to the ground. But for her litheness, she would have ended up sitting in the same puddle Captain Harris had vacated. As it was, she kept on her feet and stared furiously up at the tall figure of Alex mounted on his horse.

"You should be fighting those English muckers instead of your own!" she snarled.

"Fetch his horse!"

Sullenly Cameron retrieved the gentle mare, her anger increasing when she saw the blood on her flanks caused by the captain's spurs. Furtively she loosened the cinch and plucking a burr from the hedgerow, surreptitiously placed it under the saddle.

Captain Harris snatched the bridle that Cameron held out disdainfully.

"I'll tell the colonel," he sobbed with petulant anger as Cameron mounted, looked down at him, and spat. Luckily Alex missed the exchange as he'd wheeled his horse abruptly in the direction of Glen Aucht. He whistled without turning, and Cameron's stallion followed, much to her chagrin. They rode at a moderate pace without talking for a mile, Cameron in a pulsating red rage and Alex in a muddle as to what to do about Cameron. He'd have to send her away for her own safety, but where? He cursed his own stupidity for informing Colonel Beddington of the existence and presence of a wife. That he had at the time been unaware of the Englishman's baseness and spite was no excuse. Maybe she should be sent to the caves with the women and children. He rejected the idea as soon as he thought it. The caves had no locks or doors, since the present occupants were glad of their refuge. Cameron would not stay put, and he needed her where he could see what recklessness she was up to.

"When we reach the house, you'll go up the back stairs and lock yourself in our chambers, is that clear?" he ordered tersely.

"Why?"

"Because, damn it, I say so and have no time for explanations! You're behaving in a selfish, childish way, Cameron, endangering all around just for your own needs of freedom and enjoyment! Well, grow up and look around you; others have no time for swimming and riding, and running wild. It takes all of themselves just to survive in these times!" he lectured coldly.

"You lock me up and tell me little and then expect me to ken what is going on?" shouted Cameron, reining her horse.

"You have to do as I say without question for now. Trust me, there is no time for idle chat," appealed Alex, softening his tone when he recognized the justice in what she said. He had told her just the barest facts, not wanting even to say aloud the atrocities for fear she'd take justice into her own hands. He also knew that Beddington had a plan to humiliate and destroy him, and Cameron could be used as a prime target. Each day since his return he'd been submitted to goadings and insults designed to make him lose control and raise a hand to his superior officer, which would result in his losing rank and lands. He wished he knew how effective Beddington was, but having no spare men, he could not send couriers to London to ascertain. All he could do was assume the colonel held power. He stared hard, trying to appeal for understanding from Cameron, but her face was closed and her eyes were stormy.

"We are in the dickens of a schlorich, and for now 'tis best you help me with your obedience," he murmured, urging his horse into a canter. "And by God, Cameron, I swear to you that, whether I like it or not, I'll take a horse-whip to you if that's the only way you'll obey and keep your life!"

Cameron's face showed no emotion as she seemed to docilely sit her horse, which cantered beside his toward the stables.

"Young-MacNab," Alex hailed, dismounting in the yard. The youth limped out and took the offered bridle as Cameron sat her mount, wanting to dig in her heels and gallop away from her husband, who seemed like a dictatorial stranger. Sensing her thoughts, he plucked her from the stallion's back.

"Is Colonel Beddington about?" he asked.

"In the breakfast room, I heard tell," answered Young-MacNab.

Alex set Cameron on her feet and, keeping tight hold, led her to the kitchen door.

"Mum? Mum?" called the now Jemmy-Lad, peering around the stable door.

"Och, just the one to keep you from mischief and boredom," said Alex, scooping up the red-haired child with his free hand. The puppy danced beside, leaping and trying to catch his coat sleeve.

Mackie looked up from her pie baking as Alex strode across the kitchen floor, carrying the giggling child and the fuming Cameron under each arm, with the rambunctious dog thinking it all a great game.

"Follow wie the key and some food," he ordered tersely, taking the stairs two at a time.

CHAPTER SEVEN

Alex waited until he heard Cameron slide the bolt before turning the key in the door and pocketing it. He was so intent on trying to find a solution to the dilemma of his life, it did not dawn on him to remember that she had that very morning escaped from the locked room. He descended the central stairs toward the unpleasant interview with Beddington, wondering whether he should pass Cameron off as his valet. But then who would take her place as his wife? Maybe he should inform the colonel that she had succumbed to the pox, for he doubted the Englishman would jeopardize his own life by peering into the coffin.

Beddington sat eating in the sunny breakfast room, and Alex noted with satisfaction as he entered that Beddington looked somewhat the worse for wear from the excesses of the previous night's festivities.

"I am informed that the farms are empty, Sinclair," stated the colonel.

"Aye, I noted that myself this morning," answered Alex.

"Where are the women?"

"The last I saw them they were with you and your company of men," answered Alex truthfully with a bitter set to his mouth. Beddington continued eating noisily, snorting his exasperation.

"They will be found, or heads will roll," he promised, vehemently waving his fork. "And when am I to have the pleasure of your wife's company?"

"She is still indisposed, sir," returned Alex evenly, his handsome face calm, belying his inner fury.

"Then I should certainly pay her a visit. I am noted for my bedside manner," salivated Beddington with his mouth full of food. "It has come to my ear that your wife is famous for her unconventionality and flashing emerald eyes." Alex froze. Who under his roof would divulge such information, he puzzled. He covered his consternation well.

"I would not have you endanger your health, Colonel. As I have told you, it could very well be the pox."

"I was not born yesterday, Sinclair," screamed Beddington, furious at the tall young man's composure. "I will not be made a fool of . . ."

Fortunately the fat man's screaming was abruptly halted by the appearance of Captain Harris, whose pale face bore the evidence of tears.

"What in God's name happened to you?" exclaimed the fat man, letting fly pieces of ham and eggs.

"I was attacked," sobbed Harris.

Alex frowned, as the captain's appearance was decidedly worse than when he and Cameron had left him.

"By whom?" roared Beddington. "And what is that foul odor?"

"He was one of them," whined the captain, maliciously pointing a finger at Alex, who saw no point in deigning to answer the charge.

"Was he, by gad?" spluttered the fat man, leaning back with a triumphant sneer. "Was he?"

"Nay," growled Ian, who had entered unobserved. "I had the opportunity of seeing Captain Harris thrown not once but twice from his poor abused horse. And as to the stench, sir, he landed last in sharn."

"You lie, you cad!" screamed Harris.

"Sharn? Sharn?" inquired Beddington. "Shut up, Harris, and stand away from me."

"Manure, sir. Dung," answered Ian with a twinkle in his eye.

"He's lying, sir, lying," squealed the captain.

"There is a yardful of your own men to attest to the fact, Colonel," replied Ian calmly.

"But that was afterward. Before that I was attacked and my cinch loosened so I couldn't keep my seat," yelled the frustrated man.

"You can't keep your seat anyway! Harris, go and bathe. 'Tis hard enough to eat after last night's imbibing without you stinking of manure."

"But, sir, there's a youth with bright green eyes and

black hair. He attacked me, and Major Sinclair helped!"

Beddington swiveled his fat buttocks around and fixed Alex with a mocking leer.

"Thank you, Harris. You are dismissed," he purred contentedly.

"But, sir—"

"DISMISSED, HARRIS!" spat Beddington, holding a perfumed handkerchief to his nose.

"Yes, sir," sobbed the miserable Harris, saluting.

"Out, Harris . . . OUT!"

As the door slammed shut after the scrambling captain, Beddington pompously and slowly rose to his feet, still keeping his eyes fixed on Alex's stony face.

"Strange, is it not, Sinclair, that Captain Harris's description of the attacker fits your wife to a tee?" Ian stiffened and looked to his friend, whose face showed no emotion. Beddington laughed and rubbed his pudgy hands together with glee.

"Major Drummond, refill my plate, I feel my appetite returning."

Ian clenched his fists at the effrontery of being ordered like a lackey, but bowed civilly and did as he was bid.

"Would you like some of each, sir?" he asked, indicating the profusion of covered dishes.

"Only what is recognizable. I'll not be poisoned by your barbarous cuisine," replied Beddington, keeping his eyes riveted on Alex.

"No haggis nor brose, then," said Ian with relish, piling the plate high with beef kidneys and calves' brains.

"What devilry have you been up to this morning, Sinclair, besides spiriting away the women and children from the farms?" demanded Beddington, walking back and forth in front of the tall young man, who stood impassively like a statue.

"I made the rounds of my holdings."

"Your holdings?" sneered Beddington. "Go on."

"And found what you already know. Fields lying fallow . . . and the abused women and children gone."

"Abused? Abused? Sinclair, surely you jest. Surely not abused but used by lusty Englishmen. And surely 'tis better the fields than the females lying fallow," he giggled, delighted with his own wit. "The females will be returned, Sinclair. We must keep those loyal to the crown contented."

"I want to Crail as ordered, sir," Ian hastily interjected, knowing well what the angry ticking in Alex's lean face prophesied. "The *Edna Rae* has been sighted in Newcastle and will dock at Crail within the week."

Delighted with the news, Beddington at last removed his gaze from Alex and danced a little jig as he giggled merrily.

"Oh, the pieces fall into place. Good things in threes and there's the third. A messenger rode in this morning to inform me that most welcome guests will be arriving the day after tomorrow, so I shall expect your wife to act as hostess for me, Sinclair. I trust her disposition is of a trivial woman's nature," he chortled. "I advise you to whip your slovenly servants to order and find the females. The service in this house is appalling, but what can a refined, educated man of great sensibilities expect from this backward country, eh?" Ian and Alex both stood erect, their faces showing no sign of the fear and fury that pounded their blood. Beddington sat heavily, glowing and pleased with himself. He stared at them with great satisfaction as he rang a small bell. Daft-Dougal almost sprang into the room on his wiry old legs, emitting a high-pitched cackle.

"Yer rang, Curr . . . enell?" he asked, rolling his crossed eyes.

"Get this idiot away from me! What is the meaning of this?" shouted Beddington, rising as fast as his great weight would allow.

"Hush now, hush," warned Mackie, scurrying in. "Dinna call him such names, or he'll fix you wie his evil gley eyes and shrivel up yer manhood fer all times."

"I beg your pardon!" roared the fat man apoplectically.

"Nay, it's his pardon you should be abeggin' for calling him an idiot. He's kin to the Fairy-boy of Leith. He can conjure up a revenant at the blinking of one eye," whispered Mackie.

"A pox on this pagan superstition!" raged Beddington.

"The wandering green lady, you'll be wanting, then?"

intoned Daft-Dougal, clasping several serving platters and bounding out of the room on his bent, skinny legs.

"Sinclair, what is the meaning of this?" bellowed Beddington.

"As the womenfolk have disappeared, sir, we have to make do wie the servants we've got," explained Alex calmly.

"What wandering green woman? Is it that Milly or Tilly he's talking about?"

Mackie clucked and shook her head dolefully before hurrying out with her hands full of dishes.

"What is this wandering green woman?" screamed Beddington.

"The pox, sir, 'tis what it's called hereabouts," explained Ian. Beddington looked from Ian to Alex, his face glistening with cold sweat before clapping a pudgy hand to his mouth and exiting rapidly.

Ian and Alex watched the door swing closed. There was a tense silence. Ian looked at his friend's lean face.

" 'Tis getting stickier," he murmured.

Alex neither looked at him nor acknowledged. He stood still, staring at the door. Ian frowned, not knowing whether to quit the room quietly or make conversation. They had to talk and somehow find a way out of the net that seemed to be closing in.

"Alex?"

" 'Tis best not to speak here," said Alex quietly and evenly, still without turning to Ian. He opened the door and strode out. Ian stood a moment, frowning, before following the taller man to a small, secluded room at the rear of the house.

"It appears that once again I am in your debt," pronounced Alex stiffly after several minutes, in which Ian had examined the small windowless library with feigned interest.

"What are friends for?"

"Aye," hissed Alex, his eyes unfocused at a point to the left of Ian's ear. His friend stared sadly at him, feeling the waves of cold animosity, remembering their steadfast friendship from the age of two.

"You were always the leader of us two. 'Twas you always extricating me from some scrape or other. Now fate has gie me a chance to even the score," he said slowly.

Alex remained silent.

"Is it pride that's wounded?" probed Ian.

Alex laughed harshly. "Some, but not all," he admitted, a painful picture of Cameron being held in Ian's arms flashing through his mind.

"And the rest is Cameron?" continued Ian, determined to heal the breach.

"Dinna play the innocent wie me, Drummond!" roared Alex savagely. "The first night back I find her in her night attire wie you in the hall . . . earlier that same night in your arms rolling in the hay—"

"What?" interrupted Ian.

"Your perplexity doesna fool me! The willing savior always appropriately on hand to rescue! I can take care of and defend my own!"

"Jealousy doesna become you, Alexander Sinclair," answered Ian in stilted tones, trying to curb his own fury. "I'd think you'd not begrudge the love of a brother."

"A brother! Hah! You dinna love her like a brother! 'Twould be incest!" he snorted.

"Aye, you are right," nodded Ian. "But I'd think you'd respect your wife enow to trust her. *She* loves me like a brother and no more than that."

"Aye, and you wish it otherwise," attacked Alex cruelly.

"Aye, and I'd be a liar to deny it, but I'm not a wee babe in hippens, and I gie up wishing years ago, seeing our fathers and mothers die," appealed Ian, trying to force Alex's mind to all they had shared together.

Alex turned from him, fighting the rage that clouded his perspective. All the degradation and humiliation that Beddington had submitted him to as he stood stoically allowing no emotion to show now joined with the frustrated impotence of having those under his protection abused with no recourse. Somewhere inside he knew he was being unfair and adolescent.

"Alex, there'll be many who'll fall in love wie Cameron, but she chooses you, mon. *You.*"

"Aye and you'll do all you can to change that, won't

you? Become the hero to point out how ineffectual and unmanly I am!"

"What manner of man do you judge me as?" exploded Ian, his temper now ignited. "Twenty-three years we've known each other, and you believe that of me?"

"What else am I to believe? Always so conveniently championing my wife as though I canna protect her. The lies you tell the colonel about Harris and his horse—"

" 'Twas no lie!" interrupted Ian.

"The lump on my head to stop me taking care of my own. So cozy in the kitchen as though it were your own . . . and my Cameron clasped in your arms in the hay, and you ask me not to judge you?" raged Alex. Ian stood frowning in amazement. "Aye, well you should be at a loss for words. There's nocht to say, is there, Judas-Friend? 'Tis like kiss and betray?"

"Nay, you'll not insult me nor Cameron so!" hissed Ian.

"You'll keep my wife out of this!"

" 'Tis you dragging her through!"

Both young men glared at each other with white-lipped fury, their tall, lean bodies tensed and fists clenched, each waiting for the other to make the first move. Fergus entered and closed the door quietly behind him.

"Well, at least you had the sense to closet yourself in here before you fought like cats. But your caterwaulings are biting enough to pierce any wall, so hush yer faces, both of you!"

"You're forgetting your place, Fergus MacDonald," returned Alex, his eyes still pinned on Ian.

"Beggin' your pardon, Yer Lairdship, 'tis you forgetting yours!" answered the old steward. " 'Tis sorrowful times when Scot fights Scot wie the English listening in. Isna there enow trouble wie out you two butting your heads together like randy rams?" he asked dryly. "Can near hear your petty squawkings clear to the bothies. And atalkin' of bothies, I was in the stable when the wee puppies tumbled Master Drummond and Lady Cameron into the hay." He stared with satisfaction at the change of expression on Alex's face, and did not volunteer that he'd listened at the door.

"Aye, laddie, I see'd you storm away wie another green-eyed lady sitting on your shoulder blinding your eyes and common sense. Some things are not as they appear, *but* others are more so . . . meaning the misery here caused by Colonel Beddington."

Alex felt like a fool. He saw the censure in Fergus's lined face, and his humiliation fanned his fury further. He was no longer a boy for the old to take to task. He bit down on his tongue, wanting to release his pent-up anger and frustration by accusing Fergus of disloyalty in his defense of Ian.

"Aye, and if young Drummond hadna hit you with that bottle to save yer proud neck, I would have hit you wie the soup tureen I was carrying to the kitchens. Och, 'tis ofttimes easier to fix one's eye on a wee fanciful problem so as not to wrestle wie the awful mickle real one," he said gruffly. "And that applies to you too, Master Ian. You've lost your lands and are busy pretending it doesna hurt by going your own sweet way. Well, none can read another's mind."

"What?" exclaimed Alex, his rage at Ian forgotten. "Your lands are lost?"

"Here, swallow your stubborn prides down wie this," said Fergus with satisfaction, pouring three drams of whiskey and handing one to each. "No answers 'til pride is swallowed." Alex felt the liquor burn his throat and spread warmth to his stomach. He and Ian held their glasses out for more.

"Hard to swallow?" chuckled Fergus, refilling them.

"Aye, 'tis stuck in my thrapple," laughed Alex.

"Aye, 'tis a bitter pill, but we're going to be needing it wie the mess we're in," growled Fergus, imbibing himself and making himself comfortable.

"Your lands?" probed Alex when he and Ian were sitting. "They're lost? Why didn't you tell me?" he added when Ian looked away without reply.

"Pride, 'twas like having my manhood taken. Libbed I was by my own granny and Beddington," answered Ian lightly with a laugh to cover his pain.

"What?"

"Aye, to my shame. 'Tis a blessing my father didna live to see the day that his son was as powerless as a wee lass.

You ken my maternal grandmother is English?" continued Ian.

"Aye."

"Well, seems there's some vague connection to Beddington's family. Dinna fash, the blood doesna mix wie mine. He's her distant cousin-in-law, so thankfully I'm not tainted wie the same brush."

"Get to the point," urged Alex impatiently.

"In short, Beddington has taken over Drummonds, and it has been sanctioned by the Commission on Forfeited Estates and welcomed by my illustrious grandmother, who feels more at peace having a fellow countryman in charge, at last a civilized gentleman, to make up for the years she's been forced to stay in such a savage country."

"But your lands were returned, as some of mine were," protested Alex. "For fighting wie the Black Watch for the English in New France in fifty-four."

"Aye, but the decision was reversed. The quote 'sins' of the fathers and grandfathers for their part in the uprising are now revisited and revisited," laughed Ian harshly, pouring himself another dram. "My spinster Aunt Morag is ecstatic. She sees Beddington as a prospective bridegroom. She virtually raped him on the spot, and I had the misguided sensitivity to feel sorry for the puir man."

"If he has Drummonds, why, then, is he at Glen Aucht? Not that I think he should be at either place."

"The Lady Morag scared him off," wheezed Fergus.

"Aye, he didna like her large proportions nor the smaller proportions of Drummonds. Wasna grand enough for him. I think he has a mind to join our estates and increase his title and lands," informed Ian.

"But he canna just take lands and titles as he pleases!" fumed Alex.

"Well, he can and he has taken mine. Forfeiture for my father's part in the Forty-five and on Culloden Moor, and I think he plans the same for you. But you do not have a bitter English grandmother who hated every second of being married to a braw, savage Scot. Gie me another dram, Fergus, 'tis an awful bitter pill to swallow, and as Mackie would say, 'There's no use crying over what's done'.

. . . And dinna gie me sympathy, or I'll blubber like a wee-un," chattered Ian.

"You might not have an English grandmother to be used, but there is Lady Cameron," offered Fergus dryly. "His aunty Morag has a wide, flapping mouth, Master Alex, and wie a bit of sherry, it flaps a mile a minute."

"Aye," admitted Ian ruefully. "Beddington had her spinning tales of you and Cameron. Duncan Fraser's name was mentioned, talk of treason to the crown for harboring a known criminal, the speculations as to Cameron's identity."

"Why have you not told me until now?" raged Alex, fear clutching at his guts.

Ian bit down on his unruly tongue so as not to point out Alex's previous cold avoidance of him.

" 'Tis all a bluff. Beddington's a stupid man," he comforted lamely.

"Aye, but a dangerous stupid man," growled Fergus.

"No one in London will listen to his nonsense. He's alienated everyone, an embarrassment to the court and the Cabinet with his slanderous tales of Bute and the dowager queen. That's why he's exiled here, I'm sure," said Ian earnestly, trying to convince himself.

"He got your lands," remarked Alex dryly.

"Aye, but that was an opportune tool for his countrymen to use. There's no way he can get possession of your lands."

"He's already bled it of men, women, and children," returned Alex, his mind in a turmoil. The reference to Cameron's identity clawed at his heart.

"There is Cameron's parentage," said Fergus quietly, as though reading Alex's mind.

"No!"

Ian sat up, startled at Alex's vehemence. He looked from Fergus to Alex as their eyes locked in a battle of wills.

" 'Twill never be said aloud, MacDonald, you ken?" hissed Alex.

"Aye," said the old man reluctantly. "What of the charge of the lass harboring a known fugitive wie a price on his head?"

Alex thought of the old Highland outlaw who'd exiled himself on the bleak, isolated moor of Cape Wrath sooner than leave his native soil.

"He canna fault a bairn for her guardian," he answered.

"He'd fault a newborn babe for his first cry," muttered Fergus.

"Does he know Fraser is dead?"

"Wait," answered Ian slowly. He stared intensely from Alex to Fergus. "Something is being kept from me. You are both talking around in circles, and I am standing like the dunce in the middle. We are in this together, I have nothing left to fight for but the love and friendship I have with you and yours, Alex. To me, we are brothers. If it is not the same for you, I will go, volunteer for duty helping Pitt fight the Spanish or keeping New France for the English. There'll be nothing left for me here in Scotland."

Alex turned away from the pleading in Ian's eyes. He paced furiously.

"Ten years of swallowing my pride, keeping my nose clean, playing hypocrite and fighting for the English, tippy-toeing, making sure I peacefully coexisted and showed no opposition to the Union!"

"Whoa, lad, whoa. I've heard it said that there's nocht twa nations under the firmament that are more contrair from others than Englishmen and Scots, although they be within the same isle and be neighbors. Coexist? Hah!" laughed Fergus scornfully.

"So you'll not share wie me?" said Ian softly, turning to the door.

"Share my house and lands and friends whilst I still have them, yes. Share myself, yes," offered Alex.

"Share the secret of Cameron's parents?" returned Ian.

" 'Tis not my secret to share. She doesna even know herself." Ian stared at him sadly. "Help me, Ian?" begged Alex, holding out his large brown hand. "I need all your help and brotherly love."

There was a moment, and then Ian clasped the offered hand in his own, and the two young men wrapped their arms around each other. Fergus leaned back, chuckling contentedly.

"This is insane!" exclaimed Alex, breaking free from the embrace, his amber eyes looking suspiciously full of tears. "There has to be recourse."

"There is none, I've tried," replied Ian, gruffly wiping his eyes on his sleeve. "The local magistrates look the other way, and neither of us choose to take our seats in London's House of Lairds, if you remember."

"I sat in that Union Parliament and couldna stomach the corruption nor the derision. Watching our lairds sell their own clansmen for profit and favor in the English court. Dancing like monkeys on strings to prove they were not ignorant barbarians . . . fixing the elections of our local town councils—" exploded Alex.

"That is neither here nor there," interrupted Fergus. "The *Edna Rae* has near docked, and Master Ian has gie us some time wie his lie by telling Beddington it'll be a week. I think it best that we put our heads together, as I think Beddington has a mind to sell our women and children to the flesh-peddling captain for his whorehouses."

"Thank God they're safe!" ejaculated Ian.

"Aye, but for how long wie out food nor drink?" retorted Alex. "None has dared go near, as the countryside swarms wie Beddington's men."

"Aye, and dinna forget the visitors whom he expects the day after tomorrow," added Ian glumly.

Upstairs, Cameron sat with Jemmy-Lad in the red bed-chamber, probing the child for the answers to all the questions Alex avoided. On the hearth the pup, Maggie, attempted to get her large, shaggy sire Torquil to play, but he lay patiently ignoring her antics until the young dog tired, cuddled beside him, and slept.

"Who's hid in the attic wie Granny MacNab?" asked Cameron.

" 'Tis the maid Jeannie, the one who first come wie you from the north," replied the little girl, eager to please.

"Jeannie?" exclaimed Cameron, remembering the not-too-bright but vivacious girl of her own age that Alex had brought from the inn at Glenrothes to be her own personal maid. "Why is she hid?"

"She were . . . were . . . like what near happened to me," stammered the child, her face so white that her freckles stood out. Cameron reached out and held her close.

"Dinna keep it locked in, spit it out so it does not fester," she urged.

"I saw from the hayloft what they done to Jeannie. They held her down and showed her private parts and then put themselves in her, and she screamed. It went on and on until she didna scream no more, just lay there like dead, but she weren't. Now one of their seeds grows within her, and she's lost her senses. I near lost mine when the colonel near took me."

"But he didna get you, Jemmy, and one day when you're grown and the good times are back, you'll find a braw man, and he'll stir your blood so you'll want to be so close to him," soothed Cameron.

"Never," promised Jemmy, shaking her red hair. "I'll let no man's part inside me, never!"

Cameron smiled and stared at the bright, vivacious face. "I'll remind you of that one day. But now we must put our heads together. We are locked in, but sometimes I must go out without anybody but you knowing. 'Tis our secret, yours and mine, you ken?"

"How?"

"By the window," confessed Cameron, putting her trust in the child's wide blue eyes.

"But the laird will be very angry."

"Only if he knows, and we'll not let him know, will we, Jemmy?" The small girl shook her head doubtfully. "You must promise me, 'tis the only way we'll stop the English animals," pleaded Cameron.

"I swear, but what if someone comes when you're not here?"

"You say that I'm sleeping and keep the inside bolt shut tight. Now tell me more, so I know everything that's going on."

"A messenger came from Edinburgh this morning for the colonel, but Young-MacNab didna find any news in the saddlebag 'fore the man took it in wie him," offered Jemmy eagerly after wrinkling up her nose and searching her brain for a few seconds.

"Anyone overhear anything?"

"Nay, but Mrs. Mackie says at the noon meal that she didna think was good news, as it made the Englishman too happy."

"Tell me about the caves," probed Cameron.

"The old smugglers' caves where the others are hid?"

"Aye, where are they?"

"Dinna ken, somewhere along the coast, 'tis said."

"You've no idea?" asked Cameron. "Toward Crail?"

"I dinna ken. I was meant to go, but some of the girls from the farms know about me and what the colonel tried to do. One of them laughed, so I dinna want to go with them."

Cameron said nothing but smiled ironically, thinking that none of the other young girls would laugh or tease Jemmy now with what they had since endured.

The afternoon passed quickly with the company of the vivacious child. They chatted and laughed and played with the two dogs and shared an enormous tea with Mackie. But even though the hours passed more rapidly with company than the previous ones, Cameron was restless, feeling she was being treated like a child. The sun set, and Jemmy slept, surrounded by the playing cards and chess pieces that had helped to while away the time. Cameron stared out of the window across the firth, watching the last rays of red sink below the horizon. She debated leaving the room and inching her way along the narrow parapet but was worried lest Alex would appear. She hadn't seen him since he had roughly deposited her and Jemmy upon the wide bed before reporting to Colonel Beddington. She had questioned Mackie, who had recounted some vague story of the master riding off somewhere. Cameron turned away from the window and opened a book, but her angry, jumpy feelings would not allow her to concentrate. Coming to a quick decision, she shook the little girl gently.

"Jemmy? Jemmy? Wake up a minute," she urged. The child sat up, rubbing her eyes.

"I'm going to go out for just a wee time to see puir Jeannie in the attic. Now you remember the plan if someone comes to the door?" questioned Cameron.

"Aye," responded Jemmy as awareness flooded in and her sandy-lashed eyes widened.

"You'll have Torquil and Maggie to keep you safe, and the bolt must stay closed on the door," she ordered.

"Aye," answered the girl, watching Cameron clamber over the wide sill. She scurried off the bed and craned her head out of the window watching. Cameron reached the casement of the nursery window, waved, and disappeared. Jemmy walked slowly back to the bed and sat, her heart hammering in her chest. A few minutes later a soft rapping at the door caused her great panic.

"Jemmy . . . Jemmy . . . 'tis me, Cameron. Remember our plan, I'll not be long," came the whispering.

"Aye, oh, aye. Dinna be too long," cried the child.

Cameron quietly tiptoed to the back stairs and climbed to the attic floor. Opening the stair door, she peered along the dark labyrinth of corridors, wondering which of the rooms the maid was in and in which direction to go.

"What might you be looking for, lass?" growled a deep voice behind, making Cameron nearly jump out of her skin.

"Daft-Dougal, you scared me," she sighed with relief at seeing the whites of his crossed eyes gleaming from a shadowy doorway and recognizing the fragrance of his pipe.

"Better me than some," he returned.

"Aye," she agreed fervently. "I've come to see Jeannie."

" 'Twill nay help her now. She's gone by her own hand."

"Escaped?" queried Cameron.

"Aye, in a sort of way. Maybe it were best."

"I dinna ken."

"Her life is gone. She is no more in this life," explained Dougal, puffing his pipe so his head was wreathed in clouds of smoke.

"Dead?"

"Aye, hanged herself while the baby still kicked inside. We pulled the wretched thing from her, but it mercifully died . . . 'twas deformed . . . cursed by those rutting muckers. Two heads it had. Two heads. I've seen many a sight and heard of others, but two heads on a baby I've never seen until today."

Cameron stood silently for a few minutes watching the old gley-eyed man. "He should see. He should be haunted by our Jeannie and the monstrous two-headed babe," she said slowly, keeping her eyes pinned to his. His separately moving eyeballs focused in as one sharply.

" 'Tis meet to help the wee folks wie their games," she

continued. "The babe in his bed and our Jeannie hanging above it."

The old man clasped Cameron's face between his two gnarled hands and looked deeply into her green eyes.

"The color of the wee folk I see within thee. You believe?" he asked hoarsely.

"Of course. 'Tis said I'm kelpies' kin, spat from the sea at the witching hour."

"When the witching hour comes . . . be here and we'll teach the English mucker to mess wie the likes of us. Tell no one."

"I'll be here," promised Cameron, turning to go. She walked a few paces and stopped. "Dougal?"

"Aye?"

"Where are the caves?"

"One thing at a time, wee lass," he cackled. "One thing at a time."

"Why are you standing here in the gloom? Is that where Jeannie and the babe are kept?" she asked, indicating the door behind him.

"Aye, I maun see that the door remain shut until her spirit rests."

"Maybe her spirit'll not rest until she's had her vengeance?" suggested Cameron, well aware of Highland traditions and beliefs.

"That is not for us to decide but the force within her," chided Daft-Dougal. "Unfortunately she were not a thinking lass, so I doubt if her ghost'll rise. There wasna enow brains to allow her second life and wreak havoc in the hearts of them who harmed her. So the door will stay closed until her spirit has flown, and we'll do her haunting for her."

Cameron reached the third-floor landing and, hearing firm-booted footsteps on the central staircase, flew quickly into the dusty nursery as Alex appeared in the corridor. He stopped, hearing a faint scraping but, seeing nothing, continued to his chamber and knocked.

Jemmy, dozing on the bed, sat up in alarm, staring white-faced at the door, unable to answer. Alex inserted the key and turned it. He tried to open the door, but it would not yield. He rapped again.

"Who is it?" quavered the child.

" 'Tis me, Sir Alex," he answered impatiently. "Slide open the bolt."

"Her Ladyship is sleeping," responded Jemmy.

"Open the door at once!" he demanded.

"I canna, she's sleeping and doesna want to be disturbed."

"Jemmy, open this door at once before I'm very disturbed!"

"The mistress will be out of temper wie me, sir."

"The master will be even more out of temper wie you if you dinna!" roared Alex.

Cameron, inching her way along the parapet in the dark, nearly lost her footing in her haste as she heard the child's loyalty and Alex's deep, angry voice. She reached the window and swung herself in. She tiptoed to the bed putting a finger to her lips.

"Open this damned door!" swore Alex.

"What is all the fuss?" cried Cameron in a sleepy voice. "Open the door, Jemmy."

"I daren't," she shivered, backing away from the violent pounding.

"Slide the bolt and jump back," suggested Cameron, diving under the fluffy eiderdown. Jemmy slid back the bolt and leaped out of the way as the door burst open. Alex stood on the threshold in a thunderous rage, staring suspiciously at the sound under the bedcovers.

"Where's your mistress?"

Jemmy stood speechless. Alex strode to the bed and threw back the covers, expecting to find a bolster.

"Hello, Alex," said Cameron sleepily. He stared down quizzically at his wife, whose tousled hair covered most of her face. He was not fooled for a moment by the sleepy act, knowing her face awake and asleep. He was only too aware her mischievous, sparkling eyes were being stimulated by something. He studied her for several moments before examining the room. His eyes raked the small child, who shivered under his scrutiny, the two sleepy dogs whose tails thumped heavily in unison, and stopped at the wide-open window. Jemmy, following his gaze, sprang forward.

" 'Twas nigh on stufly, Yer Lairdship, wie the four of us locked in here," she offered, closing and latching the window. "I opened it, thinking Her Ladyship would be sleeping sounder wie a breath of fresh air."

Cameron's heart went out to the small girl who had swallowed her own fear of Alex in defense of her.

"That was very thoughtful of you Jemmy-Lad, wasna it, Alex?"

"Aye," growled the man tersely. His eyes narrowed, looking from one to the other.

Cameron stood on the bed and put her arms around his neck. "Have you come to join us for dinner?" she asked, seeing the fires kindle in his amber eyes.

"Unfortunately no, I've orders to ride to Crail with Colonel Beddington and will not be back until the wee hours."

"For what?" asked Cameron, hiding her elation. Now meeting Daft-Dougal at midnight would pose no problem.

"Nothing to worry your head about," sighed Alex wearily, igniting Cameron's rage.

"Rape, murder, and the like, and 'tis nothing to worry my little head about! You're full of hot air, Alex Sinclair. One minute you're accusing me of being selfish with suffering all around, and yet I'm expected to play children's games and not worry my silly little head! Am I your wife or your bairn?" she ranted.

"If we didna have company, I'd show you, Your Ladyship," growled Alex, raising a roguish eyebrow.

CHAPTER EIGHT

Cameron sat tensely by the fireside, straining her ears. She had no clock, but she listened for the faint chimes that echoed from a lower floor. She had lain beside the child Jemmy to sleep after Mackie had bustled out with the dinner dishes, and had wakened with a start, her heart pounding for fear she'd overslept. As though the fairy folk watched over her, she'd caught the muffled striking of a clock and held her breath, counting the chimes to ten. Two hours stretched before her. She longed to leave the suffocating walls of the room, but the vulnerable picture of the sleeping child caused her to put her own needs aside. Jemmy had suffered so much that she'd leave her alone as little as possible. She stretched her stiff body and walked to the window. The night was still, as though waiting. There was no moon, and the countryside was shrouded in velvet blackness. Eleven struck, measured and ominous, and the child stirred, crying pitifully in her sleep. Cameron sat upon the bed and stroked the smooth forehead until the girl cuddled close to her and the tiny, thin body relaxed.

Many thoughts flooded Cameron's mind about her own bleak childhood. At least little Jemmy knew who she was, but then again Cameron had never felt the sorrow of seeing parents die, not having known any but Duncan Fraser, whom for all his dour, bitter nature she had loved, and his mistress the Crazy Mara, whose jealousy had caused much pain and suffering. Cameron's mind conjured up the face of her twin brother, and she gasped, wondering how she could have forgotten him, even with all the chaos around. Would she ever find him?

She was snatched from her reverie by the distant chimes as the half hour struck. At the quarter she would leave. She carefully lifted her weight from the bed, making sure she didn't jolt the sleeping Jemmy awake. She stood thoughtfully, and on an impulse sat and removed her boots.

She'd creep barefoot and also get a better grip on the stones on her perilous path to the nursery window. She was dressed in just the tight trews and the jerkin, having taken off the white shirt for fear it would be too conspicuous. Quickly she took handfuls of soot that she had scraped from the hot chimney to cool and rubbed her face and arms with it.

The quarter hour echoed dolefully through the quiet house, and Cameron opened the window and slid lithely to the parapet below and inched her way. Reaching the nursery casement, her blood ran cold. The window had been securely locked from within. She balanced herself on the broad sill, leaning against the arched masonry. It had to have been Alex. He must have recognized the clothes she wore, she thought, her hands plucking the dirk from her waistband. Thank goodness she'd had the foresight to keep it there instead of down her boot, where it usually lay. Carefully she slid the thin blade between the two parts of the window. Bracing her back, she pulled it upward against the latch with both hands. The latch did not yield. Again she tried and was rewarded by a slight movement. Summoning all her energy, she thrust the blade upward, and the window swung open outward, nearly toppling her from her precarious perch.

Safely inside the room, her heart hammering painfully in her chest from her narrow escape, she closed the window and ran to the door. It was bolted, locked from the outside. She nearly cried with frustration. The other door from the dressing room was also locked. She stood a moment trying to calm herself to think logically. She'd go back onto the parapet and inch her way around the whole house if need be until she found an open window.

Cameron's hands were numb from gripping the cold, smooth stone. She had worked her way to the corner by the giant chestnut tree. All three windows she'd passed had been not only latched from the inside but also shuttered. She made her way painfully, her nails torn and fingers bleeding. She stepped thankfully onto the broad sill of a window and crouched, her legs shaking from the tension and exertion. She could go no further. Taking a deep breath and fervently praying, she stared at the frame. It was open. Gratefully she slid inside and huddled on the floor, trying to massage the cramps from her feet and thighs with her numb, aching fingers. The chimes of midnight bounced through the gloom, making her forget her aches and pain. She stood in the eerie room, the white dust covers on the furniture making ghostly shapes, and ran stiffly to the door. It opened with a protesting groan that reverberated down the long, dark corridor. Cameron raced like the wind to the back stairs and climbed to the attic floor.

The last deathlike chime of midnight died away, and she stood at Jeannie's open door, staring into the room lit by one flickering candle. The dead girl's face seemed phosphorescent. Her arms, stiff in death, held a small bundle to her stilled breast. Cameron froze. Although none of the baby was visible, she remembered its deformity. By daylight the mischievous plan had been a forthright act of justified revenge, but now she felt the forces of the unknown surround her. She stared, mesmerized. She'd seen pictures of the Madonna and the Christ child, and her guardian, Duncan Fraser, had scoffed and pointed them out as the yoke of the people, damning all religion. Now she felt a strange, unnatural power. Jeannie's eyes were open, seeming to blink and wink in the candlelight, beckoning her. The ghastly translucency of her skin made her appear awesome and alive in some terrifying way. Cameron's eyes didn't waver until it seemed the small bundle in the dead girl's arms moved, and Cameron stepped back.

"Death is strange to look upon," stated Daft-Dougal's voice softly from the shadows, causing her heart to beat wildly.

" 'Tis strange, aye, and I canna fathom it," replied Cameron breathlessly.

" 'Tis because what gie us life canna be seen. We know 'tis gone but canna see it . . . nor grasp it. Everything is still there. All her parts—eyes, nose, and the like—but the most precious . . . the never-seen part that binds has flown," he murmured. "Come, 'tis best to get it done," he said matter-of-factly after a pause, when they'd both been lost in thought staring at the still figure.

"How?"

"I'll carry the lass over my shoulder. I have the rope in my pocket, and a pail of pig's blood is there already. You'll carry the bairn." Cameron recoiled. " 'Tis an innocent bairn, never sinned, 'twill not harm you," said Daft-Dougal, calmly staring into Cameron's blackened face, his usually crossed eyeballs perfectly trained.

"Why the pig's blood?" she asked, swallowing hard.

"Add a wee bit of color . . . You'll see."

"What if the colonel catches us?"

"He's gone to Crail."

Cameron followed Dougal and his strange burden down the stairs, the tiny swaddled baby cradled in her arms. Jeannie's head limply banged against the old man's back with each step he took, and her long, fair hair danced as though each strand lived. She averted her eyes and kept them firmly glued on Daft-Dougal's tweed cap as they made their way to Colonel Beddington's bedchamber.

Placing their unprotesting bundles upon the bed, they both stared at the ceiling.

"There's nocht to tie the rope to," hissed Dougal.

"There's the bell cord," said Cameron, pointing to the heavy, tasseled braid that hung beside the bed. "We can move the bed over . . . and she'll be above his pillows."

"Aye, and have dropped the puir deformed bairn right upon them. 'Twill make the blood shine brighter," cackled Dougal with relish. " 'Twill make his blood run cold."

They worked feverishly.

"The wee folk are wie us tonight, young lass," remarked the old man with satisfaction as they moved the heavy mahogany bed easily. Cameron looked at him, her nose crinkled with consternation. It was unnatural, she thought, looking down at her slight body and then at Daft-Dougal's ancient, worn-out one. It would normally take three strong men to move such a piece of furniture.

"Dinna question, just accept thankfully. Now, lass, I need you to balance our puir Jeannie while I tie the knot." Cameron didn't move. She was filled with horror.

" 'Tis like killing her again," she whimpered.

"She canna feel pain no more. 'Tis yer own self you're now thinking on," chided the old man.

Cameron felt the weight of the dead maid pressing upon her as she tried to think of other things, and her stomach lurched alarmingly. Pictures of the alive, irrepressible Jeannie flashed in her mind. Oh, Jeannie, Jeannie, with her empty chatter. Tears furrowed down the soot on Cameron's face, her back and shoulders ached from the weight of the much larger girl who, on the threshold of womanhood, had taken such pride in her full breasts and hips.

" 'Tis done," panted Dougal. "You can step away." Cameron collapsed on the soft bed where she'd been standing with Jeannie balanced across her hunched back. She flinched as the body swung above her like a pendulum and leaped from the bed as Beddington's sickening pomade odor filled her nostrils from the pillow.

Daft-Dougal stood back and stared appreciatively. "Unwrap the bairn while I get the blood," he commanded.

Cameron opened her mouth to protest as the bile rushed to her throat, but the old man had left the room. She stood swaying, fighting a wave of faintness as the enormous moving shadow of the hanging body swept across the room, helped by a flickering candle. Gingerly Cameron approached the small bundle on the bed. Dougal's words of comfort were remembered.

"An innocent bairn, wie no sin," she mouthed as she unwrapped the swadlling clothes. She stared down at the minute creature and to her surprise felt none of the expected horror. He was deformed, and yet both faces were so sweet, so perfect. It was as though two baby boys shared the same pair of legs, the same genitals. Down to the waist there were two children, who then became one. Two heads, two pairs of shoulders, four small arms, two bellies with the umbilical cords long and still thick . . . and then they became one.

"Lay the puir accursed child beneath her on the pillow," said Dougal gently. Cameron obeyed, her heart aching as she held the cold baby. She longed to warm him and bring laughter to the closed little faces. She stood back as the old man poured the blood down Jeannie's legs so it streamed onto the babies and pillow below. If they had lived, would the two heads have had different thoughts? she wondered.

Daft-Dougal touched Cameron gently. " 'Tis time we

disappeared, lass. I know we should have 'til cockcrow, but 'tis after one and 'tis best we leave." Full of sorrow, Cameron stared one last time at Jeannie with her birthing beneath and blew out the candle. Dougal closed the door quietly, and they crept to the back stairs.

" 'Tis a drink I'm needing. Could you use one, too?"

Cameron nodded silently as they descended to the kitchens.

Cameron entered the warm room and, oblivious to the gasps of consternation from Mackie, Fergus, Old-Petey, and Young-MacNab, collapsed in a chair.

"What have you been up to?" clucked Mackie.

"You'll be hearing soon enow, old harpy, now gie me and the lass a guid strong drink," growled Daft-Dougal, rolling his eyes at the concerned group.

"There's blood adrippin' down yer arms!" gasped Young-MacNab. "You've not killed—"

"Nay . . . nay. 'Tis no person's juices."

"But the colonel's in Crail!"

" 'Tis pig's blood," laughed Dougal.

"But as Old-Petey just said, 'The colonel's in Crail,' " laughed Mackie, slamming down a bottle of whiskey and some mugs. "Now there's yer drink, now you tell us what the pair of you have been up to. Look at you, Miss Cameron, you look like a chimney sweep! What're you doing out of your chamber?"

Cameron stared at Mackie sadly, the tear furrows that coursed through her sooty cheeks still glistening. "We've been laying to rest, Mackie," she said sorrowfully.

"Aye, and the rest you'll have to wait on," cackled Dougal. "Here, lassy, you've earned it," he added, pushing a generous portion of whiskey toward her.

"What mischief have you been dragging the mistress into?"

"Maybe she's a been draggin' me into it," laughed Dougal. Cameron stared at him in surprise. " 'Twas your idea, lassie, na mine."

Cameron smiled. "Aye, it was but I nair thought how it would be," she murmured.

"I hear horses now," exclaimed Young-MacNab.

"Best get to the stables, lad," ordered Fergus, who had

been sitting back, quietly staring at Daft-Dougal and Cameron, speculating as to what they'd been up to. "And you, lassie, should hightail it back to your room before Sir Alex asks too many questions," he added after seeing MacNab limp hurriedly out and Cameron sit without moving.

"I'm too tired to worry. Besides, I'll not go walking that parapet safely tonight," she said, all too conscious of raw hands that now stung from sweat and soot.

"What parapet?" exclaimed Mackie. "How did you get out the room?"

The kitchen door swung open, and Ian and Alex entered wearily. There was a still moment as Alex surveyed the sooty, tear-stained face of his wife. His anger at her disobedience warred with the pathetic picture she made.

"I'll accept the offer of your brandy from Beddington," said Ian, breaking the silence. "That way I'll know where he is," he added, leaving the room.

"Is the child in our rooms?"

"Aye, sleeping wie the dogs," answered Cameron.

"I'll fetch her down," offered Fergus.

"Nay, 'tis too far to carry the hot water needed. For tonight I'll take your suite of rooms and you and Mackie will stay wie the child," Alex said tersely, not wanting to question Cameron with the curious group in attendance. "Bring up water for Lady Sinclair," he added, taking Cameron's arm in a tight grip. When she made no move to rise, he swung her up into his arms.

Cameron sat in the steaming hot water, unaware of Alex's scrutiny, her mind back with the lonely Jeannie and her babe. Alex picked up the flannel and gently wiped Cameron's face clean of the soot.

"What is it?"

Cameron shrugged, not able to explain the desolate feeling that consumed her. Alex fought his impatience.

"Wash yourself," he barked, furious with her. He had spent a painful evening with Beddington in Crail, where the colonel had made arrangements for the captain of the *Edna Rae* to come to Glen Aucht as soon as the ship landed. He'd also left several soldiers to accompany him. Ian's lie of the ship not docking for a week, which could have bought them a few days respite, had been shattered. Now the sight of his disobedient wife refusing to explain herself fanned his fury further.

"Each little fingernail was so perfect . . . except that there were too many of them," murmured Cameron sadly.

"What?" bellowed Alex.

Cameron stared at him, and then around at her surroundings. "We're in Mackie's rooms?"

"Aye, now, will you wash and prove yer not the bairn!" snapped Alex curtly.

Cameron looked at him impassively, her face tightening rebelliously, and she plunged her hands into the water to catch the soap. She winced as the heat stung the broken skin. Alex, having stripped the clothes off her, was aware of the lacerations and did not miss the reaction.

" 'Twill teach you to stay where you're put."

Cameron washed herself thoroughly, taking her time. Her anger at him was reignited, and she gloried in standing and exhibiting her nude, lithe body temptingly as she lingeringly soaped herself. Alex felt a stirring in his loins and abruptly moved to a chair behind her and turned his back, not willing to be seduced to forgiveness. But seduction was not in Cameron's mind. His references to her being a child just made her want to prove her womanhood. At last free of all the soot, she stepped out of the bath, her skin rosy from the heat of the water, as an ear-splitting scream tore the silence of the house. Alex sprang to his feet. Cameron smiled contentedly and threw herself back on the bed and laughed. His eyes narrowed, surveying her reaction, and then he purposefully strode out, locking the door behind him.

Colonel Beddington cringed against the wall of his bedchamber with Harris unconscious at his feet as the grotesque shape swung back and forth. His eyes were riveted to the blood-soaked pillow, where the deformed boy-child lay. Alex, Ian, and Fergus knocked at the door and, only hearing the colonel's terrified whimpers, walked in with lamps in hand, causing the tremendous shadow of Jeannie's body to swoop and pulsate. Beddington slid down the wall to oblivion.

The three men looked at each other and moved closer to the bed, staring silently at the fruits of Jeannie's labor. Blowing out the one candle, they left the room, disturbing nothing as tacitly each felt a macabre, triumphant joy at the thought of Beddington awaking to the nightmare.

Alex unlocked the door of the MacDonald's suite. Cameron lay awake against the pillows. She stared at him. He gazed back, marveling that such a small, young girl could help accomplish such a deed.

"Aye, each fingernail was perfect, moons and all . . . except that, as you said, there were too many," he said softly, walking to the bed. Cameron threw herself into his arms and wept. Alex held her close, wordlessly. There were no words. He too had felt an overwhelming, desolate pity at the sight of the deformed baby. We all have two faces, he thought, the one we show to the world and the one we keep for ourselves.

After a while Alex held Cameron from him and stared into her eyes. "It was a braw, terrifying thing you wrought tonight, but no more, my love. No more. 'Tis time to play the lady. Colonel Beddington expects you to play hostess for his visitors and knows how you look." He stopped her mouth with his as he saw the numerous questions flare in her eyes.

Panic flared into Cameron. She was barely conscious of Alex's warm, demanding mouth, which nuzzled and nipped, for her mind seethed with cutting, brittle pictures of herself stiffly corseted, smiling artificially as she entertained the English soldiers. A terrifying, lurid image of herself laughingly uncovering a silver salver to display the poor deformed babe with an apple in each mouth sent a shudder through her, and Alex held her close, feeling her rapidly beating heart. Cameron clung to his strength with all her might to stop herself from spinning into nameless terror. Desperately she kissed him, mingling their breaths, writhing her body to his as she tried to submerge herself and block the streams of endless horrific pictures that churned her brain.

"Love me, love me," she moaned urgently, and Alex, also in need of diversion, redoubled his efforts. And they successfully forgot time and place as they strove to meet each other, merging their frustrations, anger, and desires with exigency.

All too soon reality spun in, and Alex, sated and sweaty from lovemaking, sleepily kissed her poor blistered hands. "Not very ladylike, but they look useful," he murmured before closing his eyes and wrapping her securely to him. Cameron lay awake feeling the moisture cooling on her skin, feeling apart and very separate. It was impossible for her to sleep, and irritation at Alex's ability nagged at her. Who were Beddington's mysterious visitors, she pondered. How could she play the gracious hostess and successfully hide her hatred?

Alex's lecture rang in her ears: "You maun not indulge your feelings, Cameron. Too many lives could be lost. Beddington will provoke and goad, but we must be strong and not give him reasons or satisfaction in more hurt." His words echoed and rang in Cameron's ears, and her rage burned. What manner of men were Alex and Ian that they'd allow such a fat bully to ride roughshod over them without a fight? Rape, murder, deportation—and they let such a man live and called the poor deformed babe a monster instead of him! Well, she'd not be so cowardly, she determined, carefully wriggling out of Alex's arms. A cry of frustration burst from her mouth as she was clasped and gathered closer to his strong chest, her struggles confined as he imprisoned her further with one heavy leg.

"Och, Cameron, will you let no man rest?" he groaned. "Settle yourself. There are trying times ahead."

"I canna. I dinna ken how two braw men can be so afeared of a fat pig and his runt!" she hissed.

"You'll be conveniently forgetting the twenty men at the farms and another thirty at Drummonds. Besides, 'tis better to know what is going on before taking action."

"I know what is going on. Jemmy-Lad and Dougal told me," persisted Cameron, determined that if she couldn't be free, he wouldn't sleep.

"Then tell me why it is going on and for what purpose?" murmured Alex. Cameron lay against his chest, puzzling.

"I dinna ken. Tell me."

"I dinna ken either. That is what we maun find out," he growled, glad to feel her warm young body stilled against his, hopefully to sleep. Cameron lay quietly thinking as she traced the line of his strong jaw, her finger rasping against the day's growth of golden beard to the softness beneath his ear, where a warm pulse beat. Mischievously she pressed her body closer and moved her satiny length against him, delighting in the feel of his well-muscled body.

"Never satisfied," grumbled Alex, lazily loosening his grip to allow her more movement and access. He lay back, fighting the need for sleep and his own arousal. Alex kept his eyes closed and appeared to be still sleeping as Cameron lay full-length atop him, flicking her tongue and writhing her slim hips rhythmically. His deep chuckle welled up, and he snorted with laughter. He opened his eyes and looked into her indignant green ones. He cupped her stormy face between his large hands.

"I wasna laughing at your not-so-subtle seduction, my love," he said, grinning wickedly and capturing a small, quivering nipple, "but wishing you could have had the pleasure of seeing the colonel's reaction to your little surprise."

CHAPTER NINE

Cameron awoke and stretched. Sunlight filtered through a crack in the heavy draperies, blurring the dark velvet. She sat up and looked around at the cozy familiarity of Fergus and Mackie's chamber. She turned to see Alex watching her, his face somber and stern. She smiled quizzically, but it did not serve to thaw his icy expression. Despite their ardent lovemaking, which marked the climax of the previous night's activities, Cameron's scornful words still rang in his ears, touching a raw place: "How can two braw men be so afeared of a fat English pig and his runt?" Everything about Beddington went against his very fiber and the cost of remaining silent and passive was tremendous.

"You are sunk in the doldrums this morning, my lord," she murmured, wriggling her warm, relaxed body closer. Alex curtly swung his legs out of the bed and stood. Cameron sat up, hurt and puzzled at the rejection.

"There is no time for play nor the expending of energy in such," he informed her coldly as he dressed.

"Where am I to be locked up today? Do you have a dungeon like we had at Cape Wrath?" she challenged, her green eyes sparkling dangerously.

"Nay, today you have your wish, but in my choice of gown. 'Tis time you played the part of Lady Sinclair. I trust it will be easy after your successful haunting of last night," he returned, his worry for her safety causing him to be cruel. Her eyes softened, and her expression was one of childlike terror. Alex steeled himself against her vulnerability.

"They are Beddington's orders, and you have yourself to look to by making yourself so conspicuous. So you are now to play hostess for the colonel's guests," he hissed.

"I won't!" she determined.

"You have no choice, unless you wish to see innocent blood—more innocent blood—spilled. Cameron's face was blank with horror. "Oh, 'tis so easy to judge, but it will be interesting to see how *you* deal with the man," laughed Alex.

"I'll not be cowed by the likes of him, you'll see," she vowed with bravado.

"Well, you'll have the better part of today to practice. I'm sure that after the surprise you had waiting for him in his chamber, he'll not be rising too early."

"Maybe his heart stopped from the shock," suggested Cameron hopefully. "I've heard of that happening. Many a person has fallen dead in their tracks by the sight of a revenant."

"Nay, his voice could be heard bellowing orders well after you had gone to sleep leaving me wakeful. In fact I had to help with the unpleasant task of moving the unfortunate Jeannie. But it seems we now have our rightful chambers returned to us, as the colonel has sworn never to set foot in them more. I'll send Mackie to you to help you dress with propriety and settle in the master suite," he added, briskly leaving the room.

Cameron stared at the sharply closed door long after his footsteps had faded. She felt desolate. Once more Alex seemed a stranger, angry and displeased with her. The thought of being a lady, a hostess to the hated colonel, loomed nightmarishly in her head. She'd have to be corseted and encased so she couldn't breathe, shod so she was crippled and couldn't walk. She wished with the whole of her being that she hadn't been so caught. To be back on the wild, barren moors of the north, beholden and responsible to no one, was her aching desire. Now she was caged inside herself caring for Alex and Mackie and the rest. She couldn't just ride off and leave them to the English.

Mackie's soft knock stopped her reverie, and she embraced the round, loving woman. "I'm sorry for putting you and Fergus from your own bed last night," she said contritely.

"Dinna fash, 'twas very interesting. Musical beds it was. With the colonel's ranting and ravings and having no other rooms prepared, he ordered us to quit ours. He now has the red suite, and Fergus, myself, and the child slept in the master suite. Slept isna the word, for although I knew 'twas a mortal deed, it fair shivered my bones, as I felt the presence of the puir maid Jeannie and her wee babe all the night."

The day passed too quickly with the gleeful removal of the colonel's possessions and the installation of Cameron's and Alex's into their rightful chambers. Jemmy-Lad helped, unconcerned and ignorant of the night's happenings. All trace of Jeannie and the babe had been removed, and yet as Mackie had said, her presence weighed heavily.

As evening approached, Cameron felt chilled inside. She had been left alone to rest for the long night that stretched alarmingly ahead, but she could not. She paced the floor, avoiding looking at the gowns that hung for her inspection. A row of shoes were lined beneath, seeming to laugh and sneer at her. Panic flared, and she stared out the window across the rolling lawns to the firth.

"I dinna think your puir blistered hands would thank you for submitting them to more of the same," chided Alex, entering silently and watching her back.

Cameron turned and looked at him reproachfully. She reminded Alex of a wild, frightened bird. He could see the frantic pulse beating in her neck. It was no time to soften or comfort, he told himself, allowing a distance to be between them as he longed to enfold her in his arms. A sharp rapping at the door broke the tense staring.

"What is it?" barked Alex.

"Colonel Beddington expects you and your wife in the library in one hour," whined Harris's nasally voice. Cameron backed to the window, and her small hands clenched the sill behind her. A pervasive depression shrouded the room as they listened to Harris's brittle footsteps recede.

"Well, my lady, what'll you be wearing tonight?" asked Alex, trying to lighten the mood. "I'll have to play lady's maid, as Mackie has her hands full preparing a sumptuous repast for Beddington's honored guests."

"Who are they?" asked Cameron quietly.

" 'Tis to be a surprise," retorted Alex, furious with himself for not being able to find out. "I saw the list of dishes you and your cohorts devised for the colonel's palate," he chuckled falsely.

Cameron laughed. She, Mackie, and Jemmy had given themselves an hour's delightful play fashioning the dinner dishes.

"What did the colonel say?" she asked mischievously.

"He didna say a word, as I didna think he had the stomach to look at a list of victuals with the amount of spirits he drank to block the sight of the swinging Jeannie. So Mackie assumed he agreed and is making everything on the list," responded Alex, laughing in spite of himself. Cameron turned away, her own laughter dying, and once more panic clutched at her. She scrambled to the large bed and pulled the covers over her head. Alex stood silently for a few moments, staring at the mound under the blankets before pulling them back.

" 'Tis no time to be hiding," he cajoled, forcing cheerfulness and picking her up in his arms. "No time for scared rabbits," he teased.

"You're the scared one!" she spat, trying to wriggle free.

"Aye, you're right!" he said, stung, looking straight into her eyes. "There's much to be scared of. I'm much afraid for you," he added, setting her on her feet.

Cameron stood naked in the middle of the room, her raven hair tousled. The look in Alex's eyes and the seriousness of his tone made her feel very small and defenseless. She shivered, and Alex, realizing her desirable vulnerability, cursed under his breath and turned savagely away from the tempting sight of her.

"You're afraid I'll disgrace you and your noble name!" she accused, flinging back her thick, unruly mane.

"Nay, I'm afraid for you! 'Tis a hard thing to keep one's temper reined at the sight of injustice, even at my age . . . 'twill be much harder for you, who's still adolescent!" stated Alex, hoping to challenge her pride.

"Adolescent? Half-grown? I'm a woman!" expostulated Cameron.

"Aye, on the outside, but you've given me no reassurance about in here!" answered Alex, tapping his own head. "Cameron, this is no story book or one of Duncan Fraser's tales of long ago. 'Tis real and 'tis happening, and there's no room for heroics or tempers! You must do as I've bid tonight. Curb your tongue and your feelings, no matter what happens."

"How many times must you tell me? You repeat and repeat like the cuckoo!"

"Aye, but will you obey?" demanded Alex harshly.

Cameron glared at him, hating the word "obey," and her pride making verbal acquiescence impossible.

"You'll have to wait and see, won't you?" she answered, stalking to the wardrobe. Alex's hand itched to strike out at her saucily moving buttocks, but he reasoned that with all his lecturing on curbing emotions he'd better set the example. Cameron blindly selected a dress and wrenched it from the wardrobe.

"You'll not wear that!" stormed Alex, snatching the diaphanous gown. "That is for my eyes only! You'll not flaunt yourself, tempting rape!"

Cameron's anger mounted at his dictatorial manner and her own stupidity in her random selection.

"You'll wear this," stated Alex coldly, selecting a modest green velvet gown. "And this and this and this and these," he continued, laying out an assortment of undergarments and shoes. Cameron eyed the hated, confining clothes, feeling her breathing constrict and her feet ache.

"Oh, so that is why women have to endure being bound up tightly, is it? To save them from being raped!" she crowed sarcastically.

"Cameron, I'm depending on you . . . dinna fail me," pleaded Alex in a last bid for cooperation.

Cameron nodded, not trusting herself to speak as she wondered how she could omit some of the uncomfortable clothes without his knowing. Alex gave her a long, searching look, not quite satisfied that he'd made his point. She smiled falsely at him, increasing his trepidation, but he nodded and then proceeded to see to his own dressing in the adjoining room.

Cameron quickly stuffed the stiff corset and confining bodice between the mattress and the springs of the bed and slipped into the petticoat and dress. After tugging on the hose, she tried to wiggle her feet into the hated shoes, which she remembered as having pinched and crippled, making walking stilted and unnatural.

"They dinna fit!" she crowed triumphantly.

"What dinna?" inquired Alex from his dressing room.

"The shoes!" exulted Cameron.

Alex strode out impatiently in his breeches, wiping the shaving soap from his face. Suspecting her guilty of some trick, he knelt and tried to fit her foot into the shoes to no avail. Four more pairs of shoes were tried.

"My feet grew!" sang Cameron proudly, spinning around. "And so did the rest of me. See? Even my ankles show, which is supposedly a very wicked thing."

Alex shrugged into his shirt, scowling with vexation.

" 'Tis not my fault," cried Cameron gaily. "You canna fault me for growing."

Alex thought he could, but he didn't. Why was he so surprised to find that Cameron was still growing? She was but fifteen or barely sixteen, at the most, he raged inwardly as he buttoned his shirt and picked up his tunic.

"I'll send Mackie to you," he said tersely as he quit the room, locking it after himself.

Cameron sat dejectedly on the bed. While Alex was present to tease and provoke, she could successfully block her fear, but now it tore in with nightmare proportions, panicking her pulses and shaking her body in violent tremors. Having been raised as a boy in kilt and plaid, she felt awkward and clumsy in the fashionable gowns of convention. The heavy material twisted between her legs, tripping her, the bodice restricted her breathing and movement, and the weight dragged and sagged her shoulders and spirit. How long she sat before Mackie's knock shook her out of her despondency she had no idea. The sound of knuckles on wood caused her to jump and set her already furious pulses galloping out of control. Mrs. MacDonald let herself into the room, locking the door carefully behind herself.

"Oh, Mackie . . . Mackie," burst out Cameron, flinging herself into the woman's comforting arms. "Canna we poison the colonel . . . like Lord Randall of the song?"

Mackie quickly and efficiently let out the hem of the dress, steaming the velvet so that no line showed, and found a small pair of kid slippers that fit so comfortably it was as though she were barefoot. But even so, Cameron felt awkward and clumsy, hampered by the heavy material. Luckily the diligent housekeeper was so flustered, her usual keen eyes missed the absence of the conventional, confining undergarments as she stepped back to survey her young charge. Her eyes filled with tears at the petite girl's unusual and striking beauty.

" 'Tis a sin agin all nature that that Sassanach mucker's eyes should even rest on you!" she muttered angrily, collecting her sewing materials together and stuffing them into her apron pocket, savagely pricking her fingers in the process. Alex's impatient knock heralded his appearance. His stony expression cracked for a brief second on beholding Cameron, and he wondered if it would not be better to attempt the impossible and somehow try to disguise her incredible beauty. But already the hour was past, and Beddington was venting his impatience.

"You take my breath away," he murmured gruffly, formally offering her his arm. Cameron felt sharp desolation when he ordered Torquil to stay by the fire in their chamber. "I'll protect you, you'll not be needing your hound," Alex comforted, seeing the fleet panic flash through her eyes.

Each step they took along the corridor and down the broad central staircase increased her trepidation. Her knees threatened to buckle, and she clung to Alex's arm, grateful for the support. Several times during what seemed the interminable descent she looked up into his face, but he kept his eyes straight ahead and, except for the tic in his lean cheek, showed no sign that he was aware of her discomfort.

Now the carved oak door of the library loomed in front of them, and Cameron felt a clutch of fear that bowed her stiffly held shoulders, and instinctively she recoiled, her tense fingers digging painfully into Alex's arm. Alex stared down into her small face, recognizing the sheer panic in her large, expressive eyes.

"We'll show these English," he whispered, hoping to spark her wild Scottish pride as he bent to kiss her softly.

"How touching!" sneered Beddington, choosing that precise moment to fling open the door. "Lady Sinclair, I presume?" he continued, accenting the "lady" slightingly as he rubbed his plump hands together greedily like a small boy with a vicious secret. "I've heard so much about you," he giggled, eyeing her insultingly from top to toe.

"*Currrr* . . . nell Beddington, I presume. I've heard so much about you, too," Cameron returned. The fat man forgot his giggling abruptly and stood mesmerized by the unusual brilliance and color of her eyes.

"Well, are we to stand exchanging pleasantries in the doorway? I was not aware that that was a polite English custom," said Cameron haughtily, not shifting her gaze from the bloodshot eyes. Beddington stiffened at the effrontery but, seeing no mockery in her steady gaze, snorted and attempted to bow despite his large girth.

"Forgive me, madame," he purred. "But I was overcome by your most remarkable appearance. I have heard it spoken of, but it in no way prepared me." Cameron repressed a shudder as his pudgy pink hand took hers, lifting it toward his spittled moustache and lips. "Sherry?" he offered after leading her to a large couch.

"I care not for it," replied Cameron pertly, seating herself in a straight-backed chair behind which Alex placed himself. "I should prefer a wee dram of whiskey," she added, placing her hands primly in her lap. Beddington, alone on the couch, snorted with laughter.

"Do you find that amusing?" inquired Cameron.

"It is not the customary female drink."

"I am not the customary female," she replied.

"So I've been told," responded Beddington, giggling nastily behind his hand.

"Oh? From who?" asked Cameron politely.

"From whom," corrected the colonel pompously.

"Yes."

"I have my little birds," chortled the fat man.

"Aye, so I've heard," replied Cameron cryptically. Beddington's small eyes narrowed until they nearly disappeared into his fat folds.

"You elude me, madame."

"I do?" answered Cameron after a pause as she won-

dered what the phrase meant. "Alex, are you not drinking?" she added, changing the subject in the hope that her
ignorance would go unnoticed.

"Major Sinclair may not drink, do, or say anything in
my presence unless I allow it. I am his superior officer,"
stated the colonel, puffing out his chest. Cameron found
his stance comical and bit down on her lip to prevent
herself from giggling. To her surprise she was not afraid
of the pompous posturing man. She found him weak and
pathetic. Just the fact that he had to state his superiority
released her from tension, and she relaxed.

"You find that amusing?" spluttered Beddington.

"What? . . . That you're Alex's superior?" she responded
mischievously.

"I hope you're not playing games with me!" yelled Beddington.

"I assure you, Curr . . . nell, there is nothing I'd rather
do less . . . than play games with you. Why, thank you,
Captain," smiled Cameron pertly, accepting the proffered
glass and look straight into Harris's dumbfounded face.
The captain couldn't believe his eyes. He stood stock-still,
unable to move even after Cameron had shifted her gaze
back to Colonel Beddington.

"Harris? What's got into you? Where's my drink?" yelled
the commanding officer impatiently. Harris seemed not to
hear as he bent down almost on his hands and knees and
peered around, trying to see Cameron's face more fully.

"HARRIS?" bellowed Beddington, and the thin, pale
captain recollected himself and shot up to attention, shivering. "Are you sure that you didn't addle what little brains
you have when that horse threw you? Fill my glass!"
ordered the colonel furiously. Harris nervously slopped
liquor into a glass and scrambled clumsily to the man who
now stood by the fireplace.

"Permission to talk, sir?" he babbled. "It's important,
sir," he hissed, looking surreptitiously behind him at Cameron, who sat perfectly at ease staring at the colonel's portrait above the mantelpiece. Beddington glowered at the
white-faced, rattled young man. "Please?" whined the little
captain.

"What is it?" Captain Harris clutched at Beddington's collar, trying to whisper in his ear. "Stop mauling me! What in damnation is wrong with you, Harris? Are you a lunatic . . . afflicted in some way?" roared the colonel, flapping his hands about as though the young man was a cloud of gnats.

"It's private . . . oh, please," begged Harris, nearly in tears.

"All right," said Beddington, offering his ear. "But don't touch me."

Alex took the opportunity to touch Cameron reassuringly as the fat man and the thin man hissed conspiratorially together.

"Are we back to that boring subject, Harris?" yelled Beddington, roughly shoving the man away from him.

"But, sir——"

"Get out, Harris! Get out now! Stand in the hall and await our other guests!"

"But——"

"OUT!"

Beddington straightened his uniform and turned his attention back to Cameron.

"Captain Harris is convinced you have a brother . . . a double . . . a twin, in fact," he laughed after a pregnant pause.

Alex froze. What sort of game was being played? There was something too triumphantly smug about the fat man's expression, as though he inferred something more than the incident between Harris and Cameron the previous day.

Cameron leaned back, pressing her shoulders against Alex's hands, which gripped the back of her chair, and looked thoughtfully up at the colonel's portrait on the wall as she tried to think of a clever retort or change of subject.

"Why would he have such a notion, do you think?" probed Beddington, enjoying himself.

"Because I had occasion to humiliate him," answered Cameron, taking the bull by the horns.

"You threw him from his horse?"

"Aye."

"Alone and unaided?"

" 'Twas not difficult," replied Cameron evenly.

"Do you know the penalty for assaulting an officer of the crown?"

"Aye."

"Well, let's not spoil our festivities with matters that can wait until another day," wheedled Beddington with a look of jubilation on his face. "There's much I wish to know about my charming hostess before my guests arrive," he continued, walking excitedly on the hearthrug.

"And much I'd like to know of you," replied Cameron. "That is a most awful vivid likeness," she proclaimed, staring critically at the portrait. "And you're wearing a different uniform," she continued, looking from the painting to the colonel and back again.

"That is the dress uniform of the Foot Guards," informed Beddington, drawing himself erect and trying to hide the paunch which was not present on the canvas.

"Foot? Have they no horses?"

"The Foot Guards are the most prestigious regiment in the whole empire," stated the colonel, sneering at her ignorance. "They are the personal bodyguards of kings . . . and all are of noble birth."

Alex swallowed a snort of derision, knowing that a commission in the Foot Guards was most expensively bought and insured only that the spoiled younger sons of the court need never have to risk their lives on a battlefield but could live as gentlemen of ease in London, the only soldiering being the pomp and ceremony of glittering brass and parades.

"Why are you not guarding the king now?" asked Cameron, unknowingly touching a most sensitive nerve in Beddington, who fought for control of himself as a flood of fury threatened. He closed his loose lips tightly against the tirade that longed to be released. Cameron stared with undisguised interest as the colonel's face ballooned and bloomed with various deep hues of red and purple. He turned angrily from her and poured himself another drink.

"I'd like a drop more," said Cameron conversationally, holding out her glass.

"How old are you?" barked Beddington abruptly, maliciously glad to see her taken aback by his sudden turn of mood and subject. Cameron, after her initial shock, laughed brittlely.

"Why *Curr* . . . nell Beddington, from all I've read of English etiquette, 'tis bad manners to ask a lady such a question," she remonstrated gaily.

"A *lady*? And are you a lady?" spat the colonel savagely. Cameron leaned her body against Alex's hands warningly as she felt his tension prickle the air at Beddington's vicious attack.

"No," she answered coolly, staring directly at the obese man. "I'm not."

Beddington's eyes nearly popped out of his head.

"I beg your pardon!" he exploded after a long pause.

"And so you should," retorted Cameron promptly, purposely misinterpreting his meaning. "But you're forgiven."

"I BEG YOUR PARDON!" he splutteringly reiterated.

"I said, my pardon is granted," replied Cameron enunciating as though to someone hard of hearing.

Beddington turned even more alarming colors as he noisily sucked in a very long breath. He held it for several long seconds and then expelled it in such a rush that his waxed moustache quivered like an aspen tree.

"I expect that you'd like to go over again the dishes to be served this evening," offered Cameron, unfolding a small piece of paper while Beddington shook with stupefaction, not knowing quite how to proceed with his line of questioning. "I understand from Mrs. MacDonald that you have at least four guests, so we've made provisions for twice that number as I wasn't certain as to *who* of your staff would be dining with you." Cameron looked up from her list with surprise as the colonel started to laugh. It was a fascinating sight as each band of fat seemed to have a completely different rhythm of its own, and as the mirth increased, the rolls slapped together until it appeared that the man had not a firm bone in his body.

"Guests! . . . Oh, yes, my guests!" he squealed, tears of merriment squeezing out of his eyes and rolling over and down the folds of his face. "Oh, my! Oh, my!" he wheezed, holding his stomach as though to keep the quaking mass from falling off his body. Cameron looked at Alex quizzically, her small nose wrinkled. He frowned at her also, puzzled by the colonel's almost hysterical hilarity. Who were these guests? Why was the fat man so confident despite the obvious snubs and setdowns Cameron had victoriously battled him with?

"Are either Sir Alex or myself acquainted with your guests?" asked Cameron when the loud guffaws had slowed and quieted so she could make herself heard without shouting. Beddington opened his mouth to answer but was once again overcome by mirth. He sat upon the couch nodding his head as he drummed his feet, clinging to the curved back for support as great belching roars crackled Cameron's ears until they buzzed.

"Do you know them? I should say so," he snickered nastily, as the wave of frenzied mirth ebbed. "At least, your husband knows one of them . . . intimately," he tittered, stressing the last word lewdly and rubbing his hands together with gleeful anticipation. "Now may I see the list of dishes?"

Cameron obediently held out the slip of paper. She felt numbed. An ominous foreboding filled her, and as the fat hand snatched the paper from her, she turned and looked up to Alex. He stood like marble, the color drained from beneath his tanned cheeks. Beddington giggled spitefully, seeing the two tensed faces, and thrust the paper back to Cameron.

"Read it to me," he ordered crowingly, feeling for the first time totally secure of his superiority. Cameron stared unseeingly at the white sheet, trying to focus her eyes to read the words that swam and joined together. Painfully she stammered through the menu of five courses and three removes. "Eel!" expostulated Beddington, shocking her out of her inertia. "Eel?" he repeated, it being the only food he recognized. Cameron felt her spirit returning.

"Yes, jellied eel," she replied after rechecking her list.

"Common peasant food!"

" 'Tis what we could get at such short notice. 'Tis very fresh from the Forth," she replied, her eyes gleaming wickedly as she thought of the folk song about Lord Randall's death. Maybe Mackie had decided to poison the fat man after all, she thought, as the tune ran through her head, and she determined to give the eels a miss and warn Alex if he were at the table.

"And what are these other dishes mentioned?"

"Which ones?"

Beddington snatched back the list. "Here," he snarled, spraying her face with saliva as he poked his finger savagely at the paper. "Cabbie-claws and crappit heids?"

"Fresh cod wie a sauce of horseradish and egg, and haddock heads wie liver and oyster crappin," replied Cameron tolerantly as though talking to a small child.

"What the hell is crappin?"

"Stuffing."

"And what's that?" he demanded, his face so close to Cameron's she felt his heat.

"Hattit kit is a custard."

"And that?"

"Partan bree is soup made from crabs."

"Why isn't it written in English?" bellowed Beddington.

"I understood you were given the list earlier before the cooking was started, and as you made no inquiries then—"

"Is there no meat?"

"Pig!" spat Cameron.

"I beg your pardon!" exploded the colonel.

"Pig!" she repeated patiently. "And hough and gigot."

Beddington glared at her, livid with rage.

"Do ye ken hough and gigot?" she asked innocently. "'Tis beef and lamb."

"You're trying to make a fool of me!" he screamed, his voice breaking into shrillness.

"I am not trying," remarked Cameron dryly.

"THAT IS ENOUGH! I have borne quite enough of your confounded impudence! . . . Your brazen effrontery . . . your flippant disregard . . . your ill-bred bumptiousness . . . your . . . your . . . your audacious insolence," he ranted. "You obviously are too ignorant . . . too moronic . . . too cretinous . . . too uncultivated . . . to . . . to . . . to understand the tenuous nature . . . the . . . the extreme dubiousness . . . the very instability . . . in short the complete precariousness of your position . . . your circumstance here!" He paused and took a breath as Cameron stared at him with wide-eyed awe, not comprehending many of the words and astounded at the man's verbal fluidity "Nor do you seem to understand the weight . . . the . . . the seriousness . . . the absolute specific gravity . . . in fact the enormous magnitude of the charges leveled against both of you! The fact that neither of you is rotting in the dungeons of Edinburgh is solely due to my . . . my magnanimous benevolence . . . to my, er . . . um, charitable disposition," he continued, his anger forgotten as his pleasure in oratory took over, and he strode around the room with great assurance as though politicking for electoral office.

"I have extended to you courtesy and well-bred civility, Sinclair, so I advise you to curb your baseborn wench's mouth, or I shall forget my altruistic and philanthropic nature and take matters into my own hands," he concluded, smiling with satisfaction as tension crackled the air. But neither Alex nor Cameron made a move, although their very fibers were curled to spring. Beddington surveyed their tightly controlled faces and smirked gloatingly. He longed to provoke further, sensing that they were wound so tight that just one small spark would kindle the explosion, but he curbed his impatience, knowing that a loss of temper by Sinclair at that point would be unwise and untimely without adequate witnesses and protection.

"I can wait. Oh, by Jove, I can wait," he crowed exultantly, jiggling around in delicious anticipation of the rest of the evening's entertainment. "Randall Beddington, you shall come into your own yet."

Cameron sat stiffly, pressing her body against the straight back of the chair and Alex's clenched knuckles as the minutes tensely ticked by and the colonel's exuberance turned to irritation at the delay. Through her head ran the folk song "Lord Randall," and more than once she caught herself as she was about to rock with the melody. She fixed her eyes on Randall Beddington and mentally undressed him, imagining how his pink fat folds would sag without the support of his uniform . . . collapse into a jellylike mass around his feet. Maybe all that existed of the man was the uniform and without it he was nothing more than an obscene glistening blob with a purplish moustached face.

"What is that humming?" barked Beddington waspishly. Cameron, realizing that she was the culprit, chose to hum louder. Anything was better than the silent waiting.

"Stop it! Stop that humming!" screamed the colonel.

Cameron felt Alex's knuckles digging warningly into her back, but they just served to goad her.

". . . What were the caller of their skins, Randall my son? What were the caller of their skins, my bonny one? Speckled and spackled, mither. Speckled and spackled, mither . . ." She sang loudly, her voice clear and untrembling.

"How dare you!" thundered Beddington.

"Make my bed soon, for I'm sick to my heart and fain would lie down," continued Cameron.

"SILENCE!" he roared, his eyes almost popping out and his face turning various lurid hues.

"Where shall I bury your body, Randall my son? Where shall I bury your body . . ." improvised Cameron, not at all intimidated but seeming extremely amused by the man's frenzied fury.

"HARRIS! HARRIS!" screamed Beddington, literally foaming at the mouth. The skinny captain all but fell into the room as though he'd been eavesdropping.

"Yes, sir?" he responded, regaining his balance and saluting, although his eyes were fastened on the sweetly smiling Cameron, who sang as though giving a drawing room recital.

"Wie the eels and eel sharn, mither. Wie the eels and eel sharn, mither . . ."

"HAVE MY GUESTS ARRIVED?" bellowed Beddington, trying to drown her out.

"There are carriages approaching, sir," replied Harris absentmindedly, his eyes riveted to Cameron.

"Good, very good . . . you will show them in as soon as they arrive."

"But they'll need to freshen up, sir."

"YOU WILL SHOW THEM IN HERE IMMEDIATELY, HARRIS!" shrieked the colonel hysterically.

"Yes, sir," saluted Harris.

"AND CLOSE THE DOOR AFTER YOU!"

Cameron sat still humming and smiling contentedly.

Beddington clenched and unclenched his fists, taking small steps toward her as he fought the overwhelming urge to slap her face. The steely warning that was written across Alex's features deterred him. He breathed deeply, trying to compose himself as he straightened his tunic and dabbed at the perspiration that wilted his moustache. Just a few more minutes and victory would be his, he assured himself as he posed pompously at the hearth facing the door, ignoring the two, whose eyes seemed to bore burning holes into his shaking flesh.

CHAPTER TEN

Time seemed suspended as through the sturdy oak door muffled, unintelligible sounds heralded the arrival of the awaited guests.

"Stand over there, Sinclair," hissed Beddington, gesturing impatiently to the opposite side of the room. Without hesitation, Alex strode to the appointed place, a sardonic smile playing across his handsome features as he realized that he and Cameron now framed the pompous man. Beddington puffed himself up and stood with a tentative smile as if he were exercising his facial muscles in preparation for his most effusive expression of welcome. He giggled and jiggled nervously as though the last split seconds of suspense might be too much.

Cameron started imperceptibly as the door was sharply opened and a cold draft ruffled the poised stillness of the room.

"Lady Fiona Hurst! How absolutely, wondrously stimulating and intoxicating to be in your fascinating, enchanting and breathtakingly beautiful presence again," declared the colonel without changing his contrived stance except to extend one of his plump hands dramatically in her direction.

"The pleasure is all mine," purred a hated voice from the not-too-distant past that grated Cameron's nerve endings and sent numbing shock waves crashing through her small proudly held body. Lady Fiona Hurst, Alex's wellborn, beautiful former mistress! Lady Fiona Hurst, who could make her feel like a grubby, unformed child next to her voluptuous majesty! Lady Fiona Hurst, whom Alex had loved! The thunder pounded in Cameron's ears as she remembered the numerous humiliations and insults the older woman had subjected her to. She forced herself to appear calm and composed, clinging onto the melody that still ran through her head, although she shook to her very core.

Fiona Hurst swept magnificently across the room and carelessly placed a gloved hand upon Beddington's outstretched one. He slowly drew it to his lips, where he lingeringly kissed it. A look of pure distaste flashed fleetingly across Fiona's face, but it was quickly covered by a throaty laugh as she turned theatrically toward Alex. Cameron concentrated on the tune in her head, ignoring the tall, statuesque woman who stood seductively before Alex, her ample breasts thrust forward so that they threatened to spill out of her low-cut gown. Alex returned her look coolly, a cynical smile creasing his face with sardonic lines. Fiona's expression hardened, and she insultingly appraised his body, her steely gray eyes coming to rest suggestively on the gentle swell his manhood made beneath his tight trousers. Keeping her eyes pinned to that spot, she swayed closer to him, her mouth open and the tip of her tongue playing tantalizingly across her lips.

Alex appeared bored although fury hammered his pulses and a painful knot of panic tightened his stomach. What was Beddington's game? How could he use Fiona's spiteful jealousy against him, raged his mind as Fiona swayed nearer. Fiona drank in everything about the tall, russet-haired man, and the old hunger sparked and spread deliciously, warming her loins. She longed to feel his hardness pressed to her. Her nipples strained toward him as she stood less than an inch away, feeling the tiny space throb with excitement. She had forgotten how beautiful he was . . . forgotten how just the sight of him could stir her blood to such a fever pitch that she would do anything . . . debase herself in any way just to be possessed by him. Yes, she had forgotten how all-consuming was her need for him in the long, cold months since he'd rejected her so callously for the green-eyed slut. She whirled suddenly and fixed Cameron with a malevolent gaze, but the young girl sat seemingly unaware, a serene smile on her face as though in a world all her own.

"Sherry, Lady Fiona?" offered Beddington, who, being an avid voyeur, had been disappointed by the cessation of the sexual game with Alex. Fiona didn't answer as she still stared at Cameron, speculating on how to shatter the girl's composure.

"Have you tasted the child yet, Randy?" she asked spitefully, keeping her eyes pinned to Cameron's face.

"Lady Fiona!" exclaimed Beddington, turning his eyes anxiously toward the door. "The other guests."

"The old fuddy-duddies are in their rooms making themselves presentable."

"Nevertheless . . . it is not opportune . . . not the time . . . we must be patient," stammered Beddington. "Have some sherry."

"Thank you. Why don't you send her out of here?" suggested Fiona, indicating Cameron. "I'm sure there is plenty for her in the kitchens to busy herself with . . . and she certainly hampers the evening's enjoyment."

Beddington frowned, but when he understood Fiona's sly indications in the direction of Alex, enlightenment beamed across his face.

"Harris?"

"Yes, sir."

"You may pour two sherries and then escort Lady Sinclair," he said, looking at Cameron, "to the kitchens. Oh, and be sure you are on hand to entertain our other guests, as I shall be in conference for a short while."

"Yes, sir," saluted Harris. "Should I entertain them in the library or—?"

"I couldn't care less . . . just take her out of here! Now!" yelled Beddington.

"But the sherry?" stammered the young captain.

"I'll pour the sherry . . . just go!"

The flustered Harris grabbed Cameron roughly by the arm and yanked her to her feet. She pulled free and stood like a startled deer before picking up her skirts and running fleetly from the room.

"After her, Harris!" urged Beddington, and the skinny captain raced out, slamming the door behind him.

Fiona smiled wtih satisfaction.

"Now bolt the door, Randy, and we'll have a little appetizer," she purred, excitement trembling her knees as she approached Alex. Beddington obeyed quickly, despite his large size.

"Oh, Alex, you used me shamefully," she said as once more she stood with less than an inch separating their bodies. "You used me and used me," she continued, caressing each word.

Alex stood stiffly, his eyes focused on Beddington's portrait as Fiona undid the buttons of his tunic and shirt and ran her hands across his broad chest and down his flat stomach. Not even when she released her own breasts and rubbed their heat against him did he move. Fiona stepped back, her eyes glazed and, kneeling, blew softly against the front of his breeches. Alex felt his traitorous manhood stir. He tried to will his lust away, but Fiona knew her work well, and soon his loins were aching to thrust and pound his murderous fury into her. And yet still he stood at attention, his eyes glued to the painting of the hated man who watched and twisted his own fat thighs as he writhed with excitement.

"Oh, how you used me," moaned Fiona, greedily nipping him through the tight material that was strained to bursting. "Now, I can use you."

Cameron fled the room, pursued by Captain Harris straight into the arms of Ian, who paced the hall.

"She's to go to the kitchens, colonel's orders," he puffed.

"I'll see she gets there, Harris," replied Ian, noting with consternation Cameron's agitated state.

"Yes, sir," complied Harris with alacrity, eager to eavesdrop at the drawing room door.

" 'Tis her . . . 'tis her, Lady Fiona Hurst!" exclaimed Cameron bitterly when they were in the kitchen corridor out of earshot of the captain.

"What is that devil up to?" swore Ian bitterly. " 'Tis foul and stinks, whatever it is . . . but we must na lose our heads, or we're lost. Come sit wie Fergus and Mackie and calm yourself," he comforted, herding her into the warm kitchen, where Mackie and old Granny MacNab busily stirred and chopped. Fergus sat in conversation with Young-MacNab and Dougal.

"I want to rid myself of these hampering clothes and go outside," said Cameron, needing to release her tension by blotting out everything and galloping through the darkness on Torquod's back.

" 'Tis no time for running. Your man needs you," reproved Fergus. "Och, easy it is to turn tail and pretend 'tis not happening . . . but 'tis not the way."

"But *she's* here!"

"Och, I know who's here, but there's nothing she can do unless you let her. She's none but a bitter, jealous woman, and she has reason for jealousy. Alexander loves you. Now remember that, lass . . . and whatever entertainment they've planned, we've got some of our own, or rather it seems Daft-Dougal here has," said Fergus.

"Aye, I have that," cackled Dougal, rolling his eyes and rubbing his gnarled hands together. "Unnatural entertainment," he added enigmatically.

"His name's Randall like the song . . . and Mackie's cooking eel," giggled Cameron a little hysterically.

"Did he turn a might green around the gills when he heard?" questioned Mackie, straightening Cameron's hair and rubbing some color into her pale cheeks.

"Aye, and I sang 'Lord Randall' and made up a few words of my own," gurgled Cameron. "But what are they doing in there to Alex? I know 'tis no good . . . and hurtful!"

"Dinna fash yerself sick, he's a big, braw man and can take care of hisself. Besides, they'll not dare harm him wie those two in the house," soothed Fergus.

"Who else is here?" asked Ian.

"A judge from the lord advocate's office and another from Lord Kames," responded Fergus dourly.

"Lord Kames? The commissioner of the forfeited estates! Och, now I have some idea of what Beddington is planning," exclaimed Ian bitterly.

"What? What does it all mean? Who is this Kames man?" questioned Cameron.

"Henry Home, Lord Kames, is another judge in charge of all the lands that were forfeited after the uprising in Forty-five," explained Ian.

"And the other lord you mentioned?" probed Cameron.

"The lord advocate ended the right of inheritable jurisdiction in seventeen forty-seven . . . for rebels, that is, but they let the lairds who swore loyalty to the English throne retain their lands and called it compensation."

"I dinna ken," said Cameron impatiently. "You're using longer words than Randall Beddington."

"It means this . . . the two men upstairs are judges. They make laws and see that they're carried out. There are judges for all sorts of things, but the two upstairs deal mainly with land . . . the land that was taken from the Jacobites after the Forty-five. Now this land was taken . . . Glen Aucht, you ken? And Alex won it back by—"

"By fighting for the English!" interrupted Cameron savagely.

"Och, now, dinna you be so quick to judge!" reprimanded Fergus.

"He was a bairn no older than you! Scarce twelve years old too when he landed in the New World wie a father who'd become little more than a helpless babe. Alexander worked for three years so he could bring his father home to Scotland to die . . . and what was here for him? No family . . . no land . . . he made his decision to regain what was rightfully his so that he as a Scot could still stand proud and tall on Scottish soil, breathing Scottish air. Aye, 'tis easy to judge a man when you're not in his shoes, but 'twas not easy swallowing pride and fighting for the English cause over the seas. He asked me once what good would Scotland be without Scots and said that we had to stay so our grandchildren and great-grandchildren would inherit the earth that had been christened with the blood of so many."

"But he won this land back, so what's to fear from the judges?" asked Cameron shamefacedly after a pause.

"Seems as though Beddington wants to challenge."

"Greedy mucker, isn't he? You'd think my lands would be enough for him," laughed Ian hollowly.

"He took yours?" exclaimed Cameron with horror.

"Aye, but mine were easier, as he has a family connection to my maternal grandmother. He's going to have a hard time proving that Alex is not loyal to the crown. He didna have to prove it to get my lands."

A long, glum silence hung as all stared sorrowfully at Ian, whose usual carefree, mischievous nature was hidden by the frown that creased his brow.

"Och, this is na guid! We'll win nothing wie long faces and drooping spirits. Mrs. MacDonald, would you be letting us have a wee dram of spirits to raise our flagging ones?" wheedled Dougal.

"We'll all be needing sharp wits about us, not dulled ones," clucked Mackie disapprovingly. "Och, but I wouldna say no to a wee dram myself," she relented.

"Where's our Jemmy-Lad?" inquired Fergus as Mackie bustled around setting glasses and Dougal opened a bottle, sniffing it appreciatively.

"Dinna fash, Mr. MacDonald, she's . . . I mean he's wie Old-Petey, settling in the strangers' horses. Really picked up, she has . . . he has . . . bright and shiny like a new penny, thanks to you, milady," said Young-MacNab shyly to Cameron.

"Please, 'tis something I want to say to all of you before you drink," stated Cameron earnestly, looking from one face to another. "All of you please listen to me, for I dinna know quite how to say it. 'Tis like you are all my family. The only one I have on this earth. You're like my brothers and sisters, mother and father and grandparents . . . I'm a part of you, no more nor less. I am not your lady. Each time one of you calls me ma'am or mistress or lady, 'tis like I am cold and alone, so dinna call me anything but my name, I beg you."

"Can't say that 'tis proper," sniffed Mackie, wiping her brimming eyes on a corner of her apron.

"I'll drink to that!" declared Ian, raising his glass.

"Aye," agreed Fergus, following suit.

"Aye," chorused Daft-Dougal.

"Now, back to work, or there'll be nocht but bread and scrape and fancy words to eat," fussed Mackie, breaking the poignant silence that followed the draining of the glasses.

"Is there aught I can do?" offered Cameron.

"Nay, nay, you just sit tight and rest yourself while you can as I'm betting there'll be much asked of you before this drear night is over," replied the busy housekeeper.

"I remembers when you played the pipes . . . a sweet coronach that swelled from your soul and touched all our hearts," growled Daft-Dougal, peering intently at Cameron, neither eyeball rolling but perfectly straight and true in his head.

"Aye," replied Cameron wistfully as she thought of another supper party when Fiona, after playing the piano, had challenged her˙as to her drawing room accomplishments. " 'Twas Ian's idea, not mine."

"They were Fergus's pipes, not mine . . . and you the piper," laughed Ian.

"There wasna a dry eye in the house," added Mackie without looking up from her chopping and stirring.

"There's true pipers and there's them that just blows hot air, and, lass, you are a piper. I'll be calling on you to play again but not to stir the soul this time . . . 'twill be to call the revenant . . . he or she whose blood was spilled upon the foundation stone to guard this house from evil," uttered Dougal slowly, his eyeballs flickering up so that they hid in his head.

"Pay no heed to the ramblings of our gley-eyed friend here," laughed Fergus, noting Cameron's startled expression. "He got you into enow mischief last night."

"Gley-eyed, is it?" snapped Dougal, his eyes coming sharply into focus. "Och, you'll just be jealous of my witching powers. Beware, Fergus MacDonald, for as you well know, I can summon a glaistig wie her long yellow hair and flowing green gown to curse and bless as she sees fit! Now, young lass," he said, turning back to Cameron. "There is work for you wie your blessed green eyes . . . the color of nature and the wee fairy folk. You have the power to aid me. Och, there's folks who think green is the color of evil, but 'tis only evil to them that are so."

Cameron sat spellbound as his words triggered the rhyme that was tauntingly repeated throughout her childhood. "Witch's spawn and kelpie's kin, and your heart is black wie sin," she mouthed, remembering how mothers used to cross themselves to ward off evil as they herded their children and animals away from her.

"Och, dinna let Daft-Dougal dig up them old hurts, lass. You ken he's awa' wie the fairies, ain't you, Dougal?" chuckled Fergus, trying to break the tension.

"Aye, I'm awa' wie the fairies, but noo the way you ken. Your heart's na black wie sin, wee-un . . . but proud should you be akin to the wee people. They'll nay skaith you unless you sell your soul to them . . . and that you mustna sell to any . . . nor gie to any but always keep for yourself," informed Dougal.

"But kin to a witch? I dinna like that," responded Cameron.

"There's bad and guid of them just like earth folk. Just keep your soul for yourself and they'll not harm. There's mischief in all of us . . . and if you're unnatural, then the mischief is more powerful. When Mrs. MacDonald is in a stamash at some lazy slummock of a maid, she'll gie a headache to the rest of us wie her banging of pots and sharp tongue. A regular limmer she is when she's angry. Now, when a witch gets in a stamash and is boiling wie fury, there's real trouble. Wie out her really meaning to, she can change herself into a cat and sink a ship to the bottom of the sea . . . but to her 'tis no different than Mrs. MacDonald banging the pots wie her spurtle, you ken? And what would you say to Mrs. MacDonald, aye? You'd gie your apologies . . . and maybe say something loving and gentle. Well, 'tis the same wie a witch. You can sink her in her sieves just by smiling and saying, 'Go in the name of the best,' you ken?"

"I dinna ken if Mrs. MacDonald is flattered by the use of her name," chuckled Fergus, eyeing his wife, who stood with a stirring spoon in her hand glaring at Daft-Dougal. "Looks to me if the spurtle may be banging on you and not the pots."

"Do you believe in what you dinna ken?" asked Dougal, ignoring both the MacDonalds.

"You mean like the gruagach, the wee brownies who care for the Highland cattle?" asked Cameron.

"Aye, them and more?"

"Well, I've seen the fairy rings of the Daoine Sith . . . and many shians, but not here in the south," confessed Cameron.

"What are the Daoine Sith and shians?" asked Ian, not sure how to accept the strange conversation.

"The Daoine Sith are the wee people, and the shians are their hills," replied Cameron. "Aye, Dougal, I told you before I believe."

"You believe in magic and fairies and the like?" laughed Ian.

"Of course," she answered. "Dinna you?"

"And of course you've seen the wee folk?" he chuckled.

"Do you have to see to believe? There's many who believe in a God and have they seen him? Mara, Duncan Fraser's woman, taught me to fear the Daoine Sith. She was forever picking the Mohan herb from the mountainside where no man had trod. 'Twas all evil and darkness, she said."

"Aye, like the kirk . . . some preach of a god of love and gentleness and others of a god of wrath and vengeance . . . and all are Christians," said Dougal dourly.

"I canna believe you give credence to fairies and witches and ghosts?" pronounced Ian. "Do you also believe in the tea-leaf-reading Gypsys, speywives, dragons, and the like?"

"What's not to believe? There's more proof of them and for them than for any Christian God. The Daoine Sith leave their signs for all to see. The twisted ropes of sand that ridge the seashore . . . the ring of toadstools that spring in a perfect circle between midnight and sunrise . . . and there's many who can foretell what is to be," declared Cameron.

"My own ancestor was the Fairy-boy of Leith. Every Thursday before midnight he'd fly over the seas to meet the Daoine Sith and on his return could recount the future to those who asked," stated Dougal proudly.

"I've only heard of Daft-Jamie of Leith, who'd run as naked as the day he was born around the racetrack thinking he was both horse and rider," laughed Ian.

"Aye, I've heard of him . . . used to pour soup in his pockets to take home to his ma," chuckled Fergus.

"Laugh if you will, but the lass is right, there's too many signs and too many prophesies fulfilled," growled Dougal.

"Aye," joined in Mackie. "Think on Claverhouse of Dundee, who sold his soul to the devil . . . leaden bullets would bounce off him like dried peas. He could turn a cup of wine into clotted blood and boil cold water wie a touch of his foot. He was killed at the Battle of Killiecrankie by a silver button fired by his own gillie . . . and there were many folks who witnessed all of it."

"Duncan Fraser told me of Kenneth MacKenzie, called the Brahan Seer. He told of Culloden more'n a hundred years before it happened . . . and said Scotland wouldna be free until the black rains covered our land," volunteered Cameron earnestly.

"Aye, the black rains," murmured Dougal.

"You canna believe such gibberish stite?" said Ian, staring around the kitchen expecting to meet other skeptical eyes, but to his surprise he found all work had ceased as each and every person listened intently.

"The black rains will come, mark my words. There's many things the Brahan Seer saw. He was given the gift by the ghost of the princess of Norway," stated Daft-Dougal solemnly.

"Aye, puir wee lost soul buried so far from her home in the soil of the Black Isles, near Inverness," added Mackie.

"If Kenneth MacKenzie could foretell the future, why, then, didna he avoid the keg of boiling pitch the countess of Seaforth cooked him in?" challenged Ian.

"Foretelling the future doesna prevent it," returned Dougal.

"Granted," conceded Ian. "But there's more. He laid a curse upon the House of Seaforth, striking the laird both mute and deaf, having him outlive his own sons . . . and from what I hear they're all enjoying excellent health."

"Aye, for now. But he didna say which laird. He said the House of Seaforth would be lost in the sands of time, just a cobweb of memory . . . maybe not in this lifetime nor the next, but just like the black rains it will come to pass," stated Dougal vehemently.

"Aye," chorused fervent voices.

"Keep your mind open, Ian Drummond, even if you dinna ken . . . just keep your mind and eyes open," warned Dougal.

"Ian, one small acorn, only this big," offered Cameron, making a small ring with her finger and thumb, "contains a tree maybe as tall as, if nay taller than, this house. Can you reason it?"

"Aye, 'tis the science of nature," answered Ian.

"And what is nature but a miracle? Magic!" pronounced Dougal. " 'Tis getting late, and soon the bell will toll for Mrs. MacDonald and us minions to feed the English pigs. Here, lass, take this rowan charm and tuck it in your bodice. 'Twill keep you unafraid, no matter what you see tonight," said Dougal gravely, handing Cameron a small sprig.

"I had forgotten about the Daoine Sith since coming south. Nay, not so much forgotten but not thought on. 'Tis like in the Highlands, 'tis all around, but here where 'tis low and smoky wie so many people and buildings I thought there was no place for them to be. I thank you, Dougal, 'tis like you've given me back part of myself . . . and I hope you're right and I have some power to help you . . . for I swear I'd do anything to harm the English muckers who trespass here," professed Cameron, kissing the thin, weather-beaten face of Daft-Dougal.

"You're a bewitching wee lass. . . . Now remember, no matter what powers of darkness appear tonight, you will be safe, and no harm shall come to those close to your heart."

CHAPTER ELEVEN

The enormous dining hall was warmed by a roaring fire and lit by numerous candles branched along the massive table and sconced on the paneled walls. The reflections of the many flames flickered and licked the shining wood surfaces in ever-changing patterns of gold and red; and mischievous shadows danced across the ornate ceiling, converging into obscurity in the dark corners of the room as though they were playing hide and seek.

Cameron sat alone, isolated, staring down the long expanse of table to the five people who clustered at the distant end. The heat from the tapering flames distorted the faces, making them seem grotesque and nightmarish. As was to be expected, Beddington had appropriated the master's chair, where he sat much like an indolent king, lolling obscenely with one fat leg over the carved arm of his throne, with a bubbling, overly vivacious Fiona on his left, facing a stony, impenetrable Alex on his right. Two old, wizen men, dwarfed by the high, carved backs of their chairs, hunched over their platters of food silently, slowly and thoroughly chewing without raising their eyes.

"Sir Robert Kinkaid, I must confess to being surprised at your presence, as I expected your noted colleague at the bench, Judge Walmer. Of course I am honored by your company," proclaimed Beddington, hiding his consternation badly with an excess of joviality.

"I am an old man who respects the limitations of age," replied Sir Robert wtih cool cordiality. "I find it imprudent to sup and converse at the same time."

"Imprudent?" laughed Beddington.

"To my digestion," answered Sir Robert icily.

"Oh, come, come, now, Sir Robert, surely you'll not have us believe that you are old?" cajoled Fiona seductively.

"Allow me to be the better judge of that!" snapped the ancient man cantankerously.

"What wit! What wit!" guffawed Beddington, insensitive to the seriousness and unheeding of the sharp kick that Fiona delivered. Despite Sir Robert Kinkaid's shriveled and wrinkled appearance, his eyes were as piercing as a hawk's as he glared silently and witheringly. Beddington's irritating laugh wilted, and he sat embarrassed with an inane smile frozen across his bloated features.

"Judge Singleton, I hope you find everything to your satisfaction," purred Fiona to the other old man, hoping to ease the awkwardness. "Judge Singleton?" she repeated as he seemed totally deaf and famished for he neither acknowledged nor slowed the rapid, jerky movements of his fork to his mouth.

Cameron was glad of her shadowy seat apart. Not hungry, she idly toyed with her food, her eyes pinned to the amount of bosom Fiona displayed and seemed to push temptingly across the table to Alex, who sat steadily eating. It was too far to see his reaction or expression, but the flickering candles played with Cameron's imagination as the wicked, dancing lights grotesquely distorted the scene, seeming to elongate the breasts so that they floated teasingly nearer and nearer to Alex, caressing and dancing titillatingly away each time his mouth opened to eat the food from his fork. Cameron's stomach churned, for the very fact that Alex could eat seemed a disloyalty. She forced her gaze away toward Ian, who stood at attention like a footman, alert to spring forward to refill an empty goblet or pull a chair back for a rising guest. He smiled roguishly, hoping to reassure her, but the strange lighting and seething fury in Cameron turned the smile into an evil, gloating leer. She frantically searched the room with her eyes for one stable, unmoving shape to ground herself, but each object writhed and was distorted into constantly changing nightmarish deformities.

The meal was interminable as course followed course and Cameron hung onto her sanity, clinging to the strong edge of the table. The fire roared in the immense hearth, and the sound joined with the rushing of her blood. She was in some kind of hell . . . she was burning, suffocating . . . there was nowhere she could rest her eyes. She wrestled with herself and determinedly stared back at Fiona; at least her pain and jealousy at the other woman's outrageously seductive manner toward Alex was real . . . maybe the only real thing in the churning, writhing room. Daft-Dougal, Mackie, Fergus, and Young-MacNab silently glided in and out of the room, appearing wraithlike, their faces shrouded and impassive as they served and removed. Their sly winks and smiles of reassurance to Cameron were lost as she avoided their eyes and concentrated on the hated Fiona and her voluptuous, taunting breasts. Curses and jingles pounded with the rhythm of her thumping pulses as she concentrated, willing some force, some supernatural power to pierce the woman so that she'd collapse and shrivel. The dancing candlelight and her heightened senses caused the creamy mass of Fiona to ebb and ebb . . . shrinking and shrinking to bony, haglike lines, but just when Cameron started to rejoice, the mischievous light would reverse and enhance the hated woman with soft, swelling, ethereal lines. Cameron concentrated harder, her bright emerald eyes fixed to one breast, willing, willing pain. A sharp scream caused forks to clatter and all eyes to turn from platters to Fiona's open wailing mouth. Not caring for the shocked expressions of the two old judges, Fiona tore at her breast, exposing her nipple as she tried to scrape off the burning wax that had poured like a torrent from a branch of candles that now seemed to dance mockingly in victory.

"My breast! My breast!" screamed Fiona.

The moment seemed suspended in time as Beddington stared at her, his mouth agape full of half-chewed food. Alex sat like a golden statue, impassive, the light playing across the chiseled planes of his face, and the two old men appeared as small, motionless shadows. Cameron sat back and surveyed the tableau before her. The candlelight and firelight got brighter and brighter, throbbing with intensity, changing the once deforming scene into a harsh, frozen moment in time. Without a flicker the flames got longer and longer . . . reaching straight up like tapering spears to the ceiling. A sudden rumble of thunder broke the stillness, and Fiona's shrill scream echoed and reechoed. The candle flames returned to flickering normalcy as Daft-Dougal silently closed the kitchen door that caused the sudden draft. At the very second of unfreezing, as Fiona opened her mouth to scream again and Beddington reached out to help, a keening wind burst open one of the immense mullioned windows with a deafening crash, breaking the glass so that it smashed and shattered across the stone floor and doused each and every candle. The fire in the hearth reduced its flames to an even glow, as though cowed and afraid of the sudden invading violence. Beddington fumbled around the table, knocking over goblets and tureens as he blindly felt for the handbell.

"Service! Service!" he cried hoarsely.

The kitchen door swung open silently, and four black-shrouded shapes filed in and stood, their faces turned toward the window that was flattened back against the wall. The eerie light of a full moon flooded in, turning the once warm, golden colors to a waxen pale green.

"Fasten up that window! Pull the draperies! Relight the candles!" screamed Beddington, his face gleaming with sweat in the weird, uncanny glow, but no one moved. Fiona's mouth was wide open as though she had been paralyzed at the peak of her scream. Her hands still clutched one breast, and her head was thrown back, showing the strained, knotted sinews of her neck. Every face but Beddington's looked expectantly toward the window. He sat ranting and thumping and yelling out his orders, his voice getting shriller and shriller . . . fainter and fainter. To Cameron's eye it seemed his obese body pulsated, growing larger and larger and then smaller and smaller until he shrank to a tiny, impotently writhing, mute figure in the large, looming chair. Distantly she heard a rhythmic whooshing coming nearer and nearer . . . louder and louder like a deep steady breathing that seemed to cow the fire further so that it hid beneath the blackened logs. Nearer and nearer, louder and louder, the ominous beating of heavy wings . . . until silhouetted against the eerie light, spanning the wide window, hung suspended an enormous bird, the moon behind seeming to burn through its head and send piercing streams of light from its eyes. A crack of lightning accompanied by a resounding crash of thunder propelled the bird into the room. The flames of the fire

shot up higher and higher, dancing in exultation and jubilation, as though fanned by the dark, rushing wings.

" 'Tis death . . . a raven!" stated Daft-Dougal, and at
his words bedlam broke loose as Fiona's suspended scream
resumed, accompanied by Beddington's graceless blubbering and Harris's high-pitched wailings as they all frantically flapped their arms. As though controlled by the
emotions of the three, the bird's agitation increased. The
more they screamed and waved their arms, the more frantic
became the movements of the giant wings and the more
agonized the hoarse cawings as it flew this way and that,
trying desperately to find its way back outside. Faster and
faster the hysteria mounted, feeding the raven, who
swooped and fluttered, its wings brushing and crashing
crockery from the table to the floor. Shriller and shriller
became the human voices, hoarser and hoarser became the
anguished croaks of the bird as it flung its glossy black
body against each wall, violently seeking freedom.

Cameron stared in horror at the feverish agitation, her
heart hammering painfully in her chest as though she were
the tormented raven, She stood upon her chair, holding out
her arms, willing the bird to come to her. The raven ceased
its frantic, compulsive flight and alit on the back of one of
of the numerous empty seats between Cameron and the
rest. Beddington froze, shutting his mouth to muffle the
terror that burst out so noisily. One by one each stopped
his screams until all that could be heard was the hiccoughing sounds of sobbing breaths. Cameron crooned softly in
Gaelic to the raven, urging it to be calm, telling it that she
would give it freedom. The glossy bird cocked its head and
fixed her with two sharp eyes. It jiggled from one foot to
the other and rocked its body as though to fly to her outstretched arms.

"Your heart beats as mine, Raven," pleaded Cameron,
but still the bird sat hesitatingly, bobbing his head. "As a
child I was oft called Raven's-blood . . . for you see, my
black hair 'tis as your feathers . . . and my blood-red lips
. . . and my love of freedom."

Fiona gave a piercing scream as the bird launched itself
into the air. Beddington hastily clamped one pudgy hand

over her mouth to quiet her, but it was as though the raven saw, for it circled them mockingly before alighting gracefully on Cameron's arm. She smiled at it and longed to smooth its ruffled feathers but, knowing instinctively not to stretch the trust it'd shown her, curbed her impulse. Slowly she bent her legs, reaching with her free hand to the table for support as she stepped down from the chair. The bird was heavy on her forearm, causing it to ache with the effort of keeping it still and outstretched so as not to frighten him. As though sensing her discomfort, the bird gave a hop, landing on her shoulder.

Cameron surveyed the people at the other end of the table. They sat motionless, holding their breaths, it seemed, for fear one movement might put the raven to mad flight again. She looked at them one by one. Sir Robert Kinkaid's piercing gaze reminded her much of the raven, as did Alex's, and yet she couldn't fathom either expression. Beddington, Fiona, and Harris had their hands stuffed into their mouths as their eyes seemed to bulge in panic. The shadowy figures of Ian, Mackie, Fergus, Young-MacNab, and Daft-Dougal stood stolid and supportive, even though she couldn't see their faces. Outside, the storm raged violently, lashing the side of the house and whistling its gusty fury through the open window, drenching the floor with spitting, stinging spears of wetness. Feeling tall and calm, Cameron walked slowly to the open window, where she stood letting the fierce rain scrub her face, cooling her jealousy and anger. She stared over the countryside, feeling the energy of the storm stir her blood with excitement. Oh, to be out there defying the elements, racing with the wind, howling with the gusts that bent the trees and grasses and whipped the waves of the firth to ecstasy. The raven rubbed its glossy ebony head against her identical one, bringing her back to the present.

"Fly free," she whispered. The raven remained motionless, staring at her profile as she looked out at the shining, moving darkness. Sensing its eyes, she raised her hand, not wanting to turn her head and startle it nor to get inadvertently pecked. He carefully stepped onto her small hand, and they gazed at each other. Cameron laughed softly and gently stroked his feathers, delighting in his sleekness.

The raven flew off into the raging night-darkness, and Cameron watched until it was swallowed up in the shiny wet blackness, her heart flying with it as she longed to purge herself by also becoming part of the storm. She wheeled suddenly and walked determinedly across the room, ignoring everyone. Now she felt small and vulnerable. She had to get away from the claustrophobic atmosphere . . . she had to become part of the natural forces outside . . . she would suffocate in the social artificiality in the house . . . would become frantic and self-destructive like the raven . . . blindly hitting out and hurting herself until she knew and felt nothing. She had to get out to find peace for herself.

The door swung shut after Cameron, and the awed silence was broken . . . fragmented.

"Stop her . . . stop her. She's a witch! She's a sorceress . . . a minion of the prince of darkness. Sir Robert, Judge Singleton, you are witnesses . . . can attest to the fact," screamed Fiona in a high-pitched voice.

"Get that window fixed . . . and let us to the drawing room away from this cold draft. Wine . . . bring more wine," ordered Beddington. "Harris, move yourself!"

Captain Harris ran this way and that, not knowing what to do first before buckling to his knees and sobbing as though he were five.

"Won't no one stop her?" shrieked Fiona. "Alex, has she turned you to stone that you just sit so silently without doing anything to stop her evil machinations? He's bewitched . . . she's cast a spell."

"Madame, hysteria is not conducive to digestion," remarked Sir Robert dryly. "All that occurred, though highly dramatic and entertaining, was no more than a natural phenomenon. A draft caused by the brewing storm caused the tallow to spill unfortunately upon you. The high winds broke the window latch, dousing the candles and blowing the poor bird into the room."

"And what of that green-eyed witch?" insisted Fiona.

"Are you referring to our gracious hostess, the Lady Sinclair?" asked Sir Robert Kinkaid icily.

"You saw how the raven flew to her as though summoned?"

"There's many who have a natural affinity for wild creatures. The king himself is said to be so gifted in that way," remarked the old man, standing briskly. "Mrs. MacDonald, that was fine Scottish fare and entertainment, but I would relish a warming dram to aid digestion. Sinclair, I suggest you lead the way to a warmer, cozier place. My old rheumatic bones don't appreciate this damp, drafty room." Alex stood and bowed ironically, silently indicating with one movement of his hand that Colonel Beddington was playing host.

"By all means let us adjourn to more hospitable surroundings," proclaimed Beddington expansively. "Fiona, my arm. Now, let us lead the way. We shall partake of desserts, sweetmeats, and whatever in cozier climes."

Beddington, with a frantically babbling Fiona, exited the room. Judge Singleton, avoiding all eyes, scampered after. As the door swung shut behind them, Sir Robert Kinkaid fixed Alex with a cold, speculative gaze.

"I'm surprised to find you in residence, Sinclair. Wagging tongues had it that you'd been absconded by . . . or had deserted with . . . andor disappeared off the face of the earth with an enchanting changeling child. There's always a grain of truth in the most fantastic of tales," remarked Sir Robert Kinkaid.

Alex stared above the tiny, shriveled judge, fixing his eyes on a knot in the wood paneling on the wall and assuming an air of tolerant boredom.

"Yet here you are in the flesh, though your spirit seems to have absconded, deserted, or disappeared," challenged the feisty old man cuttingly, and was rewarded to note the silent ticking in the tall, golden-haired Scot's lean cheek. "Wouldn't attribute the absence to witchlike means . . . perhaps bitchlike, if you can grasp my drift?" he added dryly.

Alex turned his amber eyes back to Sir Robert. Was this strange little gnome of a man friend or foe? The piercing eyes, nestled at the bottom of myriads of wrinkles, met his gaze, strongly belying the time-eroded flesh, making him feel as vulnerable as if he were a half-grown truant. Alex glared back unflinchingly, furious at his urge to hang his head as shame flooded through his strong young body. Who was this old man? Was he a pawn of Beddington's brought to gain his confidence somehow? He searched the fragile, parchment face in awe of the great strength that emanated from the bright, sharp eyes.

"You are an enigma, sir," he said wonderingly, without thought.

"That makes two of us, Sinclair," chuckled the ancient judge. "I think we should suspend our judgments of each other and follow to the drawing room. I'd hate to miss the second act of this highly melodramatic entertainment. There'll be time to converse, I'm sure, when that posturing pederast, Beddington, and that miserable woman have drowned their hysteria," he added, opening the door.

"You see what we're up against, Judge Singleton? You see?" gabbled Beddington, trotting backward and forward in front of the hearth. "Nobody ever believes me . . . no one! I tell them . . . I warn them, but do they take heed? No! They laugh . . . they jeer . . . they mock and treat me like a recalcitrant child . . . like an idiotic imbecile . . . like a criminal! Exiling me . . . punishing me . . . making me a mockery!" he ranted, nearly in tears.

"But you made no mention of supernatural happenings," chattered Singleton, his nervousness causing his hands to smooth his clothes meticulously with jerky brushing movements.

"That is a bold-faced lie, sir!" screeched Beddington. "Lady Fiona, did I not mention the talk that surrounded that little black-haired chit?"

"My breast . . . I shall be scarred," sobbed Fiona, cradling her injured part.

"I give no credence to ignorant superstition of changelings and the like . . . but you also said nothing of Sinclair being here . . . said he had fled the country . . . deserted," snapped the old man, busily picking invisible lint from his clothing and avoiding Beddington's eyes.

"He arrived less than a week ago—how could I warn you, as you were already on the way from London. Unfortunately, *I* do not possess any powers of the occult! I barely had enough time to prepare Lady Fiona . . . but since she lives in Edinburgh, I managed," ranted Beddington, resuming his furious pacing but keeping a wary eye on the door.

"And Kinkaid! Of all people to thrust me with! A barbaric Scot ready to turn a dagger in me at the drop of a hat! You are the liar, Beddington. Walmer you said it was to be. Walmer a loyal Englishman . . . but Kinkaid, where's your sense? Not that I don't think what you're about is just and lawful—"

"Do you think me lunatic?" screamed Beddington, interrupting Singleton so that his busy fingers stilled for a fraction and then frantically resumed the smoothing and picking at his clothing. "*I* did not invite Kinkaid here," he hissed, lowering his voice for fear of beng overheard. "I hoped you'd enlighten me as to his presence."

"I? Me? Why me? I have avoided being in the same room with the man . . . to eat at the table with him was not a pleasant experience. You saw how he looked at me?"

"How you saw anything with your head buried in your plate the whole meal . . ." spat Beddington viciously. "But that is neither here nor there. The thing is what do we do now?"

"I think that is your concern. I know you hope to claim Sinclair's lands, and from the little you've told me, there does seem to be some doubt as to Sinclair's ownership. But as to your claiming them . . . well, there I see no legal precedent. At Drummonds there were family connections and the dowager did not oppose but supported your claim—"

"You sniveling little weasel! Backing down now, are you?"

"I must object to your insults," whispered Singleton, nearly in tears, his head sinking into the heavy clothes that hung on his shriveled frame, his fingers busily nipping and smoothing, his eyes never leaving his knees.

"Object? Object? I am the one who should object!" blustered Beddington.

The door opened suddenly, and Alex and Kinkaid entered. Colonel Beddington stopped his frantic pacing and stared malevolently at the tall, lean young man and the tiny, old one. His face was suffused with blood and his breathing heavy and ponderous.

"Object? What were you objecting to, Beddington? Please

don't let the presence of young Sinclair or myself interrupt your conversation," said Kinkaid wryly, breaking the still silence that heralded their entrance. Beddington's eyes flickered this way and that as he tried to calm himself and think of an answer.

"Brandy!" he uttered suddenly. "That was it, brandy. Your learned colleague refused, and I objected as after the trial . . . the horrendous trial that you, my most welcome guests, were subjected to . . . I offer the most delectable French brandy."

"Smuggling now, are you, Beddington?" remarked Kinkaid, lifting a quizzical gray eyebrow.

"Not me, your honor, but Sinclair here . . . it is from his cellar," smirked Randall Beddington.

"It is one of the many sadnesses about our conflict with France, the lack of good cognac," stated Sir Robert Kinkaid.

"My sister Amelia is always decrying the lack of fine lace," twitted Singleton, still intently focused on his busy hands, which meticulously fiddled with the nonexistent lint on his clothes.

"Are you not going to pour?" charged Kinkaid impatiently.

"The smuggled brandy?" hesitated Beddington.

"Until one has tasted, one cannot rightly judge, as it is easy to exchange the superior contents with an inferior," snapped Kinkaid, filling two glasses with generous amounts and crossing to the hearth, where he stood staring speculatively at the amber liquid as he swirled it around.

"Sinclair, join me," he ordered, offering one to Alex, who stood stiffly by the door.

Sinclair and Kinkaid stood with their backs to the fire, usurping Beddington's favorite spot. The fat man hovered, ill at ease, looking for support from Fiona and Singleton, who sat absorbed, their eyes turned to themselves as one picked the lint from his knees and the other nursed her breast, straining to see the extent of the damage.

"Madame, this is hardly a suitable place for such personal ministrations," pronounced Kinkaid cuttingly. Fiona looked up, startled. Her tears had smudged and splattered her carefully contrived makeup. Black lines streamed down from her eyes, taking arbitrary routes and converging like veins. The red paint from her mouth was spread, giving the appearance of an open wound. Her elaborate coiffure had collapsed, the stiffened, coarse hair sticking out in all directions much like a year-old nest after a storm.

"Alex . . . oh, Alex, look," she whimpered pitifully, exposing her breast.

Singleton's shiny forehead nearly touched his knees, and his frenetically busy fingers bumped his beaky nose as he applied every scrap of his concentration to the avoidance of the scene before him.

"Madame, I assure you that Sir Alexander Sinclair has more pressing matters consuming him than your mammary gland, and I have long since abandoned any desire to raise my weary flesh," stated Sir Robert. "As for Colonel Beddington, his tastes seem to lie in less riper orchards, and my colleague, Singleton, is aptly named and quite content with his sister."

Beddington gasped at the effrontery, Singleton's head cracked painfully against his bony knees, a smile twitched across Alex's stony face, and Fiona fled screaming from the room.

"Now I understand the custom of segregating the sexes after a filling repast," remarked Kinkaid after the door had slammed shut behind the loudly wailing woman.

"I find your manner distasteful and criminally slanderous!" spluttered Beddington finally.

"I find your slanderous tastes criminal and distasteful," parried Kinkaid. "But I am sure we are not gathered to discuss your sexual appetites, Beddington."

Randall Beddington stepped backward, struck dumb at the low blow, and collapsed gracelessly on the sofa.

"If you gentlemen will excuse me, I am an old man and have not been in good health this past winter and find that the evening plus the long journey have exhausted me," twitted Singleton, his whole body twitching and jerking.

"I happen to be at least ten years older than you," interrupted Kinkaid. "So enough of your excuses. I should like to be informed as to the reasons we are congregated."

Singleton raised his eyes from his knees and stared toward Beddington, who sat motionless, his mouth agape, still in shock from Kinkaid's insults.

"C . . . C . . . Colonel Beddington re . . . re . . . requested a representative from the lord advocate's office," stammered the man, his head bobbing and jerking in agitation.

"And?" prompted Kinkaid.

"Tha . . . tha . . . that is wh . . . wh . . . why I am here."

"You were not invited," spat Beddington, shaken out of his stupor and pointing a chubby finger at Sir Robert. "I did not invite you. How dare you invite yourself and then trespass upon my hospitality?"

"*Your* hospitality?" answered Kinkaid coolly. "That has me puzzled, but let us deal with the issues at hand one at a time. Firstly, as to my being invited . . . I was given to understand that a judge from Lord Kames's commission was requested. I am such."

"It was to be Walmer!"

"Why?"

"He has familiarity with the case in question."

"And what is the case in question?"

Beddington glowered at Kinkaid with ill-disguised hatred.

"Singleton, maybe you can inform me as Colonel Beddington seems, for a change, to be at a loss for words?"

"It is whether Sinclair has right of ownership to Glen Aucht," replied the trembly old judge all in one breath.

Kinkaid nodded thoughtfully.

"And if he does not, who, may I inquire, is the claimant?"

Singleton perused his shoes and shrugged unhappily.

"That is not the issue," shouted Beddington.

"No?" smiled Kinkaid ironically.

"NO! It isn't," blustered Beddington, lumbering to his feet and drawing himself up. The tiny old man stared coldly at him, and Beddington puffed himself up further, intimidated despite the fact he was half again as tall and weighed at least four times more. "The issue is solely Sinclair's right of ownership."

"Voice your arguments."

"Well, go on, Singleton," hissed Beddington after a pause.

"Well, Colonel Beddington is citing the act of Seventeen Forty-seven . . . the termination of inheritable jurisdiction," stuttered Judge Singleton.

"And?" coaxed Kinkaid.

"What do you mean 'and?' . . . it is obvious!" spluttered the fat colonel.

"To you perhaps. I'm a doddering old man, so humor me," snapped Kinkaid.

"You are on the bench, sworn to uphold the king's law," retorted Beddington. "You are aware that the late Alexander Sinclair was a rebel . . . a Jacobite . . . a most wanted outlaw."

"Yes, but that was, as you said, *the late,* not the present Alexander Sinclair . . . and I am sure you, Colonel Beddington, are aware that under the same act of Seventeen Forty-seven, which terminated inheritable jurisdiction, compensation was paid to those loyal to the English crown," informed Kinkaid.

"INHERITABLE!" crowed Beddington maliciously. "He is his father's son, so what right has he to INHERIT? These lands were justly forfeited in seventeen forty-seven, as were the northern estates in Caithness."

"I am informed that this young man compensated and proved his loyalty to the crown by fighting under the commands of such noted generals as Braddock and Forbes . . . in fact he was willing and very nearly gave his life in the takeover of Fort Duquesne from the French in seventeen fifty-eight . . . and for this and other valiant deeds he was given recompense, namely this estate of Glen Aucht," proclaimed Kinkaid feistily. "Recompense, Beddington, *not* . . . I repeat *not,* inheritance!"

"It is the land of his father and his grandfather . . . call it what you want, it is still an inheritance," charged Beddington.

"Not in the interpretation of the law. Inheritable jurisdiction was terminated for *all* Scots. 'Tis called compensation. The lands in Caithness from John O'Groats to Dunbeath are still forfeited estates and remain in the hands of the commission under Henry Home, Lord Kames," returned Sir Robert, serenely refilling his and Alex's glasses generously.

"Compensation for those loyal to the crown?" crowed Randall Beddington rhetorically, rubbing his hands with greedy triumph. "Well, I charge Alexander Sinclair with treasonous acts!"

Kinkaid fixed Beddington with his searing eye, waiting for him to expand further.

"Such as?" he snapped after a long pause. Beddington took his time, thoroughly enjoying himself as he leisurely waddled to the sideboard and poured himself brandy. He drank greedily, and Kinkaid snorted impatiently.

"Drink lemonade or cordials, 'tis sacrilege to treat superb cognac so!"

"Such as aiding and abetting a known criminal . . . a rebel! Such as harboring a threat to the very throne itself!" proclaimed Beddington with great satisfaction. Alex's blood ran cold. What did the fat man know? Harboring a threat to the throne itself? Was he referring to Cameron?

"There's more charges such as failure to report on command to his regiment," chortled Beddington.

"The first two charges are serious enough *if* you can substantiate them," replied Kinkaid dryly. "Have you got Bonnie Prince Charlie himself hidden in your wine cellar, Alex?"

"It is no joking matter," blustered Beddington, the wind taken out of his sails by the apparent casual acceptance of his accusations.

"Who's joking?" cackled Kinkaid, superbly covering his own consternation. "We may be getting to the bottom of that smuggled brandy . . . for if Charles Stuart, the Pretender, is being harbored here . . . he might have smuggled it in with himself."

"I will be taken seriously!" screamed Beddington impotently.

"Of course," soothed Kinkaid mockingly, his tiny frame spasming with the giggles that shook him. "We are taking you very seriously, aren't we, Alexander?"

Alex was startled from his own seething thoughts. He stared into the wise old eyes, his own amber ones mirroring his fears. No longer painfully piercing, Robert Kinkaid's caressed and comforted, reflecting Alex's own trepidation and yet reassuring, much as his own father's had done before the English had caused his pride and manhood to crumble.

"Oh, by the by," said Kinkaid conversationally, seeing the searing pain in Alex's eyes and playing for time by turning to Beddington. "Have you heard that Pitt resigned in a snit?"

"Is it a riddle? Are you making fun of me?" attacked Beddington.

"No, he was denied money and permission to enlarge the war against Spain by the Cabinet. Admirable, awesome man, Pitt . . . brilliant strategist. 'Tis a pity. I'd have liked to have played chess with Pitt, the Great Commoner. He was a brilliant war minister . . . his determination to win was absolute, yet he lost his objectivity. Well, maybe now that he has more time on his hands, he'll have more time for parlor games," rambled Kinkaid.

"Has his resignation been accepted?" asked Beddington.

"Not officially, but it will be."

"How can you be so sure?"

"Even the English are tired of war. Constant victory can be tedious, especially when it is the sweat of their brows that is paying," replied Kinkaid.

"Who's to replace him?" asked Beddington suspiciously.

"Whom do you think?" replied Kinkaid mischievously.

"No . . . no . . . not John Stuart, Earl of Bute?" gasped the fat man incredulously.

"Aye, that's the one," chortled Sir Robert.

"I knew it! I knew it! I warned them about him," expostulated Beddington, sitting heavily.

"Aye, I heard rumor of that . . . tried to discredit Bute with bedtime stories about the king's own mother, didn't you? Tut, tut, Randall, you should learn from Pitt and plan your strategy along less offensive lines," snickered Kinkaid. "Well, it has been a long day of travel and enlightening experiences, so I'm for retiring, as I expect another long, tedious day full of words tomorrow. Good night, gentlemen. Would you be gracious enough to show me to my chambers, Sir Alexander?"

Alex placed his brandy glass on the mantelpiece and stiffly nodded his head in assent.

"Good," replied Kinkaid, briskly rubbing his hands together.

"Major Sinclair is under my command, and I have need of him. Captain Harris will escort you to your room," informed Beddington hastily. "HARRIS? HARRIS?"

Captain Harris made his usual clumsy entrance by nearly falling into the room and sprawling across the floor as though he had been leaning upon the door with his eye to the keyhole and his hand on the knob. Singleton stood surreptitiously and prepared to scuttle out unseen to hide in the darkness of his own bed.

"Judge Singleton, I'm in need of your counsel," barked Beddington, causing the frantically nervous man to wring his hands and entwine his legs together as he twitched and bobbed.

"I feel very unwell," twittered the extremely agitated old man. "Very, *very* unwell," he repeated, looking very green and nauseous.

"Run along to bed, Singleton, I'll sacrifice my rest and counsel the colonel," said Kinkaid warmly, patting the other old man on his bent back and opening the door for him.

Before Beddington could open his astounded mouth to protest, Singleton was gone and the tiny leprechaun of a man stood before him grinning roguishly as he rocked forward and backward on his heels with his gnarled hands clasped behind his back. Harris stood cowering by the door, and Alex, resembling a statue, stared impassively into space, his face expressionless as though carved of marble.

CHAPTER TWELVE

Cameron tore through the raging darkness on Torquod's glistening bare back. She was at one with the seething elements . . . a part of the howling, rampaging wind that whipped her cheeks and streamed her tumultuous hair . . . a part of the stinging, driving rain that scoured, purging her of the cloying staleness of the nightmarish supper . . . a part of the slashing lightning and crashing thunder that liberated her pent-up emotions, elating her blood so that she cried out with jubilation. This was freedom, the wild, abandoned freedom she had craved for so long. The freedom she had reveled in as a solitary child on the stark moors of the Highlands. Unbound, unfettered, unrestrained, answerable to no one but the natural, furious ecstasy that exploded outside and within herself.

Jemmy-Lad crouched in the hayloft clutching her squirming, cowering puppy, her eyes glued to the silhouette of the coastline where the fleet, black shadow seemed to race with the wind. The little girl's freckled face shone with wonder at the flying figure, and she forgot her own fear of the raging storm.

"I'll be just like that, Maggie-Pup," she whispered comfortingly to the frightened dog. "I'll be braw and fearless and ride with the wind so none can catch me."

From an upstairs window, Judge Singleton in his nightshirt peeked through the heavy curtains out at the frenzied, furious night. His eyes widened in shock, and his pale complexion blanched as from out of the dark, thrashing shadows flew what seemed to be a phantom rider. Each sharp shattering of lightning lit the world for a pulsating split second, illuminating the ghostly figure and shuddering the old man's emaciated frame. Each ominous roll of thunder reverberated through his violently shaking body, quivering his bowels, and yet he stood staring as though hypnotized, unable to move or unfocus his eyes.

Fiona huddled in her bed as the wind howled and wailed like tormented voices, causing brittle tree-fingers to scrape the panes of the windows and chills to dance eerily up and down her spine. She hugged the covers to herself, her blistered breast forgotten as she rocked and moaned, her racing imagination whipped to panic by the vehemence of the raging storm.

Colonel Randall Beddington and Captain Harris were closeted behind the heavy draperies in the drawing room. The fat man was buffered from the screeching gale, which threw its full force upon the house as though demanding entrance, by an excess of brandy. Filled to overflowing with his own exacerbation, he was insensitive to the savage turbulence outside as his own inner fury pounded and seethed. Harris swayed drunkenly on his feet, his nerves frayed as he gave way to high-pitched, ragged giggles, fanning the flames of his commanding officer's rage.

Alex impassively watched his wife from their bedchamber window, heedless of the violently shaking panes that threatened momentarily to shatter from the furious battering of the wind and rain. His face betrayed no emotion. It was as though he were carved of cold granite, a counterpoint to the passionate intensity that raged, shaking the large stone house to its very foundations. A soft tapping at the door caused Torquil to raise his shaggy head and look expectantly toward Alex, who stood like a statue, his eyes glued to the speeding shadow that raced the wind and dared the lightning bolts. The rapping continued persistently, getting louder, and the large hound barked.

"Come in," intoned Alex without moving.

Sir Robert Kinkaid entered, quietly closing the door after quickly peering up and down the long hall to see whether or not he was being followed. He pursed his thin, pleated lips and surveyed the tall, broad back of the young man for a few moments before crossing and standing dwarfed by his side.

"The gods are angry," he stated conversationally and, with the lack of acknowledgment, turned his eyes to the scene outside. He knew what Alex watched, as he himself had spent some time fascinated by the sight of the graceful rider. He had felt his own departed youth and vitality surge back and had rejoiced that there still existed some spirit and spark in his own weary bones. They stood side by side, the tiny, fragile man whose old face glowed alive with exhilaration and the tall, strong man whose young face was shrouded, devoid of emotion, both silently gazing out over the tempestuous night. Robert Kinkaid turned and scrutinized Alex's expressionless face.

"It is the pain and passion of the whole universe within one small girl," he remarked. Alex did not move. "Is it stoicism, numbness, or indifference?" he added, hoping to goad Alex to react. Not a muscle twitched in the young man's face. "How can you stand amid such unrestrained foment with such apathy, Sinclair?"

"To what are you referring?" replied Alex coldly, his eyes still riveted to the coastline for sight of the impetuous, unbridled figure who raced with the shadows and then became part of them, reappearing against the foaming waters of the firth.

"It is analogous, is it not?" answered Kinkaid cryptically.

"To what?"

"To your inner turmoil . . . the gnawing away at the very roots of yourself, your home, family . . . native land," said the old man slowly and softly, hoping to see some crack in the young man's impenetrable façade. Alex continued to stare impassively out the window, which rattled violently as if reflecting his inner turmoil. With a sigh Sir Robert Kinkaid turned away and, rubbing cold, gnarled hands, stood with his back to the fire. He looked down at Torquil, who lay at the hearth by his feet, his large, shaggy head pillowed dejectedly on his massive paws, his mournful eyes glued to Alex's back.

"Even that huge, dumb beast shows his soul's torment in his eyes," remarked Kinkaid thoughtfully after a long pause. "Maybe I judge too harshly. If one of a pair is wild, impulsive, and without discipline . . . the other is robbed of the luxury in order to maintain a balance."

Alex turned suddenly.

"You'll not speak of my wife, sir!"

"I was not attacking," laughed Sir Robert, holding up his hands in mock terror. "I was but fishing . . . trying to fathom a way to reach beyond your forbidding exterior. Will she ride out the storm?"

"To the bitter end," answered Alex shortly.

"Both of them?"

"If you'll excuse me, Sir Robert. I am in no mood for idle socializing," retorted Alex sardonically.

"Neither am I."

The two men stood with their eyes locked in a battle of wills. Once again Alex felt intimidated by the old man's searing gaze.

"What do you want of me? You are here by no invitation of mine," said Alex harshly.

"Nor Colonel Beddington's . . . call me an uninvited guest. I am here at Lady Kames's request," informed Sir Robert, satisfied to see a look of puzzlement crease Alex's brow. "Do you know her?"

Alex shook his head.

"Before her marriage to Henry Home, Lord Kames, she was Agatha Drummond," informed Sir Robert, deliberately taking his time.

"I have no interest whatsoever in the society marriages," returned Alex.

"Nor in the predicament of friends?" answered Kinkaid, his own eyes flashing. "But that is to be expected from one who expresses no concern in his own."

"You seem to take pleasure in playing word games," spat Alex hoarsely.

"And you, young man, need a lesson in civility. Lady Agatha née Drummond is a kinswoman of your friend Ian Drummond. Ah, now I see that you are beginning to see the light."

"I apologize for my abrupt manner, but in the scant week I've been home, I have found it best to be on my guard. I was not sure if you were part of Beddington's greater plan to wrest Glen Aucht from me," confessed Alex bitterly.

"Understandable," murmured Kinkaid warmly, seating himself in one of the two comfortable chairs by the fire. "Sit down, Sinclair, I find you too tall, and craning my old neck is not conducive to communication."

"Are you representing Lord Kames?" asked Alex guardedly, seating himself opposite.

"Unfortunately I'm not. I am here on no authority but my own, and I'm afraid I have no authority, neither has Lady Agatha, except maybe to cause Beddington aggravation and doubt. There does not seem much to be done about Drummond's estate, as his grandmother sanctions the transferral, and the Cabinet prefers the muckraker Beddington far out of earshot. In other words it is a political convenience to them," explained Kinkaid sadly.

"Then what is the use of your presence?"

"To cause aggravation and to see that young Drummond is not transported on some trumped-up charge, which is one of Beddington's methods of ridding himself of inconvenient opposition to what he wants."

"Surely the Cabinet . . . the Ministry . . . the House of Lords does not condone him? It canna be that a man can just avariciously take another man's house and lands! There has to be legal recourse!" raged Alex.

"Usually, yes, but sadly there is unrest against Scotland in England. The drain on the English taxpayer due to this long war has created great animosity. Do you realize that before the Union English customs, excise, and land tax yields were more than thirty-eight times greater than Scotland's? And that was when the population ratio was only five to one—"

"What has all that to do wie—" interrupted Alex impatiently.

"Hold your horses!" shouted Sir Robert sharply. "From what I understood, you have been cut off from political news for some time, and it's best you understand a few facts! Now, sit back and listen. The union of the two countries is a complete drain economically on England . . . and now with this war the anti-Scottish feeling is rampant. The Highland regiments that are returning from their victories for England are being stoned at the docks! The King's friendship with John Stuart, the Earl of Bute, is fanning the animosity . . . and to top it all off it seems the Earl of Bute will very likely be appointed prime minister."

"Then that's to our favor," remarked Alex.

"What is? Having a Scottish prime minister? It is like

fire to a powder keg right now. In order to appease, the Cabinet and the bench must tread very lightly. Public opinion in London would be cheering Beddington on. At this time there is no way a stand can be taken against an Englishman when it concerns support of a Scot. Which brings me to you. What are these charges of treason against the throne?"

Alex stared back at the old man without answering.

"Is there any foundation to them?" probed Sir Robert impatiently.

"No, but I can see how malicious, graspling people could come to that conclusion," answered Alex evasively.

"Either tell me it's no concern of mine . . . or come to the point!" growled Kinkaid irascibly.

"Do you know of one Duncan Fraser?" said Alex after a long silence as the two men sat, eyes locked, summing each other up.

"Yes, there is quite a price on his head . . . dead or alive."

"Scarce nine months ago I received word from him instructing me to go to Cape Wrath," informed Alex and then stopped as he realized that those nine months seemed like years.

"So you went?"

"Aye, I'm not sure why. After the death of my parents and sisters it seemed a door had closed on that part of my life. His message opened it . . . reminding me of my father. They were very close friends, you know. I went, I suppose, to say good-bye to the old ways . . . the Scottish ways. To make my peace so that I could coexist with the English . . . accept the Union and live a productive life."

"I can understand that."

"He was dying when I arrived. So if that's treason to the crown, then I'm guilty. I suppose I could have profited from the reward and brought his carcass for the English to degrade and thereby prove my loyalty . . . but I did not. I stayed to see him interred beneath the cold stones of a cairn overlooking the sea. He's now part of his native soil."

Sir Robert Kinkaid waited for Alex to continue, but the young man just raised his hands. "That's it."

"Is it?"

"Well, I didna inform any authorities of his death. His lawyer was there as were several of the citizens of Durness, and I supposed that they might—" improvised Alex.

"Might what? Put their own necks in an English noose?" volunteered Kinkaid. "For surely they knew his whereabouts for much longer than you."

"Possibly," returned Alex noncommittally.

"And there's possibly more that you're not telling me."

"Such as?"

"Why did he send for you?"

Alex wrestled with himself, wanting to reach out somehow and trust the tiny, gnomelike man who gazed at him so intently that it seemed the old eyes burned into his turbulent brain.

"He had something for you?" suggested Kinkaid. "You can trust me," he added, seeing a fleeting change of intensity in the young man. Alex didn't answer.

"Let me help you, Sinclair. It was the lass, the one named Cameron?"

"Why would you think that my wife had anything to do with Duncan Fraser?" answered Alex curtly.

"Oh, from several slighting, vindictive comments that henna-headed virago entertained me with," chuckled Kinkaid.

"Fiona, as you so aptly described her, is nothing more than a vicious, jealous woman," hissed Alex, standing and returning to the window. The storm had reached its peak and ebbed, leaving a litter of strewn branches and leaves in its wake. A soft, misting rain and a gentle breeze soothed the distantly shuddering sky.

"Don't underestimate her. She's here to do mischief, and she has a most avid ally in Beddington."

"She has no proof, just spiteful suppositions," remarked Alex casually without turning.

"Then Beddington's spies will find nothing incriminating at Cape Wrath . . . no evidence to tie Cameron to Duncan Fraser? That lawyer or the people of Durness will know nothing of a girl of such striking complexion?" probed Sir Robert mercilessly. Alex turned, his face pale beneath his golden tan.

"You'd best trust me, Alexander. Two heads are better than one," said Kinkaid softly as the young man stood dumbfounded.

"Cameron was Fraser's ward," volunteered Alex stiffly. "But children cannot choose nor be blamed for the guardian thrust upon them," he added savagely.

"No, children cannot be blamed for the parents who spawned them, either," stated Sir Robert.

Alex felt the shock reverberate throughout his whole body. He stared incredulously at the frail little man, unable to speak.

"Sit down before you fall," gestured Kinkaid fussily. "I'm getting bored playing cat and mouse . . . 'tis late and damp and my bones ache. Now, let us cut through all this word mincing. I know you're protecting your wife . . . and I wish I had such a one to protect. I'll tell you what I know. About twelve or so years ago twins, a boy and a girl of about two or three years old, were spirited away from a convent high in the Pyrenees on the border between France and Spain. Cameron looks much like her mother, Dolores. Oh, how I loved that woman—from afar, mind you—for who would take such a tiny mannikin seriously when every tall, handsome buck on the Continent was willing to pay court?" He laughed sadly. "But we were friends . . . she talked, and I listened. Each time one of her handsome suitors hurt her, I would be there to listen and have the knife turned in my own heart. Oh, not that she was a cruel woman. On the contrary . . . she did not know how I felt, for pride made me keep silent. A false pride much like yours, young man . . . for had I spoken, maybe . . . just maybe she might have lived . . . or I might have known a requiting of my love. As it was, her own quest to be loved grew desperate . . . self-destructive, until it consumed her, and many an animalistic male fed upon her until she was a shell. Even then I didn't show my love for fear I would be thought like the others. Unable to bear her pain and my own, I fled like a coward back to England and immersed myself in theoretical abstractions, denying my own feeble flesh. I hated my small physical stature and even more my small, cowardly one. I heard news of her death with a deaf ear, refusing to open my

senses. It was three years later, when I felt I was hardened
. . . inured . . . like a dusty old volume full of blank pages,
that I made a sort of pilgrimage to Olaron Sainte-Marie,
that little convent high in the mountains where Dolores
had been raised. She's buried there, and it was strange to
see such a serene cemetery . . . so serene and orderly . . .
not a sign that the tempestuous Dolores rested there . . . as
if such a spirit can ever rest. She had given birth to twins
in forty-six, a boy and a girl . . . no day . . . no names."
The old man sat silently lost in his sad memories.

"Who was the father?" asked Alex softly. The sharp,
hawklike eyes zeroed in on him keenly.

"You know?"

"Aye," affirmed Alex. "Do you?"

"I have my suspicions, and if I'm right, that lass is in
danger."

"There is no way Beddington can prove it, nor yourself
for that matter."

"Does the lass know?" asked Kinkaid.

"Nay, she's rebellious enough without fanning the flames
of futile patriotism."

"What of the boy?"

"Duncan separated them at about the age of seven or
eight. And from something that was said I have reason to
think him somewhere in the Colonies or New France fighting with the Indians for the French, but there again 'tis
something that I did not see fit to confide to my wife."

"Then 'tis no wonder you are wound so tight. Some
secrets weigh more heavily than others. It can be no easy
task hoarding such vital knowledge, especially from one
close to your heart. 'Tis her very family you keep from
her . . . twin brother and father," said Kinkaid sadly,
shaking his head.

"What else would you have me do? As you said yourself, 'tis a threat to her very life . . . she's wild and impulsive, no more than a child," retorted Alex savagely.

"She's grown enough to be your wife."

"Aye, and that was not of my choosing but a product of
her impetuous nature," replied Alex, remembering the
naked, defiant Cameron with hands on her hips declaring
to an irate landlady and clustering, curious guests that she

and Alex were legally man and wife. Public declaration, undenied by him, made the marriage binding under Scottish law. He had no choice but to agree with her, the marriage being infinitely preferable to jail for child molesting, although it had been the child who had been molesting him.

"You mean it is not a love match?"

"It is a love match despite my intentions. I love that bewitching little wildcat with all my heart," professed Alex. "But if I'd had my way, I'd have waited until she was older and knew her own mind."

"There's many a child married much younger . . . and that young lass seems strong-minded enough already," chuckled Kinkaid.

"Aye, she is that," brooded Alex. "But 'tis now that she chooses me . . . needs me. She has little frame of reference, being raised on that solitary promontory of land with Duncan Fraser. I fear there will come a time, when she is more formed, that she'll regret the choice and I'll have to let her go," he added somberly.

"Surely that applies to all people. I still think you should trust her," urged Kinkaid.

"Trust her? How?"

"With the knowledge that her father is Charles Stuart, the Young Pretender."

"Hush, never say that aloud again," hissed Alex. " 'Tis easy for you to say, not knowing Cameron as I do. Her fervent loyalty would put her neck in a noose, and if I ever let her go, it will be to let her fly like the natural, free spirit that she is . . . not to close her in a dark coffin and imprison her 'neath the cold stones of a cairn."

"What was Duncan Fraser's plan for the two bairns?" asked Kinkaid, changing the subject.

"That is buried with him under his cold cairn."

"You think he hoped to raise the clans with the two?"

"Maybe. Who knows what the old Highlander hoped? But he must have realized the futility of such dreams. Scotland is fragmented, the clans dispersed to the four corners of the earth," replied Alex bitterly.

"And buried beneath the purple heather," added Kinkaid sadly.

"And far, far from home on foreign battlefields." Alex

returned to the window and gazed across the now serene countryside of his estate.

"Have you any suggestions for the coil I'm wound in?" he asked after a pause.

"It would seem that if you choose to fight for Glen Aucht, you must once more prove your loyalty to the crown and dispel the rumors that Beddington has been busily spreading. Unless there is incriminating evidence at Cape Wrath . . . in which case I advise you to flee," suggested Kinkaid.

"They'll find no tangible proof at Cape Wrath. Duncan's mistress, Mara, burned all his papers and possessions in an excess of grief. Och, he'll find plenty of wagging tongues about a changeling child spat out of the sea at midnight . . . kelpie's kin and witches and the like . . . but that's about all," answered Alex.

"Well, if you're truly confident of that, then I suggest you volunteer for active duty. I doubt if it'll be for long, as Pitt has resigned and Bute is a man of peace," replied Kinkaid. "But that is, of course, if Glen Aucht is that important," he added with significance.

"Important?" ejaculated Alex. "Of course it is important!"

"There's a brave, new world to conquer . . . times are changing . . . machines that can do the work of eight. Let go the old and carve for yourself and future generations a new life. You're young and strong . . . everything is ahead of you . . . everything is behind me," pleaded Sir Robert.

"Aye, I've been to that brave, new world, and why should I have need to conquer and carve out a piece of another man's land? I have my own, and 'tis here in Scotland. My father and grandfather and their fathers before gave their lives for this birthright, and I'll not let a fat English lunatic rob me of it!" vowed Alex vehemently.

"Then your path is evident, is it not?" responded Kinkaid wearily. "Well, it has been a long, grueling day, and my old bones ache for sleep. I hope I helped, if only as a sounding board," he added, rising stiffly.

"Aye, you have, and I thank you," said Alex gruffly, offering his hand. Kinkaid clasped it warmly, and once again the young man was surprised at the feeble-looking old man's apparent strength.

"Think on it. Make no rash decisions. We can talk more on the morrow if you wish it," murmured Kinkaid at the open door.

Cameron rode her weary horse toward the dark, silent house, delighting in the sweet freshness of the newly washed earth. The storm inside herself was spent, and she was soothed and rocked by the steady, plodding rhythm. A hoarse cawing caused her to rein, and the giant raven circled out of the darkness and alit on her shoulder. Cameron sat quietly, and through the black of the night she heard the eerie strains of the pipes. Who would dare to wail the bagpipes with the English army quartered so close? she wondered. Was it Fergus or Daft-Dougal keening a pibroch for the poor Jeannie, she puzzled, urging her horse in the direction of the sound. Muffled voices caused her to halt silently again. Straining her ears, she recognized Harris's frightened whine, slurred from an excess of spirits.

"I'll not be treated like a common minion," hissed a strange voice. "Who does Beddington think he is, sending a drunken sissified subordinate to tell me what to do? Where is the cargo he promised me?"

"There's been a slight setback, Captain Loving, but the colonel swears he'll have it all ironed out if you'll just stay at the Sign of the Boar in Crail. He has seen to your accommodation there," pleaded Harris.

"I was aiming to set sail for Skye on the morrow's noon tide and was promised my cargo would be waiting. I demand to see Beddington at once. Now stand aside, you sniveling excuse for a man," roared the irate Captain Loving in no endearing terms.

"The colonel said if I could not dissuade you, I was to have you wait for him, as there are certain people at the house who are dangerous."

"Oh, that's the way the land lies, does it?" sneered the seaman. "Well, you tell your precious colonel I'll wait no more'n one hour, but I'll be damned if I'll wait outside in this wet, inhospitable weather."

"The stables are warm and dry, and there'll be none who

can overhear," offered Harris apologetically, leading the way.

"Stables?! Pah!" exclaimed Loving, reluctantly following.

Cameron felt a surge of excitement rush through her at the mention of Skye. Alex had promised to take her to the Isle of Rona, off Skye, where she supposed her twin brother to be. She sat her horse, watching Harris and Loving disappear into the stables. The raven shifted his weight, bringing Cameron back to the present. What should she do? What was the cargo that Beddington had promised the sea captain? From the shadows she watched Harris scurry fearfully into the darkness toward the main house.

Colonel Beddington blessed the storm that had covered Captain Loving's furious knocking from the ears of Alex and Kinkaid, who he trusted were soundly asleep in their respective chambers. He sincerely hoped that Harris had sent the rough seaman packing back to the Sign of the Boar in Crail, as he was loath to tell the man to his face that all the women and children had somehow disappeared into thin air and that he had no cargo except possibly for one small, green-eyed girl, Cameron Sinclair. She hadn't been part of the promised bargain, as Beddington felt her a useful tool with which to bring the arrogant Sinclair down on his knees.

Harris rushed into the room, sobbing and blubbering.

"He's back in Crail?" Beddington hissed.

"He wouldn't go. He's in a rage. Wants his cargo. He's in the stables, and if you don't go out, he'll come in," cried Harris hysterically.

"What did you tell him?"

"That there were unexpected guests . . . dangerous . . . and he wouldn't listen. He wants to sail tomorrow on the noon tide. You have to go out, sir, or he'll come in," begged Harris. "What'll we do? There is no cargo!"

"I'm well aware of that, you blithering idiot. Shut up and let me think!"

"But, sir, just one hour and he'll come in," screamed Harris, who was rewarded by a brutal cuff that sent him sprawling.

*　*　*

Cameron quietly tethered the horse Torquod and crept in through a window in the back of the stables, the raven still perched upon her shoulder. Captain Loving stalked about uttering curses beneath his breath. Jemmy-Lad stared down at him from the hayloft, her eyes wide with panic. Cameron edged her way in the darkness toward the ladder when a shape stepped silently from the shadows. She stifled a scream, her heart pounding fiercely. It was Daft-Dougal. He bent and placed his face close to hers and put a finger against his lips. Cameron nodded. The raven launched himself into the air, and Loving turned at the sound of the heavy, rushing wings. Jemmy screamed.

"Who's there," hissed the sea captain, peering up through the gloom, catching sight of the shrinking figure of the child. Cameron and Daft-Dougal froze, hoping Jemmy was hid, as they'd recognized her voice.

"What is it, Jemmy?" asked the sleepy voice of Young-MacNab. With a snarl Loving reached for his cutlass. The raven cawed a warning harshly, but the lame youth emerged, rubbing his eyes, unaware of the slashing sword, which caught him squarely, nearly severing his neck. A bloodcurdling scream shocked the night as Cameron leaped with her dirk in hand. She was unaware of danger to herself as she sprang, her clear, young voice howling her rage.

Beddington, cautiously approaching the stables, froze in his tracks at the bloodcurdling scream and backed away, certain the ghost of Jeannie had returned again to haunt him. Again and again Cameron plunged her knife until she fell half conscious on the inert man beneath her. Daft-Dougal's wiry hands pulled her from him, and Cameron stared, dazed at what she'd done. Jemmy, her eyes glassy from all she'd witnessed, quietly climbed down the ladder from the hayloft and stood staring blankly at the body of Young-MacNab. Fergus entered the stables with a lantern in hand and stopped abruptly at the carnage that met his eyes. Cameron, her hair wild, stood with a dripping dagger in hand over the corpse of a large man in rough seaman's clothes. The red-haired child stood silently, with round, haunted eyes, over the sprawled body of the youth. The stunned silence was broken by the rushing of wings as the raven circled and then landed upon Cameron's shoulders.

The melancholy, faint wail of the pipes drifted with the breeze.

Fiona lay between cold sheets, her heart racing beneath her burned breast at the ghostly lament of the phantom pipe that seeped into her lonely bedchamber. Unable to be alone in the eerie darkness, she crept out of her room. The corridor stretched unwelcomingly before her, each dark doorway seeming to contain threatening shadows. She was cold and miserable, and comforted herself thinking of Alex's tawny, warm strength. She let her mind remember the scene with him and Beddington in the study. At the thought of Beddington she shivered with repulsion. She had been able to successfully block him out as she had filled her senses with the sight and smell of Alex. She had played with him, teased him, and he had grown hard and straining beneath her hands. He still wanted her. Fiona's pace quickened as she remembered. She would find him and finish. Her nipples were erect beneath her sheer nightgown as she tiptoed up the stairs to the floor where she knew him to be housed. Absentmindedly she kneaded her straining breasts, taking delight in the pain of her burn as she remembered the scene in the study. Heat and aching spread in her loins, and her hands sweated, still feeling the rigid member beneath the fabric of Alex's tight trousers. She had stroked and tried to grasp despite the restriction of the cloth, and his immobility as he stood at attention had fanned her hunger. She had slid her hands so slowly down the waistband, feeling his body heat until she had, with her fingertips, touched his throbbing part. She had knelt and breathed hotly, increasing his desire, wanting him to break . . . wanting him to unbend and crumple. Wanting him to beg . . . but he had stood still at attention, his face impassive as though carved from stone.

Fiona watched Sir Robert Kinkaid leave Alex's chamber. She hid in a recessed doorway, excited to fever pitch, aching to her very core, and when the old man had made his way, oh so slowly, out of sight, she silently crept to the bedchamber door, which stood ajar.

Alex slowly unbuttoned his shirt as he stared broodingly into the fire. Torquil, dozing on the hearth, raised a shaggy head and growled. Fiona's passion was too inflamed to be deterred by her fear of the large dog. She had convinced herself that Alex wanted her, and her eyes saw only him as she floated toward him, her lips moistly parted and her voluptuous breasts exposed. Alex turned, his thoughts still on his interview with Sir Robert Kinkaid. He stood still, watching the woman approach, her eyes glassy and her breathing heavy. He was detached, as though seeing her from a great distance.

Fiona refused to see Alex's impassive face. Her eyes were fixed to his tight breeches. Her hand reached out, only to be caught in a steellike grip, and she raised beseeching eyes and an inviting mouth. Alex's brain flooded with furious thoughts and feelings. He and Fiona had had a long liaison. She had been his mistress for a number of years, and even though he was now repelled by her, he remembered and recognized the heated musk of her arousal, and it joined with desire and fury. He fought with himself as rage enveloped him, recalling the humiliating scene in the study where he had been toyed with. Thunder roared in his head, and he savagely pushed her against the wood-paneled wall, wanting to kill her. Fiona struggled. He had her hands pinned to each side and stood in front of her, glaring with undisguised hatred. She could smell the nostalgic scent of him. Her face was but several inches from his bared chest. She tried to edge her body closer, wanting to rub against him. She arched her back, thrusting out her breasts. Her mouth, open and lusting, beckoned, but he just stood staring down at her. She licked her lips and writhed her hips, wishing he'd release her hands so she could pull all of him to her, crushing her soft bosoms to the firmness of him.

Alex held himself in check, knowing how pleasurable it would be to debase her . . . pin her to the wall . . . impale her and hammer out his fury, not heeding the bruises she would receive from the carved oak molding behind. Unable to control himself he thrust out his pelvis as though his member was a weapon that could rive the woman in two . . . crucify her. It was as though all his fury became centered in his manhood, which she had trifled with . . . and he thrust, getting savage satisfaction as her head and back cracked against the wall.

Despite the pain Fiona stood on tiptoe, trying to connect, wishing he'd release himself and enter her.

"Let go my hands," she whimpered, spreading her legs and ignoring the painful bruises in the small of her back as she thrust to meet him. Alex bucked his rage at her like punches, punishing himself in the process.

Fiona delighted in the brutal punishment. She was consumed with passion, unconscious of the furious hatred that burned from Alex's eyes as her whole being was centered on arching her aching core to meet his pounding. She moaned in frustration as Alex suddenly stopped. She whimpered, thrusting her breasts and pelvis toward him, but he held her hands against the wall, his body out of reach.

What the hell was he doing? raged Alex, trying to control his own arousal. He glared at the bowed head of Fiona, whose eyes were pinned to the object of her desire, which strained the material of his tight breeches. Disgust welled within him, and releasing her hands, he stepped back, not wanting to touch any part of her.

"Get out!" he clipped.

Fiona stood, dazed from the pounding her head had received and the sudden iciness that cut through her aching heat. She raised her eyes and gasped at the undisguised disgust that curled Alex's lips. She stepped forward hesitatingly.

"You still want me, I know you do," she whispered, trying to cover her apprehension and fear as she noted Alex's clenched fists by sweeping across the room and posing in front of the fire. "You must be so hungry for a mature woman after the skinny child," she cajoled huskily.

Cameron was unaware of anything as she was herded to the kitchen by Fergus, leaving Old-Petey and Daft-Dougal with the body of Young-MacNab. She entered the warm kitchen oblivious to the still-dripping knife she held and Mackie's consternation.

"Gie her a little something to dull the pain," ordered Fergus gruffly, but Cameron walked like a zombi straight through the room to the back stairs.

"What's been ahappening? What is that blood?" fussed the old woman.

"Young-MacNab is dead, and the lass avenged it. Gie me your dirk, child, 'tis no use brandishing the deed," added Fergus, taking the knife from Cameron's unresisting hand before she turned the corner to the stairs.

"What?" exclaimed Mackie, sitting heavily. "Young-MacNab?"

"Aye," replied Fergus, putting Jemmy onto her lap. "Take care of the bairn. She witnessed all," he said, following Cameron up the stairs. "I'll just see she gets to the master safely. 'Tis like she's sleepwalking."

Fergus followed Cameron to the second floor and, confident that her feet knew where they were taking her, returned through the kitchens to the stables.

Cameron was cushioned, her mind not allowing her to think of what she'd done. Outside the door of the master suite her hand reached numbly for the ornate handle, somehow knowing that inside was safety and comfort. Before her hand could grasp the knob, a warning growl prickled the hairs on her neck. Fiona's shrill scream knifed through the blanket of numbness. Cameron stood stock-still, staring at the closed door as though turned to stone.

Inside, Alex stared contemptuously at the scantily dressed woman, who shrank against the wall of the bed-chamber, terrified of the large hound's sudden movement when he'd recognized Cameron's almost imperceptible tread. Alex threw open the door and stared at his wife, who stood motionless, her face drained of all color. He assumed that Cameron's pained expression was jealousy, and his accumulated frustration, humiliation, and impatience built.

Cameron stared at his harsh face and attempted to shake off the dreadful inertia that seemed to weigh her limbs, determined to stalk away haughtily as though she didn't care.

"You'll not turn tail and run," stated Alex roughly, as if reading her intentions. Cameron fixed her eyes on Fiona, who stood seductively in the center of the bedroom, aware of the firelight that flickered through her nightgown, silhouetting her ripe body. Cameron allowed herself to be firmly steered into the room toward the hated woman. Nothing seemed to matter anymore.

"*Lady* Fiona Hurst, my wife and I would like some privacy, so I suggest you find yourself a more welcoming bed," hissed Alex as Torquil bared his teeth. "Before the hound vents his spleen," he added, watching Fiona's sensual posing slump as she backed away from the snarling dog and ran from the room. Alex slammed the door emphatically and turned to his wife, who stood staring at him with what he read as censure. The firelight played across his features, highlighting and accentuating the stern, uncompromising cast. Cameron felt nothing, her naturally proudly held body erect and dignified, her shoulders thrown back. Hidden beneath her dark cape her hands were sticky with blood. She stared unseeingly at the tall, handsome man as though he were the wall. Alex forced himself to lean against the doorjamb nonchalantly, his expression grim, and his amber eyes not leaving the pools of her deep green ones.

"I apologize for interrupting," droned Cameron expressionlessly.

"Dinna act the jealous child," retorted Alex coldly. "And get out of those wet clothes before you catch a chill," he added, seeing the steam curl off her damp cape as she stood like a small, proud statue before the fire.

"Aye, I'm a child," she intoned. "Then you had best follow the full-blown whore."

"I said to get out of those wet clothes," repeated Alex, unnerved by Cameron's strange mood and pointedly avoiding the reference to Fiona. Cameron made no move to comply. With an oath Alex stepped forward, meaning to force her obedience, when a strange tapping came at the glass of the window. He wrenched the heavy draperies back, and there sat the large raven, the firelight dancing in his beady, seemingly all-knowing eyes.

Alex stared mesmerized at the large, glossy creature as Cameron quietly opened the window and stretched out her hand. Alex was stung out of his inertia by the blood that covered her fingers and ran congealed into furrows down both wrists.

"What scrape have you got into now?" he groaned, covering his concern that she be hurt.

Cameron didn't answer as she stroked the shiny head of the raven.

"Cameron, are you hurt?" he insisted.

"Nay, not where you can gie comfort," returned Cameron coldly. "But maybe he can . . . and has," she added with a strange little smile. The raven cocked its head to one side and then launched itself out of the open window, and Cameron felt an easing of her horror, as though the black bird had rid her of the sin of killing a man.

Alex closed the window and pulled the drapes viciously, not knowing how to deal with this new, distant side of Cameron. She was removed from him as though an invisible barricade had been erected. Unable to help himself, he gathered her unresisting form to him and picked her up like a baby, burying his face into her fragrant, rain-drenched hair, but she lay limply submitting to his embrace, not caring. Alex wrenched his head back and stared into her impassive eyes.

"You mean to punish by withholding yourself from me," he mocked bitterly, depositing her roughly on the bed, where she lay with no change of blank expression.

"There's one who'll not withhold any part of herself from you. I smelled and felt the heat of the she-animal in season," stated Cameron unemotionally, increasing Alex's suspicions as to her strange behavior, and his fury as her words evoked the humiliating memory of Fiona toying with him while watched by the drooling colonel.

"Aye, you're right!" he roared. The week's toll of forcing himself to keep his emotions in check while being forced to submit to usurpation, debasement, and countless other outrageous injustices was ignited by what he judged to be Cameron's petty jealousy.

Cameron felt a cold, sick fear snake through the numbing armor. She felt herself trembling like jelly, her guts curling, sticking to her spine. She was a quivering mass of nauseous horror. She stiffened her muscles, trying to will back the nothingness she'd felt before. She closed her eyes tightly, unable to bear the sight of Alex's burning intensity as he seemed to look at her with such loathing, making her skin crawl. A paralyzing pain welled within her, which seemed to rob her of her very self.

"Look at me!" ordered Alex, goaded by her closed, set face, but Cameron lay, teeth clenched. He shook her savagely, but no sound of protest or expression crossed her frozen features.

"I will have obedience!" he hissed, needing release from the days of degradation he had been subjected to. He felt impotent and self-abased. He had humbled himself, allowing unpardonable monstrosities in order to retain his lands. "Is it worth it?" Sir Robert Kinkaid's wry voice re-echoed in his mind.

"Of course 'tis worth it!" howled Alex aloud, throwing Cameron back against the pillows like an inanimate object. "Everything, even my sex, my manhood, my pride, my very soul is worth my family house and lands!" he averred, vehemently trying to quell the niggling doubts that assailed him.

A furtive knocking at the door saved Cameron from more of Alex's flowering rage.

"Who is it?" he snarled.

"Fergus," was the quiet reply.

Alex knew that Fergus would not disturb unless it were a dire necessity. He opened the door and went out to the old man in the hall. Cameron sprang from the bed and turned the key in the lock, then slid the heavy bolt.

Alex, hearing the sounds, turned back to the door. Fergus touched his arm.

"Did the lass tell you?"

"Tell me what?" hissed Alex impatiently. Fergus put a finger to his lips.

"Obviously not, so 'tis best I show you, as the walls may have ears," whispered the old man, leading the way to the back stairs.

"More glaistigs and ghoulies in the witching hour, is it?" mocked Alex.

"Young-MacNab is dead," returned Fergus cryptically, hushing Alex's tongue, and no words were said until they entered the stables.

"Do ye ken the devil, Your Lairdship?" cackled Daft-Dougal, rolling his eyeballs as Alex stared down at Captain Loving's corpse.

" 'Tis the captain of the *Edna Rae* the braw young lass killed, and her no bigger than a peewit," he chortled when Alex silently shook his head.

"Cameron killed him?" he uttered blankly.

"Aye, a whirling dervish . . . a true Highlander. The salty brute slashed Young-MacNab's thrapple, and before the blink of an eye she dished out his just deserts," informed Dougal with relish.

Cameron's expressionless voice and face haunted Alex's mind. No wonder she behaved strangely; she was in shock from such violence. His gall rose. A sorry state had come to pass when he couldn't even protect his own, that his sixteen-year-old wife showed more courage. His eyes raked the large body slumped at his feet, and from the numerous, bloody knife slits he knew that Cameron had struck again and again.

"Who knows?" he asked harshly.

"All of us, including the bairn who witnessed all," replied Fergus tersely.

"Where's Young-MacNab?"

"In the attic. Mackie's laying him out. Young Master Ian's keeping the deathwatch."

"I think it were best that he be brought back here. Then it looks like a fight between the lad and the seaman," suggested Alex.

"To protect the lass?" questioned Fergus.

"Aye, Young-MacNab has no more to lose," replied Alex. "Will you see to it, Fergus? Then we'll all to bed and apprise the colonel of it in the morning."

The two old men watched him leave.

"The lass didna tell her own man?" said Daft-Dougal wonderingly.

"Nay, I wonder if the Lady Fiona had a hand in that. I see'd her, near-naked, gliding down the hall from his rooms," thought Fergus aloud. "And the way that bedroom door got locked as soon as Sir Alex come out to me, I dinna think our lass will be letting him sleep in their bed tonight."

"Sad that. They should be getting together agin the muckers, not letting the muckers divide them."

*   *   *

Cameron lay, planning dispassionately. She'd go to Skye on the *Edna Rae*. Somehow she'd convince Fergus and Daft-Dougal to tell her where the women and children were kept in the caves, and sail with them away to safety. She'd find her brother and make her home far away from the English. She was so intent on her scheme, she didn't hear the pounding on the door until Alex's voice demanded entrance.

"You'll open it, or I'll raise the English."

Cameron didn't answer. She knew the sea at Cape Wrath and had sailed small fishing ketches, but she was not confident about a larger ship. How big was the *Edna Rae*, she wondered as she fell asleep.

Alex hurt his fists upon the door. He had no wish to raise Beddington, despite his threat to the contrary. He fumed. He was master neither of his own house nor of his own bedchamber. He stood trying to calm the murderous rage, determined he would sleep in his own bed or he'd have no pride to salvage. He stormed into an adjacent room, flung open the casement and stepped out onto the narrow ledge.

Alex hauled himself in through the window, his hands sore from the perilous inching along the narrow parapet that afforded Cameron's slight, lithe figure little foot room and his height and size even less. He stared down at her, noting the bloodstained hand that was curled by her cheek, and curbed his desire to shake her awake. He sat heavily on the bed, but she didn't stir. What did he feel? he wondered. He was filled with awe. She was so petite, her tiny features so feminine and refined, and yet she had single-handedly just killed a man three times or more her size and strength. His lips curled in a bitter, sardonic line as he felt emasculated and ineffectual. What sort of husband was he who pushed his wife to such lengths and was unable to manage her or his own household? He gazed at her, and the magnitude of the love he felt welled and choked him, mingling with his intense rage. He cursed her for lying there looking so vulnerable and innocent, and savagely turned away to sleep on the hard cot in the adjoining dressing room.

CHAPTER THIRTEEN

For Cameron, the three days following her killing of Captain Loving passed in a detached gray fog, all thoughts of her plan to sail the *Edna Rae* forgotten. Her mind was a comforting blank, her senses numb, seemingly impervious to the mounting chaos that the frightened and hysterical colonel engendered. Dressed in a demure gray silk gown, she had stood the following morning blankly watching as Colonel Beddington and Harris were ushered into the stable, somewhat the worse for wear, both nursing pounding heads and nauseous stomachs due to the previous night's intoxication. Ian, Alex, Cameron, Fergus, Daft-Dougal, and Old-Petey stood silently in a semicircle around the remains of Loving and Young-MacNab. The raven sat unseen on an overhead rafter peering at the odd tableau with cocked head and beady eyes.

The fat colonel stared in stupefaction, fear and relief mingling with his hangover and causing him to be at a loss for words for one of the few times in his life. Harris's bloodshot eyes bulged in terror. He frantically swiveled his skinny neck around, staring from one to the other of the quietly still people. Every face appeared to him to be evil and threatening in the eerie sunlight that filtered through the rafters from the hayloft. The raven emitted a sudden raucous cawing that to Harris's ears sounded like an unearthly chuckle. He screamed and backed into a dark corner, where he slowly slid down the wall and slumped, a pathetic, sobbing bundle in the hay on the floor.

Alex kept his eyes on Cameron, wishing he knew what was occurring beneath her seeming poise. His eyes had narrowed suspiciously on waking in the small, narrow dressing room on the hard cot. Hearing a rustling, he'd entered their bedchamber to find Cameron already dressed in the demure gray gown instead of the accustomed breeches. He'd lifted an eyebrow quizzically as he'd noted that her newfound propriety had not stretched to her small bare feet and had opened his mouth to inquire sarcastically as to the wearing of undergarments, but she had whirled out of the room without a word or nod of acknowledgment.

"Where is everyone?" cried a petulant voice as Fiona stumbled across the stable yard. "Alex?" she called, recognizing the back of his tall, lean frame. "Alex, what is going on? I've been ringing and ringing . . ." Her voice petered out as she stared at the strange circle of people. She followed the direction of their eyes and recoiled.

The subsequent chain of events made no impression on Cameron. She stood silently by the graves watching the remains of the men covered with moist earth. An hour later she stood silently on the broad stone steps of Glen Aucht for Fiona and Judge Singleton's hurried departure for Edinburgh, and despite the threats of bringing the authorities to prove their claims of witchcraft and evil happenings, which were maliciously directed at Cameron through the windows of the departing coach, she seemed to hear and feel nothing. It was as though Cameron mirrored nature, for the following days were gray and overcast, without even a sprinkling of rain or a glimmer of sunlight to disturb the monotony.

For three days Sir Robert Kinkaid stood apart watching the strange, strained household. He sadly noted the rift between Cameron and Alex; she seeming totally unaware of her husband's existence, while his amber eyes were hard and narrowed to suspicious, speculating slits as he made no move to touch or break through the icy wall but watched her like a hawk. Sir Robert had a fair idea of the atmosphere in their bedchamber, as they behaved toward each other like two strangers. Unable to stand apart longer and despite his better judgment, which told him not to be meddlesome, he finally drew Alex aside.

"You'll not reach out to her?" he ventured, indicating Cameron with a slight incline of his head. Both men watched the girl sitting upright in a straight-backed chair, her hands clasped in her lap, dressed in yet another gray gown, her face pale and her eyes blank and staring. Alex didn't answer. He had tried, but what does one say to one's wife after she has killed a man? He felt powerless and lonely. Cameron was wrapped up in her own secret world, not seeming to need anyone. Each night he lay beside her in their bed. At first he'd tried to talk to her, to touch her, but she was silent, unresisting, yet unresponsive.

Sir Robert glanced up keenly and caught the sadness that softened Alex's harsh features.

"You've tried? Well, maybe time," he comforted.

"Aye, so Fergus said."

"Was she uncommonly attached to the lame groom MacNab?" probed Kinkaid gently. Alex looked at him sharply. "Well, surely she had no dealings with that salty flesh peddler, Loving?" added Sir Robert, seared by the scathing look.

"Nay, neither," hissed Alex.

"Did she kill the man?" asked Sir Robert quietly.

"What makes you think such a thing?"

"Old man's intuition and many years on the bench," sighed Kinkaid. "Don't fash yourself, young man, I'm friend, not foe, and I'll not do anything to jeopardize Dolores's child."

From across the room Ian Drummond had concerned eyes on Cameron. He longed to encompass her in his arms and comfort her, and he wondered angrily about his friend Alex's humanity that he could seem so detached.

Beddington's tiny eyes gleamed with anticipation. He reveled in the icy rift that he noted between Alex and Cameron and determined to turn it to his advantage as the detached young beauty swept from the room in her cloud of gray.

It was like three days of mourning, and nothing seemed to disturb the numbness Cameron had shrouded herself in. On the third night the moon pierced the blanket of the sky, and she awoke to an insistent tapping. She lay staring at the crystalline light that streamed across her bed. Shocked to awareness, she turned to the pillow beside hers in the bed. It was empty. Dimly, as though from a dream, came a vague recollection of Alex riding off with a group of soldiers. She sat up abruptly as the persistent rapping broke through her muddled senses. Absentmindedly she rose and opened the window, allowing the raven access. It glided to the bedpost and roosted, watching her intently as she sat trying to get her thoughts in order. Memory flooded in, and yet she was bewildered as to whether this was reality or dream, as all seemed to have a nightmarish quality. Coming to a quick decision, she rummaged around the wardrobe until she found her breeches and jerkin, which she hurriedly shimmied into. The raven bobbed up and down silently as though giving its approval of her shaking off the inertia that had enclosed her. Torquil raised his sleepy old head and, on seeing that his young mistress was about to go out, raised his heavy body reluctantly and stretched, stifling a yawn as though he sensed silence was in order.

Cameron, with the raven perched upon her shoulder, silently crept barefoot down the long, polished corridor, her nerves stretched to screaming by the scratching sounds of Torquil's nails on the hard wooden surface as he skittered in his effort to keep up. The muffled chimes of the library clock penetrated the thick walls of the back stairs as she made her way to the kitchens, determined to find Fergus, Mackie, or Daft-Dougal. It was midnight, and she shivered as she grimly remembered carrying the body of Jeannie's poor baby.

Daft-Dougal sat at the kitchen table, lit by one candle that streamed steadily upward, causing the whites of his cross-eyes to throb with an intensity as though lit from behind. To Cameron's confusion the old man seemed to expect her. She stood with her brow wrinkled with consternation.

"I'd almost gie you up, lassie," he chuckled, delighting in her bewilderment.

"You expected me?"

"Aye, for three nights now I've asat, but all's in threes or circles or the like," he answered enigmatically.

"Where's Alex?"

"Rid off on some fool errand of the English. He'll not be back for a day or so, as he's to keep the crew of the *Edna Rae* entertained so that'll nay miss their captain. But it gies us space to work. So put your self-pity from you and let us gie our heads together," returned Daft-Dougal, rubbing his leathery palms together.

"Where has he gone?" persisted Cameron, unable to

bear the thought of Alex leaving her without so much as a good-bye. But did he? The thought teased her mind. Things seemed so hazy and indistinct.

"You've been hiding your wounds by dulling your feelings, young mistress. You killed, and it canna be undone, so you must go on," informed Dougal, as though reading her befuddled mind.

"Where is Alex?" demanded Cameron, stung by the old man's bluntness.

"Sent to Crail to get him out of the way," snapped Dougal.

"The *Edna Rae!*" exclaimed Cameron as the events flooded into her brain. "My plan," she added, thinking aloud.

"Sssh!" warned Dougal as a stealthy creaking issued from the stairs. Ian Drummond popped a tousled head around the corner.

"What's this? A black mass?" he teased, causing Cameron to giggle at Daft-Dougal's indignation.

"Where are the caves?" asked Cameron, but Dougal's mouth pursed in a firm, angry line as he stared at Ian with undisguised antagonism, his eyeballs dancing in different directions.

"What are you doing here, when you rode off wie the others?" demanded the old man suspiciously.

"We doubled back after a night of heavy drinking with the crew of the *Edna Rae.* We'll not be missed until tomorrow noon, I reckon, wie their pickled brains," answered Ian lightly .

"Alex is wie you?" asked Cameron eagerly.

"Nay, he took a fishing boat across the firth to get a message to someone in Edinburgh."

Cameron felt as though she'd been punched in the heart. She shivered as a coldness drained the blood from her. Alex had gone back to Fiona, for who else lived in Edinburgh for him to take such risks for? Neither Ian or Dougal noticed her draining of color in the dim candlelight.

"Where are the caves?" strove Cameron, fortifying herself with Dougal's past references to self-pity. " 'Tis not idle curiosity, but it seems to me that the *Edna Rae* could be put to good use putting the women and bairns far from Beddington's reach." She was pleased to see both men stare at her incredulously. She had their total attention.

"Cameron, you canna be serious?" gasped Ian. "How do you propose to wrest the vessel from her crew? Wie one slip of a girl, one gley-eyed old man—"

"One gley-eyed old man!" bristled Daft-Dougal.

"You told me yourself that you got them drunk so you and . . . well, so you could slip away," returned Cameron, loath to mention Alex's name or where he'd slipped away to.

"And who'd crew the vessel? 'Tis enough that their captain's not returned to them, and they don't seem to believe Beddington's story that he had to go to London," explained Ian patiently.

"He went to London to visit the queen, pussycat, pussycat," sang Dougal.

"They dinna ken he's . . . dead?" asked Cameron hesitatingly.

"Beddington is afeared, as he promised them a cargo that somehow got spirited away to the caves. They're a rough group of men, and there's no telling what might happen if they suspect foul play," explained Ian, ignoring Daft-Dougal, who continued singing the nursery rhyme.

"There's kin of the farmers on the fishing boats. They'll help," persisted Cameron.

"I'll think on it, but I have a message for Kinkaid that I must gie. Cameron, dinna do anything rash. Tomorrow or the next day Alex and I will return, and I'm hoping things will be much different."

Cameron and Dougal heard Ian's furtive footsteps recede. They sat as the candle flickered and dimmed with just the heavy ticking of the dining room clock breaking the silence. Dougal stood suddenly.

"I'll take you to the caves, lassie. Grab a cloak. 'Tis near time for the Beltane ceremony, and yet 'tis like the daft days before Hogmanay. Maybe 'tis nature herself trying to drive the English out, and that great raven an omen."

"Omen, that shall be its name," said Cameron softly.

"What date is it?" she added, unsure of how many days she'd detached herself from the world.

"Tomorrow 'tis the last day of April, and Mrs. Mac-Donald is already preparing the cakes for May first to sacrifice to the birds and beasts of prey so that the herds, flocks, and harvest might be protected. Took a lot of persuasion, as the good woman seems to have fair given up the ghost, what wie you in your doldrums and the fields not yet sown," chattered Dougal as they quietly let themselves out of the house, leaving the large hound by the kitchen hearth, the raven still perched on Cameron's shoulder.

"May first is an awesome day," remarked Cameron, remembering Duncan Fraser, her guardian's words. " 'Twas the day of the Union between Scotland and England."

"Aye, May first, 1707. Did you ever hear of the second duke of York?" cackled the old man.

"Nay."

"Well, he begat an idiot son, who on that very day, May first, 1707, killed and roasted a small kitchen lad," recounted Daft-Dougal with obvious relish.

"How terrible," recoiled Cameron.

"Nay, 'twas judgment on the duke for supporting the Union!"

Ian Drummond and Sir Robert Kinkaid stood at the older man's chamber window watching the shadows of Daft-Dougal and Cameron move steadily toward the coast of the firth.

"That old man will keep her safe," comforted Kinkaid. "He's as much a part of spirited Scotland as the lass herself, and there's naught they can do tonight. 'Tis good to know she's shaken off her lethargy and is out of Beddington's reach, at least for a while. Now, you say Sinclair managed to get a message to my old friend Judge Talbot, who's attached to the military in Edinburgh?" he added sharply, drawing the heavy drapes decisively and turning to the young man.

"I know he obtained passage on a fleet fishing vessel, and I last saw him crossing the firth. What is his plan?" asked Ian.

"He did not confide in you?" •

"Only to say he'd do anything to save his house and lands, including returning to that savage country in order to prove his loyalty to the crown."

"He's volunteering for a post at Fort Detroit," explained Kinkaid.

"I remember when he returned in fifty-six after General Braddock's defeat. He was cruel and embittered, unable to resign himself to the savagery he had played a part in. Braddock had encouraged his men to take Indian scalps, even offering two hundred pounds for the scalp of Shingass, the Delaware Indian leader. To Alex it was wrong, not just the scalping but the taking of another man's land."

" 'Tis ironic that in order to save his own, that is what he'll do," remarked Sir Robert. "I hear many of Braddock's men claimed the reward for Shingass's scalp . . . seems the man had many heads. I think he also entertains hope that by getting Cameron away, they may come together in harmony."

"In the midst of a war in a strange, wild country?" ejaculated Ian.

"If he'd just trust her wie the truth," thought Sir Robert aloud.

"What truth?" inquired Ian sharply.

" 'Tis not mine to divulge," returned Kinkaid wearily. "Now, I'm an old man who needs his sleep much like a baby. I've got the old gillie Petey wie his eyes peeled as I'm expecting a messenger if Sinclair has been successful. Hopefully 'twill be his appointment plus an arbitrator in the sad affairs of your estate as well as this one. Also I have filed a complaint against Colonel Beddington's atrocious behavior, but as things stand in London, I don't hold out much hope on that score. As I informed Alexander, anti-Scottish sentiment is rampant in England." The old man nodded sadly and sat staring at the closed door long after Ian had gone.

"Sad times," he sighed.

Cameron stared around at the shivering bundles of women and children in the cold, damp cave. Because they did not want to give away their location, no fires could be lit, and the freezing people futilely huddled against each other for warmth. Mackie and Fergus were quietly collecting pots and bowls, having carried hot broth and fresh bread along the two miles of rugged coast as soon as the big house of Glen Aucht was quiet each night. Mackie's eyes lit on Cameron, and she clucked indignantly and then melted when she saw that the girl was free of the terrible lassitude that had bound her. She impulsively hugged Cameron and rocked her before remembering her place and busily turned to collect her bowls.

Cameron walked out of the cave for fresh air, overcome by love for the old woman and her husband, who every night put their lives on the line to trudge the long, cold, windy distance to feed the women and children hidden in the dank cave. She stood with her bare feet in the waters of the firth, noting that the cove was free of rocks.

"Can bring a boat in?" growled Daft-Dougal's voice from the darkness.

"Depends on the size. How big is the *Edna Rae*?" The old man shrugged in the darkness.

"Dougal, can you steer a vessel?"

"Nay, I'm not a witch nor warlock. 'Tis said witches in the shape of cats can sail any ship. There's many a cat prowls the stables and the bothies feeding off the rats," cackled Dougal.

" 'Tis no laughing matter," chided Cameron.

" 'Tis no use acrying neither."

Two hours later Cameron kissed Mackie's soft cheek and Fergus and Dougal's leathery ones and quietly left them sitting at the kitchen table. She climbed the stairs thoughtfully with Torquil at her heels. The raven had whirled into the shadows of the night before she'd entered the house, leaving her feeling oddly bereft. On the long trudge home Mackie and Fergus had filled her in on much her cushioned state of mind had missed. She was relieved and somewhat guilty to learn that Jemmy-Lad was safely with Old-Petey and Granny MacNab in the south attic. Cameron walked quietly along the corridor, shaking her head in consternation that she could have so successfully blocked out her surroundings, especially all those she'd learned to love. Thoughtfully she let herself into her bedchamber and sat in an armchair by the fire, not wanting to climb into the cold, empty bed. Where was Alex now? she thought, torturing herself with a ghastly stream of lurid images of him coupling with the voluptuous Fiona in Edinburgh, across the firth. She tried to stop her vivid, hurtful imagination, but her mind refused and probed the pain much like a worrying tongue on an aching tooth.

Colonel Beddington also couldn't sleep, he hugged the bolster to his corpulence as he imagined thrusting into Cameron's lithe body. Strange animal-like whimperings from Harris in the adjoining dressing room disturbed his fantasies. With an oath Beddington sat up and threw the pillow at the door.

"For godsakes shut up!" he screamed but the pitiful yelps increased. He stuck his fingers in his ears and tried to reconjure his erotic dreams, but Harris's whimpers increased in intensity. Harris, the only person he'd trusted not to laugh at him, had turned into an idiot as a result of the strange goings-on and recent murders at Glen Aucht. Harris, the only person who didn't make him feel inferior and stupid, had rounded the bend to lunacy. Self-pity welled in the colonel. He had no one. As large, self-indulgent tears welled, an idea germinated.

"You sound like a demented mongrel curr, Harris," he sniffed, blowing his nose on the bedsheet and clambering ungracefully from the high bed.

"Woof woof wooooof," Beddington imitated, unlocking the dressing room door and gleefully splashing cologne all over himself. He combed his moustache and twirled the ends with wax as Harris yelped and pulled at his nightshirt like a worrying puppy. "That's right, good doggie. Woo, wooo, wooooo!" he howled like a wolf and giggled with anticipation.

They made a strange duo, the fat colonel waddling in his nightshirt wearing his army cap and sword, leading the prancing skinny captain. At Cameron's bedchamber they stopped and Beddington pushed Harris at the door.

"Woo, woo, woo," he whispered and to his glee Harris resumed his hurt dog noises and clawed at the door.

Cameron awoke at Torquil's warning growl. She sat

sleepily hearing the frantic whines and scratchings. Was it Maggie? Had something happened to Jemmy? Her limbs were stiff and cold as she'd fallen asleep in the chair, her clothes soaked with the night's dampness. She flung her cape off and cautioning Torquil to stay, opened the door.

"I couldn't calm him," purred Beddington, freezing Cameron's blood. Torquil bounded to his feet, his hackles raised and teeth bared. The fat colonel backed away in terror drawing his sword. Harris clutched at Cameron in fear, whimpering and mewling.

"No, Torquil, no!" ordered Cameron trying to disentangle herself from the captain's clutching hands, but it was too late. Her loyal hound had summoned youth into his old aching muscles and had launched himself into the air. He leaped like a lithe pup to defend his mistress and impaled himself on the poised blade, to die instantly. To Cameron the moment seemed suspended in time. One second vibrantly alive and the next devoid of life as his tremendous weight wrenched the sword from Beddington's terrified hand and the valiant hound fell with a strange deadly thud.

"No, no," Cameron intoned dully, shaking her head, unable to believe. She stood like a statue, refusing to acknowledge the death of her oldest, truest friend as the tragic scene replayed and replayed in her mind's eye. "No! No!" she stated vehemently. It was not possible. It had not occurred. She stared at the inert body of Torquil, seeing his blood and the sword thrust deeply into his shaggy coat where she had pillowed her head since her first rememberings. The full, terrible horror swept in, and she found herself a small child again, full of infinite pain, needing her only friend to give her comfort, but he lay dead at her feet . . . slain so quickly that there had been no last look between them, no growl or bark to bid farewell. There were no buffers. The full pain coursed in. All she saw and felt was the full, crushing impact of Torquil's death.

Cameron was oblivious to Harris who cowered against the wall, yelping and urinating like an abused animal, his eyes fixed on the thick red blood that spurted and congealed on the carpet. She was oblivious to Beddington who stared in stupefaction at the dead hound at his feet. As his fear receded, amazement at his prowess soared. He puffed out his chest victoriously. He had the ridiculous desire to pull the erect sword from Torquil's belly, and stand with one foot on the vanquished foe as a portrait in honor of his victory. He crowed. He was in command, really in command for maybe the first time in his life. He was superior to everyone else in the room. The dog's blood sickened him and he turned his eyes to Cameron, who stood like a vulnerable child turned to stone. He felt his maleness rise. Full-grown women threatened him, but she was not full-fledged. She appeared half girl and half boy in her tight breeches and shirt.

Cameron vaguely felt herself pushed backward onto the bed but it didn't seem to matter. Greedy grasping hands cruelly pinched and pulled, but it seemed a far way off. Her clothes were torn off her but she lay unresisting, her mind and spirit crushed by the enormity of Torquil's death; nothing else was real.

Beddington flung his obese body on the slight lifeless girl as he clumsily tried to lift his cumbersome nightshirt. In his greedy haste he became entangled in the folds puffing with excitement and exertion. In frustration he struck out at Cameron's still face.

"Don't you laugh at me, you bitch!" he snarled, cruelly backhanding the silent mouth. "I'll show you what a man is! I'll mount and master you . . . break you . . . ride you until . . . you beg for more and more," he hissed, his saliva flying to spatter Cameron's frozen face. Unnerved by the open green unblinking eyes that showed no sign that she heard, he maliciously bit her breasts, drawing blood. But still no emotion, no fear was exhibited.

"I'll teach you to mock me. I can hear you laughing, you whore, you harlot!" he sobbed, punching at her unresisting head and getting no reaction. He bit, punched, and clawed, his eyes bulging alarmingly. He licked his lips, tasting the salt and seeing the livid marks he made on her body.

"There see my brand, my claiming mark," he crowed, and laughed raucously and insanely. "I can jeer and laugh louder, drowning you out!" He felt confident and virile. He knew he could enter and thrust into her. He could for the first time in his life consummate. Still laughing he fumbled for his stiff organ as he cruelly kneed her legs apart and to his horror felt himself shrink.

"Whore . . . whore . . . whore!" he screamed, punching with one hand and kneading himself with the other as his whole unsupported weight crushed her.

Cameron felt the pain of the blows penetrate her numbness sharply and she began to kick and bite, trying to dislodge the suffocating body that pinned her down and cracked her head over and over again. She howled out her rage and pain for Torquil, unaware of the blood that streamed from her lips, nose, and breasts.

Kinkaid, hearing terrible cries cut through the still night, ran as fast as his old thin legs could carry him, meeting Fergus, Mackie and Daft-Dougal on the way. Nearing Cameron's open chamber door they saw the body of the dog with the sword plunged deeply into the belly. Beddington, his moustache and nightshirt smeared with blood, stood flattened against the wall holding the pathetic mewing Harris in front of him like a shield. Cameron, dirk in hand, stood poised. She was naked, her face bloody and her ebony hair wild. On her shoulder perched the raven, and the glass of the window was shattered.

"The whore can summon the forces of darkness, of evil . . . she is of the devil," screamed Beddington, his right eye streaming blood from the raven's attack. He had thought the thunderous pounding of the giant wings to be the angry beating of his own blood, and then, with the smashing of the glass, everything had become black and red, a whirling vortex of insanity.

"Pluck his eyes out, Omen," commanded Cameron. "And then I'll rip his fat flesh from thrapple to bollox as he did my Torquil."

"Lassie, drop the dirk," said Fergus quietly.

"Get back, or I'll hurt you, too," hissed Cameron, her lithe body stiffening so that all were threatened by her knife.

"Unarm her. That is an order," barked Beddington.

" 'Tis better you shut yer mouth and get yer fat mucker self out before she sets the raven Omen on you again, sir," cackled Dougal.

"How dare you address me with such insolence!"

"What occurred here, Beddington?" asked Kinkaid, his quiet voice edged with steel.

" 'Twas the idiot Harris. You've seen how she tried to seduce him with her whorish, evil ways. She stole his wits with her wicked spells and then led him on . . ." lied Beddington.

"There'll be a full inquiry, but for now I suggest you withdraw quietly and discreetly," stated Kinkaid coldly.

"Nay!" spat Cameron. "I'll kill the murderer! He killed my Torquil." Her voice broke as she said the words, and sobs tore at her throat. She fought to still them and keep her threatening stance, but since she was drained of energy, the tears poured down her face, mingling with the blood. She threw herself down and buried her face in Torquil's shaggy hide, trying to give her own body's warmth to the still-warm corpse. Beddington took advantage of the situation and sidled out of the room backward, still holding the unfortunate Harris before him like a shield.

"I'll fetch warm water and liniments to soothe," cried Mackie, wrapping a blanket around Cameron's nakedness as she lay hugging her dead friend. "Did you see her puir wee breasts bitten and mauled by those animals!"

Daft-Dougal deftly kindled the fire to a cheery blaze as Fergus herded his weeping wife from the room. Dougal stood stiffly, his old bones creaking, and exchanged glances with Kinkaid before both old men turned to look sorrowfully at Cameron.

"Come, lass. Let me lay your loyal beastie to rest," growled the gley-eyed man.

"Nay!" shouted Cameron, leaping to her feet and throwing the blanket from her shoulders. " 'Tis for me to do. *Me!*" she stated as she frantically rummaged in a wardrobe and brought out a bundle wrapped in paper and twine. Daft-Dougal and Sir Robert watched the young girl, who, without embarrassment and still bleeding from Beddington's savage beating, walked naked in front of them. She slowly, almost reverently unwrapped her precious bundle and withdrew the kilt and plaid of the Fraser hunting tartan.

"I'll need Fergus's pipes," she ordered, and Dougal bent

his elbows like rooster wings and crowed jubilantly before strutting from the room. He nearly collided with Mackie, who entered with old Gran MacNab, laden down with warm water, herbs, salves, and a jug of whiskey.

" 'Tain't decent looking at her bareness, even though yer old enough to be her great-grandfather," clucked Mrs. MacDonald indignantly to Sir Robert, purposefully avoiding looking at the large black bird that perched on the top of the wardrobe. "What in heaven's name is she doing?" she added as Cameron covered her naked, raw body by donning the kilt and plaid. "Any responsible man would stop her. She should be in bed!"

Sir Robert Kinkaid didn't answer Mackie's contradictory chatterings. He sat silently watching Cameron finish her dressing and kneel beside her great, shaggy beast. The round housekeeper followed his gaze to the girl, who cradled Torquil's head on her knee and placed her shiny black head on his as the tears poured down her face. Mackie stopped her fussings as her ample bust heaved and choked with sorrow.

They all stood silently watching the young piper, whose kilt and plaid streamed in the wild night wind as she piped a coronach for her oldest, dearest friend. Fergus and Daft-Dougal dug a deep grave and piled a cairn on a promontory overlooking the firth where many a time Cameron and Torquil had sat staring across the waters toward Edinburgh. All night they stood until the first rays of morning softened the eastern horizon, consumed with grief as the lament keened with the wind.

At cockcrow, the raven flew from Cameron's shoulder and alit on Torquil's cairn. The pipes dropped from Cameron's hands, and Fergus picked her up in his arms and carried her to the house.

Cameron slept from emotional and physical exhaustion, unconscious of the two old women who bathed her body and tucked her into bed. Sir Robert sat by the fire, staring into the deep embers. The old man's thoughts were far away, back in the past with another emerald-eyed, ebony-haired young woman.

CHAPTER FOURTEEN

Both Cameron and Sir Robert slept until late morning under the sharp eye of Omen the raven. The heavy drapes were drawn and pinned together to thwart the draft from the shattered window. Sir Robert was nudged awake by the raven's insistent pokes, and before he opened his eyes, pain flooded his old body from the uncomfortable position in the fireside chair. Slowly and carefully he moved each part, finding his bones and muscles aching and cramped. He opened his eyes as imperceptible whimpers issued from the small mound in the large bed. He rose stiffly and stared down at Cameron, her small face swollen and bruised by the previous night's abuse. She seemed in the throes of a nightmare. He sat on the bed and gently bathed her forehead with a damp flannel Mackie had left on the nightstand. Cameron's eyes flew open, and Sir Robert felt a lump of aching tenderness catch his throat by the depth of pain he saw in her haunted green eyes. The raven stared down at them from the headboard of the bed.

"Who am I?" asked Cameron softly, looking up into his old wrinkled face like a tiny lost child. "I dinna ken myself. I'm lost. Wie Torquil. 'Twas like he was a part of myself who'd always been. Like my twin . . . a place to put my feet . . . and now there is nothing. There is nothing before . . . just a space and I canna find myself," she struggled, still half in her dream but the torments of her mind so very real. The raven's eyes seemed to burn intensely into Sir Robert's brain as though urging him to divulge all he knew.

"Your mother, Dolores, had such a hound. A Russian wolfhound. A giant she-dog. 'Tis said by the nuns where you were born that the bitch whelped on the day you and your brother were born." Cameron lay without moving, her eyes fixed to his face. She seemed spellbound.

"Where was I born?" she asked softly, her eyes not leaving his face but her small brown hand reaching and holding his old wrinkled one with trust.

"High in the Pyrenees where your mother, Dolores, is buried. A small, peaceful Eden far from the rest of the world's strife. Olaron Sainte-Marie," he answered, his voice husky with emotion and his own rheumy old eyes brimming with tears.

"You loved her."

"Oh, yes."

"Are you my father?"

"Oh, I wish, but no."

"Who is my father?"

Sir Robert didn't answer. He longed to tear his blurred eyes away from her also streaming ones but was unable to do so.

"Do you know?" insisted Cameron quietly. Unable to lie or to talk, Sir Robert nodded.

"Gie me myself, please?" she begged.

"Charles Stuart, the Young Pretender," he intoned.

"Bonnie Prince Charlie?" exclaimed Cameron.

"Aye."

"The Bonnie Prince," she whispered with awe.

They sat silently, their hands clasped. Sir Robert thought that she slept, propped against the pillows, as her thickly lashed eyelids were closed. His rage surged at the violent purple and red welts that marked her face, and he gently tried to disentangle his hand from hers.

"Am I a bastard?"

Her sharp question shocked him, and he stared at her without answering.

"They were not married, if that is what you mean," he responded slowly.

"Was she a whore?"

Sir Robert recoiled from the hardness in Cameron's tone.

"Nay, she was a beautiful young woman like yourself," he replied gently.

"Then why did not my father claim us when she died?"

"Maybe he didn't know of your existence," lied Sir

Robert. "Maybe your mother had pride much like your own and did not tell him for fear it would entrap him into marriage."

"He did not love her?"

Sir Robert's tired, age-weary brain was on the spot. How could he tell this vulnerable, bruised young woman that Charles Stuart had tired of Dolores and thrown her aside like a used doll.

"There's many forms of love, Cameron . . . and Charles had much else upon his mind. His pride and hopes were in ashes after Culloden in forty-six."

"The year of our birth?"

"Aye, many deaths and twin births," mused Kinkaid.

"And my brother? Where is he?"

"I do not know."

"Does Alex know of this?"

"What?" parried Sir Robert, not wishing further antagonism between the two.

"Of my father?"

"Cameron, many things are not as they seem. Alexander was protecting you, as there are many who'd use the name of Stuart for their own ends. Greedy lairds, romantic Scots, embittered English—"

"So he knew!" stated Cameron, her small face hard and set on rebellious lines.

"He thought only of your safety," pleaded Kinkaid.

"That he'd not trust his own wife with the knowledge of her own father," she spat bitterly.

"He would have told you, I'm sure, when he thought you old and understanding enough . . ." struggled the old man, whose poise from many eloquent years on the bench was being shattered by a sixteen-year-old.

"I'm old enough to bed and rut with . . . to be a wife . . . to kill . . . but not to know who sowed the seed of my beginning," she sneered, pulling her hand from his and quitting the bed. " 'Tis not just one man I've killed, Sir Robert. I thank you for giving me purpose to my life. I have no bonds to hold me now. You've freed me to do what I must," she added, pulling on breeches and throwing off her nightgown with no thought of modesty. "I'm now free to find my brother. I owe Sir Alexander Sinclair nothing at all," she threw at him as, with the raven on her shoulder and her dirk in her boot, she lithely quit the room, despite the excruciating pain of her sorely abused body.

Sir Robert Kinkaid sat dejectedly on the bed listening to her sharp footsteps recede. He questioned his own wisdom in divulging her parentage, knowing he'd now helped to widen the gap between the young married couple. It would have been easy for her to slip back into the gray lassitude that had bound her after the killing of Captain Loving, he musod, but she had strode from the room with fire in her eyes, her spirit wild and rebellious. A much more encouraging frame of mind than the previous inertia, he brooded, trying to console himself. She was a young warrior, a survivor, and young Sir Alexander would have his work cut out trying to handle and guide her, he decided, raising his creaky old bones and making his way to the comfort of his own bed. He was determined not to face the world that day but to sleep through 'til the morrow, fortifying himself for the eventual stormy meeting with the bridegroom.

Alex and Ian sat in a dark corner in the Sign of the Boar tavern in Crail as Ian recounted Cameron's plan.

"Has merit," ejaculated Alex with a laugh. "I know of three fishermen, kinsmen of the MacFarlanes, who'll crew the *Edna Rae* just to extract their pound of flesh for the damage wreaked upon their families. How was Glen Aucht last night?"

"Peaceful. Nary a peep from Beddington or the puling Harris," answered Ian, not sure whether to divulge Cameron and Daft-Dougal's excursion to the caves.

"It sets my mind to rest that Cameron has shaken off that depressive humor. There was another time, after accidentally killing a horse thief, when she sank so low and lay for hours unseeing," remembered Alex aloud. " 'Twas when I brought her south from Cape Wrath and she eluded me on her giant stallion. The horse died trampling the miserable man to a bloody pulp, and it was as if part of Cameron died with her steed."

"How did you break through to her?" asked Ian softly.

"I held her naked against my own nakedness and lowered her into an icy mountain stream," replied Alex, huskily remembering how her young body recoiled away from the cold water, pressing against him. "Enough of remembrances. We only have a short time before we must return. You keep Beddington's escort and the crew of the ship here under your eyes, plying them with more spirits to mend their hangovers, while I ferret out the MacFarlanes. I'm eager to see my wife now that she's returned to the land of the living." And with that Alex strode out of the gloom of stale ale into the bright sunlight.

As Alex rode off along the coast to Saint Andrews and Montrose hoping to find the MacFarlanes' kin, Ian sat despondently in the dark, shadowy tavern, trying to dispel his jealousy, which had been aroused by his friend's intimate recollections. He was jerked out of his dark brooding by the entrance of Fergus.

"Is there trouble at Glen Aucht?" he exclaimed, seeing the seriousness in the old wrinkled face.

"Aye, Beddington and Harris tried to rape the young mistress last night . . . killed her hound," answered Fergus shortly. "Where's Sir Alexander?"

"Rode north along the coast to raise the MacFarlanes," responded Ian, his face white from shock. "Is she all right?"

"Aye, battered and bruised . . . keening for her faithful old beastie. She's sleeping . . . the old judge Sir Robert and that great black bird keeping watch. I rode out at first light. Why would the master be raising MacFarlanes' kin?"

"To crew the *Edna Rae*. We're to spirit the bairns and women to safety up the coast," explained Ian.

"I'm athinking we'll have to be spiriting the young mistress somewhere, as Beddington would like to see her burned as a witch, and I'm not trusting that Judge Singleton or Lady Fiona after they threatened to press charges. I'm sure they're up to mischief in Edinburgh. I'm surprised we've had no word as yet."

"Aye," sighed Ian morosely. "But do you think it wise to apprise Alex of Beddington's attack? He'll kill the fat pig. Did he—?"

"Did he what?"

"Rape her?"

"He smashed her face, her wee breasts are bitted and bruised—"

"But did he—" interrupted Ian harshly.

"And what if he did? Is the rest not enough?" retorted Fergus.

"I'll kill that debauched lecher myself. I've nothing more to lose!" swore Ian, leaping to his feet as the full import of Fergus's news penetrated his weary brain.

"You'll do no such thing," barked Fergus, pushing him down. " 'Tis not your honor or your place."

"I love her!"

"Aye, so do I, but I'm not her man, and neither are you. I love them both, and I'll not cut Alexander's man hood like that. Think on him. 'Tis for him to do, or he'll have nothing left, and a man canna live wie out pride."

Ian slumped dejectedly in his chair, weighed down by the truth in the old man's words. They sat in silence as the sounds of groans and the heavy creaking of the stairs heralded the bedraggled and ramshackled group of redcoats and the crew of the *Edna Rae*.

Cameron rode her horse, Torquod, along the coast road to Crail, impatient at the slow pace of Daft-Dougal on his swaybacked old gray beside her.

"Ain't you heard about the tortoise and the hare?" he cackled. "More haste, less speed."

"I just want to see the *Edna Rae*, how big she is. How many men it will take to sail her."

"She's not going nowheres at low tide wie no captain, so you'll save your puir wee bruised bones some jolting if you keep a slow, even pace like my old nag Duchess here," chided Dougal.

"Duchess?" laughed Cameron, looking at the droopy, unregal-looking old horse.

"Watch your mouth, mistress. 'Tis not the outside of a thing you should be judging but the inner, and my Duchess is all and more than her name implies. As gray as the cairns on the moors and as steady and true, ain't that right, you ole lass?" he crooned, at which the dappled head tossed, and she whinnied, showing crooked yellow teeth as though comically smiling.

"You shouldna have rid your showy piece, mistress. 'Tis sure to cause a stir wie you dressed like a stable lad.

They'll be remarkin' and thinking you stole him. I'll have
a visit wie Old-Petey's sister and hide yer black beastie in
her bothie this side of Crail, and you go the rest of the
way on my old Duchess, unless she'll offend yer proud
bottom?" suggested Daft-Dougal, laughing and showing
yellow, crooked teeth identical to his old nag's. " 'Twill gie
Old-Petey's sister a thrill, her being after to drag me to the
altar since she tried to seduce me at haying time when I
was a wee innocent bairn of no more'n ten. Silly old slummock is Old-Petey's sister, but she can cook, so she has
her uses." Daft-Dougal kept up a steady stream of chatter
despite Cameron's brooding silence. Later, he himself
strode silently, looking after her as Old-Petey's sister prat-
tled on and on about the girl's battered appearance.

Cameron's body protested as she rode into Crail on the
swaybacked old nag. She rode bareback and barefoot, as
Dougal had remarked dryly on the showiness of her boots
and hair as he crammed a filthy old straw hat over her
glossy curls.

The waterfront at Crail was busy and noisy as fishing
boats unloaded and women haggled over crates and nets,
screaming as they cleaned, sorted, and sold the silvery
fruits of the sea. Gulls swooped and fought over the guts
that were thrown back into the lapping, shimmering waves.
Cameron slumped into the curved back of the nag, mesmerized by the loud, colorful activity before recollecting
her mission and scanning the odd collection of boats hoping
to find the *Edna Rae*. One vessel was anchored offshore
apart from the motley assortment. Although sadly in need
of paint, she rode the waves proudly straining against the
thick, rusty anchor chain that bound her. There seemed to
be no activity on board, and Cameron debated swimming
out. Skirting the busy wharves, she rode to a small beach,
dismounted, and sat on the pebbles, sucking on a blade of
grass and watching the bucking boat. Coming to a sudden
decision, she unbuttoned her jerkin and was about to remove it when she realized that if she was discovered, the
wet cotton of her shirt would cause her breasts to be no-
ticeable. She rebuttoned the tight leather and waded into
the icy water. She gasped as the salt bit into her numerous
abrasions, unaware that she was watched by a solitary

horseman as she swam strongly to the vessel and lithely shinned up the anchor chain.

Cameron crept across the splintery boards of the deck, trying to stop her teeth from chattering. She was frozen to the core, and her muscles jerked and shook. She glanced back in dismay at the sharp imprints of her wet, bare feet on the bleached wood floor and then shrugged, thankful for the warmth of the sun. She carefully climbed down a metal ladder into the bowels of the small vessel. A terrible stench of unwashed bodies and human excrement caused her stomach to heave, and peering through a narrow grill at the end of a long corridor, she was horrified to see a small group of people chained in rotting, rancid hay. They seemed like skeletons, the flesh shrunken on the brittled bones, clawlike hands drooping resignedly in the rusty manacles. A sudden rustle and a squeaking made her heart beat even faster, and a fat rat ran across the body of a child, who stirred and moaned softly. Cameron spied a large ring of keys hanging on a hook, and she quietly took them down, trying to still the jangling. As the metal rubbed against metal, the chained people stiffened and strained away from the door, their eyes wide and staring with terror.

"Sssh!" whispered Cameron, putting a finger to her lips as she carefully inserted the largest key and tried to turn the rusty lock. The door swung open with a loud scream of anguish, the hinges sore in need of oil. There were seven people, three women and four small children. They stared, their eyes still wide with fear. As Cameron approached them, her bare feet squishing in the foul straw, they tried to back away, the rusty manacles ripping into their pale, emaciated flesh.

"Dinna fear me. I'll set you free," she comforted, frantically trying to find the right keys to undo the dreadful chains that forced the people to a half-sitting, half-lying position. The terrible smell churned her stomach, and her heart beat triple-time with each creaking, shuddering moan of the vessel as it strained protestingly against its own confining mooring. Her fingers were numb with cold, and she sobbed with frustration in her efforts to turn the large, rusty keys. The first manacle dropped off with such a heavy thud that the brittlely thin arm it had imprisoned seemed to snap.

"Help me wie the other," Cameron implored, but the freed woman stayed motionless as though still chained. Systematically Cameron worked, bruising her hands and ripping her nails. She lost track of time as she methodically tried each key until the opened manacles hung empty.

"You're free," she panted, but the skeletal people lay as though still confined regarding her with terror. Cameron stared at them uncomprehending. They were alive, and yet something was missing in their wide, hollow eyes. "Get up," she implored. "Get up!"

A loud clatter of feet and the low rumble of burly voices overhead announced the arrival of the crew. Cameron froze, staring at the pathetic row of people, who had not stirred since each frail arm had dropped like a disembodied limb. Cameron slowly backed from the room into the corridor, beckoning as she went. The sound of heavy boots ringing the metal rungs of the ladder caused her to duck into the shadows directly below it. She sat shivering with fear and cold watching a man descend.

"What's this?" roared a deep voice. "The brig's unlocked!" Several other booted feet hurriedly scraped the iron ladder, and Cameron pressed herself against the wall, watching the feet and legs slithering by her as a mob of men rushed down the narrow passageway to the wide-open door. Hearing no sounds from above, she took a chance and quickly climbed the ladder, thankful for her bare feet. She burst into the sunlight as raucous laughter burst from below at seeing the pathetic cargo of the *Edna Rae* unlocked but still there.

"So the unsold dregs were too pitiful to steal," boomed one jovial soul. "When Captain Loving returns, we'll dump this lot in the open sea to feed the fish."

Cameron furtively looked around and, keeping to the shadow of the gunwales, edged her way to the rear of the boat, away from the loud activity that erupted as men searched for intruders. She crouched behind a large coil of rope, wondering if she should wait until the hue and cry had died down or risk being seen by diving overboard. As she debated, two large, powerful legs stood before her, blocking her means of escape. How had the man moved so silently, she puzzled? She held her breath, hoping he couldn't hear the furious pounding of her heart.

"Nothing down here," boomed a deep voice above her that reverberated through her bones.

"Whoever they were are probably long gone now that they've found there is nothing worth stealing," answered another voice. Cameron's body ached as she crouched, afraid to move a muscle, and she listened to the grumble of men's voices recede as they called off the search, but the enormous legs still stood before her like two great bars of a jail.

"The coast is clear," murmured a low, rumbling voice. "They're all below deck."

Cameron didn't move. Could he be talking to her? Was there someone else with him? To her horror she saw the large legs bend and an enormous torso and bearded face loom in front of her. She gasped and tried to elude the monstrously enormous hand that reached to grasp her chin. Cameron stared into steel-gray eyes that narrowed. She glowered defiantly. The large man whistled through his teeth with surprise as if something about her was familiar and then nodded with satisfaction before frowning.

"Someone's sure gie you a beating, young-fellow-me-lad." he growled, staring at her cut cheekbones and the blackened circles about her eyes. Cameron felt his hand relax as he stared at her as though mesmerized. She took advantage and fleetly sprang by him, determined to leap over the high side of the boat into the sea. A loud shout went up as she was seen.

"Catch him, Goliath," yelled a voice as heavy feet pounded the deck.

"I'm trying, but he's as slippery as an eel," returned the huge man, grasping the back of Cameron's jerkin so that she hung suspended, staring into his massive, hairy face.

"Squirm, lad, squirm . . . kick and fight," he whispered as though Cameron needed encouragement. "Aye, that's the way," he added, swinging her over the gunwales. "I've got him!" he roared, flinging her into the sea. "Darnation!" he bellowed for the benefit of the rest of the crew as they ran up. "He'll not survive. He was no bigger than a mouse." He laughed as a couple of men took out their guns and their eyes raked the sea. "Not worth good powder. 'Twas nought but a half-starved sprat. A wee dock rat. It's time we were getting ourselves all spruced up as we's to be guests of Colonel Beddington in his fine house. Soft beds, good food, wenches and all the rum we can guzzle."

Cameron plummeted through the depths of the deep gray-green water until her ears buzzed and her lungs felt as if they would burst. She pushed up from the bottom and despaired of her head ever breaking through the murky water, when the sunlight filtered down, and she strove toward the surface as the thunder pounded in her ears. She broke into the air and gasped, not caring if the crew of the *Edna Rae* saw. Without turning, she dived like a seal back beneath the waves and headed for shore.

Ian sat in the public house in Crail for three hours, drowning his heartache and depression with mug upon mug of dark ale. Fergus had left him there, eager to be back, not wanting Cameron and Mackie to be alone when Colonel Beddington arose. Ian's fuzzy mind had played for time, trying to keep the crew of the *Edna Rae* and Beddington's redcoat contingent amused while he waited for Alex's return. He finally hit upon the brilliant notion of extending Colonel Beddington's heartfelt invitation to the crew. At the time it had seemed a stroke of genius, but after three cups of strong coffee and the departure of the raucous crew to collect their gear, he'd questioned his sanity.

Alex entered the dim, noisy tavern and listened silently to Ian's rueful confession and lame explanation that by having the crew of the *Edna Rae* under their noses at Glen Aucht they'd have clear leeway to steal the vessel away. Alex blew heavily through his nostrils and shook his head.

"Puir old Mackie and Fergus will be run off their feet. There's not enough hands at the house to suffice the few housed there already, nor tend the folks hidden in the cave," he answered, his mind still on the small, lithe figure he had watched shinning up the anchor chain of the *Edna Rae* on his way back to Crail from Saint Andrews.

"I'm sure Colonel Beddington will be intimidated by their arrival and make sure some of his troops are put to good use," offered Ian, realizing that his idea had been rash but not knowing how to reverse it.

"Aye, you've a point there. He'll probably jump to the conclusion that they've come for their cargo, and he'll be bending over backward not to antagonize," Alex returned thoughtfully. "However, 'tis best we reach Glen Aucht before the crew. We'll leave these lads to accompany the colonel's most welcome guests," he added with a laugh, indicating the drunken redcoats who lay sprawled around the tavern.

Leaving word with the innkeeper, the two young Scots set off toward Glen Aucht, each lost in his own thoughts—Alex's mind teased by the familiar lithe figure climbing the ship's chain and Ian's on how to inform his friend of the rape of his wife.

Teeth chattering, the wind sharply blowing through her drenched clothes, Cameron shivered on the back of the gray nag, her cuts and bruises stinging sharply from the crusted salt. Daft-Dougal hailed her from the hedgerow beside Old-Petey's sister's cottage, but she didn't hear him, for she was sunk in the painful, plodding rhythm, *Charles Stuart's my father . . . Charles Stuart's my father . . .* that beat in her brain in time with the hooves.

"Whoa, me Duchess," shrilled the old man, and the nag stopped suddenly, nearly toppling the half-conscious girl. Dougal narrowed his gley eyes so that the balls focused straight and true.

"What have you bin up to, young lass?" he growled, sniffing the salt spray on her wet clothes.

" 'Tis this old bag of bones, she has fair rattled mine," returned Cameron spiritedly, shaking off her aching fatigue. "Gie me my Torquod and let's get home," she ordered, giving a piercing whistle and sliding painfully from the old swayback.

"Looks like you need a wee drop to warm you."

"Nay," refused Cameron, welcoming the idea but afraid lest she succumb to the warmth and sleep. "Where's my boots?" she asked as the sleek black stallion trotted up, his tail and head held proudly. She took a deep breath and agilely leaped upon the tall, glossy back, hugging his muscled warmth with her cold legs. "Follow wie me boots," she shouted as she dug in her heels and raced toward Glen Aucht, leaving the old man scratching his gray head.

"What?" exclaimed Alex incredulously, his bronze face lightening at Ian's news. "Why did you not tell me before instead of your fool notions and pranks of inviting the *Edna Rae*. Tried to rape her? Beat her?"

Before Ian could answer, Alex urged his mount into a thunderous gallop. At that moment the silhouette of another racing horse was imprinted against the red horizon as Cameron sped along the coast road. Ian's voice was lost, and he resignedly slowed down, knowing he was unable to overtake his friend. Hearing the pounding of hooves behind, he halted and turned in time to see Cameron fly by. He had a brief glimpse of her bruised, set little face before she was gone.

Cameron's heart lurched for a beat as she recognized Alex, but she closed her mind and dug her small, bare heels even more sharply into the firm black girth and galloped by. Neck and neck raced the two horses for the four miles to Glen Aucht. For a while Cameron forgot her hatred, thrilling at the competition, every nerve atingle and every bruised, aching spot calmed as the wind streamed her ebony hair. She halted her sweating mount sharply in the stable yard, and the horse reared triumphantly, having won by half a length. Cameron sat victoriously on Torquod and then, as remembrances of what Alex had withheld from her flashed, she sneered, swung herself down, and led her horse into the fragrance of the stable. Alex stared in horror at her bruised, gashed face, as fury pounded his pulses. He dismounted and followed her into the stable.

"Cameron?"

She gave no indication that she heard as she watered and fed her horse. With a snort of rage Alex grabbed her arm, turning her to him. He caught his breath again at the violence reaped upon her face and seized it between his strong brown hands, his amber eyes hurt and troubled. Cameron felt the traitorous tenderness well and for a moment she stared back at him, mirroring his love, but when she remembered his excursion to Edinburgh the previous night, she broke free and ran toward the kitchen door.

"Where have you been? We've been aworried sick," fussed Mackie as Cameron entered the warmth of the kitchen. "And you're soaked through to the skin," she added, clutching at Cameron's sleeve. Alex strode in, his booted feet ringing sharply on the red clay tiles. Cameron quelled the desire to cower behind Mackie's comforting girth but stood straight and proud, glaring defiantly at her husband.

"I'll have my things moved to the green suite, Mrs. MacDonald, and please to bring up warm water for washing," commanded Cameron imperiously. Mackie looked from one to the other, not knowing what to do.

"Do as my wife says, Mrs. MacDonald," ordered Alex curtly, after a tense silence before striding from the room and slamming the door. Cameron listened to his footsteps recede. I'll be subject to him no longer, she vowed again, trying to firm her resolve and fight the desolation she felt.

Later ensconced in the green chamber, Cameron lay in a blissful tub of hot water scented with lavender before a roaring fire. She kept her eyes averted from the hearth, knowing her beloved hound would not be lying there lazily watching her. She kept her mind busy planning how she could take over the *Edna Rae* and sail her away to find her brother, so that together they could go to their father, Charles Stuart. Sleep weighted her bruised eyelids, and she fought the languorous waves. Her neck prickled, her eyes flew open, and she sat sharply spilling the water as she became aware that she was watched. Alex leaned against the closed door, his mouth in a firm stern line.

"Get out!" she spat.

"NO!"

" 'Tis my room, you've no right—"

"I have the right," he stated, purposefully striding toward her and hauling her upright so that she hung dripping. He lifted her over the rim of the bath and carried her to the hearth, where he examined her breasts, the purple crescents of toothmarks angry and violent. Silently he noted the welts on her slim arms and flat belly. He turned her about, taking in every abrasion. Cameron's rage smoldered at his callous treatment. She felt like a piece of meat. She endured silently, her thighs firmly closed, her lips pursed in a bitter line.

"Finished?" she asked sarcastically.

Alex didn't know what to say, he wanted to knead and kiss each abused spot on her beautiful young body, but her attitude kept him on guard.

"There's one place you've missed, my lord," she hissed spitefully, opening her lithe young thighs. The inner parts of her legs were red, black and blue from Beddington's impotent pummeling, where he'd grabbed handfuls of the firm young flesh and cruelly twisted. The angry bruisings ran clear to the triangle of blue-black hair. Alex's gut clawed.

"He raped you?" he whispered.

"He killed my hound, which is worse by far," answered the girl coldly. "Now get out!"

"Cameron?"

Cameron stood her ground, fanning her already ignited rage as she reminded herself of how he had withheld knowledge of her own father and had furtively crossed the firth to Edinburgh. There was only one reason he would court such danger, she told herself—Fiona. Her jealousy welled. They deserve each other, she decided, sneering with undisguised malice. How could she ever have thought she loved this hard, unyielding dictator? she fumed. How could she ever have trusted him? Felt safe with him? He was no better than Beddington.

"Cameron, let me help you," said Alex softly, noting the emotions that played across her abused face.

"I hate you! 'Tis not Beddington, the fat fool, I hate but you. He tried to take something from me I had not to gie . . . but you . . . you . . ." Cameron's voice quivered as she tried to control herself. "I gave to you, and you twisted and used. You're worse by far. Get out!"

"Nay! I must know," roared Alex.

"Know what?"

"Did he have his way?" hissed Alex with anguish. Pain knifed through him at the thought that the English colonel's flesh might have lain where only his had. Cameron

stared at him, recognizing the agony in his face. Her eyes
narrowed with speculation, and she regarded him silently
with her small hands on her slim, naked hips.

"Did he have his way?" she repeated mockingly. "Did
you have yours?"

"Cameron, I must know," pleaded Alex.

"Why?" she asked, genuinely puzzled. "Why is it so important that you know? Torquil is dead, my puir body
sadly abused, and yet all you are interested in is whether
he had his way? What is his way?"

"Cameron, you ken my meaning surely."

"Explain to me, my lord."

"I canna say it better. Did he enter you?" cried Alex
hoarsely.

"Which part?" asked Cameron, getting a cruel delight.
"His male part? His tongue? His hand?"

"Stop it, Cameron!" roared Alex, lifting his hand to
strike. Cameron pushed her bruised face closer.

"You, too? 'Tis numb, but I'm sure you'll find a place
unabused to place your own claiming mark," she challenged.

"Oh, Cameron, don't," groaned Alex. "Let me reach
to you . . . Dinna shut me out."

"I dinna need you," resolved Cameron. "I dinna need
what you can gie me."

"I'll not go. I'll not let you shut me out," returned Alex,
not knowing how to deal with her and seating himself
firmly in the fireside chair. Cameron regarded him, at a
loss herself, and then shrugged into her nightgown, got into
bed, and turned away from him. She lay staring at the
flowered patterns on the wallpaper, wishing he'd leave so
that she could succumb to grief. She hugged the pillow
thinking of Torquil's shaggy coat and Alex's warm, strong
body, feeling desolate. A brisk knock at the door heralded
Mackie's bustling in with a laden tray. Steam curled above
several dishes with the most delicious aroma. Despite her
despondency Cameron's saliva ran and her empty young
belly churned with hunger. How could she chew with him
sitting there?

"I brought both your suppers up," chattered Mackie,
unpiling several dishes on the table by the fire.

"We'll serve ourselves, Mackie. Oh, and have the crew of the *Edna Rae* arrived yet?" asked Alex cordially.

"Nay, a couple of outriders rode in awhile back with notice that they're on their way. The colonel's in a rare taking, and Sir Robert is wishing to have a word wie you, but he says the morning will suffice," answered Mackie, withdrawing discreetly.

All thoughts of hunger were instantly dispelled by Alex's inquiry as to the crew of the *Edna Rae*. She suppressed the desire to turn impulsively to him with numerous questions. If the crew were at Glen Aucht, then she and Daft-Dougal would have free run of the vessel, she planned.

Alex forced himself to eat, even though the thought of food was repugnant. He chewed slowly and methodically, his eyes not leaving Cameron, who lay turned from him, her mind trying to think of a way to find Dougal.

"I'd wish you'd have the civility to leave me to my privacy. A more sensitive, considerate person would see that I am feeling far from well and not sicken me with his noisy eating," stated Cameron, sitting up demurely and doing her best imitation of a society matron. If Alex hadn't been so deeply steeped in torment, he might have roared with laughter, but as it was, he just fixed her with a cold, steely eye and commenced forcing the food into his stomach.

"Will you leave!" screamed Cameron, her composure shattered and dangerously near breaking into a childish tantrum. Alex did not answer but kept chewing stolidly. Cameron beat the bedclothes with rage.

"Get out!"

The pulses roared in her neck and wrists, and Cameron felt she would explode with fury. Her breath was labored as she tried to control herself. She glared at the seemingly calm man who ate, his eyes never leaving her for a fraction.

"Then I will go," she stated, throwing back the bedcovers, her glance resting on the pile of wet clothes that she'd flung in the corner. Alex followed her gaze and in one lithe movement he picked up the damp bundle. He smelled the sea and turned back to her. It *had* been her shinning up the anchor chain of the *Edna Rae*, he realized, wondering if he should confront her with the knowledge.

"You'll not wear wet clothes. There is enough to worry about without you becoming even more troublesome by falling ill with lung inflammation," he said tersely, opening the window and flinging the clothes out.

Cameron gasped at the effrontery. "How dare you!"

"Easily, for although you seem to have forgotten, you are my wife and subject to me," he stated in a dangerously low tone. Many furious responses flashed through Cameron's mind as she regarded him, wishing her eyes could pierce him. Her whole body was rigid, tensed to attack. Her small hands unconsciously twisted the bedclothes maliciously until her fingernails dug into her numb palms.

A discreet knocking echoed through the still-brittle tension between them. Neither acknowledged nor shifted their glaring eyes from each other's. The rapping persisted.

"Come in," barked Alex, still keeping his glowering amber eyes on her flashing green ones. Sir Robert Kinkaid entered, clutching a letter.

"This has just arrived from Edinburgh. Your orders, Sir Alex—"

"Let me see," exclaimed Alex, taking his eyes from Cameron, who grabbed at the opportunity and fled the room. With an oath he started to his feet, but the old man detained him.

"I must have words wie you. I thought they might wait until the morrow, but they'll not rest easy within me."

"I'll not have Beddington harming her more!" shouted Alex, pulling forcefully away from the clawlike hand.

"He'll not go near her."

"And what gies you that assurance?"

"Her raven, Omen, will pluck his eyes out next time," said Sir Robert.

"Her raven what?" ejaculated Alex.

"She's named the bird so. 'Twas that large shadow of the night who came to her defense last night against Beddington's attack. Flew through the glass of the window and near fed on the fat man's right eyeball, which was fortunate for the lass but unfortunate when you read this dispatch, which contains not only your orders but tells of a warrant soon to be prepared for the arrest of the witch Cameron. Lady Fiona Hurst and Judge Singleton have been extremely busy and seemed to have bent the ears of some greedy churchmen. Evidence is being collected, not just from Glen Aucht but also from Cape Wrath, where it seems our black-haired lass is held in awe, able to converse with animals, swim with seals, and . . . fly with the bats. There's also a claim of murder."

Alex sat heavily.

"The lass told me Loving was not the first man she'd killed," continued the old man.

"There was a horse thief last summer who beat her with a whip . . . would have killed her if she hadn't had her horse trample him to death. But this talk of witches and witchcraft is insane. There has been no such barbarism since the burning of the poor, unfortunate woman in Durness forty years ago," protested Alex, trying to clear his head.

"Public burning . . . but don't you think there might have been other, not-quite-so-publicized persecutions since? Burnings and stonings have given way to incarcerations, transportations, or furtive killings," informed the old judge.

"Oh, God! Was there ever such a tangle! Each time that it seems it can get no worse, we're plunged into more hell," cursed Alex.

"Maybe this will supply some of the answers," said Kinkaid, handing him a folded sheet of paper. "There's a ship, the *Earl of Winchester*, sailing from Fort William at Loch Linnhe a week from tomorrow, the seventh day of May. I took it upon myself to accept and send the messenger on and reserve a cabin for you and your wife, as I doubt any warrant can be issued by then. That's one good thing about bureaucracy—it takes time for the creaking wheels to take action."

Cameron made her way furtively to the nursery rooms to hunt for appropriate clothes from Alex's boyhood wardrobe. Fitting herself in tight-fitting black breeches, shirt, and vest so that she'd blend in with the night, she crept

down the back stairs to the kitchens in the hopes of finding
Daft-Dougal. Mackie and Old Gran MacNab busily
scampered around basting and stirring while Old-Petey,
Jemmy-Lad, and Fergus grumbled as they chopped and
pared at the kitchen table. The small red-haired girl's
freckled face broke into a broad smile, which quivered
tremulously waiting for Cameron's reaction. The black-
haired girl hugged the younger one impulsively.

" 'Tis good to see you. I've quite missed you," she
laughed.

"But I was here, I've been nowhere," puzzled Jemmy-Lad.
" 'Twas you so strange, looking through me as though I
were not there. Your puir face 'tis all the colors of the rainbow . . . so was mine after the colonel . . ." The child
stopped her chatter, her blue eyes sad at remembering.

"If Mackie can spare you, I'm looking for Daft-Dougal,"
said Cameron gently.

"Aye, what's one pair of hands more or less when trying to do the impossible? And when you find the gley-eyed
codger, tell him to bring his laziness here to help," panted
Mackie without a pause in her bustling. "And keep yer-
selves hid from the redcoats and that murderous crew
who'll be arriving any minute," she warned as the two
seeming lads slipped out followed by the gangly pup Maggie.

Cameron breathed appreciatively of the crisp night air.
A hoarse cry above their heads caused Jemmy to shiver.

"Dinna fear, 'tis only Omen," comforted Cameron as the
large black bird swooped out of the darkness and landed
on her shoulder.

"Omen?" stammered the child, flinching from the eerie
eyes that seemed disembodied in the blackness.

"The raven," explained Cameron as they stepped into
the lantern-lit stables. "Here, raise your hand and stroke
it," she added, seeing Jemmy's fear. Tentatively the girl
raised her trembling hand, and the glossy black bird gently
rubbed its iridescent feathers against it.

"He's nay black but many, many colors. There's sparks
of blue, purple, and green," exclaimed Jemmy.

"Aye, like my face," laughed Cameron, and the bird
bobbed up and down, joining in their merriment.

"What's all the frolicking?" growled Daft-Dougal, emerging from one of the stalls.

"Go look in on the other pups, Jemmy," ordered Cameron, wanting to talk to Dougal alone. "Have you heard that the crew of the *Edna Rae*'s expected?" she whispered when the girl had appeared reluctantly to obey.

"Aye, I've had my ears to the keyholes, and 'twas that rapscallion Drummond who stole our plan and put it in the master's ear, I reckon. Your man rid off to Saint Andrews and Earlshall today to find the MacFarlane kin who fish the North Sea."

"I'll nay go wie them, I'll stay wie you," cried Jemmy, launching herself at Cameron. "They dinna like me. 'Tain't my father's brothers but their wives wie ten bairns each who think I'm a bother."

Cameron frowned, unable to comprehend what had put the young girl in such a pucker.

"Jemmy MacFarlane, mind yer manners," growled Dougal. "The wee lass thinks we're for sending her away to her kin. That's what happens when you listen to that which don't concern you! You get the wrong end of the stick!"

"*You* eavesdrop, you just said so yerself," challenged Jemmy with an unusual display of spirit.

"Och, red hair always tells," cackled Dougal. "We need yer uncles to sail the vessel to spirit the lassies and bairns in the caves away."

"Can I help?" asked the girl eagerly.

"Aye, by doing as yer told and tending to the pups. Which brings to mind something, mistress. Jemmy-Lad, bring out the strapping black-un."

Cameron looked inquiringly into Dougal's cross-eyes, but he cackled and nodded his head up and down.

"If you're thinking any will take the place of Torquil—"

"Hush up," interrupted the old man as the girl clucked encouragingly, trying to coax something from the shadows.

"He will nay come," she complained. "And he's so big, and black that I'm a wee bit afeared of him."

The raven gave a sharp caw, and from the darkness

stepped the largest of the litter. Although not full grown, it was plain to see he'd equal the size and weight of his sire. The proud young dog walked steadily to Cameron and sat staring up at her and the raven. Pain churned in Cameron, and she fought the emotion as it seemed as though she looked into Torquil's dark brown eyes.

"Spirits never die, lassie. Some are so loving and noble they canna desert or betray, even in death, those they protect," murmured Dougal. "Last night I came to fetch shovels to dig a resting-place for your noble beast, and this young fellow had changed. Lost his innocence, it seemed. He stood apart from the rest of the litter. He is father and son."

Cameron dropped to her knees and, holding the young dog's head, stared deeply into his eyes. The biting sorrow that filled her was calmed by the seeming warm wisdom in the clear darkness.

"Torquil?" she whispered. "Nay, there shall only be one."

"You'll claim him?"

"Aye," nodded Cameron. "But his name shall be Tor like the highest mountain crag. Half his father's name, and I hope he can live up to that much, for it will more than suffice," she decided, brushing away a tear.

"Now to business," said Dougal sharply. "Young Drummond and the master plan to move the folks from the caves the day after tomorrow. Apparently there are two men keeping watch on the vessel whom they aim to lure away for fun and games in Crail and then the MacFarlane brothers will sail the boat to the cove, which is deep and free from rocks."

"Tomorrow night is Beltane Eve . . . the first of May and cause for celebration," thought Cameron aloud. " 'Twill be best to use their plan a day earlier. If you gie me a map, I'll ride to the MacFarlanes now."

"You'll nay need a map, I'll take you there," volunteered Jemmy.

" 'Twill be better," growled Dougal, seeing Cameron hesitate. "Them MacFarlanes is a surly, suspicious lot. The wee lass will gie credence, them knowing she is a ward, so to speak, of the master. Now 'tis best to get a move on, as that salty bunch will be riding up any moment," he said, leading out Cameron's black stallion.

"And what am I to ride?" asked Jemmy.

"There is none that you could master who'd keep pace wie this prince of darkness," cackled Dougal. "He'll carry you two wee-uns as though you were mere feathers."

Jemmy clutched Cameron's waist from behind. Dougal smartly slapped Torquod's glossy rump, and the great horse sprang forward. Jemmy's pup, Maggie, whined, but Tor sprang after the galloping steed as the raven flew above. Dougal watched the fleet, dark trio vanish into the night.

CHAPTER FIFTEEN

The din of revelry echoed through the large house as Beddington plied his soldiers and the crew of the *Edna Rae* with victuals, drink, and bawdy tales. Alex stood silently throughout the grotesque festivities, curbing his desire to kill the lecherous colonel. He would kill him, he vowed, but not until Cameron and the cave folk were safely out of reach. He contented himself with going over and over his plan. Cameron would be put aboard the *Edna Rae* even if he had to put her in irons stark naked. The MacFarlane brothers would sail the vessel north to Inverbervie, where he would meet it after dealing with Beddington. He'd then ride with her to meet the troopship at Loch Linnhe, even if he had to tie her across the saddle. If for some reason he lost his own life or was captured, the MacFarlanes would keep her hidden and send word to Sir Robert Kinkaid. Alex was furious with Sir Robert for divulging to Cameron the secret of her birth, and yet he also felt relief at the lifting of the heavy burden. It had been a torment to keep her father's name from her, and he understood her rage. He chafed against the long, arduous meal that kept him apart from Cameron, as there were many things he wanted to explain in the hopes of mending the breach between them. Hopefully she would have had time to simmer down and be in more of a conducive mood to listen. He desperately hoped she was safely sleeping as he fixed Beddington with what he intended as an evil eye. Nauseated and unable to bear the man's bloated face, he turned his attention to assessing the crew of the *Edna Rae*. They all seemed a scurvy lot except for one man, who towered above the rest. A giant in height and width of shoulder who sat eating silently. Feeling Alex's eyes, he stared back unwaveringly. Alex frowned. The man did not seem to belong with the rest of the crew, and yet they accepted him.

Were in fact a little in awe of him. He determined to find out more.

As the sun rose, so did the drunken revelry wind down. Those that could, staggered up the broad stairs to find beds. Others drifted off to snore sonorously where they lay. Alex searched for Cameron and, not finding her either in the master suite of rooms or in the small green chamber where she'd moved her things, he made his way to the kitchens, where his few servants, nearly dropping from exhaustion, cleaned up the remains of the long night's festivities.

"She's up in the south attic wie Jemmy-Lad. Daft-Dougal's keeping watch," said Fergus, thinking it best not to inform Alex that the two young girls had ridden in just an hour before. There was a coldness in his young master's expression and a tension that crackled, so it was best to let things be, he thought sagely. Alex narrowed his eyes before curtly turning on his heel and making his way to a cold, empty bed.

Cameron slept late the next morning and, in throwing the curtains wide, cursed herself as she saw that the sun stood high in the sky. Jemmy lay curled on a small cot at the foot of the bed. Bone-weary, they had accomplished all they set out to do and had arrived back at Glen Aucht to find Daft-Dougal waiting for them. He had carried the sleepy Jemmy up the stairs in his wiry old arms to the small attic room, where they had slept. Cameron shuddered, thinking of a similar room in the gabled eaves where Jeannie had spent her last days.

"'Tis May first, Jemmy, stir yourself," sang Cameron, trying to dispel the dark, heavy shadow of Jeannie and shaking the small, red-haired child. "We have to help Dougal make the Beltane cakes for the birds and beasts of prey. He'll be putting many a strange potion and herb into the ones for the two-legged buzzards housed under this roof," she giggled, pulling on her clothes.

"Did I hear my bonny name mentioned?" cackled Daft-Dougal, prancing in. "'Tis time you sleepy heads awoke, for I've much to do," and with that he strutted out of the room.

The two girls padded down the stairs, followed by the

two dogs. To their surprise the kitchen was empty, and no smell of baking nor Beltane activity was in evidence.

"Where is everyone? 'Tis past ten," puzzled Cameron.

"They're not all dead, do you suppose?" whispered Jemmy, her face turning alarmingly white so that her freckles sprung into prominence.

"Nay, they're having a well-earned sleep," offered Ian, entering from the pantry while munching on a large hunk of cheese.

"While you were soundly dreaming, they were working their poor fingers to the bone. Dinna stop until cockcrow," he continued cheerfully. Cameron glowered at him.

"Traitor," she hissed.

"Me?" laughed Ian, covering his concern for her bruised face and her hostility.

"Aye, you. Stealing my plan for your own and tattling it," she accused, knowing that now she'd not sail with the *Edna Rae* but had to ride across country to Rona as she was unable to part with her horse and hound.

"Well, who is this handsome fellow?" asked Ian, changing the subject and kneeling beside the large black pup.

"Come, Tor," ordered Cameron, curtly leaving by the back door with her dog obediently at her heel. Jemmy scampered after.

"Jemmy, stay and help Mackie wie the Beltane baking. I need time to myself." Jemmy hung back at the kitchen door, her mouth turned down at the rejection.

"Wie all the fuss around here I near forgot the day," said Ian, trying to cheer the young girl. "D'ye think Mackie'll let me lend a hand?"

"Lend a hand wie what?" fussed the old lady, out of breath from her rapid descent downstairs.

"The Beltane baking."

"Oh, my lord, I clear forgot!"

Cameron entered the stables and was rewarded by an eager whinny as Torquod kicked against the confines of the box stall.

"Who have we here?" rumbled a familiar voice, and Cameron stared up into the unshaven face of the seaman who'd dropped her overboard the *Edna Rae* the day before. The black pup tensed and growled low in his throat, staring up at the enormous man who'd obviously just woken from sleep in the hayloft. Cameron stood frozen, wondering what her course of action should be, when she heard the welcome rush of heavy wings and Omen glided through the open door and landed on her shoulder.

"And what have we here?" repeated the man with humor in his deep voice.

Cameron chose to ignore him as she purposefully strode to release Torquod. The enormous man swung his legs over the side of the loft and sat bemused, watching the ebony-haired youth with the raven, black hound, and horse. He grinned happily as the seemingly lithe boy swung himself upon the high back and seemed to fly off, followed by his two companions. The man was still sitting, his legs dangling, when in ran a red-haired lad followed by a red-haired dog.

"Have you a red-haired horse, too?" he chuckled, causing Jemmy to back away in terror. "Or perhaps a robin redbreast or some great red falcon to perch on your shoulder?" He leaped down, surprisingly agilely for his enormity, and Maggie-Pup took an instant liking to him, wagging her heavy tail and licking his hand.

"Come away, Maggie, you fickle bitch you," chided Jemmy. " 'Tis one of them from the ship that sells flesh. Come away." The large man laughed jovially, seeming to shake the stable rafters as Jemmy ran away as fast as her legs could carry her.

Cameron rode back from the cave, hoping that with all the celebrations for Beltane, Alex wouldn't visit the cave and learn of her plans. She had readied the people for midnight, lying and saying that her husband had sent her as he couldn't get away from the English.

She entered the busy kitchen to the delicious aroma of baking and giggled as Daft-Dougal slipped her a cross-eyed wink as he sat concocting a strange assortment of herbs. Ian sat at the table with Jemmy, both their faces smudged with flour and their faces full of cake. Cameron smiled at the warm merriment and joy that seemed to pervade. She caught her breath as another large shape sat absorbed in rolling out pastry. The giant seaman sat with Mackie at another table. His enormous girth dwarfed the little housekeeper. Cameron frowned and was about to beckon Dougal to her, when the door opened and Alex strode in. A sudden tension cut through the warmth, and each busy person looked up and stared at the small, dark figure and the tall, golden-haired man. The seaman looked from face to face and then back to Alex and Cameron. Tor whined, looking from one to the other, not knowing quite what to make of the strained silence.

Alex did not want to make a scene, but he desperately wanted to comfort Cameron, yet noting her stance and spitting green eyes, just stood mesmerized, aching to hold her and yet kept at bay, somehow knowing the time wasn't right. She was impervious to the tenderness he felt, just recognizing his stony, dictatorial features and seeing distrust and censure. She wished he'd leave so that the small glimmer of normal happiness in the busy kitchen could resume. Old Gran MacNab and Jemmy started to fidget as the long, tense moment stretched. Cameron turned sharply on her heel, not knowing where she was going, and walked out of the kitchen door. Alex debated following but instead turned and surveyed the still tableau. Released, the hive of activity resumed with fervor as each became aware of and embarrassed at their staring. Daft-Dougal chuckled softly and then louder until he choked and was pounded on the back by Old-Petey.

Alex stared speculatively at the large seaman, who nodded noncommittally.

"Mackie, I think our Dougal needs some help," said Alex softly. The little woman stared up bewildered, and when she saw him nod meaningfully at the seaman, she scurried to the other table, leaving the two men to talk. Alex lowered his rangy frame into the vacated chair and summed up the other man as he wondered why he was drawn to him, in fact instantly liked him.

"Sir Alexander Sinclair," nodded the seaman, feeling it best to break the silence as he stared frankly back at the younger, russet-haired Scot.

"You have me at a disadvantage, as I do not know how you are called," responded Alex.

"By many a name and label. The wee, red-haired lad over there calls me flesh peddler, others bastard and worse," answered the enormous man enigmatically. "But I'm known by the crew as Goliath, and it seems as good a name as any."

"Are you a flesh peddler?" asked Alex directly.

"A man is known by the company he keeps."

"Aye," agreed Alex ironically.

"Seems to me there's more here than meets the eye. That English colonel didna seem overjoyed by our company and yet extended an invitation?" remarked Goliath in a mellow tone. Amber eyes pierced the steel-gray ones, and neither man wavered as they summed up each other's worth.

"The black-haired lad near lost his life yesterday on the *Edna Rae*."

Alex froze and forced his voice to an evenness.

"And?" he probed.

"Is he your son?" queried the seaman and, at no reply, "Your brother? Young ward?" and at still no reply shrugged. "Aye, 'tis no business of mine, but it turns my guts to see a wee-un so abused."

"What saved his life?" asked Alex.

"I flung him overboard, not knowing if he could swim or not before his distinct coloring could be remarked. 'Twas a relief to see him swim like an otter."

"I'm in your debt," answered Alex stiffly.

"Nay, he might be . . . 'twas his young hide not yours. What is he to you?" probed Goliath.

"As you previously remarked, 'tis not your business. But your cut seems different from the rest of the crew, and I do wonder at the company you keep," returned Alex.

"And, to quote the much-quoted, 'tis none of your business either. Now, if you'll excuse me, I think your housekeeper has need of these large but inadequate hands if she's to feed us scurvy crew plus the English soldiers, who seem to be devouring your home," he stated.

Alex sat fuming, watching the large man gracefully wend his way through the busy activity. Who was the enormous, enigmatic stranger? He spoke too well to be a mere seaman. What was he doing among the crew of the *Edna Rae*?

Goliath, Jemmy, and Ian sat kneading and rolling, listening to Daft-Dougal's tales.

". . . and then there was Molly MacLeane from the Isle of Rum in the Hebrides, who'd prophesy wie a well-scraped blade bone of mutton, and Kenneth Oaur of Sutherland."

"Och, are we back wie the wee folk, Daft-Dougal?" laughed Ian from the far side of the room.

"Guard yer tongue, or you'll rue yer words tonight around the Beltane fires."

Alex, unable to join in the forced merriment where it seemed that all involved deliberately ignored their oppression, let himself out quietly into the stable yard, hoping to find Cameron. Her horse was neither in his stall nor prancing in any of the neighboring fields. He wondered if she'd taken time for a quiet swim and debated riding out to find her when a movement behind caused him to turn. Goliath leaned his huge frame against the outer stable wall. Not wishing to be followed and deciding that Cameron would be in his company soon enough in the confines of a ship, Alex sought out Sir Robert Kinkaid.

The sun was setting as Cameron rode back to Glen Aucht. She had spent a day of solitude swimming and sleeping in the sun, hidden from the world. She felt slightly guilty at leaving all the busy preparations for the night's Beltane ceremony to others but told herself that she'd be working throughout the long night and then have a gruelling ride across the width of Scotland to find her brother. She swung off her horse's high back and was grasped by two strong hands, who swiveled her in the air so that she stared into the steel-gray eyes of the seaman. He stared long and hard before setting her gently on her feet.

"Salt in your hair again?" he laughed gruffly. Cameron appraised him with her own vivid green eyes, wondering why the raven in the rafters above hadn't cawed a warning and why her young hound sat calm and relaxed.

"They trust me . . . so should you," growled the man, following her gaze.

"Why?"

"I held your life in my hands yesterday, and didna I save it?" he returned.

"You could have broke my neck flinging me so," retorted Cameron.

"Aye, 'twas a chance I had to take. Would you have preferred to be left to the others?"

Cameron didn't answer but led her horse to a nearby pasture.

"Night is coming and you're not stabling him down?" remarked the man, raising an eyebrow. "Perhaps you're keeping him free in readiness."

"He values his freedom as I do mine!" she retorted hotly, furious with herself for giving the stranger cause for suspicion.

"Aye, as does another I know."

"Meaning?" asked Cameron, sharply turning on him.

"Nothing quite yet."

They walked in silence through the apple orchard, Cameron strangely unnerved.

"What other?"

"We all like freedom," came the irritating reply. "We'll be seeing much of each other later," he laughed as he strolled away from her. Cameron watched him go as the spent petals of apple blossom whirled around her in the breeze. Omen landed on her shoulder, breaking her puzzled reverie.

The rest of the day afforded no time for contemplation as coachloads of squealing wenches from the neighboring towns of Leven, Wemyss, and Kirkcaldy spilled into the house to be pinched and fondled by the seamen and soldiers. Beddington sat and sweated, forcing himself to be gay and yet keeping an ever-watchful eye on Alex and the crew of the *Edna Rae*. Laden tables were placed on the well-manicured lawns, and a large bonfire was prepared. Alex and Ian stood apart, watching on the fringes, while Daft-Dougal, Cameron, and Jemmy peered down from a high attic window.

"I wish the sun would set. 'Tis the longest day ever," complained Cameron.

"Patience," chided Dougal. "You nay want to miss the entertainment. The small green cakes have a powerful spell. 'Twill gie such a thirst that they'll nay be able to find enough spirits to drink. The wee pink ones will gie them visions and change their way of looking so even their own loved ones will seem like gargoyles."

"Tell about the heather-colored ones, Dougal," urged Jemmy.

"You tell," cackled the old man.

"They'll turn their bowels to water so that they soil themselves like babies," giggled the young girl.

"But when? When?" asked Cameron, not joining in their hilarity, just wanting to be away sailing the waters with no temptation. She stared down at the setting sun's reflections like fire on Alex's golden head, and her heart betrayed her. She turned away, unable to bear his tall, lean figure as her nose remembered his musky body smell and she tried to still the deep need for him by reminding herself of his betrayal with Fiona and the withholding of her father's identity. Daft-Dougal looked at her long and hard.

"Awa' wie thee, lass. Hightail it to Crail. Young Jemmy and me will meet you and the *Edna Rae* at the cove. All the power of nature go wie you."

Cameron beamed and hugged both of them before running fleetly down the stairs. Mackie and Fergus bustled about the kitchen preparing large platters. She stopped and felt an aching huskiness blur her eyes and tickle her nose. Impulsively she threw her arms around them both.

"I love you as though you were my mother and father," she cried before dashing out of the kitchen door, leaving them bewildered.

" 'Tis though we'll never see her more," sobbed Mackie, her old knees shaking and holding onto her husband for dear life. Neither old person saw the enormous shape of Goliath glide after Cameron as she made her way silently through the orchard to the meadow beyond.

The deep red sunset reflected off the ebony trio as they seemed to fly with the wind toward Crail. Goliath smiled and urged his not-so-rapid mount after.

* * *

Cameron stood at the rail of the *Edna Rae,* delighting in the icy salt spray that burned her cheeks. It had seemed so tame after the expectation of a bloody battle, she pondered. She had waited an hour for the MacFarlane brothers, despairing that they'd ever arrive. They had been dismayed to find her but had resentfully taken her in their small dinghy as they'd rowed taciturnly out to the *Edna Rae.* Silently they had shinned the anchor chain and crept about the vessel and to their surprise found the two watches missing. Only the silent, thin people in the brig lay staring at them with wide, haunted eyes.

" 'Tis a ghost ship," shivered Chakie MacFarlane.

"Nay, not so," boomed a deep voice, causing the two fishermen to reach for their weapons as Goliath stepped out of the shadows. "I've just saved you a might of energy. Put down yer knives, or you'll lose yer heads," he added, the large claymore in his huge hand belying his humorous tone. As the two fishermen hurriedly disarmed, he sheathed his sword and offered each some rum.

Now they sailed inland down the Firth of Forth toward Glen Aucht and the cove where they were awaited.

"You'll be missing your pets, young lad," growled Goliath's deep voice.

"Nay, they'll meet me there," returned Cameron.

"But how will you get the horse aboard?"

"I'm not sailing wie them."

Goliath pondered this a moment.

"Where are you bound?"

Cameron didn't answer. She'd trust no one with her plan to ride across country to Rona to find her brother. Goliath tried a different tack.

"How will the horse and hound meet you there?" he asked.

"The raven will guide them," answered Cameron simply. The huge man roared with laughter and beat his hand upon his thigh.

"Of course, why did I not think of that? You are more like the other, each thing I learn," he chuckled, ruffling her ebony hair.

"What other?" demanded Cameron.

"We're nearly there, keep yer young eyes peeled for a warning light."

The next hour was filled with confusion as screaming children were hauled aboard the vessel. She embraced Dougal and Jemmy excitedly. She stood silently as Goliath coaxed and carried the poor imprisoned skeletal people from their foul jail into warm, clean cabins to be cared for by the simple farm folk, who clucked concernedly and forgot their own misery when they saw the less fortunate.

" 'Tis time to cast off for Inverbervie if we're to make the tide, but where is the laird with his lady wife?" worried Chakie MacFarlane. "He was to be here."

"The plan was changed," interjected Cameron quickly, taken by surprise to hear she was to be shipped off with the rest. The last dregs of remorse at her betrayal of Alex were successfully put aside as she fumed at his presumption. After a few grumbles and suspicious remarks the MacFarlanes had no alternative but to set sail or be stranded until the next tide.

"Here's fresh rowan to keep you safe," growled Dougal, tucking a sprig down her shirt.

"You're not going wie us?" exclaimed Jemmy.

"I canna, I have things to do," said Cameron gently.

"You'll not leave me," cried the child.

"Dougal will see you safe."

"Nay!"

But the red-haired child's protest was lost as Cameron dove over the side into the dark waters of the firth. She didn't see the two splashes that followed as Jemmy and then Goliath followed suit. The raven circled overhead.

Cameron swam strongly to shore without looking behind at the departing vessel for fear her own solitude would cause her to swim after. She became aware of a rhythmic splashing and, treading water, stared around, trying to pierce the darkness.

"Keep swimming. I'm counting on you to guide me," panted Goliath's deep voice. "And I'm not alone, as there is a wee-un here who forgot she canna swim." There was nothing else for Cameron to do, but swim strongly to shore.

Out of breath, Cameron, Goliath, and Jemmy lay on the stony beach. A sharp wind blew.

" 'Tis best we change clothes, or we'll be dead afore morning," volunteered the seaman. "I have a change in my saddlebag, but they'll be a might big for you two wee-uns. 'Tis either that or return to the big house before we have a dead bairn on our hands," he added, looking at Jemmy, who shivered and choked.

"Is that your plan, to take me back?" accused Cameron.

"Nay, your wish is my command," laughed Goliath, holding his hands up in mock terror.

"Aye, and I want my Maggie," chattered Jemmy.

Cameron gave a piercing whistle and was rewarded by a snort and heavy rustling as Torquod and Tor made their way down the steep cliff to the small beach.

"Seems you're horseless," sneered Cameron.

"Nay, not so," laughed Goliath. "I tied my horse to yours."

"And mine and old Duchess are in the cave wie Maggie," shivered Jemmy.

Cameron lifted down her saddlebag and withdrew her change of clothes, tossing them at Jemmy.

"All mine are on the *Edna Rae*," confessed Jemmy.

"Then there's only two things to do. Dry what we have or return for more," suggested Goliath.

"You two can do what you wish, but I travel alone," resolved Cameron, mounting her horse and prancing him up the steep bank.

"You're as strongheaded and willed, too!" chuckled Goliath, catching her foot and hauling her down.

Cameron kicked and struggled to no avail as she was easily tucked under the massive arm. She went limp, her hands reaching to her waist for her dirk.

"Same tricks, too," laughed the giant, snatching the knife from her cold fingers.

"Who are you and what do you want from me?" demanded Cameron after being set down in the dank cave. The large man did not answer as he lit a small fire.

"I'm athinking there'll be none in their right wits to be suspicious of a small smoke after your Dougal's sorcery," he chuckled. "Except maybe Sinclair and a wizen old judge, but they'll just suppose 'tis the folks waiting for passage on the *Edna Rae*."

* * *

At Glen Aucht Alex, Ian and Sir Robert Kinkaid sat alone in silence in the library. Across the hall with the door opened wide sat Beddington, eyeing them malevolently. Feeling edgy and nauseous, he'd not eaten but filled himself with brandy as he kept looking from the seamen to Sinclair. Why hadn't the tall Scot made a move? he worried. He must have known what had occurred? Alex stared across at him, noting the fat man's agitation as the apoplectic eyes shifted nervously. Suddenly Beddington lumbered to his feet, the brandy dripping off his drooping moustache.

"Ahoy, crew of the *Edna Rae*!" he screamed, a drunken plan forming in his mind to pit them against the tall, silent man, whose long, sinewy body seemed coiled to spring at his throat at any second. "Captain Loving is dead! Murdered by Sinclair!" he proclaimed. Alex uncurled his rangy body like a snake and stood. Beddington waddled as fast as his bloated body allowed, and the young Scot strode calmly toward him, not hurrying his even pace. Sir Robert watched beneath hooded lids, bemusedly thinking it was like watching a graceful golden eagle stalking a fat rat.

"Help, crew of the *Edna Rae*," squealed the colonel, his boots slipping on the highly polished floor of the great hall as he lumbered on his stubby, fat legs. His frantic eyes darted across the rolling lawn where the Beltane fire flickered and licked the dark night sky with hungry, leaping flames and an ominous low crackle. Lit by the deep orange tongues, bodies lay higgledy-piggledy like thrown dolls, white clothing in the eerie light fluttering about the still forms. Beddington's eyes popped in horror, believing them all dead. He turned and made a mad, graceless dash for the broad, sweeping staircase as Alex's calm, measured stride neared relentlessly. Scrabbling and sobbing for breath, the colonel reached the first landing and drew his sword. Turning to his silent stalker, who stood feet apart looking up at him and appearing like a statue carved from gold, he laughed uncertainly.

"I am your superior officer, Sinclair. Tell him, Sir Robert, you are encumbered to uphold the king's law. Tell him!" he shrieked at the small, shadowy figure who stood with Ian Drummond like an unearthly monk, watching the proceedings with gnarled hands held before him as though in prayer. Alex withdrew his own sword, and the two men faced each other.

"To threaten a superior officer of the king is punishable by death. Tell him, Sir Robert!" squeaked Beddington. Alex stood frozen, sword in hand, as thoughts of Cameron raced through his mind. He supposed her safe in the south attic with Jemmy, guarded by Daft-Dougal and the raven. He was being impulsive, undisciplined, and once more putting her life in danger. True he meant to kill Beddington by any means he could to avenge his attack upon Cameron, but not now. Not before she was safely away from Glen Aucht. He stood deliberating, his stolid face showing none of his inner confusion. To Beddington the silent tension was agony as the seconds seemed to stretch unbearably and his sword arm ached and shook. It wasn't even his ceremonial sword but Harris's, his own having been interred with the wretched dog. His eyes flickered this way and that, hoping for a flash of redcoat to come to his rescue, but nothing broke the interminable suspense. His frayed nerves throbbed to an excruciating extent and snapped. Giving an awful, whining howl, Beddington lunged toward the motionless figure below him. He tripped, his obese girth unbalancing him. The rushing movement broke through Alex's thoughts, and he instinctively thrust the sword before him to protect himself, impaling the colonel in much the same way the colonel had impaled the dog. He stared down in amazement, the sword still held in his hand and plunged deeply into the man, who lay facing him propped up by the stairs. Several seconds passed, the sword like an umbilical cord connecting the live and the dead man. Beddington's face stared back at him, the eyes seeming detached from their sockets, the bloated, broken-vesseled face slowly deflating until the purplish skin folded and hung like blue drapes.

Ian and Sir Robert stood motionless, shocked by the sudden violence, bewildered that death had occurred in what seemed like a blink of an eye. Alex slowly withdrew his blade from the flesh, which seemed to shrink and cling to the cold metal. He stared at the brightness of the blood that streaked the steel and then commenced methodically to wipe it clean upon the red fabric of the dead colonel's uniform. Ian gasped at the cold cruelty, confused as to his own compassion. There had been no malice nor spite in the slaying, and yet Alex's subsequent action of cleaning his blade appeared more terrible than a cold-blooded killing.

Alex Sinclair methodically polished his sword to its original unsoiled state, using the corpse much like a cleaning rag, and then sheathed the blade. When his muddled brain realized that Beddington lay dead by his hand, he was filled with rage at the rapid, unthinking disposal. He had wanted to debase, hurt, and humiliate the man. Had wanted to vent all his rage, hatred, and contempt before he killed him. Savagely, with hatred bursting in him, he had smeared and soiled the colonel with his own life's blood, his fury mounting when he acknowledged that the man was beyond awareness and had gone to his death painlessly.

Alex turned and looked at Ian and Sir Robert, waiting for their judgment. He noted the younger man's white, drawn face and the older noncommittal one. A slight movement caught his eye, and clustered by the kitchen door stood Mackie, Old-Petey, and Fergus, witnesses to the whole. No one spoke to break the heavy silence for a long time.

"We are in a pickle," breathed Mackie.

"When the redcoats wake and find him dead, all hell will break loose," remarked Ian softly.

"Thank goodness for Daft-Dougal's concoctions," growled Fergus dryly. "Well, there's no use standing around waiting to be found out. Let's haul his blubber up the stairs and put him to bed. He's inclined to stay abed late on account of his drinking. By the time they go alooking for him, we can be gone."

"There will be an investigation. He's an officer of the king, not a flesh-peddling sea captain like Loving. His body canna be hid and lies spread of his being in London," worried Ian as they carried the loathsome burden up the steep, ornate staircase.

" 'Twas at my hand, and no one else shall shoulder the blame," swore Alex.

"No one will if you leave it to me," said Sir Robert enigmatically. "Go ahead wie your plans for the *Edna Rae* and be at Fort William on May seventh. Carry your lass to safety from the would-be witch-hunters and leave the rest to me. I promise that no one other than yourself will suffer for what has occurred this Beltane night."

CHAPTER SIXTEEN

Cameron rode her horse ahead of the others as the sun sent heralding streaks above the lavender-gray horizon. Her mind wondered how to lose her persistent companions. Above flew the raven, and by her side loped the young dog. The night had dragged interminably, and to her self-disgust she had fallen asleep, lulled by the steady, crackling warmth of the small fire Goliath had kindled. The giant man had not endeared himself to her the hour before when he'd gently shaken her awake. It had sparked anger at herself, as she had planned to steal away while they slept. She headed due east toward the rising sun knowing that the Isle of Skye and the smaller Isle of Rona were situated in that direction after studying Alex's maps. She would find her twin brother and together go to their father, Charles Stuart, she promised herself, despite her unwelcome company. She stared down contemplatively at the sleek hound, knowing that she was inexplicably bound to him and he would slow her pace. Without him, she and Torquod could race, leaving Jemmy and the seaman on their slower mounts far behind.

Goliath grinned at Cameron's erect back. She'd not said one word to him since the night before, but the hostility that sparked in her wide-set emerald eyes was eloquent enough. Beside him the red-haired child chattered on and on, hiding her nervousness at embarking toward the unknown, with humorous anecdotes and remembrances that unfortunately made her more and more homesick for Mackie's warm, fragrant kitchen and loving arms.

Cameron was oblivious to the emerging spring beauty of the May morning as the sun rose higher, dappling the vibrant verdancy as it filtered through. Goliath rode, appreciating all with great snorts of delight as he breathed in the crisp freshness. Jemmy's constant flow of words had trickled to a stop and she sat her horse, her mind lulled to nothingness by the steady rhythm, her eyes pinned to a spot between her mount's ears.

It was past noon when Alex felt himself being shaken awake. He sat abruptly, certain he'd not closed his eyes for more than a second as Fergus sharply wrenched open the heavy drapes to the brilliant sunshine of the afternoon.

"They're gone," informed the old man tersely.

"All," added Mackie as she hovered near the door. "All from the cave, and Daft-Dougal, the MacFarlane lass, and her pup Maggie."

"And Cameron?" asked Alex, his heart leaping painfully in his chest.

"Aye."

"Are you sure 'tis not for her usual ride and swim?" he inquired hopefully, springing out of bed naked, so that Mackie withdrew hurriedly, even though she'd held him so as a baby.

"Could be just coincidence, the others being also gone, but I dinna think so. She didna sleep here last night, and the giant of a seaman they call Goliath has also vanished," growled Fergus, helping Alex shrug into his shirt.

"And Drummond? Has he also conveniently disappeared wie my wife?" snarled Alex suspiciously.

"Nay," responded Fergus softly, frowning at his young master's renewal of his previous jealousy. " 'Twas he who found the cave empty when Mackie couldna find Dougal. Our gley-eyed friend had the feeding of the unfortunates, we being busy wie the Beltane feast. She wanted to ask him about the condition of one of the wee lasses, who was burning wie fever, and couldna find him. Me and Master Ian rode out to find them all gone. There's many footprints in the sandy cove, pointing to them being spirited away by some vessel."

"The *Edna Rae*?"

"Master Ian rode straight on to Crail."

"Why was I not wakened before?" roared Alex, stamping his heels into his high riding boots.

"I have this minute ridden back from the cave, where I had accompanied young Drummond. There was no use awakening you on a mere suspicion," returned the old man dryly.

"Is my horse ready?" barked Alex.

"For what? Seems the only thing to do is sit tight and wait for Master Ian Drummond's news."

"You think I should sit tight while another man has the finding of my wife?" hissed Alex.

"There's your lawns littered wie moaning and groaning redcoats and pirates. There's an English colonel lying dead in the red suite of rooms. There's a host of screaming, screeching wenches from the neighboring towns, and too few hands and tongues to deal wie them all," said Fergus sharply. "Besides, if you ride out missing Drummond, you'll have lost time," he added gently.

Alex savagely opened his chamber door and strode down the long, polished corridor, his boots ringing and echoing off the walls.

"Sir Robert is up and awaiting you in the kitchen," offered Fergus, keeping up easily, with his long, lean old legs.

"For what?"

"Seems as though a messenger arrived from Edinburgh this morning."

"It seems I'm the last to know the workings of my own house," retorted Alex, descending the stairs two at a time.

"He had an arrangement wie Old-Petey and the gatekeeper so the colonel couldna intercept."

Alex swore loudly at the bedraggled, moaning people who clustered in the central hallway.

"See to their carriages and send them on their way," he ordered Fergus.

"The wenches, aye, but I dinna think you'll want to send the crew of the *Edna Rae* packing until we find out about their vessel. We'd be in an even greater schlorich wie the authorities on account of a certain missing captain and a ship," hissed Fergus, following the tall young man into the kitchen.

"Send the wenches to their homes and the redcoats to the farms and make the crew comfortable wie food and drink," spat Alex impatiently.

"Good afternoon," greeted Sir Robert, sparking Alex's inflamed temper at reference to the lateness of the hour.

"You received a messenger this morning?" he demanded, roughly turning to Sir Robert. "Would you be so kind as to accompany me to the library so that we might discuss your news in private?"

The tiny old man regarded the young man who towered above him, his eyes sharply piercing Alex, who abruptly turned away and exited, uncomfortable under the silent stare. Sir Robert watched the door swing closed behind and listened to the ringing footsteps recede before wearily rising and, with a bemused nod of his head, following.

Ensconced in the wood-paneled library, the noises of the house muffled behind the heavy oak door, Sir Robert sat silently watching the tall, broad back as Alex stared out the window trying to control his rage. His lawns were littered like a public ground after a fair. Bottles, platters, and broken tables and chairs lay strewn in every direction. Pieces of torn clothing and complete garments were tossed and hanging obscenely. Several people still lay sleeping wrapped in the damask tablecloth hand-embroidered with the Sinclair crest. He wrenched his eyes from the debasement of his land and faced the small, wizen man.

"I trust you're to share your news with me? Or do you think me too cowardly and incompetent?" he challenged harshly, fury marbling his chiseled features.

"Don't be childish, Sinclair," chided Kinkaid impatiently.

"So you equate me with Captain Harris, Sir Robert. You obviously have little respect for me. You see fit to arrange my life, inform my wife of her parentage despite my objections, use my servants without my consent to intercept your messengers," he ranted, turning away from the penetrating old eyes to survey again the still scene outside. "I canna blame you. Seems I dinna deserve respect. I canna keep order even in my own bedchamber," he added bitterly.

"You have six days before your ship sails to New England from Loch Linnhe. Here is the confirmation of your orders," said Sir Robert briskly, offering a roll of parchment. Alex took it and silently read.

"I have less than six days to find Cameron."

"I doubt you'll find her until she finds herself. Sail, and with your permission, I'll stay here at Glen Aucht—"

"I'll not sail without her! Stay here bringing wisdom and order to my much-abused lands if you want, but I'll defy these orders if she's not beside me!" roared Alex, interrupting the old man.

"Read this before you act in haste," said Sir Robert softly with pain in his eyes. Alex took the proffered paper.

"Seems the wheels of bureaucracy spin rapidly when oiled with spite and greed."

"There is no warrant or formal charges of witchcraft yet, but as my dear friend writes, within the week there will be. For Cameron's safety she must not travel as your wife. If you find her, she must be well hid until I have had a chance to undo this terrible mischief," returned the old judge.

"How? With Beddington dead and the wretched Harris out of his wits? 'Twill point to Cameron's guilt. Who's to defend her except my own household and Drummond, whose lands were taken? It will be said that they are prejudiced and that we string together lies to protect ourselves. Judge Singleton witnessed the raven alighting on Cameron's arm, and to many he'll seem an unbiased man of the law—"

"Aye, seems a sticky web, 'tis true, but not impossible to untangle. 'Tis important you not offend the crown by desertion. To do so would be to sign and seal your wife's guilt," interrupted Sir Robert Kinkaid. "You made a decision to hold your family lands at any cost, and 'tis too late now to back down without bringing disaster upon all under your protection."

"Not until I learn that Cameron is safe," promised Alex. " 'Tis but one day's hard ride to Fort William. That gies me five to find her."

Alex paced the floors waiting news from Ian, his nerves stretched to screaming. He had just determined to order his horse saddled, when a red-haired youth rode up.

"Come quick, Master Alex. 'Tis a young MacFarlane lad, son of the fishing brothers. Master Ian sent him wie news," panted Mackie.

After hearing that the *Edna Rae* had sailed the night before and that Ian had rode on to Inverbervie, Alex saddled his horse and galloped across country, hoping that Cameron had been detained on board as he had planned. The sun was setting as he pressed his sweating mount, impatiently weaving his way through the throngs of people on the narrow bridge that crossed the Firth of Tay at Dundee. He muttered furiously at himself for not keeping alert and allowing a whole day to pass without keeping tabs on his rebellious wife. He prayed that Cameron had sailed with the ship and wondered if he could curb his temper when he finally met up with her.

Galloping in the opposite direction, Cameron was brought up short by a large hand grasping her arm.

"The wee lad is exhausted and needing of rest," growled Goliath benignly.

" 'Tis your concern, not mine," retorted the ebony-haired girl, struggling to free herself from the iron grip.

" 'Tis time we talked," he responded good-humoredly, lifting her from Torquod with ease and setting her on her feet. Cameron bristled. She glared at him, her chest heaving as she fought to control her rage. "And ate," he laughed, taking out bread and cheese that he'd stowed in his saddlebags. Cameron stood watching him, determined to leap back on her horse as soon as his back was turned. Jemmy slid wearily off the back of her small rusty mare and staggered with fatigue. Cameron instinctively reached out to steady her, and the smaller girl wrapped her skinny arms around her waist.

"All my bones are like jelly," she said bravely, staring up with her blue eyes suspiciously sparkling with tears. Despite Cameron's rage she was touched by Jemmy's courage as she sniffed and dashed the wetness from her freckled cheeks. "We're like sisters now, aren't we?" she stated.

"Hush yer mouth," hissed Cameron, and the red-haired girl clapped a hand over her traitorous mouth as Goliath roared with laughter.

"*Both* of ye females. Well, I'll be!" he chuckled. "Well,

Jemmy, you had me hoodwinked. I'd swear you were a braw lad."

"You didna think Cameron was?" exclaimed Jemmy.

"Nay, I knew," he growled, his gray eyes twinkling with mischief as Cameron stared at him, her face a picture of puzzlement. "Always knew," he added cryptically.

"Always knew?" repeated Cameron.

"Aye," he responded cheerfully, holding out food.

"How?" she demanded.

"If you're intent on finding yourself on Rona, I suggest you take sustenance and not twist up your tired brain."

Cameron froze. Her eyes narrowed. How did this large brute of a man know where she was going? She had told no one. The shock of his words rendered her speechless. She silently munched, watching him as her befuddled mind tried to fathom the mysterious seaman. Who was he? What did he want from her?

"You mentioned something about talking?" she challenged after washing down the coarse bread and hard cheese with water from a nearby stream.

"Aye, you're heading too sharply west when we should be going due northwest," he answered infuriatingly.

"There's more on your mind than that," retorted Cameron as Goliath ignored her and traced a map in the mud with a pointed stick. "Here we are, about there, between Loch Katrine and Ben Lomond, and we're wanting to be here at Kyle of Lochalsh to cross to Skye, unless you're athinking of riding further north to cross straight to Rona at Loch Torridon, which I wouldna advise, it being a fair stretch of water," he informed.

"How do you know that's where I'm for?"

"Could cross at Glenelg to Skye."

"What makes you think I'm going to Skye?" she persisted.

"That's where the Bonnie Prince landed!" exclaimed Jemmy, revived by the food and drink and joining in on the strange conversation. Cameron was made acutely uncomfortable by the steel-gray eyes that locked into hers by the mention of Charles Stuart. Her heart hammered in her chest, and she tried to appear disinterested.

"Is that why you want to go there?" inquired Jemmy excitedly.

"I dinna ken what he's on about," hissed Cameron, her cheeks stained fiery red, and turned away from them both. "I'll be leaving you now," she decided, stalking to her horse, who grazed peacefully among the young shoots on the bank of the stream.

"Leaving?" cried Jemmy, staggering to her feet, her sore, cramped muscles protesting. "No! You canna leave me and Maggie, you canna."

Cameron stared at the red head that burrowed into her and made no movement to rid herself of the thin arms that embraced her. Tor sat, his mournful brown eyes looking up at her, and the desolation and sadness in their velvet depths reminded her of Torquil when he seemed to chide her. Her conscience prickled, and her own loneliness ached.

"If it were just you, Jemmy, I'd not, but 'tis him I do not trust," she said, gently disentangling herself and staring into the freckled face.

"Goliath? But he's kind and strong and saved me from drowning," she stammered, confused.

"Why?" demanded Cameron.

"Why did he save me from drowning?"

"Why did he make his business ours? Why does he follow like a hawk after a mouse? Why is he not back with his own kind from the *Edna Rae*?" challenged Cameron, hoping to put the younger girl's confusion to her own advantage.

"He's not like the others of the *Edna Rae*. I dinna think he'd peddle in flesh as they do," whispered Jemmy, her eyes wide as she wavered between the comforting bulk of the enormous man who made her feel safe and Cameron, whom she loved.

"How do you know? By his own admission he knew us as female. He aims to lead us to Skye and steal us away on another boat that deals in human suffering," pressed Cameron.

"He didna ken I was a lass," returned Jemmy lamely.

"Said to butter you up for the skillet, no doubt. Ask

him why he is here. See if you can get more assurance from his evasive answers than I can. He skirts around each question, never giving satisfaction."

Jemmy looked from the rebellious Cameron to the huge man, who lay seeming to enjoy the exchange.

"Why are you here?" she asked, her voice trembling.

"To protect you," he answered laconically.

"See?" smiled Jemmy, turning back to Cameron.

"Ask him on whose authority," and, when Jemmy frowned, added, "Who sent him?"

"Surely his own. No one asked you to help me—It came from yourself, your own goodness. Maybe 'tis the same for him," offered Jemmy earnestly.

"I doubt that."

"How did he know where I was going, then?" battled Cameron, betraying herself impulsively by the frustrating conversation.

"Then you are going to Skye!" exclaimed Jemmy, and Goliath threw himself back on the soft, springy grass roaring out his merriment at the dismay mirrored across Cameron's face. "How long will it take us to get there?" asked the excited girl, insensitive to Cameron's throbbing fury and throwing herself beside the prone man, whose broad chest rumbled with his laughter. Goliath sat up, wiping his streaming eyes, and ruffled Jemmy's red hair.

"Forever wie all this time wasting chattering," he growled, noting Cameron's proud, warlike stance and trying to swallow his mirth. "Och, yer so much like another in yer faults as well as yer virtues. A bit of humor about oneself is in order, Cameron."

"What other?" demanded Cameron, her anger breaking. "What other? 'Tis many times you've made remarks of another," she yelled, but Goliath turned away and busily repacked the remains of the meal in his saddlebag. "You'll avoid again! See it, Jemmy, he'll nay answer my question. I dinna trust him!" she yelled impotently, further riled by his calm, unharried movements. "You're none but a flesh-peddling bastard trading on others' misfortunes."

Goliath turned, his face stern and harsh. "I'll not trust a petulant, willful young miss with any things of import," he stated softly, his gray eyes hard and disciplinary. "Now, mount up. There's a few good miles to be traversed before we rest for the night."

Cameron made no move to obey. She smarted from the censure. She watched Goliath toss Jemmy into her saddle and then swing his own large body lithely into his.

"Let her temper cool. She'll be along," growled the seaman as he noted the frightened blue eyes. "Her stubborn pride will keep her rooted to the same spot for a while, and I bet you a crown she'll reach Rona afore us."

"Skye," corrected Jemmy.

Cameron watched them go, seeing Jemmy straining her head and looking back at her beseechingly. Her limbs shook with fury, but she refused to move a muscle until they had been swallowed up by the trees. Then she sat burying her face in Tor's glossy black coat, her mind whirling with confusion.

Later a cawing overhead penetrated her dozing state, and she looked about at the darkness that surrounded her. She had fallen asleep pillowed on her young dog. She whistled, and nearby she heard the answering whinny of her horse. She was alone, exactly what she had desired, she reasoned. She needed no one except the animals who chose to be with her. She stood and stretched and, after plunging her face to awareness in the icy stream, mounted her horse, and they picked their way carefully through the dark forest.

Alex reached Inverbervie when all the lights in the small fishing village had been doused for the night. His horse's hooves clattered noisily through the narrow cobbled streets toward the harbor. The moon rippled its reflection with the waves that gently swelled and caused the many small crafts to creak and strain against their moorings. His eyes tried to pierce the dim light in his effort to spot the *Edna Rae*. Several larger vessels seemed to be anchored beyond the cluster in the cluttered harbor, of which he got brief, frustrating glimpses as elusive shapes loomed out of the sea mist that rolled off the surface of the water.

"Alex?" hailed a voice.

"Ian, where is she?" he asked, recognizing the low tone.

"Didna sail wie them. I fell asleep waiting for you," returned Ian, his boots crunching in the wet sand.

"Didna sail wie them?" ejaculated Alex, seizing his friend's shoulders as they loomed out of the darkness.

"Seems she dove overboard and was followed by that giant of a crewman from the *Edna Rae* and the wee, red-haired MacFarlane lass."

"Where? When?"

"Before they sailed from the cove."

"Where are the MacFarlane brothers?" snarled Alex, shaking Ian, wanting to pound his frustration out on someone. "Why did they not obey my orders?"

"Cameron said she brought a message from you, and they believed her. I'd prefer you strike me than shake me like a rat as you're doing now," returned Ian. Alex looked at his hands, which bit into the other man's shoulders, and relaxed his hold.

"She could be back at Glen Aucht, maybe never have left," he said hopefully, but even as the words were said, his tone belied his belief in them. "Where are the Mac-Farlanes?"

"They've dropped the people up and down the coast and are now sinking the *Edna Rae* out there in the mist somewhere," informed Ian. "What'll you do now?" he asked after a long silence as Alex stared over the dark water that merged with the night sky.

Alex didn't answer but trudged along the beach. He wished he were alone so that he could roar out his anguish across the silent North Sea, but instead he locked his emotions away beneath a steely exterior.

"Return to Glen Aucht. There's nought to do here," he intoned as he swung himself into the saddle and headed his horse south. Ian followed suit, and the two young men, silently rode a numb, steady rhythm.

Mackie and Fergus exchanged worried glances as Alex strode through the central hall, his face set in stern, uncompromising lines. He had returned from Inverbervie in the small hours and, refusing food or rest, had paced the remainder of the night away as his mind wrestled with the task of finding Cameron. Fergus stayed awake hearing the restless, echoing beat of the rhythmic strides, wondering how to melt his young master's frozen features, and put hope and warmth back into his heart. He ached as he recognized the cold expression, knowing Alex's propensity to cover pain with harshness. Even if he were to find Cameron, his steeled eyes would be cold, offering no tenderness and love but probably driving her further and further away with icy, autocratic discipline.

After several hours' sleep Mackie arose and scurried downstairs and looked tenderly at her husband's haggard face.

"Get to bed, my love. I'm here to watch, and I heard Sir Robert stirring," she said softly. Alex's sharp footsteps neared, and the door was swung open.

"See to the packing of my trunks and the sending of them to the vessel at Fort William," he ordered harshly.

"Master Alex, I'll do as you say, but you need some sleep," suggested Mackie.

"Mrs. MacDonald, I'm grown out of hippens and can tend to my own bodily needs. I dinna need a nursemaid anymore," he stated coldly and evenly.

"Daft-Dougal's old gray nag, Duchess, returned to the stable last night," informed Fergus hurriedly, seeing the battle light spark in his wife's eyes. "Dougal canna live wie out his gray mare, so I'm reckoning we'll be seeing him shortly."

"It better be very shortly as I'm riding out within the hour," returned Alex.

"To where?" asked Mackie, forgetting her anger at his snub.

"To Rona?" answered Fergus quickly, at last able to suggest his idea without sparking Alex's stubborn pride. The tall, golden Scot turned his hard amber eyes to the old man, his steady, penetrating gaze not mirroring his surprise as he stood in awe at his own stupidity. Of course, Rona. His mind had been locked like a rusty vise, unable to have the freedom really to reason. Fergus noted with dismay the tightening of the lean, stolid face as Alex swung curtly on his heel.

"All night 't'as teased my mind, but the young master gave no opening wie his rage. I know the lass has headed to Rona to find her brother," growled the old man to his wife when they were alone.

"Go wie him," begged Mackie.

"Nay, he's right, he's grown. Best pack some food for him."

"But the cruel mood he's in, he'll just drive her away," fretted the old housekeeper.

"Then that's the way of it," he responded wearily. "I'll see to the packing of his trunks, you see to the feeding of his belly and leave the feeding of his heart and soul to himself."

"Whose heart and soul?" asked Ian entering, his usually cheerful face drawn.

"The master's to Rona to find the lass before sailing to the savage New World," explained Mackie, wiping her eyes on her apron.

"Why Rona?"

Fergus exited to the main staircase as Alex strode abruptly through the kitchen carrying his saddlebags.

" 'Tis none of your concern, Drummond. This time you leave the finding of my wife to me."

Ian reeled back as the icy words were thrown at him. He frowned, recognizing the murderous black mood of his lifetime friend.

"I've food for your travels, Sir Alex," spat Mackie with censure. "You aim to sail away to the New World wie out returning here?" Alex didn't answer but stood glaring at Ian, who glowered back.

"Leaving your home and those about you, maybe forever, and yet no word of warmth or love do you bestow on those who care," she ranted angrily, cutting bread, meat, and cheese. Alex's amber eyes turned, and he surveyed the round, small woman who had always been there for him, from the first moment he drew breath. He felt a terrible aching well inside of him. Mackie looked up and recognized the hollow agony. Tears burst and coursed down her round, rosy cheeks, and she flung herself at his hard, lithe body, and Alex encircled her with his strong, golden arms.

"Make your peace wie them who love you," she sobbed, and Alex stared across her neatly bunned hair to Ian, who stood tall and silently crying without shame. He steeled himself as aching desolation swept through him, blinding his vision.

"Help keep Glen Aucht safe, my friend," he growled huskily, "and forgive me for leaving such a mess in your brotherly hands."

"What mess?" returned Ian mischievously through his tears. "A wee schlorich, 'tis all. One dead English colonel, who'll be stinking to high heaven if you dinna get yourself to Rona to find that raven-haired hellion you've wed. You're the one in the mess, my dearest friend, married to that free, wild kelpie."

The two young men embraced and searched each other's face long and hard, knowing they might never meet again.

BOOK TWO
THE JOURNEY

May 1762

In every cry of every man
In every infant's cry of fear
In every voice, in every ban
The mind-forged manacles I hear

WILLIAM BLAKE, *London*

CHAPTER SEVENTEEN

Goliath and Jemmy rested comfortably in a small tavern in Portree on the Isle of Skye. Warm and well fed, the huge man relaxed contentedly, but Jemmy paced, worrying about Cameron.

"Hush yourself, you're like a little midge," growled Goliath.

"But what if we never see her again?"

"We will. 'Tis as certain as the sunrise and sunset. We'll be meeting up wie her on Rona if not before," laughed the jovial giant.

"But what if she's been and gone?" fretted Jemmy.

"Cameron wouldna ride the busy roads as we did but keep to nature. She's the mirror of another and would also travel under darkness of night wie that great black bird and beastie to guide her," he comforted. "Now to sleep wie you. I'd like to start wie the sun and be on Rona afore her."

"Won't she be surprised to see us?" giggled Jemmy, snuggling down in the small cot beside Goliath's larger bed, which was still too short, so that his feet and calves dangled over the end.

"Aye and not too pleased, I reckon," rumbled the immense man with amusement, but Jemmy had already succumbed to the exhaustion of the past two grueling days.

As Goliath and Jemmy lay sleeping in warm, comfortable beds on Skye, Cameron sat her horse, looking toward the island across the narrow strait. She had circled Glenelg and ridden up and down the coast trying to ascertain the best way to cross over and now debated swimming with her horse. It could not be more than a half mile, she decided as she rode Torquod carefully down the steep escarpment. At sea level the distance seemed much greater, but not allowing herself to dwell on it, she purposefully led him into the cold water. The moon sailed high in the clear sky, and Omen seemed to position himself dramatically so that he was silhouetted against the bright orb.

Cameron despaired of ever reaching dry land as the icy water weighed her limbs. She forced herself to kick her legs and held tightly to Torquod's rein, unable to see anything as the salt stung her eyes and rasped her numb face. Unable to feel anything, her entire body numbed, she attempted to roll onto her back so that she'd float, pulled along by her tiring horse. Her body wouldn't answer the commands of her brain, and she closed her eyes, beyond caring whether she lived or died. A hoarse cawing overhead pierced her frozen apathy, and she kicked her heavy feet, touching shifting sand. She tried to stand, but her legs buckled, feeling like jelly, and she went limp, allowing her horse to stagger up the beach pulling her from the water. Tor lay beside her licking her face, and her horse shuddered, stomping his hooves impatiently, eager to gallop and warm his frozen muscles. Cameron pulled herself on to his high back, her own muscles screaming with agony, and, bending low so that she grasped his sleek neck, urged him into a brisk canter.

"We're on Skye, where the Bonnie Prince . . . where my father landed," she whispered through bloodless lips. "And we must to Rona where my brother waits," she added to herself.

As the first rays of sun tinged the sky, Cameron dismounted wearily at an abandoned croft where Omen roosted, cawing loudly. She led her horse inside and lowered her cold, aching body onto a mound of fetid hay and stared up through the broken roof at the emerging dawn. Beside her, Tor curled up in sleep, and Torquod noisily chomped on the makeshift bedding. Though completely drained, Cameron's mind was a whirl of excitement. According to the maps she'd furtively studied, the Isle of Rona lay off the coast less than ten miles away. Her thoughts wandered to Glen Aucht, and she tried to block out the image of Alex, but his tall, golden body seemed etched on her mind. She rolled onto her side and embraced her sleek hound, breathing the fragrance of his salty coat as loneliness and fear insidiously crept in. Doubts assailed her. What if her brother was not on Rona? What if he were dead? She pushed the terrible dread from her, her tired brain illogically reasoning that by thinking him so, she could possibly make it happen. She dozed and, forgetting where she was, reached out for warmth and comfort, yearning to curl herself in the curve of Alex's strong, protecting body.

She woke with a start as the prickly emptiness penetrated, and she sat staring around at the filthy croft. The sour smell of rotting hay offended her nostrils, and she leaped to her feet, scratching and itching. The sun beat down through the broken rafters, and she knew she'd had but a few hours of sleep. Tor stretched reluctantly, his reproachful eyes eloquently pleading for more rest. Cameron stared across the treeless moorland from the open door of the croft. It reminded her of the rolling heather of her childhood home on Cape Wrath, and she hoped it prophesied that her brother was near.

Her excitement soared, and she led her horse out into the brisk, bright springtime, determined to get to Rona as soon as possible and end the terrible suspense. Tor panted and her horse blew through parched lips, but Cameron ignored her own thirst and, not seeing a sign of fresh water, pushed on along the coast. Three islands met her eyes, and panic surged as she wondered which of the three was Rona. She tried to remember the map she thought she had imprinted on her memory as she rode blind to the majestic, breathtaking scenery. Gulls swooped and wailed in the reflected shimmer of the sea, causing Cameron to squint her eyes.

Wishing to clear her foggy head and stop the irritating itching of what she supposed were insects from the croft's hay, she stripped off her clothes and plunged into the sea. The icy shock reminded her of the long, tortuous swim of the previous night, and she quickly and briskly rubbed her young body and exited, running up the sand to the horse and dog, who stood patiently waiting. A warning caw froze her goose-bumped body, and she quickly dove toward the protective shelter of a clump of bushes, the only vegetation of any substance on the barren coastline. Unfortunately it was a clump of gorse, the bright yellow flowers nestled in the lush green, camouflaging the sharp spines. She muffled a scream as her flesh was torn and stared in dismay at her large black stallion, who stood proudly and obtrusively, the sunlight glinting off his shining coat. Hurriedly she pulled on the tight breeches, unmindful of the insects that still hid there as the murmur of voices neared above her on the crest of the coast.

Goliath saw the ebony stallion and successfully pointed to another direction, hoping to avert Jemmy and the old crofter's eyes as they trundled by in the rickety old cart. They had left their horses and Maggie on the mainland in care of a tavern keeper in Glenelg, as the small fishing vessel in which they had crossed to the island had little room and a ferocious dog.

Cameron, her heart racing beneath her bared breasts, released her breath as the rumbling voices and wheels faded into the distance. She quickly donned her shirt and jerkin and stopped, listening as a familiar deep, mocking laugh was borne back on the breeze. Straining her ears and hearing nothing more but the jeering cries of the gulls, she decided it was her imagination.

She rode the shore, hoping for sight of a person to ask directions of, but there was no sign of another living soul. Rona was the northernmost of the islands off Skye, she told herself, as her horse plodded through the cobwebs of the thinning sea as it receded, leaving patterns in the fine sand. At early evening she sat dejectedly, staring across the dark, misty strait, loath to enter the icy water. Storm clouds gathered, and the sky was angry shades of purple and gray that melded with the heather-tinged, illusive island, so that she was unsure whether it existed or not. Should she rest and wait out the impending turbulence or should she cross? She debated, her blood tingling in the deadly calm as all nature seemed to wait for the first roll of thunder. So deep and ominously low reverberated the gathering rumble that it seemed to come from Cameron's very bones. It shook off her dejection, and as the lightning rent the sky illuminating the Isle of Rona, she stood and, leading her agitated horse, walked into the sea. The raven circled, cawing excitedly, seeming to herald the bobbing black heads that swam steadily despite the raging storm that howled, whipping the waves to a foamy frenzy.

Cameron was thrown onto the rocky shore with such violence that she welcomed the darkness that obliterated her pain. She opened her eyes, feeling her body cramped and shivering, and saw nothing. She lay marshalling her thoughts, trying to remember. A low whine and a warm tongue caused her to roll onto her back and survey the dark sky. The storm had passed, leaving a light drizzle and the distant echoes of the violence shuddered the air. Where was she? Had she managed to swim to Rona or had the strong current thrown her back onto the Skye shore? she worried. She sat and whistled for Torquod and was rewarded by a gentle butting as the horse lowered his great head. Her eyes strained through the darkness, and she wished the clouds would part and uncover the moon. A biting wind blew through her wet clothes, and she stood leaning against her stallion's warm flank. How long had she been unconscious, she wondered, her teeth chattering painfully. There was no point staying there without shelter from the inhospitable elements, she decided, hauling herself with difficulty upon Torquod's high back. A cawing came from the thick darkness, and the stallion moved steadily toward it, followed by the tired young hound. Cameron leaned forward, hugging Torquod's strong neck to avoid the biting chill wind that seemed to whistle clear through her as the raven led the way.

It had been three days since Cameron had left Glen Aucht, and she was weak from hunger, thirst, and exposure. She entwined her hands in Torquod's long mane and slept, rocked by his sure, steady gait as he wended his way through the intense blackness.

Goliath and Jemmy spent the night on Rona in a croft, where a witchlike old crone expressed joy and elation at seeing the immense man. The red-haired girl watched, her blue eyes round with surprise in her freckled face at the strange reunion.

"Goliath MacLeod! Goliath MacLeod!" she cackled,

leaping around on spry old legs and reminding the girl of Daft-Dougal. "Thought you'd been dead these last two, or is it three years, resting your great whale bones wie Davy Jones." She stopped, it seemed, in the midst of her wild Highland fling, cocked her head to one side, and fixed Jemmy with a piercing stare. "Who's this rusty-haired runt?" she asked sharply, pointing a bony finger, and the small child backed away with fear.

" 'Tis wee Jemmy, and you'll not be scaring her wie your witchifying, Great-aunty Jennet," laughed Goliath.

"Great-aunty Jennet," mocked the old crone with one hand on a thrust-out bony hip. "Dinna remind me of my age . . . 'tis plain Jennet or just Aunty, you saucy lad. 'Tis safe to talk in front of . . . 'tis a lass, you say?"

"Aye, 'tis a lass who needs food and a warm bed and, I'm thinking, a bath, but that can wait, so dinna scare her, me dawtie, but feed us both. 'Tis a drear night," chided the large man as the wind howled and shook the small croft.

"Me dawtie, is it now? Och, you've not changed for all your world traveling. Always trying to charm a woman wie his treacle tongue. Dawtie, I'll be damned," she returned, banging pots and pans around.

"Me da called me dawtie daughter," murmured Jemmy, her tired eyes filling with tears, which succeeded in melting the old crone's cutting tongue.

"To each mon his daughter is his darling and can soften een the hardest of them," she cackled, softly brushing the red hair back from the freckled young brow. "What's your name, bairn?"

"Ailsa MacFarlane, but I'm now called Jemmy."

"And where's thy da?"

"Dead."

"And thy ma?"

"Dead birthing a brother."

With Jemmy sleeping full and warm in the loft, Old Jennet and Goliath sat at the well-scrubbed table. He pushed his large girth back and belched contentedly.

"Where's our lad?" whispered the crone after noting that the child slept soundly.

"In the New World, across the ocean."

"Safe?"

"As safe as a wild one can ever be. Angus is wie him," responded Goliath wryly.

"And how is my Wee-Angus?"

"Wee-Angus is fine and still larger than me," he laughed.

" 'Tis like prying winkles. Tell me all. I thought you took the lad to France?'

"Aye," responded Goliath, his face frowning and his usually merry eyes glinting like steel.

"And? Dinna tease me so. Did he find his sire?" hissed Jennet impatiently.

"Aye, but royal blood does not recognize a bastard son, especially if he's busy playing at court," muttered the large man, standing suddenly and nearly cracking his head on a rafter.

"You'll nay be saying such words about the Bonnie Prince!" exclaimed the old crone. "He's a fine man and he'll be back."

"Aye, anything you say Great-aunty Jennet," responded her large great-nephew wearily. "But that is not why I've come. I've come for the other."

The crone froze, her wrinkled face becoming ashen in the dim light.

" 'Tis never to be mentioned, or you'll have Duncan Fraser's wrath upon your head. 'Twas signed in blood the promise," she hissed.

"He's dead near a year and a wee book sent. Our lad sent me back to Cape Wrath, where I found the other had been spirited south to an estate on the Firth of Forth. At Durness I ran across a certain Captain Loving, who also was asking suspicious questions, and so I signed on his boat the *Edna Rae* hoping to glean what information I could."

"Whoa, laddie, yer setting my puir old brain atangle. What wee book? What suspicious questions? What is this Captain Loving and the *Edna Rae*? Och, was that evil-eyed witch, Mara, there?" babbled Jennet, not able to make head or tail. "Start at the beginning. You and our lad set sail for France and found the Bonnie Prince?"

"Aye, and from there set off for New France wie a covey of priests, arriving amidst the bloody Indian war agin the English. Our lad summed up the two sides and, having nay love for the English and loving the free, natural ways of the red men, joined Pontiac on the Maumee River near Fort Detroit," explained Goliath, pacing with his head bent low to avoid the sharp rafters.

"Joined who?"

"Pontiac is a fierce Indian chieftain, a native of the New World. He took a liking to our lad's prowess wie knife and horse, sort of adopting him into the tribe. A tribe is like our clans. They were somewhat afeared of Wee-Angus and myself, us being head and shoulders above them and three times as wide," recounted the large man.

"What wee book?"

"Seems as though on the death of Duncan or perhaps before, when the old warrior knew he was coming to the end, he sent a wee book to the lad. 'Twas a miracle it arrived and even more of a miracle that it was deciphered. 'Twas those priests on that interminable ocean voyage with their Latin, I suppose. Our lad was bored, and you remember how like dry wool he was for soaking up knowledge? Well, he learned the strange tongue and was able to read what was writ."

"A wee book in Latin?"

"Aye, writ by Dolores MacLeod, our kin, to her children."

"Go on," urged the crone.

"I did not see it, but it seems it told feelings and the like and what the lad already knew. His father's name. Well, it stirred memories of another, and on his bidding I immediately signed on a ship and set sail for Scotland. The castle at Cape Wrath was silent and gray. Only the black crows nested and one lone raven, who followed and roosted on the spar of the *Edna Rae,* scaring the cowardly flesh-peddling crew.

"Flesh peddlers?"

"Aye, in the employ of Loving and a certain Colonel Beddington, bound for Glen Aucht, where I learned the other had been taken as ward to a Sir Alexander Sinclair."

"I remember that bonny mon, friend of Sir Duncan, a

lean, golden god of a lad," remembered Jennet, smiling lasciviously.

"Nay, that 'twas the former. He and his bonny wife and daughters died more'n ten years past. 'Tis the son who has the other in his keeping. Wed her he has, but things seem strange and unloving betwixt them, so I'll bring her to her brother as he bid me. If I found her safe and happy, I was to return wie just such news, but if I found her in danger and chafing, I maun bring her to him."

"Then where is the other?"

"Patience, the raven will bring her. She comes to find him. She'll smother you with the pain of the past when you see her riding her stallion, Torquod," smiled Goliath, tenderness aching his nose.

"She comes to find him? But he's not here. You have led the bairn on a wild-goose chase?" queried the old woman.

"She's as like him as himself, she'll not be told. So I thought it best to gie her free rein to find for herself," laughed the large man good-naturedly, ceasing his pacing and sitting heavily, so that the chair creaked in protest from his weight.

"When?"

"Passed her on Skye well past noon."

Jemmy kept her eyes tightly closed and her breathing even, as her heart hammered at all she was hearing. Her thoughts were a whirl of confusion. Who was this "other" they repeatedly referred to? Whose father was the Bonnie Prince? Obviously Cameron was one of them they spoke of, but why did Goliath make mention of the pain of the past? Unable to sort out the maze of information, Jemmy drifted off to sleep, and the voices receded to a low, meaningless rumble.

Alex also took the main roads east-west toward the Isle of Skye, reasoning that speed was more important than discovery. His black rage beat with his horse's hooves as he cursed the day he'd ever laid eyes on Cameron. His fury closed his memory to the wonderful golden times they had shared, and he dwelt on all the pain and turmoil that had entered his life with her appearance. He was determined to close his heart, vowing never to be so weakened and shackled by a woman again. Then why was he racing at this breakneck pace to find her? questioned a traitorous part of his brain.

"Duty!" he roared in answer to the pacing trees.

Duty, duty, duty, beat out the rhythm of gallop as an even more illogical answer came to mind. He'd promised the dying Sir Duncan Fraser that he'd protect Cameron, and he, Alexander Sinclair, was a man of honor. He'd fetch the raven-haired witch and carry her with him to the New World by hook or by crook, but never again would he weaken, allowing her to rule his heart or head. He'd resist her charms and play just the role of guardian, not husband. But she's your wife, his traitorous mind niggled, and at the thought an ache surged through his loins, and he steeled himself against the image of his exquisite elfin bride.

"Aye, she's my wife, but in name only. She'll have her uses keeping me so bound, so I'll not succumb to another female web, and I'll be doing the rest of my sex a favor by binding her so that no other can be so entangled by her!" he vowed aloud, oblivious to the curious stares of fellow travelers, who eyed the tall, golden man on his sweating, foaming mount.

Alex cursed as he neared Glenelg and the violent thunderstorm broke. He sat his horse, staring toward Skye, not heeding the flashing lightning and lashing rain. For a moment he forgot his cold, murderous rage as his mind pictured Cameron atop Torquod, battling the elements. He had first seen her so on the barren moor at Cape Wrath the night Duncan Fraser died. He had stood mesmerized by the small, valiant figure in kilt with plaid streaming as she raced with the wind, defying the deafening thunder and challenging the sky-rending spears of light. He angrily blocked out the memory and forced his mind to assess the boiling sea logically. Deciding that no boats would be leaving or going to Skye in such a storm and that anyone who chose to swim would not survive, he made his way to the nearest inn.

As he wearily approached the warm, welcoming lights, he heard a frantic barking. Not waiting for an ostler, he headed straight for the stables behind the main building.

Dismounting, he led his weary horse inside the dry fragrant housing. Maggie, tied by a length of thick twine, strained toward him, pawing the air and wagging her long, heavy tail in welcome. Alex looked around for Tor and recognized two horses from his stable at Glen Aucht. The small rusty sholtie the young MacFarlane lass used and a large-boned gelding, which, he ascertained, could carry the seaman Goliath's tremendous weight easily. There was no sign of Cameron's ebony friends. Reasoning that he needed rest and sustenance to keep his wits about him, Alex decided to spend the night at the inn.

Later, Alex lay in a hot bath soaking out the rain's chill and the ache of the grueling ride. He had learned from the innkeeper that the giant and the small red-haired child had no other companions except the animals now boarded in his stable. They had crossed to Skye the previous day and not returned. Alex's body relaxed in the heat, and yet his mind was still tense as he debated what to do. He could stay in the relative comfort of the inn, waiting, and yet it was obvious Cameron was not part of their party. Had she gone on to Cape Wrath? he wondered. If so, for what? There was nothing left for her there but Duncan's solitary cairn and an empty-eyed ruin of a castle. Should he cross to Skye as soon as the weather calmed? But if he did so, he'd chance missing her. Outside, the storm beat to a frenzy, rattling the windows of his room and dashing the waves against the rocky coastline. His heavy eyelids drooped with fatigue, releasing his pounding brain, and he dozed in the rapidly cooling water as he pictured Cameron with her black hair streaming and melding with the night, racing out her rage across the barren moorland of Rona.

Cameron awakened in her uncomfortable position stretched forward over her stallion's neck as his steady plodding ceased and he stood motionless, staring up at the raven, who roosted upon a small, stunted tree. The clouds had parted, and now the moon illuminated a small dory pulled high on the shore away from the sea's reach. Cameron stretched her cramped body and blearily looked around. She stiffly slid from Torquod's high back and clambered into the small boat, pulling the heavy fishing nets over her for warmth. Tor agilely leaped in beside her and curled against his young mistress, and they slept.

The new day dawned watery and dismal, the sun shrouded with impenetrable gray clouds that dipped their darker undersides drearily down, seeming nearly to touch the disconsolate, monotonous expanse of sea. A crunch of footsteps and murmur of voices caused Cameron to sit up and stare around her with confusion. Omen cawed loudly, and Torquod pranced toward her, tossing his shining black head and whinnying a warning. The young hound growled and, leaping from the shelter of the small dinghy, advanced on the two old fishermen who approached. With his front legs splayed before him and his hind quarters raised, Tor snarled and bared his teeth as Cameron hauled herself onto her horse's high back. Her head throbbed and her eyes burned and watered, causing their greenness to be even more pronounced. The old men gaped, their homemade pipes falling from their slack lips as they watched the small ebony-haired figure on the enormous black horse, which reared and pawed the air before galloping away, followed by an equally black hound and an enormous raven. Silently the two old men crossed themselves, their wrinkled weather-beaten faces ashen.

" 'Tis the changeling . . . spat agin from the sea at midnight," trembled one.

"Aye, and never growed since last we saw."

"And above, the shadow of the bird of evil and darkness."

Cameron thought her head would split from the pounding of Torquod's hooves over the heathered land. She slowed his pace and tried to think what to do. Why had she run from the two old men? she wondered. She should have asked them for her brother's whereabouts. What did the fishermen's incredulous expressions mean? Was it fear of her dog, she puzzled, realizing that their old eyes had been fixed on her. It was as though they had seen a ghost, she thought, as a cold dread came over her. A ghost was of one dead. She dug her heels into her stallion's firm sides at the anguished thought, sending him once more into a head-splitting gallop.

* * *

"There!" breathed Goliath at the open door of the croft. Jennet scurried to his side and stared across the gray and purple vista at the streaking black horse. The old crone twisted her hands in her homespun skirts and drew them to her sunken, dried breasts, exposing bare feet and sinewy old legs as her rheumy eyes were transfixed.

"'Tis Cameron!" yelled Jemmy excitedly, thrusting her small body between the two who blocked the door. "Cameron? Cameron?" she squealed, running across the moor, waving her arms toward the dark trio. Jemmy's high, childish voice pierced the deafening thunder that filled Cameron's ears, and she reined suddenly, causing her horse to rear. Goliath and Jennet watched the magnificent animal silhouetted against the gray sky and gasped as the lithe figure atop fell backward and limply toppled to the ground. There was a shocked pause, and then Goliath and Jennet ran toward the prone figure.

Alex could not contain his impatience and, at first gray light, crossed over to Skye. Refreshed, he and his horse cantered across the moorland toward Rona. Crossing to the small isle, he was immediately aware of great consternation, as it seemed all the inhabitants of the tiny spot of isolated land were gathered in front of the church. He walked among them, frowning, as mothers held children suffocatingly close to their breasts and men shook fists and talked angrily among themselves. A small, round priest trembled, his hands clenching a large cross.

"The son of the De'il has returned and no bigger than before."

"We should have burned him and the witch Jennet long years ago."

"The great beastie that runs by his side has turned to pure black, 'tis said, and a giant black bird flies above."

"Then 'tis time we rid ourselves once and for all," roared a voice.

"Peace, peace," trembled the small priest. "He hasna hurt no one."

"Aye, not yet, but think on the good harvest of the sea we've had these past three years wie out his evil presence."

"Aye, and the weather has been kind, and yet last night many boats were broken and dashed to the bottom of the sea. 'Tis a sign. This time we maun burn the young warlock," and the pronouncement was greeted with a roar of approval.

"Aye, driving him out willna suffice. 'T'as been proven that he'll just return as he first came. Spit from the sea at midnight astride the giant black fairy horse wie the monstrous hound of Satan aside."

Alex's eyes narrowed and he watched the priest's efforts to calm the crowd, and when the small man picked up his surplice and scurried in the church, he followed.

"Where is the lad?" he asked roughly.

The priest, kneeling at the altar rail, looked up in surprise. "I'm looking for guidance. They are peaceful, God-fearing folk and are suspicious of what they dinna ken. The boy is good, for I taught him all I know, but he rejected the Christian way, saying it made no sense to him. From age eight to ten I spent much time wie him away from the good folks' eyes, but then the boy withdrew from me . . . became solitary and brooding. He'd swim wie the seals and play wie the wild animals, striking fear in the hearts of them who saw. He'd run naked over the heather, shocking many a lass and good mistress, and ride wie the storms that shook our small island. When he vanished near three years ago, it was as if a calm descended, a tension ebbed. So you canna blame the good people of Rona for wanting their bit of peace," chattered the frantic man of God.

"Nay," returned Alex dryly, thinking that Cameron's brother was of as turbulent a nature as she herself, able to turn everything around him into total confusion.

"But burnings and bloodshed I canna condone."

"Where's the lad?" repeated Alex.

"At old Jennet MacLeod's croft."

On the priest's tame gelding Alex quietly slipped away from the crowded church and, following the directions given, made his way to Jennet's croft, his mind pondering the coincidence of the name MacLeod. Cameron's mother had been a MacLeod, but ignored and not acknowledged by her grandfather the laird, as his oldest son's marriage to a Spaniard had offended and, in his prejudiced eyes, tainted a long bloodline. The truth had been that he had arranged marriage for his oldest son to the daughter of a neighbor, expecting to increase his lands. Alex shrugged. There were many MacLeods and the isles of Skye, Raasay, Scalpay, and Rona all part of the clan's holdings. The priest himself and most of the agitated villagers probably all bore the selfsame name.

Alex dismounted at the croft, the gray stone walls seeming to rise naturally from the rocky, heathered land. The roof was straw, silvered and weathered with time, and atop the spine, beside the smoking chimney, sat the raven. The man and the bird seemed to lock eyes for a second, before Alex roughly opened the wooden door without knocking.

Jennet and Jemmy gasped with dismay, Jemmy from the anger that tightened Alex's face, and Jennet always wary and distrusting of strangers, especially those who pushed their way into her crude abode. Alex noted cynically that she earned her name of Witch Jennet. Goliath did not let his surprise mark his features. His gray eyes met Alex's unflinchingly as the two men took stock of each other. Though Alex stood six feet in height, Goliath was half a head taller and twice as wide. Alex's broad shoulders tapered to slim hips and long, lean legs, whereas Goliath's kept the same vast circumference clear down to his enormous feet.

"Where is she?" asked Alex sharply, breaking the silence. When no answer came from the three, he turned and raked the small room with his eyes. The young black hound sat staring toward a small loft, and Alex, following his gaze, saw a small brown hand hanging limply.

"Dinna wake her, she's in a fever," protested Jemmy as he rested one booted foot on the rung of the ladder. "Jennet has gie her herbs to break the sickness."

" 'Tis better I wake her than the witch-hunters, who plan to burn her," snarled Alex.

"They'll not come before sunset, because of their superstitions," growled Goliath, "so there's time for talk."

Alex stood with his back to them, his foot still resting on the ladder debating what to do. Obviously the large seaman was no stranger to these parts, as there seemed to be a fellowship between him and the old woman. He turned.

"Get us some whiskey, Aunty Jennet?" asked Goliath softly, keeping his steely eyes fixed to the glinting amber ones. "Jemmy, take up more cooling rags to the loft and keep your young mistress comfortable," he added, lowering his weight onto a chair at the table and indicating that Alex should join him. Reluctantly Alex sat, uncomfortable standing with his head bent to avoid the low-hanging ceiling.

"What are you to my wife?" inquired Alex after draining the small tumbler of fiery liquid that the old crone dashed onto the table disdainfully before him.

"What are you to your wife?" returned Goliath. Alex didn't answer but returned the long, searching look. The man's questions dug deeply. Although enigmatic, it seemed directed to a place deep inside of him, and he was at a loss for words.

"We can sit and spar, fencing backward and forward until sunset," he responded slowly, "neither of us giving the other satisfaction. I am here to protect her from the many who would harm her, and from herself."

To his surprise the large man chuckled. "Aye, especially from herself," he laughed, refilling Alex's glass. "What are your plans for her?" he added, his tone changing sharply.

"I have orders to report to Fort Detroit. That is in the New World, far from the reaching hands of those who would harm her," responded Alex stiffly, even more uncomfortable stating his private business to the mysterious stranger.

"I'm aware of the location of Fort Detroit," grinned Goliath, overcome with mirth and tipping the frail-looking chair back so that it creaked and groaned in protest, threatening to collapse into splinters. Alex stared with narrowed eyes at the quaking enormous man who tried to control himself but gave up, shaking his head as tears of hilarity streamed down his face and great guffaws of laughter spurted from his mouth. Alex sat silently, a tic beating in his lean, tanned face, waiting for Goliath to curb his merriment.

"Of all the places in the wide, wide world . . . Fort Detroit!" wheezed Goliath, pounding an enormous hand on his tree trunk of a thigh and gasping for breath. Still keeping his eyes pinned to the subsiding tremors as the seaman righted his chair, Alex took a deep swallow of the spirits. When the last spurt of deep laughter had finally calmed, Alex broke the silence.

"I have answered your questions, obviously to your great enjoyment, and expect some answers in return."

"I'm not at liberty to divulge anything, but to say I have your wife's happiness and safety on my mind," returned the giant.

"Why?"

"You must just trust those words, for there is no more I can tell you. I know not how much you know, and I would cut out my own tongue sooner than betray the secrets locked within me."

.Alex stared long and hard into the gray eyes. It was a vicious circle. If this man knew Cameron's parentage, then which of them could utter first? If he didn't and was angling after such answers, then Alex himself would be putting Cameron in greater jeopardy.

Much the same thoughts were passing through Goliath's mind. Here was an arrogant young redcoat on his way to Fort Detroit to fight for the English, while he, Goliath, served Cameron's brother, who fought with Pontiac on the other side. No, he'd not divulge anything to this proud, tall man, even though he instinctively liked and admired the golden-eyed Scot.

"I'll help you get the lass aboard the vessel to the New World with conditions," stated Goliath suddenly. "That you sign me and the red-haired child on as part of your company."

"Why?"

"Jemmy-Lad seems to have no one left who cares whether she lives or dies in this sad land, and I'd not even leave a dog to starve for food or affection," growled the man, deliberately misunderstanding.

"Why would you want to be part of my company when you obviously don't trust me?"

"We seem to have an investment in the same raven-haired lass."

"Aye, but my investment's obvious, as she's my wife, and of no concern to any other man . . . except maybe her brother," said Alex evenly, his hawk eyes not leaving the other man's face. He noted with satisfaction the whitening around Goliath's nostrils and detected the sharp intake of Jennet's breath. Alex leaned nonchalantly back in his chair, feeling somehow that he now held the upper hand. After a frozen moment, during which he stared around languidly at the still tableau noting Jemmy's small face peering down at him from the loft and Jennet's corded old hands clenched together, he resumed.

"So Duncan kept the male twin hid here?" and, at no answer from the tensed people, went on. "But the lad left, it seems, near three years ago at what I'd guess to be the age of twelve or thirteen, and now the folks of Rona believe he has returned from the sea, exactly the size he was before. Unfortunately a storm heralded my wife's arrival, and they superstitiously attribute the turbulence of nature to her and wish her dead so that this time there will be no return."

"Then she was seen and thought to be the other," hissed the old crone.

"Aye, Méron," returned Alex calmly, remembering the name the old soldier Cathcart had put to the green-eyed, black-haired young savage. Goliath sat bolt upright.

"You know the name!" he ejaculated.

" 'Tain't his name!" screeched Jennet.

"Aye, 'tis now, Aunty," said Goliath softly. "Cameron MacLeod is nay more."

" 'Twas never MacLeod, and well you know it," hissed the old woman.

"It was Stuart," intoned Alex, taking the bull by the horns and deciding to trust the mountain of a man who stared at him intently.

"Nair say it aloud," whispered the hag.

"Camerona Sinclair lies ill up there. When does your vessel sail, Sir Alex?" asked Goliath.

"The earliest tide on the seventh," replied Alex tersely, his mind back with Fraser. So the Highland outlaw had named the twins for two isles of the same name, Rona and North Rona, Cameron and Camerona, and hidden one upon each tiny, isolated scrap of land guarded by the sea.

" 'Tis late on the fifth," remarked Goliath, with a worried frown creasing his burly face. "If we leave in the morning, we'll gie the lass chance to mend. 'Tis but a short day's ride to Fort William on Linnhe."

"You're forgetting the witch-hunters," remarked Alex. "It seems it will be more than a fever burning her if we wait."

"Aye," pondered the other man, his mind wrestling with the problem.

"They'll nay set foot near enow to fling their burning roods. I'll weave my spells and frighten them wie my incantations until they piddle their breeks and soil themselves," threatened Jennet, opening the door and peering out over the dusky moor. "Here they come, the sniveling bunch of them."

Goliath, Jennet, and Alex watched the bobbing lights approach through the drizzling gloom.

"Better start weaving, Aunty."

Torquod pawed the ground and screamed out in an unearthly cry that echoed, shivering the spines of all who heard. The approaching line of people stopped still in their tracks, their lighted crosses wavering in trembling hands, as the raven cawed as though summoning help. From the sea-lashed gray rocks came an answering chorus as gray seals lifted their shining, glistening heads and a flock of gulls circled and uttered their mournful, lonely laments. Jennet cackled and leaped around with glee at the awesome sight. The gulls swooped and dived at the cringing people, as their cries joined those of the seals, crescendoing until eardrums and nerves frayed at the persistent, horrific sound. Burning crosses were dropped as the people fled back to their own houses.

Goliath's hearty laugh echoed with the shrillness of the gulls as the last burning rood spluttered out in the wet heather. The scrambling shapes disappeared into the gloom, and silence reigned but for the sound of the waves. Jennet's wild leaping ceased abruptly, and she stood holding her skirts, a comical picture of stunned disbelief.

"Och, you've more power than you thought, Aunty Jennet," gurgled her great-nephew.

"Aye," agreed the old crone, hastily gulping down a full glassful of whiskey.

"There'll not be a living soul daring to put a toe across this threshold tonight, so maybe 'tis best we steal away under the cover of night," remarked Goliath, also helping himself to a liberal amount of spirits.

"You've just returned, and you're awa' agin," complained the crone. "Canna you leave that great black bird? 'Twill create more respect for me in these parts," she asked hopefully.

"You'll hae all the respect you need 'til the end of your days after tonight," laughed Goliath gently. "The bird watches over his lass, whose hair is the color of himself," he added, watching the tall, golden-haired man lithely climb to the loft.

Alex stared down at his wife's sleeping face, and for a moment forgot his firm resolve, as his stern expression gentled. He felt a clutching at his heart as he recognized her bruised vulnerability, and he reached to pull her into his arms. Jemmy cowed in the corner watching and she saw his expression of loving tenderness change once more as he tightened the sinews in his softly reaching arms until his fists clenched and he presented a hard, forbidding exterior, remembering his vow not to weaken.

"I trust she came clad," he uttered harshly, noting the bare breast that gently swelled with her breathing and the long, bloody scratches that raked her flesh.

"Aye, washed and drying by the hearth," responded Jennet.

"Well, at least she learned one bit of discretion," he replied sarcastically, and was surprised at Goliath's burst of amusement.

After a supper of mutton pie they left the croft. The enormous man made his way agilely through the darkness, seeming to have the eyesight of an owl as he helped himself to boat and wagon. Alex rode Torquod beside the trundling farm cart, wondering what he was doing trusting the man named Goliath.

The dawn was breaking, and the gulls wheeled noisily

over their heads as Alex and Torquod swam strongly beside the dory that the large man rowed toward Glenelg on the mainland.

At the inn, where Maggie greeted her black brother and red-haired young mistress with excited yelps and frantic wiggles, the two men decided to spend the night. Their faces were gray with cold and weariness as they bid each other a terse good night, even though it was morning, before disappearing into their adjacent rooms, each with a hound and a small, bedraggled urchin.

CHAPTER EIGHTEEN

Alex leaned back on the large bed listening to Goliath's sonorous snores, which rhythmically shuddered the thin connecting wall. He stared dispassionately at Cameron, who tossed and turned on the small cot across the room, where he had placed her out of temptation's way, and noted the young black hound's concern for his young mistress's distress as small whimpers burst from her dry lips. He turned away from the sight, blocking his ears, determined to sleep and not soften his harsh resolve. The events of the last hour flashed through his mind as he'd firmly laid her sleeping body upon the small bed. Her clothes had been damp, and not willing to be responsible for a worsening of her illness, he had coldly and efficiently stripped her, hardening his heart to the desirable lithe body that still bore the marks of Beddington's brutality. Long, angry scratches now striped the mottled bruises, and finding his hands softly tracing the lines, he'd covered her abruptly and now lay on his larger bed, alone. He turned back and watched her restlessness.

Fiona's jeering painted face haunted Cameron's nightmare. She tossed this way and that as the mocking, grating laughter filled her ears and taloned hands pried her eyelids open to watch the voluptuous, sensuous woman fondle Alex's strong, golden body.

"No," she moaned, pulling away from the steel hands that grasped her head. "No, I dinna want to see," she cried.

"Open your eyes. 'Tis but a dream."

"No, I dinna want to see!" she repeated frantically, trying to loose the firm grip from her head. She screamed with alarm as she was forced to sit up.

Cameron opened her eyes and stared straight into Alex's golden ones. With a small whimper of relief she burrowed her hot face into his strong, bare chest and, wiggling, curled herself like a small animal into the safety of his warmth. Alex stared down at the glossy dark head nestled into him, his arms instinctively wrapped around her, and wavered. Taking a deep breath, he grasped her slight shoulders and wrenched her from him. Murmuring soft, sleepy protests, Cameron groped toward the warmth and blindly flailed the space between them until she opened puzzled eyes. The rigid, angry set of his face woke her like a splash of icy water. She stared around at her surroundings in bewilderment, unable to bear the hostility and rejection mirrored in those hard eyes. She struggled against the iron grip that still held her away from him.

"Lie still," he ordered tersely, forcing her back against the pillows, where he held her pinned as he unemotionally sponged her body as though she were a china ornament in need of cleaning, before flinging the wet flannel into a basin of water and getting into his own bed. Cameron listened to his breathing as she forced her mind to awareness. Snatches of the previous day filtered into her memory. An old crone with the giant seaman, a rumbling, creaking cart. She sat up carefully and, leaning on one elbow, reached down to stroke Tor. She had been ill from all the sea swimming and lack of dry clothes, she reasoned, but where was she now? She had to find her brother.

Quietly, she swung her legs over the side of the bed and tiptoed to the window. Parting the heavy drape, she peered out into bright sunlight and down into the busy courtyard. She gasped, recognizing the inn at Glenelg that she'd furtively skirted before crossing to Skye. She was back on the mainland. Alex watched the naked girl through half-closed lids as she turned, white-faced, to stare at him with undisguised hatred. He opened his eyes fully and lay on his back, pillowing his head on his forearms. Cameron wrenched back the curtains, allowing the light to flood the room. She stood motionless, her small fists clenched, her small uptilted breasts heaving as the rage consumed her. With a cry of fury she launched herself onto his seemingly relaxed, long body, intent on biting, scratching and kicking. Alex grabbed her, but not before a small, sharp fist had struck him squarely on a high cheekbone. Silently he pinned her arms with one of his and stilled her wildly kicking legs with his hard thigh. Cameron couldn't move as he ineffectively tried to muffle her loud curses and screams with his free hand. He stared down coldly at the flashing green eyes, ignoring the persistent knocking at the door. Finally Goliath burst in and surveyed the scene. His eyebrows lifted whimsically at the tangle of nakedness upon the bed, then lifted even higher at the trickle of blood and large, swelling bruise that decorated Alex's face.

"She's healed, I'd say," he remarked.

Alex shifted his gaze to Goliath, and Cameron, feeling a lessening of the pressure on her mouth, bit down hard. Alex swore at the sharp pain and clamped his hand down harder, but Cameron did not remove her teeth. Releasing his other hand, he quickly turned her, smacking her sharply across her bared buttocks. Cameron scrambled across the bed, her eyes flashing this way and that as she sought a weapon. Goliath leaned his great weight against the door, blocking her escape, as Alex, not heeding his aching hand, climbed into his breeches feeling somewhat at a disadvantage.

Cameron looked from one to the other, feeling trapped. Her young dog whined his concern but seemed at a loss as to what to do, as his instinct told him neither man meant harm to his young mistress.

"Since we're all awake and there's sure to be someone curious at the ruckus, I suggest we make our way," suggested Goliath genially. "But seems as you've your hands full," he added conversationally to Alex, indicating Cameron, who stood proudly in all her naked glory, an immovable expression of rebellion on her face.

Alex's fury pounded at the seaman's open stare at his wife's naked body.

"Can you manage?" quipped the older man, sparking even more fury, before nonchalantly whistling and exiting through the adjoining door.

"Get your clothes on," barked Alex, and at no obedience, the lines of his lean face tightened even more as he advanced toward her. Cameron had noted his knife tucked into the waistband of his breeches, and as he neared, she reached out, only to have her small fingers squeezed in a painful grip.

"I'll mark you, Cameron, if you resort to your old

tricks! Now get dressed, or I'll parade you naked to Fort William, and that I promise!" he roared, flinging her toward the hearth, where her clothes hung drying. Cameron dressed silently as Alex sat on his bed staring at her. He pulled on his riding boots and buttoned his shirt. "Now if you've a mind to listen, I'll inform you of some things, but if you persist in behaving like a reckless brat, I'll spare myself," he stated coldly, as she stood fully dressed with her stiff, proud back turned toward him. Cameron made no motion that she'd heard. "Then hear from another," he added, knocking on the connecting wall. Jemmy and Maggie burst into the room, followed by Goliath, who closed the door discreetly behind him. The young red-haired child stopped her headlong rush toward Cameron as the older girl's hostile stance deterred her. Even Maggie shied at the tension, looking from one to the other before sitting beside her brother.

"Ask your questions, Cameron," demanded Alex of the raven-haired girl, who had her eyes pinned to the rolling sea through the window. Beyond the haze she saw the shadow of Skye and remembered the long, cold swim. It had all been for nothing, she wept inwardly as her eyes filled with tears. Why couldn't they leave her alone to find her brother? she screamed inside.

"Your brother left Rona more'n two years ago, lass," said Goliath softly, as though reading her thoughts. Cameron turned suddenly to face him, tears pouring down her face. Alex felt compassion and a draining of his anger for his bruised cheek and bitten hand as he realized once again that her violence stemmed from real fear and a fighting for her own survival. He reined his emotions, remembering that her willfulness threatened her own survival.

"Where is he?" asked Cameron, her voice breaking.

"In the New World, where we'll all soon be if you don't lead us on any more goose chases," returned the large man.

Cameron rode numbly beside Jemmy, unaware of the rumble of deep voices behind her as the two men conferred. Once again she had blocked all emotion. The young red-haired girl beside her seemed either to respect or to be cowed by the silence and stilled her usual excited chatter. The two hounds, each the color of their young mistress's hair, loped gracefully beside the black and red horses.

"Then the warrant has not been issued?" asked Goliath rhetorically after listening intently to all Alex imparted.

"Sir Robert Kinkaid has friends in high places and will suppress the foul document until the ship sails, but even so he has warned me not to travel wie Cameron as my wife."

"Well, to see her now, no one will suspect she could be any man's wife," chuckled the giant, watching the girl's straight back. "But I canna see her as a valet neither. A cabin boy or drummer, aye, but not even a young male ward wie her distinct coloring. That's been my bain wie the other. There's ways to change hair but not the unnatural vivid green of their eyes."

"Are they that much alike?"

"Aye, and more, but I'm thinking you may have the harder chore. The other is a proud young stallion and will never be broken, but yours is a mare, and how does one gentle her wie out breaking her spirit?"

Alex didn't answer, not willing to face his interest in such a proposition. He'd tried many ways, the last of which had been to open his heart. Nay, he'll not try that way again. He turned his mind to more practical problems.

"Whatever I decide to pass her off as, she stays wie me," he uttered.

"Aye, and those looking for ebony hair and emerald eyes will find her like the moth to a candle," responded Goliath after a weighty pause. "Take the red-haired lass as ward or whatever and let me sign on the vessel wie Cameron. They'll not seek her belowdecks wie us common sailors. As an officer you'll have berth for your horses and hounds. She can watch over them wie the animals that gie her comfort as no man or woman can."

Alex looked into the gray eyes sharply. It was like the meeting of gold and silver, sun and moon. "Give her comfort that no man or woman can?" he intoned, himself knowing the truth of the words and yet remembering the small, burrowing Cameron who had curled for comfort against his belly many nights before.

"Aye, they are as alike as peas in a pod," returned the

gruff voice, stilling his tongue before he compulsively informed Alex of Méron's affinity with the natives and the natural solitude of the wilderness of the New World. Nay, he'd not divulge his young master's sympathies to this soldier of the king, no matter how much he liked Alexander Sinclair.

Goliath's suggestion rankled Alex. He heard the sensibleness of it, and yet to have Cameron under another man's protection burned him. He didn't allow himself to think it was jealousy but felt that his honor was slighted.

"There's no time for jealousy or possessiveness when one's very life is at stake," growled Goliath, instinctively reading Alex's mind and challenging his very resolve.

"Your plan seems sound," Alex intoned after a pause as he reasoned that a ship in the midst of an ocean gave Cameron no chance of escape and that the temptation of her seductive body in the close quarters of a cabin could very well shatter all his intentions. "However, she'll be no common sailor among a crude crew, where, if her sex were discovered, she'd surely be used. You and she will be part of my staff to take care of my stable. You shall be my valet, and Cameron shall at all times be guarded by you."

"Nay, 'twill be the same. There should be no connection to bring curious eyes or suspicion. In this you maun trust me, Sinclair. I took an oath thirteen years ago when I first beheld the wee bairns. Old Duncan held one in each arm as I sailed the boat out to North Rona and swore I'd lay down my life for either of the puir motherless wee-uns. My brother, Angus, also, and he still stays like a shadow next to the other."

Alex rode silently, digesting the information. "And what assurance do I have that you'll not spirit her off, leaving me to sail alone wie the red-haired brat?" he asked hoarsely.

"My word. Cameron will sail on the same vessel to the New World wie you, and by my enormous girth and persuasive manner I shall see to it, and in no way shall I be connected with your entourage."

Alex probed the large man's eyes silently before nodding his assent. He had no recourse but to trust the enormous stranger.

* * *

Cameron stood rebelliously as Goliath hacked through her long ebony tresses, and yet made no move to pull away from the knife. Alex leaned against a tree watching, his stolid countenance mirroring none of the pain he felt as the glossy hair fell limply to the ground to mix with the red curls of Jemmy.

"There. You're done," growled Goliath, cramming a black, broadbrimmed hat over Cameron's shorn hair that, released from the weight, now sprung into a confused halo of curls around her face. "Here we will rest, giving you time to report to the ship. We'll be along shortly to battle our way through the docks to the front of the line of them waiting for employment. Go. You have my word that we'll ride the same vessel o'er the waves," he promised, extending his huge hand to Alex, who, after a searching gaze into the steel-gray eyes, grasped it firmly.

Cameron watched the tall, russet-haired man and the small urchin beside mount up. She refused to feel anything but the rage that filled her.

"Take the black hound as well," roared Goliath, and pain shot through Cameron as she saw Torquod and Tor tied and being led behind. The enormous man easily stopped her headlong rush to free her animals. She fought him, but he held her as though she were a tiny child, ignoring her swearing and kicking as he watched the two riders pass out of sight. Still he held her until he judged the distance too far for her to follow.

"Hush yourself and find your pride," he chided, setting her on her feet and pinning her with one enormous hand to the broad trunk of a tree. Cameron stared venomously up at him, her mouth in so firm a line that her lips were bloodless. He looked kindly into her small, bruised face, seeing her brother.

"Och, you are a pair of trouble wie yer uncurbed tempers," he chuckled softly, but her ears were deaf to his tantalizing words as her angry, pounding blood roared. "Look above you," he added, cupping her chin and forcing her face upward. Omen, the raven, perched motionless like a sentinel against the clear blue sky. Goliath took his hands from her, and she remained leaning against the tree, her head upturned.

Cameron felt as solitary and desolate as the great black bird seemed to her eyes. Aching, hollow sorrow took the place of the pulsating fury, and she breathed deeply, calming herself as though taking strength from the tree that supported her. Goliath watched the changes cross the young, uptilted face and saw the angry pulse still in the hollow of her neck. The sun glinted on the brimming green eyes, and he turned away, somehow knowing how like her brother she really was in hiding any sign of sadness and despising it as weakness. He whistled tunelessly allowing her privacy as he pretended to be rearranging his saddlebag.

"Time we were on our way," he said softly, turning to see her still leaning, looking up through the branches of the tall tree. He watched her a few moments. "Have you ever thought what you'd like to be if you had a chance after death to visit this troubled earth again?"

"A bird," she answered without moving, her eyes glued to the topmost leaves that bent back and fro with a gentle breeze. "To soar straight up from the heather, singing my lungs out like the lark. To be able to vanish above the clouds and be carried with the wind like the hawk. To fly alone where no man can reach."

"The hawk flies in twos, and the lark soars to defend the nest or mate," informed Goliath gently. "There's none that fly always alone."

"He does, my Omen," challenged Cameron, standing straight and looking at him.

"Aye, so does the albatross, another omen," agreed the man gruffly.

Goliath walked briskly and was amazed that Cameron walked beside him, not lagging or skipping to keep up. He strode with the saddlebag straddled across his shoulders, choking in the dust that was stirred by their fellow travelers on the busy thoroughfare to Fort William. At Glenfinnan they caught a ride from a jovial farmer, who enjoyed a ribald conversation with the jolly giant. Cameron sat silently, the broad brim of her hat covering her face.

"So you and your boy are looking to work passage to the New World at Fort William, are ye?"

Cameron debated exposing her companion as a kidnapper. It would be easy, she thought. All she would have to do was cry "liar" and unbutton her shirt and exhibit her breasts. But if the strange giant really knew her brother and could take her to him, then she would have lost the opportunity. But what if it were not true but just a ruse to get her aboard the vessel with Alex? She stared straight ahead and kept her mouth shut as she spied the comforting shape of the raven, languidly flapping his wings.

"Your best bet would be to go straight to Ballachulish. 'Tis there that they are loading the vessel and hiring, as I've been told," informed the farmer. "I can take you near there, as I'm bound for just south of Ben Nevis."

"Are you sure?"

"Aye, the troops assemble at Fort William, but the strait is too narrow. The large boats are moored at Ballachulish or Oban, down Loch Linnhe at the Firth of Lorn. I know, for I sold flour to the redcoats two days ago. Has to be the one at Ballachulish. 'Tis the only one seaworthy enow to be sailed on the morn's tide," chatted the rotund man.

"What is she called?"

"I dinna ken. One boat's like another, just like my cows, and my lazy slummocks of daughters. Thirteen of them have I and not one fine son. Och, was ever a man so cursed?"

The painfully slow cart trundled and labored, with the fat farmer not giving peace until Cameron thought she would scream.

"Aye, see, what did I tell you? Can you see a vessel braw enow to sail the ocean wide?" pronounced the irritating man, waving a hand toward the harbor at Fort William, where only small fishing smacks and dories were moored. "Wouldna get me floating on the water. If the good Lord meant us to swim, he'd have given us scales, webfeet, and whatnot."

Goliath and Cameron silently endured the monotonous, grueling, bumping ride along the east bank of Loch Linnhe.

"There's my farm turn now, and there through the evening mist you'll be catching a glimpse of the vessel you're looking for," he chuckled, pointing a pudgy finger. "But you're welcome to the hospitality of my home. A widower are you wie a child to care for? Well, there's thirteen strapping maidens around my table, and you're welcome to any of them, wie the blessing of the kirk of course," he offered expansively.

Goliath declined politely and lengthened his stride to catch up with Cameron, who had already walked ahead toward the distant shape that loomed through the mist, unable to bear another second in the company of the farmer.

The dockside was a screaming hurly-burly, and Cameron stared around with eyes wide at the wasted, ragged people who pushed and scrambled, their few belongings tied in pitifully small bundles. A group of cackling, painted women were herded by seamen, who pushed and prodded them like cattle up the bouncing gangplank. The women answered the filthy jeers and epithets in kind as they kept their heads high and swayed their hips lewdly, pathetically clinging to whatever dignity they had.

"Food for the hungry redcoats' appetites," growled Goliath, following Cameron's eyes. "Those who will survive will be sold in New England on the auction block. 'Tis the same as the cargo on the *Edna Rae.*"

"I killed Captain Loving," stated Cameron baldly, hoping to shock, but the large man just shrugged.

"I believe it. He didna deserve to live."

"There's many here before us. We'll never get on the vessel," she observed, staring down the long line of wretched people. Goliath chuckled and shouldered his way methodically to the front of the line, keeping a firm hold on the back of Cameron's jerkin.

" 'Tis unfair," she whispered, embarrassed and ashamed of such behavior as the thin, hungry people turned to complain and then, at seeing Goliath's great size, backed away without a sound.

"Use the eyes you were born wie and not a pious brain," challenged the large man. "Go on, look, and tell me, of all you see, which of the unfortunates would survive two days? They can barely lift their small bundles, let alone the crates and sacks to be loaded. Now hush yer mouth and stay close," he cautioned as three armed men strode down the small gangplank surveying the line of people in the gathering gloom. Goliath, already head and shoulders above the others, stood on his toes and puffed out his already massive chest.

A frightened whinny and a horse's panic-stricken scream tore through the low rumble of voices. Torquod, held by two ropes, a man on each side, shied at the thin wooden bounding strip that joined the busy wharf to the grim-looking vessel. Unable to contain herself, Cameron twisted from Goliath's grip and fleetly wended her way through the mass of people. The great black stallion reared, and the hubbub was hushed as they gazed as one at the seeming small boy who stood beneath the raised iron hooves. Goliath swore softly beneath his breath and pushed his way through the gawking mass.

Quietly Cameron gentled the frantic horse, stroking and soothing until he stood nuzzling her. She wrenched the two restraining ropes from the limp hands of the two astounded handlers and rode the proud horse aboard ship. Immediately the noise resumed, even louder than before.

" 'Tis my son, sir, has a knack wie animals, and I'm a farrier," pronounced Goliath to the three armed men, who still gazed in awe, their job of hiring extra crew forgotten.

"Take on the lad and this hulk of a man too," barked one of them. "What are your names?"

"Abraham and Isaac," responded Goliath. "The lad's Isaac."

"No other name?"

"MacLeod, sir."

"More of these pious Catholic Highlanders. Any women?"

"Lord, no, sir," chuckled Goliath.

"That's a blessing. Take this wie you," stated one of the seamen crisply, handing him a slip of paper and indicating that the enormous man should climb on board.

Cameron rode Torquod across the broad, busy deck of the boat, following the other horses to a large, gaping hole in the wooden flooring. She stared with terror into the dark bowels of the ship where the stables were, hearing the terrified cries of the frightened animals. Torquod's nostrils flared and his eyes bulged, white-ringed, as he pranced backward. A young mare was suspended with a sling under her belly. She kicked frantically as three men lowered her into the dark hold by a creaking pulley. Her thin, flailing forelock snapped with a sickening crack against one side of the hatch, and her screams were abruptly halted by the sharp report of a pistol.

"That's the third," shrugged the man through the acrid fumes of the gun. Cameron sat fighting the nausea that welled as a loud splash committed the young mare to her watery grave over the side of the vessel.

"Lead him over, lad," growled the voice in her ear, and she stared wide-eyed into the face of the man who had now tucked his gun into his broad waistband. Cameron, on Torquod's sweating back, crooned to him as she urged him toward the sling. She shook her head mutinously when asked to dismount.

"Well, 'tis your miserable young life," laughed a burly man leaning against the iron wheel of the pulley. Goliath pushed his way to the front of the hushed crowd that stared up at the giant black stallion suspended in the air with his frail rider. Oblivious to the awed audience, Cameron leaned over the great horse's neck crooning in his ear as the sling swung them achingly slowly into the dark, smelly depths. A loud cheer was raised as the sling was hauled back empty.

"Come back up, lad," ordered the man with the gun, who was overseeing the loading of the animals. "Lower the sling for him, mates. What's his name?"

"Isaac," boomed Goliath as he stared down into the darkness. "He's my son. Come up, boy, and do as you're told." Cameron stared up into Goliath's whiskered face, her hands still resting on Torquod's flank. She reluctantly let her horse be led off to be stabled and grabbed the swinging sling above her head.

"Haul the lad up," barked the loader. "He'll ride them all down, and maybe we'll save a few."

Goliath fervently prayed that Cameron was as adept at communicating with all animals, like her brother, when a large war horse foamed at the mouth, flickering his eyes in terror at the gaping hole. The small, lithe figure fear-lessly approached the enormous frenzied animal, uttering soft, strange words of comfort. He shuddered violently as she agilely leaped upon his broad back, his girth so wide her legs could not encompass it. She stretched out upon his length, hugging his muscled neck, as the men gingerly approached and fitted the sling beneath his sweat-soaked, trembling belly.

Alex stood upon the bridge with some fellow officers watching the tiny figure upon the broad back of the horse.

"If anything were to happen to my Galahad, part of myself would die," came a gruff voice beside him.

The old general and Alex watched, holding their breath as the enormous animal was lifted into the air. The wide sling hid most of Cameron from view, but two small hands could be seen caressing and gentling the sinew-strained neck. Foam flew from the extended nostrils, and the panicky eyeballs danced, but the animal kept his great body still as the creaking wheel lowered his tremendous girth belowdecks. An enormous wave of relief was heard as held breaths were expelled and Alex turned to the tall old man beside him.

"Who is the lad?" bellowed the general.

Goliath looked toward the cluster of uniformed officers. His blood ran cold as he recognized General Ramsbotham. The Old Turkey Buzzard survived Méron's arrows, he thought, but he relaxed himself, gentled his expression to one of a simple man, and strode toward them, hat held respectfully in hand.

" 'Tis my son, Isaac," he stated humbly, his gray eyes sparkling mischievously at Alex, who stared dumbfounded as he realized the identity of the small figure gentling the frenzied animals.

"And you must be Esau?" mocked a dandified young English officer.

"Call me as you see fit, although my name is Abraham," answered Goliath.

"Sacrificing your son as in the Old Testament?" remarked the old soldier dryly.

"The Lord saw fit to spare him, if you remember?" returned the large man, and the old white-haired warrior laughed.

"Well, Abraham, you and your Isaac will have charge of the horses of those under my command. But if harm comes to them, I'll not be as merciful in sparing either of you."

Goliath bowed his head respectfully and backed away. Again surrounded by the crowd on deck, he gave his great strength to the wheel of the pulley as Cameron soothed and rode each frightened horse into the deep, dark pit.

Alex's hawklike features tightened and, after tersely asking permission to leave, made his way to the cabin he was to share with Jemmy and the two dogs. He strode in, ignoring the pale, freckled face, and sat at a desk, the flickering lantern light reflecting on the chiseled, harsh planes of his face. Jemmy sat on a bunk clutching her hound and staring at the stern seated man as the deafening noises of the loading ship filled her ears and the vessel rocked, straining against the chains that held it.

Throughout the night the noise continued, the pace increasing despite the fatigue, as the tide rose and the excitement of casting off across the wide ocean toward the New World surged with the incoming water.

Cameron's bones ached with fatigue as she watered and fed the now calm horses stabled in the dark hold. The air was close and suffocating, and she yearned to be above deck in the fresh sea breeze under the dark night sky. Goliath noted the weary slump of her shoulders and took the heavy buckets from her.

"Rest yourself awhile. You'll not want to miss the casting to. It'll stir the salt in your blood as it does mine. 'Tis like flying to ride the waves."

Cameron stared up through the square hole above to the stars that twinkled like diamonds against the velvet-black night sky.

"Wait 'til the animals are settled and we'll go up . . . but you maun not alone, you ken?" he stated firmly, seeing the flash of rebellion in her mutinous eyes. Cameron nodded silently as the heavy tramping of feet shook the deck overhead, and took up currycomb and brush to groom the matted hides of the horses. She worked methodically beside three youths and one old man, who shied away from Torquod and the battle-scarred war horse.

" 'Tis best you tend them two great devils," croaked the bandy-legged old man, who whistled tunelessly, a straw between his sunken, lined lips. " 'Tis a jockey you should be, my lad, wie your light weight and horse sense. Be you bound?"

Cameron kept brushing the caked mud and sweat, not realizing that the old man addressed her, until a sharp, bony elbow jabbed her aching back. She turned, her body tensed against attack. Goliath, noting her warlike stance, strode forward putting his great girth between the two.

"Nay, neither my son nor I are bound. We are free men working our way across," he rumbled.

"What's wie his tongue that he canna answer for his-self?" wheezed the old man, the straw bobbing up and down in his mouth as the three strapping youths stopped work and circled curiously. The last thing Goliath wanted was antagonism, as the six of them had to share close quarters and jobs throughout the long voyage. Neither did he want close friendship, but preferred a respectful cordial distance.

"He's a might homesick already. 'Tis his first voyage," he improvised.

"A little mamma's boy, have we?" jeered a youth. "Well, we'll have to toughen him up."

"Aye," agreed another. "But we'll have to wait until he's stopped hiding behind his pappy."

All the rage that had culminated and been suppressed surged up, and Cameron lithely sidled from behind Goliath, ducking under the belly of the nearest horse. She faced the two bullying boys with her dirk in hand, silently daring them to lunge at her. The old groom chuckled, his laughter wheezing through his toothless mouth, which still held the ever-present straw. Goliath was powerless to reach her, as the horse separated them.

"Cam—" He stopped himself from revealing her name. "Damn it!" He roared, hoping the sounds were similar enough. "Isaac, put your knife away!"

"What's amiss here?" barked an authoritarian voice, and

the two louts stared at the autocratic old general, who surveyed the tense scene. His old eyes beneath shaggy white brows took in the smallest of the youths, agilely crouched ready to spring, the knife glinting in his hand.

"Two big, strapping bullies harassing one small hero, I see."

"We're not armed," protested one boy with a nasally whine. The old soldier ignored the cowering youths and limped stiffly toward Cameron, who still stood frozen, ready to attack.

"Drop the dirk, Isaac," repeated Goliath, trapped between the broad flanks of two large horses and not wanting the frightened girl to attack, nor for the white-haired campaigner to see her features too closely. Cameron watched the steady approach of the tall old man.

"Obey your father, lad!" he ordered.

Cameron stared at the grizzled face that neared, and something in the old man's eyes stopped the wild pounding of her heart. She straightened and tucked her knife back in its sheath and stood unflinchingly as a weather-beaten, large hand grasped her small, pointed chin in a firm but warm grip. The lined face stared into hers, and an audible, sharp intake of breath quivered the white moustache as the bright emerald green of her eyes glowed, even in the dim light. The blood froze in Goliath's veins knowing that this old campaigner, having spent long spells of duty in the New World, was aware of the green-eyed young savage who rode with Pontiac against the English.

"Seems you've had more than your share of bullies, young lad," remarked the old man evenly, dropping her face and turning to Goliath. "Who marked the boy so?" he asked in a quelling voice, referring to Cameron's blackened eyes.

"He canna speak, sir, so therefore canna tell me," improvised Goliath hurriedly, hoping Cameron was listening.

"He spoke to my steed, Galahad, for I was told."

"Aye, but it were meaningless mumbo jumbo. He canna speak as to be understood by people. Just strange sounds and noises. 'Tis maybe why he can be at ease with natural animals," explained Goliath.

"I've heard of such," cackled the old groom.

The old general stared silently and intently at Goliath, his eyes not mirroring what he thought, but an air of speculation raised one shaggy eyebrow before he turned and strode to the scarred war horse, whose coat gleamed with Cameron's attention. He silently examined the noble old animal for signs of harm and then turned to the proud, small figure, nodding his appreciation.

"If there's one new mark upon that lad, all the rest of you will be clapped in irons, and that also goes for you, his father," he stated imperiously. They watched him stiffly stride to the door. "I want that lad safe and healthy with me at Fort William," he added cryptically before leaving.

Goliath remained motionless, the old soldier's parting words sending icy shivers of fear through his guts and curling his bowels. The man had noted Cameron's features and, having come face to face with Méron in combat, possibly realized they must be kin.

A loud shouting and a shuddering signaled that the time of departure had arrived. Orders were sharply barked and echoed above, and the tortured rasping of the anchor chain reverberated as it was labored up from the muddy depths. Goliath picked up Cameron and hoisted her onto his shoulders, determined to flee the ship despite his promise to Alex, for his oath to protect Cameron's life came first. The girl stood lithely on his broad shoulders, reaching for the edge of the open hatch. She agilely pulled herself up upon the deck, breathing the crisp near-morning air as Goliath clambered clumsily up a rope.

Cameron stared around at the lightening sky and the throng of people who stood on the land. All around was confusion.

"You'll see better from over there," remarked a voice, and she stared up into the old general's gaunt face. Panting, Goliath hauled his enormous bulk onto the deck and sat gasping for breath, his thick legs dangling as he looked around for sight of his young charge. His breathing stopped with dismay as he watched the tall, limping old soldier shelter her under a protecting arm and lead her to the prow of the boat. The clustered people parted, acknowledging the man's rank, and then closed behind, blocking sight of them from Goliath's view. He swore, knowing that escape was impossible now as the vessel cast off and the great ship proudly sailed down Loch Linnhe toward the protecting Isle of Mull, accompanied by three frigates. It would be a while before they were out of sight of Scottish soil, he planned. Cameron had proved herself a strong swimmer, and the islands of Jura and Islay and the smaller Isle of Colonsay lay within reach of the vessel's route. Once the ship had cleared the Firth of Lorn, the old soldier would doubtless want his rest, leaving time to jump ship and swim. But as if he suspected Goliath's plot, the general kept Cameron beside him until the majestic boat had lost all sight of land and sailed like a giant white bird across the open water.

Cameron could not fathom her intense feelings as she stood beside the erect, gaunt old man watching the coast of her beloved Scotland fade into the misty horizon behind her. An aching loneliness welled, and the sea sprayed salt to mix with the silent tears that coursed down her cheeks. She stood, a tiny figure beside the taller one, unaware of the grief that she exposed to his eagle eyes. As his constant gaze pierced her, she turned proudly to face front. The land had been swallowed leaving a vast emptiness. She stared straight ahead, her eyes blurred and unseeing, as she tried to conjure up her brother's face as she'd last seen it nearly eight years before. He was her future, she must cling to that, she vowed, and pain welled up in her as though she had been ripped forcibly from the womb of her beloved Scotland.

Goliath kept vigil, as did Alex. Unknown to each other, both men's eyes were fixed on the solitary two figures standing like proud statues at the prow of the boat as the sun rose high above them and the graceful ship parted the waves and streamed toward the New World.

CHAPTER NINETEEN

Alex kept apart from the camaraderie of his fellow officers, his face displaying none of the seething fury and turmoil that consumed him. What was wrong with Cameron that she could not be inconspicuous but became the center of attention wherever she went? he raged inwardly, as the redcoats chattered among themselves about the child that had calmed the old general's horse. He drank deeply of the glass of rum he held and felt the burning sear his throat and spread, joining with the heat of anger. It was evening, and after the excitement of the casting off, when all land had disappeared from view, the soldiers had retired to their cabins to sleep the day away. Now they were gathered socially to eat and drink. Alex stared distastefully at the ribald group who, refreshed from their sound sleeps, now hungered for food, drink, and companionship. He had spent the day silently sitting at his desk, unaware of the red-haired child who sat clutching her dog, regarding him with fear until she had given in to exhaustion. The sound of her slumping had caused him to turn, and for a moment the sight of the slim, limp legs had made him think it was Cameron. He'd towered over the small, prone body and, noting the red curls, had remembered. The freckled, sleeping face broke through his harshness, and he'd tenderly removed the boots and tucked the child gently into the bunk, reminding himself to order food and drink for her before buttoning his tunic in preparation for the officers' dinner.

General Ramsbotham watched the tall, arrogant-looking man who stood apart from the rest. He seemed like a young Viking, he noted, with his golden skin and hair. Feeling an intense gaze, Alex turned lithely, and his amber eyes connected with those of his commanding officer. He sharply stood at attention and saluted.

"At ease, Major," drawled the old man, as he whimsically changed his first opinion. Not a Viking but a young lion with no extra flesh, just sinew and muscle, his movements catlike, quick, and fluid. He needed scouts, not uniformed, pompous marionettes to strut and display themselves. This tall young man who stood alone seemed, to his experienced eye, to be the stuff a frontiersman was made of.

Alex's steady gaze did not waver under the examining eyes.

"Name?"

"Alexander Sinclair, sir."

"Is this your first time over?"

"Nay, I was under General Braddock in fifty-five and with Forbes at Fort Duquesne in fifty-eight."

The old general looked closer into the young man's face. "How old are you?"

"I'm in my twenty-sixth year, sir," responded Alex.

"Where are you bound?"

"Fort Ponchartrain du Detroit."

"Hah, Major Henry Gladwin is commandant there. Do you know him?"

"No, sir," answered Alex stiffly.

"You seem uncomfortable, Sinclair. Do you find the company of your fellow officers distasteful?"

"I am not for pomp and ceremony nor social chit-chat, sir."

"Sit down and discourse with me," ordered the old man cordially, and due to his superior rank, Alex had no recourse but to obey. "I'm looking for likely young men who'd doff their scarlet coats and wear the fringed buckskins of the red man to fight them and the French for the king. You seem such a one to me," explained the general slowly, not taking his eyes from the lean young man.

"I have orders to report to Major Gladwin at Fort Detroit, sir."

"I may be old, but I'm neither deaf nor absentminded, young man. I myself will be visiting Detroit to confer with Gladwin about the Senecas."

"There is trouble?"

"Nearly, but the Ottawas, under their wily chief, Pontiac, apprised us of the Senecas' plot."

"What of the other tribes in the area?" asked Alex, intrigued.

"The Hurons, Chippewas, and Potawatomis seem in alliance with the Ottawas."

"Then that seems in our favor."

"On the surface, yes, but I would prefer to have no alliance between tribes. Together they make a silent, deadly enemy. 'Tis better for us if tribe fights against tribe. Divided they are weaker, much like your Highland clans."

"You have no love for the red man, it seems," said Alex dryly, ignoring the bait.

"I have great respect for them, but neither love nor great hatred. They are as most men, some weak, some greedy, some stupid, and as a whole they are an enigma . . . somewhat like you Scots. Appearing to be uncultured and almost childlike in your simple needs but never to be underestimated," returned the gaunt man. A long silence ensued.

"What say you, Sinclair? Will you choose the perils of the mountains and forests or the perils confined to Fort Detroit?"

"Surely it is for my commanding officer to relegate my duties," answered Alex noncommittally.

"I can arrange what you decide. I may look like a doddering old fogy, but I assure you I still hold power. This very vessel has an escort of frigates, one of which is named for me."

"What is your name, sir?"

"General Maximilian Ramsbotham," stated the old man pompously. Alex had a wild desire to burst into laughter at the ridiculous name and the pride with which the general stated it. He had never heard of the man and yet, feeling pity at a certain vulnerability in the arrogance of the old campaigner, he forced an expression of being impressed to cross his face.

"Come up top, for the air is stale down here, and I'll point out the frigate *Ramsbotham* to you," offered the man, standing and stiffly limping to the door. Alex had no alternative but to follow.

Alex breathed deeply of the fresh sea air, his eyes scanning the decks for sight of Cameron but not noticing Goliath's vast bulk gracefully merge into the shadows. The general stared across the dusky expanse of sea at the escort of frigates that protected the larger vessel that carried them.

"I thought I hated the wild New World. First landed there in seventeen thirteen as a raw youth of nineteen. The main fighting was over, but I stayed four years. I was recalled again in thirty-nine and was with Oglethorpe when he led the victorious campaign from Savannah against the Spanish. We took Fort George and Fort Saint Francis and Picolata. In fifty-four I was under Washington against the French in the battle at Fort Necessity . . . and before that with Pepperell in forty-five," rambled the old soldier with a boastful air. "Each time when I was ready to return to my estates to marry and sire me a legitimate heir, another skirmish came along and I'd tell myself just one more. . . . So you served under Braddock?"

"Aye."

"He made a bloody mess of it."

"Yes, sir," agreed Alex politely.

"I was on the Plains of Abraham," he bragged. "Wounded by two arrows." He unbuttoned his tunic to show a ragged scar on his aged but still taut belly. "The other barb got me lower, didn't sit for some time, I can tell you. They sent me home expecting me to die, but I fooled them. They tried to pension me off, giving me sops . . . calling me general after forty-seven years of being a mere major. At first I was content, but then I missed the challenge of that wild, open land, so here I am."

"How is it that you are so familiar with Fort Detroit?"

"Was there in sixty with Rogers and his Rangers. Was part of the taking of the fort from the French. That's where I received those arrows."

"Not on the Plains of Abraham?" puzzled Alex, mightily confused by the mass of information the general was firing at him.

"I came out of the taking of Quebec unscathed," bragged the old man, buttoning his tunic and puffing out his chest. "I've a score to settle at Fort Detroit. I've permission to recruit healthy young men and harden them, teaching them the ways of the red man so that we can foil them and the French at their own games."

Alex leaned over the rail of the ship as the sunset and darkness covered the sea, listening to the lonely old man drone on and on. He calculated the general to be nearly seventy and marveled at his proud, erect bearing and yet wondered as to his ability in training and leading such a force. If he accepted the man's offer, what then of Cameron? The idea of being without the constraints of fort life appealed to him, but regretfully he realized he'd have to turn down the offer. He toyed with the idea, unwilling to voice his refusal. Maybe Cameron could be recruited also? An outdoor life in the wilderness would probably also appeal to her. As the idea germinated, so did the many drawbacks. He'd have to hold her on such a tight rein, never knowing from one minute to the next what she was liable to do. How long would it be before her sex was discovered?

"You've permission to recruit from enlisted men and officers as well as the general populace?" he asked, interrupting the old man's reminiscences. The general looked at him with confusion.

"Enlisted men, officers, and all those true to the king fought. After Quebec we marched down toward Mont Royal under Murray—oh, there was a canny Scot—while Amherst approached from the southwest and Haviland from the south—"

"I don't mean to presume, but I do not think you ken my meaning," responded Alex with a frown.

"I am describing to you the brilliant strategy of the taking of New France in seventeen sixty, to what were you referring? Ah yes, your're anxious to get back to the present and the future. Well, young man, there is a lot to be learned from the past, and if you choose to serve under me, you must learn patience." Alex met the cold, chastening eyes steadily.

"Now as to your question. I am a law unto myself. As I said, the War Ministry and the military thought to give me a sop. Expected me to sit beside the hearth draped in a shawl like an old spinster waiting for death or salacious daydreams. I devised my plan, and as they had seen fit to confer the rank of general on me, assuming my retirement . . . I pulled rank on them. I'll not be put out to pasture with my noble steed Galahad. We will die as we lived, in service to my king and country."

Alex wondered as to the old man's wits as he saw the gnarled hand tremble with emotion during the pronouncement.

"I assure you, young man, that I'm neither senile nor inept. I have earned the respect of all I've fought with and against, and there are not many who can say the same," barked the gaunt man.

"I assure you, sir, I have no doubts as to your competence," lied Alex.

"I am called Old Hawk by the red men, which I infinitely prefer to my family name of Ramsbotham. I would have liked that frigate to be called such, but then none would have known except some naked savage out of sight of the sea," droned the man, his eyes fixed to the faint outline of the smaller, more graceful vessel.

"You and your recruits will be stationed at Detroit?" asked Alex after a long silence.

"We will use the fort for supplies, reporting what we find to Major Gladwin. The silly young pup trusts Pontiac. 'Tis what happens in this modern age, when adolescents are promoted to commanding ranks for some flamboyant feat on the battlefield that usually endangered all. 'Tis the task of the seasoned soldier silently and unobtrusively to cover for such. We are the unsung heroes," proclaimed Ramsbotham bitterly.

"There sails the frigate with your name, General," replied Alex gently. "So your worth has been acknowledged." He felt great sadness for the old man who had to boast and brag of his accomplishments, a lonely man at the end of his life who had chosen to deny himself friends and family.

"Aye, given when they thought I had two feet in the grave, Ha, ha! But I fooled them, and by God I'll show them!"

Goliath had silently moved downwind, his ears straining. Learning of the old general's plan, he smiled wryly as he thought of the ironic circles in life. He had heard the boastful mention of "Old Hawk" and choked back a laugh at the prevarication. "Old Turkey Buzzard" was the Ottawa name for Ramsbothom. The Indians looked on him with affectionate ridicule and yet admired the old man's tenaciousness and ability to keep up with even the youngest of his men. He stifled a laugh, remembering one story where the old man had managed to creep deep into Indian territory only to sabotage himself by loudly regaling his men with a list of his accomplishments and alerting all around to his presence. Quietly Goliath crept back to the longboat, where he'd left Cameron sleeping. He had followed her there and watched her crawl under the tarpaulin, the fetid heat of stabled horses making it impossible for her to rest belowdecks. His heart lurched at finding the small boat empty. He had been gone less than an hour and she had not slept for two nights. He had assumed she'd sleep for hours.

Cameron, however, had feigned sleep until she heard Goliath creep stealthily away. She agilely climbed out of the longboat and onto the deck, making her way to the stern. A heavy fluttering of wings heralded Omen's descent from a high mast. She crouched down in the shadows and caressed the raven's glossy feathers, wondering if it had eaten and making note to save food for it.

"I must find Jemmy and Tor," she whispered to the giant black bird, who cocked his head to one side.

Cameron stared into his beady eyes, wondering if he knew where they were. The ship was vast and carried fifty-two guns as well as numerous cabins and salons. The officers' quarters were on the second level and off limits to crew members except for stewards. She crept to the stairway and listened intently to the raucous English voices that rasped her nerve endings. No footsteps were audible and, taking the chance that the soldiers were safely closeted behind closed doors, she descended.

Cameron padded barefoot down a long dim passageway on the second level, her heart beating painfully as she passed each closed door. A mournful whine caused her to stop. It was Tor, and yet what if Alex was inside? Taking a deep breath, she softly whistled. A joyful bark answered, and carefully, after hearing nothing else, Cameron turned the handle and peered into the cabin. It was a larger room than she had expected. She quietly closed the door behind her and sat on the floor as her hound licked her face in greeting and took stock of her surroundings. A hammock swung lazily with the vessel's movement, a desk with quill and ink, a bunk large enough for two, and in the dim light she saw a form beneath the covers. Was it Alex? She sat still, watching, unable to approach. The raven bobbed up and down as though encouraging her, but she seemed frozen.

Jemmy yawned and turned in sleep, then sat up suddenly as the rocking of the ship caused her to remember where she was. She gasped in astonishment at the dark, silent figure with the bird that sat in the middle of the cabin floor. She felt ill, her skin clammy and moist, and she fought the nausea that welled.

"Jemmy?" came Cameron's quiet voice, but all she could do was nod as great heaves shook her and she leaned over the side of the bunk. Cameron quickly scanned the room and, spying a basin firmly anchored in a hole cut in a board, wrenched it out, spilling the water all over the floor before carrying it to the sick child.

"Oh, Cameron, I think I'm dying," gasped Jemmy, lying back exhausted against the pillows.

"Nay, 'tis just the motion of the sea, you'll get used to it," she comforted. "Does Alex rest here wie you?" she asked after a pause in which she had noticed several of his possessions. Jemmy nodded silently as another wave of sickness overcame her. As Cameron digested this disturbing fact, sharp, booted footsteps neared the cabin. She lithely flew across the cabin to hide behind the door just before it was thrust open.

Alex sniffed the acrid odor of vomit and, with a curse, crossed to the porthole. Cameron slipped out into the corridor followed by Tor and Omen. Alex turned, hearing the sudden movement and rushing of wings. He stood at the open cabin door watching the dark shapes of Cameron, hound, and bird in the dim light.

Cameron forgot the need for caution as she raced through the endless corridor looking for the stairway to the open deck. She had to get away from Alex. She had

been unprepared for the emotions and need that burst
through her at the sight of his tall, lean body. An aching
hunger coursed through her, and she fought against the
desire to press against him and for a while submerge herself, forgetting all her fury, hatred, and fears.

" 'Tis a bat! A giant bat!" screamed a panic-stricken
voice, and suddenly Cameron's escape route was blocked.
The raven flew back and forth against the walls of the
narrow space as people waved brooms and jackets, converging on the three dark figures in the middle. Cameron
watched Omen's frenzy and heard Tor's frantic barks of
agitation. She wanted to calm the bird and failed to see the
tall figure of the old general shouldering his way through
the excited mob, which had stopped fearfully six feet each
side of the three. Holding her arm out to the raven, she
fixed her eyes on it and spoke in her head, willing it to
come to her as it had done that stormy night at Glen
Aucht. Omen dashed himself against the wall and fell like
a stone. Cameron rushed to it, and to her relief it regarded
her with a rueful beady eye. With a gentle, practiced hand
she examined it. No wings were broken, which was a
miracle, but one leg hung limply. She was so intent on
helping her feathered friend that she was unaware of the
crowd that surged closer until Tor gave a menacing growl,
trying to hold the mass on either side at bay.

"Get back and let the lad have room. 'Tis no bat, just
a poor land bird that's lost its way at sea," barked the old
general.

" 'Tis a raven, an omen of death!" shrieked a voice.

"Stuff and nonsense! You are meant to be civilized
soldiers of the crown, not superstitious savages like the
ones you are sailing to fight," roared the old man. "Now
get to your bunks and do not show your cowardice. If one
small boy, a dog, and a bird can strike terror into your
hearts, what are one hundred naked savages and the
French army going to do?"

Alex and Goliath exchanged glances from opposite sides
of the narrow passageway. Each had heard the loud confusion and, suspecting that Cameron would somehow be
involved, had raced to the source. Between them crouched
their charge, cradling the large bird and guarded by Tor.

"There is a ship's surgeon aboard, Isaac, who'll tend your friend," informed the general. Cameron looked up into his sharp eyes, set deeply among the wrinkles, and shook her head.

"He's set many an animal's limbs, sir," interjected Goliath, hoping that Cameron possessed the same healing skills as her twin brother.

"What is that thieving urchin and his father doing on the officer's level? If I have anything missing, we know who's responsible," stated an officious voice.

"And what is that mangy cur?" joined in another voice. Alex opened his mouth to claim the dog, but the old general beat him to it.

"The dog and this boy are under my protection!" he roared in a voice that brooked no argument. Alex exchanged worried glances with Goliath, whose rugged face was wrinkled in consternation for quite a different reason. The old soldier had an investment in Cameron, and the giant man was now sure that it was solely due to the striking resemblance to the Indian renegade Méron. Alex stood still, his brain tied in knots. What did the old man mean by protection? Hopefully it was just a warning to those who would try to harm him.

"Abraham?" barked the old man, and it took Goliath several seconds to respond to his fictitious name.

"Aye, sir," he stammered, recollecting himself.

"You'll have your son's possessions, if he has any, moved to my cabin. There is a hammock. He'll still perform his duties with the horses, but he'll eat and sleep under my protection, is that clear?"

"Aye, sir," responded Goliath, breathing deeply.

"Sinclair, accompany us," ordered the old man, catching sight of Alex's lean countenance.

"I have a sick child under my care, sir, and was looking for someone to swab the cabin floor when I heard the confusion," he replied.

"A sick child? Seems, Sinclair, we're both to be nursemaids on this long voyage," chuckled the old man. "Come along, boy, bring your pets, and we'll take a gander at Major Sinclair's young charge."

"The . . . er . . . aroma is not pleasant, sir," protested Alex.

"You think my stomach too weak for vomit? I, who have lain beside corpses as the sun beat down until the putrefaction would have killed a lesser man? I, who have held suppurating limbs that the maggots feasted upon as the surgeon cut them off?" challenged the general. Alex had no recourse but to open the door of his cabin hospitably to the imperious old soldier. A hot, stinking blast issued forth, but the old man strode in undeterred and surveyed the small red-haired child, whose face glowed greenish white. Maggie-Pup barked welcome.

" 'Tis best to get the child atop in the fresh air. Wrap him warmly against the chill and give him a shot of rum. Keep him outside until he has his sea legs. Another hound? This vessel becomes more and more like Noah's Ark!"

Cameron took a strong uncut quill from Alex's desk and, tearing fabric from her shirt, splinted and set the raven's leg, unaware that the conversation had stopped and that she was being watched by the two men.

"I'll have that lad, too, as part of my company, despite his tender years," hissed the general softly, not willing to break the concentration nor disturb the deft fingers. Alex let the import of the old man's words sink in and clutch his guts before turning to the pathetic Jemmy and wrapping her dispassionately in unsoiled blankets to take her on deck.

Goliath hovered outside the door, his own mind in turmoil at the whispered words. He held Cameron's saddlebag after quickly removing the kilt and plaid. It contained nothing else but a change of shirt, breeches, and her boots.

"A son's place is with his natural father," he stated.

"I see no similarity between the two of you, and a natural father surely has more discipline over his son than you seem to exercise," returned the old man.

"He takes after my dearly departed wife, his sainted mother," strove Goliath valiantly.

"Doing it a bit thick, aren't you?" the general countered.

" 'Tis wrong to separate kin, sir," insisted the large man.

"I seek solely to protect your . . . er, son."

"What say you, Major?" said Goliath, turning to Alex, who stood with Jemmy bundled in his strong arms.

"It would not be good for morale on this vessel for families to be split," he answered evenly.

"Let it rest with the boy, then," responded the old man, turning to Cameron, who looked from one to the other. Her rage boiled as she thought of the manipulations of both Goliath and Alex. She felt also a sense of power. She stared insolently into Alex's amber eyes and then down at the swaddled girl in his arms. Even though she knew that nothing existed between them, her jealousy was fanned as she noted his golden hands tighten on the roundness of Jemmy's body through the blanket. Taking her time, she turned and stared at Goliath. How many times had he laughed, ridiculing her, talking in riddles, peaking her curiosity and then hiding behind enigmatic answers? Sharing a cabin with the old man would give her more freedom and more privacy than the open deck or the confined stables. She had already found out the drawbacks of living as a male on board, as the men could openly urinate over the side of the vessel, making sure first that the wind blew away from them. She had been to near bursting before she found a secluded spot and then hung her naked rear end precariously above the waves.

"Who will you choose?" growled Goliath, his gray eyes boring into her, but she just gave a triumphant stare. Food would be better. She could also bathe, she rejoiced inwardly. Tentatively she looked up into the old man's face. There was something indefinable that reminded her of Duncan Fraser. What was it? The eyes of a proud warrior coming to the end of his days? At the thought, she instinctively reached out to him, seeing the loneliness and vulnerability despite his imperious and arrogant manner.

"The lad has chosen, Sinclair," he crowed victoriously. "Give your puling ward to him to tend on board as your substitute, and find us some food," he ordered, shepherding Cameron out of the suffocating sickly atmosphere of the cabin. "And have water brought so that the lad can bathe," he added as an afterthought, causing Cameron's blood to chill as she wondered about her decision.

To Cameron's relief, the old man took himself on deck to smoke a cigar, leaving her to bathe hurriedly, guarded by her dog. As his footsteps limped away, she had noted with dismay that the cabin door could not be locked and assumed the general kept the key upon his person. She longed to lie in the hot salt water but reasoned it was a luxury she couldn't afford. She hastily leaped from the tub and enveloped herself in a towel as the door opened after a cursory knock. Alex stared at her coldly as he deposited a tray of food upon the general's cluttered desk. Mesmerized by his eyes, she stared back, hiding her tumultuous feelings beneath a defiant expression.

" 'Twill be a long time before you can rid yourself of your newest protector," he stated harshly. "It will be interesting to see how you can disguise your sex, living in such intimacy for such a time."

Cameron stood silently digesting his cutting challenge, not allowing him to see how it released a torrent of new problems.

"How will you explain your monthly bleeding?" jabbed Alex cruelly and noted with satisfaction the imperceptible flicker that he'd learned to recognize flash in her green eyes.

"Maybe he'll be delighted at the discovery and enjoy the meeting of our flesh," spat Cameron, goaded. Alex's eyes narrowed, and the hard lines of his face tightened. He ached to tear off the flimsy towel and thrust into her, showing who was master of her lithe young body, but he remembered his resolve and laughed cynically.

"Better his flesh than mine," he chuckled before striding out and slamming the door.

CHAPTER TWENTY

The days seemed as gray and endless as the water that stretched to each horizon, meeting the sky in a nearly imperceptible line of the same endless color. Cameron despaired of ever seeing land again, imprisoned as she was on the cramped vessel amid the sea's vastness. She paced the deck of the ship like a caged animal with the raven on her shoulder and her black hound at her heels, much to the awe of the superstitious seamen, who gave the silent, dark trio a wide berth. Jemmy, finding her sea legs and her natural exuberancy, bounced back and thoroughly enjoyed the ship's company, and the small, vivacious red-haired child and her rusty-coated animal soon became a favorite with the crew and the officers. Her mischievous, impish ways, however, in no way mollified Alex's grim countenance as he also silently paced, his rage and pent-up frustrations kept in firm check.

Whether she knew it or not, the voyage was teaching Cameron patience. For the first time in her life there was no alternative but to wait out the voyage. There was no place to run to and no choice but to keep her awesome temper on short rein. Alex ironically smiled at the thought, knowing the tremendous effort it must extract from her, and at the same time prayed that there would be no violent storm on the voyage that would ignite his own thundering rage.

Each day Cameron would perform her assigned jobs, methodically raking out the fetid stable area and grooming the listless horses, whose coats had lost their glossy sheens. No amount of brushing seemed to change the dull, matted look. She would stare into Torquod's eyes and see her own hopelessness mirrored there, and her panic would well. It was like being suspended in a rocking nightmare that would never stop. She would hastily climb out of the suffocating quarters to breathe the fresh sea air, only to be exposed to more of the terrible dream as her eyes frantically searched around for some solid, unmoving land to ground herself to. But all around was the gray sea, seeming to stretch to infinity, as though that was all that existed in the whole world.

Cameron could not abide to sleep in the forever-swinging hammock in the general's cabin. Each night she lay in the too-warm, stale closeness, unable to stretch her arms as the heavy, rocking canvas bundled and swaddled her much like a baby. She lay stilling her wildly thumping heart, fighting the fear of her own suffocation as the old man droned on and on like the endless ocean, retelling countless tales of his exploits until rumbling snores would punctuate his epic and finally submerge the whole. Then she would steal out to lie in the brisk night air, staring up at the breathtakingly enormous arc of sky with its myriad of stars that dwarfed the world, making her and her problems seem insignificant.

Both Alex and Goliath had occasion to observe Cameron's nocturnal routine and had at first worried for her safety among the rough crew and undisciplined soldiers, whose limited opportunity for pleasures of the flesh now made them less particular whom they slaked their lust on, but the crew's obvious avoidance of Cameron caused them to relax their nightly vigils as they reasoned that the raven gave more adequate protection than they could possibly provide. Alex kept Jemmy under a constant eagle eye, sensing a change in a number of men's friendship with the chipper child. He often firmly removed her from ribald company and forced her to sit for hours listening to general Ramsbotham's sagas, knowing the child would not disobey him and hoping to ease the old man's smarting at Cameron's avoidance of him.

Each morning the general would wake, his sleepy, foggy mind fantasizing that he now had a semblance of a son, or grandson, as he gazed at the gently swinging hammock that caused the light from the porthole to flicker the gloom of the cabin. It would take several minutes for the realiza-to dawn, and he'd sit up stiffly, noting that Cameron was not there. Each morning he would methodically perform his ablutions, scorning any thought of a valet, as he resolved that the boy would not elude him again. He prided himself on his ability to sleep like a cat, instantly awake and aware at the tiniest of sounds, and yet the ebony-haired lad could not only swing out of the high hammock but cross the floor and leave by the door without waking him. He pushed aside any thought of his own age causing an inadequacy as he remembered the green-eyed savage, Méron, who could silently melt in and out of the shadows, and blessed the fates that had placed the miraculous existence of another such one in his hands. The boy, Isaac, would be used to discredit Méron. He also cursed the fates that made the child mute, for there was much he'd like to learn. He voiced this frustration to Alex, who shrugged nonchalantly and remarked, " 'Tis said we each have a double who roams the earth somewhere." Not content, the old man sought out Goliath and received a mundane story of no account that made mention of Cameron's mother, "Abraham's" dearly departed spouse being dark like the boy—a black Scot, caused, very likely, by the Spaniards, who'd sowed wild oats in the Highlands centuries before.

"And I suppose her name was Sara?" replied the old man with exasperated irony.

"How did you guess?" was the innocent surprise from the enormous man's mouth, and the gaunt general stiffly limped away, determined he would give "Isaac" lessons in speech.

For hours before bed Cameron was forced to sit next to the old man at his cluttered desk, where he made exaggerated shapes with his mouth. She watched him dispassionately as he exhibited sparse yellow teeth that his moustache usually hid.

"Aaaaaah!" pronounced the general, but Cameron's own mouth stayed firmly closed.

"Ooooooh!" he strived, his jaw muscles aching, but to no avail. The general gave up, his old eyes drooping beneath his hooded lids. He leaned back in his chair and warily surveyed his young charge.

"Get me some rum," he ordered softly, and Cameron started to obey, but as she passed him, she found her small wrist caught in a viselike grip. Anger flared in her eyes for an instant.

"Usually the ears are similarly afflicted. How is it you can hear a pin drop and yet not speak?"

Cameron returned his sharp gaze, keeping her expression blank before looking down and fastening her eyes on his gnarled hand that imprisoned her small, brown wrist. Reluctantly the general withdrew his hand, releasing her, and she lithely fled from the cabin. He didn't see her except from a distance for three days.

The old man cursed his action. The wild child obviously resented being touched and was instantly on guard when any note of anger was expressed. He knew that, and yet his fatigue had caused him to act hastily. He stood erect on deck watching her shin like a monkey up the high rigging, where she'd sit with her bird for hours on end, often 'til darkness fell, and none but her hound's keen eyes could distinguish her from the dark shadows of the sails.

Cameron felt a modicum of peace high up on the center mast. The flapping of the taut sails and the wind lifted her from her gray depression, and she could imagine she was a bird. From her vantage point, she also reasoned, she would spy land at the same time as the watch in the crow's nest and could dive into the sea, making good her escape. The fact that she perched four stories high did not deter her. She had many times at Cape Wrath leaped and dived from similarly dangerous places. She felt a pang as she realized she would have to leave Tor and Torquod, as she couldn't get them over the high gunwales, and wondered if she'd have the strength to venture forth in a strange land without her loyal companions, with just Omen between her and complete aloneness until she found her brother. Could she find her brother in the alien land that she had heard tell was even vaster than the ocean she now was helplessly confined upon? She thrust her terrifying thought from her mind, determined not to allow herself such awful imaginings, and stared at the white-tipped waves that rolled, increasing with the velocity of the wind. The turbulent air sang against the taut rigging, twanging it with eerie sounds, and drummed against the sails, billowing them so that they ballooned, speeding the dangerously rocking vessel. Through the darkness men ran hither and thither

over the lurching deck, shinning up the rigging to loosen
and drop the straining canvas before it ripped.

Cameron, hearing the confusion below, was loath to
leave her high perch. The storm was a welcome change
from the monotony, and she rode the mast delighting in
the increasing fury of the elements much as she did her
steed Torquod. Through the gloom she watched the crew
like ants, rushing about the deck. The sudden thunderous
roar of a large sail released from its taut mooring caused
her to duck instinctively, saving her from being dashed by
its weight to the deck below. She clutched the mast for
dear life while all around her the majestic, billowing sails
deflated as the frantic crew obeyed the barked-out, re-
echoed orders. The intricate patterns of the rigging ropes
jumbled like torn cobwebs and became hard, swinging
weapons that struck out. Cameron was lashed by the wet
cables, which seemed to hang free for a moment and then
turned to cutting, vibrating saws as the winches groaned
and labored. Cameron's scream, when one such straining
rope seared her arm as she reached out during her perilous
descent, was lost in the howling wind, and she was thrown
to the deck.

Ignoring the orders for noncrew to remain below hatches,
Alex made his way across the bucking deck, grabbing on
for support and being dashed against immovable objects.
Through the deafening din of man and nature he heard
the frantic barking and whining of a dog. He despaired of
ever finding the hound, as he would progress a few feet
only to be thrown back by the incredible force of the
storm. The rain fell in torrents, and the deck was slippery,
causing his boots to slide as he made a zigzag approach,
allowing the lurch of the ship to propel him at an angle.

Tor covered Cameron's limp body with his own, buffer-
ing her as they were rolled with each sharp lurch of the
vessel to crack into the gunwhale and back to be dashed
into the main mast. Alex bent over the still form, adding
his strength to keep her from further buffeting and pinning
her under the arced gunwhale as he realized the futility
of trying to carry her back to the comparative safety
belowdecks. There was no way he could do more than
ascertain that she lived, as all his strength and wits were

put to use in seeing that they were not pounded to death. He anchored his body, bracing his legs, as he lay holding both dog and girl. The boots that he had cursed he now was thankful for as he wedged his foot between two beams. For three hours the storm raged at its most ferocious and then gradually tempered to a brisk breeze and steady drizzle. Several times Cameron stirred, but Alex could do nothing except make what he hoped were reassuring sounds, as all his energy was being expended. As the deck subsided back to a less agitated roll, Alex relaxed his aching legs. He rolled off Cameron and sat up, allowing the blood to return to his limbs. Massaging his feet, he found both boots to be cut, the thick well-oiled leather severed across each toe. He stared down at Cameron, unable to see her features clearly in the dark. She looked back alert and awake, although one arm burned and pounded, sending pain through her whole body. She sat up, and Alex expelled his breath with relief. All through the ordeal he had worried about the extent of her injuries, not knowing if she had toppled from her high hiding place, not knowing if her back, neck, or the bones in her whole body had been broken.

Cameron pulled herself to her feet, not showing any of the agony that streaked through her. She turned her back on Alex and stared across the dark sea, fighting to keep conscious as waves of dizziness threatened to engulf her.

"Are you of one piece?" growled Alex, hauling himself to stand, and hiding his concern behind gruffness. Cameron nodded, unable to turn to him and keeping her injured arm firmly by her side.

"Are you all right?" he repeated, grasping her head and turning her to him. Cameron tried to swallow the cry of pain as she pulled away. She wanted to creep away and nurse her own wounds, determined not to be in a weak position with Alex, whom she had vowed to be free of. Her stifled cry and stiffening of body were not lost on the man who had spent nearly a year in her turbulent company. With a snort of impatience he swung her into his strong though battered arms and made his way through the drizzling darkness, his torn boots squishing and slipping on the wet deck.

Cameron stared frantically around for Omen as she was carried slowly and purposefully. She knew struggling was useless as well as painful as she stared around in the thick, wet darkness. She pursed her lips and whistled, and out of the night came an answering caw. Heavy, languid wings descended, and Alex didn't lessen his laborious pace as the raven alit on his shoulder.

Cameron was gently set down on Alex's bunk, and he turned and locked the cabin door.

"Got out of those wet clothes, and I'll find you some of Jemmy's. They'll be a mite small, but beggars canna be choosers," he said harshly as he lit a lamp.

"Where is Jemmy?" asked Cameron, despite her resolve not to allow one word to pass between them. Alex didn't answer, he himself wanting no conversation between them. He had given Jemmy into the general's keeping, hoping to divert him when the old man had grown frantic with worry about Cameron since he knew her to be high in the rigging at the onset of the storm. His stiff leg, due to the wound from the Indian arrows, had made his movements on the storm-tossed deck impossible.

Cameron sat up and stoically swung her legs over the side of the bunk. She had no intention of stripping in front of Alex. "I'm quite capable of seeing to myself," she hissed, standing slowly, unaware that blood dripped down her arm and mingled with the water from her rain-drenched clothes, staining the bedcovers and the floor. Alex's brows creased in concern and vexation as a loud hammering came at the door.

"Sinclair, the general wants to know if the boy Isaac has been found?" answered a voice to Alex's inquiry as to who was there. Cameron stared back at the set, chiseled face that seemed both to censure and mock her.

"Aye, tell the general the boy is fine and resting and that he and Jemmy should do the same," he responded. " 'Tis a pretty fix you'd be in now if I hadna found you," he laughed harshly after the footsteps had faded into the distance. "Now climb out of those clothes, and let's see what your injuries are."

Cameron refused to make a move but stood resolute, her face rebellious and her green eyes flashing. Alex surveyed her for a moment and then with an oath grabbed a towel and knelt on the floor, rubbing the shivering hound.

Cameron's blood boiled as somehow his action rankled her, implying her callous insensitivity to her dog. She was trapped and she knew it. Even if the door had not been locked, where would she go to tend her wound and put on dry clothing? Where would she obtain such clothing, her own being in the general's cabin? She couldn't very well yell and beat on the locked doors with her fists, when it was believed she was mute.

Alex had her at a disadvantage and he knew it as he briskly toweled the dog dry. He had noted that her clothes were torn and through the rends had seen welts and abrasions. Her face, now clear of Beddington's bruises, displayed a prominent lump, which he ascertained had been caused by her fall. The arm that she held protectively to her side still steadily dripped blood. Alex's face, intent on the dog, showed nothing of his thoughts as he delayed attending her, too weary for a battle and not willing to have curious ears hear what promised to be a loud, verbal scene. He felt as trapped and cornered as Cameron did.

Alex stood, throwing the wet towel from him, as Tor, no longer shivering, curled thankful to sleep. In two quick strides Alex crossed to Cameron and proceeded to divest her of the soaking clothes. To his surprise she stood, passively submitting. He felt a melting of his firm resolutions as his hands touched her smooth skin, and he longed to kiss her rainwashed face. He hardened himself as he stared into her stormy countenance and addressed himself to coldly examining her bared body. She certainly had received the whipping he had often wanted to give her, he thought grimly, as he noted the long raised welts. Her left forearm, however, bore a deep, long gash, which needed stitching if the skin was to grow together. He chewed his bottom lip as he cleaned the cut, wishing she'd break the agonizing silence with a scream, as he was aware of how much it hurt, and wondering how to get it sewn without exposing Cameron's female charms.

"You're lucky," he hissed. "Like a cat, forever landing on your feet. You've taken a beating and will be black and blue for a week or so about your back and legs, and it's no more than you deserve. Your arm, however, needs to be stitched and at once, and I'm afraid you'll have me as a seamstress, as the ship's doctor would no doubt insist on examining the whole of you." Cameron bit down on a corner of the pillow, silent tears of pain squeezing from her tightly shut eyes as Alex painstakingly drew the sides of the deep gash together and sewed. He had forced her to drink two full glasses of rum and also fortified himself before embarking on the loathsome chore. Each time he pushed the sharp needle through the living flesh, he felt his gorge rise. Perspiration beaded on his face, and his eyes burned from the concentration. She'll forever bear the mark of my clumsiness with the needle and the mismanagement of her life, he thought. Bungling stitches and abungling all around.

"There," he sighed with relief after biting off the length of thread and looking down at his handiwork. Cameron welcomed the cessation of the torturous process and, keeping her eyes still closed, relaxed her body. Her arm throbbed, but nothing nearly so bad as the sharp pain of the sewing. Alex covered her and sat at his desk, fortifying his shaking hands with another shot of rum, and watched her. The heat of the drink relaxed him and allowed the warmth to spread glowingly to his loins. He had missed her satiny softness, and there she now lay in his bed. He stood and stripped off his own clothes, blew out the lantern, and climbed in beside her.

Cameron slept, unaware that she nestled into the warmth of Alex's chest as he lay loosely holding her for fear he'd jar her injured arm. Although drained physically, he lay staring at the glossy ebony head, feeling complete and content for the first time in weeks. He was completely relaxed; and aware of a mellow happiness, he dropped into a sound sleep.

They slept for several hours, their breathing even and in harmony. Through the deep, muffled layers of sleep, Cameron reached to be closer to the golden strength, trying to merge with the heat that encircled her. In her dream she lay naked on the furs in front of the hearth at their honeymoon hunting lodge, high in the mountains away from the rest of the world. She felt the flames of the wood fire flickering and tingling every inch of her body. She stretched, arching her back, thrusting her breasts toward the warmth; her hands flexing and stroking as though to absorb the heat; her lithe legs reaching to entangle and entwine; her flushed, inflamed cheeks nuzzling. She felt like a cat writhing sinuously and sensuously before a roaring fire that kindled and rekindled until it blazed.

Alex's pulses raced, and his hands caressed hot silkiness. He opened his eyes and stared bemusedly at Cameron, who, though sleeping, thrust hungrily against him. He lay still, trying to marshal his sleepy mind, watching as Cameron played with his body until his breathing matched her own. She was abandoned and open to him in sleep. All her defenses were down, her desire for him naked and exposed. Could he be just any man to her? he questioned, not wanting to be vulnerable, as her urgent mouth nipped and nuzzled his chest, traveling lower to his firmly muscled belly, which quivered involuntarily with anticipation. Oh, God! The witch, he groaned inwardly before letting go of all reason and surrendering to the flood of exquisite sensations as his straining manhood was encompassed and suckled hungrily.

Cameron's eyes flew open as she was firmly lifted and positioned against the pillows. She stared into the smoldering eyes that flamed with a matching passion, trying to reorient herself as her body compulsively arched to meet his. She gasped aloud as they joined and closed her eyes to become one with a rhythm that built, consuming them both.

Bright sunlight streamed through the porthole, and the noises of the crew on deck awoke Cameron. She stared into Alex's sleepy eyes, but he grinned, enfolded her, and settled himself more comfortably to sleep. She tried to wriggle out of his embrace, causing her arm to throb. She lay still, at war with herself. It would be so easy to relax and curl contentedly in the warmth of his strong golden body. She remembered their lovemaking of a few short hours before and felt weak. How could her body betray her so when her mind was firmly resolved to leave him at the first opportunity? Even as she thought, a pang went through her at the possibility of never seeing him again, never being held so safely and warmly, never feeling him deep inside of her, their breaths, heartbeats, and flesh mingling and merging, wiping out all fear, worry, and pain. She had to leave him, she determined. She didn't trust him. He didn't trust her. She forced her mind to calculate the list of grievances coldly, the largest being his keeping her father's name from her. Why, even when she had been beaten and nearly raped and her dog killed by Beddington, he had remained subservient to the English colonel, as though nothing had happened. Alex didn't care about her, she realized, remembering how he had taken a risk by going to Edinburgh. He had taken no other risks, even though all the people under his protection had been abused. He obviously still loved Fiona, she concluded, trying to ignore the feel of his flesh against the length of her.

Alex watched her through half-closed lids, feeling much the same tangle of emotions as well as a resumption of his desire. He could not have enough of her. He ran his hands down her satiny back and, cupping her firm buttocks, pulled her to his aching groin as his lips encompassed hers. His tongue probed her moist mouth, and he felt her erect nipples against his chest, although she seemed to be passive. He moved his lips tantalizingly, wondering how long she could remain still.

Cameron battled with her traitorous body as Alex's mouth moved down her cheek to her neck. She was determined to have some control over herself and even when his lips captured her quivering nipples, she lay still, trying to keep her breathing even. He is my husband and owes me satisfaction, she finally compromised, and her whole body strained toward him, aroused to fever pitch, but he refused to be hastened as he savored each part of her all the way down to her small brown feet. Cameron bucked against him, wanting to be taken, but Alex held himself away, knowing full well what she craved, and glorifying in his mastery. His mind refused to acknowledge the love he felt for her. He felt anger, lust, and a need to dominate, and he took a sadistic delight in her frustrated writhings. Goddamnit, he'd tame her one way or the other. Through his head flashed the humiliating scenes with Fiona and Beddington, the debasement he had been subjected to, the loss of his home and lands, the red uniform that hung at the end of the bunk, and blind rage took over, and he thrust himself into her burning core to pound out the fury that melded with his passion.

At the point when Cameron thought she'd go insane, Alex spread her legs and entered her roughly. She rose to meet him, heedless of any bruising, and quickly climaxed, but Alex continued, and she opened her eyes to see his face above her suffused with rage as he stared down at her with undisguised hostility. She shut her eyes quickly as pain streaked through, not so much from the brutal hammering but from the contempt she read in his stern, determined face.

Alex saw the hurt flare in Cameron's eyes, and it pierced his anger. He gentled his movements, trying to rekindle her appetite, but she lay enduring, and to his horror he felt his manhood shrink. Still coupled, he rolled to one side, holding her. He gently kissed her, played with her breasts, coaxed her in all her favorite places, but she didn't respond. He felt himself slipping from her and, encountering her mocking green eyes, wrenched himself away as though burned. She lay, seeming to smile triumphantly, her lips curled cruelly. He sneered back and coldly quit the bed.

Cameron smoldered as she watched him stand naked, washing himself all over as though the scents and essences of her might contaminate him. Her head and arm throbbed, and she felt her own stickiness between her legs as a burning evidence of their rutting. She made herself lie still with what she hoped was a nonchalant expression on her face until he had finished his ablutions and stood with his back to her as he dressed, staring through the porthole at what looked to be a sunny day, and then she stood scouring her own body with her sound arm. She tried to scrub all evidence of their mating from herself as she cursed her femaleness, which could harbor the juices of man, whereas he could erase every vestige, retaining none of her. Her clothes lay sodden on the floor, and she picked them up, noting the tears and lost buttons and wondering how she could obtain spare garments, when Alex coldly threw some onto the crumpled bunk.

"These were a mite large for Jemmy," he informed

tersely before turning away. Cameron dressed in the seaman's clothes, finding the harsh canvas pants a good fit
but scratchy and the woolen tunic bulky enough to hide
the swell of her breasts.

Alex held open the door of the cabin mockingly for her
to pass. With the raven on her shoulder and followed by
Tor, she stepped into the corridor and came face to face
with the general, who immediately grabbed her arm thankfully.

"You're all in one picoe!" he rejoiced and was silenced
by the sudden pallor and cry of pain. "What is it?" he
asked, still holding onto Cameron's injured arm.

"He has a gash in his arm," informed Alex, gently removing the offending hand. "I have sewn it, and the boy spent
the night under my protection. I seem to have some control
over the brat," he added as they made their way toward
the galley. "So if it pleases you, sir, I suggest that he
share cabin with me if the younger redhead in no way
inconveniences you?"

The general looked thoughtfully at Alex. "I hold you
personally responsible, Sinclair. It is true your legs and
arms are younger and better able to keep up with the
young savage. Firstly I should like the ship's surgeon to
examine our young charge. Why was it you sewed him
yourself?"

"All hands were full with the storm," improvised Alex.

In the infirmary Cameron stood silently with her wide
left sleeve rolled to her shoulder as the surgeon and the
general clustered, looking at the gash that tore her arm
from elbow to shoulder joint.

" 'Tis evident you were never taught embroidery, Major,"
remarked the ship's surgeon dryly. " 'Twill suffice, as
'twill do more damage resewing. Well, 'tis well you're not a
lass, lad, as you'll be carrying that mark for the rest of
your life."

"It has the look of a feathered arrow," observed the
general. "See there the point and up there the wings?"

"The major's stitching improved from start to finish,"
laughed the surgeon. "I bet you started at the bottom near
the elbow, aye?"

"I did."

"And at the top had no notion of how to finish?" Cameron stood displaying none of the seething she felt at the men regarding her as an object of curiosity and ridicule. She remained silent as they bound up the wound, but when she made as if to flee, she was stopped by Alex.

"You will remain with me and eat," he informed her firmly as the general nodded his satisfaction.

"You will remain with Major Sinclair and obey him, Isaac. My bones are too old to go chasing after you."

"The boy works with the horses?" asked the surgeon.

"Yes, he has a way with them," replied the general.

"Not just with horses, it seems," returned the surgeon, eyeing the raven who roosted and the black hound who watched. " 'Tis better he stay away from the stables until the wound has healed. The excrement of animals has been known to bring illness and infection."

"That giant of a man who claims to be the boy's father can tend my Galahad and that great black beast of yours, Sinclair," stated the general as they made their way out of the ship's infirmary with Cameron being guided firmly by Alex.

"I think 'tis best the boy rest for a few days, as there'll doubtless be infection," called the doctor after them, ducking as the raven launched himself and swooped through the low cabin door.

To her fury Cameron now found herself confined in an even smaller space. She stood staring out at the endless sea, now reflecting the blue of the sunny sky, through the porthole in Alex's cabin. A tray of unappetizing food had been hurled by her at the locked door, causing little damage as the now meager fare consisted of hardtack and ship's biscuits dotted with the black specks of baked-in weevils. On board she heard the crew singing as they worked, glad for the fine weather and the passing of the storm. Overhead, gulls wheeled and cried for scraps as several men trawled fishing lines in the hopes of supplementing the boring, monotonous diet. She turned from the window and paced the small room as she wondered frantically if she was to be confined for the rest of the voyage. Would she ever be able to escape from Alex's hold? Unbidden, thoughts of his hard, golden body and amber eyes flooded her mind, and her pace quickened as her anger at herself grew. So quickly she had submitted and now to be closeted with him in such close quarters. She sat suddenly on the rumpled bed, which seemed to taunt her with the abandonment of herself the previous night, her heart thumping painfully and her breath labored. What had she done to him? she wondered fearfully. Alex had never grown soft within her before. Terrifying thoughts of Daft-Dougal's concoctions, his wilting mixtures, flashed in her head.

"No more'n he deserves," she said out loud, remembering Alex's remarks about her lashed body. Was she really a witch, she wondered, able to strike a man's manhood down? She thrust the horrendous thought from her and looked around for an alternate place to sleep. A hammock was neatly rolled and tied to give more space in the cramped quarters. She unfolded it and, with great difficulty and a lot of pain to her injured arm, managed to string it across the cabin. Clambering onto Alex's desk, she rolled into the swinging canvas, jarring her throbbing wound in the process. She lay gently rocking with the rhythm of the boat, staring through the porthole at the endless expanse of sea. The large bolts that held the porthole in place came closer and receded, came closer and receded, and she eyed them speculatively. The porthole was not able to be opened, being too near the waterline, but maybe she could loosen the bolts so that when they were in sight of land, she could slip through like a seal and swim to freedom. She could push Tor through first, and Omen could fly through. It meant leaving Torquod, her horse, but at least she wouldn't be completely alone. Her mind busily planning, she fell asleep, lulled by the motion of the waves.

CHAPTER TWENTY-ONE

Cameron had lost all track of time as May turned to June and still there was nothing but the empty sea. Alex had made no comment at her desertion of his bed and had not approached her, except for the first three days, when he had laid a cursory hand on her forehead to ascertain if she ran a fever. She was well, and yet he still kept her locked up like less than an animal. Even Tor and Omen were allowed fresh air, she seethed, as she feverishly worked on the enormous bolts of the porthole with anything she could find. Alex's manicure set was rather the worse for wear, and as she carefully replaced the instruments each night, she hoped he would not notice in the dim light. She rarely saw him by day. She would awake at the first light and, without acknowledging his presence, would listen to him dress. She played a game counting how long he took and what he was putting on. Five booted steps and the staccato sound of him unlocking the door, a brisk three count, and he was out, with the door locked behind him. She still would not climb out of the hammock as she had done the first day, for she had felt at a disadvantage when he had returned abruptly to stride across the room, place a tray of food on his desk, and stride out again. At the count of five hundred and ninety-nine her straining ears heard his distinctive footsteps nearing and again the staccato sound of the lock, the door latch, the opening, the closing, the slam of the tray, and the reverse as he exited. Only now could she clamber out of her swinging bed knowing that she was free of his disturbing presence for hours.

Cameron froze upon hearing footsteps approaching, and hurriedly replaced the manicure instruments into the leather case embossed with the Sinclair coat of arms. She tossed them onto his desk and clambered into the hammock where she lay still, placing a steadying hand on the ceiling to try and halt the violent swinging.

Alex entered with the ship's surgeon and frowned seeing the rounded canvas of the hammock, as he had expected her to be up.

"Isaac, 'tis time to remove the major's stitches," stated the doctor briskly.

Cameron, not bothering to sit, rolled up the wide sleeve of her tunic and thrust her arm over the side.

"Down you come, lad, I'll make a botch of it with that wild swinging."

Cameron withdrew her arm and made no motion to comply. She'd not stand at a disadvantage with the two men towering above her, making her feel puny and vulnerable. She gave a gasp of surprise as Alex placed a strong, broad hand under the hammock and pitched her out, catching her with his other arm.

"It will be the merest pinprick after the sewing, I assure you," comforted the surgeon, assuming that her recalcitrance was due to fear.

Alex sighed with relief seeing that she was fully clothed and proceeded to dump her like a sack of potatoes onto his bunk.

"He's very pale," frowned the doctor, feeling her head. "Not feverish, though."

Alex frowned also at Cameron's wan looks. Her usual berry-brown face was white and drawn, though the emerald eyes flashed with fire at the surgeon's implication that she was afraid.

"Has he been out into the sea air?"

"I thought it better to confine him this last fortnight, not knowing what fool prank he'd get into his willful head," responded Alex.

"Maybe that's all it is, then, but it also appears that he has lost weight. Is he eating?"

"Some, but he leaves most."

" 'Tis no wonder with all the ship's larder holds," returned the doctor, bending over and concentrating on removing the black stitching in Cameron's flesh. "Well, 'tis nothing that some sun, fresh air and fish won't cure. There, that weren't so bad, was it lad?" he said, ruffling the ebony curls and straightening. She stared at him sullenly, refusing to look at her arm.

" 'Tis said he's mute and yet he hears. The general has spoken of this lad at great length. Sometimes in infancy high fevers cause a child not to speak, but usually 'tis because he canna hear. I must speak to the father, Abraham, and see what befell this young fellow. It intrigues me," chattered the good-natured surgeon, stowing his paraphernalia into his black leather bag and taking his leave.

Cameron kept her eyes on the closed door, knowing Alex's eyes were on her and wishing only that he leave. He walked into her range of vision and stood with his hand on the door. She turned her gaze to the porthole, then quickly to the washstand as the chipped paint on the bolts revealed what she had been about. She heard him move across the cabin and swear beneath his breath. She kept her face averted, knowing well that he had found out her handiwork. All those days and her minor triumph had been one loose bolt. The minutes passed, tension increasing, yet no words were said as Alex stared at his wife's profile. He was appalled at her pallor and furious with himself for not noticing it before. Two weeks had passed since he had last laid eyes on her face, even though they had been sleeping in the same room. She had obviously avoided him, and he had been grateful at the lack of temptation, remembering the icy scorn mirrored in her eyes as they had lain coupled together. He felt a sharp pain at the recollection and felt used and abused. His anger surged. A man was at his most vulnerable when his manhood lost its hardness and lay limply nestled inside a woman's warmth, he fumed. And she knew so, he concluded furiously, wondering whether, with all his other troubles, he was also impotent.

"The door is open," he stated harshly and left.

Cameron listened to his receding steps before turning to stare at the half-open portal. She felt almost afraid of the freedom that beckoned her after weeks of confinement and a vast, aching hollowness engulfed her at the sight of open space. She shook her head and gingerly approached the door, peering out along the long dim corridor to the stairs that were flooded with light from the sun that beat down on deck.

Tor barked encouragingly and pranced toward the stairway. Omen, still with its leg splinted, landed heavily on Cameron's shoulder as she hesitatingly ventured down the dim expanse. Why was she so afraid? she wondered as her heart pounded. She felt like a mole she'd seen once who emerged from the dark depth of the earth and sat, stunned and amazed, before groping this way and that and hurriedly returning back into the darkness from whence it came.

The hot, blinding sun beat down on her as she, anxious to see Torquod, furtively crept onto the curiously still deck and made her way to where the horses were stabled. Goliath watched her embrace the listless stallion, who whinnied gently and tossed his head in welcome. He had been worrying about the proud horse, who had seemed to pine for his young mistress, and now hoped the animal's flagging spirit would revive and see him safely through the long voyage.

"Oh, if you only had the great wings of Pegasus in the myths, we could fly from this hell in the midst of the water," crooned Cameron softly in Torquod's ear.

"He can talk, I heard him!" cried the old groom, the ever-present straw bobbing excitedly from his puckered mouth.

" 'Twas meaningless sounds," intervened Goliath, stepping from the shadows.

"I heard him distinctly say, 'Fly to hell'!" insisted the old bandy-legged man vehemently.

"So did I," joined in one of the large louts who couldn't possibly have heard a word.

"He's from the devil hisself!" screeched the groom through the hatch to the curious seamen, who thronged on the deck looking down. "With my own two ears I heard him say to that black beast that they would fly to hell. Told you he should have been put overboard with his bird of death and devil-dog!"

"Has been four days now without a wind. We have a jinx on board!" yelled a sailor, and Cameron realized the unearthly silence had not been from being locked below but that the sails hung deflated and dead without a breeze to charge them.

The crowd grew larger as the crew stopped their jobs and clustered, muttering in low, angry tones. The volume increased to a roar as they blamed the storm and the idle sea on the black-haired changeling and his companions.

Alex and the general stared with consternation at the rumbling crowd as orders were barked from the bridge for them to return to work, but the angry mass stood immovable, as one, staring down into the bowels of the boat.

" 'Tis a mutiny, you think, at no wind and the meager food supply?" asked the gaunt old man as a shot was fired over the heads of the seamen.

"I hope that is all," returned Alex.

"That is all!" ejaculated General Ramsbotham. "Is that not enough?"

"The surgeon pronounced the boy Isaac well today," informed Alex tersely, drawing his saber and lithely leaping down to the deck and advancing on the furious mob.

Cameron stared up through the hatch at the angry faces silhouetted against the bright sky. Her feet squelched through the fetid manure of the dark stable, and she looked around for a place to hide, only to see more threatening shapes loom out of the shadows, their hostile eyes fixed unwaveringly on her. The low rumble of voices built to a roar, and she backed away, appalled by the undisguised hatred she heard and felt. Her head throbbed as the horses, unnerved by the impending violence, kicked and screamed. Everything became a loud vortex of confusion as the voices built to a roar and shots were fired. She was unaware of Alex and Goliath battling their way through to her. The sharp sounds of metal cracking against metal as swords were brought into play were lost in the thunderous, whirling madness that spun her head and senses as she crouched, frozen with fear and rooted in the suffocating stench between Torquod's forelegs. She was picked up roughly, and the pain of her nearly crushed ribs brought some awareness as all around her the scene was etched with nightmarish clarity. She felt herself thrown upward, and her head broke out of the close gloom into the bright sunlight, where clawed hands reached to grab, curled lips spat hatred, and eyes contorted with malice. She was unaware of who carried her, for she was mesmerized by the distorted faces of the mob. There was a bright flash, and a blade caught Alex's stolid face. The blood spurted vividly in the bright sunlight, and mercifully Cameron lost consciousness.

Once more Cameron found herself confined in the suffocating heat of Alex's cabin. She watched dispassionately as he removed his manicure case, her dirk, and any other object that could be used as a tool to pry open and unscrew the porthole bolts. She stared at his set face, noting that new, cynical lines were etched, and felt remorse at the jagged cut that ran from one golden eyebrow to his jaw. A fraction of an inch closer, and he would have been blinded, she thought, and turned away so that her tear-filled eyes would not be noted. Alex, Goliath, and the old general had battled their way through the threatening mob to save her as she huddled beneath Torquod's forelegs. She had been carried under Goliath's massive left arm so tightly that she thought her ribs would crack, but she had never been so glad to be so brutally handled, for she had been unable to close her eyes, mesmerized as she was by the venomous hatred directed at her by the seamen. Why did she generate such hatred and hostility? she wondered. It had been the same since childhood, as far back as she remembered, when the people of Durness would taunt her and shepherd their children away, warning them never to look straight into her eyes. Even Colonel Beddington and Fiona thought her a witch. At the thought of Fiona, Cameron felt a lessening of her sympathy to Alex, remembering how he'd dared disobey orders and had taken a boat over the Forth to Edinburgh to be with her. He'd never stood up to Beddington for his own wife, not even when she'd been beaten and nearly raped by the Englishman, she fervently reminded herself. Her blood boiled, and she wondered at herself for even caring whether Alex was hurt or not in her defense. He wouldn't have bothered but for the old general, she raged inwardly, remembering the orders addressed to Alex that he keep her safe or he'd be answerable. Why did the old general care? Why did her resolve keep softening? she wondered as she mentally made a list of all the injustices

Alex had subjected her to, the largest being her own
heritage. Charles Stuart was her father, she repeated to
herself, puzzled that she felt none of the rejoicing she
should expect to feel. A year ago the knowledge would
have fired her blood. Why didn't it now? Why hadn't she
sought him out? Surely one's own father would protect
one? But as she thought about it, she sadly realized that
that was very improbable from all she had pieced together.
What if her own twin didn't want her? came the paralyzing
thought. Instead of thrusting the idea away in her usual
manner, she forced herself to face the very real possibility.
After all, how could she trust any man? Alex, for whom
she had broken down all her defenses, had lied and tricked
her. She had opened her heart, giving of herself until
she felt she couldn't exist without him, and for what?
Cameron firmly resolved never to trust anyone again, even
her own twin. She'd find him but would stand alone,
needing no one.

Alex kept his eyes on Cameron as he sat allowing the
surgeon to sew up his face. " 'Tis a regular sewing circle
in this cabin," the doctor laughed, cutting the thread and
standing back to survey his work. "Have a look in the
glass, Major. You'll find my dainty stitches preferable to
your clumsy ones. All right, lad, let's see if you suffered
damage to your wound."

Cameron docilely rolled up her sleeve.

" 'Tis a wonder you don't boil to death in that woolen
tunic in this heat," remarked the surgeon, running a practiced eye over the still-angry scar on Cameron's arm. " 'Tis
no social society except for uniformed officers of the
crown. You'd be more comfortable and less inclined to
rashes if you stripped down to your breeches." His sharp
eyes noticed Cameron's tension, and he leaned over further
as though to examine the healing wound yet watched the
small hand that crept up to her neck to pull the fabric
tightly together. He whistled soundlessly in amazement,
noting the soft shape of her breasts as she pulled the
fabric too tightly in her nervousness. Cameron stared up
into his startled but kind eyes and followed his gaze. She
glanced at Alex to see if he had noticed, but he was
staring moodily over the still sea. She shook her head

beseechingly at the doctor, silently begging him not to divulge her secret. There was a pause, and the good-humored man then nodded slowly.

Orders echoed from topside for the crew to assemble to witness the floggings of the men who had taken arms against the officers of the king. Cameron tensed at the whistling sound of the whip as it spun through the air, and she recoiled at the crack when it met living flesh.

"I shall take the lad to the infirmary to clean his wound. I have not the right bottle here," said the surgeon, noting her pallor and frantic eyes at hearing the punishment administered. Alex turned.

"He shall take the bird and hound and will be safe wie me," reassured the doctor.

"I think you'll be having your hands full shortly, and the boy can wait until evening, when the animosity has calmed a bit," stated Alex stiffly, finding it painful to talk.

"As you wish. 'Tis a barbaric custom to flog a man until he falls, but discipline must be maintained, I suppose," agreed the doctor. "Our particular captain prolongs the torment, leaving the men to remain tied until sunset, so 'tis then my hands will be full and the infirmary crowded with those you wish the boy to avoid."

Alex stared at the kindly man skeptically and, seeing nothing but warmth and professional concern, he nodded and waved his hand as a signal for them to go.

Once there, Cameron watched the doctor lock the door of the infirmary behind them. For a moment he didn't speak but stared speculatively at the seeming child with the raven on one shoulder and the young hound that sat panting in the still, hot air, by his side. He didn't quite know how to proceed. Even though he recognized that the feisty lad was female, his experienced eye saw that she was like a young wild animal, poised and tensed for flight.

"It has been near a month since your bird broke its leg. Will you permit my examination?" he asked gently.

Without taking her eyes from the kindly face, Cameron raised her hand and offered it to the raven, who unhesitatingly stepped upon it. Setting the bird on the runged back of a chair, she unwound the cloth from the splint.

"Will it permit me to touch its leg?"

Cameron nodded and stroked the glossy black head as the surgeon gingerly reached out to the bird, conscious of the large, sharp beak that could tear flesh from any living animal. Relaxing as he saw the bird controlled, he felt the length of the scaly leg.

" 'Twas a clean break, and you aligned the bones to a tee. A good job. I have need of such skill as yours," he remarked, stepping back and smiling at her. "The leg is completely healed." Almost as if the great bird understood, it hopped to the floor and did a comical but triumphant dance. The surgeon laughed heartily and stopped short as he heard a peel of bright merriment issue from the up-to-then-silent lips of Cameron. A clear, bubbling laugh like spring water rippling over the pebbles of the streams in his beloved Highlands.

"Och, look!" she exclaimed as the large bird strutted.

"You can speak, child," he said gruffly, and she turned, her eyes mirroring her alarm. "Hush, you have nothing to fear from me. 'Tis for the best dressing as a lad stranded aboard this vessel full of lusty men. I understand 'tis the best protection. I'll not betray your secret. My name is Will McAllister. And yours?" he asked extending a large hand. "Surely not Isaac?"

Cameron grasped his proffered hand but did not answer.

"Be as you want. If you would rather not converse with me, 'tis probably safer, as who knows what curious ears are oft pressed to doors. I have some clothes that are more suitable for this heat and will keep hidden what you would not wish to reveal," he said gently.

Cameron stood silently watching the man kneel before a large trunk. The smell of camphor rose from the garments he reverently picked up. She frowned, recognizing dresses neatly folded.

"These belonged to my wife and daughter, and underneath are my son Douglas's clothes. Some say I'm a sentimental fool for keeping them, and maybe I am, but to throw them from me would be like losing the last vestige of their presence."

"They are dead?" whispered Cameron.

"Aye," answered the man sadly, not betraying his surprise and joy at hearing her voice. "Taken from me by the pox, and there I was a doctor unable to save my own. We left Inverness bound for the promise of the New World, and they never reached it. Somewhere under this vast ocean is their resting-place, and so I pay tribute to their graves by constantly crossing and recrossing them, making my home nowhere, as there is no home without them."

Cameron's pity welled for the kneeling surgeon, but she could find no adequate words with which to comfort him. He gave a burst of embarrassed laughter and stood, holding some neatly folded garments.

"I canna take your son's clothes."

"He needs no clothes where he is now," answered the doctor, delighting in her familiar, lilting Highland brogue but still making no comment for fear she'd return to her muteness. Cameron reached out and took the proffered garments.

"I thank you," she said softly.

"And I thank you for trusting me," returned the kindly man. Silently they returned to Alex's cabin with the dog and raven. Alex was stretched across the bunk, sleeping soundly, and didn't stir when a hand was laid on his brow to ascertain whether he was feverish.

" 'Tis just exhaustion. I doubt many have had a decent night's sleep in this oppressive heat," whispered the doctor, quietly tiptoeing to the door. "Bolt the door behind me, as I must get back to tend the lashed backs that soon will be presented to me."

He strode back to the infirmary, wondering how it was possible for Major Sinclair to live in such close contact with the young elfin lass without being aware of her gender.

Cameron hastily dressed in the lighter, more comfortable clothes of the doctor's dead son. There was an eerie silence, broken by just the occasional shuffling of feet or rent violently for a minute by an anguished scream as seawater was dashed against a lacerated back, the salt biting sharply into the abused flesh. Cameron shivered, feeling sick and responsible. If it hadn't been for her presence, those men would not have been so cruelly punished. She stood at the porthole staring across the molten sea that mirrored the late afternoon sun on its flat, unmoving surface. She thought of the kindly doctor and remembered his neatly laid-out instruments. Alex had removed her knife and all tools with which to pry. She acknowledged the futility of further work on the porthole and yet felt defenseless without a weapon. She debated with herself whether to steal back to the infirmary and help herself to several of the shiny, sharp-looking knives, but the sounds in the corridor of doors opening and closing deterred her.

She turned and stared at Alex. He was deeply asleep, and his cynical facial lines had softened so that he appeared almost boylike. She sneered, remembering his harsh and cruel disposition as she quietly searched his bags and desk, recovering two daggers, both her own. One had been used to kill Captain Loving, she remembered. Fergus, after cleaning that one, had obviously given it to Alex. They were a pair of matched blades, the hilts embossed and the steel wrought with intricate designs. She had always possessed them, like her horse, Torquod, and hound, Torquil, and Alex had no right to remove them from her, she raged bitterly as she tucked one down the bandage on her left forearm and hid the other behind the washstand.

Goliath stood at the rail watching the sun set until it seemed to descend slowly into the water and bleed, the blood thickening until the horizon was a deep red bar. Behind him were the anguished groans of the beaten men, who were being cut down and dragged below. Wherever he looked, wherever he went, there was bloodshed, he thought bitterly, from the tiny isle of his birth, Rona, to the vast wilderness of the New World. And there it was all reflected and exhibited in the setting of the sun. He cast his philosophizing aside and tried to concentrate on the immediate problem of Cameron. There was no way she could be safely brought into harbor in Boston with such a superstitious crew—if they ever got to Boston, he thought savagely. Here they were, as though soldered to the still, metallic ocean. No movement, not the merest whisper of a breeze. It was uncanny, as though time stood still, and they were suspended in a hellish, burning limbo. A limping footstep neared, and he turned as the old general approached him.

"Your son and Major Sinclair seem little the worse for wear. How are you?"

"Fine, sir."

"You acquitted yourself well, Abraham, and after much thinking I have decided to enlist you as one of my scouts. You move lithely and quickly for one of such large size," stated the old man. Goliath listened quietly, without comment, as the general informed him of his plan to infiltrate the Indian encampments surrounding Fort Detroit. He had lived with Pontiac and the Ottawas on the Maumee River, and it was with wry amusement and some consternation that he heard the offer of fighting for the king against the people he had learned to coexist with.

"I feel I can trust you, MacLeod," continued the general. "There is a certain young savage who rides at the left hand of Pontiac, like his son, and he might well be except for his unnatural green eyes." The old man stopped and gazed piercingly at Goliath, waiting for him to make surprised comment.

"Unnatural green eyes?" intoned Goliath slowly, not being an accomplished actor but knowing that some reaction was expected.

"And hair as black as the night."

"Like my son?" rumbled Goliath.

"Just so. The young savage Méron is taller and older than Isaac, but the resemblance is amazing."

Goliath waited for the old campaigner to continue and, as the silence lengthened, knew he was expected once more to make comment.

"We have no relatives that I know of in the north. Many of our clan sailed to the Carolinas, and they swore allegiance to the English king. I can also vouch that there is none that I know of who'd breed with a red man," he returned innocently.

"That is not my point, MacLeod. 'Tis obviously a miraculous coincidence of nature that can be turned to our advantage," said Ramsbotham excitedly.

"Oh?" returned Goliath blankly. "How?"

"Oh, those savages are a pagan suspicious lot, for all

their cunning, but I have a brilliant, absolutely ingenious plan in which your young son can be of service to his king and country. Be a hero for England."

Many humorous thoughts ran through Goliath's head at the irony of the general's words, but he held himself in check, doing the best he knew how to appear suitably proud and in awe of such an opportunity as he hoped to hear the specifics of the plan. But the wily old man was not as openmouthed as Goliath expected. Both men gazed silently across the dark, still ocean to the horizon, which was delineated by the merest blood-red line. The stillness was almost supernatural, and Goliath felt his spine quiver, knowing that if no wind filled the sails soon, there would be more violence. He could sense its inexorable building. The thick, suffocating night air was stretched and charged. It would be turned once again against the one who was different, enigmatic, and mysterious—Cameron—but this time with even more hatred and vehemence. He had to get her off the vessel.

He thought back to Méron as a small boy. He remembered clearly the first time he had held the child. He had gone with Duncan Fraser to Olaron Sainte-Marie to a secluded valley high in the Pyrenees. He had stared in awe at the perfection of the whitewashed convent and gardens dwarfed by the harsh, towering peaks of the mountains. It had seemed like Paradise, and he'd wondered at Duncan's fervent desire to remove the two beautiful, vivacious children from such an Eden. The old Highlander's hatred of Catholics blinded him to the mellow love and gentleness that flowed from the nuns. He had ranted about silken cords that bind, cutting off all feeling, until a living heart, spirit, and soul were poisoned and suffocated. "They shall be free . . . totally free of such restraints and guilts!" raged Duncan Fraser.

Goliath smiled ironically in the darkness, realizing that the Highlander's very philosophy also had its deadly silken cords. He let his mind return to the island of North Rona, where he had left the raven-haired twins and returned to his home on Rona, not to see them for six years. Later he had marveled at the eight-year-old children, burned berry-brown by the wind and the sun, able to run, swim, and climb like natural animals. He had been summoned by Fraser to return to North Rona and, on arriving, he felt incredible pain at the realization that he was to be an instrument of severing the precious connection between the two children. He laughed sadly in the darkness and rubbed his forearm that still bore the crescent scars of the boy twin's strong teeth. He had sailed away, and his blood had chilled at the anguished keening and hollow agony that wailed with the screeching circling gulls. The young lad had led him a merry chase, but with strength and time Goliath had managed to gain his trust. There was still part of the boy that was unapproachable, kept locked away and private, preferring the company of the elements and animals to that of man.

The old general cleared his throat, breaking through the strands of time, and Goliath started at being brought so suddenly back to the present predicament.

"The captain feels 'tis best to head for Acadia or Nova Scotia for supplies before attempting to land in Boston," informed Ramsbotham.

"If there's a wind," responded Goliath, once more smiling at the ironies of life. Of all places, Acadia or Nova Scotia—those distant spots of land to which Scots had run, hoping to build a new life away from the English, only to be plucked from the earth they had worked and tilled to be sold as bonded slaves to the English colonies so that they would not ally themselves with the French.

"Yes, if there is ever a wind," replied the old man wearily. " 'Tis time to sleep, even though 'tis impossible in this stifling heat. Good night, MacLeod, think on what I've said."

"Yes, sir."

Goliath watched the tall, gaunt shape limp stiffly away in the dark humidity and sighed deeply. Irony or no irony, it would be fortuitous if the vessel did dock in Nova Scotia or Acadia for supplies. Usually it would take several days, allowing the crew to drink and wench so that they'd settle down more productively once again under sail. The horses would be brought ashore for exercise, and escape with Cameron would be easier if she was with her hound and horse.

"Blow you winds, blow," he hissed, even more determined to flee the ship with Cameron, despite his promise to Alex, as it seemed obvious to him that General Ramsbotham meant to pit one twin against the other.

CHAPTER TWENTY-TWO

Cameron lay half asleep in the hammock watching dawn lighten the dark to a monotonous gray. Everything seemed as suspended as she was. No time, no motion, no color, just an eerie limbo. Disturbing remembrances shattered her drowsy half awareness. The past seven days of no wind had seemed to create a persistent drone, but she realized that momentum had actually been gathering as a deadly friction increased. Wherever she went on board, no matter how unobtrusively, she felt watched by malicious eyes. At first she thought her pent-up state had made her feel too self-conscious, but as she noted Tor's hackles raised and sleek young body tense, she realized that she was indeed being watched by many angry, silent people. She confined herself to the cabin by day and prowled the deck restlessly at night, but even that seemed dangerous. She shivered as she remembered the men standing in the shadows and Omen's warning caw before it had flown at the menacing shapes and they had run, damning and swearing at her.

Cameron opened her eyes fully and stared dismally out at the black sea, wishing she could pull a numbing cover over her misery.

"I'm dying," she whispered.

Alex stared at the hammock, his ears hearing Cameron's quiet statement. He didn't move but just let the whispered word penetrate deeply into his own despondency. Part of him wanted to comfort and reassure her, but he thrust that urge away purposefully and willed himself back to sleep. His dreams were haunted by a small, piquant face, vivacious and brimming with sensual mischief, that slowly lost color and vibrancy. Its vital glow waned until a drawn, masklike face regarded him, the green eyes fading as they accused. He reached out to comfort and found his hands full of dust. He awoke and sat up with a hoarse cry, blinking his eyes at the sharp, flickering light that moved rhythmically back and forth. He remained motionless, his brow furrowed, not realizing what the swinging hammock and lurching floor denoted. The reflection of the waves flooded the cabin in measured flashes as the vessel tore through the water, her sails full-blown. Alex laughed aloud, the tight lines of his face softening. He pulled on his breeches and, forgetting his military position, left the cabin barefooted and bare-chested to get topside and feel the healing wind on his flesh.

Topside, Cameron stood high up on the mast, her hair streaming, her body straining with the enormous sails that were filled to sating. She stared ahead at the ornately carved prow that cut through the shimmering water purposefully. Below, the crew sang joyfully, the lines of fear and hatred erased, blown away by the precious sea breezes that propelled them to the New World. Alex watched Cameron as the brisk, almost lacerating salt air scrubbed and scoured his golden torso clean of the gray mood that had shrouded him.

"Let's hope 'tis clear sailing from now on," growled a voice in his ear. Alex turned to Goliath, who watched the small figure high above them.

"Isn't it wonderful?" piped Jemmy's voice excitedly as she raced across the deck, followed by the stiff, limping stride of the old general. Alex hardly recognized the small, shy girl. She was golden and freckled from the sun, her shorn red hair haloed around her wide-eyed, merry face. All she wore were white cabin-boy trews, cut just below the knees. He stared at the flat, bony chest in consternation before he realized that all breasts appeared the same before maturation. For a moment he imagined Cameron similarly attired, and the exultant madness all around that was stirred by the driving wind was whipped to fever pitch. He threw his head back and, despite the stiffness in his cheek caused by the long, jagged wound, he laughed rejoicingly for a moment forgetting the troubles of his home, wife, possible murder charge, and having to fight for the English. Taking Jemmy's small freckled hands in his, he spun her around, and they danced a jig, accompanied by a seaman's pipe and several burly men, who joined their rough voices in song.

The old general stood apart, watching the tall, lithe, golden man. He noted the sinews and muscles that rippled across the broad shoulders and down to the narrow waist and nodded with satisfaction, a small smile of contentment on his gaunt face. The young man was like a Greek god, he observed, well formed, with none of the softening of laziness and debauchery to weaken. He had chosen well. Young Sinclair would be able to endure the rigors of wilderness life. He watched the red-haired child, whose face was flushed with happiness and exertion, and his expression softened. He had become very fond of the little imp who had kept his loneliness at bay with his merry chatter. Here was the family he had never had time to form. If only Jemmy was a girl, it would be ideal, he mused. The child had a feyness about him more suited to females, which he unfortunately saw as a weakness in a male, no matter how young.

Cameron stared down at the festive scene below her, as hands clapped and feet stomped in time with the music and dancers as Jemmy was whirled from one arm to the next. Her eyes were pinned to the tall, golden figure of Alex. She had never seen him so free and uninhibited, she thought. Except in bed with her, she added to herself. Who was he really? she wondered, her brows furrowed, her eyes not leaving the shining, smiling man who sang and laughed and lithely danced as though he had not a care in the world. The face and manner he had shown to her was very different from what she gazed upon now. Where was the autocratic, enigmatic, tightly controlled Alexander Sinclair that she knew? Where was that set, chiseled face that betrayed nothing of what he was feeling? Cameron agilely climbed to a lower place on the mast to get a better view of the joyful stranger. She straddled a cross-boom, feeling none of the pervading happiness that billowed with the wind filling the sails, as she instinctively knew not to leap down and join in the dancing and singing. For a moment she had wanted to, and then doubts assailed her, and she imagined what might happen. She saw her presence like a dark cloud dousing the celebrations, each person becoming rigid and fixing her with a hateful eye and Alex losing his golden joy, the fluidity of his body draining until he became the cold, arrogant man of the previous months. Cameron's shoulders hunched as though she bore the weight and responsibility of the entire ship.

Alex, out of breath but still laughing, leaned against a gunwale. He stared up at the small, crouched figure and, noting the hunched shoulders and pained expression, his open smile faded until his white teeth were hidden behind the tight line of his lips. He watched Cameron turn from him and quickly climb higher and higher until she was lost from his view among the full-straining sails. He stood still, his heart beating painfully in his chest, as the joyful noise of the celebration became harsh and jeering. God damn her, he raged, why did her presence have such an effect on him? Why couldn't she grab happiness where it was? The wind was blowing, the animosity toward her had died down, why couldn't she rejoice? All she could do was huddle like a wounded bird. Well, she'd not dampen his spirit; she'd not have such a hold on his life. Her pain would no longer sear into him like a hot knife, he resolved, as he purposefully leaped back into the dancing throng, determined to forget her. But the previous golden release had been soured, and he knew that his laughter was forced. The captain beamed contentedly from the bridge and ordered a keg of rum to be opened for the soldiers and his commanding officers, and Alex took liberally of the offered spirits to boost his sagging one.

Cameron climbed until she could get no higher, but even the distance and the roar of the wind in the sails didn't drown out the ribald revelry below as the captain ordered yet another barrel of rum to be drained for the crew. Cameron wondered cynically who was left sober enough to sail the vessel, for the wind celebration continued well into the night as each watch was relieved and each duty roster joined in. Laughter and drunken singing ran through the darkness as she quietly shinned down the rigging and made her way belowdecks to the cabin, determined to bundle her few possessions together and make her home in one of the tarpaulined longboats that were lashed to the outer sides of the gunwales. She had noted Alex on deck liberally partaking of the proffered rum and hoped he would remain until she had finished.

As she entered the cabin, her nostrils filled with the scent of him, and she tried to quell the traitorous feelings that surfaced. She purposefully avoided looking at the bed and his uniform that hung, seeming to mock her, as she busied herself rolling up her few belongings. She felt watched and turned to see Alex leaning nonchalantly against the doorway with what appeared to be a sneer on his face. She froze in his presence, her pulses hammering, her mouth dry, and her throat constricted, as she waited for him to stop her. The silence was unbearable but was finally broken by his harsh laughter.

"Before you leave my bed and board, there's something I must prove to myself," he said carefully, as though measuring his words, as he purposefully bolted the door and strode unsteadily toward her. Cameron backed away, realizing he was drunk.

"Prove what?" she asked apprehensively, but Alex didn't answer as he concentrated on putting one foot in front of the other until Cameron was pinned against the wall and his hot, liquored breath suffocated her.

"You are my wife," he stated, trying to separate the words so they didn't slur and nearly toppling down on her as he bent over to kiss her mouth. Cameron instinctively knew what he was referring to, and part of her wanted to assure him that he wasn't impotent. Yet the thought of making love to this drunken, angry man repulsed her. Her indecision kept her rooted to the spot, unable to run or fight off the arms that squeezed her painfully as he half-carried her to the bunk. She lay on the blankets where she had been flung, making no effort to disrobe as he tore at his own garments. She just watched him sadly, as though from a great distance.

Cameron's hollow stare pierced Alex's stupor, causing his anger to rise. The urgency he had felt in his loins diminished. Once again it seemed she had robbed him of his virility with her hurt, pathetic look. He plucked her roughly from the bed and deposited her on her feet, giving her a push that caused her to stagger against the door. He threw her pitiful bundle of belongings after her.

"Och, an' dinna forget this wee toy," he mocked savagely, reaching behind the washstand for the dirk she had hidden from him and throwing it so that it pierced the wooden floor by her bare foot and quivered. Cameron had no way of knowing that the rash action had sobered Alex like a plunge into ice water. He stared in sick horror, seeing the fraction of an inch between the razorsharp blade and the small brown toe. All Cameron saw were the harsh, hating lines that set his face instead of the golden, happy, carefree countenance she had seen that afternoon. Her eyes mirrored her pain and concern for a brief flash before she contemptuously wrenched her knife from the wood and stowed it efficiently in her waistband.

Alex's rage ignited with his guilt, and he grabbed her shoulders and turned her to face him. Cameron forced herself to glare at him without flinching, trying to hold onto her dignity as she hung suspended, her feet dangling. He breathed heavily through flared nostrils, and she felt the spurts of hot, angry air against her cheeks as his flashing amber eyes seemed to sear into her brain. Her silence goaded Alex. He was sick of holding himself in check, sick of being constantly on guard, sick of behaving in a controlled manner while she behaved wildly, indulging every impulse. His life stood in ruins. Everything he had fought so hard to retain, swallowing nationalism and pride in the process, had been wrenched from him, and now he fled to an alien, unwelcoming land to do the same once again. He was a fugitive, on the run, as his own father had been after the Battle of Culloden Moor. For all he knew, at the end of this torturous endless voyage they were waiting to arrest and execute him for the murder of Colonel Beddington as soon as he set foot on shore. A committee of witch-hunters also could be waiting to throw both of them into the nearest jail or pyre. His furious stream of thoughts joined with the rum, loosening his tongue.

"To think I killed for you! Sacrificed my home, land, and friends for you!" he hissed into the face that seemed to regard him with loathing. Cameron stared at him with amazement. Killed for her? she puzzled as she was flung back onto the bunk.

"And ran like a coward, leaving faithful, appreciative, priceless people to face the authorities in my stead . . . and for what?" he ranted viciously, enjoying the release. "To save your miserable neck from officers of the church and crown who would burn or stone you for being a witch. Well, by God, I think they are right. You manage to entangle me, weave your spells luring me into this damnable predicament, robbing me of pride and manhood, but no more, no more! Get out!" he roared, opening the door, unable to allow her hurt bewilderment to penetrate his resolve. "You'll not fool me with your air of hurt child anymore. You are no child. You've proven that in many ways."

Cameron sat in shock, unable to move. Alex approached her menacingly, and Tor's hackles rose. He growled deeply in his throat, causing the girl to reach for her knife instinctively. Alex stopped, aware that he was losing control of himself. It was the first time Tor had ever bared teeth to him. He stood still while sanity took over, almost instantly appalled at the violent invective he had hurled at Cameron.

He remained motionless long after the door had closed behind her and then sat on his bunk, burying his head in his hands.

Cameron had many sleepless nights in the longboat as she stared up at the stars, which surprisingly seemed the same despite her location and all that had happened to her. Whom had she made Alex kill? She knew how precious Glen Aucht and its people were to him, and yet somehow she had robbed him of his ancestral home, causing him to run like a coward. It was all her fault, no wonder he hated her. No wonder he could not be relaxed and happy in her company. No wonder his face closed and became harsh and frightening. As the long days and nights passed, Cameron used Alex's words like an armor, turning them to her advantage. She was able to admit that she loved him and so therefore would protect him by relieving him of her presence. She had plenty of time to reflect upon the nearly sixteen years of her life and, after examining her encounters with most people, decided she had an adverse effect on everyone. She would keep to herself.

She thought of Mackie and Fergus, who had so briefly become the loving parents she never had. They had loved Alex first, from birth, and now because of her he might never see them again. Neither would she, she thought, with uncharacteristic self-pity. The rebellious side of her noture rose as she struggled with her feelings. Was it her fault the English occupied Glen Aucht? She had to admit that it was, however unmeaning or indirectly. It probably had to do with her father, Charles Stuart, Pretender to the Scottish throne, and her guardian, Duncan Fraser . . . and also Lady Fiona Hurst's relationship with Alex. Once again she realized that Alex had loved Fiona first and that it had been Cameron's intrusion that had soured the union. But she hadn't willingly come south with Alex, she fumed. She had been dragged from her solitary wildness on Cape Wrath, kicking and fighting the whole way. Why couldn't she have been left alone where she hurt no one? From what she had gleaned and overheard, the New World was vast and wild, with ample space to hide . . . so vast and wild she'd never find her brother, came the unbidden fear.

One night, remembering Goliath's sly references, she climbed out of the longboat to seek the large man. She had no idea where to look first, but he loomed out of the shadows when Tor skittered around, wagging his heavy black tail in welcome. Unknown to Cameron, Goliath kept watch over her every night, and often the young hound curled beside him, sharing his supper and vigil.

Cameron was loath to break the silence, as she felt dwarfed next to the shadow of the huge man. She stared across the dark sea watching the mist, which danced for several minutes.

"Where is my brother?" she hissed abruptly.

Goliath weighted his answer before replying. "You are grown now and have chosen your man, so should you not leave childhood and brothers behind?"

"I did not choose, 'twas done for me," whispered Camerson hotly. "I choose to be with my own kind," she continued.

"It has been nigh on eight years, and maybe you've grown apart from your twin," responded Goliath gently.

"I would see him and judge for myself."

"Aye," he acknowledged. "But what of your husband?"

"I have none," stated Cameron firmly. "The little lust there was is cold between us."

" 'Twas surely more than a little lust," replied Goliath with a chuckle.

"Aye, maybe—but even of that I'm not sure. 'Tis a closed book now, and I have no wish to speak or think on it. I hear how vast the New World is . . . every living thing larger than at home . . . birds, trees, animals."

"You've been listening to the crew swapping tall stories?" laughed Goliath.

"Aye, are they true?"

"Aye, for the most part. What have you heard about the red man?" probed the man softly.

Cameron had heard many conflicting stories about the near-naked savages who painted their bodies and wore clothing made from the skins of animals and feathers of birds. It wasn't so much that the stories were conflicting, most of them being recollections of a strange bloodthirsty race, but that her mind had dwelled on the descriptions of their life-style. Although the stories had been told sneeringly and in derogatory terms, her eyes had lit up when she heard that they lived like animals with nature. She sensed that the warlike Indians were harmonious with natural things, and she didn't blame them for their hostile acts against the English, in fact she applauded them. However, she cringed inside remembering the yarns of scalpings and the tying up of live bodies under a blazing sun. She could understand killing in the heat of rage, but not cold, calculating torture.

"Is it true that they cut the hair and the scalp from the living?"

"Aye, 'tis a useful trick taught them by the French. Bounty hunters abound in all countries, and in the wilderness of the New World 'tis impractical to be burdened with a whole body, dead or alive. You must have seen reward posters saying, 'Wanted Dead or Alive?' responded Goliath.

"Aye, there were many for Duncan Fraser. He'd laugh over them saying a man seemed to gain more value with age. The price on his head was one hundred crowns."

"There it is in a nutshell . . . 'the price on his head' . . . the bounty for his scalp. 'Tis a gruesome thing, but white man and Indian do it alike. What else have you heard?" he probed.

"That they rape women and children before killing them, ofttimes slowly."

"Does that sound familiar?"

Cameron nodded, thinking of Colonel Beddington and his soldiers. "Why are you talking of the Indians when I asked about my brother?" she asked after a pause. Goliath didn't answer but took her small, upturned chin in his large hand and stared into her eyes. "Is he—?" His palm muffled her words as he looked anxiously around him. No matter what he felt for Cameron, the female counterpart of Méron, he'd not allow her question to be spoken aloud. His action answered her query, and she nodded mutely until he removed his hand and stared away from her into the darkness. He knew none were near enough to hear or the hound and raven would have given warning, and yet he'd take no chances with Méron's life.

"We'll reach land in a few days to take on supplies, and then we'll disappear into the shadows. I'll take you to him," whispered Goliath. "But no questions . . . no talk between us until we are away. No anxious or inquiring looks. You'll tend the horses and keep to your routine until 'tis time."

Cameron felt him leave but didn't turn. Excitement filled her and, unable to contain herself and knowing sleep would not claim her, she crept to the front of the vessel to spend the night mesmerized by the parting water.

For two days Cameron forced herself to contain the anticipation. Each night she was now aware of Goliath's large, shadowy bulk stealthily creeping toward her, but each time, he settled himself silently to keep vigil while she slept. She longed to ask him numerous questions but realized the wisdom in the man's orders not to speak to him. Up until this time playing the mute had been easy, but now she was bursting with curiosity and the constraint was painful. She docilely groomed Torquod and Galahad and raked at the fetid straw, which could no longer be replaced, but all the time her eyes had a wild sparkle. Alex watched her from a distance and, knowing her of old, wondered what schemes she was plotting. Her face was no longer drawn and wan but tanned and filled with suppressed excitement. Her shoulders were held proudly, her head up, her eyes defiant and confident. General Ramsbotham shrewdly watched Alex's preoccupation, noting the creased brow.

"He's healed well," he remarked as they watched the small, lithe figure, the ever-present raven and hound keeping her company.

"Aye, too well," growled Alex without thinking.

"Meaning what, Sinclair?"

"I think the lad smells the land breezes—"

"And may take it into his headstrong head to jump ship?" interrupted the old man, filled with panic that he might lose the master key to his plot to infiltrate Pontiac's camp.

"Aye," replied Alex tersely, wondering why the old man cared and then coldly reasoning that two pairs of watchful eyes were better than one.

"Why would he?" asked Ramsbotham.

"Maybe he's in trouble with the law?" improvised Alex.

"And the father also? I have approached Abraham MacLeod to be one of our party. Do you trust the man?"

"I hardly know him."

"Come, come, Major, I think you a good judge of men. Do you trust him?" demanded the old man.

"Do you, sir?" countered Alex evasively.

"I did until you stirred this hornets' nest in my head. Well, 'tis obvious that you think like father like son, so both bear watching. I'll not have that lad slip through my fingers now."

Cameron noted the profusion of birds that circled the ship and roosted on the rigging. Although there was still no sight of land, she felt the impending excitement sweep through the vessel. She anxiously checked Torquod's hooves, cleaning and waxing them to stop the perpetual, stinking dampness from rotting them. She massaged his muscles to make up for the lack of natural exercise. His head still hung listlessly, but he opened his nostrils, as though sensing the nearing land. She longed to whisper in his ears but, remembering the other time, refrained and concentrated on trying to share her thoughts silently. He regarded her with soulful dark eyes and nuzzled and butted her belly. It won't be long, Torquod, I promise you. Soon we will be free of this dismal prison on the water and racing across wild countryside with no one to contain us again, she told him in her head. He seemed to look at her wearily, one large eye drooping as though he knew it was impossible.

Despite her resolve to stay awake, Cameron fell sound asleep. A gleeful call from the watch in the crow's nest awoke her. "Land ahoy!" was echoed and reechoed. She sat up, rubbing the sleep from her eyes, and stared eagerly toward the approaching horizon. But to her disappointment she saw nothing but the interminable sea. She lithely shinned up the rigging, straining her eyes. A group of dolphins playfully leaped out of the water as though racing with the speeding vessel, but there was nothing else that resembled firm ground. She climbed higher until she spied what seemed to be a darkening cloud on the horizon. Was that land? She sat hours, her eyes fixed to the misty gray that seemed to play tricks, dancing and disappearing until she could make out a consistent, unbroken line. She was about to clamber down and search out Goliath, when she remembered his warning. She scanned the deck below her. A cold fear snaked through her. From her vantage point she could see the old general and two uniformed soldiers watching Goliath's every movement. Three pairs of eyes also were trained on her. She argued with herself, chiding herself for being fanciful, but as the day wore on and the coastline became sharper and more distinct, so did the scene below her. The three pairs of eyes trained on her did not waver, even when she changed position. Alex and the two soldiers simply moved until she was within their sights again. When Goliath went belowdecks, the old general motioned for his two aides to follow.

Hungry and thirsty, sweating from the sun that beat down mercilessly, Cameron slowly climbed down the rigging. Standing on the deck, she forced herself to measure her steps and appear nonchalant. How did she normally move, she wondered frantically, her body feeling disjointed and obtrusive. Alex and the men watching would certainly be aware that she knew she was being spied on. She patted Tor, who greeted her exuberantly, and she was glad for the moment to hide her face in his shining coat. Each step jarring her tense body, she made her way to the horses, where she tried to still her nervous excitement by steadily and methodically grooming the lifeless coats. Out of the corner of her eye she was aware of the watchers, and her arm felt heavy and unnatural as she brushed and brushed, all the time wondering frantically if Goliath was aware of how intently they were being observed.

Goliath was very cognizant of the fact. He whistled in his usual cheerful, relaxed manner and chatted good-naturedly with the crew as he inwardly prayed Cameron wouldn't panic and take it into her wild head to dive overboard. He was further disturbed at overhearing a conversation between two officers at the rail a few moments after land was first sighted. The men were grumbling at the captain's decision to anchor outside the harbor limits of Canso, Nova Scotia, denying all shore leave because he couldn't afford to lose more time. Apparently six longboats were to be sent ashore to obtain just enough supplies for the week it would take to sail to Boston. How to separate Cameron from her horse puzzled Goliath. They would have to make their escape while the ship lay at anchor, and yet Canso was much further north than he had anticipated. Maybe they should bide their time and disembark at Boston, to lose themselves among the crowds that thronged the docks and streets of that busy port. Conscious of how closely he was watched, Goliath surmised that Alex and the general were expecting a move to be made at Canso, so maybe it was better all around to disappoint them, hoping that they might be reassured and relax their vigilance. The vessel would probably sail along the Nova Scotian coast and then in a straight line as the crow flies to Boston, meaning that they would not be in sight of land for several days.

Unable to bear the constant eyes that followed her every move, Cameron retreated to her high perch above the busy deck. The coastline now loomed, thickening as they approached. She could discern what seemed like three distinct land masses, the cliffs sheer, reflecting the late afternoon sun. She quivered with anticipation, watching Goliath's large, recognizable form out of the corner of her eye, waiting for some sign. As darkness fell and a heavy dew beaded her clothes, she stared toward the twinkling lights onshore, hearing the groaning chains lower the longboats into the water. Maybe Goliath was looking for her, she thought frantically. She should be on deck, available to him. Cautiously she slid down a rigging rope close to the broad mast. The deck was a hive of activity, bobbing ship's lanterns spreading a warm glow. She slipped into the deep shadow under the bulwarks on the upper deck, where she had a good view of the busy scene as her eyes searched frantically for the giant man. There was no sign of Goliath, and her heart hammered in her chest as she realized she'd seen no sight of him for more than an hour. Maybe he had slipped off the ship already? she worried. Maybe he was in league with Alex, and it was all a plot to keep her from escape? The long voyage had sorely tried Cameron, teaching her patience as there had been no alternative, but this agonizing wait, with the smell of land filling her senses, tested her new virtue until she felt every fiber of her being straining. What if the large man had been lying to her about her brother? How weak and fickle she was, she berated herself. She had made herself promises of trusting no one, only to turn around and the next second break her very resolve. What did she know of the giant anyway except that he'd been part of Captain Loving's crew on the *Edna Rae*? What was she anyway but a stupid bairn to trust him, believing the stories he hinted at about her brother? What had he in fact told her about her twin? Nothing, just sly innuendos but nothing of substance that could prove he could take her to him, she concluded. She silently watched the longboats row steadily toward the mass of winking lights on the now dark outline of the coast. When the rhythmic chanting of the seamen and creaking of the oars had faded into the distant sea mist, a keg of rum was brought on deck to appease the crew, who yearned to go ashore to kick up their heels and wench away the two months of enforced denial. She would wait until they were drunk and swim toward land, she resolved, pushing away the nagging fears of being without Torquod and being swallowed up by the strange New World. She crouched, unaware of Alex's eyes trained on her hiding place, feeling nauseous. She swallowed hard, trying to suppress the violent retches of her stomach, and took deep breaths. She hadn't eaten or drunk all day and reasoned that that was the cause of her discomfiture as she tried to take her mind off her cold, clammy illness and concentrate on the revelry on the lower deck. Unable to keep down the rising bile, she staggered to her feet, intent on leaning over the gunwale to vomit into the sea. As she leaned, a hard hand gripped her, spinning her around. Cameron vomited all over Alex's breeches and boots, unaware and uncaring of who he was as the seizure gripped her. With an oath Alex spun her back to face the sea, lifting her so that she dangled helplessly and placing his broad, hard hand behind her neck to bend her head down. Cameron felt so wretched it didn't matter. All that existed in those minutes was the violent heaves that spasmed her belly.

"Always have to be different, don't you," he said sardonically. "Two months sailing the sea with no *mal de mer*, but the moment we reach port, up she chucks."

Cameron felt decidedly better despite the burning sourness in her mouth and nose. She stood beside him trying to appear dignified.

"I think it better you go below," he said tersely, keeping his hand firmly on the back of her neck and propelling her toward the stairway. Cameron debated fighting and fleetly racing to throw herself over the side but, seeing her proud hound loping by her side, knew she could not leave both Tor and Torquod behind.

Once more she was locked in the stifling humidity of Alex's cabin. She felt drained and defeated. She looked at the gently swinging hammock and averted her gaze quickly as the constant motion once more made her gall rise. She stretched herself full-length on the bunk and closed her eyes.

She awoke some time later to the low rumble of voices and a hand being placed on her brow. She sat up suddenly and opened her eyes, to be blinded by the sunlight that poured in through the open porthole. She heard the steady drumming of the waves against the hull and the creak of the yardarms as the wind billowed the sails. It was morning, and the ship had raised anchor. As the realization dawned, she stared into the faces of Alex and the ship's surgeon, panic flaring her nostrils and widening her emerald eyes. She had avoided the kindly doctor since the day he had given her his dead son's clothes, reasoning that if they were seen together, the animosity of the crew would be leveled against the man, and that would have been a poor reward for his keeping her secret and for his generosity. She leaped from the bunk and across the tilting floor to the porthole and stared at the rolling water, unable to see sight of land from the cabin near water level. The two men watched her leave through the open door, followed by the raven and hound, and did nothing to detain her.

"There is no fever. 'Twas probably the excitement of being near land or the stale and weeviled food we've been forced to eat," informed the doctor. "Well, 'tis said we dine on the fat of the land tonight," he added, making his exit. "Lamb and beef sides are hanging in the galley alongside of fresh fruits and vegetables, which will set us all to rights before long."

Alex remained, with a skeptical look on his face, for several minutes after the doctor had gone and then, without change of expression, strode up to the deck.

Cameron was perched in her usual high roost, savoring the cherries and peaches that she had liberally helped herself to from the baskets that lined the deck. She kept her eyes glued to the coastline that skimmed by on her right. She would be free, she said over and over again to herself. That night she would haul Tor over the side and then dive into the sea to swim beside him. She caught her breath as she spotted several gray seals fluidly weaving up and down through the waves. Nostalgic remembrances tore through her at the sight, joining with the salt spray and the gull's cries. This New World seemed like Cape Wrath, with the perilously steep, rugged cliffs and harsh scrub moor atop, the gray sea and seals, and the wheeling, lamenting white birds. Lost in the past for a moment, she stared hard at the skimming coast looking for a castle that seemed to thrust out of the rocks, but nothing denoting a man's hand met her straining eyes.

As the sun stood high overhead at noon an excited clanging joined the sonorous ship's bell, and the fragrant aroma of roasting meat filled Cameron's nostrils, causing her mouth to fill with saliva. Surprised, she stared down to the deck, where fires burned, and spitted carcasses were being turned and basted. Intent on the beckoning coast, she had been all but oblivious to the vessel's activity. Recollecting the watchful eyes of the previous day, she scanned the deck, but all eyes were hungrily and firmly fixed on the succulent meats that teased the senses. Cameron's belly growled in protest as she perched, watching generous slabs of meat cut off and devoured. Fingers and tongues were burned, and the juices ran down arms and chins. Enormous platters were carved and taken below to the officers' mess, from which loud cries of appreciation could be heard. The noises of smacking lips and grunts of satisfaction were torturous to Cameron, but still she sat waiting for the men to eat their fill.

She smiled as she observed Tor slowly sidling toward the hacked carcasses, drawn like a magnet to the fresh meat, a welcome change from the diet of rats. Above him circled Omen. The young hound made a sudden dash and closed his strong teeth around a dangling limb. With a great wrench he freed the leg, severing the few tendons, and quickly bore his prize away to a private spot. There was a halfhearted shout of objection but no action as the crew lazily sprawled, their bellies full to bursting. Omen perched upon a fresh-cut carcass and, ignoring the furious screams of consternation, savagely ripped at the still-bloody flesh. Cameron laughed aloud at the futile antics of several galleymen, who tried to shoo the large bird away. Terrified, they stood a few yards back waving aprons and dishrags.

But then a sharp report shattered Cameron's laughter. She froze in shock at the anguished scream of the raven as black feathers flew detached from its sleek body. Omen tried to fly but lost balance and fluttered to the deck. The raven managed to land on its talons. Cameron was relieved that it was still alive.

"Stand back and let me get clear aim at the devil bird!" yelled an excited voice.

"No!" screeched Cameron at the bandy-legged old groom, who still had the ever-present straw between his mean lips. She drew her dirk from her sleeve, and as the man aimed once more, threw it with all her might. "Fly, Omen, fly," she yelled at the top of her lungs, ignoring the bellows of pain from the groom, who was pinned to the forecastle, the dagger through the back of his hand. The large bird summoned all its energy and launched itself into the air. It wavered in flight and landed on some rigging just below Cameron. The crew forgot their full stomachs as they lumbered to their feet.

Alex, followed by several officers, raced onto the deck from the officers' mess at hearing the pistol shot. He stood blinking in the bright sunlight, trying to discern what was happening as more shots were fired at the bird. All was noisy confusion but, following the angrily pointing fingers, he swore loudly. Goliath, on the scene from the beginning, ingeniously using all his strength, heaved over one of the huge metal braziers used to cook the meat. Fortunately he was unseen, as all eyes were turned on the dark figures of Cameron and Omen. He quickly sidled away toward the gunwale, where Tor, his precious meal forgotten, whined and pawed the mast in consternation.

"Fly, Omen, fly," pleaded Cameron as the shots whistled by them. One pierced the full-straining sail, and it ripped with a thunderous, rending sound. The raven once again summoned up all its strength, blood dripping onto the scrubbed white of the deck below, and, flapping heavy wings, flew toward the coast. Cameron watched it anxiously as it keeled and veered, any second expecting it to drop like a stone into the sea, but the valiant bird gained strength and soon flew evenly out of range of the guns. She stared

down at Tor, silently bidding him farewell, knowing it was
time to take her own freedom.

"Fire! Fire!" screamed many voices as smoke billowed
and hungry tongues of flame were fed by the fatty meat
drippings. All attention left Cameron and the small spot
of the raven, still visible, flying toward the coast of Nova
Scotia. She froze as she saw Goliath pick up her dog in his
enormous arms. He looked up at her, but she was too high
to see his expression, and then threw the frightened young
hound into the sea. Cameron held her breath, waiting for
the sleek black head to break through the churning gray-
green water in the wake of the vessel, before diving from
her own high roost.

Alex's heart was in his mouth as he saw her lithe,
graceful body launch into the air. She was diving from too
high, and he was sure she would snap her neck. He
sighed with relief as she curled her body into a tight ball
before impact. He hastily unbuttoned his tight tunic,
preparing to go after her.

"All hands needed," barked a voice in his ear, and there
stood the old general. Alex's mind was a mass of confusion.
From the corner of his eye he saw Goliath's large shape
disappear over the gunwales after Cameron. He stood
staring at the gaunt old man as though in a daze.

"What's the matter with you, Sinclair? Take a bucket,
unless we're all to burn to a crisp!" ordered Ramsbotham.
Not wanting to alert the general that something was amiss
with Cameron, he felt it best to comply. Alex was soon
swept away into the swirling mass of confusion. The air
filled with the screams of the panic-stricken horses trapped
belowdecks. Men clambered up the rigging through the
dense black smoke to frantically lower the sails so there
would be no added motion to fan the savagely leaping
flames that roared and spat, eating into the dry timber.

For hour upon hour Alex worked alongside the blackened crew and soldiers, not daring to raise his smarting
eyes to the sea. He felt torn in two, not knowing whether
Cameron was alive and free or dead and free, her lifeless
body moving with the seaweed, her green eyes wide and
staring, only to turn milky and sightless. If she lived,

would Goliath bring her back, and if he did, for what? he worried. This blazing inferno would surely be blamed on her. Maybe it were best if Goliath could keep her safely in the vast wilderness where she could be a part of the natural order as she had been as a child, scarcely a year ago, when his presence and possessiveness had robbed her of her dignity and home. What had he ever given to her but humiliation and confinement, he raged inwardly, as he hauled the heavy buckets of seawater over the gunwales to dash upon the dancing flames. They mocked and jeered, consuming the water hungrily as though it were oil. What had *she* ever given *him* but heartache and anxiety, he reminded himself savagely. He was best off without her, he convinced himself, trying to block the vibrant thought of her from his memory as his body rhythmically labored. He groaned aloud as the image of her lithe, satiny skin prickled the hairs on his arms. Never again to hold her, never again to wake to her flashing emerald eyes, never again to hear her infectious, gurgling laughter, never again to embrace the whole of her. The acrid smoke stung his eyes, and tears furrowed his soot-blackened face, mingling with the streaks of sweat, as he methodically worked, swinging the heavy buckets as part of a human chain.

Had he ever embraced the whole of her? There had always been an elusiveness, an intangible something, withheld even at their closest moments. Even at her most abandoned, something undefinable had seemed to be withheld from him, he puzzled. Was it elusiveness or unpredictability? Was she woman or child? Sometimes she seemed older and wiser than he and then in the blink of an eye could skip over the border into carefree childhood. Had her childhood ever been carefree?

"What the hell does it matter now?!" he roared, trying to free himself of thoughts of her. His voice was drowned out by the screaming, frantic confusion as the inferno raged on board. "I'm finally free of her! Free to regain my pride, my manhood, and what is rightfully mine!"

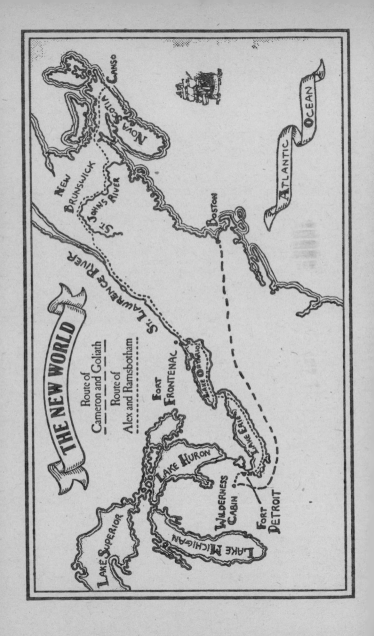

THE NEW WORLD

Route of
Cameron and Goliath
Route of
Alex and Ramsbotham

LAKE SUPERIOR

LAKE MICHIGAN

LAKE HURON

WILDERNESS CABIN

FORT DETROIT

LAKE ERIE

FORT FRONTENAC

LAKE ONTARIO

ST. LAWRENCE RIVER

BOSTON

NEW BRUNSWICK

ST. JOHNS RIVER

NOVA SCOTIA

CANSO

ATLANTIC OCEAN

BOOK THREE
THE NEW WORLD

Summer 1762

Then let us pray that come it may,
As come it will for a' that,
That sense and worth, o'er a' the earth,
May bear the gree, an' a' that.*
For a' that, an' a' that,
It's comin yet, for a' that,
That man to man, the warld o'er,
Shall brothers be for a' that.

ROBERT BURNS, "A Man's a Man
for A' That"

* "Bear the gree": Have the prize.

CHAPTER TWENTY-THREE

Goliath paddled the canoe methodically down the Saint Lawrence River through the land of the Hurons, his eyes firmly fixed to Cameron's back. She looked like a young brave, dressed in fringed and beaded leather. He allowed his mind to drift back to the beginning of their month-long trek across the Nova Scotia Peninsula to Acadia, on the mainland, where they had paddled down the Saint John River. At the beginning he had worried at her seeming frailness. They had lain exhausted after the long, icy swim, watching the leaping flames from the burning vessel stab the night sky and reflect on the dark ripples of the sea. Not a word had passed between them, and somehow he had been loath to break the silence. He had slept for several hours intuitively feeling she was waiting for Alex to claim her, that some unaware, unthinking part of her mind expected him to walk from the sea with his strong golden arms outstretched. He had awoken to the sunlight on the empty sea, the smooth water broken by blackened debris nearing and then receding gently with the tide. There was no sign of the ship or its escort of frigates. Only then had Cameron spoken.

"He is dead to me," she had pronounced as she rose stiffly to her feet, her eyes dry and hard. He had felt chilled to the marrow and unable to move, but sat in a frozen stupor watching her walk away with her young hound. She stared up at the rocky cliff that towered above them, looking for an easy place that her dog could scale. He stopped paddling a moment as he remembered how her proud bearing had faltered and she'd collapsed, hugging a large rock for support. She had been vomiting and continued to do so at least once a day for two weeks. He stared at the lithe figure who now knelt before him in the dugout, expertly paddling the canoe as though she had been born to it. He wished he knew some of what was in her mind as she kept a passive face despite the breath-takingly majestic scenery, the like of which she could never have seen or even imagined before. He grunted content-edly, feeling complete. It was the only country he had ever felt in proper proportion to, the size of the moun-tains, trees, and rivers dwarfing him to a more comfort-able height and breadth.

"This New World keeps me in perspective," he sang, but Cameron did not acknowledge his words. Goliath frowned, his contentment marred. It was as though she were a machine—feeling nothing except the rhythm of the paddle. All she seemed aware of was the necessity to put one step in front of the other. He stared thought-fully at Omen, and he smiled, remembering Cameron's search for the raven. They had been fortunate in meet-ing up with a small band of Micmac fishermen, and quickly Goliath had spoken French, knowing where the fishermen's alliance lay, hoping that Cameron would un-derstand and not speak English. He need not have wor-ried, for the only sound to issue from her mouth had been a hoarse cawing as she ignored their hospitable hosts and wandered around scanning the scrubland. The Mic-macs had been excited at the bright emerald eyes and had chatted together in an obscure Algonkian dialect that Goliath had had a hard time following. His young ward Méron's fame had traveled to even this isolated corner, he realized, as he pieced together the hastily gabbled words and gestures. Apparently one young brave had heard of the green-eyed warrior who rode at Pontiac's left hand. They had treated Cameron with awe for the first two days, laying out food and clothes with reverence but as her hoarse cawing continued, they had backed away with fear, believing her possessed of evil spirits. Goliath knew that there was no likelihood of an Indian harming a person thought to be insane, as they firmly believed that the evil spirits would travel from the afflicted along the arrow, spear, or knife and enter their own body. Their antagonism was directed at him as they made angry ges-tures to show Goliath that he and his companion were no longer welcome.

He smiled ironically to himself at the fix he had been

in, because he had dared not talk to Cameron in English for fear of being overheard and yet he didn't know if she still spoke French as she had done as a small child. He had pantomimed, drawn in the dirt, but she had totally ignored him and proceeded to roam around, cawing hoarsely. It had been a nerve-straining time but had somehow served a purpose. The Micmacs had given them a canoe and provisions, anything to be rid of them. Goliath chuckled aloud remembering the day Cameron, dressed in the doeskin clothes, appeared with the raven on her shoulder. The Indians had backed away, their eyes wide with terror at the smiling, joyful figure who thanked them in perfect French.

Cameron's thoughts also returned to her first meeting with the native inhabitants of the enormous alien land which had made her feel like an ant—insignificant, almost humble. How could she even be presumptuous enough to have feelings of pain or fear when she felt no bigger than a speck of dust? The first few days had seemed detached and dreamlike. All she had been aware of was her need to find Omen. She had been haunted by the image of the raven laying wounded and alone, knowing somewhere inside of her that the bird still lived. Upon finding it she had felt a lifting of the heavy inertia, and the whispy, dreamlike images of the previous days had sharpened as she welcomed the brown, lithe people, thanking them for the intricate, beautiful clothes. She had wanted to embrace them and apologize for her remoteness, but she had recoiled from the fear and panic in the Micmacs' dark eyes.

Theirs was the same reaction as that of the crew. The same reaction that spiraled back to childhood's first rememberings. She had doused the sparkle in her eyes and turned from them, not understanding—or caring—what Goliath said in the strange guttural tongue to the wildly gesticulating Indians. She had turned away as bile rose in her throat. The Micmacs had immediately broken camp, certain that Cameron was not only insane but carried one of the dreaded white man's diseases that had been known to kill whole tribes of strong, noble warriors. Within less than an hour they had mysteriously disappeared, leaving no trace of their encampment except a dugout canoe and food for the crossing of the wide bay that separated Nova Scotia from Acadia, on the mainland.

Cameron had seen the worry in Goliath's eyes at her frequent illness and she had hated herself for such a graceless weakness. She didn't let her mind dwell on what could possibly be occurring in her body. The nausea had thankfully passed, and yet she was aware of changes in her. She forced her mind to block the barrage of nagging questions that tormented her as the realization of the cessation of her monthly flow tore in. Her small, firm breasts felt bruised and swollen, and there were times when a deadly lassitude crept over her. When she bathed in the river alone, she minutely examined herself, but her belly was flat and smooth, and for a while she laughed at her silly imaginings. By the time they had paddled deep into the Acadian interior along the Saint John River, she felt healthy, her appetite had returned, and her skin glowed. They had been greeted distantly but respectfully by the Malecites and Passamaquoddies, but Cameron, remembering the fear and panic in the eyes of the Nova Scotia Micmacs, kept silent and apart from them, leaving Goliath to communicate.

Another roving band of Micmacs had stopped them as they trudged through the thick forest toward the mighty Saint Lawrence River. The Indians had circled, taunting, pointing at the raven. Cameron's heart beat rapidly in fear as their voices sounded threatening and cruel, and her hand inched toward her dagger, the only one remaining, the twin blade being left on board piercing the old groom's hand. But to her surprise Goliath had doubled up roaring with laughter. Between his great guffaws of mirth he had uttered guttural words to the Micmacs, who soon joined in the merriment, slapping their bare brown thighs, as they derided their ocean cousins of Nova Scotia.

So far their trip had been fairly uneventful. There had been one instance when fortunately Goliath's keen ears and sense of danger had alerted him before they stumbled into a camp of renegades, an odd mixture of tribeless natives who had no allegiance to any but themselves, mostly outcasts, men driven from their own camps. Unfortunately he had not been aware soon enough, and they had been forced to take cover in sight of the gory entertainment, as trying to steal away might have made their presence felt. Goliath frowned, remembering the horror on Cameron's face as she watched a small, emaciated Beothuk Indian, his naked body smeared with red clay, being tortured and then scalped. The other Indians had been dressed in a motley array of white men's clothes, French and English uniforms, and when they had sprawled drunk around their fire, Goliath had forcibly to restrain Cameron from going to the ochred body that lay limp.

"He's dead, mercifully . . . he is from the far north, a distant place called Newfoundland. He is a Beothuk, a race of quiet, timid people who will not survive, as they have no warlike skills. The French have a bounty on their scalps, and to the coward it is easy money," explained Goliath, answering the silent question in her eyes.

"He still lived," hissed Cameron. "I saw his body twitching."

"Aye, but he'd made his peace," returned Goliath softly.

" 'Twould have been more merciful to put him out of his misery than leave him there to suffer a slow death at the hands of those animals," she attacked.

"Cameron, there is much you must understand about this strange land. To the red man, this life is but a part. They have belief in an afterlife . . . a happy hunting ground. The Beothuk was not afraid to die. Did you hear him cry out once?"

Cameron refused to answer. She was appalled at his callousness. The poor creature had no energy to cry out, she ranted inwardly. She had never seen such emaciation on a human being. In comparison the wretched poor on the streets of Edinburgh seemed robust, even fat.

Goliath called out and waved toward shore, breaking Cameron's reverie. On the bank huddled a group of Indians.

"Hurons," explained Goliath. "Once a mighty nation of the Iroquois, called the Good Iroquois by the Catholic priests who sought to reform them. 'Huron' is a French word meaning 'slob'—ironic is it not? They were part of what was called the Five Nations until France pitted them against their own. Huron against Iroquois . . . Iroquois against Iroquois . . . weakening and slaughtering until many were scattered to the four winds, dying of cold and starvation or joining the conquering tribes. The mighty Hurons are but a shadow now."

"Why do you call them Hurons? What is their real name?" said Cameron savagely, furious at Goliath calling the pitiful, huddled people on the banks "slobs."

"That is what they call themselves also."

"Do they know what it means?" challenged Cameron.

"I doubt it, but them I dinna ken," he returned, averting his eyes from the bent, hopeless bodies. "Wendats or Wyandots, as the English call them."

"What does Wendat mean?"

"I dinna ken, but usually the Indian tribe names mean 'Man,' 'Human Being,' or the like. 'Man of the forest' or '. . . the river' or '. . . the plain.' "

"Then it seems that maybe the English are more merciful than the French," puzzled Cameron.

"Nay, 'tis but the same from both sides. All is fair in war. There is no right side, neither French nor English. Both are greedy for land or souls to convert, and many tribes are greedy for the white man's tools, guns, and trinkets."

Goliath was pleased that her long silence was broken, but she did not acknowledge his words, and soon he talked just to keep himself company, his eyes pinned to her straight back as she methodically paddled down the mighty Saint Lawrence toward Lake Ontario.

"When the French came to this vast land, they were not farmers eager to harness and control the wilderness but were mostly priests, missionaries out to herd and harness souls, or trappers who saw the wealth in the pelts of the wolf, beaver, and other animals that roamed free. The trapper learned much from the red man and learned to survive in this untamed world. The English and Dutch were more interested in acquiring land, cultivating and farming. The red man resented the changing of the earth, for he accepted it as it was. To them it was inconceivable that the ground could be owned . . . as incon-

ceivable as owning the sea, river, and sky . . ." Goliath
trailed off, feeling awkward as he heard his voice sounding like a boring preacher in a kirk on Sunday. He
smoothly and rhythmically dipped the paddle into the
swiftly flowing water, unaware that Cameron not only
heard his words but felt and examined them silently.

Harnessing land and harnessing souls, there was nothing
much to choose between each as far as she was concerned.
In fact wasn't that what she herself railed against? she
fumed. Had not she been expected to be tightly reined,
to trot docilely upon the manicured lawns of Glen Aucht,
where nature had been molded and redesigned by man's
arrogant hand? Even though the red men, who didn't appear to be red but a beautiful brown, were strange and
frightening to her, she felt a kinship, a loyalty toward
them. For a moment she thought of the Beothuk whose
body had been coated with an artificial red color and of
Goliath's words about how their gentleness and timidity
were causing their extinction. She would never be timid
or gentle, she vowed. One couldn't afford to be in this
huge country if one was to survive.

The once-proud vessel with her escort of frigates limped
into the busy Boston harbor. Listing badly, her holds full
of water, it was a miracle that she reached her destination.
The old general had also lost his arrogant, erect bearing,
and he watched the approaching land with his shoulders
bent. The loss of the dark-haired boy with whom he had
hoped to infiltrate the Ottawa camp weighed heavily, and
his shrewd mind was unable to accept, as the captain had
done, that he, his father, and animal companions had died
in the fire. There had been burns, but no others had lost
their lives except for the usual and expected demises from
illness and poor diet. A mere twenty people had been
entered in the ship's log as having expired on the long
voyage, despite the storm, the unnatural calm, and the
fire, and for this the captain celebrated by throwing a
rousing party, which did nothing to lift the old soldier's
sagging spirits. He turned sharply and eyed the tall, golden
Scot at his side, his gaunt face suspicious and bitter. Alex

continued staring straight ahead toward the approaching shore, ignoring Jemmy's excited chatter and the general's hostility.

Jemmy did not believe Cameron dead for one second. She had secretly grieved at the loss of her friend, but on hearing there was no sign on board of either Tor, Omen, or Goliath, she comforted herself that they were together. Maggie whined at her side, sensing that soon she'd be on firm ground instead of on the steeply listing deck. Jemmy stared up at Alex's chiseled features and shivered. Since the night of the fire he had not changed his expression and although she filled the tense silences with her steady stream of observances, she had not dared ask what was to become of her. The old general, who had become rather like a grandfather, had also withdrawn into a bitter shell. She now stood between the two tall, lean men feeling afraid, as neither one seemed aware of her presence. She looked ahead at the people who swarmed like ants, milling around the busy harbor, and panic clutched her. If only Goliath had been on board, she knew she would never be forgotten. Terrible thoughts flashed into her head as she saw herself left alone, pushing through the towering, pressing throng of people, not finding one familiar face or any that cared. She wound her fingers into Maggie's shaggy coat, clinging on for dear life.

The ship was guided into berth, the clamor of the orders and machinery becoming deafening and frightening as Jemmy desperately looked up to the two hard, set faces for comfort. Burly laborers and ragged people screamed and screeched from the dock. The gangplank was lowered, and uniformed soldiers marched off. The horses screamed as their listless, emaciated bodies kicked pathetically in the grasp of the creaking crane that swung them out onto dry land. Two of the horses died in mid-air and were callously dumped like dead meat, the lifeless legs buckling like straws. Only then did the old general stir.

"Galahad," he cried hoarsely and limped quickly away, to be swallowed by the mass of pushing, shouting people. Jemmy watched his departing back, torn about whom to stay with. She glanced from one man to the other, her heart hammering in her small chest until she could not see the old man anymore. Alex turned away to collect his gear from the cabin and was conscious of a frantic tugging at his sleeve. He looked down dispassionately into Jemmy's wide, scared eyes.

"Please? Please?" she pleaded.

"What?" he replied impatiently.

"I'm sorry I can't be like Her Ladyship," stammered the child, her blue eyes filling up with tears. Alex frowned as his anger rose at the reference to his wife.

"Thank your lucky stars for that," he responded harshly.

"But . . . but I canna . . . I canna be so brave. I've tried, but I canna. What will I do?"

Alex stared long and hard at the upturned, tear-streaked freckled face as his rage receded and he saw the red-haired child as no threat but a small waif. He snorted mirthlessly for a second when he recognized that she looked just as he felt: lost, abandoned, with no one to care whether he lived or died.

Jemmy froze in the long silence. His snort of laughter caused her spine to stiffen, and she swallowed her tears and resolutely turned away, her hand on her shaggy hound's head. She took a deep, sobbing breath as she saw the frightening crush of people and prepared to disembark. Thunder roared in her ears, and she closed her mind to the thoughts of what would happen to her. Stoically she put one small foot in front of the other. A strong pair of hands picked her up, and she whimpered in alarm before looking up at Alex's resolute chin as he carried her like a bairn. She relaxed against his broad red-uniformed chest, hearing his heart beat strong and steady. She looked down at her hand, which clutched one of his shiny buttons, unable to see the expression on his face from her position as she was carried below deck. She was deposited on his bunk, and as he silently and efficiently collected his gear, she watched him nervously. For the few minutes in his arms she had felt safe, but now his forbidding exterior frightened her. She had to stay with him, she thought frantically. She had to or she would be swallowed up by the strange New World full of screeching, grasping people. How could she ensure it? raced her mind. Her twelve-year-old brain was flooded with ideas, none of which could possibly affect such a tall, wellborn, educated laird.

There was one thing, she realized. The long voyage in male company, disguised as such, had made her privy to much that she would have normally been protected from as ribald tales were swapped. It seemed as the weeks had gone by that each man had dwelt upon just one subject, dreamed about one thing to do when he got on shore. Fear snaked through Jemmy at the thought, and she remembered her near rape at Beddington's and Harris's hands. They had torn her clothes off and spread her legs, their stinging, cruel fingers prying into her body and burning deeply inside of her as though their nails were brined. To be stabbed to death, to be rent in two, as the terrifying remembrance of Beddington's swollen, awesome organ tore into her mind. She had tried to recall the prayers taught her by her dead mother as Harris had pinned her legs open and the fat colonel had knelt between them, aiming the throbbing, bulbous point. She froze, her eyes riveted to the weapon that would surely kill her as it neared and then oddly collapsed and shriveled. He had hurt her then as he tried to squeeze and push the nauseating softness into her.

But Alex was different. She stared at his muscular body and frantically reasoned that it was not ugly and fat like the colonel's. In fact there was a smoothness she felt would be comforting to touch. She had loved the feel of his strong arms about her, and she let her mind go back to the carefree days when her father was alive, sitting on his lap and smelling the musk of his body and of the countryside, the rasp of his day's growth of beard, and the corded, satin texture of the back of his hands. For a second her eyes filled with tears as a picture of her small, freckled hand lying trustingly in his large, weather-beaten one flashed into her mind. Angrily she dashed the tears away. Childhood was gone, her father and mother dead. Obviously Sir Alexander Sinclair was not old enough to be her father and had no need of a dependent child.

Jemmy did not look up at Alex's face as she slowly crossed to him, but kept her eyes riveted to a point past his high shoulder somewhere, but as she neared, his shoulder filled her sight, as did his chest. She stopped scarcely a yard from him, and Alex stared down onto the top of her red, curly head, not knowing what to make of the strange performance.

Jemmy felt strange pulses beating all through her. She tried to keep her eyes pinned on the middle button of his tunic, but somehow a curious part of her made them fall lower, to the front of his tight breeches. What was she supposed to do now? she wondered, wishing he would make the first move instead of standing as still as a statue. Tentatively she raised her hand, reaching toward him, but leaving it to hover midway in the space between them.

What was the child about? Alex stood mesmerized and confounded, and then sharp horror cut through as the small, hovering hand made a sudden movement and landed softly like a butterfly on the swell of his genitals beneath his tight breeches. He snatched her hand away savagely, imprisoning it as a quicksilver flash ran through his starved groin.

"Oh, your mistress taught you well," he snarled, throwing the child against the bunk, where she collapsed, sobbing, her thin body rolled like a ball, her arms clutching her bent knees tightly, feeling that all was lost. Now she would certainly be abandoned. She calmed her crying and held her breath, waiting for him to leave.

"What were you trying to do?" he barked, after a long silence. He surveyed the white-faced child. She did not answer, but her eyes shifted with embarrassment. Alex had sensed the child's stark fear when she stood hesitant before him. He was consumed by conflicting emotions at his own responses to the child's touch and an instinctual understanding of her action. He had wrestled with himself, staring at the pathetic, waiflike picture that she made, knowing that he wanted no one to hamper or tie him down, as he told himself that soon he would rid himself of the pain of Cameron. He needed no one, he resolved vehemently as he saw the faces of his two young sisters mirrored in Jemmy's vulnerable, pleading eyes.

"Why, Jemmy, why?" he asked softly, and at the tender tone the dam burst.

"There's nobody for me more except my Maggie," sobbed the child. "My da is dead and my ma also birthing a brother. Goliath has gone, and so has Lady Cameron, and I'm not as brave and fierce as Her Ladyship, tho' I try to be, and I dinna ken what'll become of me."

"But you are but a child of eight or nine?"

"Twelve in May, sir. It is after May, is it not? . . . I've lost all track of time," sobbed Jemmy. "All track of everything, and I'm afraid to be alone, and you dinna want a child, for many is the time I've heard you tell Her Ladyship to behave like a grown-up lady . . . and every man on the boat talked about . . . about . . . so I thought since Her Ladyship . . . well, that maybe you would . . . you would take me, and then I could stay with you." Jemmy forced the words from her quivering mouth and exploded into uncontrollable sobs. Alex picked her up in his arms and sat with her, rocking both her and himself for comfort. The storm of tears subsided, and Jemmy lifted her her face and sniffed.

"Jemmy, I hold myself responsible for you. I will not abandon you but will see that you are properly taken care of. You are all I have left of Glen Aucht."

"Not all, there's Maggie," hiccoughed the child.

"Aye, there's Maggie," agreed Alex. "But you'll not do such a thing more, you ken? To offer yourself like that to any man until your body and mind are full-grown, understand?"

Jemmy didn't answer but snuggled closer to his strong body, arousing many feelings in Alex. "You ken?" he repeated harshly. "There are many men who would have taken you . . . frightened you like this," he shouted, firmly raising her chin so that her face looked straight into his. He crushed her mouth to his and then as quickly set her away from him. Jemmy cringed, terrified. "Aye and that is only a small example of the risks you take."

"I know," whispered the small girl, cowering against the wall. "The c . . . c . . . colonel."

Remembrances of the child's near rape flooded into Alex's mind, and he swore inwardly at his harsh action.

"Then why, Jemmy? Why?" he uttered after pacing furiously. "Were you so afraid that you were willing to face

something your whole being shuddered at?" he added as
there was no answer from the cowering shivering small
figure who backed from him in terror. Knowing that his
presence frightened her and that any attempt to undo his
unthinking action was futile, he threw her small bundle at
her, picked up his gear, and abruptly opened the cabin
door.

"Come along unless you prefer to be left behind," he
ordered, striding into the narrow corridor. He walked the
length to the stairway before realizing she had not followed.
He leaned against the wall feeling guilty and uncomfortable,
knowing that what he had done to Jemmy had been too
harsh and was the result of his own painful and frustrating
situation, a culmination of his sense of impotence to handle
the reins of his own destiny. What did he need with a
twelve-year-old child? he raged as his booted feet walked
reluctantly back to the cabin where Jemmy still huddled
with a nervous Maggie at her feet.

Alex strode on deck, followed by the hound, the listless
child slung over one shoulder as he planned her future.
She'd be his anchor, his conscience, his reality, he decided.
He'd dress her as was fitting for her sex, certain that there
would be women at Fort Detroit who would watch over
her when he was out in the wilderness with the old general.
She would be a ward, a young sister, a link to his past . . .
someone to come "home" to, to be responsible for so it
would not be easy to throw his life away in a rash, suicidal
accident as he had seen so many lonely and embittered
soldiers do before. Yet she would leave his emotions free
from conflict, would not weigh his spirit down with complex feelings as his wife had done.

An angry line of people met his eyes, near the gangway
and several official men checked papers and examined the
impatient crowd one by one as they jostled and complained,
wanting to disembark.

"There is Major Alexander Sinclair now," shouted the
old general, his color heightened as though he had been
in a furious argument. "Sinclair? Sinclair?"

"I have a warrant here," intoned a pompous-looking
man. Alex felt the new resolve drain from him. He was
to be arrested for the murder of Colonel Beddington. He

debated trying to escape, but the weight of the exhausted child deterred him.

" 'Tis for a Lady Cameron Sinclair?" expostulated the old general. "I have been informing the idiots that your good lady did not accompany you. Didn't know you were married, Sinclair."

"My wife and I are no longer . . . together," answered Alex stiffly.

"Are there charges against the major?" queried Ramsbotham. "I am his commanding officer . . . I have the king's favor. There you see a frigate named for me," he bragged, waving his gnarled hand toward the harbor.

"No, 'tis just for the said Lady Cameron Sinclair. But I'm sorry, sir, each and every passenger and crew member must be examined, including the person the major is carrying."

Jemmy regarded the noisy assembled officials with frightened blue eyes, ran a hand through her red curls, and pretended to go back to sleep, unwilling to deal with the raucous confusion.

"We have rooms at the Blue Feather, where we are to assemble and be prepared to make our way to Fort Detroit within the next few days," informed the old general when they were at last allowed out of the harbor yard, leaving the loudly complaining non-uniformed and less fortunate common folk to wait. They strode through the narrow cobbled streets of the Boston waterfront toward the inn, with the old general eyeing Alex suspiciously.

"Should we hire a carriage?" asked Alex, conscious of the weighty silence and the uneven, limping bootstep of the old man.

" 'Tis but a stone's throw," answered Ramsbotham shortly. "The Lady Cameron Sinclair? 'Tis strange, Major, that you made no mention of a wife," he added after a significant pause.

"It did not seem pertinent. As I previously stated, my wife and I no longer cohabit," he answered stiffly.

"Would seem the separation is recent and causes pain," remarked the old man shrewdly. "Well, here we are. I am well acquainted with this inn, and I trust you'll find the food and beds at the Blue Feather to your liking. After we have been shown to our rooms and refreshed ourselves, you'll be good enough to meet me in my private parlor so that we might discuss our long trip to Fort Detroit. You will keep the child with you?" he added as they followed a young maid up the stairs, and Jemmy stared around with puzzlement.

"Yes," answered Alex, setting the child on her feet as they reached the broad, sweeping landing.

"I shall expect you in one hour," clipped the old general decisively, shutting the door to his own suite of rooms. Alex felt his hackles rise at the terse order, so like Beddington, he thought, these pompous Englishmen with their arrogance.

Jemmy walked unsteadily into the large bedroom. The floor felt strange beneath her feet after the long voyage on the rolling ship.

"Cute little honey, ain't he?" giggled the buxom young maid, chucking Jemmy under the chin and eyeing Alex with evident appreciation.

"She liked you, will you . . . er . . . you know?" stammered Jemmy after the door had closed on the saucy wench who had tipped Alex a knowing wink. Alex snorted his disapproval at the young girl's improper words. He had been casually toying with the very idea that Jemmy implied and did not like it expressed on her young lips.

"You shall sleep in here," he said, opening the door to a small dressing room. "I shall have food sent up to you."

Jemmy sat in the tiny room hearing the noises of Alex washing and changing his clothes. She heard the throaty giggle of the serving maid as she brought the water and offered to render service to the tall, golden Scot. Alex curtly dismissed her, all too conscious of the young ears in the dressing room.

"Here," said Alex opening the door and handing her a tray of food. "I must meet with the general, and you'll remain here. Keep the door bolted and have a wash. There's water in my chamber."

Jemmy obediently bolted the door after his tall figure and, after listening to him sharply rap on the general's door and enter, she sat and ate ravenously of the savory rabbit stew.

A sumptous repast was spread on a trestle table in the general's private parlor—meat pies, a large roasted wild turkey stuffed with forcemeat and surrounded by cranberries and apples, a ham, and several cheeses. Alex nodded silently at the three young soldiers whom he vaguely remembered from the voyage. He nodded silently again in appreciation as he was handed a large tankard of deep, rich wine.

The old general was in his element. He stood, his bearing once more erect at the head of the table, with his own pewter mug raised, and surveyed the four, tall, healthy young men.

"I have selected the cream of the crop," he crowed. "I drink to you."

Standing uncomfortably the four young men drank, ill at ease and embarrassed.

"Sit down, sit down," clucked Ramsbotham. "As we eat, I'll inform you of my lastest plan. Dig in, we must stoke the fires after that abominable voyage. Must regain our strength for what we are about to undertake." For a good ten minutes no words were spoken as the old general noisily ate, slapping his lips together and grunting his appreciation. Alex and his fellow soldiers ate stiffly and politely, waiting to be informed as to what General Ramsbotham had in mind.

"You have been selected by me to be part of a group of scouts. You will not be marching to Fort Detroit with the rest of your detachment. You will shed your conspicuous uniforms and, led by me, we will make our own way, learning as we go. Your horses are stabled here, and your trunks, of which you'll have no need, will be placed in storage. Major Gladwin will be apprised and knows I have full authority to select those of his men who I feel are fit for such rigors."

The general's dinner lasted for hours, the young men, with the exception of Alex, loosening up with the effects of the earthy red wine, so that they chatted excitedly as they pored over the map that the old soldier had spread over half the table when the platters and covers had been collected by servants.

"We shall spend such time as I see fit honing our

bodies and those of our horses and outfitting ourselves . . .
as minimally as possible. Now, here we are in Boston
in the king's colony of Massachusetts . . . and here is
Fort Detroit. The distance is about four hundred miles
of rough, wild terrain."

The general droned on and on until it was difficult for
the sated, wine-filled men to keep their heavy eyelids
from drooping. Only Alex remained alert. He had eaten
and drunk sparingly, his thoughts far from anything the
old man rambled about. In 1755 and 1758 he had traversed the New World's wilderness. At first with General Braddock and later with General Bradstreet during
his defeat at the hands of the French at Fort Duquesne.
After the battle he and several other young soldiers had
been dazed and lost. Afraid of the conspicuousness of their
bright uniforms, they had stripped them off and had
wandered half naked, living in the forests much like the
Indians they feared, until they found their way back behind
their own lines. Only two of them had survived. Would
Cameron survive? he wondered. A scraping of chairs and
a shuffling of feet brought him back to the present as the
general shepherded out his sleepy recruits. Alex stood to
leave also but was detained by the old man's gnarled hand.

"I have not finished with you, Sinclair."

Alex stood patiently waiting while the door was closed
firmly and the general leaned against it, watching the tall
Scot with an inscrutable expression.

"Well, Sinclair?" uttered the old man harshly after an
interminable pause. He was irritated by the younger man's
apparent calm and dignified silence. Alex raised his eyebrows but did not answer.

"You sit at my table in a world of your own, neither
asking questions nor showing interest. Those other young-
sters are still wet behind the ears, but you have been in
this country before. I obtained your records and was
surprised to find that you already have experience as a
scout and in that capacity earned your commission under
Bradstreet in fifty-eight. Why did you not apprise me of
those facts?"

"You did not request them," responded Alex cooly,
ironically thinking that the old soldier was so full of his

own exploits, he left no room or space for another's. "I have decided after much consideration that I have to withdraw from your operation," he added. The deeply etched face of the general sagged incredulously.

"Withdraw? Poppycock! You cannot. What is the reason for such infernal impudence?" he spluttered.

"The child, Jemmy," answered Alex shortly.

"Time that young pup was hardened. We'll have need of such smallness to wriggle and hide where a full-grown man can't."

The thought of the tiny red-haired girl without shelter in the vast forests, dodging angry and hostile Indians brought a cynical smile to Alex's steely features.

"That ward of yours is too soft and almost feminine by far. Nice enough lad, but obviously mollycoddled," ranted the old man, incensed by the smile.

"Soft and feminine?" asked Alex softly.

The old hooded eyes looked sharply into the amber ones. The young man was like a lion, he thought, almost purring.

"Yes, decidedly soft and feminine," attacked the old man, challenging the lazy nonchalance.

"Aye, decidedly soft and feminine," agreed Alex, thoroughly enjoying himself. The old man stepped back with a bewildered and then almost horrified look.

"By Jove, man, you cannot . . . no, you cannot be saying . . . implying what I think. . . . No, tis outrageous," he stammered.

Alex smiled and nodded victoriously, assuming that the old man had guessed Jemmy's sexual gender. He frowned as Ramsbotham's face lost all color and his lips gaped in disgust and horror.

"A sodomist," whispered the old general weakly, sitting heavily.

"I beg your pardon!" exclaimed Alex, himself now totally bewildered.

"I thought myself, nay prided myself on being a good judge of character . . . and to think that you were capable of such unnatural acts and on a mere boy . . . your ward under your protection? 'Tis unthinkable!"

At the realization of what the old man assumed,

Alex roared with laughter, heightening the poor man's consternation.

"I have never professed to be virtuous, but there are some practices I draw the line at, sir. My ward, as you see fit to call her, is much too young for my taste. My appetites run to more mature women."

"What are you saying, man? 'Tis late, I'm old and tired," spat Ramsbotham after a suspicious pause.

"Jemmy is a lass . . . a twelve-year-old lass, the daughter of one of my estate men who was unfortunately killed."

"Why was she dressed as a boy?"

"It started as a caprice . . . her own, I assure you. She should have stayed behind at my home of Glen Aucht, but rashly she followed me. I kept her so clad for reasons I'm sure you respect," explained Alex, taking liberties with the truth.

"Yes, a female, no matter how young, has no place on a vessel with lusty men. But he . . . er, she lived with me closely in my cabin, and I never once suspected. By gad, Sinclair, you knew all along and allowed me to be alone with a female in my cabin . . . which amounts to my bedchamber! Living in close, intimate . . . personal proximity? That beats all! How many times I stripped off my clothes, assuming I was in the company of my own. 'Tis immoral! 'Tis downright embarrassing! 'Tis utterly humiliating!" expostulated the incensed man.

"I'm sure she was discreet. As you previously said, General, you had no idea of her sexual composition so she obviously was circumspect," replied Alex with a hint of mischief in his warm tone.

"Circumspect!" howled the intensely irritated old man.

"Yes, sir."

"Get out, Sinclair! Get out! I shall speak to you of this at some length in the morning."

"As you wish, sir," purred Alex, trying to suppress the laughter that welled up. Letting himself out, he strode, whistling tunelessly, to his own rooms, his face now set and worried. After pounding several minutes on his door, he remembered instructing Jemmy to bolt it from the inside. There was no way she could hear if she'd closed the door of the small dressing room and lay soundly sleeping, he realized. Unless he was to wake the whole inn with his pounding.

"Can I be of some assistance?" came a low, seductive voice, and Alex turned to see the busty serving wench, whose charms were now exhibited to better advantage. Her amble bosom welled over the low-cut bodice of a nightgown. Alex impudently allowed his hands to cup both full breasts, his thumbs flicking the large nipples that strained erectly through the coarse fabric. The woman's breath heaved her chest excitedly and came out in small, hot pants.

"Not here, sir. Let's go in?" she urged breathlessly, indicating the door.

"I seem to be locked out by my young ward," whispered Alex huskily, bending and burying his nose into the cleavage offered to him. She was clean and fresh smelling and had obviously prepared herself for him. "Do you know of an empty bed?" he asked, his voice constricted as he flooded with desire, the exquisite ache and throb in his loin causing him to cup her ample buttocks and lift the central heat of her to grind against his own pulsing core. He yearned to be consumed, thrusting inside her, his pain and worries obliterated for a short while.

For several searing minutes he lost himself in the sensations that flooded him, as mouths met and tongues probed and sucked. Clinging tightly, she backed with him into a deep alcove, a window seat behind thick velvet drapes to one side of his bedroom door. As the curtains dropped behind them, Alex let go of all sense of the propriety and fear of being found rutting like a barnyard animal in a public corridor. He pulled his straining hips back, allowing her greedy hand access, and sighed with relief as his manhood was released from the painful restriction of his tight trousers. He closed his eyes as experienced fingers grasped him, his own hands busy lifting the homespun nightdress. All he wanted to do was plunge into oblivion in the depths of her. She thrust her tight nipples toward his panting mouth, and he suckled them hungrily, biting and nipping as he positioned himself. She moaned in pleasure, reluctant to let go of his hard organ. His hand closed over hers, his other hand placed strategically on her lower back.

"Not yet, not yet," she whispered hoarsely, wanting to prolong the exquisite suspense. Alex released her breasts and covered her protesting mouth with his, then drove himself into her. He lost himself in the unthinking, rising thunder of sensations as he thrust and thrust inexorably toward his climax, unaware of the woman who writhed beneath him or of her uncomfortable position, forced backward on the window seat. His two strong hands gripped her heavy buttocks, lifting as he rammed himself faster and faster as though to submerge and purge himself totally of his pain, rage, and accumulated frustrations by placing them in the soft body of this anonymous woman.

Jemmy had been awakened by his persistent knocking. She had padded to the door, rubbing her sleepy eyes, and her hand was about to draw back the heavy bolt when she heard the deep sultry voice of the serving wench. She stood frozen, her hand on the bolt, hearing the muffled sounds, her small, shivering frame trembling at the implication of lusty violence and setting off strange, aching feelings in herself. A sharp knock caused her to pull back the bolt.

Alex had pushed several crowns into the dazed woman's hand, unable to look at her face. He had left her still sprawled in the curtained alcove, deciding to try to awaken Jemmy one last time before descending to sleep on one of the benches in the public room. He entered his chamber and stared with eyes narrowed at the child. He knew he had lost control and sense of time and place for too short a span. At the climax of his blind surge of passion, he found himself as angry as, if not angrier and more frustrated than, before. Now he was facing the shocked face of his young charge, who had obviously heard him rutting in the hall like a prowling tomcat. Ignoring her, he strode across the room and, tearing off his tunic and shirt, lay morosely on his bed staring up at the ceiling. He faintly heard the child tiptoeing to her own bed before exhaustion overtook him and he slept, his mind full of pain at the loss of himself and Cameron. At least he wasn't impotent in all ways, he consoled himself.

CHAPTER TWENTY-FOUR

Alex awoke the following day and lay without moving as the weight of all his problems bombarded his mind. He had no desire to traipse through the wilderness with a crazy old man on his last glorious campaign. He had no desire to be dressed like a puppet of the king parading around a fort either. He had no desire to do anything, he concluded, turning over onto his stomach and burying his head in the soft pillow so that the sunlight was blocked. A stealthy creaking reminded him of Jemmy's existence, and he groaned, realizing that neither had he a desire to be wet nurse to a female child. A sharp rap at the door caused him to groan again and fix the pillow more securely over his ears. He ignored it, tried to be deaf to the hoarse whispers as Jemmy explained that he still slept. The door was slammed, and brisk, limping bootsteps shattered his vague hope that he was to be left in peace. A hard, bony hand prodded him, and with yet another groan, this time of resignation, Alex threw the pillow aside and sat up in the bright sunlight that seemed to mock his thunderous mood.

"I have word there is a warrant for your arrest," barked Ramsbotham without preamble.

Alex snorted cynically as he wondered why the English did not have diplomacy as part of their military training. He smiled as he envisioned a course in bedside manners.

"For questioning in regard to the death of Colonel Randall Beddington," informed the old man, furious at Alex's apparent wry mirth at the news.

"An answer from the gods," laughed Alex, offering his wrist. "A way out of this cursed dilemma. . . . Take me away, General Ramsbotham, or surely you'll look like a horse's arse."

" 'Tis no time for adolescent tomfoolery."

" 'Tis surely prime time for it. What better time than when a man is hounded to the four corners of the earth and finally acknowledges his defeat?"

Jemmy stared at the golden, naked torso that rumbled and shook with laughter. "You killed the fat English colonel?" she exclaimed.

"Aye, and proud am I to admit it. 'Tis probably the only truly noble act I have performed on this earth," chuckled Alex.

"Aye, that mucker deserved to die," shouted Jemmy at the old general. "And the laird wouldna kill but in fair fight."

Alex's mirth increased at the feisty, skinny child who stood with hands on hips defying the tall, gaunt man. "Oh, I've acquired an awesome champion, it seems," he sputtered, lying back and roaring with laughter, feeling the oppressive tension flood out in the release of humor.

General Ramsbotham looked from the rebellious child to the shaking young man with irritation before deliberately sitting in a straight-backed chair.

"I'll wait out this demonstration of what I hope is temporary insanity," he stated, trying to appear dignified and patient. "I happened to be acquainted with the late Randall Beddington."

"Was he a friend of yours?" asked Jemmy suspiciously.

"I was fortunate enough not to be numbered among his friends. I did not say, however, that you are to be charged with murder but merely to be questioned in regard to the unfortunate man's fortunate demise. You, young, er . . . um . . . lady have too loose a tongue in posing so leading a question to your guardian, who obviously has a blatant disregard for his own life," stated the old man sternly.

"I admit my guilt, so call in the guard," said Alex cheerfully. "A holiday in a jail cell, the reins of my life taken over, no responsibility for myself or any other, no decisions to make . . . 'tis all very appealing to me at this time."

"No! They'll not take you . . . 'tis not fair. The fat colonel tried to rape me and Her Ladyship," shouted Jemmy.

"The man's foul ways are well known, and I'm sure there would be no inquiry but great sighs of relief if it wasn't for his older brother, who has considerable power in the court. Not that I'm saying Sir Jonquil Beddington is not also relieved of the embarrassment of having such a brother, but in his position he's obliged to make righteous indignation. Now, Sinclair, if you've finished with your self-indulgence, I suggest you pull yourself together sufficiently to discuss the welfare of your ward. I'm sure there are many good women hereabouts who will take care of her for a sum."

"No!" objected Jemmy.

"Quiet! Well, Major, whether you throw yourself into jail or accompany me, the child must be taken care of."

"I have just successfully cleared my mind of such nagging cobwebs, and now you have to blow them back in my ears," complained Alex. "Why not send her on to Fort Detroit with one of the officers' wives?"

"Because they left first thing this morning. That is how I happened to obtain the news of Beddington's death," replied the general testily.

"They cannot be too far ahead?" answered Alex airily.

"Have you any idea of the time?"

"No, and it doesn't much interest me."

"It is four in the afternoon."

Alex hid his surprise at sleeping the clock around by yawning widely.

"I have spent most of this day on your behalf, Sinclair. Lying has always been against my moral fiber, but today I lied on your account, and all you can do is lie there yawning and cackling. You may have nothing to lose being so casual about your life as you seem to be, but I do. I've lived most of mine and hold it sacred and precious. I am nearing the end and will not expire in a rocking chair by the hearth like a neutered cat but in a blaze of glory."

"Be my guest," offered Alex, mockingly spreading his palms wide.

"If you want to die, does it matter how? Surely an arrow in the back is less painful than the hangman's noose?" ranted Ramsbotham, losing patience. "I'm counting on you, Sinclair. You may think me a fool but I know it would be sheer suicide for three green cadets and an old buzzard like me without your courage and expertise."

"Courage?" exploded Alex, giving way once more to laughter at such irony. "General Ramsbotham, you see lying prone before you the most uncourageous, inept wreck of a man," he added when he could speak.

The old man's shoulders slumped, his erect, dignified bearing seemed to crumple in defeat. Alex stared at him, seeing the pathos. He watched the general age twenty years as he stood and limped to the door.

"I'm sorry to have wasted your time, Major Sinclair," he said numbly. Alex swung his long legs over the high side of the bed.

"What lies did you tell on my behalf?" he asked.

"They're of no account," replied the old man wearily, with his gnarled hand on the doorknob.

"You are right, sir, when you state I have nothing much to lose. I will be honored to be part of your party," stated Alex with a slight bow.

"Mock me no more, you impudent cub!" hissed Ramsbotham.

"I mock myself, General," replied Alex. "When do we leave?" The general's eyes lit up, although he regarded the young man skeptically.

"As soon as we are ready," answered Ramsbotham noncommittally, still uncertain of Alex's rapidly changing moods. "And have made arrangements for the child."

Jemmy stared from one to the other in horror. She was to be dumped with strangers, probably never to see anyone she knew again.

The next morning the general and Alex left Jemmy to her own devices at the inn for the day. She watched them ride down the twisting cobbled streets and, ignoring the taunts and jeers of several ragged boys, sat disconsolately in the stable yard with Maggie, who bared her teeth and growled when one of the teasing young bullies got too close. Suddenly a familiar shape appeared.

"Goliath! Goliath!" she screamed in welcome, rushing toward the enormous man.

"Och, now, what is this?" growled a deep voice as she

was caught in large hands and picked up as though she were a feather.

Jemmy stared in dismay at the strange face. She squirmed and wiggled, trying to free herself, but to no avail.

"I mistook you for a friend," she explained.

"Och, 'tis a fellow Scottish lad. And what's a wee Scot like you doing knowing my brother, Goliath?"

"Are you Wee-Angus?" asked Jemmy, her eyes wide as she remembered the conversation in the croft on Rona between Jennet and Goliath.

"Aye, where is that little brother of mine?"

"Went off the ship when it caught fire off the coast of Nova Scotia wie the Lady Cameron and Tor, brother to my Maggie," chattered Jemmy in a rush.

"Whoa, now, who's Maggie?"

"There she is," pointed Jemmy to the large, gangly hound. "But Tor is as black as Omen the raven and Lady Cameron's hair." Angus set the chattering child on her feet.

"Nova Scotia," he said thoughtfully. "Och, all this way for nocht. They'll be acoming down the rivers and through the lakes."

"Do you know where they're going to?" asked Jemmy eagerly. "Then take me with you, please, and Maggie and my pony, for I dinna have anyone except Goliath . . . and the laird'll nay take me along, and I do so want to be back with Cameron. . . . 'Tis all right she said I could call her so."

"Describe your Cameron," probed Angus gently.

"She's wild and free and can ride a horse like the wind. Her horse is here, a giant black stallion named Torquod." She led the large man into the stable.

"What color are her eyes?" questioned Angus, idly stroking the horse, who was still listless, his coat dull from the long voyage.

"Very, very green . . . 'tis shocking how bright."

"And she is with my brother, Goliath?"

"Aye, well, I hope so, because they disappeared at the same time. So if we are going to find her, we should take her Torquod, because she'll sorely miss him. But we should hurry up before the old general and the laird return," urged the excited child.

Angus frowned. "Where are your parents?"

"Dead," answered Jemmy simply.

"Who's responsible for you?"

"They went to find some woman to pay to be . . . the laird and the general," explained Jemmy impatiently. "I was on the boat with Goliath and Cameron, but I canna swim or I'd be wie them now."

"Have you any possessions to collect before we're on our way?" asked Angus, deciding to take the child with him.

"Nay, just my Maggie and the pony Cameron gie to me."

"Then let's be off," laughed the giant, swinging the girl onto one broad shoulder.

"But my pony and Torquod?" protested Jemmy as they stepped out into the warm late-afternoon sunlight.

"They need to rest and would just hamper us on our journey. 'Twill be a time before they can be ridden. What are this laird and general to Cameron?" he asked as he carried her down the winding cobbled streets and out of sight of the inn.

"The general's very old and he was on the ship, and the laird is Cameron's husband. But Torquod and my pony will be taken to Fort Detroit," protested Jemmy. Angus stopped in his tracks.

"Taken where?" he uttered, letting her down and staring into her freckled face.

"Fort Detroit," she repeated.

"Why Fort Detroit?"

"That is where the laird, who's also a major, is to be stationed, but the old general has formed a special group of scouts, and so they didna leave wie the rest of the soldiers."

Angus roared with laughter and hoisted the child back onto his shoulder.

"No wonder Goliath spirited Cameron off the ship before Boston. What a pretty kettle of fish," he chuckled. "Well, wee-un, I'll guarantee you'll be seeing your pony afore long."

Jemmy stared around at the busy streets of Boston from her high vantage point. Once more she felt safe and protected. She totally trusted the enormous man, brother of Goliath. Her young eyes could now take in her strange, new environment. She had never seen a large town, having spent all her short life on the Sinclair estate at Glen Aucht. The busy fishing town of Crail had been an exciting place to visit on special occasions but had in no way prepared her for what she gazed upon now. The sun dipped deeply as Angus strode through the outskirts, and Jemmy watched, fascinated, as the houses thinned with more spaces between until they entered a thickly wooded area, where she was pulled down from the high shoulder and cradled in strong arms, but still the vibrations of the steady, unceasing strides went on, and her sleepy eyes closed.

Jemmy awoke as strange, guttural voices barked. She sat up disoriented. She was lying on a prickly blanket in the darkness. Her heart beating triple time, she swiveled around in the direction of the voices and emitted a small shriek of terror. Around a campfire sat three near-naked men, the flames reflecting on the copper planes of their faces and down their long dark hair. They stopped their conversation and turned in her direction as she backed away, her hand pulling Maggie's neck hair in a painful grip. Angus's enormous shape rose from the shadows.

"Hush now, laddie, there's nocht to fear," he growled, motioning the other men to remain still. "Come and join us. Have a bite to eat."

Jemmy stood hesitatingly, but as the other men ignored her and resumed conversation in their strange tongue, she tentatively approached, skirting the fire in a wide arc to reach the safety of the enormous man. She hastily sat facing him, keeping her eyes averted from the near-naked bronze bodies but feeling their curious eyes boring into her. The firelight danced upon her vivid red curls, giving the appearance of a halo of flames, which fascinated the three young braves, one of whom stood silently and, mesmerized, crossed without a sound to touch. Jemmy gave a wild scream as she felt something brush her head. She leaped to her feet, whirling her small thin arms, but was caught by strong brown hands. She breathed deeply and stared up into the laughing bronze face of the Indian, who spoke over his shoulder to the other braves.

"He says the lion cub's hair is not hot, but his spirit is," translated Angus. "It seems my friends have already given you an Indian name. That is a great honor."

"They are savages?" whispered Jemmy.

"We are all savages. These young braves are our traveling companions."

Jemmy ate hungrily with her fingers of the meat and fish that was roasted on pointed sticks thrust into the fire. She relaxed and stared curiously at the Indians, who gazed back just as fascinated.

"Where are we going to?" she asked.

"Would it mean anything if I told you?" replied Angus evasively. "It will suffice to say that hopefully you'll be reunited with your Cameron and my brother. Now, sleep, as we'll be setting off before sunrise."

Jemmy lay awake staring into the burning embers of the fire. Strange rustlings in the underbrush and the eerie call of an animal caused her to shiver. A blanket was wrapped around her, and she looked up into the face of the young brave who had touched her hair. She smiled shyly, and once more he tenderly fingered a bright curl before sitting cross-legged and chanting a low, soft sound as he rocked back and forth. Jemmy felt soothed, as though the young brave sang a lullaby, and soon she slept.

Alex and General Ramsbotham returned to the Blue Feather with a round, cheerful matron in tow. They seated her before a laden table in the general's private parlor and went to find Jemmy. A search of the inn and grounds and the questioning of a number of staff brought the news that the missing child had disappeared atop the broad shoulder of an enormous man.

"Abraham?" exclaimed Ramsbotham. "But he was presumed killed in the fire, and even if he were swept overboard, there is no way on God's earth he could have managed to get here in so short a time."

"Unless he was picked up by a passing vessel. Obviously at least one has docked since we did, or else how did the news of Colonel Beddington's unfortunate demise reach here?" remarked Alex, surprised at the elation he felt that Cameron might be near.

"Jackson? Jackson?" roared the general through the open door. "I shall send a man to inquire at the harbor asking if Abraham and his son were picked up. There should be no mistaking the pair of them," he added, turning back to address Alex.

The fat matron sat consuming a vast amount of biscuits and cakes, seeming unconcerned that the child she had supposedly been brought to meet was not in evidence.

"It is doubtful that they would have remained on the vessel. And the tight cordon of police around the harbor yard examining all will surely remember such a giant and the green-eyed lad with his ferocious companions," said Ramsbotham excitedly. A cold pang smote Alex at the possibility that Cameron could that very moment be languishing in jail or, worse still, be in the hands of fanatically pious witch-hunters. He paced the room knowing there was nothing he could do until the young soldier, Jackson, returned.

The fat, cheerful matron, after consuming the heaping plates of confection, lost her pleasant humor. Her merry façade melted away after four glasses of sherry when she realized the loss of the child meant the loss of a goodly sum of money. She gathered herself together and pulled her large bulk from the deep comfort of the overstuffed chair.

"It appears there is no child. I've wasted my time . . . my very precious time, and I want payment," she demanded, crumbs sticking to her once-pleasant mouth that now was flattened against her yellowing teeth in a bitter, cruel line.

"Madam, it would appear that you've consumed enough food for several days, which, it would seem, is compensation enough," stated Alex coldly, glad that Jemmy was out of the greedy clutches of the two-faced matron. "But nevertheless, I'm sure this will be adequate," he added, flipping a coin so that it landed on the armchair seat that still bore the deep impression of her more than amble buttocks. He watched, cynically sneering as she scrambled for the coin, bit it, and stowed it away between her enormous breasts.

"Am I expected to return home unescorted?" she quavered.

"Of course not, madam," replied Ramsbotham with a hint of irony, once more opening the door and summoning one of his young soldiers.

Alone at last, the tall old man and the tall young one paced the parlor, each trying to contain his rising excitement, hoping Cameron was near at hand. Each for very different reasons. Late that night an exhausted Jackson returned with no news. Both Alex and Ramsbotham grilled him mercilessly, but the conscientious young soldier had left no stones unturned, having made persistent and thorough inquiry.

"They did not arrive by vessel, it seems," stated the old man wearily, his disappointment evident from the more pronounced limp and the bending of his usually stiffly held shoulders.

"Maybe we both jumped to a hasty conclusion. The large man could have been any extraordinarily large man. 'Tis a gross assumption that it was the man we know as Abraham," offered Alex, feeling deflated after such a long, anticlimactic wait.

"That red-haired boy . . . er, girl would not take off with a stranger. He . . . er, she didn't strike me as the sort. Dashed too much of a coincidence," expostulated the old man. Alex didn't answer as he recognized the truth in the man's words. "I must find the boy Isaac. If Abraham's alive, the boy is too, and I've a feeling in my old bones that he's near at hand. We shall delay our departure for several days and make more inquiry."

The next two days uncovered nothing but a vague description of a giant of a man with a red-haired boy followed by a large, gangly hound heading west through Boston. Supplies obtained, the old general, dressed in fringed buckskins like a trader, rode out accompanied by four young men dressed in similar fashion. Fresh horses had been bought, and those still recovering from the rigors of the ship were led, carrying the lightest of loads divided between them. Torquod had bucked with some of his old spirit at the effrontery, but the general's old war horse, Galahad, accepted his burden resignedly.

Alex snorted with laughter as he rode easily beside Ramsbotham. Clothes don't make the man, he mused, noting that despite the fringed leather the old man sat his horse like a soldier on parade at Whitehall and clipped out orders becoming a sergeant at arms. It was obvious suicide, he concluded, as they rode through Massachusetts toward the Connecticut River on the start of the long trek through the wilderness to Fort Detroit.

Cameron stared in awe at the enormous waterfalls that spilled the torrential contents of Lake Ontario into Lake Erie. She was mesmerized by the boiling, seething foam that dashed itself down giant steps. She and Goliath had beached the canoe before the rapid white water in order to avoid the English-held Fort Niagara and, with Goliath carrying the boat, had taken to the thick forest. The enormous man smiled as he watched Cameron's face. She was finally thawing and able to appreciate the splendor of this New World. He allowed her to have her fill as he kept his ears strained and eyes peeled. The thunderous roar of the falls and the awesome majesty took his own breath away, despite the fact that he'd witnessed it many times. It was yet another reminder to him that kept him in perspective; seeing the incredible force made him feel like a mere wisp of straw.

Cameron felt much the same as the thunderous pounding joined with her life blood. One drop of water by itself was nothing, but joined and joined it could culminate in what now she gazed upon. Her life seemed dominated by water. The endless ocean, then the long, swiftly flowing rivers and placid inland lakes that were so vast that often there was no shoreline to see, all emptying into this wondrous sight. Reluctantly she turned away and silently followed Goliath into the relative coolness of the forest. Many insects buzzed and bit, and even the juices of the leaves that the large man showed her to rub on her skin did not seem to help. The heat of this strange country was like nothing she had experienced before.

They camped that night on the east bank of Lake Erie.

Although exhausted, Cameron could not sleep. Many questions buzzed in her head, like the legion of mosquitoes whose voices crescendoed in her ears, and the chorus of crickets, who seemed much louder than the ones in Scotland.

"Is everything of double size and sound in this New World?" she asked of the man who sat contentedly staring up through the trees at the stars.

"It appears so," he answered laconically as he wondered when she would ask about her brother. He had evaded her questions on board, suspecting listening ears, but now with just the trees, insects, and animals, he was prepared to answer directly. Yet in the six weeks they had been traveling, she had asked nothing.

"Even the sun is bigger and hotter," she remarked.

" 'Tis near the middle of August."

Cameron fell silent as she realized that over three months had passed since they set sail from Fort William. On the one hand it astonished her and on the other it felt even longer, as the time imprisoned by the interminable sea had dragged by so slowly. The six weeks she had been traveling with Goliath had sped by at an alarming rate, by day that was. Nighttime passed slowly as she remembered nights wrapped in Alex's golden arms, but she fortified herself with the thought that she would soon meet her brother.

"The winters are just as extreme. Snow above even my tall head," volunteered Goliath, breaking into her thoughts.

"Where are we going?" asked Cameron, the night and her fatigue causing anxious pangs. Had the large man really said that he would take her to her twin, or was it just her wishful thinking? she worried. Everything had an unreality, as though she lived and walked in a dream.

"To Méron," responded Goliath, deciding to open the subject.

"I do not know a Méron. I only know Jumeau," answered Cameron, hiding a sharp pang of fear as she acknowledged that even though they had shared the same mother's womb and at the same time, her twin was now a stranger.

"Your French is perfect, so surely you know that the

word *jumeau* means only 'male twin,' " answered Goliath.

"And my name, Jumelle?"

"Is 'female twin.' "

"We must have spoken French when we were together on North Rona, but when he was taken from me, it was as though I forgot the language. Locked its meaning away in my mind. It confused me," professed Cameron.

"French was the language of your birth."

"I am Scottish, not French."

"By blood, not by birth. Duncan Fraser named you both Cameron and Camerona. Your brother's name was shortened to Méron, as it sounded more French and was less of a mouthful."

"Where is . . . Méron?"

"Waiting for you. By now he should have heard of your arrival on these shores," replied Goliath.

"How?"

"By Indian runner. News travels like the wind and as swiftly and silently between tribes, and all whom we've met have allegiance to the French."

"But where is he? How long before I see him?"

"In a week or so, if all goes well."

"On the ship it seemed as though you said . . . he was an Indian?" ventured Cameron.

"Lives as one, 'tis true. He is like the adopted son of the Ottawa chief, Pontiac, who at the moment is torn between loyalty to the English and loyalty to the French," explained Goliath.

"He lives with this tribe of Ottawas?" asked Cameron. "Is that where you are taking me?"

"Nay, he has his own lodge. He spends time in solitude away from the squabbles of the tribe. Often he winters with them, but in the summer months he prefers his own company. He'll ride out with them on hunting parties, but Méron, despite his youth, is his own man."

"How old are we?"

"Past your sixteenth year. Just starting your seventeenth, I reckon," responded Goliath, not surprised by the question.

"Tell me about him," asked Cameron, getting drowsy but wanting the picture of her brother in her head.

"You'll see for yourself soon enough," laughed Goliath softly, not knowing how to describe the youth whom he had taken care of and protected since he was eight years old. How could he tell Cameron that their roles were now reversed and it was the tall, lithe youth who seemed now the guardian and protector. A sixteen-year-old boy who looked much older than his age. A silent, unpredictable shadow, who showed little joy. It had not always been so, remembered Goliath, wide awake and hearing Cameron's steady breathing. It had been the meeting with his father in France that had robbed the youth of his childhood. The decadence and carelessness that Bonnie Prince Charlie submerged himself in, wallowed in, thought Goliath savagely. The hope of Scotland, no better than a pig in a barnyard. Actually the pig was better, he amended, as at least it took care of its own. Goliath turned on his side, trying to block out the painful expression that had crossed Méron's young face as Charles Stuart had mocked him by pronouncing to all assembled, "Come meet yet another bastard who claims to be my son!" The look of pain had passed, taking with it vibrancy and the hope of youth. A stony, impassive face flashed into Goliath's mind. Emerald-green eyes that could harden to a gemlike sharpness. The boy had disappeared, and a hard man had prematurely taken his place. Maybe the reuniting with his twin sister would bring back some of the youth their father had stolen, he mused before falling asleep.

CHAPTER TWENTY-FIVE

It was the end of August and the sun beat down, turning the grass to brittle straw. They had left the waters of Lake Erie after paddling more than thirty miles following the northwest bank and struck due north on foot. The grasslands and forest had been riddled with the flash of redcoats, and although the going was rugged, Cameron never complained.

Goliath now watched her ride beside him, glad he was able to obtain the horses, even though it had cost him several precious items—his watch and chain and most of his clothes—as well as considerably lightening the money belt he wore hidden at his waist. He had been reluctant, knowing word could possibly leak out to Fort Detroit, which lay too close to the west for comfort. He kept the proximity of the fort from Cameron, not knowing what her reaction to having Alex so close would be and feeling that Méron should be the one to apprise her of the facts. He laughed aloud and dug in his heels to catch up with the lithe figure who galloped before him, a very different picture from the wan, spiritless person on board. She now glowed with health, her face, arms, and legs the color of mahogany. In the blazing summer heat she had shed her leather leggings, choosing to wear just a breechcloth and sleeveless leather vest. Her feet were bare, and her raven hair hung to her shoulders in a glossy blue-black cloud. Around her forehead keeping the hair from her eyes was a beaded band. His horse labored under the tremendous weight of his body, unable to keep up with the galloping figure that streaked ahead in the golden sunlight. He swore furiously, kicking the poor, heaving sides of his overburdened mount as Cameron was lost from view.

Cameron reveled in the so-long-denied freedom, wishing it was Torquod's body beneath her. The air was hot, still, yet tense, as though gathering strength. Not a breeze touched the treetops, and she knew it was that incredible moment of calm before a storm. She wondered if the New World's storms could equal the exhilarating violence of Cape Wrath. She was unaware of eyes watching her as she raced, her hair streaming. The whistle of the air rushing past her ears and her own horse's hoofbeats thundering, throwing up dust from the dry earth and pounding with the blood in her body, covered the sounds that were approaching and gaining.

Topping a rise, Goliath reined and stared down at the two racing figures. "Well, old nag, they've found each other, we can take our time," he growled with relief, patting the wet neck of the exhausted horse before urging him slowly down the hill, keeping his eyes glued to the riders who kicked up the dust on the dry plain below them. The thunderclouds gathered and swelled, becoming purple and deep gray, rumbling and threatening.

Cameron sensed the other rider as the sky darkened. She didn't look behind her but bent over the horse's head, urging him to go faster. Lightning rent the air and she felt the other rider drawing abreast of her. She once again wished it was Torquod beneath her, for surely then nobody would be able to catch her. As she was about to veer her mount sharply in another direction, she was yanked from her horse. For a dizzying minute she thought she was to fly through the air to come crashing to the ground, but she felt her bare flesh contact warm skin, and then she was facedown with the wind knocked out of her, seeing the rain-spattered earth moving beneath her as she was carried like a sack across the other rider's horse. A muscular brown thigh extending to a moccasined foot caused panic to mount, and summoning all her energy, she shifted her head and bit. Her hair was grasped and the horse halted sharply so that he reared, but still she hung on with her teeth dispite the pain. A frantic thought of being possibly scalped like the Beothuk flashed through her mind as she tasted the salty tang of blood. The hard, muscular leg afforded little hold, but she hung on to the skin as she blindly fumbled for her dirk. A strong hand reached the hidden weapon before hers did, and she stiffened, waiting for it to be plunged into her. The Indian seemed to freeze, and the moment was long as Cameron lay across his thighs, her teeth still buried in his flesh. Her eyes were tightly closed as she waited for her own death. The blood pounded in her ears, and she thought she was imagining the hoarse whisper drowned out by the ferocious thunder overhead.

"Jumelle?"

Cameron opened her eyes, but all she could see were the blur of brown thigh and the now wet ground. The rain beat down on her body, and her ears strained.

"Jumelle?"

What was happening? she wondered. Was she losing her mind? She released her numb, aching jaws and was immediately turned over. She stared up into the dark face above her, unable to see in the dim light and sheets of rain. She lay in strong arms, gazing, her face frowning in the effort to recognize. She struggled to sit, to see at a closer range as lightning flashed, illuminating the emerald green of the eyes that seemed to devour her face.

"Jumeau?"

Brother and sister stared mesmerized at each other, unaware of the violence of the storm that tore the heavens and earth. Cameron did not know what she felt. She wanted to reach up and touch the planes of his face but was unable to move. After what seemed an eternity, she felt the horse moving steadily beneath her, although her brother's eyes had not left her face. Embarrassed, she wrenched her gaze away and looked about her. Her own mount had disappeared, probably terrified by the violence of the storm.

"My horse," she said lamely, but the stranger who was her brother did not respond but continued staring at her. She once again looked away from him, pinning her eyes to the passing scenery as they left the plain and entered thick forest. No words passed between them as they traveled for nearly an hour, at an even, steady pace. The storm abated, leaving a misty drizzle to water the sunset, which occasionally bled through the thick cover of pine trees that soared above them. Cameron felt suspended, her heart hammering out of step with the plodding hoof-beats and her brother's pulse. She sat sideways in front of him, her bare arm against his chest, unable to look at him but conscious that his eyes never left her profile. Her mind was a blank, no thoughts, no exhilaration at the final reunion, just the clashing rhythms of her, horse, and him.

The horse stopped, and as though in a dream, Cameron looked around at the small clearing. The waters of a crystal lake reflected the pale, ebbing rays of the sun, and the light rain ruffled the shimmering surface. As though sleepwalking, she numbly slid to the ground, vaguely feeling the cramping of her muscles at riding in the unaccustomed position. She felt her legs move until she stood with the cold water lapping at her bare feet, staring blindly across the lake, which seemed to be tightly embraced by tall, thick trees. Dimly she heard the horse moving and then felt a presence beside her. She hadn't heard his footsteps. How long they stood side by side she didn't know, but darkness fell, and the still, deep waters turned to black and melded with the sky and trees. From far away, as though she was out of her own body, she felt him take her arm and knew she allowed herself to be led.

Goliath looked up from his cooking as the door opened and the twins entered. He frowned, seeing Cameron's blank expression as Méron led her in rather like a docile mare. The two stood silently before him, and he breathed heavily through his nose, shaking his head in disbelief. He had known Méron for nearly nine years and Cameron for four months and should be used to their appearances, he mused, and yet in each other's company their distinctions were heightened. The two sets of unnaturally green eyes that regarded him from their placement in golden skin set off by blue-black hair were disconcerting, to say the least.

Méron towered above his diminutive sister, who barely reached his shoulder, and yet each was perfectly formed and long of limb. Goliath knew he was standing gaping and once again shook his head, trying to read what was in Méron's eyes as they seemed to burn into him. He felt loath to break the shrouding silence as he cleared his throat nervously.

"Supper's ready," he said hoarsely, finding it strange to speak, as though he had been struck dumb. He turned away and busied himself, crashing the tin plates together as somehow he felt his voice had jarred something undefinable, almost mystical. He set the table, feeling awkward and clumsy, and Méron sat Cameron down in a chair and placed himself facing her. The three sat together, and Goliath did not take his eyes off the two. Méron's eyes did not leave his sister's face, and hers did not leave her plate, nor did she attempt to eat.

Cameron stared at the mass of congealing food, hearing the sounds of Goliath and Méron eating. The noises were no longer muffled but steadily grew sharper and sharper until the scraping of the plates and forks tore in painfully so that she wanted to cover her ears and drown them out by screaming and screaming. Her body stiffened, and her small brown hands grasped the edge of the table as she prepared to flee out of the cabin. Goliath watched in consternation as he saw Méron stand staring down at Cameron's bowed head. Poised for flight, Cameron felt the weight of her brother's towering shadow. Her heart hammered. Why was she so afraid to look at him? she puzzled frantically. Why was she acting in this strange way? Tightening her jaw, she took a deep breath and threw her head back and stared at him. Green eyes flashed, and her nostrils flared, her mouth set in a rebellious line.

Goliath leaned back in his chair and folded his arms, intensely interested in the scene unfolding before him as he realized that Cameron was afraid even as her eyes blazed back at the ones that so mirrored her own. Méron was also afraid, he concluded, knowing well the hard, unyielding expression. Should he tactfully leave the fiery twins to work out their differences? he wondered, or should he remain as a buffer? His shrewd eyes traveled the length of Méron's lithe brown leg and, noting the shape and pattern of Cameron's teeth on the firm thigh, decided to remain. Maybe Duncan Fraser knew what he was about nine years ago when he separated the wild twosome, he mused.

Cameron wrenched her gaze from Méron's as she remembered Tor and Omen. In her wild, uncurbed dash across the plain she had forgotten them completely, having been caught up in her need for the purging gallop. Seeing no sign of them in the cabin, she stared accusingly at Goliath, who laughed to find himself now the object of her flashing eyes.

"Och, dinna vent your wild rage on me," he chuckled, holding up his great paws in mock alarm.

"Tor," pronounced Cameron.

"Outside sniffing around," he replied, waving his hand toward the door, which Cameron quickly opened, emitting a piercing whistle. Tor responded with a distant answering bark, but Omen hopped down immediately from the rafters, from where he had been watching the proceedings with a beady eye. The raven perched on the back of a chair between the twins, looking from one to the other and shaking his great black head with such apparent disapproval that Goliath could not contain his mirth any longer. He leaned back further in his chair and roared, slapping his large girth, and was joined, it seemed, by Omen, who bobbed up and down, cawing loudly. Cameron felt her anger rise and looked sharply at her brother to ascertain if he also thought her an object of ridicule, but his face was tightly controlled, showing nothing of what he felt. It was then she realized what she felt, and sadness welled up. She turned, hiding her emotions, as Tor loped into the cabin, his long tail wagging a greeting. Cameron threw herself down on a pile of skins and held her hound close, burying her face in his damp coat. This was not as it was supposed to be, she raged inwardly, as her brother's hard, set face flashed in her mind. In his stern expression she saw no love, joy, or welcome, just cold censure, much like Alex's.

Goliath noted the softening of Méron's expression as he stared at the curled back of his sister, who lay hugging her hound, facing the wall. He saw sadness melt the stern features of the youth, and he shook his head and clucked his tongue before heaving his enormous girth from his seat and noisily taking the plates from the table. Silly young fools, he muttered to himself. How could two such courageous bairns be so cowardly at showing emotions such as love? He felt dejected that there was nothing he could do, and that they had to work their conflict out themselves. Méron shattered Goliath's inner dialogue as the young man wrenched the plates from Goliath's hands and dumped them noisily back on the table.

"Nay! Let the squaw do it!" spat Méron savagely.

Now we are in for some explosions, thought Goliath, chewing the inside of his lip. "It has been a long journey, lad, and the lass is tired," he attempted softly, knowing as he tried the futility. Méron was hurt and bridled with a stubborn temper to equal if not surpass his sister's.

Squaw? Cameron thought to herself and suddenly felt a hard toe dig into her back and ignored it, not turning, although her muscles tensed. She knew the word "squaw" was woman in Indian, but Méron said it sneeringly and with disdain.

Méron looked cunningly at his sister's body. Her slim arms, encircling the large dog, made it impossible to lift her alone. He crouched down on his haunches and scratched behind the dog's long, sleek ears. The hound wriggled around, adjusting his position to sniff at Méron's hand, and as Cameron's clasp loosened to allow the animal freedom of movement, Méron picked her up in one lithe movement. Cameron seethed. For a moment she had allowed herself to feel a closeness with the stranger, who petted her dog with seeming affection. The heat of his body as he squatted next to her on the soft pile of fur as they both caressed the soft coat of the young hound had joined with her own, forming a kinship between them. She debated fighting his strong arms, which felt like steel bands, but realizing the futility of it, allowed her body to go limp. As he set her on her feet in front of the messy table, she deliberated whether to let her legs buckle, but not trusting his hard foot not to kick her inert body, she stood. She felt nausea rise in her throat as she stared at the glutinous cold stew. It had been weeks since she last sickened, and now the paralyzing horror of her possible condition poured in as she fought the waves of faintness.

Méron watched in alarm as he saw the beads of perspiration cover her face, which paled beneath her sun-bronzed skin, and quickly picked her up and carried her into the fresh night air. Cameron was conscious of his firm hand on her forehead as she heaved. She lay back exhausted on the pine needles, staring up at the dark sky as he bathed her face and neck with cold water.

"I am sorry, little sister," whispered Méron, and Cameron rolled away from him to hide the tears that were released by the warmth and tenderness in his voice, so she didn't see the flare of rejection and hardening of his face. She lay smelling the fragrance of the wet pine forest, willing her tears away before turning back to him.

Méron was gone. Cameron sat up and stared around in the darkness, but she was alone. She hugged her knees and looked across the dark lake, which was now illuminated by a half-moon, feeling lost and very deserted. Angry at her vulnerability and weakness, she chided herself sternly. She needed no one, especially not this strange brother. What if she was with child? When was it conceived? Her mind coldly calculated the months since her cycle. April, May, and it was now, according to Goliath, the end of August. She had no frame of reference as to the gestation time of women, having been brought up in isolation with an old Highland outlaw, and she wondered why her belly did not show the emergence of new life as a dog or wild animal's did. It could not be possible that she was with child. She didn't want to be, she resolved angrily, and feeling grimy and sour from the long, hot day and from her sickness, she stood and stripped off her few clothes.

Cameron floated in the clear, icy water staring up at the equally clear night sky that, washed by the rain, now sparkled with crystalline stars. The coldness of the mountain-spring-fed lake soon seeped into her tensing her muscles, and she swam vigorously to the shore. As she waded through the shallow water, she stopped, aware of being watched. She saw Méron sitting silently, and after her

first startled faltering, she walked bravely toward him,
appearing like a young goddess or Indian legend of a
moon woman emerging from the dark, illuminated pool.

Not knowing what else to do, and, betraying no sign
of her confusion, Cameron stalked past him with her small
nose in the air and entered the cabin, much to Goliath's
consternation. His usual ability to cope with the unexpected deserted him as he gaped, with slack lips, at the
naked, wet girl. Méron leaned against the doorpost, his
green eyes brimming with laughter as he watched his sister's dignified entrance and his large guardian's expression
of shocked disbelief. Cameron stood haughtily looking
from one to the other, covering up her feeling of being
trapped as she seethed at her stupidity, knowing that her
clothes hung limply from Méron's shaking hand as he
tried to control his amusement. She would not ask him
for them, as that would be lowering herself, and so, finding nothing better to do, stood trying to appear superior
in the English-lady-of-the-court tradition, with her small
clenched fists on her hips. Méron could no longer contain his mirth. He howled, his eyes streaming as he acknowledged that his twin had not changed very much
from the eight-year-old girl he had left on North Rona.
Cameron watched her brother's face, trying to summon
up her rage, but to her surprise she felt a nostalgic, aching warmth spread through her, as though they were
tiny bairns again with no one but each other. His face
was no longer harsh and forbidding. It was not a stranger's closed suspicious mask but Jumeau's, alive and
happy. Her laughter joined his, and soon was joined by
Goliath's deep rumble. With arms about each other, the
twins sank down on the pile of furs, still gasping and
hiccoughing their free, untrammeled amusement.

Their laughter died away, and they stared at each other,
searching each other's eyes, tentatively touching each
other's features before Méron pulled her close to his
heart. Goliath sniffed and tiptoed out as he saw Méron's
proud face with tears coursing down his cheeks as he
stared above Cameron's cradled head. She was unaware
of her brother's wet cheeks as she closed her eyes, smelling the musky scent of pine and man, feeling safe and

at peace with the steady beating of his heart close to her ear.

"We are no longer children, and you are my sister but arouse unbrotherly feelings in my male parts," said Méron huskily, standing. "I love you, as you are a part of me and will always be . . . but, as I said, we are no longer carefree, innocent bairns, but man and woman."

Cameron watched him take some skins and leave the cabin. She tried to puzzle out his words, but soon sleep claimed her exhausted body, and she cuddled into the soft pelts.

Cameron awoke as the first light tinged the sky behind the thick fir trees. She felt a happiness spread through her as she remembered the previous evening, and sat up quickly looking around the large wooden room, which was decorated with objects from two great clans, one Scottish and the other Indian. A set of bagpipes hung with native drums; intricate woven blankets hung with the tartans of Stuart and MacLeod; and iron skillets and wooden spurtles hung with the painted earthenware pots of the Native Americans. The roughhewn table and chairs and the stone fireplace used for cooking were offset by the blankets and mats of pelts that lined the walls for sleeping and sitting. On one wall was a rifle surrounded by bows, arrows, and spears. She got up to examine these when she turned, aware of being watched. Goliath cleared his throat nervously, wishing she would cover herself.

"I should like to learn to use this," said Cameron gaily, twanging the taut gut of the bow.

"Should you not cover yourself?" responded Goliath, averting his eyes and busying himself.

Cameron looked down at her naked body with surprise. Alex's words of censure spiraled into her brain and, covering her breasts, she scrambled for her clothes and, clutching them, raced out of the cabin unable to dress in the suddenly charged atmosphere. She stood in the morning sun looking over the lake as she tied the breechcloth around her loins and covered her tender breasts with the tight leather vest. Why did her breasts feel so swollen and sore, as though they might burst? she wondered. She longed to plunge into the icy water to rid herself of her momentary depression. Deep in thought, she walked along the narrow shore that was ridged by the giant veins of tree roots. A colony of beavers distracted her from her own problems, and she stared with fascination at the busy, strange animals. As she watched, an otter surfaced and, clowning, put on a performance, it seemed, just for her. She laughed aloud at his antics, remembering her past enjoyment of those playful, mischievous creatures. She cautiously looked around, not wanting to offend either Goliath or her brother, who had both seemed as censuring and disapproving about nudity as Alex, before removing her clothes and joining the otter in his play.

She swam, and the fearless, friendly animal spiraled and flipped over and around her floating body. Tor barked from the shore before plunging into the water to join his young mistress. Regretfully Cameron watched the otter swim swiftly away, and she headed back toward her hound.

Méron made his way into the cabin, smiling at the memory of his sister and the otter. "She surely is a child of the forest," he remarked to Goliath. "Unspoiled by civilized life."

"Too much a child of nature, and not such a child when she's as old as yourself," replied Goliath dryly. "I need a lusty woman, for your young sister's exhibiting of all her charms sorely tests a man."

"Then go and leave us to refind each other," said Méron slowly after a long, thoughtful pause. "Angus set off to Boston two months past to meet up with you, but it would seem you missed each other."

The two men had spent much of the night talking under the trees, and Goliath had briefly filled in Méron as to how he had found Cameron at Glen Aucht and the circumstances surrounding that. The young man had sat silently listening, no emotion crossing his face until the large man was done.

"And this Alex Sinclair?" he had said.

"A good man but as lost as the lass herself. Hamstrung

by the English and fights to save his family estate by
fighting for them at Fort Detroit. The Old Turkey Buzzard has collared Sinclair and nearly got Cameron also,
as he marked the similarity between you two," informed
Goliath.

"Old Turkey Buzzard still lives?" ejaculated Méron.

"Not only lives but has translated his name to Old
Hawk, which he proudly boasts," laughed the large man.
"That old Ramsbotham might be a fool, but he certainly
leads a charmed life. They made him a general and
named a frigate after him, expecting him to rock the
remainder of his years away in an old soldiers' home,
and now he's back and after your young neck with
your own brother-in-law by his side."

"Does Sinclair know of me?"

"Of your existence, yes, but not of your alliance with
the Ottawas. But I'm thinking he'll be putting two and
two together shortly."

Silence then had fallen between them, only to be punctuated by a snort of cynical laughter.

"A free translation, don't you think? Old Turkey Buzzard to Old Hawk?" spluttered Goliath, but Méron just
stared broodingly up at the stars, not wanting to ask
if his sister loved this man whom Ramsbotham had enlisted to destroy him.

After breakfast Goliath whistled cheerfully as he
stowed his gear onto one horse and mounted another.
Cameron watched, infuriated, as the two men chose to
talk in the guttural grunts of the Indian tongue. She
looked from one to the other suspiciously.

"Leave us in peace for at least one moon," stated
Méron in Algonkian.

"You'll return to the Maumee?" asked Goliath in kind,
referring to Pontiac's camp.

"If we are not there shortly after, come find us."

Goliath tipped his hat to Cameron and rode off at a
leisurely pace. Méron turned and surveyed his sister's
stormy face and smiled engagingly.

"Now there'll be no secrets between us, as we will
be alone."

"You do not trust me?" she challenged.

" 'Tis not you I have distrust of but your ignorance," said Méron gently and, at seeing the indignation on her face, amended his words hastily. "No, not ignorance but lack of knowledge. This land of conflicts must be strange to you, and until you are aware of all, there are many things I cannot share. Now I have much else to share with you if you'll clear your brow of those thunderclouds."

Cameron looked at him solemnly, hearing the strange mixture of Scottish brogue mixed with another element. "This land is not as strange as the south of Scotland . . . for instance Edinburgh and the social whirl," she answered rebelliously.

"This spot here is not the world or land I speak of but a small resting-place free from conflicts," said Méron patiently, indicating the lake and forest. "A hiding place, if you will, to which I retreat when I feel pulled in too many directions, seeing faults in all . . . but it is not the land of conflicts I speak of."

"Explain to me, then, what you mean."

"Not now. 'Tis not time. We must get to know each other again," he smiled, taking her hand in his.

For three weeks Cameron and Méron lived an idyllic existence as he introduced her to the animals that used the lake as a watering hole. Deer, bear, raccoon, opossum, skunk, and stately heron, as well as the beaver and otter and countless other large and small inhabitants of the lake, forest, and plain. Riding side by side on the parched flat land, Méron pointed out the tawny mountain lion whose color stirred up in Cameron painful thoughts of Alex. She shivered at the chilling scream of the sinewy feline as he pounced upon a young deer. For the first time in a long while, the twins were together again as they had been as children so long ago on the windswept island of North Rona with just each other, the elements, and the wild animals for company. At night they sat filling in the experiences of the lost years. Méron translated the small book of Latin, reading the words their mother Dolores had written to her children and although the words brought choking sadness, Cameron rejoiced that she had been given a second chance. She admitted to Méron that she had also had such a book, which she had destroyed in a swift spurt of anger, rejection, and disillusionment.

"I dinna ken why I did such a thing," she confessed. "It was as though a dream was broken. A dream I had always had without really knowing I had such a dream. Then to know my mother was dead and that I'd never find her . . ." Cameron struggled to explain, her eyes filling with tears and the words strangling in her throat, making it impossible to go on. Without a word Méron enfolded his sister in his arms and together they cried for themselves and the mother they never knew, except through the faded words in Latin in the small, leather-bound book.

"But we have a father," exclaimed Cameron, pushing herself back so she looked into her brother's face.

"NO!" shouted Méron.

"But . . ." protested Cameron, trailing off in bewilderment at the intensity of her brother's vehemence.

"We have no father!" Méron stated coldly, disentangling himself from his sister's arms and stalking across the room to stare through the window across the dark lake. Cameron watched him silently for a while and then her eyes drifted to the Stuart plaid on the wall.

"Aye, we do," she said softly, stroking the woven fabric. "We're royal Stuarts and our father the Bonnie Prince," she added, but her words were drowned by the slamming of the door as Méron stormed out.

The next morning Méron acted as though nothing had occurred and for a while Cameron did not press the issue.

"You said there'd be no secrets," she ventured as they sat tranquilly fishing. She noted Méron's hand tense and the fish that had been about to take the bait sped away.

"Keep your dreams!" he spat.

"You don't even know of what I was going to speak," protested Cameron to his retreating back.

Méron's refusal to talk about their father shattered the harmony between them. Twice more Cameron had broached the subject with the same response, and even when she said nothing about it a taut string seemed stretched between them that underscored all they did together.

It was the middle of September and Cameron feasted her eyes on the incredible blaze of autumn that was mirrored in the clear lake. The nights had grown chilly and she smelled the frost that stung her nose, and yet the days were hot and sunny and she marveled at the contrasts of the strange New World. She sat seeing Alex in the golden and red leaves around her, wondering if he was happy. Despite the hot days she wore a long, loose shirt of Goliath's, the tremendous sleeves rolled up, leaving the too-long tails to fall to her knees. She now knew positively that something grew in her belly and yet could not bring herself to tell her brother.

Méron, back from fishing, stood watching her from a distance, loath to disturb her solitude and yet knowing instinctively that some part of her cried out. But to whom? he asked himself as he approached silently. He paused as she stood and smoothed anguished hands down her stomach, and his breath hissed in his throat as he recognized the swollen outline and what it portended. Unable to deal with the knowledge, he turned and noiselessly walked away to the cabin, where he sat puzzling the new turn of events. The month was nearly up, and if he didn't return to the Maumee, Angus and Goliath would be appearing within a week or so. He had told Cameron about life in Pontiac's camp, editing out tactfully certain aspects of it, namely those having to do with women. He could not see his high-strung, impulsive sister passively submitting to the chewing of hides for leather and the everyday female labor of the tribe. He had resolved to introduce her as his younger brother, keeping her close by him in his tepee until he could fathom what to do with her.

There was an uneasy peace between the Ottawas and the English, but the undercurrent of tensions on both sides guaranteed no lasting cessation of the hostilities. Both the French and the English wooed and bribed the tribe and its allies with petty trinkets, which appeased them for less and less time as the Indians began to hold out for guns, powder, and metal tools.

Darkness fell, and Méron remained motionless, unmindful of the fish that lay by his side losing the brightness of their eyes and scales.

Cameron entered and watched him from the door for a moment before picking up the fish.

"There is a secret you wish to keep from me?"

The harshness of Méron's voice stopped Cameron in her tracks. She turned and instantly knew to what he referred. No words were needed. She splayed her small hands across her belly and nodded.

"How many moons?" asked Méron, rising to his feet and gentling his tone. Cameron shrugged unhappily.

"You do not know?" he said incredulously.

Cameron shook her head sadly, and then her expression brightened. "Do you?" she asked hopefully.

Méron sat down at the table with a thump, regarded her with stunned astonishment, and then proceeded to clean and gut the fish.

"When was the last cycle of the moon?" he said after a long pause. Cameron frowned, wondering how she was supposed to know and then, seeing his serious expression, tried to remember when the moon was last full.

" 'Tis ebbing now," she ventured.

"What is?" exclaimed Méron impatiently.

Cameron fluttered her hand toward the night sky through the open door.

"The moon cycle of woman . . . the blood that flows!" Méron almost shouted. "When was the last?"

"In April, I think."

"You do not know?"

"I did not bleed on the vessel, and it sailed on May seventh. I did not think of it," professed Cameron. "But should not have the baby come by now?"

"I'm sorry. I remember now there was no mother to tell you of such things," replied Méron, ashamed for his impatience.

"There was no mother for you either, so how do you know about such things?"

"You forget, I've lived for two winters with the Ottawas. I saw my own son be born and die, taking his mother with him," informed Méron sorrowfully, his eyes haunted by the memory. They sat silently, Cameron empathizing with her brother's pain.

"It seems my nephew will be born with the snows of the New Year, but don't worry, little sister, I'll stay by you, and this child and his mother will live," he pronounced, not showing the cold fear that pierced him as he remembered the helplessness of watching the life drain from the young Indian girl, still attached to the baby by the thick, engorged umbilical cord. He had beat ineffectually at the stony-faced squaws who barred him entrance and had been borne away by the braves, who excused his behavior as ignorance of their ways.

Méron became conscious of the smell of cooking as Cameron placed a laden plate before him. He thrust away his past pain and concentrated on the future, deciding to brave the harsh winter in the small cabin. It was autumn, and they must make haste to provide for the long, cold siege, he thought, as they ate.

Nearly two weeks later, as Cameron worked drying meat and fish to store away, she heard the rumble of voices. She hid and peered out, wishing Méron was back from checking his traps. He hated snaring animals, preferring to hunt them one to one, but he explained that they were in a race against time, and she had felt guilty, knowing that he compromised himself on her behalf. Three young braves dismounted, and behind them towered Goliath with a man of equal size. Her green eyes widened in disbelief at Jemmy's flaming red hair.

"Up into the loft," hissed Méron, who had, in his usual silent way, entered without her knowing.

" 'Tis Jemmy and Goliath with another giant," she protested.

"Do as you're told," he replied, pushing her toward the ladder. "I am not ready for the Ottawas to know you are here. You will not come down or show yourself to any until I come up for you."

Cameron crouched in the loft, trying to see through the rough planking floor. The unintelligible language drifted up from outside, but none of them entered. There seemed to be a heated argument, with Méron's voice raised in anger.

"Dinna fash yerself, laddie," comforted Goliath's burr. "'Tis just a bunch of boys having their usual argument. So, Jemmy-Lad, go look at the water and watch the beavers getting their winter home ready."

Cameron heard hoofbeats ride off and wondered at the sudden silence. She debated descending despite Méron's orders, but when she peered down into the empty room, she saw he'd taken the precaution of removing the ladder, and to spring down in her cumbersome condition was pure suicide. Her heart thumping as she imagined them all scalped and dead, she strained her ears to hear nothing but the birds and crickets and an occasional splash. What would she do if she were the only one left alive? she worried, knowing she was not equipped to survive in the wilderness. If the winter was as extreme as the scorching summer had been, she and her baby would surely perish. She lay down, paralyzed at the terrifying thought, the pounding of her pulses covering the low hum of nearing voices. No matter how fervently she told herself she needed no one, the full truth flooded her mind. In her clumsy, vulnerable condition she was as helpless and useless as the babe she carried in her belly. The rumble of male voices punctuated by Jemmy's excited treble entered the house, and Cameron's rigidly held body relaxed with relief. She lay prone, her stomach silhouetted, feeling weak and overcome. She still lay in that position when Méron mounted the ladder. For a moment he feared she was in labor, but there were no spasms of the smooth, round belly. He touched her face, and she looked at him.

"I thought I was alone," she whispered, tears of relief pouring down her face. Méron held her in his arms, vowing he would let no harm come to this precious part of himself, not allowing thought of Alex to enter his mind. Cameron had hidden the man's existence away in a locked part of her mind. He, Méron, would lock it away also.

Later that night, after an extravagant celebration feast, which Méron justified by the fact that now there were more hands to work, Jemmy slept peacefully beside Cameron in the loft, her small, freckled hand clasping Cameron's thin, brown one. Angus and Goliath sat beside the still-dark lake hearing the plop of the frogs and the eerie call of the owls. Méron listened impassively to Goliath's news.

"Sinclair has made something of a name for himself, and the Turkey Buzzard is strutting and gobbling up the praise. Pontiac was put out but accepts your need for solitude. I added a few things of my own in order to convince him. Something about needing to test your manhood after the death of Little Doe," he explained, not willing to bring up the cause of Méron's grief the past winter but feeling he had to, as Pontiac had offered a choice of substitutes, which he had to use all of his persuasive and verbal powers tactfully to refuse from the autocratic Indian.

"I suppose he had a string of young squaws to keep me warm this winter?" said Méron with irony.

"You know him well, but as he said, he wants to breed strong warriors. Well, I told him you had a vision, and with a lot of colorful elaboration, which bored me so much that I won't bore you with it, he bade me embrace you in his name and keep you safe. There was a bit of a schlorich, as word had come down about Cameron . . . already called Little-Green-Eyes. I had to do a might of quick thinking there, I can tell you," confessed Goliath ruefully.

"Go on?"

"I said 'twas part of your vision . . . a brother from the same mother's womb who had descended with a giant raven from the sea," professed Goliath with embarrassment. Méron nodded with satisfaction. "So she is with child," added the large man after a weighty pause. "I suspected, but then she seemed so lithe and well. When is the bairn due?"

"She isna sure, seeming ignorant of woman's workings, but I am thinking 'twill be in January or late December. You think it is his?"

"Sinclair's?"

"Aye."

"Aye," responded Goliath slowly. "I've seen her wie no other."

"But this English Colonel Beddington . . . you said he raped her?" said Méron harshly.

"He wasna normal. I know the type. He couldna even stay stiff enough to rape the wee red-haired lass."

"Lass? Jemmy? 'Taint a lad?" queried Méron.

"Nay, I forgot to tell you. 'Tis also a lass, and a rare time my brother Angus had keeping it from his traveling companions when he found out hisself, I can tell you," chuckled Goliath, remembering Angus's vivid description of being nursemaid and protector to the young girl, who after a few weeks of traveling still refused to bathe. The large man, used to the company of men, had stripped bare and turned to Jemmy and, ignoring her protests, removed her clothes, offended by her rank stench, as he so crudely put it. "I'd have given anything to see his face when he beheld her. He didna trust the lusty young braves, who were already fascinated by the red-gold curls, so Angus took it upon himself to see to her cleanliness and bodily functions like a nanny," Goliath laughed.

Méron didn't join in Goliath's mirth. He silently waited until the large man's rumbling guffaws had growled away.

"How is it the child is not at the Maumee?" he asked.

"I used the old noggin, having met up wie Angus before seeing Pontiac, and just slipped in the red-haired child as another part of your vision. Incidently Jemmy is a spunky young lass and is called Lion-Cub by the Ottawas. 'Tis ironic, as Sinclair is named Mountain Lion . . . for his total disregard for danger and his own life, and the scar that claws his face from eyebrow to jaw."

"I want to hear no more," pronounced Méron firmly. "I close the door to all not in this circle, and like the bear we will rest a season in our winter home."

Goliath grunted grimly, knowing it would be a long, grueling winter for all of them, further complicated by the birth of the child. He looked up, but Méron had glided silently into the deep, thick forest. He snorted. The youth was more a part of the wild country than a lot of the natives, who, influenced by the invading Europeans, were hungry for the clothes and possessions of the white man.

"A country of Ishmaels," he grumbled. "All of us displaced." He sat brooding, homesick for his own land of Scotland, where the natives were also scattered and disbanded, wandering, trying to assimilate themselves not only to the invading English culture but to the cultures of alien territories all over the world. A season of peace would be a blessing, he mused, and chuckled as he wondered what tranquillity there could possibly be when they were snow-bound in the small cabin with the turbulent twins, whose wild, impulsive natures caused havoc and turmoil wherever they went.

CHAPTER TWENTY-SIX

As the first large, fluffy snowflakes teased the earth, floating languidly and far between, Alex and Corporal Jackson reached Fort Detroit dragging General Ramsbotham on a travois. The old man's eyes were sunken into his face, now even more gaunt from poor diet and the travails of the wilderness. His parchment skin was stretched, giving his face a skeletal appearance, and the once-sharp eyes were now dim and weary. As the old general had crumbled, seeming almost to have turned to dust, so had Alex flourished. He stood tall and strong, exuding a golden virility. His tawny hair was long and shaggy, bleached and streaked by the elements, his amber eyes were keen and hard, and his full beard did not disguise or hide the strength of his face.

Major Gladwin assessed the bearded woodsman who stood silently appraising him. "I see why the savages call you Lion, Major Sinclair," he said slowly.

Alex nodded and turned to the old general. He knelt and took the withered hand, looking silently into the sad eyes.

"I am Corporal Jackson, sir," informed Alex's young companion, saluting his commanding officer.

"At ease, Jackson," replied Gladwin with humor at the earnest soldier in stained, ragged buckskins before looking around for the rest of Ramsbotham's contingent. "Where are the others?" Jackson, about to answer, hesitated and looked toward Alex.

"Major Sinclair?"

Alex heard his commanding officer's voice but did not stand or remove his eyes from the emaciated old man who seemed to be trying desperately to communicate. The sunken mouth struggled, opening and closing. Alex leaned nearer, raising a large hand, cautioning Gladwin and Jackson to be silent.

"Méron," was forced like a small explosion from the

pleated, bloodless lips, and the old general panted painfully from the effort and then made strange sounds in his throat, trying to form another word. "Ker . . . ker . . . kill."

Alex felt the sharpness of the old man's dying word cut through him. Why had the general such a hatred for the youth? he wondered. The boy was his own wife's twin, his brother-in-law, he recalled with an ironic twist to his lips as he stood and stared down at the lifeless figure. He had grown to have some affection for the fanatical old soldier, who had proved to be courageous. Old Turkey Buzzard, he thought warmly, having picked up enough Algonkian to realize that the old man had translated freely to suit his own pride. Well, better a Turkey Buzzard than the name you were born to. Ramsbotham, he said to himself, covering the still face with a blanket.

"Where are the rest?" asked Gladwin after a pause, not wanting to show disrespect for General Ramsbotham but feeling a sense of relief that the old man would not be meddling around his fort all winter.

"Dead," answered Alex shortly. "Here is the full report," he added, reaching into his saddlebag and handing a sheaf of papers, which Gladwin quickly scanned.

"He was always a stickler for paperwork, I'll say that for him."

Alex did not reply for a moment. His amber eyes scanned the fort, thinking it looked like a toy, the brightly uniformed soldiers like the small lead ones he had played with as a child. How ridiculous it all seemed after the harsh reality of the wilderness beyond the walls. Sergeant majors strutting pompously, barking out orders to shiny-faced recruits with shining buttons, who marched as though they had been wound up with keys.

Gladwin eyed Alex shrewdly, truthfully ascertaining that the tall, golden man could not be cooped up within the fort. He would only prowl and pace like a captured wild animal, causing disruption. Their two strengths would be at odds, he concluded, deciding that Major Sinclair would be more useful as a scout outside the fortress walls. He turned his attention to the young soldier Jackson, whose schoolboy eyes shone with a respectful fervor.

"Jackson, would you prefer fort life or to continue under Major Sinclair on the outside?"

Alex smiled a slow, lazy smile and nodded at Major Gladwin. Though the commandant looked like a painted toy soldier, he was obviously a shrewd judge of character. Gladwin returned the smile, thinking that at any other time the two of them might have been friends.

"I mean no offense but . . ." stammered Jackson uncomfortably.

"Speak your mind, Jackson," said Gladwin impatiently.

"Well . . . er . . . um," stuttered the embarrassed soldier.

"He prefers the comforts of fort life and canna wait to shed his stained and tattered raiment to don the glorious red coat," helped out Alex humorously. " 'Tis all right, Jackson. I am mortally offended but I will strive to survive."

"Report to the sergeant at arms," dismissed Gladwin and laughed as Jackson saluted hastily and scampered away. "You were hard on the boy?"

"Nay, 'twas not I but the going. He needed prodding and pushing, but I got him here alive, and there's the thanks I get," returned Alex as the two men walked to Gladwin's quarters. Many titters and giggles were snorted through fingers as girls and women regarded the tall, golden man. Several Indians sat wrapped in their blankets watching, and small children played in the dry, cold dirt.

After a bath and change of clothes, Alex relaxed with Major Gladwin in his comfortable quarters.

"Most of the Indians here are from the missions, but, Christian or pagan, I don't trust them. 'Tis a strange, uneasy time. Last year the Senecas tried to cause trouble. They sent the red wampum belt to the Delawares and Shawnees, also to the Chippewas, Potawatomis, and Ottawas, trying to get the tribes to assault all our forts simultaneously. Here at Detroit, also at Pittsburgh, Presque Isle, Verango, and Niagara. It was a good plan, but fortunately for us the Detroit tribes informed me, and I was able effectively to sabotage the Senecas' plot," informed Gladwin with satisfied pride.

"What made the Senecas plan such a thing?" asked Alex.

"Greed. The French refused them certain requests and so they swore allegiance to us. Then they demanded more than we could afford to give them, and so they were angry. Like spoiled children."

Alex listened to the gross oversimplification, not volunteering his own knowledge. The Senecas were angry at not receiving the rum and gunpowder that the French had been so generous with—in that Gladwin spoke truthfully. However it was but a grain of truth, as the Indians also claimed that the English were disrespectful of their people and way of life. He contemplated his glass of rum as he thought sadly of the Indians' growing dependency on the white man and his weapons. Gunpower was needed for hunting, as the tribes that lived in the shelter of the forts had become almost crippled, relying on the sophisticated guns and tools in order to compete for meat.

"What are you thinking?" probed Gladwin, noting Alex's somber expression.

"We have just returned from Pontiac's camp on the Maumee," answered Alex, deciding he would have to know the major much better before sharing his philosophical thoughts. "He wishes you well, and I have several gifts in my saddlebag as proof of such."

"What do you think of the chief," asked Gladwin eagerly.

"As much as his inscrutable face allowed me to. He's an intelligent man," returned Alex, thinking of the tall, solidly built man with whom he had spent several days. "Cordial, extending every hospitality despite General Ramsbotham's lack of . . . er . . . tact," he added.

"Ramsbotham was never known for diplomacy," returned Gladwin. "I expect he was after the savage Méron?"

Alex nodded, and the Englishman roared with laughter. Alex watched him silently, not joining in the hilarity.

"It cost him his life," he added dryly when the commandant's mirth had died down.

"How?" asked Gladwin shortly, smarting under the unspoken censure.

"As I said, Pontiac greeted us with open arms. The general for some reason would not ask the chief directly about this man Méron but preferred instead to sneak around the camp." Once again Alex fell silent as Gladwin roared with laughter.

"The image of Ramsbotham trying to sneak furtively

around destroys my sense of seriousness. I'm sorry, Sincliar, but it's like trying to imagine a rooster pretending to be a mouse and yet crowing and preening every few seconds," he spluttered. Alex stood patiently waiting. What Gladwin said was true; it was humorous, but tragically so. "Of course Pontiac was aware of the general's sneaking?" added Gladwin and once more Alex nodded silently. "Well, go on," the Englishman insisted, wiping his streaming eyes.

"Inept at sneaking or not, apparently Ramsbotham was given news of the whereabouts of Méron and took off like a man possessed. We found him several miles from the Ottawa camp. His horse Galahad was dead . . . pushed beyond his limits," informed Alex stiffly.

"That's it?"

"That's it."

"Did he injure his head when the horse died beneath him?" probed Gladwin and, at Alex's shake of the head, added, "Then what accounted for his condition?"

"I can only surmise it was the loss of his war horse. They seemed uncommonly attached."

"That's all the old man had left, I suppose," replied Gladwin soberly.

"That and a fanaticism about this man Méron. Maybe you could enlighten me?" asked Alex carefully.

"Méron is a half-grown young savage who rides at Pontiac's left side. He has strange green eyes, so is probably a half-breed."

"Pontiac's son?"

"He appeared about three years ago. I suppose he could be Pontiac's son whelped from some captured white woman, but I doubt it. Those eyes are too strange not to have been remarked on before, and the savages are a superstitious lot. They hold the youth in awe as though he has some magical powers. He is a devil, seeming more silent and deadly than most . . . can appear and disappear into the shadows . . . and it's said those eerie green eyes can glow in the dark like a cat's," informed Gladwin.

"Why was Ramsbotham so obsessed with him?"

"Méron shot him in the bollox . . . destroyed his manhood. Mind you the general couldn't have had much left at his age. It was that injury that had him shipped back to

England and earned him the rank of general and the naming of the frigate."

"No wonder Ramsbotham wanted to even the score," said Alex quietly. "Old man or not, I would prefer to come to the end of my days intact. Now, what are my orders?"

"Rest a day or so. Winter will soon be on us, and there'll not be much Indian trouble when the snow comes. They'll be too busy trying to stay alive. From what you saw of Pontiac did you trust him?"

"I didn't made a judgment either way. He's no fool, though, as far as I could ascertain. Why?" answered Alex.

"I don't trust him. He seems to have a lot of influence with the neighboring Detroit tribes. The Ottawas, Chippewas . . . Potawatomis. I sense he's a very dangerous man," replied Gladwin thoughtfully.

"Where do the Hurons stand?"

"Oh, they're no threat. Their numbers have dwindled to nothing thanks to the French missionaries," explained the commandant, refilling Alex's glass. "Actually it's good that Pontiac accepts you, as I'd like you to keep your ear to the ground . . . approaching winter or not, tensions are building . . . nothing that I can put a finger on . . . just soldier's instinct, I suppose. You'll rest up for a few days and get to know the non-uniformed men around here. You'll find a motley group in the common room . . . trapper, half-breeds, woodsmen, and the like, take your pick as I allow no man to work alone."

"Because you don't trust them or because you are concerned with their welfare?" asked Alex cynically.

"Both," answered Gladwin. "You'll find some accommodating women about, to take the edge off abstinence. I doubt you'll have to search them out . . . more likely have to fight them off."

"Things have changed since I last experienced fort life," remarked Alex, thinking of a long, pure winter when he was a randy youth.

"It is not for public proclamation, and I do not condone it, but for officers I feel it keeps the morale high."

"And the morals low," quipped Alex.

"Speaking of morals, here are some letters for you," said Gladwin, rummaging around in a drawer of his desk.

"I also received a rather disconcerting one in reference to your wife, who I believe is wanted by the law and church for unnatural practices, namely witchcraft?" he added with one eyebrow raised.

Alex didn't reach for the proffered letters or answer.

"Where is your wife, Sinclair?" pursued Gladwin, his voice sharp and authoritarian.

"Flew off on her broomstick," shrugged Alex airily. The commandant stared shrewdly at the apparently nonchalant man.

"It's a serious charge, Sinclair. So is harboring a fugitive, whether she be a wife or not," he stated evenly.

"I am very much aware of that, Major Gladwin," answered Alex lightly. "Rest assured I harbor nothing but possibly fleas and some lice and request permission to leave so that I might remedy the matter."

Gladwin glared long and hard for several minutes before handing Alex the letters and dismissing him with a wave of the hand.

Alex kicked off his boots and lay full-length on his hard bed to peruse the letters. One was from Sir Robert Kinkaid informing him that Beddington's demise had been satisfactorily taken care of, the verdict reading accidental death while under the influence of spirits. There had been a touchy situation for a while at Alex's and Cameron's absence, but when it was made known that he, Alex, had volunteered for active duty and furthermore undertaken a dangerous mission with General Ramsbotham, who incidentally had given a glowing report on young Major Sinclair's loyalty to the throne, all accusations and suspicions had been laid to rest. Alex laughed, thinking with affection of the old gaunt soldier.

"You certainly did lie for me, Old Turkey Buzzard," he said softly. "How ironic life is. Little did you know, old man, that you saved my neck so that I'd help you wring my own brother-in-law's." Unwilling to think of Méron, who could conjure memories of Cameron, he picked up the letter again and read it to the end. Glen Aucht was being overseen by Ian Drummond, whose own estate had not been returned to him but had been grabbed greedily by Beddington's older brother, Sir Jonquil. Many of the farm women and children had returned, and Mackie, Fergus, Old-Petey, and Daft-Dougal had the estate well in hand. Alex thought of all those people on his land by the waters of the Firth of Forth and wondered why he at this moment felt nothing, not even a twinge of homesickness. Glen Aucht seemed unreal, another world, another lifetime. What was that tiny scrap of land compared with the vastness of the New World? he mused unemotionally. His estate seemed inconsequential and insular, and yet he was lying on an uncomfortable cot in the middle of the wilderness fighting people he had no quarrel with in order to retain that land. Glen Aucht was all that was left of his family's holdings, to be passed down to his sons and to their sons, he told himself, trying to break through his numbed senses. What sons? He closed his eyes and pictured each room of his house but couldn't eradicate Cameron's presence. He tried to force his mind to imagine another woman, a calm, obedient young lady with propriety who would docilely breed the sons he needed to carry on his line, but each pale face changed to the green-eyed rebel he had sworn to forget. A green-eyed rebel who now was a fugitive from the law and church, wanted for witchcraft.

He let his mind wander, remembering bits of news about Little-Green-Eyes, who was accompanied by the Great-Bird-of-Death. Ramsbotham had listened, his excitement growing at the incredible story, which must have passed from tribe to tribe building in intensity, from the Micmacs to the Abnakis to the Ottawas, the story having been grossly embellished as it traveled west by word of mouth until it sounded like an ancient myth or legend. Ramsbotham's eyes had shone fanatically. It was as though the old man had just one purpose left on earth, to find Cameron to use as a weapon against the renegade Méron. How, Alex had never really understood. Maybe the general hadn't thought it all out, and if he had, he wasn't trusting anyone, so his plan died with him. Alex had a shrewd idea that it probably hinged on the superstitious nature of the native people. That fanaticism had cost him two lives. First Galahad, the old war horse who was pushed beyond his limits, and, at the loss of his last true friend, Ramsbotham's own life had drained away. Such a lovable old codger to be ruled by such hate, thought Alex, and yet he was forced to admit that if his manhood was struck down as Ramsbotham's had been, he wouldn't rest until he had vengeance. Like brother like sister, he snorted viciously as the unwelcome memory of his own impotence flashed into his head. Cameron hadn't shot arrows as her brother had done, but she might as well have for all the pain she caused. Maybe the Indians' extravagant tales of Little-Green-Eyes and her Great-Bird-of-Death weren't so farfetched, he fumed. The things Cameron managed to get up to in the year that they had been together made any story possible, although he seriously doubted she could change shapes and fly to the sky cawing like a raven. Yet she had managed to bewitch him until he had lost judgment and control over himself and his destiny, he raged unfairly, no longer unemotionally detached.

"Damn her!" he swore aloud. He knew she was alive and had survived the long trip from Nova Scotia. He would find her and eradicate her from his heart, head, and groin. He would divorce her and remarry a conforming, civilized young woman. Cameron would not have any more power over him or his life, he vowed. He would sire sons and daughters and return to his birthland to claim his ancestral home. Nobody would hold the reins of his future, especially not her.

Cameron stared out morosely at the white world. Everything was covered with thick snow. Even the tall fir trees were bent by the weight, and there was no sign of the lake, just high drifts. At first she had rejoiced and felt exhilarated at the seeming magical change of the earth, but now she railed against its confinement. There had been several weeks in early winter when, bundled in furs, she had taken walks and learned to cut holes in the ice of the lake and fish. They had played like carefree children, throwing snowballs and making effigies, but now the snow was too deep and her shape too cumbersome. She had felt a spurt of energy and warm happiness as they all pitched in together making things for the baby, but now everything was done and lay patiently waiting. A crib that rocked made by Goliath and Angus, tiny clothes stitched by Jemmy, and little moccasins made by Méron. What had she made? she had worried, suddenly feeling inadequate when she had realized that she had helped with all things but had not initiated any of the presents, and to her own surprise and shock she had burst into tears. She stared out the window remembering how Méron had held her close as she cried out her concern.

"But you are making the baby," he had laughed.

"And who will make the baby a man or a woman able to exist in this world?" she retorted.

Cameron felt a clutch of fear remembering her brother's answer.

"You, his mother, and I, his uncle," he had replied lightly. There was no mention of the word "father," and yet the unspoken name hung between them.

Cameron waddled about trying to show a cheerful face so she wouldn't dampen the happiness of Jemmy, who had decided to have a Christmas celebration. Goliath and Angus had cut down a small fir tree, watched by the two girls, who laughed until their sides ached, as the two giants in snowshoes had clowned for their benefit in the deep drifts. The tree now stood decorated with anything the red-haired girl could find, fish bones, fur scraps, fir cones, strung corn, and it was topped with a star made from intertwined reeds. A wild goose roasted noisily in the open fire, patiently turned on the spit by Goliath and Angus. Méron watched his sister, painfully aware of the forced gaiety. He knew it was a trying time for her impulsive nature, confined by the snow and the child that grew large within her.

Cameron sat at the table watching the goose carved as Jemmy sang Yuletide hymns, making Goliath and Angus sorely homesick. Having been raised with no religion except the laws of nature, Cameron's mind was back in a hunting lodge with Alex the year before. She smiled, sadly remembering how she had been ignorant of the word "Christmas" and had felt that he mocked her. He had gently told her that it was the time a certain child was born. A shiver ran through her at the memory of his warm, amber eyes caressing her, seeming to turn her blood into liquid honey, and she suddenly felt a rush of wetness run down her legs.

She stared in horror at the spreading damp that dripped down from the chair to the floor as a deep spasm tightened her belly. Méron's sharp eyes followed her startled gaze, and he lithely sprang up.

" 'Tis the child!" he shouted.

"Calm yourself, Méron, or you'll scare the puir wee thing so it'll not want to poke its head into the world," cautioned Goliath, lifting a large cauldron of water onto the hob to heat. "Your water has broke, which means the bairn will be pushing out soon. How many birthing pains have you felt?" he added, taking calm control of the situation.

"Just one, and 'tis gone," replied Cameron.

"Then, as the saying goes, a watched pot never boils. Sit and eat Jemmy's Christmas fare, Méron. We'll all need our strength before the night is out," said Goliath, tucking into the crisp, golden goose with its dried-apple dressing.

Cameron giggled watching the three men try to eat as they pretended a nonchalance to cover up their mounting nervousness. She drank liberally of the precious hoard of rum, seeing finally an end to her ungainly awkward state. Another pain hit her, and she held her breath as Jemmy, Angus, and Goliath froze, staring at her, their forks suspended in midair. She expelled her breath with relief as the pain died away and resumed laughing at the ridiculous picture they made. Méron stood up angrily and removed her glass of rum.

"Nay, lad, she'll need it before the night's out," said Goliath gently.

Jemmy did not resume eating but sat with her eyes round and the freckles pronounced in her pale face remembering her own mother's death less than three years before. There had been three tiny brothers born dead, to be baptized and buried in the small kirkyard at Glen Aucht before the one that had taken her mother's life. She heard the anguished screams ringing in her ears from behind her parent's bedroom door. Her father had paced the kitchen, barred by the midwife from the birthing. Cameron noted Jemmy's anguished look.

"Dinna look so afeared, Jemmy, I'm fine," she laughed,

and another spasm caught her. Jemmy backed away and was caught by Méron's strong brown arms as he too remembered a loved one's death in childbirth. The red-haired girl burrowed her face into the dark youth's firm chest, hearing his heart hammering like her own as Cameron stood shakily, smiling bravely.

"My body wants to lie down," she said breathlessly, and Goliath led her gently to the pile of furs near the roaring fire. Cameron sank down thankfully, but then her body immediately arched as another pain consumed her. There was no sound except for the crackle of the fire and her labored breath. She relaxed, still panting, and looked at the row of anxious faces.

"'Tis a birthing, not a wake," she laughed, her eyes bright and sparkling from the pain.

"Aye, 'tis best we clear the table, for if the bairn is as impatient and headstrong as his mother and uncle, there's no saying how soon it's to pop its head out," stated Goliath gruffly, shaking himself free of his gaping inertia and busily removing the remains of their Christmas dinner. Angus helped him, but Jemmy and Méron remained motionless. The two large brothers glanced worriedly at the dark youth and small, red-haired child and silently communicated to each other their concern. Although Jemmy's face showed fear and great alarm, Méron's was blank, his green eyes unfocused in his handsome young face. Knowing Cameron's twin as they did, they recognized his pain and knew that his mind was back with the Indian girl who had died bearing his child.

"Play something, Angus," begged Cameron as the night dragged on. When the incredible pain shook her, she was aware of nothing but the tearing agony, but in the spaces between, the tense stillness in the cabin made her want to scream and howl with the moaning wind outside that blinded the small windows with thick, driving snow. Angus reverently took his bagpipes from their resting place. After a few lamenting squeals and shrieks the pipes settled down into a rousing Highland reel, and Goliath, despite his enormous size, nimbly danced.

"Come on now, Jemmy, kick up your heels," he chuckled,

taking the small child from Méron's unresisting arms and
whirling her about in his own. "Cameron is right, 'tis a
time for celebration, not ghosts from the past."

At the nostalgic and beloved sound of the pipes, Cameron
felt a bitter sadness sweep through her. The pain of the
loss of her homeland joined with the pain of the emerging
life. She closed her eyes against the onslaught of tears and
saw the grays and purples of the moors and sea. Below the
treble, lilting melody was the constant, deep drone of the
pipes, a Gaelic lament. No matter how gay and carefree a
Scottish tune may be, she thought, there was always the
profound haunting sadness. She opened her eyes as her
body was freed from another paralyzing paroxysm. Méron
squatted at her side and gently brushed the damp tendrils
of hair from her sweating brow. She smiled tremulously
at him, but another pain came fast and furiously. She felt
herself lifted in strong arms despite her violent stretching
and stiffening. Pain upon pain hit her until she was unaware of anything but pushing and pushing to rid herself
of the pressure.

"Angus, take Jemmy into the loft," whispered Goliath,
rolling up his sleeves.

"Nay, I will stay," said Jemmy, standing resolutely by
Cameron's dark head, which was pillowed by Angus's
arms so she wouldn't injure herself on the hard wood of
the table. Méron scrubbed his hands as Goliath gently
folded back Cameron's full skirt, reasoning that it would
disturb her less than undressing. He gasped in surprise to
find himself unceremoniously pushed aside by Méron.

"Sit her up," ordered the young man harshly, and silently, Angus complied. Cameron, supported by strong arms,
cared not that efficient hands stripped her until she was
naked, so intent was she on riding with the pain of birthing. She lay back against Angus's arms, moving with the
natural rhythm as she obeyed the primal forces within her.
Jemmy forgot her fear and was fascinated by the rounded
belly that contracted and strained. Méron stood between
Cameron's raised and parted legs, his face intent, his own
fear forgotten as he instinctively knew what to do. As the
baby's head appeared, the youth smiled, his strong hands
grasping the emerging life to guide and protect it. Jemmy

saw the sun rise in Méron's face and moved to stand beside him. Goliath placed a fatherly hand on her shoulder, and together they watched as the child was expelled from Cameron's young body. Jemmy felt a pang of horror to see her friend's female parts so terribly stretched, but the awe of the moment took over as each part of the child became visible, a thick cord still joining it to the inside of the mother.

Cameron lay back exhausted, the terrible, gouging pressure finally relieved. The watery wail of the child penetrated her fatigue, and she smiled as a wriggling, wet warmth was placed on her belly, her arms instinctively embracing her child.

" 'Tis a fine boy," proclaimed Goliath, and Cameron raised her head and stared into her brother's eyes as another pain hit her. Méron frowned with concern.

" 'Tis the afterbirth," comforted Angus as his brother neatly cut and knotted the umbilical cord and swaddled the baby.

" 'Tis twins!" gasped Méron, his strong arms guiding another child into the world. "Another boy!"

Cameron lay laughing weakly with happiness as Méron stood proudly before her holding a scrap of humanity in each hand. Angus efficiently cleaned the blood from her legs and thighs and wrapped her nether regions in a large clean old sheet.

"You'll be having to wear hippens like your bairns for a while until the blood from your nest dries up," he said awkwardly, but with a smile of satisfaction on his large, good-natured face.

"It must be written down," said Cameron. "I'll nay have my bairns wie no birthday like Méron and me. What is the date?" Méron looked blank, and so did Jemmy.

" 'Tis about Christmastide, we reckoned. That's why the tree and the goose," puzzled Angus thoughtfully.

"Nay, 'tis later, but I didna want to spoil your merriment nor steal young Jemmy's Christmas. 'Tis the daft days after," chuckled Goliath, pulling a small book from his pocket and flipping through the pages. "Och, 'tis Hogmanay . . . and there's nay one dark stranger but two to bring in the New Year of seventeen sixty-three."

Cameron slept peacefully with her twin sons nestled in the furs to each side of her. Jemmy sat on the floor mesmerized by the tiny babies as Méron carved into the wooden wall of the cabin the date, December 31, 1762.

"Makes sense," chuckled Goliath softly. "When else would our Cameron birth her bairns but on Hogmanay, the daftest day of the year?"

"She must name them. They maun be nameless as we were," worried Méron.

"Gie the lass time, lad. 'Tis mighty hard work that she's been adoing, and she needs her rest," chided Goliath. "You did well, Méron. I didna expect you to be witness to the birthing, let alone midwife."

" 'Tis best to face one's greatest fear," smiled the youth. " 'Tis the only way to conquer it," he added softly as he looked down at his sister and two nephews.

"I canna see who they look like," whispered Jemmy. "Except for the hair like yours and Cameron's. They'll nay open their eyes."

"If they do, they're likely to be tinged wie the blue of their mother's milk for a while," answered Méron.

"I've never seen such great heads of hair on a newborn," stated Goliath proudly.

"And the size of them! Neither runtish nor puny from sharing the womb, both well formed and of equal and identical size," boasted Angus, as they stood with their massive arms around each other, glowing with grandfatherly satisfaction and pride.

Cameron awoke feeling achy and sore but elated. Her eyes accustomed themselves to the warm darkness of the cabin, which was dimly lit by the fire's red embers. She pulled herself to a sitting position and smiled with affection at the large shapes of Goliath and Angus, who snored lustily across the room. She swung her legs to the floor and sat looking at the two babes. Her breasts prickled and felt swollen. She unbuttoned the flannel shirt and, picking up one of her sons, held him close, guiding his blindly searching mouth to her engorged nipple. She wanted a son on each breast and as she sat wondering how to manage it, Méron, who had been watching her silently, glided up and, as though reading her mind, picked up and placed the other babe in her free arm. As the babes sucked hungrily, Cameron felt pain and joy as the sensuous feelings swept through her, joining with an echo of the agony of labor. Neither she nor Méron said a word. They sat in harmony, bathed in the warmth and glow of the fire.

"You must name them," said Méron as together they unwrapped the tiny boys and Cameron explored and wondered at the perfection of each tiny part of them.

"Not yet," answered Cameron drowsily as she reswaddled her sons and cuddled them close. Méron waited until she was deeply asleep and then gently picked up his nephews and returned them to their cradle. He had heard of children, both Indian and white, who had been suffocated by a sleeping mother. He sat alert as the sky lightened and the sun shone brightly reflecting off the virgin snow, keeping watch over his twin and her twins.

Cameron regained her strength at a surprising rate, not content to rest in bed. She was in awe of her infant sons, whose wrinkled faces soon became smooth and rounded. Their eyes, though tinged with the usual baby blue, bore traces of gray-green, and in one month it was apparent that both boys had inherited the unusual color and intensity of Méron's and Cameron's eyes, under thick thatches of raven-black hair. Still, much to Méron's distress, the children had not been named, and the carving proclaiming their birth was unfinished.

"They grow aware and knowing," he remarked as identical green eyes regarded him solemnly and two small hands grasped his brown fingers firmly. "They should be named."

"There is time," returned Cameron softly. Each night she lay puzzling over what to call them. When she had been heavy, feeling the strong kicks within her, she had called the baby Raven, but now that there were two, she was in a dilemma. She firmly closed her mind from any thought of Alex as the babies took on some of his looks. She chided herself angrily for her imagination as she stroked their soft cheeks remembering his hard features.

Late one night she sat beside her sleeping sons watching

the contented rise and fall of their peaceful breathing, pondering the problem of their names. She became conscious of Méron's steady gaze and thought of their father, remembering her brother's swift darkening of mood at the mere mention. It had been months since she had last broached the subject as she had been unwilling to break the harmony, but now she felt her anger well. Why did Méron deny her such knowledge in much the same way as Alex had done? At the thought of Alex her fury built as a picture of his golden face sliced painfully through her.

"I shall call my sons Charles and Stuart, for their grandfather," she stated deliberately, her eyes fixed challengingly on her twin.

"You'll not insult innocence so!" hissed Méron vehemently and although Cameron expected anger she was shocked by his vicious intensity.

"Insult?" she questioned, but Méron had turned away to indicate the subject was closed.

"Nay, Méron, you'll nay shut me out. You maun trust me," she whispered. "The Bonnie Prince is my father, too," she added beseechingly, and at no reaction she goaded, "Then I shall so name my sons!"

"Bonnie Prince!" sneered Méron bitterly. "Grow up, Cameron, you're a woman, a mother now. 'Tis time to throw away romantic dreams of glory. We have no father. Aye, there's Bonnie Prince Charlie, the stud who serviced our mother—but no father."

"He is our father," insisted Cameron.

"Angus, Goliath, aye even Pontiac are more father to me than that ugly, fat, debauched Pretender!"

"You have seen him? Been with him?" asked Cameron softly after a lengthy pause in which her own anger had fled seeing pain burn in her brother's eyes.

"Aye!" answered Méron shortly, the word seeming to be wrenched from his body.

"Please tell me about it," she urged quietly.

"There's nothing to tell."

"Please?" she pleaded. "Or I shall have to go find him for myself."

"Are you sure you want your dreams broken?" said Méron harshly.

"I have no more dreams," replied Cameron sadly. "All I have is you and my sons. Our mother is dead. . . ."

"Wish that our sire was too!" interrupted Méron with a cruel laugh. "I went with dreams to find our father and found nothing!" spat the youth savagely. "He's not worthy to have grandsons like these. He has many whores, Cameron, and even more children. He's like a diseased breeding bull. He doesna care that we or our many half brothers and sisters exist. He throws his seeds to the wind not caring that they take root. Not caring if they grow in muck or wither in arid places. Aye, he throws his seeds as though they were piss!"

Cameron couldn't say a word. Her brother's violent tirade deeply marring the picture of the dashing prince riding, plaid flying, as he gathered the clans against the English, and a grotesque protrait of Beddington filled her mind. She shook her head mutely wishing he would stop, but Méron grabbed her chin forcing her to stare into his hard green eyes.

"You'll hear me. You begged to be told, now hear me!"

"Whether he's fat or not, debauched or not, he's still the rightful king of Scotland!" she said firmly, trying to cling to her dream.

"RIGHT-ful? RIGHT-ful?" mocked Méron. "What's *right* about him?"

"Aye, by blood!" she retorted.

"Nay, a man should be fit to rule . . . prove himself. It shouldna be an accident of birth."

"You think then 'tis *right* that the English king George rules Scotland and calls it Barbarian Northern England?"

"Nay, 'tis wrong. No country should take over another, changing the way of life and bowing people's pride and spirit, forcing them to forsake their own ways," returned Méron wearily. "You have yet to see the noble natives of this great country. All over the world people such as we are being beaten and bowed. I watch invaders with skin the color of ours use much subtler means to break the red man's ties with the earth. Once proud warriors now huddle like old women in the shadows of the English and French forts, begging for scraps . . . whining and groveling like mangy curs."

"But surely you fight for the French who have been Scotland's allies against the English for generations?" probed Cameron, wanting to resume conversation about their father but also relieved that no more invectives about him were being hurled.

"I did but am now confused. There seems no difference in their disregard for the people of the land. Both French and English want to conquer and reap a rich profit without thought for the rightful owners of the country. There is no respect for custom and ceremonies, except to use the same to their advantage, to wrest from them land, and dignity."

" 'Tis strange to think we have brothers and sisters we shall never know," ventured Cameron, breaking the ponderous silence that enveloped them. Méron surprised her by a sharp bark of laughter.

"Aye, 'tis a pity Duncan Fraser didna find more of us," he chuckled.

"I dinna ken. Find more of us for what?"

"You've never wondered why we were hidden even from each other?" asked Méron.

"Nay, why should I when it was all I ever knew?" replied Cameron.

"Even when you learned you were royal Stuart?"

"I was glad to know I had a name and thought to find my father and you. What should I have thought?"

"We both were an old Highland outlaw's dream. He thought to keep us safe and one day to use us to raise the clans, but isolated as he was he didna ken that the clans were beaten and dispersed. He lived in his dream world to the end, not knowing Stuart bastards had swelled in numbers."

"Stuart bastards," echoed Cameron.

"Aye," replied Méron, "but luckier than most. We at least weren't born of diseased seed as the others who came after us. We're not twisted, blind, or moronic, tainted by the green lady."

"Daft-Dougal spoke of the green lady. Who is the green lady?"

"The pox. Syphilis, disease of the debauched."

Cameron shuddered. "Where is he?"

"Playing in the courts of Europe with no thought of the thousands of Scots that laid down their lives for his cause and who are still paying. And that's who you'd name your bairns for?"

"Then shall I call my sons Blood and Tears," said Cameron sadly after a long silence. She felt weighed down and depressed by Méron's bitter words. It triggered the deep void within her that the twins' birth had not dispelled. Although the cavity within her belly where the boys had grown was now flat and smooth, it was as though there was an aching chasm, which haunted her nights and tinged her happiness and peace with a constant, droning pain. She felt incomplete and yearned for the high snowbanks to melt so that the ghost that stalked would be blown away by the wind rushing past her ears as she galloped through the untamed country. She refused to allow herself to put a name to her deep hurt, and when Alex's face appeared in her dreams, she forced herself awake.

The frowning youth gave a bark of laughter and eyed his brooding sister thoughtfully.

"I'm sorry. Sometimes it seems that there is a great dam inside of me against which the waters of emotions thrash. Sometimes I forget to hold fast, and I am swept away in a torrent that roars and pounds my blood, deafening me to my own sense. It should be a peaceful time for you, calm and without strife, so that your children are well grounded to this earth and without fear," he confessed huskily.

"There is also a tempest inside of me, Jumeau," she replied softly, reverting to his childhood name. "But 'tis not as noble or as selfless as yours, which embraces all people. 'Tis just the pulling and tugging within myself until I am torn in two . . . not whole," she struggled to explain.

"Torn in two by what?" asked Méron, somehow knowing she was at last going to talk of her husband, the father of her sons, the man respectfully called Lion by the Indians who had met him.

"Alexander Sinclair," pronounced Cameron, her mouth forming each syllable with whitened lips, stabbing the sounds with a bitter hissing. "I hate him. He holds my dreams. My skin still burns in his grasp. He holds every place of me, and I want to cut him out of me, but I dinna ken where to start. Even the children from my body are haunted by him!"

Méron sat silently, pursing his lips against the obvious question that rose in his mind. To state to Cameron that she loved the man would only accomplish added agitation and vehement denial. It was something she would have to wrestle with herself if she was ever to find peace, he thought.

"It is strange the power of this great country," he said at last, tactfully changing the subject. "It gives perspective. Everything falls into place, and kings and queens and glory become laughable. On Rona I dreamed of raising the clans . . . of freeing Scotland . . . I gloried in being a Royal Stuart. But here I've learned it is more important what one man does with his life. Before leaving for France I rode across our country, seeing complacency and a numb acceptance in our people for their lot in life. Nonthinking, like yoked oxen plodding before the plow. Tired and drained by war, families rebuilding, filling the gaps of dead fathers, mothers, and sons. Bairns born after who knew nothing of before. Of course there were rebels, but they seemed to me men who were concerned with just their own glory. The old ways of Scotland are gone for a time, and, just like you and your bairns, a time is needed to recoup strength so that you can look around you and see where you stand in relation to all things."

Cameron did not answer. Méron's words echoed Alex's, and as she stared at her brother during his reflective monologue, her eyes played tricks in the dim lighting and the youth's dark face became a tawny, chiseled one.

"No!" she shouted after a pause. "Heritage and nationality are important. We must never forget who we are and what we come from. I am a Scot before all other things."

"I didna say to forget what we have sprung from. 'Tis always there and canna be changed, but 'tis the future, not the past, that is important," returned Méron gently.

"And yet you talk of the red man's way of life . . . surely that is their past?" challenged Cameron.

"Not yet, but I fear it soon will be unless they hold on to it for their future," he said, turning away from her.

Cameron knew that she had attacked her brother so that she would not have to dwell on her own pain about Alex. Suddenly feeling very alone in the darkness, she leaned over the cradle. She lay holding the warm, milky, fragrant babies to her breasts throughout the long night and silently cried for all her lost dreams.

CHAPTER TWENTY-SEVEN

The March winds shrieked and howled like a hungry lion, and, weary and bent in spirit, Alex returned to Fort Detroit alone. He was numb to the cutting, icy gale that tore at his clothes and swirled the thick snow as he methodically trudged in the cumbersome snowshoes, his mind full of the emaciated bodies he had seen covered in what the French called the Death of Roses. Such a romantic name for such a wretched disease as pellagra, he thought. Each raven-haired, emaciated corpse he had found alone or huddled with a number of others had caused a clutching at his heart as Cameron's flashing green eyes and vivacious face haunted his waking and sleeping hours.

Reaching the crude shanty huts that had grown like toadstools around the stockade walls of the fort, he removed his snowshoes and strode stiffly through the slushy, filthy lanes, noting the smell of abject poverty that even the cold couldn't hide. He snorted cynically as he recognized the broken dreams of the whites who had fled from their own country's poverty and persecution. This land of promise, where each man, woman, and child had hope for a better life, he thought sardonically. Except of course for the convicts and bonded servants caught stealing food to ward off starvation as long as it was no more than fivepence, for fivepence farthing ensured the gallows.

"Hope? Promise? New life?" he sneered out loud as he saw the huddled shapes of three blanketed Indians sheltered against a shanty wall out of reach of the howling wind. Through a rent in the sacking that covered the window of the miserable hovel he could see a wretched, ragged white woman feeding her two shivering children. Slops were thrown out of the window, narrowly missing the Indians, who reached for them hungrily.

"Well, she has one of her dreams in this promised land," muttered Alex, striding by. "Someone to feel superior to," he added with a snort of bitter laughter, remembering a small Indian encampment where the once proud and independent people had sold their warm fur clothing to passing trappers for cheap white clothing and jewelry. He had found their bodies frozen in grotesque positions, hideously dressed in thin gingham dresses and bonnets and bedecked with ridiculous trinkets. An ironic, prophetic death, he mused. How could the native people who lived near the intruding white man hope to compete against guns in hunting for meat? he railed inwardly, not acknowledging the guard who opened the gate of the fort to him.

He walked across the parade ground directly to the commandant's quarters, ignoring the lines of uniformed soldiers, not feeling the cold as his blood boiled. He had nothing to report except death. Those of white settlers, Indians, and his own companion, who had sat down in a blinding blizzard, unable to go further. Alex with his head bent against the driving snow had not noticed his absence for several minutes, and when he had done so and retraced his nearly invisible footsteps, it had been too late.

Major Gladwin eyed the tall man whose moustache and full beard were caked with ice. He listened to the unemotional report.

"You realize, Sinclair, that that is your second scout who has not returned. You are fast earning yourself the name of Jinx. There was General Ramsbotham, Lesvesque, and now . . . what the hell was the man's name?" he ranted.

"Jones," answered Sinclair shortly. "What is it you imply, Major Gladwin?"

"I imply nothing, Sinclair. It is purely an observation, which you'll do well to think on. Where is Jones's body?"

"Lost in a blizzard. The man sat down . . . gave up . . . and I had no way to return the corpse to the fort unless you wished me to end my life trying," explained Alex with bored patience.

"Did you bring his effects?"

"Nay, I had no shovel to dig him free, and my hands were near frozen. The place is marked, and I can map it if you would like to send troops out to recover him. The snow should preserve his body well, so you will see there are no marks of foul play."

"I was not implying foul play. I apologize if my shortness has caused you offense, Sinclair, but I rail against this accursed snow. Winter seems to go on forever. It is nearly April, and I am homesick for an English spring with crocuses and daffodils. Here, warm yourself with this," he offered, pouring a stiff drink. "And get some food and rest. When did you last sleep?" he added, noting for the first time the dark circles around the hard, amber eyes.

Alex drained the glass swiftly, welcoming the burning sensation, tersely inclined his head, and left.

Later he lay on the hard cot in his barren quarters, which resembled a monks cell, possessing only the essentials of bed, washstand, and closet, and closed his eyes. He had not slept for thirty-six hours, but sleep eluded him. For two months he had trekked the frozen wilderness searching for news of Cameron, but it seemed she had disappeared without a trace, buried beneath the thick, beautiful blanket of treacherous snow. He had, however, learned one interesting fact while sharing a campfire with a hunting party of young Ottawa braves. The Green-Eyed-One who normally rode at Pontiac's left side was not spending the winter with the Ottawas but was secluded in his retreat. One young brave spoke of Lion-Cub, a child whose head appeared to be like flames, but when he would have spoken further, he had received a swift kick from one of his companions and had fallen silent with a sharp grunt. Alex had not pursued the topic but had feigned a casual disinterest, although his blood had quickened. He made a mental note to separate this talkative young brave from his wary companions and probe him for further news, but it wasn't fated to be. The following morning the deep prints of a lone bear were marked with excitement, and the impulsive brave, despite the warnings of his companions, was determined to prove himself to his tribe by such a kill. His obsidian eyes had shone with thoughts of himself striding into the winter camp with such a trophy, to be feted and acclaimed. The bear, as hungry as the youth himself, had charged, killing him instantly and staining the white snow with the brave's red blood.

Alex opened his eyes to stop the grisly remembrance and contemplated the beamed ceiling, willing his mind into nothingness as he consciously forced his long limbs to relax. His eyelids drooped, and he sank slowly and comfortingly into sleep, only to jerk himself to awareness within less than a minute as Cameron's open, laughing face seared into his mind. With a curse he sat up and reached for the bottle of rotgut whiskey on the floor next to the bed. As he drank deeply, he debated seeking out some compliant woman of easy morals. The fort seemed full of them. Even the wives of many of the men had offered their services to him at one time or another. As he drank and brooded, he heard a hissing argument outside his door and then the sounds of slaps and squeals of pain and anger. He opened the door and surveyed the two disheveled women. He stared at them in silence before mockingly bowing and inviting them both in. With two women in his bed he would have no opportunity to think of Cameron, he reasoned as he watched them strip, each competing with the other as they bared breasts, bellies, groins, and limbs.

The twin boys had no lack of loving arms as their mother, bundled in thick furs, walked with her brother through the still, snow-covered wilderness learning to read the tracks of animals and hunt with the spears and arrows of the Indian. Her young, lithe body showed no sign of her motherhood except for her rounded, milk-filled breasts. With her once-cumbersome belly now flat, it was possible for her again to wear leather breeches, and she reveled in the freedom they afforded her long legs. She watched the crisp, shrinking snow, impatient for it to be melted enough so that she could ride a horse. The times out in the open with Méron were precious. For hours on end they could be two carefree children making up for their lack of childhood as Méron taught his agile sister how to skate upon the ice of the lake as the Indians had taught him. Cameron struggled to learn the guttural language of the Algonkian and Iroquois, and as they checked the animal traps, they conversed, albeit haltingly.

Goliath and Angus watched them from the cabin as

Jemmy crooned and sang to the baby boys. Méron's carving was still incomplete, and the twins still were unnamed. At four months old they were happy, active infants, able to turn over and lift inquiring identical faces over the edge of their cradle to survey their first home.

" 'Tis good they have no names, because who could tell which was which?" laughed Jemmy one day. The red-haired girl fell silent as Méron had glared, and a tension shrouded everyone for some minutes before Goliath had tactfully changed the subject. Angus had once tried to bring up the subject of naming them at the table as they ate, trying to make a game of it.

"Cain and Abel," he had chuckled.

"Romulus and Remus," joined in Goliath.

"Esau and Isaac," offered Jemmy.

But their merry voices had died away as they became conscious that Cameron sat silent and that Méron, after glaring, turned from the table and stared out the window.

Cameron did not know why she could not name her sons. She told herself that she did not know them as people and that soon she would just know their names by some natural instinct. She tossed and turned at night, blocking out the thought of Alex when she found herself wondering what he would call them. Many names flashed into her mind only to be rejected as she thought of Fergus MacDonald, Ian Drummond, and Duncan Fraser. She would not name her sons for any other person, she decided. They would be who they were going to be, not a shadow of someone else. She knew that Alexander was named for his father and his father before him and angrily told herself that he would arrogantly name one of them for himself. That would not be, she vowed vehemently. At one point she decided to name her sons for trees, whose leaves were green like their eyes, but none of the names, whether Indian or English, satisfied her. Pine was sad, like a lamentation. Fir was confusing. Maple, Willow, Cedar, and Cypress sounded like female appellations. She seriously pondered Juniper, Oak, and Ash and then discarded them.

One night, when she sat hugging her knees staring up at the night sky, she thought excitedly that she would name her children for the firmament, putting them above the

earth. She lay back searching her mind for the names of
the stars that shone in the clear darkness and to her frustration realized that she could only recognize the moon.
Goliath had been a sailor and he would know, she remembered, and eagerly raced back to the warmth of the
cabin to search him out.

Goliath and Cameron sat beside the lake as he pointed
out each star and named it. "There is the collection of
stars called the Plow or Spurtle . . . or Big Dipper," he
informed.

Cameron could not envision calling her sons any of
those names.

"It doesna seem right to call stars such earthy names.
Dipper and spurtle belong in a kitchen and a plow in the
field," she retorted.

"Och, they have fancier names . . . usually Latin.
There's Orion, the hunter of the sky . . . and Canus, meaning dog, and Pisces, meaning the fishes," he said, pointing
out each cluster.

Cameron listened, making a note of Orion the hunter
and waiting for another name in the long list Goliath
droned, but all the others were inappropriate words, such
as Pleiades, Cetus, and Andromeda. She considered Ursa,
the bear, and Gemini, the twins, and even Taurus the bull,
but none of them struck a chord.

"There are many other stars that cannot be seen in the
northern sky this time of year. Ursa is one. In Gemini the
twin stars of Castor and Pollux are not yet visible," remarked Goliath, suddenly realizing her interest.

"Castor and Pollux," repeated Cameron with distaste,
the names sounding ugly to her ears. "Tell me more stars,
whether I can see them or no."

"Leo, Virgo, Libra, Lyra, Hercules," struggled Goliath.
"Lynx, Draco, Hydra—"

"Say that one again . . . Li . . ." interrupted Cameron
excitedly.

"Libra?"

"No, another."

"Leo? Lyra, Lynx?"

"Lynx," breathed Cameron. "Lynx and Orion. Orion
and Lynx."

"Do you ken what a lynx is?"

"A star."

"The constellation of Lynx is a collection of stars. Five to be exact, and because of their placement they look like a cat about to spring. A lynx is a wildcat, a savage, wild animal that roams this country."

"I will call my sons Orion and Lynx," proclaimed Cameron.

"That is like naming them Cain and Abel," remarked the large man dryly.

"Who were they?"

"Two brothers from the Bible. One slew the other. Orion, the hunter of the skies, stalks the Lynx."

"No, I canna name them so, then," agreed Cameron, feeling deflated. She sat in silence for a while. Hearing the beat of heavy wings, she looked up as Omen circled above them and remembered. The name she had called the first movement in her belly had been Raven. Lynx and Raven, she decided, waiting for the niggly, uncomfortable feeling to come upon her, but the names rang true and strong in her head. As though understanding her decision, Omen landed on her shoulder and nuzzled its dark head against her own.

"You always know the moment I do, don't you?" she said laughingly to the bird as she stood. "I have decided, Goliath, but I will tell you all together because first I have to be with my sons so that I name them properly."

In the cabin Cameron laid her twin sons upon the bed of furs, examining them minutely. Although they were mirrors of each other in face, already their individual characters shone forth. Both tiny boys regarded her solemnly. The first one that looks away, become more curious about what else is happening in the room, I shall call Lynx, decided Cameron, who could not label either child. The minutes ticked by, and one of the boys gave a gurgle and impatiently heaved himself onto his stomach and watched the brightly burning fire with interest. Cameron laughed and hugged the children to her. She stood triumphantly upon the bed.

"I have something to tell you all. Méron?" she called to her brother, who was busily sharpening arrowheads. "I have decided on my sons' names. Here is Lynx and here is Raven, and so that they will not get confused by your own confusion, I shall mark my impetuous and not-so-patient Lynx with a tiny headband of blue and my solemn Raven with one of red." Méron quietly nodded his approval.

Cameron rejoiced in the emerging spring. Méron had fashioned two slings, and the tiny boys accompanied them wherever they went. Their magnolia faces became brown and ruddy as they stared wide-eyed at their untamed world. Raven definitely seemed the more wary and cautious of the two as he would solemnly and silently gaze upon each new thing, whereas Lynx would cry with delight, reaching out with chubby hands toward a branch moving with the wind or a brightly colored flower.

Toward the end of April several Indian braves rode up to the small cabin in the woods. It was unseasonably warm, although patches of snow still lay here and there and loose slabs of ice floated idly in the shimmering lake. Cameron sat with her sons, watching the beavers and otters, raccoons and deer, in the warm sunlight. She heard the hoofbeats and instinctively lay flat next to the naked, sleeping bodies of the twins as she watched Méron converse with the four braves. She was too far away to hear the content of their words. After several minutes they all entered the cabin. Cameron hastily covered her own bare body, wondering whether she should stay hidden from the Indians as Méron had made her do the autumn before. A long shadow blocked the sun from her, and she stared up in surprise to see her brother. She wished he wouldn't move so silently. He squatted beside her and softly touched each warm velvet cheek of the sleeping children before turning to her.

"I must go for a while to the Ottawa camp. I'm afraid the peace of winter is over, and with the spring Pontiac has ordered my presence at a council," he informed her quietly.

"Ordered?" challenged Cameron.

"Aye, I am part of the council, and it is my place to obey."

"I want to go with you," said Cameron eagerly.

"No, women are not allowed in the council."

"I am dressed as a man," protested Cameron. "And can hide my full breasts with fur clothing," she added, following her brother's eyes.

"And let your small sons go hungry?"

"How long will you be gone?" she asked, knowing he was right and yet the disappointment showing plainly.

"It depends. It seems Pontiac is assembling the Ottawas and Potawatomis to introduce them to the Delaware Prophet and to proclaim himself a disciple," explained Méron.

"Delaware Prophet?"

"I have met him before, and though somewhat of a fanatic, he is a man who speaks with a great deal of wisdom. He claims that the Indian will perish unless he returns to his old ways of before the white man. He tells us to forsake our guns and powder and take up once more the weapons and tools of yesteryear, or the sky and land will be stained with the blood of the red man, who will cease to walk the face of this earth." Méron deliberately avoided telling her that the Delaware Prophet wanted to kill and expel all the white men. Although he was a blood brother of Pontiac, chief of the Ottawas, he, Méron, was a white man and knew that sooner or later the Delaware Prophet would be apprised of the fact. By his sitting in on the sacred council, even though it be at Pontiac's command, Méron was endangering his own life.

"This prophet is like our Brahan Seer, who said Scotland would not be free until the black rains," said Cameron wonderingly.

"I must be going, as the council meets on the twenty-seventh of this month of April, which gives two days. 'Tis but a days ride, but I should like to be in the camp beforehand to ascertain the feelings," informed Méron, standing and looking down at his sister and her twin babies. "Stay hidden until we have ridden off. Angus will accompany me, and Goliath will stay to guard you."

Cameron watched her brother ride away looking as much Indian as the Ottawa braves. She stripped off her clothes again, stretched out in the warm sun, and closed her eyes. It was the latter part of April, she mused, less than a week before the Beltane feast. Her mind drifted back to Glen Aucht. Was it nearly a year since she had left Alex's estate on the Firth of Forth, she thought, astonished that it seemed a lifetime ago and yet had sped by so quickly. The sun pierced her closed eyelids, reminiscent of the Beltane fires that had burned on the rolling lawns of Glen Aucht, an ancient rite to ensure a good harvest. It was nearly May first, and what should she do with her life? she wondered. Would she be content to live in the small cabin in the wilderness with her brother and sons? Was it not infinitely preferable to the artificiality of society? Her reasoning mind told her that it was, yet a lump rose in her throat, and she rolled over and pulled her warm, sweet-smelling sons into her arms, where they nuzzled her breasts sleepily. Would there ever be arms to hold her again? she wondered.

Alex had followed the four Ottawa braves, somehow knowing that they would lead him to Méron. From his hiding place he had at last seen Cameron's green-eyed twin as he rode away from the small, secluded cabin. The resemblance was remarkable, and yet, except for the vivid eyes and blue-black hair, every other aspect of the two was a contrast, a counterpoint. Méron was decidedly masculine, with strong, aristocratic features and long, muscular limbs. Cameron was petite and lithe, her features finely drawn. He had sat high in the branches of a fir tree until the sound of hoofbeats receded and he fell in a reverie, mesmerized by the thought of the twins. Male and female of the same mold, striking in their similarities and in their differences. Having a reasonably good idea where Méron and his Ottawa companions were heading, he decided to investigate the youth's forest retreat further. He circled the small cabin and silently threaded his way through the tall pines. The lake winked and shimmered between the hairy trunks, reminding him of the loch at Lochearnhead, where he and Cameron had spent a winter in seclusion from the rest of the world. Dreams were meant to be broken, he thought bitterly, remembering the trust and love that had grown between them but that had been so easily destroyed.

Alex caught his breath at the scene that met his eyes.

In a small clearing by the lake sat Cameron, naked, with two small naked babies at her breast. For a moment he was transfixed by the tranquil beauty of the sight, and then blinding jealousy tore in. His blood pounded, and he was filled with murderous rage. He noted the red and blue beaded headbands that the infants wore and the golden skins and irrationally concluded that his wife had mated with an Indian. His face lost the tender softening of first witnessing the sight and hardened to uncompromising, sardonic lines. He silently turned his back and retraced his steps.

He fumed as he walked into the forest to calm himself. He lay under a large tree, lost in thought, waiting for his turbulent pulses to still. He sat up with a start as a cold, wet nose was pushed against his clasped hands. Tor whined a welcome, and a hoarse cry overhead caused him to look up and see Omen perched on a limb above him. The presence of Cameron's two dark shadows did not lessen his pain but seemed to grind it further into him. He buried his face in his hands to block them out, trying to make sense of his jumbled thoughts and emotions. He had vowed to eradicate Cameron from his heart, and yet sight of her caused the collapse of every resolve until he felt like a callow, trembling youth. Having no point of reference on the age of infants, as all babies looked alike to him, his spinning brain assumed they were newborn, conceived in August after she had quit the ship. Heaving a great sigh, he stood and stared dispassionately toward the small glade. This time he would imprint the scene upon his mind and use it to harden his heart completely, use it to tear Cameron's graspings from the whole of him. He retraced his steps.

Cameron lay flat on her back with her eyes closed. The babies were nestled in the crooks of her arms, gurgling and kicking tiny feet. Relaxed and content, the sun bathing her body with golden, comforting warmth, her mind was at peace. The noises her sons made were like music to her ears, joining with the songs of the birds and the splashing of the beaver and otter in the lake. A sudden cloud seemed to block the sun, and her skin goosebumped, the hairs on her arms and legs standing erect.

Lynx continued his reaching and kicking, and Raven lay still. Cameron opened her eyes and froze with shock. Alex stood above her staring down, his amber eyes hard and riveting, his chiseled face harsh and seeming to hate. Cameron was sure she was dreaming. She closed her eyes tightly, and when she opened them again he was gone and the sun once more shone brightly on her prone body, but she felt cold and chilled. She sat up and stared around her. Everything seemed as it should be, but the joy and comfort of the day were gone. She pulled on her clothes and dressed her babies, her face sad and solemn, and returned to the cabin.

Alex returned to his horse and was about to mount, but the black of his steed's glossy coat once more re-kindled his anger. Torquod pawed impatiently, eager to gallop.

"I shall rid myself of all reminders," muttered Alex. "You shall be returned to your tempestuous mistress."

Late that night Alex stole into the small lean-to at the back of the cabin and exchanged Torquod for a large raw-boned bay. He silently led the horse over the carpet of thick pine needles through the forest before mounting and riding toward Ottawa's camp.

Cameron was unable to sleep. The moonlight streamed in across her bed of furs, and Tor whined uneasily. Across the room Goliath snored rhythmically, and in the sleeping loft, the gentle swell of Jemmy's breathing mingled with that of the twins in their cradle. Cameron got up and opened the door for Tor and followed him out into the clear night to the makeshift stable in the back. There stood Torquod, pawing and butting his great black head up and down in greeting, unable to get near to his young mistress, as he had been tied.

As though sleepingwalking, Cameron approached her horse, afraid he was a figment of her imagination and would disappear when she reached out.

"Torquod?" she breathed as she buried her disbelieving face into his hard, corded neck and ran her hands gently over his shimmering coat, feeling his strong muscles.

Quickly she raced back to the cabin with Tor at her heels to pull on her breeches. Leaving Omen roosting in the rafters to watch her sons and wake Goliath if they needed something, she returned to her stallion and, leaping onto his tall, bare back, kicked him into a gallop through the crisp moonlit night.

Cameron halted Torquod's wild pace as she saw a movement approaching from out of the long shadows. The moonlight glinted on the leonine, thick hair of the rider, and she knew that it was Alex who had returned her horse. It had been him by the lake that afternoon, too. Her heart pounded in her chest as she sat motionless atop Torquod, waiting, it seemed, for agonizingly slow minutes. It was as though he had seen that she waited and had slowed his own horse's pace to a walk. She fought against the urge to race toward him to break the agony of waiting. Everything had a dreamlike quality. The full moon caused long, dark shadows across the plain, and Cameron closed her eyes, expecting the slowly approaching horseman to disappear. The figure steadily neared, and Cameron held her breath, certain that the frantic beat of her pulses could be heard in the still night. She sat her horse motionless as the rider reined his horse scarcely two yards in front of her. The moonlight reflected on the high, definitive lines of his face so that he appeared a figment of her imagination. What was the matter with her? Was she losing her mind? She tore her eyes away and shook her head. She clenched her knees, feeling Torquod's girth, and stared down at his blackness. Wake up, she implored herself.

Alex stared straight into Cameron's confused eyes. He noted her breasts, which rose and fell quickly. She seemed so childlike and vulnerable. Everything seemed so suspended, so ethereal, that when she looked away shaking her head, he was afraid she would disappear like a phantom. He urged his horse forward and grasped Cameron, lifting her from her horse so that he cradled her in his arms. She didn't resist but stared up at him wonderingly, her lips soft and inviting. He slowly bent his head and touched his mouth to hers and felt her tremble, as though it were her first kiss. He savored the sweetness of her pliant lips, which quivered beneath his as her small hand caressed his face as though tracing each plane. He gently explored her mouth, softly probing it with his tongue as she allowed him entrance. He increased the pressure as her tongue flicked into action and she pressed her breasts against his chest and, keeping her mouth glued to his, swiveled her body so that she sat astride his horse facing him. Alex lifted her so that her legs curled around him and their sexes were pressed together as their mouths made love, their tongues vying for dominance.

Alex clasped her tightly and swung one long leg from his horse, dismounting as she clung agilely to him, her eyes tightly closed, not wanting to awaken from the dream. She buried her face in the fragrance of his shirt and she felt his hand slide beneath her clothes. Her chin was grasped, and once more his mouth captured hers and she parted her lips eagerly as she thrust her aching body against his, her hands delighting in the feel of the hard muscles of his back and buttocks. She felt herself pushed back and lay still, her eyes closed, mourning the loss of the warm pressure, wondering if she was to wake up alone in her bed, but then hands undid the lacing of her shirt, freeing her breasts. Exquisite sensations streaked through her as she was sucked, and her hands caressed the thick mane of hair. Again her mouth was captured, but this time in a way that savagely bruised her lips, and she tasted the sweetness of her own milk. Now there was no gentleness and she fought the heaviness of the body that pinned her to the prairie floor.

Alex had been caught up in the mystical moonlit fantasy. But the gentle savoring of each other had curdled to savage rage at the tasting of her mother's milk, reminding him that she had lain with another, bearing children. The urgency in his loins coupled with his jealousy and rage, and he was determined to possess her any way he could. He raped her mouth with a hard, merciless tongue, goading her to fight him, and she did as he tried to knee her thighs apart. This was how it should be with her, he told himself. A battle. No gentleness, no softening. Despite his brutality, Cameron was aroused, like a bitch in heat, he was sure of that. Not just her flaming temper but her lust. Her nipples were erect beneath his harsh fingers, and although her body tried to pitch his off, her movements were rhythmic, as though more than their mouths were coupled. He raised his head and stared down. In the moonlight her nostrils were flared, her breasts heaving, but her eyes remained tightly closed. He thrust himself against her, and she thrust back, her thighs wide. He rocked back so that he knelt between her legs, not touching any part of her. Without opening her eyes, she arched toward him, trying to connect, her hands busy trying to shimmy down her trousers. Alex watched her coldly, curbing his desire, which raged against the confines of his own breeches. He wanted her to open her eyes. What was she doing, pretending he was someone else?

Cameron was cold. She had bared herself, and there was no one there. She felt the rough ground on her naked skin. She opened her eyes, and for a second all was dark. Then she saw his shape against the moonlit sky, kneeling before her, his face in darkness so that she couldn't see his expression, but she could smell and feel the charged sexuality emanating. She made no movement, although she longed to tear off his clothes so she could feel the warmth of his flesh. Every part of her ached, and yet she willed herself to be still. She kept her eyes open and pinned to the dark shape of his face. Neither of them moved for several minutes, and then slowly and deliberately Alex leaned forward, pressing her back against the hard dirt. Cameron welcomed the contact but was frustrated by his clothes, which were uncomfortable on her bare flesh. She tried to slide her hands between them to undo the buttons that dug into her breasts, but Alex made that impossible. She writhed in frustration against him, trying to capture his mouth, but Alex even withheld that from her. What had started as a delicious dream was now a nightmare. Cameron closed her eyes and willed her body to be still as she wrapped her arms around Alex's muscular back and buried her face in his shirt. If this was all, she would be content. Memories of another time flashed into her head, and she wondered if maybe she really had cast some terrible spell, destroying his manhood forever.

Similar thoughts were coursing through Alex's mind. He knew he wasn't impotent with other women. It was just with Cameron. Maybe his male member was telling him what his brain already knew—that he was best off without her. One last time, he told himself as, keeping her pinned under him, he released himself from the tight confines of his buckskin pants and positioned himself. As he thrust into the heat of her, he lost all sense of reasoning. He recaptured her mouth, determined to possess her thoroughly. Her willing compliance and passion that matched his own infuriated him. He was trying to teach her a lesson, and yet she matched him stroke for stroke. However punishing and bruising his thrusts, she rose to meet him until they climaxed, arching together.

Cameron held Alex tightly to her as her sensations exploded, and she lay back exhausted, feeling the deep, echoing ticking of her orgasm slow with her heartbeat. She was not conscious of the hard, stony ground nor of the sweat that dried on her body. She felt complete and wanted to lie forever in his arms, possessed by his manhood. She breathed deeply of the fragrance of him as she felt him still hard within her. She gave a cry of alarm as he curtly unsheathed himself and stood buttoning his pants.

"Now we both are free," he stated harshly as he mounted his horse. Cameron lay naked, looking up at the shadow of the mounted man who towered above her.

"Free?" she repeated dazedly, but Alex wheeled his horse away, and the vibrations of the hooves jarred her prone body.

Cameron lay unmoving long after the hoofbeats had receded, and then humbly sat up and dressed herself. She listlessly mounted Torquod and rode slowly back to the cabin. Everything felt unreal, and yet the horse beneath her and the stickiness between her legs proved it was no dream. She plunged into the iciness of the lake, trying to clear her head, but it seemed only to numb her senses more. She crawled between the pelts on her bed and, with her mind a merciful blank, fell fast asleep.

She awoke the following morning to the whimpers of her hungry sons. The sun streamed across her bed, and she opened dull eyes as the events of the previous day flooded her brain. She took her hungry children into her arms and fed them, staring sightlessly out the window at the lake.

Goliath, already up and puttering around, frowned at her blank look but made no comment before stomping out to feed and water the horses with Jemmy at his heels. He returned several minutes later, his burly face the picture of astonishment.

"Your stallion Torquod is here, and my gelding gone!" he exclaimed. Cameron did not answer but just remained staring out the window as she suckled her babies.

"'Twas a full moon last night," offered Jemmy nervously.

"Aye, and the madness made a fool of one," said Cameron bitterly.

Alex rode furiously through the night, not allowing himself to think of the puzzled hurt in Cameron's eyes when he had left her half-naked on the prairie dirt. He felt cruel but justified as the painful memory of the time on board ship stabbed him. She had stared at him with such mocking hatred as his flesh had lain vulnerable and soft within her warmth. Now I am free of her; I will be free of her. These words rhythmically pounded in his head, as though that final act of coldly coupling could erase his need for her. Let her live with her bastard children any way she chose, and he would live his life, he thought grimly. "His life" had a hollow ring, and at the knowledge, he determined to start legal steps to rid himself of his unwanted wife. It shouldn't prove to be too difficult, as after all she was a fugitive from justice and couldn't show herself in Scotland again. As soon as he had finished his tour of duty and proved his unquestionable loyalty to the throne, he would return to his estate in Scotland. He drove his horse faster as his cold calculations cut painfully, making his future seem bleak.

"Damn her!" he howled to the passing trees as he raced toward the outskirts of the Ottawa camp where he hoped to glean news of Pontiac's tribal council.

CHAPTER TWENTY-EIGHT

Méron rode back to the cabin, deep in thought about Pontiac's council. He had sat in his customary place at the Ottawa chief's left side, aware of the hostile, jealous glances of a number of braves, particularly one named Crooked-Nose, who felt that the honored position should rightfully be his. Four hundred and sixty Potawatomi and Ottawa warriors had listened to Pontiac's long diatribe against the English before adding their own angry grievances. Méron had agreed with all that was said, his own fury ignited by the eloquent chief, whose proud, imperious bearing had the ability to make all present feel awed. A magnetism emanated from the tall Ottawa chief, which caused white man and red man alike to revere the man's physical presence alone.

Pontiac spoke of the meeting over two years before with Major Robert Rogers, who, with two companies of Rangers, had entered the land of the Detroit tribes. The Ottawas, Hurons, and Potawatomis had welcomed the English soldiers, believing their promises and allying themselves with them against the French, thus making it possible for the English to capture the forts on the western Great Lakes. Scarcely a year before, when the Senecas had sent the red wampum belt to several tribes denoting war against the English, he, Pontiac, had been as gullible as a child, still holding onto the English promises. But now it was apparent that the Senecas had been right. The red man was being driven further and further away from his hunting grounds as land was being parceled out to deserving officers. When complaints had been made, the red man had been informed that it was the white man's land. The issue of trading was ranted about for hours when the Indians realized that the English were not as generous as the French. There was now no official trading except at the forts, which made them prey to many ruthless cheats who

visited their camps. There were no longer gifts of ammuni-
tion or provisions, and it seems as though their very movements were now to be restricted.

Pontiac had allowed the surge of fury as many warriors
added to the list of outrages, but then he had raised one
hand, and the hundred voices had been silenced. He then
had spoken to them of the Delaware Prophet, of whom
he had become a disciple. All through the autumn and
winter he had meditated on the Delaware's vision of driving the white man from the face of the earth. This an-
nouncement had been met with a great roar of approval,
which the chief had allowed to crescendo before once
more, with one motion, ensuring silence and complete
attention. His next statement had caused Méron's blood
to rejoice. The red man could only accomplish his own
survival by forsaking all the white man's ways and returning to his original life-style. Only by self-sufficiency
could the Indian make effective war. Pontiac repeated the
Delaware Prophet's words to the hushed assembly.

Méron frowned and felt a clutch of fear in his belly as
the chief praised the French. It seemed that the Prophet's
words only applied to driving the English from their land.
The youth had sat confused throughout the rest of the
council, remembering the generous flow of rum and powder
that had crippled the Indians even more than had the tight-
fisted English. "Why," he wondered "would Pontiac trust
the French?"

Angus, who had been excluded from the council that
had taken place at Pontiac's camp just across the river
from Fort Detroit, had watched from his hiding place the
hundreds of Indians who had filed into what had been
meant to be a secret meeting. He now rode beside the
silent, intense youth, knowing better than to ask what had
occurred as he wondered whether the council had just
been meant as a show of strength to the English, who
could not possibly have failed to see the activity.

Méron rode thinking of the first part of Pontiac's plot,
which was planned for May first. It was now April twenty-
eighth, and although the chief had offered hospitality, the
youth preferred to return to his isolated retreat, even
though it meant he would have only a few hours before

returning. He needed time to sort out the jumbled mass of emotions that tore into his head and caused an uncomfortable clawing in his gut. He had waited out the long feast and ceremony that concluded the council, determined to talk with Pontiac alone, but once in the tall man's presence, he had been tongue-tied and unable to speak as he was warmly embraced like a long, lost son. The Ottawa chief had noted Méron's reticence and shown his disapproval when told the youth would not be spending the days and nights before May first in the camp. Méron had impulsively promised he would be part of the party that entered the fort, and now he regretted the rash decision. He kicked his heels savagely into the mount's sides, remember how callow and ignorant he had felt standing in front of Pontiac. He had wanted to shout that the French were white men, too, and not to trust them but to do what the Delaware Prophet said and drive all white men from their land, including, if necessary, himself, but instead he had felt cowed and trapped. How could he, a sixteen-year-old, unproven youth, presume to tell a great chief what to do? he realized. Maybe what he thought he saw so clearly was not so. Pontiac had to be aware of what he was doing, he told himself as his horse galloped across the treeless plain, but no matter how he reasoned with himself he could not dispel the nagging unease.

Méron's inner dilemma increased as he dismounted outside his cabin and looked down into his sister's drawn face. He frowned when he saw the closed, set expression, which, though eradicated by the long, quiet winter, was now re-etched, her green eyes seeming hollow and unseeing.

"What has happened here?" he asked harshly, but she just shook her head blankly and turned away.

"The bairns?"

"They thrive," she answered dully, her voice sounding toneless and dead.

Méron led his horse into the lean-to and stopped suddenly in his tracks at the sight of the enormous black stallion. Angus, who followed, whistled softly in astonishment.

"Who's here?" hissed Méron.

" 'Tis the horse I saw stabled at the inn in Boston where

I found Jemmy," said Angus, appraising the stallion critically. "Aye, 'tis one and the same. There's no mistaking that beast, even wie the shine back on his coat. Wonder how he comes to be here? Perhaps Sinclair is visiting?" he added and turned to find he was talking to himself as Méron had noiselessly left for the cabin.

"Where is he?" demanded the youth, bursting into the small wooden house.

"Who?" asked Goliath, busily stirring beans in a large pot.

"Sinclair?"

"I've not seen hide nor hair. Och, you mean the animal? I dinna ken how he got here, and the lass isna talking. Let's see now. 'Twas the night you and Angus left. The next morn Cameron was strange and silent and hasna smiled since. Not even the chuckles and antics of the bonny babes can crack her sorrowful mood," explained the large man.

"Cameron?" called Méron.

"She went for a walk," informed Goliath, gesturing toward the lake with a wooden spoon.

After a brief glance at the peacefully sleeping babies, Méron lithely strode outside in search of his twin. He found her staring dully into space, her arms wrapped tightly around her drawn-up legs as though holding herself together. He sat silently, mirroring her position.

"He came?" he asked after a long pause.

"Aye."

"And?" probed Méron.

"And there is nothing."

"So, the spring is here and the ice is thawing, but you will remain frozen?" teased Méron softly. Cameron didn't answer. "Is he that important to you?" he added challengingly.

"I am not important to him, so therefore he is not important to me! I do not need him!" she spat.

"Aye, that is better. I prefer you fighting and hissing than sitting shrouded like an old woman in self-pity," laughed Méron, rejoicing that her eyes now sparkled with anger and tears.

"I have no self-pity!' stated Cameron rebelliously. "You

were gone four days," she added after a short silence wishing to change the subject, ashamed that her brother had found her in such a dispicable and pathetic mood.

"Aye, and I must be away again before morning," he responded, his own depression and worries surfacing. He stared gloomily across the shimmering expanse of water at the busy activity among the reeds where the marsh birds and waterfowl frantically built their nests. He felt removed from Pontiac and the Ottawas, and part of him wished he had spent the autumn and winter with them so that he could have been part of the planning process that had culminated in the council. Maybe then he would not have this awful premonition of disaster clawing into his guts.

"Where are you going?" asked Cameron. "May I go wie you?" But Méron did not answer as he thought about Pontiac's conspiracy to wrest all the forts in the western Great Lakes region from the English. If only the Indians would not rely on the French, he raged inwardly.

"Will you be back by May first?" persisted Cameron. "We can bake the Beltane cakes and light the Beltane fires."

Méron shook his head without looking at her.

"Then I'll ride wie you," she said firmly, knowing she did not want to be alone to brood.

"Nay, you cannot come," he said harshly. "But be sure you wash your face in the first dew to ensure a bonny complexion," he teased, gentling his tone as he referred to the Scottish custom of Beltane morning. "You can bake the scones, but I dinna think you should burn the Beltane fires. 'Twill bring too much notice."

Cameron stared scornfully into her brother's face, knowing he was forcing gaiety. She was not a child, to be so teased and cajoled, she fumed.

"How do you think Alexander Sinclair found me?" she asked sharply and was rewarded by a fleeting concern that crossed her brother's face, quickly hidden as he shrugged feigned indifference. He had reasoned that the man had followed the Ottawa braves when they had come to collect him for Pontiac's council. He stood knowing there was not much he could hide from his twin as he wondered what Sinclair wanted.

"Well, you need not fash yourself, he'll not be return-ing," said Cameron bitterly. "He said we were now free of each other. He is free of me, but how can I be free of him?"

Méron looked down into Cameron's upturned face, which, despite the mutinous expression, showed deep pain.

"You wish to be free of him?" he asked.

"Aye! You'll have your own twin married to a man who wears the red coat of the English, forgetting what they did to Scotland?' she ranted.

"I admit it is not a comforting thought, but suppose he didna wear the red coat? What of the man underneath?"

"I hate him!" she spat. "But how can I be free of him?"

"Time," said Méron softly, squatting on his haunches beside her. "When Little Doe, the mother of my child, died with him, I thought I would never be free of the sharp, cutting pain, but gradually it softens with time."

"But she is dead, and he still lives," cried Cameron.

"Yes, Little Doe and my son are dead. Do you want Sinclair dead too?"

Cameron stared up at him with horror paling her face. "No, not like that!" she gasped. "But dead inside of me, yes! Torn out of every part of me, yes! So that I am free!" she tried to explain.

Méron nodded with a chilling smile crossing his set face before silently sliding away. Cameron felt fear snake through her as she watched him until he was swallowed up by the tall pine trees of the thick forest.

Méron was now glad for his impulsiveness in agreeing to enter Fort Detroit with Pontiac. He wanted to see this Sinclair who could cause his twin such heartache. His usually acute senses were muffled by his thoughts, so he did not feel the eyes of several Ottawas who watched his every movement.

Pontiac, who would hear no word spoken against the Green-Eyed-One, had been bitterly disappointed by the youth's absence during the long months of the autumn and winter. He had understood the boy's need for solitude as he grew to manhood, but Crooked-Nose's jealous tales now seemed to have credence as he noted Méron's detachment at the council and refusal of hospitality. He ordered the youth followed from the camp, not willing to believe that he would betray him but also wanting to take no chances or leave himself open to criticism. With the help of the Delaware Prophet he had united the tribes, and soon more would join him, and with many Indian nations banded together under his leadership the red man would be victorious.

Supper was a gloomy meal. Jemmy's cheerful chatter about Lynx and Raven soon petered out as Goliath and Angus looked anxiously at Méron and Cameron, who methodically ate, their faces expressionless. Cameron was worried about Méron. Although she was immersed in her own unhappiness, she sensed that something was bothering her brother. A fear seemed to emanate from him, and she wished she had not been so wrapped up in herself when he had returned. She remembered the fleeting expression that had crossed her twin's face when she had asked how Alex had found her. What was Méron going to do? Did it have anything to do with Alex? There had been a hardness in her brother's eyes when he had asked her flatly if she wished Alexander Sinclair dead. She chewed slowly, watching Méron's face, but he ate without looking up. Why had Méron ridden back just for one meal? Where was he going and why? The more Cameron thought about it, the more she was convinced that Alex was somehow connected. Remembering the cruel rejection on the moonlit prairie, she filled with rage at her own weakness and at Alex's brutality. Vengeance was hers. It was her battle, not Méron's. She had hidden away licking her wounds long enough. It was spring and it was time she learned the ways of the new country. As Goliath and Angus cleaned up the remains of the meal and Méron sat outside staring over the darkening lake, Cameron took the red-haired girl aside.

"Jemmy, I'll be leaving you wie the bairns for a while. I know you'll be a good little mother and feed them the boiled crushed corn and boned fish. They'll miss my mother's milk, but I must go for a wee bit. Goliath and Angus will know what to do . . . but you're not to say a word until after I've gone, you ken?"

Jemmy's mouth fell open, and she stared wide-eyed at Cameron, unable to say a word.

"You ken?" repeated Cameron, giving her a little shove. Jemmy nodded, her heart beating painfully in her thin chest.

"When?" she asked fearfully.

"Before morning. Jemmy, there's nought to feel afraid of. I will not be gone long, and I'd not leave my sons if it would hurt them. They are braw, lusty lads and not content just to suck anymore, as you well know, but eat food as we do, but carefully mashed," she said, more to convince herself than the wide-eyed girl.

" 'Tis not for the bairns I'm afeared but you," whispered Jemmy. "Do you ride wie Méron?"

"He must not know. I'm trusting you. None must know."

"You ride alone?" gasped Jemmy.

"Only for a while until 'tis too far to turn back, and then I shall join Méron. Tor, Omen, and Torquod will be wie me, so there's no need for alarm."

Jemmy nodded doubtfully, and together they bathed and fed the active, gurgling babies.

Cameron feigned sleep as she watched Méron noiselessly glide out of the cabin after stroking the cheeks of the twins. She waited a few minutes and then threw back the fur blanket that hid her fully dressed state, following him out into the dark, still night. She hid in the shadows as he mounted up and rode into the darkness before leading Torquod out of the lean-to.

The three Ottawa braves led by Crooked-Nose watched with amazement as a seemingly smaller edition of Méron appeared with a giant black bird on one shoulder. Crooked-Nose was a tall youth several years older than Méron, who until the Green-Eyed-One's mysterious appearance three years before had, by his prowess in marksmanship, combat, and riding, been the leader of the emerging young braves. His hatred and jealousy toward Pontiac's favorite knew no bounds, except the superstitious fear that somehow Méron was immortal. He had tried in many ways to bring about the rival youth's death. Unwilling to do the deed himself, he tried to bribe and make promises to lesser braves, but all stood in awe of the magical green eyes. Crooked-Nose's companions shrank further into the shadows as Cameron mounted the giant black stallion and, followed by an enormous hound that seemed to be conjured up from the night's darkness, with the menacing bird circling overhead, rode almost silently until they were out of sight. Crooked-Nose, seeing his alarmed companions, shook himself free of his own panic, gesturing toward the silent cabin. The other braves backed away, shaking their heads, the whites of their eyes piercing the velvet night.

Jemmy had not been able to sleep. She had seen first Méron and then Cameron leave the cabin. When the cabin door opened, she sat up in the sleeping loft, certain that Cameron had changed her mind and was returning. Her hopeful expression turned to one of horror as the red light from the fire silhouetted the tall, large-nosed Indian, whose head was shaved but for a ridge from forehead to crown decorated with several feathers.

Crooked-Nose knew that by harming Méron and the strange shadow that followed him he could harm himself, either by angering his chief Pontiac, with whom he hoped to curry favor, or by some powerful spirit. He would harm the white men, friends of Green-Eyed-One, he determined as he stared curiously around the small cabin. A movement and soft whimper caused him to creep curiously toward the cradle, hatchet in hand. Jemmy screamed, and Maggie growled deep in her throat. Angus and Goliath leaped out of their respective beds.

Crooked-Nose kept his dignity, standing imperiously in the center of the room, making no motion although he felt frozen with terror as lamps were lighted. The two enormous giants who had appeared with Méron three years before and who towered over him by more than a foot did not cause him to falter in his proud bearing, nor did the enormous rusty hound, who bared large teeth and barked ferociously. It was when Jemmy scampered down the ladder and rushed protectively to the cradle and he gazed down upon the ebony-haired, green-eyed reflections of each other that Crooked-Nose fell apart. His eyes rolled with terror, and he fell to his knees shaking.

Goliath opened the door, knowing that the young brave would not travel alone. His keen eyes spotted the huddled group, and he opened the door wider, pointing toward Crooked-Nose, who rocked back and forth emitting strange, lamenting cries. Warily the young braves approached, amazed to see the strongest of them so stricken. They hesitated at the doorway, afraid to enter. Jemmy, intuitively realizing that the identical appearances of the babies had caused the lone brave's strange, fearful reaction, picked up the twins in her thin arms with difficulty and carried them toward the three Indians. Angus, understanding what she was about, held up the lamp, lighting the boys' faces. Raven stared at the shrinking braves without blinking, his bright green eyes seeming to belong to a much older person. Lynx crowed a gurgly welcome, his identical eyes twinkling joyfully as he reached out toward the feathers in their short hair.

"We have a pair of lucky charms," laughed Angus, hiding his consternation at the nocturnal visit after the retreating hoofbeats had died away.

"Where's Cameron?" puzzled Goliath.

"Gone for one of her midnight rides, it seems," observed his brother with a worried frown as he hoped she would not meet up with the strange party that had just ridden out as though chased by a coven of witches. Jemmy pursed her lips tightly, remembering her promise as she tucked the twins back into their cradle, which they had nearly outgrown.

Méron rode through the crisp night air toward Pontiac's camp trying to relax his body and mind, but his head buzzed with nameless anxieties and his belly was still clutched by a nagging fearful premonition. He slowed his horse's pace, breathing deeply and opening his ears to the tranquil night sounds, trying to ease his tensed muscles. He stared overhead at the night sky. The moon was a fragile, thin crescent, and the stars shone with crystalline intensity. Suddenly he was filled with an aching sadness, and he rode, loose-limbed, through the dark wilderness, a solitary boy filled with the suffering of a man. He saw Little Doe's dark eyes staring at him for love and protection and was filled with a sense of guilt and hopelessness. They had both been children playing in an adult world that had eventually brought her a painful death. Maybe it was all for the best, he thought, savagely sweeping the wetness from his lean cheeks. What right did he have to bring new life into such a world where one man was not content to allow another to live in peace? he raged. He thought of his little nephews, Lynx and Raven, destined to be raised without a father as he and Cameron had been, and smiled as he imagined them growing strong and tall under his watchful eye. His smile faded when he thought of his sister, who still seemed to be consumed by Alex Sinclair, the tall, golden Scot, called Lion by the Ottawas. He had not even met the man, and yet his hatred burned deeply, knowing how much pain had been inflicted upon his twin. His previous feelings of being inferior because he was a callow youth, not even truly yet a man, were swept away as a flood of exhilaration coursed through him. He would take charge of both his young nephews and his twin. He would quit this land of bloodshed, making his way across the vast continent deep into virgin territory, where the proud red man still lived with nature as he should, and there among the birds and animals make a home for them all—Cameron, Lynx, Raven, Jemmy, Angus, and Goliath. First he would repay Pontiac and the Ottawas for their acceptance and their teachings, which had made it possible for him to survive off the earth in the dense forests and sweeping plains. He would carve out a life free of the insidious graspings of society, politics, and religion, he determined, his eyes shining with the excitement of his planned future.

Méron's long, lithe body tensed. How long had he heard the pulse of the following hoofbeats without being aware of what they portended? he wondered as he reined his horse to a halt and listened intently. Quickly he kneed his mount, urging him into the thick shelter of some trees as the rhythmic, thudding hoofbeats neared. He heard the horse slow down until it walked and then stopped as the rider obviously scanned the long, dark shadows. Stealthily his hand reached for the knife at his waist, and his young lean body was coiled to pounce from the high back of his horse.

"Méron?" whispered Cameron as her eyes tried to pierce

the impenetrable blackness. Tor whined and ran toward the shadows, stopping anxiously as though he sensed the youth's poised tension. Méron kicked his horse so he walked forward and, without any expression on his lean face, stared at his sister. Cameron, unable to see in the darkness, felt the waves of anger exuding from the tall figure of her twin. For several minutes not a word was said as she apprehensively noted the straight, stern line of his back.

"What manner of a mother are you to leave your young?" spat Méron.

"Like our own, it seems," returned Cameron, his censure joining with her own guilt. "I will go with you or alone."

Méron wheeled his horse without a word, dug in his heels, and galloped into the night. Cameron waited for several seconds and then followed, determined she would not lose him in the darkness.

The sun streaked the eastern horizon, and brother and sister rode side by side. Méron surveyed her and nodded, trying to keep his expression stony and set, but Cameron saw the spark in his matching emerald eyes and grinned mischievously at him.

"You approve?" she quipped, referring to her tightly laced leather-thonged shirt hung with fringes.

"They may be flattened for all times," he answered roguishly, relieved that her female attributes were securely hidden. She wore the doeskin clothes that he had taught her to make, and he laughed remembering her distaste at having to chew the leather after curing. She wore leggings, also fringed, and breechcloth, her feet encased in soft moccasin boots. Her lustrous black hair, identical to his own, was parted in the middle and secured by a beaded headband.

"I thought to shave my head at the sides and wear feathers, but as you yourself dinna observe the custom of your Indian friends, I decided against it," she said airily. "And I brought you this," she added, throwing a similar headband to him, which he deftly caught. He stared at it a moment and then with a laugh ripped off the leather thong that tied his hair back from his face and replaced it with the beaded band.

"We shall not speak from now on, as we'll be watched," he cautioned, motioning her to precede him. He watched her critically, noting her graceful ease atop the huge black stallion. She was an imposing sight, although seeming to be no more than a lithe young brave of scarcely twelve or thirteen. There was a quiet, impressive dignity in her bearing, which was helped by the large black bird and enormous hound. He nodded, amusement glinting his green eyes, as he thought of the reception they would receive at Pontiac's camp.

Cameron's heart pounded painfully in her chest as they entered the Indian encampment riding side by side. She kept her head high and her eyes straight ahead, not looking to either side, hiding her terror and apprehension. The twins halted as one before a very impressive man, tall and strongly built, his skin a shade lighter than the other braves who surrounded him. For several minutes no words or movement passed between them, although behind Cameron could hear a babble of excited voices as tepees opened and curious Ottawas poured out. She kept her eyes on the man before her, knowing he was the chief, Pontiac, her teeth gritted painfully together so that her nervousness would not be betrayed by a quivering cheek.

Pontiac was also a master at hiding what he felt. He stared into the bright, unnaturally green eyes that met his without wavering. With one sweeping gesture of his hand he broke the stare, turned, and entered the tepee. Méron dismounted, and Cameron, not knowing what was expected of her, remained upon Torquod's high back waiting for some sign from her brother, but he disappeared into the chief's lodge, and she was left feeling the curious stares boring into her.

She thrust her shoulders back and lifted her head proudly as she felt her face suffused with blood. Omen's weight became heavier each second, and numerous flies buzzed, irritating her face and neck, but she made no movement as she pinned her gaze to the painted designs on the skins of the tent. Behind her she heard the thudding of hoofbeats and guttural yelling. She felt the crowd of watching Ottawas move toward the disturbance, and although she longed to ease her position and turn around to see what was happening, she kept herself ramrod straight and made no indication she heard anything. Half-starved, mangy dogs sniffed around Torquod's feet, and he stamped them away as Tor growled menacingly. The shouting and confusion behind her grew louder, and finally, after what had seemed at least an hour, the flap of the tepee was thrust aside, and Pontiac and Méron emerged into the bright sunlight. The chief gave her a cursory though admiring glance before yelling harshly to the clustered people.

Crooked-Nose gestured wildly, pointing first at Méron and then at Cameron, who froze, as she was able to decipher something about babies. Her brother's lessons in Indian dialects had been rewarding, even though the young Indian ranted and stammered. She turned and looked at Crooked-Nose as she heard the other braves defensively telling their chief that they had meant no harm to Méron's giant friends or the tiny babies with the green eyes.

Cameron did not stop to think. She launched herself agilely from her stallion's high back, causing Omen to swoop and glide into the air just above the assembled Indians' heads. She recognized the hatred and cruelty in Crooked-Nose's face and the knowledge that he had meant her loved ones harm made her lash out against him. She straddled the tall brave, whom she had toppled backward into the dirt, with her dirk in hand, but to her amazement the young man just lay inert, his face a mask of fear. Unable to plunge the knife into the unresisting body beneath her, she sat feeling silly, not knowing what to do. She gasped in astonishment as she was plucked off Crooked-Nose, who scrambled away to the jeers of his tribesmen. She looked up into Pontiac's laughing face and realized she was held like a toy in his strong hands. Her eyes met his, and his expression sobered, but the humorous line of his mouth remained.

The rest of the day passed in a whirl of color, sound, smell, and taste as the twins sat beside Pontiac watching dancing, drumming, and displays of valor between young braves. Glancing around at the many warriors, who, she noted, gave her and Méron a wide berth, Cameron realized there were no other females present except those who brought in steaming bowls of a pungent stew. The celebrations went on well into the night and finally tapered off. She stood dwarfed by Pontiac and her brother as they stared across the broad river toward a cluster of lights on the far shore. She had not spoken all day, and it seemed that Pontiac approved of her silence. Méron had just made several grunts of assent throughout the long hours but now, staring at the misty, distant lights, he spoke quietly and intently to the tall, imposing chief. Cameron was glad that the dusk hid her expression as she pieced together what was being said and understood that they looked toward Fort Detroit, where on the first day of May, Pontiac and fifty men would gain entrance to get information. Her excitement built and, throwing caution to the wind, she touched the Ottawa chief's blanketed arm. He looked down at her set, mutinous expression, noting the vivid green eyes that seemed to penetrate the dewy dusk as she pointed to herself and then to the fort. Méron, quickly understanding her meaning, spoke rapidly to Pontiac, shaking his head, and Cameron realized he was saying she was too young and inexperienced, which made her blood boil. The chief looked from the tall youth down to the smaller replica with amusement. Cameron stood firm, glaring at her traitorous twin, refusing to allow any weakening of resolve. Taking a deep breath, she spoke in a halting mixture of Algonkian and Iroquois.

"I have heard that spies are needed to slip through the shadows while Ottawas entertain the hated redcoats with dance. I am small and can fit into many places in the fort unseen. I can defend myself . . . watch?" she pleaded, taking her dirk from the sheath on her belt.

Pontiac watched the seeming young brave select a target and, despite the fast-approaching night that made visibility difficult, hit it squarely. No expression crossed his face, so Cameron picked an even smaller, more distant object to show off her prowess, the feather in the short hairs of a brave who kept watch by the river. All she could see was the white of the quill as she concentrated and aimed. She felt Méron stiffen, but Pontiac placed a hand on the youth's shoulder, warning him to be still. Cameron deftly flung the knife, and there was a startled cry from the shadowy figure, who found himself pinned to the tree. The Ottawa chief barked out an order, and the terrified warrior froze at the command as Pontiac strode slowly and silently to regard Cameron's handiwork. The dirk had struck the feather, splitting the central spine, and Pontiac nodded his approval as he wrenched the blade free and handed it back to her.

Across the river at Fort Detroit tensions were high as reports flooded in about the increased activity at the Ottawa camp. One officer casually mentioned that it could be nothing more than a pagan spring festival, and Major Gladwin had laughed harshly with his eyes pinned on Alex as he made comment of the barbaric Scots and their pagan rituals of the Beltane. Alex felt his gall rise, but knowing that the commandant was deliberately trying to rile him, he just stared back with studied indifference. The unspoken tensions between the two men had built to a crackling intensity. Everything about Sinclair now irritated Gladwin —the tall, golden Scot's graceful, lithe bearing, his obvious appeal to women, his silence, and most of all the eloquence of the amber eyes set in his impassive face. He felt Sinclair to be disrespectful and insolent, standing in judgment, and above all laughing at him in some indefinable way. He strove to break Alex's dignity by making many derogatory remarks about the Scots, enlisting the other English officers as a jeering chorus to applaud his jibes.

Alex recognized his commanding officer to be an ambitious empire builder, fanatical in his serving of his king and country, with that absolutely presumptuous superiority that seemed to say that just being English meant one was always right. He also recognized that anti-Scottish feelings ran very high in the fort, reflecting the same animosity in England, where ironically a Scottish prime minister had been appointed after Pitt resigned. He was the only Scottish officer of any rank at Fort Detroit at that time, his fellow countrymen relegated to the most menial positions. He stood in the commandant's office, seeming oblivious to the snickers, his long, hard body relaxed and graceful.

"You are confined to the fort, Sinclair," stated Gladwin, indicating an unwieldy pile of paperwork on his desk. "I'm hoping I am not presuming too much in expecting you to be able to read and write?"

A chorus of ill-disguised snorts bore witness that the sycophantic junior officers enjoyed the slighting of the taciturn Major Sinclair. Gladwin was rewarded by a lazy smile and a nod of assent that made his blood boil.

"I hope you don't take it amiss, Major, but we cannot afford to lose any more scouts. You must admit you do have a penchant for somehow bringing about their unfortunate demise," goaded the commandant, determined to break Alex's natural dignity.

" 'Tis hard to know whose side these northern English are on," stammered a young officer. "They wear eagle feathers in their bonnets and skirts much like the red savages."

"And fight much the same way," volunteered another, encouraged by the commanding officer's expression of amusement.

"And, as you said yourself, they also observe pagan festivals and believe in fairies and spirits," joined in another.

"I fought the Highlanders on Culloden Moor—whirling dervishes with no sense of fair fighting, much like the screeching, bloodthirsty Indians here."

"Let me assure you, men, that those papers contain nothing of import," responded Gladwin after watching Alex's unchanging expression of amused nonchalance. "Unless laundry lists and various bills for edible supplies can be sold or traded with the enemy."

"No disrespect intended, sir," said another officer, "but I've never understood why Pitt would send Scots to help fight the French when it is well known the two countries have conspired against the English throne for countless generations."

Alex sat at Gladwin's desk sorting out the messy pile of papers, seeming impervious to the goading insults, which caused the commandant to grit his teeth and clench his fists. He ached to shatter the man's easy grace, and yet Sinclair was just obeying his very orders and, no matter how insulting he felt him to be, there was nothing to point a finger at.

"You may take those papers to your own quarters, Sinclair," he barked, wanting to be free of the mocking amber eyes. Alex crossed the room with the lithe, easy grace of a cat and, nodding humorously to the assembled officers, left the room.

Alex sprawled across his hard cot feeling an impending excitement prickle his skin. He ran his strong, golden hand through his tawny mane, staring blankly into space as he tried to decipher the rising feeling. Something was due to happen. He felt it in every fiber of his being. He snorted mirthlessly and chided himself for being superstitious as he thought of the Beltane feast. Tomorrow would be May first, he thought, one year since Cameron had quit Glen Aucht, leaving his hopes and dreams in dust around his feet. It had been one year since he had killed Colonel Randall Beddington and fled his ancestral home to accept a commission in Fort Detroit in order to prove his loyalty to the English king so that he could retain his heritage and his birthright. The irony of it rang in his head, and Kinkaid's dry old voice echoed in his ears. If he had it to do all over again, what course would he have taken? he mused. He shook his head from side to side, knowing there was no easy answer. His Scottish roots ran deep, embedding him in the soil of his land, and the pain of the separation coursed through him, angering him to his very core, and yet would he ever be content having to compromise and kowtow to the English? Would he be able to stand silent and impassive watching the incredible corruption and injustice? What would he gain other than land won by another's blood and pride? If he and Cameron had by some miracle managed to stay together, living as man and wife at Glen Aucht, bearing children to carry on his name, what heritage would they have been able to pass on to their sons?

Alex sat up with a curse as the memory of Cameron with the babes nursing at her breasts tore into his mind. She had seemed in her element, naked in the sunlight beside the tranquil lake, the newly emerging foliage mirroring the clear green of her eyes. He tried to imagine her suitably gowned, modestly feeding his children secluded behind the four walls of a conventional nursery before delivering them into the capable hands of a nurse. He snorted derisively at the thought. How could he ever have thought for one moment that the wild, raven-haired girl could have docilely accepted the conventional social existence that he had unthinkingly mapped out for her?

He allowed his mind to wander further back, to their mountain retreat in the mid-Highlands of Scotland where he thought he had gentled and brought her to trust him. Far from the busy world, secluded by the mountains and tall trees, they had come together, delighting in each other, but the seemingly strong attachment had been too frail to survive entrance into the outside world. Would he have been content to remain in the wilderness with her, he wondered, and immediately banished the wistful question from his mind as he acknowledged it was too late for such thoughts. She had obviously found solace in another's arms, bearing a child—no, two children, he amended savagely, astonished that the presence of twin babies had not amazed him more. She could do nothing without fanfare and exaggeration, even birthing, he remarked to himself cynically as the painful image of another man possessing her body caused a violent shaft of jealousy to stab him.

He stood abruptly, banishing all thought of her, and sat before the pile of papers that demanded his attention, determined to dispose of them as quickly and efficiently as possible, as deep in his bones he knew with certainty that the following May Day morning would bring surprises and an end to the boring, gray days.

CHAPTER TWENTY-NINE

Alex stood with Major Gladwin and several other officers watching the approaching Ottawas.

"How many do you estimate?"

"Forty or fifty," returned a guard.

They silently observed the blanketed braves, who filed in on foot toward the stockade walls. Alex's eyes narrowed with speculation, noticing two shining, unshaved heads conspicuous among the bristly feathered crests. A tic moved one lean cheek as he noted the small size of one of them.

"Let them in," ordered Gladwin, knowing that his troops outnumbered the Indians, and the heavy gate was opened to the silent, proud group, who, despite their tattered blankets, strode with quiet dignity.

"What do you think they are up to?" hissed one of the officers.

"We can only wait and see. Meanwhile double the guard," returned Gladwin crisply, and despite Alex's intense dislike for the pompous, ambitious major, he grudgingly had to admire the other man's shrewd tactics.

The Ottawas formed a circle in the parade grounds and, to the beat of a large buffalo-hide drum, began a noisy ceremonial dance. Soldiers' wives and children edged out of their quarters and watched curiously.

"By Jove, I was correct," chortled one officer. " 'Tis the rites of spring or some such pagan festival."

Soon most of the occupants of Fort Detroit sat enjoying the entertainment. Major Gladwin sat beside Pontiac, glad for his cologned handkerchief that offset the strong odor of bear grease that emanated from the imperious chief. He stared into the impassive, inscrutable brown face of the Ottawa leader, aware of the fleet forms that detached themselves from their dancing, chanting companions and skillfully blended themselves into the shadows, and a smug smile flattened his lips.

Alex's eyes never left the two shining black heads, and when the smaller of the two departed, leaving the tall youth to sit cross-legged at Pontiac's left side, he followed. He knew without doubt it was Cameron, even though the eyes were lowered, hiding the telltale color. There was a certain lithe bearing he knew so well that no seedy blanket could smother or conceal it. He followed at a distance, thankful he had forsaken his uniform and boots for the more comfortable buckskins and moccasins, as he was able to move as silently as she.

Pontiac had instructed his spies well, having drawn countless maps in the smooth mud by the side of the river. Cameron had memorized the drawings, and although never having set foot in that fort or any other before, she felt she could find her way blindfolded. It was nothing more than a square stockaded town of wooden houses, the four corners and regular spaces in between punctuated by watchtowers, from which peered armed sentries, who were now lulled by the hypnotic throb of the ceremonial drum.

Tension prickling her scalp and excitement pounding her heart, Cameron silently slipped from shadow to shadow, intent on reaching Major Gladwin's quarters, where she hoped to find written orders and accounts of munitions that would let them know how long the fort could hold out under siege. It had been her own idea, readily accepted by Pontiac when he learned that she could read and decipher the white man's writings. Behind the quite large house she shrugged off the blanket in preparation to shimmy herself through a narrow window. She looked both ways, her blood chilling at the sight of a man leaning casually against the building, watching her with a hard, cynical expression. Alex! She forgot her intention as her pulses beat thunder in her ears and her legs quivered like jelly. She was captured by the amber eyes, which locked into her with such intensity she felt she would drown. A small animal whimper burst from her mouth, shocking her back into the reality of the situation as the monotonous beat of the drum reminded her of what she was about. Her small brown hand

sidled slowly to the dagger at her waist, but in one lightning movement Alex wrested it from her, knowing all to
well her intention. She quivered in his strong grasp, confused by the flood of emotions that gripped her and not
daring to meet his eyes for fear she would betray her weakness. His large hand forced her small chin upward, and she
tried to steel herself as his eyes seared into hers. His face
showed savage amusement, more painful than the cold contempt she expected.

"Would you like a leg up?" he asked in the cordial tones
of one offering a glass of sherry.

Cameron stared up at him with numb confusion, not
comprehending his meaning.

"You did mean to gain entrance to the commandant's
quarters, did you not?" responded Alex wryly. "Unfortunately you'll find nothing but laundry lists and the like,
as news of this day has been reported from many sources."

Cameron tried as hard as she could to regain control of
herself, but the close proximity to Alex tore at her senses,
making havoc of all her resolves. The sight of him, the
musk of him, the warmth of the strong hand that held her
almost cruelly created a turmoil of aching confusion. She
felt tiny and vulnerable, at war with herself as she strove
against the desire to bury her pounding head into the
safety of his broad, hard chest.

"Let go, Sinclair," purred a soft voice.

Cameron came out of her daze as she saw Méron
crouched, knife in hand. "No!" burst unbidden from her
lips, and she instinctively shielded Alex's body with her
own, much to his surprise. He stared down at his wife, who
scarcely came to his armpit, and frowned before the humor
of the situation caused his chest to rumble with mirth and
he put her aside as though she were merely a feather.

Cameron could not understand her impulsive reaction
in trying to shield him. She saw the puzzlement on her
twin's face and then the deep sounds of Alex's mirth before
she was cast aside. She felt fury at herself for once more
putting herself in a position to be ridiculed and rejected.
She took a sobbing breath and, picking up her discarded
blanket, rushed blindly away, forgetting her ornate dirk,
which Alex still held. Her headlong rush was stopped in

one little movement by Méron, who, not removing his eyes
from the amused amber ones, reached out a strong brown
arm to catch his sister in a protective embrace. She thankfully hid her burning cheeks and welling eyes in her
brother's chest, trying to control herself as the two males
took stock of each other.

Méron was also confused. He had built up such hatred
for this unknown man, and now in his presence he found
the emotion hard to retain.

"You are Méron?" drawled Alex, not moving as he saw
the tall, lean youth's tension. The bright green eyes so
much like Cameron's stared at him without wavering, and
he saw indecision and puzzlement in their depths. He was
just a raw boy, and yet the promise of a commanding
man emanated, acknowledged Alex, instinctively liking and
admiring Méron. He was little more than a child and yet
had proved himself in many ways like a man and been
accorded the honor of riding at a chief's left side.

"Go back to the ceremony," growled Méron huskily,
pulling his sister back so that he looked down into her face.
His heart constricted with pain at the sight of the tear furrows on her cheeks. Rage filled him, and savagely he turned
Cameron to face Alex. "See? See?" he hissed, his lean
fingers tracing the wetness. He held his tear-stained fingertips toward his sister's husband. "For these I could kill
you, and for these I cannot."

Alex stared into the blazing eyes of the youth, his face
mirroring his concern. Cameron wrenched herself free,
feeling exposed and humiliated. She glared at her brother,
glad that her fury beat stronger than her pain before turning on her heels and gliding away.

"Have no fear, I shall take care of her and her sons.
You are free. I shall be their guide and keep them all safe,"
intoned Méron, standing straight and pulling himself up
to try to equal the taller man.

"Who is their father?" asked Alex hoarsely, but the boy
stared at him contemptuously for a few seconds before
smiling diabolically, turning his back and walking away
from him. Alex watched him go, making no movement to
follow. He stared down at the ornate dirk he still grasped
in his hand and snorted. Yet another reminder of Cameron,

he thought, and although he had the urge to throw it with all his might over the high stockade wall, he thrust it into his belt before idly strolling back to the parade ground to watch the conclusion of Pontiac's tribal ceremony.

Alex stood high in a watchtower as the silent procession of Indians filed out of the fort at sunset after Pontiac had promised to return in a few days to pay Gladwin a more formal visit. He was oblivious to the banter that went back and forth among the observing officers about Pontiac's more formal visit as he went over the scene behind Gladwin's house countless times. Why did Cameron affect him so? The feel of her, his hand encircling her slim waist. The heady scent of her was still in his nostrils, and it had taken his iron will not to crush her to him. He remembered the tears on her soft cheeks that Méron had savagely pointed to, and they burned their salty sting, touching off a deep pain within himself. Why couldn't he stop loving her? Why couldn't he stop hating her? The unbidden questions increased the ache within him. Why couldn't he cut himself free of her?

He stared around with narrowed eyes, recollecting where he was as his fellow uniformed officers spoke derisively about the proud, tattered people who now steadily paddled their canoes across the wide river to their camp. What was he doing standing in this watchtower with these redcoats, he seethed, as though waking from a dream. A madness welled within him as he debated diving from the high rampart into the swirling brown waters below. He held himself back, knowing the pure suicide of such an action, which would make him a target for not only the English guns but the Indian arrows. Reason flooded his brain, and once again he cursed himself for weakening. How could he give up everything for Cameron, who could turn around and reject him out of hand, who, for all he knew, had found another man, the father of her children. To be with Cameron meant he had to turn his back on Glen Aucht and give up all hope of ever returning to Scotland. At last he could admit he loved her, but the admission only caused even more pain and anger.

* * *

Cameron sat silently with Méron as the other Indian spies reported to Pontiac, who was painfully aware he had been betrayed. He ranted furiously, knowing that Gladwin had obviously expected him and got little solace from the information of number of guns, barrels of powder, and edible provisions inside the fort. He suspected that Gladwin had let his men know just what he wished them to know to lull the Ottawas into a false sense of security.

Runners were sent to the neighboring tribes of the Potawatomis and Hurons with an invitation to meet with the Ottawas on May fifth. Determined not to be betrayed again, Pontiac announced that all women would leave the camp and that sentries were to ring the area.

Cameron's breasts were heavy and aching with milk, which seeped out, running down and making her belly sticky. She wanted to be with her sons, hugging them close. They would be an anchor so that she wouldn't be swept away by the desolation that gripped her. She listened intently to the proceedings, realizing that if she was to leave, she would have to make her escape from the Ottawa camp before the sentinels were posted.

Méron was instinctively aware of Cameron's feelings. He, too, wished her safely back in the secluded cabin under the watchful eyes of Goliath and Angus. Pontiac was angry and, seated by him during the ceremonies at the fort as the drumming and dancing proceeded, Méron had heard the exchange between Major Gladwin and the chief. The commandant's reaction to the complaints of high prices and poor quality of traded goods had been met with a shrug, and the notification of Indian deaths from disease, starvation, murder, and exposure had been met with another. To the youth it had seemed that the English major was happy with the knowledge, a fact borne out several minutes later when Gladwin had turned to a fellow officer and, not thinking he would be understood by the Indians around, had said, "What use are these savages to us? They expect us to mourn for them, and it's difficult not to shout for joy."

Méron vowed to stay with the Ottawas, helping them any way he could to bring about the destruction of the English, and yet he was equally determined to secret Cameron from the camp that night. He debated asking Pontiac but thrust the thought aside, knowing that permission would be denied as security was now tightened. Let the Ottawas think Little-Green-Eyes had been spirited away by unnatural magical means, he decided, knowing that they were in awe of the large raven that accompanied her. The whole time they had been at Fort Detroit, Omen had roosted on top of Pontiac's lodge, greatly pleasing the chief, as he saw it as a sign of victory. Méron thought of various Indian legends describing the beginning of the world when there was nothing, no light, no animals, no man . . . but Giant Raven created light by throwing glittering particles into the sky. Some tribes called the raven the Thunderbird, whose wings created the wind and thunder, whose eyes sparked with lightning, and from whose phosphorescent back rolled the life-giving rain.

As Méron sat lost in thought during the droning council, Omen flew into the air and circled over the assembled Ottawas, coming to light upon Cameron's shoulder. The voices hushed as the small figure stood, and when the small green-eyed brave started to leave the circle without Pontiac's permission, a gasp was heard. Méron's blood chilled, and he reached out to detain her. To his surprise the Ottawa chief stilled his hand. Cameron was unaware of the silent eyes pinned to her as she whistled shrilly. All she wanted was to ride through the night to find comfort with her children. Protocol and possible insult to the chief did not occur to her. She leaped up on the tall, glistening back of the giant stallion, who reared a welcome, pawing the air with his powerful hooves. For a dizzying minute she surveyed the stern features of the tall Indian who stood before her as the full realization of her action burst in. She saw the shocked drawn face of her brother. Omen raised his beak and cawed raucously. Pontiac raised his arm, and Cameron galloped out of the camp followed by the enormous hound. Méron expelled his bated breath slowly, aware of the awed silence surrounding him until the black horse was out of sight. Feeling Pontiac's piercing gaze, he kept his face impassive, knowing enough not to make excuses or explanations and hoping she knew her way back to the forest retreat. The council was disbanded, and

Méron alone sat with the chief smoking the calumet silently.

"One day you too will disappear back into the shadows from which you came," said the chief sorrowfully. "You are not of our people, and yet you are."

"I will stay longer," promised Méron.

"Even though the female mirror of yourself has flown into the night?"

"I will stay longer," repeated Méron, not showing his surprise at Pontiac's shrewd observation.

Alex was at war with himself. He paced the confines of his small, bare room, not knowing what to do. If he followed his instincts and love for Cameron, he could be rejected by her and left with nothing. Such an impetuous action would certainly be regarded by the English as treasonous, resulting in the loss of his lands. Thoughts of Fergus and Mackie and their incredible loyalty to him assailed his brain, and he knew he could do nothing that would cause reprisal against them and the other people who cared for Glen Aucht in his absence. Alex felt impotent, and his fury boiled as there seemed no answer to his dilemma. As usual Cameron was at the heart of it.

Trying to calm himself, he sat and wrote letters to Fergus, Sir Robert Kinkaid, and Ian Drummond, thanking them for all they did on his behalf. He felt a hollow wave of homesickness for the peaceful rolling estate so far away, and his nose could almost smell the fragrance of Mackie's comforting kitchen. He leaned back and let his mind trace the tranquil, cultivated countryside of his home, which was such a contrast to the untamed wilderness of the New World. His lands were harnessed and controlled, as were the plans for his life before he had met Cameron, whom he had tried to gentle. But she fought against the restrictions until a chasm yawned between them.

He faced their differences honestly and realized he had expected her to be the docile wife, leaning on and trusting his decisions and actions without question. How could she have understood his behavior at Glen Aucht? She who understood nothing of politics, the military, or diplomacy?

She reacted to injustice, brutality, and attack instinctively, and he had been so wrapped up in the problems of the English occupation of his estate, he had had no time or opportunity to teach her. What *would* he have taught her, he wondered. How to be a wife? A genteel society matron? Able to trot sidesaddle on the manicured lawns of Glen Aucht? Able to pour tea and converse gracefully, curbing her tongue? Able to bear and raise conforming sons to be educated in the English universities of Oxford and Cambridge? Able to provide him with pretty, mannered, simpering young daughters to be exhibited like pet ponies at debutante balls? Alex snorted derisively. Yes, without thinking, that had been the plan mapped out in his mind. That had been the conforming life he had planned on. Now, it all seemed trivial, brittle, and meaningless. What did he want? He wanted Cameron. He wanted to unlearn . . . to untame himself so that his life wasn't a flat, charted course but rather an aware one, a challenge with real choices.

He sighed deeply and resumed writing to the dear people so very far away. He reread his words, which contained mundane, comforting news, really a web of white lies, informing them of Cameron's good health and the birth of twin sons. Let the people at Glen Aucht assume that the children were his and that no rift existed. The fabrication had a twofold reasoning. Besides obviously giving joy to Mackie his old nurse, there were now heirs to his estate if he died or was presumed dead. Heirs, he thought cynically as he sealed the letters. Whose children were they? And although the question caused him pain and jealousy, he realized that if he and Cameron could be together, he would embrace and accept the children as his own. He smiled softly, caught up in the happy possibility, but then all the impediments tore into his head and he pounded the table with his fist. How could he be with Cameron who was now an outlaw, without endangering the lives of Mackie, Fergus, Ian, and Sir Robert? If only Gladwin hadn't confined him to the fort. If he had his freedom, he could disappear into the wilderness, leaving his clothes and some possessions to be found ripped and bloodied, with him presumed slain by a wandering bear or Indian.

Alex was exhausted by the events of the day and by his emotions. He lay back on his hard bunk, knowing that the following days before Pontiac's promised "more formal visit" would pass very slowly. He would then see Cameron again, and hopefully be able to start healing the breach between them. An unbidden fear surfaced. What if she truly loved another, the father of her children? He shook his head, unable to accept such a thought as the memory of the green-eyed youth comforted him. What had Méron said? That he would keep her and her sons safe? Surely the boy wouldn't make such a statement if Cameron had another man to protect her. With this small glimmer of solace Alex closed his eyes and resigned himself to the next few days of waiting with only laundry lists and derogatory statements to fill up his boredom. There had to be a way to get to Cameron without endangering all those at Glen Aucht.

Cameron reached the cabin as the first morning rays dispersed the darkness. She had traveled through the thick blackness of the moonless night, guided by Tor and Omen, without incident. Anxious to see her sons, she leaped from Torquod's high back to the lush, dewy grass and, leaving the stallion to graze peacefully, rushed to the door of the cabin. To her surprise it was locked, and no amount of knocking could arouse the occupants.

Hides covered the windows so that she could not see inside. Standing back, she observed that no smoke curled from the chimney. There were also no horses in the lean-to, and the canoe was not pulled high on the bank in its customary place. The cabin was deserted, and Cameron stood fatigued and emotionally spent as terrifying thoughts assailed her. Maybe she had not understood correctly and Crooked-Nose had in fact hurt or killed her friends and children, instead of trying and being repulsed. Why had she not plunged her dirk into the cruel brave? she raved, and her hand went to her waist but encountered nothing. Where was her knife? she wondered frantically, and the image of Alex's large golden hand flooded her brain. She collapsed on the wet ground, unable to think logically, the desperate aching for her babies joining with the pain of her full breasts and overburdened heart. Guilt at leaving her children, Alex's rejection and laughter, and the loss of her friends flooded in until she burst, howling out her anguish like an animal in pain. Consumed by grief so that her ears were deaf and her eyes blind with tears, she was oblivious to Tor, who at first ran back and forth wanting her to follow and then sat back on his haunches and joined his voice to hers.

Jemmy shivered at the unearthly cries that woke her at dawn in the damp shelter across the lake. She held Lynx and Raven close to her, and they whimpered, their hungry mouths nuzzling her flat, immature breasts.

"Goliath? Angus?" she whispered as their immense shapes loomed out of the mist that rose from the lake's surface. "Is it wolves?"

"Hard to say," replied Angus, scratching his head. "Could be, and yet I canna be sure."

"Whatever it is, 'tis surely lamenting," remarked Goliath. "Comes from the direction of the cabin. Stay wie the bairns, Angus. I think it best I go see," he decided, and he pushed the canoe down the slippery bank into the water.

"What if it's the Indians come back to get us?" shivered Jemmy, as Maggie raised her own shaggy red head and joined her howling to the eerie keening that spiraled with the wisps of mist that hung over the dark lake.

"Then it is good we are where we are," remarked Angus, squatting beside her and relieving her of one of the hungry, protesting babies. "You'll be hungry yet awhile, little Lynx, as I dare not light a fire until your uncle Goliath sees what's amiss. Jemmy, maybe you best soak sucking rags in water and maple syrup so we can keep these wee-uns quiet," he suggested, relieving her also of Raven.

Cameron huddled on the ground. Her cries had diminished until she just shuddered with dry sobs, an echo of the past tempest. Tor answered the ghostly howls that had joined his from across the lake, but Cameron was unaware of him as she sat wrapped in her own miserable desolation. Tor sprang to his feet barking excitedly and ran to the shoreline as his keen ears heard the faint splashings of an oar.

Beaching the canoe a distance from the cabin, Goliath, with rifle in hands, furtively edged his way up the bank. He had heard the excited barkings but still was not sure if he was destined to meet a pack of hungry wolves. In the eerie morning mist it was difficult to know if one's ears played tricks, he thought grimly. Tor's large, lithe body emerged sharply from the gray gloom, and Goliath rubbed a hand across his eyes, wondering if they also were deceiving him. The dog launched himself, nearly knocking the enormous man backward in an excess of welcome before running a little way ahead and then returning as he begged the man to follow him.

Cameron sat motionless as her dog and the large man loomed out of the mist. She stared uncomprehending, not knowing if she dreamed or not as there were no sharp, defining lines but a hazy, ethereal quality.

Goliath squatted beside her, peering into her red-rimmed eyes, and he was gripped with a sharp pang of fear.

"Méron?" he asked, thinking that her grief was due to something that had happened to her twin.

"My sons?" she asked, frantically pulling at his clothes to anchor herself by proving he really did exist and was not some fanciful figment of her imagination.

"Fine, but hungry. Where is your brother?"

"With the Ottawas. You were not killed? You are all alive?" she babbled, delirious in her relief. "When I found the cabin deserted, I thought you were all dead. Why did you leave no message?"

"We thought you safe wie Méron. Jemmy told us of your plan too late for one of us to follow. And after the strange visitors we had the night you disappeared, we thought it best to hide away. I left signs for Méron, not realizing you would return alone," explained Goliath.

"Crooked-Nose will not return. Pontiac will see to that," informed Cameron wearily, stiffly rising to her feet.

"Well, I'm thankful for that, as it hasna been too comfortable wie the babes camping in the dampness," replied Goliath, fitting the blade of his knife into the slit of the cabin door and raising the inside bar.

* * *

Cameron, now in dry clothes, sat before a blazing fire, impatiently waiting for Goliath to return with her sons. What had made her follow Méron? she wondered. It was almost as though she had a premonition that she would meet Alex. What had been the purpose? she puzzled. Why was she so drawn to being hurt? Had he not made it very clear that he no longer wanted her in that moonlit coming-together on the plain, when they had clawed at each other in all-consuming passion only to have him use and discard her, lying vulnerable in her nakedness? Could there ever be an action that so decisively showed his contempt of her? An hour before, she felt she had lost everything, not only him but the sons of their union, and she had been swept by such hopeless desolation that there had seemed no reason to exist. Now she waited, her breasts prickling with anticipation, vowing that the two tiny boys would totally fill her life. They would be her whole reason for existence. She would be self-sufficient and strong for them and not yearn for anyone else.

She also resolved to quit this land where the white man preyed upon the rightful inhabitants, destroying their dignity and traditions as they drove them from their hunting grounds, disbanding the tribes in much the same way they had destroyed the clans and scattered them to the four corners of the earth. But where could she go? she wondered. She wanted her sons to grow up free, unfettered by convention, religion, and fear of oppression. Where was such a place? Her mind lit on Cape Wrath, isolated with its miles of hearthered moorland where she as a child had raced, playing with the wind and rain, rejoicing with the sun and moon. Her lips curved into a soft smile as she thought of the high, craggy cliffs where the birds nested that fell to the sea in jagged teeth. There were ledges and caves where she had often sat, watching the play of the gray seal in the waves. The surf echoed through the natural caverns, exhilarating her ears like music. The castle where she had spent much of her childhood with Duncan Fraser surged purple and gray from the heather and rocks as though it were forged from nature and not by man's hand.

She would return to that haven, she decided, as Angus entered carrying her sons and followed by the beaming face of Jemmy, whose Maggie greeted her black brother with a flurry of boisterous affection.

CHAPTER THIRTY

Gladwin surveyed the ragged, shivering brave, unable to make head or tale of the stammering youth's dialect. Wishing for an interpreter, he swore, remembering he had sent most of them out to glean news of Pontiac's activities. He had kept the Ottawa camp under close scrutiny and was puzzled, as all seemed peaceful. The large-nosed young Ottawa who now cowered before him, babbling without stop, had mentioned Pontiac's name several times, and the commandant was fast becoming impatient.

"Jackson?" he roared through the open door. "Is the trapper Racine sober?"

"I have no idea, sir. I've been on duty here for five hours," replied the young soldier.

"Send him to me and also Major Sinclair," he ordered curtly, hating himself for having need of the tall Scot whose taut self-control nearly made him lose his own.

Alex and the old trapper Racine met outside Gladwin's quarters and entered together. The young Ottawa froze at the sight of Alex and babbled some more.

"He calls you Lion," laughed the bewhiskered trapper, who smelt strongly of spirits and sweat. "Says his name is Crooked-Nose. I myself have been given the most unfortunate name of Woods Pussy . . . skunk . . . 'tis probably due to my hat," he chortled, pulling off the skunk-skin cap with long tail.

Alex's eyes twinkled in his set face, but Gladwin showed no humor as he assessed the old trapper's sobriety.

"Decipher this savage's news," snapped the commandant, deciding that Racine was not too drunk but that Sinclair should remain just in case.

Crooked-Nose had not stopped his incessant babbling, and Alex's blood ran cold as he heard references to green-eyed ones, many multiplying out of the night. Racine grunted loudly and lifted his arm in a threatening gesture to quiet the nearly hysterical youth.

"You're wasting your time with this one, Major. He's touched in the head, talking of spirits of evil and the like," drawled the old trapper.

"He spoke of Pontiac. Ask him where he is," clipped Gladwin, not wishing Sinclair to see him at a disadvantage. The trapper rolled his eyes heavenward as if to convey that the commandant was also touched before asking Crooked-Nose the question. The Ottawa frantically ranted, waving his arms, and Racine's expression grew thoughtful.

"What does he say?" shouted Gladwin impatiently.

"Pontiac is in war council at the camp of the Potawatomis. It appears this young savage angered his chief and was sent away with the squaws. He snuck back and listened. Shut up, yer red dog!" roared Racine as the brave babbled on, drowning out his words. "He says his chief tells the usual lies about trading and stealing their land. Pontiac says the English are not like their French brothers, who have sent the great wampum belts. He says Pontiac calls the French Our Great Fathers," recounted Racine with a touch of malicious joy.

"You bear a French name yourself, Racine, although you have no accent of that land," challenged Gladwin.

"Given me by some pious priest. I have no notion of the nationality of my father, never met him. If you're questioning my loyalty, then that's a different kettle of fish," drawled the cunning trapper, who had no loyalty except to who paid him the highest price.

"I have no need of biographies!" said the commandant testily, feeling that he had lost face in front of the sardonic Scot.

Once again Racine grunted, and the frightened Indian let forth a torrent of frenzied sounds. After several minutes the old trapper cut him off and sat cogitating what he had heard.

"For God's sake, man, what does he say?" fumed Gladwin impatiently.

"Apparently Pontiac has sent messages and wampum belts to the Chippewas of Saginaw and the Ottawas of

Michilimackinac and the Thames River to join them but will attack in the meantime," drawled the old man, clearly enjoying his power.

"When?"

"He has not got to that yet."

The painfully slow interrogation continued for several hours, with Gladwin losing more and more of his self-control and very conscious of the gracefully lounging Sinclair, who seemed to derive wry pleasure from the whole proceedings.

"So on the seventh of May Pontiac plans to enter this fort with sixty armed men for a formal council with me?" recapped Gladwin and, at a nod from Racine, continued, "He will be followed by the remainder of his tribe, who are to wait for a signal? Meanwhile the Hurons and Potawatomis will prevent any reinforcements and provisions coming to Fort Detroit?"

"That's what I deciphered, didn't you, Sinclair?" returned the trapper.

"That'll be all, Racine. Take this helpful savage with you and see that he's put under guard."

Gladwin sat at his desk lost in thought, forgetting the presence of Alex for several moments. As he pondered his best course of action, he became aware of the lazy amber eyes. He swiveled around in his chair and surveyed the tall, rangy man.

"What would you do, Sinclair?" he snarled.

"You are the commandant," answered Alex evenly, thinking of all he had heard about Gladwin—a typical bulldog who would tenaciously hang on to any post until the last man was killed, never for a minute doubting the right to do such a thing in the name of his king and country.

"That will be all, Sinclair," dismissed Gladwin.

On May seventh, Alex stood in a watchtower observing the approach of Pontiac and his warriors. Gladwin had not entrusted Alex with his plan, but the Scot's keen eyes had noted the armed, alert garrison. He had an awful premonition that the commandant might open the stockade gate, allowing the Ottawas entrance only to shoot them

down in cold blood. Anxiously he scanned the long, ragged
line searching for the smaller figure of Cameron, but to
his relief and disappointment only her tall twin walked at
the chief's side.

The order was given to swing back the heavy gates, and
Alex held his breath as the unsuspecting Indians filed in
and were met with a silent show of force. Tension crackled
the still air as brown fingers grasped hatchets, knives, and
muskets beneath the cover of their ragged blankets and
uniformed soldiers stood tensed with guns aimed ready to
fire at the first movement. Everything was suspended,
coiled to explode. After what seemed an excruciatingly
long time during which Alex's fingernails dug painfully
into the palms of his hands, Pontiac softly grunted to his
warriors, whose proud, tensed bodies sagged and brown
arms fell limply to their sides. Dejectedly they turned on
their moccasined heels and streamed out of the fort, heads
bent and several hands clutching the insulting presents of
six white man's suits, bread, and tobacco. Alex's relief and
grudging respect for Gladwin's strategy turned to fury at
the humiliating parting gesture.

The next few days saw the Ottawas filing back, determined to enter and attack, but each time, Gladwin only
permitted entrance to a few. Each time, Alex anxiously
scanned the long, ragged line looking for Cameron only to
see her twin brother, Méron. He felt the anger and tension
building in the native people and knew it was only a
matter of time before things came to a head.

Méron kept his face expressionless as he heard the
grumbles of dissension among Pontiac's followers. He
knew the chief was extremely sensitive to any criticism
about his leadership and was aware that such comments
had not gone unheard by the tall, broad man at his side.
His worst fears were realized when Pontiac ordered the
killing of every white man outside the fort. Although
Méron understood that Pontiac's action was a measure to
ensure and regain confidence in his leadership as the Indians raged against the injustice, hurt, and humiliation,
his gall rose at the brutal murders of white farmers and
their wives and children. In a cabin by a tranquil lake

were his own family—his twin sister, her sons, his two guardians who had raised him from childhood, and a small, red-haired girl who had become very dear to him. All were white, as was he. He warred with himself, reasoning that he meant no harm and could peaceably coexist with the rightful inhabitants of this vast New World, and yet he was forced to realize that his very presence was somehow symbolic and a threat to the red man's way of life.

"As you are all aware, we are under siege," pronounced Gladwin to the assembled officers. "I want the guards doubled in the storerooms, and rationing will be instituted. I doubt that we shall be inconvenienced long, but 'tis best to be prepared. Pontiac has the misguided notion that soon the French army will come to his support, but I'm afraid he is due for great disappointment. I have received a very interesting notice today by one of the French go-betweens." The commandant stopped, taking a weighty and significant pause as he eyed the officers, an ironic leer crossing his features. "I am most happy to inform you, gentlemen, that the war between France and Great Britain has ended, the peace treaty signed in London this past February twentieth," he pronounced.

"By Jove that is good news indeed!" proclaimed an officer joyfully, and an excited murmur of voices elatedly built as homesick men eagerly envisioned the return to their families in England.

"Unfortunately," roared Gladwin, interrupting, "unfortunately, those ignorant savages are unaware of the fact and unaware of the refinements of war. They have no rules, as this news I'm about to impart bears out. Fort Saint Joseph, Fort Miami, and Ouiatenon have fallen to the Indians. You will all, I hope, remember that Fort Sandusky fell on May sixteenth to a surprise attack by the Hurons and the Ottawas. The tribes of the Weas, Kickapoos, and Mascoutens have now joined the Ottawas, Potawatomis, and Hurons."

Alex listened, his stern features not mirroring the fear he felt clawing his gut. Cameron was out there somewhere with her babies, a target for the marauding bands of abused people who had finally snapped, their need for revenge fired to fever pitch. He now wished he had dared take the plunge into the swirling river, for with the fort under siege there was no way he could escape alive to find her.

May turned to June, the summer marched on, and Alex's face was gaunt from sleepless nights as he worried about Cameron, not knowing if she were alive or dead. News came from the hands of tht French traders and trappers that Fort Michilimackinac had fallen to the cunning Sauks and Chippewas, who had also joined the Ottawa chief. The humor of how that strong fort had fallen caused no smiles from the assembled soldiers. Apparently the commandant and his troops had been invited to watch a friendly game of lacrosse between the two tribes. The fort's gates had been opened, allowing squaws to stroll casually around as the game was played with fervor outside the high walls. The ball had been hit, arcing over into the parade ground, and the Indians had streamed through the gates after it. At a signal they had dropped their lacrosse sticks and taken up the rifles that their squaws had concealed beneath their blankets. All had been massacred or captured except the French traders and trappers.

Fort Edward Augustus had been abandoned, leaving just Fort Detroit as the sole British post on the western Great Lakes. Indian tribes from beyond the Detroit region joined with the victorious Pontiac, spreading the Indian uprising into Pennsylvania. The Delawares and Mingoes swept down the Monongahela River and laid siege to Fort Pitt. The Shawnees and Senecas rose, and Fort Verango fell leaving no survivors. The western Iroquois felled Fort LeBoeuf, and warriors from four tribes united to bring about the defeat of Fort Presque Isle. Only Fort Pitt and their own Fort Detroit were not taken, but both were under siege.

"Why don't they just attack?" raged one young officer, the months of unbearable tension breaking his control.

"Because they sit waiting for the French," retorted Gladwin, and Alex breathed deeply, furious that the man had so little knowledge and insight of the proud people whose country was being wrested from them. He knew the red man valued each individual and had no concept of sacrificing lives. To attack the fort would mean death for many of them, and although their numbers were far greater than the troops, it would be inevitable that many warriors would fall.

"Why aren't they informed that the French will not come?" ranted another young soldier.

"It is best this way. We can hold out, but can they? Soon they will have to hunt for the winter, or they'll not survive. Already they have lost a lot of time. Meanwhile I have news that help is on the way."

The assembled officers grew silent waiting for Gladwin to continue, but he did not. He would trust no one but himself.

The August sun blazed, and Cameron and her children were protected from the bloody war that raged as they lay naked by the lake under the trees. No sounds of strife reached their ears, just the peaceful call of the birds and animals. At eight months old Lynx and Raven, their chubby bodies tanned bronze from the sun, crawled, vigorously exploring their environment. They would pull themselves upright on stocky legs, crowing with delight at their accomplishment and, to the amusement of their loving audience, would attempt to take their first shaky steps, only to end up on the ground once more. Lynx would immediately try again, getting more and more frustrated, his green eyes flashing angrily. Raven would sit for a moment, astonished and puzzled before taking his time and with a very serious expression, trying again.

Cameron delighted in her sons, who each day embraced life with such curiosity and fervor. She would swim in the lake with one or the other clinging on to her back. She had patiently taught Jemmy to swim, and sometimes, each with a child, the two girls would play with the friendly otters in the languid water. Summer was a time of great healing, and although they all worried about Méron's safety as his absence stretched, they busied themselves with play and providing for the winter, which would once again cover the hot golden land with cold, white snow.

Angus and Goliath kept the news of the war from their young charges, reasoning that nothing could be accomplished by all of them fretting. They took turns venturing from the safety of the retreat to glean news of the happenings in the outside world, returning with deer and other game to explain their absence. Cameron anxiously awaited Méron's return, wanting to share her decision to return to Cape Wrath. Although she worried for his safety, she knew instinctively that he was all right. Often at night she would awake with a feeling of panic and lie in the darkness hearing the steady breathing of her young sons, who now slept on mats of fur on the floor by her side. She would be comforted as though their soft breaths were a lullaby, and she would smile, gently remembering their antics of that day. Sometimes she would fill with a great sadness as her sleepy mind relaxed and thoughts of Alex came tumbling in. She saw many of Alex's traits in Raven's steadiness and quiet observation as he assessed each new thing before dealing with it. In Lynx she saw herself, wild and impulsive, tumbling into anything and everything in his excitement. If thwarted, the small boy's eyes would flash furiously, and he'd roar out unintelligible sounds in protest, whereas Raven's small face would set into serious lines, and his eyes would stare up at her with grim reproachment. At those times Cameron would feel a clutching at her heart, and for a moment it was as though amber eyes stared, not the emerald-green ones of her little son.

As Cameron spent the hot, lazy August lulled by the busy, droning bees, Fort Detroit suffered a setback. Major Gladwin, his face mirroring the drawn, gaunt lines of his officers, heard news that the reinforcements from Niagara had been ambushed by four hundred Chippewas and Ottawas led by Pontiac. Twenty soldiers had been killed and thirty-seven wounded before their retreat. News that the commandant at Fort Pitt had caused a smallpox epidemic among the Delaware Mingo, and Shawnee tribes by giving them contaminated blankets from the hospital

caused Gladwin savage delight. He believed in victory at
any cost. He was determined to hold out, knowing that
each week that passed brought the certainty of more reinforcements and stores nearer.

Alex paced his small quarters like a pent-up lion. Every
nerve and sinew in his body screamed for release from the
confined waiting. His nights were haunted by thought of
Cameron's face pitted and scarred by smallpox. By day
he'd catch sight of Méron's glossy head and long to leap
from the fort's high wall so that he could ask his young
brother-in-law for news of his twin.

That very day news had arrived that on August tenth
Fort Pitt had been saved. Alex had felt a mixture of
emotions when he heard that two Highland Scottish regiments, including his old one of the Black Watch, had been
responsible. There had been a bittersweet delight in watching Gladwin's face when the fact had been exposed, but it
had been quickly doused as the irony flooded in. Scotland,
defeated by the English, now fought for them to destroy
another race similarly, changing customs, religions, and
their whole way of life. Suddenly the troubles and injustices of the world did not matter as he acknowledged that
Cameron was his whole life. He threw himself on his bed
and morosely stared at the beamed ceiling, realizing that
there was not much difference between what he had tried
to do to Cameron in their relationship and what one
country was trying to do to the other. Had he not, in much
the same way, tried to rein and curb her nature, insisting
that she embrace his life? Maybe the conflicts between
two individuals were symbolic of the larger conflicts between nations, one trying to dominate and suppress the
other, he thought philosophically. If only he could be free
to rejoin her so that they could start over again, he yearned
as he envisioned her and himself by the tranquil lake
surrounded by the tall trees. At the thought of the enmity
that had been stirred now involving the whole of the
western frontier in a conflict of deadly hatred between
Indians and frontiersmen, Alex's hopeful feelings were
dashed. He sat up abruptly, trying to dispel the horrific
picture of Cameron and her babes as lifeless corpses floating in the bloody waters of the seething lake. Dressed as

she was the last time he had seen her, he knew she was not safe from the white settlers who were equally capable of killing and scalping any Indian, whether fearsome or peaceful. She was not safe from either side in the war that raged ferociously, as her bright green eyes belied her Indian appearance to any marauding red man with the scent of blood in his nose.

Unable to bear the constricting four walls of his room, he strode outside into the hot, night air. He gazed from the high wall of the fort toward the campfires that burned, ringing the fort on three sides, as he thought of the words Gladwin had read that day from Sir Jeffrey Amherst, commander of the British troops on whose orders the smallpox epidemic had been spread: "We should try every method that can serve to extirpate this execrable race." These words rang in Alex's ears, and hidden by darkness, his usually proud bearing slumped dejectedly. There seemed no hope for anyone, he thought dismally, remembering the edict that had been sent from England drawing a line on a map to establish a western boundary between the Indians and the whites along the crest of the Appalachian Mountains. He snorted as he imagined His Majesty's ministers, who within the safety of their English stately homes could no more envision the situation than they could the man on the moon. The western frontier was settled by fugitives from justice, army deserters, and the like—angry, embittered people, the dregs of a society, beaten and abused from childhood by the rich, many of them deported from English slums as bonded slaves, who then escaped the clutches of their masters, spreading their hatred and dissatisfaction upon the red man by atrocious acts and swindling, which the Indians answered in kind. For the isolated English ministers to think for one moment that such white frontier settlers would obey the imaginary line on a map was totally ridiculous, raged Alex, his head pounding as he realized that soon a completely lawless state of annihilation would exist.

September ran its course, and the leaves changed to the browns, reds, and golds, a reflection of the long, hot, bloody summer, and one by one tribes made their peace with the

English, aware that the winter was fast approaching. But still Pontiac stood firm, waiting for the French to help him.

Méron stared at the chief, whose face betrayed no inner feeling, knowing that despite his anxiety for feeding his people during the cruel snows, he still expected the French to arrive ensuring his victory. On October twentieth in desperation another council was called, but the tribes were no longer swayed by Pontiac's charismatic presence or gift of oratory. Méron, who loved the tall Ottawa like a father, wept inwardly as each blow seemed to erode the stern, stony face, knowing that Pontiac's pride and confidence were turning to gray dust. Four inches of snow fell, and the ground was frozen hard, yet no hunting had been done to provide for the long months ahead. The most crashing blow came with the arrival of a messenger from the French commander at Fort Chartres in the Louisiana territory.

Méron stared down at the paper that Pontiac had silently handed him to translate. The irony of the first two words was like a dagger thrust.

"French children," he read aloud, not Indian men but French children, he seethed inwardly. Pontiac gestured at him to continue, and with his eyes full of angry tears, Méron read huskily, his voice breaking and stumbling. "What joy you will have in seeing the French and English smoke the same pipe, and eating out of the same spoon and finally living like brethren. . . ." Méron trailed off, not able to look at the tall man beside him. The French urged the Ottawas to bury the hatchet and stated they had sent supplies to Fort Detroit as a peace offering, breaking the siege.

"It is over. You will help translate my message to Gladwin," intoned Pontiac after a long silence. "Then go with the French courier to see that it is delivered to Fort Detroit."

Gladwin surveyed his assembled officers, his bearing denoting his victory. His eyes shone with a fervor that had been missing during the long siege.

"I have just received the following from Pontiac," he

stated, self-satisfaction gleaming from every pore. "He begins: 'My Brother.' "

There was a burst of laughter.

"A dubious honor," quipped one man.

"Rather an insult, I should say," chorused another.

"He states that he and his warriors have buried the hatchet and wishes us to forget all the bad things that have taken place, in which case he will forget the bad things that we have done to him. He also asks for a meeting between us, himself, the Chippewas, and the Hurons."

Alex's fervent wish for a dignified end to the hostilities was dashed when he heard the answer sent back to Pontiac stating that as he, Gladwin, had not started the hostilities, he could not end them. General Amherst, the British commanding officer, was responsible and he would forward Pontiac's message to him.

The commandant, in a convivial mood and bursting with pride at his military prowess, magnanimously broke open a bottle of French brandy he had been hoarding. Sending away the junior officers, he invited the senior officers to join him in a victory celebration. As he dismissed half of the men, his eye paused speculatively on Alex, who was equal in rank to himself, although not in command. The tall, golden man seemed unaware of his surroundings, lost in a world of his own, a fact so unusual that it took Gladwin by surprise, as he was used to the amber eyes watching him enigmatically, much like a cat. He shrugged, feeling he could afford to be generous as he handed Alex brandy in a cut-crystal glass.

Alex stared at the delicate crystal wondering what such a piece of refined English tableware was doing in such a rough, savage country. He was roused from his reverie by a shout of laughter as Gladwin gleefully read aloud his letter, which would accompany Pontiac's to Sir Jeffrey Amherst.

". . . but if Your Excellency still intends to punish them further for their barbarities, it may easily be done without any expense to the crown by permitting a free sale of rum, which will destroy them more effectively than sword and fire."

Alex quelled the desire to smash the cut-crystal glass by dashing it in the midst of the reveling redcoats. Taking a deep breath, he carefully placed the untouched drink on the nearest available surface.

"Permission to retire, sir?" he asked stiffly, his voice cutting through the ribaldry.

"You'll not celebrate our victory?" asked Gladwin jeeringly.

"As you yourself stated, 'tis not yet ours," Alex responded, dousing the commandant's happy mood with his civil, yet icy tone.

"Permission granted, we need no dour, skinflint Scot to steal our well-earned merriment. 'Tis obviously true what is said about your race, Sinclair," jibed Gladwin viciously.

"Yes, sir," agreed Alex all too cordially.

"A niggardly, miserly barbaric lot who would sell their own clansmen into slavery for a few crowns and some land," goaded the commandant.

"Sounds much like the painted savages here," joined in a voice, and Alex's blood thundered in his ears, though his face betrayed nothing but bemused interest. That grain of truth in exaggeration stung as he recalled the many Scottish lairds who pandered to the English hoping to gain favor and riches.

"Why are you hanging around when you were told to leave?" shouted Gladwin, infuriated by the unwavering eyes.

Alex raised a protesting arm, saluted his commanding officer and quit the room, followed by jeers, mocking laughter, and choice epithets about his nationality. Why was he still in the midst of such barbarous, insensitive, cruel people, he raged as he strode through the snowy compound unwilling to face the four confining walls of his barren room. Because he lived by the rules, he told himself. Whose rules? he debated, and the answer was of little consolation. He leaned against the stockade wall in the long shadows trying to calm himself, remembering his father's words to him as a boy, which at the time had seemed so right and indisputable: "If there isna rules, there's nocht but chaos. 'Tis nay guid fighting against something wie nothing to replace. We fight the English for the right to live our lives the way we believe . . . for the freedom and dignity of what we are," the deep, rich brogue haunted the night, bringing an aching nostalgia. Alex realized he had been shackled and chained to one small spot, Glen Aucht. To retain that land of his forefathers, he had sold himself, losing all he held most dear, robbing himself of freedom and dignity.

At that illuminating thought he eased himself from the wall he leaned against and made his way to his room, determined to be free of the fort. He whistled tunelessly to himself as he stowed a change of clothes in his saddlebag. He would find Cameron and the children and make a home together where they could live in freedom and dignity. But where, he worried. What if they were dead? He still would be better off than he was, he resolved savagely. A lone refugee, a solitary deserter from society. But what of Fergus and Mackie? What of all the people at Glen Aucht? He threw his saddlebag across the room knowing he couldn't take his freedom at their expense.

Méron stood in the shadows outside Fort Detroit. He had accompanied the French messenger who had delivered Pontiac's letter to Gladwin. A circle of his life had ended with such finality, and he knew that the English commandant would deny any vestige of pride and dignity to the Ottawas in their defeat. He huddled in his threadbare blanket like an old woman, showing none of the rage that consumed him waiting for the French courier. He stared at the four Indian warriors who had accompanied him and, despite the darkness, saw that their eyes were listless and their once-proud bearings were as limp and hopeless as his own. They looked like shabby beggars, derelicts huddling together for warmth in the shadow of the English fort. The return of the Frenchman with Gladwin's message bore out his worst fears, and he wanted to scream out his futile outrage. His face had been impassive as he watched the raggle-taggle group climb into their canoes and paddle dejectedly back to deliver the message to their chief. He knew he was no longer a part of them. He squatted in the snow staring across the river toward Pontiac's camp, knowing he would never see the proud man again, silently keening as though at a wake for the death of a way of life. He rocked, mindless of the cruel, biting wind and thick snow.

Several hours later, before dawn had tinged the sky, he stood stiffly, his thought full of Alex Sinclair. One phase of his life was over, and it was time to continue, to start anew with no ghosts. He thought of his sister and her babies, and his heart lurched. Were they safe? They had to be, or he was sure he would have felt something, their connection was so close. Angus and Goliath would have kept them safe and well cared for, but was that enough? Would he be enough? There was a painful void in his twin that he couldn't comfort or heal. Nobody except the person responsible could, and despite her denial, until his sister faced it, she would never be peaceful and free. He would take Sinclair back with him anyway he could, dead or alive, so that he could lay to rest the ghosts of the past. On that thought he slid down the wall of the fort until he once more squatted, huddled in his blanket, to sleep the remainder of the night away.

CHAPTER THIRTY-ONE

Alex was exhilarated. His horse's hooves crunched cleanly through the crisp snow and the brisk, biting wind scoured the staleness from his face. Gladwin, full of the triumph of victory, preferred to be free of the enigmatic, cynical eyes that could dampen his spirits. He had sent Alex on a mission to ensure the final humiliation of the Indian tribes, who, defeated and hungry, with no provisions for the long, cold months ahead, were being driven to their winter camps. Alex glanced at Jackson riding beside him and wondered how he could lose the fervent young officer in such a way that it wouldn't look like he was deserting. At the rapid sounds of hoofbeats behind, he halted and wheeled his horse around.

"It's a savage, sir," grated Jackson's high-pitched voice as he tugged at his rifle trying to pull it from the cold leather of his saddle holster.

" 'Tis only one. Hold your fire," barked Alex, recognizing Méron's flying ebony hair and lithe form as he watched the youth slow his wild gallop and approach them warily.

"That horse is one of ours," hissed Jackson, noting the embossed saddle and raising the rifle.

"Hold your fire!" clipped Alex.

"But he must have killed one of ours to get it," protested the young captain.

"It would seem so, but maybe not. Maybe he's friendly and has come to warn us of an ambush or some such thing, but we won't know from a dead man, will we, Jackson?" said Alex evenly eyeing the young soldier's twitching fingers and shaky arm. "Put your firearm down before you shoot off your own foot. I have him covered," he added.

"What does he want?" whined Jackson, unnerved by the Indian who sat on his horse silently staring at Alex. "What do you want?" he shouted when the silence stretched.

"Maybe there's more of them sneaking around us," he added, staring around nervously.

"On this flat, snow-covered plain with no trees to hide them?" answered Alex dryly without taking his eyes from the unemotional face of Méron. The boy was thinner, his face gaunt, new lines of suffering eched into his young features. Had he a message for him from Cameron? Was Cameron dead? Many terrifying thoughts flooded into his mind, but his face remained as impassive as Méron's.

Jackson's nervousness was transmitted to his horse, who pranced, fighting the bit that cruelly dug into his tender mouth as the young soldier's hands gripped the bridle too tightly.

"Let's just scare him away, sir," he panted, trying to control his mount and clutching at his rifle. Before Alex could stop him, Jackson fired into the air. Another shot echoed, and the young soldier fell to the ground, blood from his arm staining the white snow.

"You fool!" roared Alex, looking from Méron's smoking gun to the man who writhed in agony.

"Look out, sir!" screamed Jackson as Méron leaped from his horse, dagger in hand, and launched himself at Alex. Alex's lightning reflexes warded off the lithe shape by holding his rifle in both hands like a bar. Méron somersaulted agilely to the ground and threw himself on Jackson, putting the dagger to the young soldier's throat.

"Drop your gun, or he dies," spat Méron. Alex stared into Jackson's eyes, which bulged with terror, and threw his rifle down. "His life for yours," added the youth, and Alex's eyes narrowed. Here was the very opportunity he had been waiting for but only if Jackson lived to return to the fort with the tale of his capture. He nodded slowly, throwing down his own knife and the small, ornate dagger that belonged to Cameron.

"Bind his wound," ordered Méron, easing himself from Jackson's prone body and aiming Alex's own rifle at both of them. Bandaged, unarmed, with his wrists tied together, Jackson clumsily mounted his horse. "If you speak to anyone before you reach Fort Detroit, Major Sinclair will die," intoned Méron, indicating Alex, whose wrists were also bound. Alex watched the mounted figure of Jackson trot across the plain, the young man moving from side to side like a sack of potatoes as he tried to keep his balance.

"We go," said Méron, kicking him so that he'd stand. "No horses," he added as Alex made to mount up with difficulty. The youth yelled and shooed the horses away, and they streaked across the virgin-white snow. "Come," he grunted, poking Alex with the rifle and indicating a direction. No words were spoken as they jogged across the snowy plain. What had Méron in mind to do with him? wondered Alex. Was he being taken to a secluded spot to be killed? Or was he to be taken hostage by Pontiac? he mused as the river came into view. If so, the Ottawas were in for a cruel surprise, as he seriously doubted Major Gladwin would want his disturbing influence back at Fort Detroit. Although Alex admired Méron's ingenuity in freeing the horses so that they'd make tracks in the opposite direction, he wondered at the boy's wisdom in traveling on foot in the wilderness with what looked like a blizzard rising. The sky was deep gray and threatening, and the wind was increasing in force, stinging his eyes.

Ignoring the rough jabs of Méron's gun butt, Alex stood still on the riverbank, refusing to move into the water with his wrists tied. The current ran rapidly, so ice only formed on the shallow pools by the shore. It would be sheer suicide to enter that raging cold, watery grave without two free arms. The sound of hoofbeats and voices broke the wintry silence, and Méron sprang into action, pulling a canoe from the underbrush and propelling it down the icy bank. Instinctively Alex helped, entering the freezing water as his bound wrists clung to the birched sides of the small boat. Keeping to the reeds beneath the drooping branches of willow trees, Alex and Méron floated beside the canoe, allowing the swift current to take them away from their telltale footprints on the bank before hauling their heavy, cold bodies into the boat.

With his wrists still tied, the wet rawhide biting painfully, Alex paddled methodically, his eyes resting on the dark, enigmatic shape before him. A strange tension emanated from the youth, and he longed to confront him. Méron had a deliberate air about him as though he was carefully carrying out a finely delineated plan. Alex decided to be led for a time, wordlessly accepting but alert and aware.

Despite his deliberate manner, Méron was confused. Why had the tall, golden man suddenly become his ally when they had heard the voices and horses of an English patrol? He could have easily cried out for help and thwarted Méron's chances for escape; why hadn't he done so? Méron purposefully paddled to shore, painfully aware of the amber eyes that burned into his back. His movements felt unsure and self-conscious beneath the unwavering gaze of the tall adult man, who seemed tuned in with his every intention, wordlessly helping him guide the canoe to the bank, beach it, and hide it under the underbrush as though his hands were not bound. Part of his young being was still wrapped in a numbing sorrow. He felt callow and ignorant and somehow lost. He stared at Alex's wrists, which were now bloodied by the rawhide that cruelly bit. He was the leader, and yet something disturbed him. Alex's presence made him feel like a child. He would dispel the heaviness of his uncomfortable emotions, he decided, suddenly sprinting into the thick forest.

The overhanging pine branches kept the carpet of needles free from snow, so that no tracks were left by his fleet, moccasined feet. Méron did not know why he ran. Was it to shake off his despondency or was it to rid himself of the tall, golden man who made him feel inadequate just by his presence? He was all too aware that Alex kept up easily with a graceful lope.

The clouds darkened, and the wind increased its ferocity, and still the youth kept the same grueling pace. The sweat poured from their faces, and their labored breaths misted the crisp air in little groaning puffs. It was as though he were being tested, thought Alex, knowing he had no intention of dropping first, despite his protesting muscles. The sky was nearly as dark as night as they ran, twisting and turning through the trees. Alex noted with grim satisfaction the slowing of Méron's pace and guessed that the raising of each moccasined foot took as much effort as the raising of his own. Enough is enough, he decided, lengthening his stride until he ran abreast of the youth. As if by unspoken mutual agreement, they stopped together and

sank down to lie full-length on the pine needles of a small
glade, oblivious to the snow flakes that whirled, settling
on their clothes. Alex closed his eyes and relaxed, ignoring
the youth, whose labored breathing echoed his own. He
felt his exhausted body drifting to sleep and sharply forced
himself to sit up and lean against a tree trunk. He stared
at the accumulation of snow on his person in surprise and
then looked at the thickly falling precipitation with concern. Méron lay with his eyes open, the worry and pain
of the last months etched in premature lines upon his
young face.

"It seems we are in for a blizzard and had best keep
moving," said Alex gently, but the youth made no attempt
to rise. Méron stared objectively at the face above him,
noting that the eyes were just a different shade of the same
golden color of the man's skin and hair, the warm hues
offset by the sharp planes of his cheekbones and jaw.

"Are you a spy sent to gloat about and further humiliate
the red man?" he spat, fighting the attraction and grudging
respect he had for his brother-in-law and savagely cutting
through the leather thong that bound Alex's wrists.

"I thought I was your prisoner," replied Alex tersely,
flexing his stiff hands.

"You could have escaped," challenged Méron.

"Yes," acknowledged Alex. "In truth, I'm a deserter
using you as my cover," he added wryly, the word "deserter" tasting bitter and unpalatable.

"That I know only too well," hissed Méron, thinking of
the pain in his sister's eyes.

"Then why ask if I'm a spy?" responded Alex slowly,
knowing they were talking at cross-purposes.

"There are many kinds of deserters."

"Your sister and I deserted each other," replied Alex
grimly, not willing to continue the verbal sparring as the
snow fell heavily. Soon visibility would be almost nil, with
poor prospects of reaching shelter and food.

"That is what you say," retorted Méron hotly.

"And what does she say?"

Méron did not answer but glared up at the tall man
who towered above him, his green eyes flashing venomously.

"Whatever is between Cameron and myself is our concern. At this moment my only concern is getting to her and her children without you adding more impediment. Things are strained enough, with many things to clear up between us, without bringing her the frozen corpse of her twin," pronounced Alex evenly, grasping the youth's forearms and hauling him to his feet.

"Leave her in peace and go your own way. I shall take care of her and her children," hissed Méron. "Go back to your redcoats."

"Neither of us will be taking care of anyone soon," replied Alex, not wishing to get into a futile argument and wanting to make the boy aware of the immediate danger of the blizzard. Méron stood indecisively, knowing that Alex was right and furious that it should be pointed out to him as though he were an ignorant child.

"I'm relying on you and your expertise to save us," said Alex gently, knowing how Méron must be warring with his pride. He and his twin were much alike, he conceded, wishing he had been as diplomatic in his relationship with Cameron.

"Why should I save you?" responded Méron, his green eyes narrowing suspiciously as he sensed Alex's patronizing tone.

Alex regarded him frankly. "Because not to do so would make me very important, as you'd have to live with it on your conscience for the rest of your life," he quipped.

Méron turned away from the lazy, mocking eyes. He felt torn. Something told him to return to the cabin with the tall, golden man, and yet he was now reluctant to do so.

Alex sensed the boy's conflicting emotions. "Well, I found my way there before, and I'm sure I can do it again," he breathed.

"How do you know she is still there?" challenged Méron, covering up his own fear for her safety.

"How do you know?" parried Alex. "I've watched you nearly every day through the summer and autumn, and you've not left Pontiac's side." He saw the telltale panic flare for a brief split second before Méron recovered and set his face to hard lines. "It seems we both love her, you as a brother and I as her mate," he added, hoping to reach through the stony façade.

"You as her mate," jeered Méron savagely, making a vicious, unfair attack. "You think her sons the product of your mating?" Alex did not flinch from the cruel jab directed at his manhood. He felt excruciatingly deep pain run through his aching, chilled body as he nodded in acknowledgment.

"I still regard her as my mate and, if she will allow, will embrace her sons as my own."

Méron was not immune to the deep pain he saw reflected. He felt ashamed of his angry, cruel words. His own throat constricted, and he cursed himself for his impulsiveness before abruptly turning away, unable to look at the set face.

As the first snow fell, Angus and Goliath stood back and looked at their handiwork. The small cabin had easily accommodated the needs of three bachelors but had become sorely cramped with the added presence of Jemmy, Cameron, Lynx, and Raven, not to mention the two enormous hounds. They had set about adding three more rooms plus a stockaded compound, not only to protect them from renegade whites and Indians but to contain the rapidly growing twins, who now toddled around on unsteady legs.

Cameron had tried to stop them from building, knowing that she would be leaving for Cape Wrath as soon as Méron returned, but the two friendly, gruff giants had gently informed her that winter was fast approaching and any plans for leaving would have to wait until spring. She had thrown herself into the planning and hammering as the anxiety for her brother's safety built. The larder and root cellar were filled to overflowing as Jemmy and Cameron had methodically cured and smoked meat and fish, salted vegetables, and made preserves of wild berries and fruits. Warm fur clothing and blankets had been sewn, and all was in readiness for the long, cold isolation. They had all been cut off from the outside world by choice, and soon it would be by the elements.

Cameron now had nothing to do to fill the long hours of waiting. It was November, and there had been no news of Méron. Unable to bear the suspense, she badgered Goliath and Angus, threatening to ride to the Ottawa camp, and they had sadly informed her of Pontiac's defeat and his self-exile to the Maumee River.

"Where is the Maumee? Maybe Méron is there?" she cried, frustrated that there was nothing she could do and no way to find him.

"He has been gone longer before and always returns. I should know if he were hurt or in danger," comforted Angus, feeling inadequate, but Cameron stalked away into her new room and threw herself down on her bed. She felt wound up and did not know how to release the tremendous pressure of the waiting. There was nothing to busy herself with while her children slept. She would spend hours staring at the perfection of their sleeping faces, eager to start a new life. But everything hung suspended and her body rocked against the forced inertia.

Cameron lay in the darkness watching the reflection of the fire through the open door of her room, wishing she could sleep. The long night hours stretched interminably, punctuated by an occasional gurgling sigh from her sleeping children and the haunting call of the nocturnal birds and animals. Goliath's and Angus's sonorous snorings were successfully muffled as they were now ensconced in their own quarters at the back leaving Jemmy and Cameron the privacy of the main room.

Unable to sleep, Cameron prowled around, fingering Méron's carving on the wall that announced the birth of Lynx and Raven, knowing that in the spring she would leave and wondering who would read of their births and care. She had successfully blocked out all thought of Alex, concentrating only on Méron's return and her plans for the future. She sat by the fire staring into the red embers, feeling restricted and confined. She yearned to leap astride Torquod and race out, releasing the pressure inside her, but the snow was thick and she was bound by her sons. No longer could she make impulsive dashes for freedom, she acknowledged, thinking of their bright green eyes that conveyed absolute trust in her. She was no longer free to be a wild, impetuous child. She was a mother, she was grown. And yet she did not feel adult, just aware of her responsibility.

Tor growled, his hackles rising, breaking her reverie. She put her hand on his neck to soothe him, listening intently. She heard the faint shuffling and crunching of feet and quietly took a rifle from the wall, checking it to see if it was loaded before throwing a fur rug around her shoulders and opening the door. The snow glistened in the moonlight of the enclosed yard. Tor sprang barking at the wall as Goliath and Angus, struggling into their clothes, came, also armed, to stand by Cameron.

"Who's there?" yelled Cameron, her gun cocked and ready, but the weak reply was drowned out by Maggie's and Tor's barking.

"Must be Méron," growled Angus, noting the hounds' frenzied joy.

"Careful," warned Goliath. "Hush those infernal dogs. There is no sense taking chances."

Cameron knelt in the snow quieting the excited animals, who obediently sat their bodies, wiggling as they tried to suppress their eagerness.

"Méron?" called Angus.

"Aye," came the weak reply.

Goliath and Cameron aimed their guns as Angus swiftly pulled off the bar and stood back, musket trained, in case of a trap. The heavy door was slowly pushed open, and two stiff, snow-covered figures staggered in, their faces covered by thick fur parkas. Like zombies they walked toward the warm, inviting light of the open cabin door, watched in amazement by the three. The dogs hurtled themselves in welcome against the two dripping forms, who swayed before the fire, the snow thawing and puddling around their feet.

"Get them back from the fire before there's harm done," ordered Goliath tersely, taking the guns and racking them on the wall. Angus propelled the unresisting figures into two chairs, where they sat motionless. Angus poured two generous portions of liquor and placed them in the still hands.

"Och, they're frozen to the marrow," he cursed, pulling

the frozen, snow-encrusted hoods back from the two faces.

Cameron was backed against the closed door. She smelled his presence, felt it in every pore, although his large, rangy shape and proud bearing were muffled and disguised by the clothes and weariness. The buried pain flashed sharply, shocking her to inertia.

"Cameron, gie us a hand here," shouted Goliath, knowing well what the tawny head was doing to her emotions but also knowing they had to work quickly if they were to save fingers, ears, and noses from frostbite.

Cameron shook herself free of her paralysis and numbly and methodically rubbed snow on the exposed parts of the now-unconscious men.

"We maun warm them slowly," informed Angus, filling a large hip bath with cold water and snow. "Get their clothes off." For several hours they worked side by side, watched wide-eyed by Jemmy, slowly restoring the circulation to the colorless, clenched hands and white, blotched skin. Cameron forced herself into a nonthinking state as she impassively administered to the naked bodies of her husband and her brother. She refused to look at the still face, fearing that the amber eyes would open and stare mockingly at her.

Méron and Alex slept peacefully on each side of the fire, their skin tingling with a healthy color beneath fur blankets. Exhausted, their arms aching, Goliath, Angus, and Cameron sat at the kitchen table as the run rose, reflecting off the bright snow through the window. Cameron was very conscious of her hands, which still throbbed with the feel of Alex's firm, muscled flesh. Now that the emergency was over, her fatigued mind was unable to remain detached. She sat with her back to the prone figure, who lay with the firelight enhancing his golden skin and hair, and stared blankly at her brother, noting the gauntness of his face. He had aged in the months since she last saw him and lost the boyishness that was still rightfully his. They were man and woman now, being seventeen or thereabouts, she reckoned, so why was she surprised at her brother's mannish appearance? It was not so much the emerging man but a quality of aging which made him seem older than his years. It was as though he had been drained. She ached to turn around and appraise her husband but knew she would weaken and find herself as defenseless and vulnerable as before. In fact she would be more so, she realized.

"Here, lass, drink this and try to sleep before the two wee-uns awaken and demand your motherly attention," said Angus gruffly, pushing a glass toward her. Cameron smiled gratefully and drank, enjoying the harsh burning in her throat that spread its heat to her belly.

"Dinna try to sort anything out now. You'll not make head or tail of it, and it'll just cause you pain," said Goliath softly, his heart going out to the girl who sat looking like a frightened young doe. Cameron nodded, unable to talk for the storm of tears that threatened to burst from her. She stood carefully avoiding looking at Alex and went into her room and softly closed the door. She sat upon her bed staring down at her sons for a long time until they finally awoke, cooing and reaching up to her. She lifted them up and lay with them on the bed. Raven, sensitive to her mood, regarded her almost sorrowfully before burrowing his dark head into her belly. Lynx, full of the joys of the new day, pranced and crawled, trying to get them to play with him.

Goliath tiptoed in, hoping to get the boys before they woke Cameron, knowing that she needed her sleep, and was surprised to find her lying inert on the bed, not resisting the rambunctious Lynx, who clambered and leaped on her. Thinking her asleep despite the boisterous child, he was even more surprised to see her wide, staring green eyes.

"I thought to let you sleep," he said gruffly. "I was meaning to feed the young-uns and take them out so that their noise dinna wake Méron and . . ." he trailed off.

"I canna sleep, and 'tis best I keep busy," stated Cameron, propping herself up and staring into Raven's melancholy expression. "Och, what am I doing to you, my wee-un?" she cooed, feeling guilty for inflicting her dejected mood onto her small, solemn son. " 'Tis up we maun get and very quiet, for there are sick men sleeping," she whispered, brightening her tone and making a game of tiptoeing. Lynx backed off the bed and toddled into the main room, where he was quickly swung up into Angus's large arms before he could playfully tumble onto the sleeping men. Goliath suppressed a laugh as Raven toddled from his mother's room and squatted quietly beside Méron, gazing solemnly into the sleeping face before examining the golden-haired stranger.

Cameron took a deep breath and bravely stepped into the warm central room, only to stop short in dismay at the sight of one of her sons sitting on the floor by Alex like a puppy keeping watch. One small, chubby hand gently touched the thick russet hair, and the other traced the scar that ran from bushy eyebrow to jaw. Quietly she bent to lift him, but Raven firmly shook his head, not taking his eyes from the sleeping man. Fearing that loud protests would wake Alex and not ready for any sort of confrontation, Cameron let Raven remain there and set about making breakfast in the hope of wooing him away.

Lynx splashed his small hands joyfully into his porridge as Cameron deftly slipped the spoon between his happily crooning lips. The oatmeal ran down his sturdy brown chest, pooling on the seat of the high chair that Angus had made. Cameron gave a sigh of relief seeing Raven put two hands on the floor and hoist his small bottom into the air in preparation to stand. Gaining his feet, Raven smiled in triumph, only to lose balance and fall heavily onto Alex's chest. She held her breath, the spoon suspended in the air out of reach of Lynx's open mouth, but there was no movement from the sleeping man. Raven once more regained his feet and toddled purposefully to the table, where Angus lifted him into his high seat and removed his deerskin shirt so that it would not be caked with oatmeal. The boy struggled to get down, and Cameron frowned at his unusual behavior. Angus attempted to feed him, but Raven glowered, pursing his mouth in a firm, closed line as he grabbed a fistful of the oatmeal and tried to clamber to the floor. Lynx stood precariously on his chair, clapping his own mucky hands together gleefully.

"We should have put Méron and Sinclair in your room at the back," whispered Cameron, for the first time feeling an inability to cope with her small sons. She felt drained by the sleeping presence of Alex and furious with the emotions that streaked through, aching her heart and groin at the sight of his long-limbed body.

"I dinna think anything can wake them yet awhile,"

reassured Goliath, lifting the struggling Raven before he toppled to the floor. The small boy silently beat on the broad chest, the oatmeal squishing through his fingers.

"What are you fashing about?" growled the large man, eyeing the rebellious face and his smeared jerkin ruefully. Raven waved a clenched fist frantically toward Alex. "Your dad needs his sleep, wee mannikin—"

"NO!" hissed Cameron furiously, and Goliath cursed his unruly tongue as he saw the hurt flare in her eyes. Raven and Lynx froze at the vehemence and regarded their mother with wide, frightened eyes.

Alex and Méron slept through the whole day despite Lynx's noisy rambunctiousness and Raven's stubborn decision to squat by the golden-haired man. Cameron had bundled up the twins, and she and Jemmy had taken them out to play in the snow. It had taken quite a while for Raven to settle down, as he strained to return to the cabin, somehow inexplicably drawn to Alex. Cameron seethed with many emotions, most of all rage at the smashing of the peace and harmony of her life. She wished Méron would wake so she could attack him for bringing such an unwelcome visitor, the relief at his safe return and the agony of the months of waiting quickly forgotten. All she was aware of was her incredible fury. Leaving her children with Jemmy, she walked into the forest that ringed the lake.

Once again her world was in turmoil. She slithered and slipped in the snow, feeding her consuming anger, not acknowledging the pit of stark terror that ached inside her. How dare he destroy her life? she raged inwardly. He was a trespasser, who now turned her only sanctuary into a hell, a place she could not relax and be safe and comfortable in. Although cold, she procrastinated about returning to the cabin, where his very presence, whether sleeping or awake, seemed to turn her inside out, making it impossible to act or think effectively. She sat dejectedly under a large tree with Tor huddling to her for warmth and Omen in a branch above, complaining raucously. Goliath watched her from a distance, guessing much of the turmoil in her mind. He had followed her, keeping her always in sight and now, shaking with cold, he cursed her stubbornness as his large, empty stomach growled for his supper. He strode forward, his massive feet crunching the icy top of the snow.

" 'Tis near past dinnertime, and your children need you," he said tersely.

"You'd gie them away to him!" attacked Cameron, glad of a person to release some of her fury at as remembrance of his words at the breakfast table tore in painfully.

"What?" ejaculated the large giant of a man, stepping back a step at her violence.

"Your dad needs his sleep," mimicked Cameron spitefully. "How dare you say such a thing! How dare you!" she wept frustratedly, unable to find strong enough words to rid herself of the overwhelming anger and pain.

"I was wrong, and I'm sorry," replied Goliath. "I didna think," he added after a long silence, staring sorrowfully into the flashing, brimming eyes.

Cameron nodded stiffly and turned away, feeling deflated. What should she do? she wondered, feeling no lessening of her intense emotions.

"I will not be forced from my home," she resolved aloud as she stood decisively and brushed the snow from her clothes. She stopped and froze at a sudden thought. "But 'tis not my home, is it?" she asked, staring up at Goliath. " 'Tis yours, Angus's, and Méron's."

" 'Tis also your and the wee-uns," he replied gruffly, amazed at her mercurial changes of mood. One minute an aggressive, spitting wild animal and the next a tragic waif bundled in thick furs staring up at him so forlornly. "Let's go home for supper?" he said gruffly, offering his enormous hand, which Cameron clasped fondly.

They walked back through the darkening woods toward the welcoming lights of the house, with Cameron's imagination torturing her with thoughts of Alex awake and playing with her children before the fire. What would she do? What would she say? she thought fearfully, hanging back, her feet dragging. But Goliath firmly held her hand. By the time they reached the door to the large main room, terror pounded her pulses, and she thought she would faint. Her relief at seeing the still-sleeping figure was so enormous that she panted for breath. Raven squatted near Alex, absorbed in the still face, and Lynx busily played with pots and pans around Jemmy and Angus, who busily cooked.

Cameron stripped off her outer clothes and set the table. She was thankful that Raven made none of his previous objections as he toddled to his chair and lifted his hands trustingly to be picked up. Cameron sat across the table, smiling lovingly at the two bronzed little boys, who were naked in preparation for their messy eating. She blew on their plates of rabbit stew to cool them as they greedily stuffed bread into their mouths and then reached out hungrily for their bowls. As usual Lynx splashed his hands joyfully in the mixture of vegetables and meat as Jemmy filled his mouth. Raven looked thoughtfully from the bread to the stew as he opened his mouth obediently for the spoon Angus offered.

"What are you thinking so seriously about, little fellow?" laughed Goliath, echoing Cameron's own thoughts. Raven carefully picked up a slice of bread and, after much solemn consideration, dipped it into the bowl before standing and holding out his arms to be lifted down.

"You've hardly eaten anything," remarked Angus, sitting him back down in the chair.

Cameron was mesmerized by her small son as his face scowled and he tried to climb down, his hand clenching the soggy slice of bread. He knelt and carefully slithered his short legs into the air, reaching and then dropping to the floor, where he overbalanced and sat sharply. He laboriously picked himself up, retrieving the bread that had fallen into several unappetizing pieces. Angus moved to pick him up but was stopped by his large brother, who, like Cameron, stared with fascination at the purposeful child.

Raven squatted by Alex, making eating sounds and motions with his mouth before shoving the soggy bread onto the sleeping face. Alex opened his eyes and regarded the small, solemn face. He was amazed at the intensity of the green eyes and shut his own, not sure whether he dreamed or not. There was a quick flurry as Raven was scooped up by Angus and deposited back in his chair at the table, and with a cooling rag Goliath washed the stickiness from the again-still face.

Alex lay in a golden haze as his mind became aware of the domestic sounds around him. He was so comfortable and relaxed, a peaceful, languorous suspension that he did not want to wake from. He was content to lie still, with his eyes closed, and he vaguely wondered if he was lying in deep snow dying, as he remembered the grueling, arduous trek with Méron through the blizzard that had lasted for days, leaving them hungry and lost. The smell of food made him aware of hunger pangs, but he was loath to open his eyes, expecting to see nothing but white snow for miles and miles with no landmark to guide them home. He had no home, came the hollow thought.

"I told you nothing will wake those two, not even a face full of soggy bread," chuckled Angus softly. "You're a clever wee lad, Raven . . . och, and you too, Lynx," he added diplomatically as small hands splashed the stew for attention.

"Do you ever think they'll learn to eat without making such a mess?" said Cameron, trying to appear relaxed and happy, with her back purposefully to Alex.

" 'Tis good they are naked," replied a low, warm voice, and her back stiffened. She was unable to move, and her eyes stared blindly at her two small boys, who stood on their chairs clapping mucky hands. The color drained from her face, and she tried to calm her rapidly thumping heart. Vaguely, as though from a great, muffled distance, she heard Goliath administer to Alex as she numbly unset the table and boiled water to wash her babies and the dishes.

Alex noted Cameron's instant frigidity at his softly spoken words. He felt tired and hopeless as he sat eating, watching her methodical movements from his bed. His eyes took in every detail of the warm, roughhewn room, pausing thankfully on the sleeping figure of Méron. It was a miracle that they were both alive, he thought, or was it some ironic jest of the gods? The hopeful possibility of somehow forging through the mass of resentments and past hurts to find love and understanding with Cameron had kept him going through the murderous snowstorm, had given him the will to live, to survive. But now he felt drained and despairing, noting her obvious avoidance of him, her movements strange and disjointed, with none of her usual graceful ease. He felt alone and displaced watching Jemmy, Goliath, and Cameron tend the children. It was as though he were an alien who did not belong in the pattern of their existence. He was an outsider, a trespasser, beyond the circle of their warmth. He closed his eyes as the mere act of eating and trying to cope with Cameron's obvious rejection fatigued him. All he wanted to do was sleep and not think.

Cameron bathed her children, feeling none of the usual joy in their mischievous antics as they splashed and tried to wash her face. Lynx, not understanding his mother's withdrawal, got wilder and wilder, trying to break through her cold reserve as Raven soon sat motionless, regarding her sadly.

"Let Jemmy and me finish them up," offered Goliath, and Cameron looked up at him with a startled expression and then at her children's woefully sad faces. "You need time to get your feelings in order, and you didna sleep last night, lass," he added gently. Cameron nodded numbly and stood undecided about what to do and where to go. She was disoriented. She yearned for solitude but at the same time was afraid that she would be too immersed in her fear, anger, and despondency.

"No, I'm all right," she decided, dropping down to her knees again before the tub and trying to smile brightly. Lynx and Raven howled, tears pouring from their eyes as her tension communicated itself wordlessly. Reaching her arms out to them, she pulled them from the water, rocking their wet nakedness to her, their grief tapping into her own.

Goliath became aware of being watched and turned to see Alex propped up on one elbow, his face reflecting the sorrow of the rocking, sobbing mother with her children. He silently gestured to Jemmy and Angus, and the three of them left the room. Cameron and the children's crying tapered off, but she remained kneeling on the floor, rocking their wet sleepiness to her as though to let go would cause her to fall apart. She was not aware of Alex standing behind her nor of the tactful departure of the others. Strong hands cupped her elbows, helping her to stand, as her thin arms held the sturdy babies, who hiccoughed in their sleep, snuggling to get closer to her body.

Alex swung them all into his arms which, although considerably weakened by the long weeks of exposure, were strong enough for the few paces to what he assumed was Cameron's room. He deposited them all on the large bed and sat beside them, somehow knowing not to try to relieve her of the weight of the sleeping children. She lay, refusing to see him, holding the boys closer, smelling the fragrance of their glossy heads until, exhausted by the emotions of the long night and day, she drifted off to sleep.

Alex sat beside Cameron's still figure watching her eyelids droop and her arms relax and fall limply from the sleeping boys. He blew out the lamp and stretched beside them, his body forming a barrier so that the children could not tumble off the high side of the bed. One of the boys snuggled up to his body and curled his warm softness against his bare chest. Alex held him close and to the sound of the rhythmic breaths they fell asleep.

CHAPTER THIRTY-TWO

Alex awoke to warm wetness, and opened his eyes to bright sunlight and the stolid gaze of a small boy. He returned the look before searching out the reason for his discomfiture. Raven's solemn expression changed to glee as he dabbed at the dampness he had miraculously created and stood on unsteady legs proudly to show the small part of his anatomy that had caused such a thing. At a peal of laughter Alex turned to see Cameron convulsed with mirth. She had awakened feeling relaxed and safe, only to tense with shock at the sight of the rangy, golden man who lay beside her on the bed, her sons nestled between them. She had jealously noted Raven curled trustingly in the curve of one of Alex's brown arms and, as she had longed to wrench her child free, had realized the boy was awake. Usually the children wore hippens, but now they lay in all their bronzed nakedness. She had watched the small boy urinate and seen the amber eyes open in surprise, and despite her resolve, Raven's obvious pride in his accomplishment had broken a barrier.

Alex rejoiced at Cameron's free, untrammeled laughter. His amber eyes brimmed with mischief as he savored her lithe, young body shaking helplessly with mirth. Lynx awoke, and Alex, recognizing the signs of another full male bladder, picked up the young boy just before Cameron was similarly drenched. The child crowed with delight, and Alex felt a strange exhilaration in the tiny but sturdy child between his broad palms. Cameron's mirth redoubled as Alex held the dripping child. She did not know what she felt, she did not even care. It seemed so long since she had laughed, and she clung onto it. Alex deposited Lynx back on the bed and stretched himself out, enjoying the rambunctious child, who immediately pounced on his chest.

"What are their names?" he asked when Cameron's laughter had ebbed.

"Lynx and Raven," answered Cameron, wishing she could have laughed forever, her anger rising at his presumptuous presence on her bed.

"Which is which?" responded Alex softly, feeling awkward and afraid.

"Does it matter? Don't they look the same to you?" challenged Cameron.

"No," replied Alex, looking from one to the other. "Aye, they are identical twins, there's no doubt about that, but this young one is much like his mother wie his wild, irrepressible ways," he laughed, holding Lynx high in the air, where the child crowed and kicked his legs and arms in delight. "And the solemn wee-un here has a manner quite distinct."

Cameron lay still, with her emotions in turmoil. It would be so easy to let her defenses down and trust this seemingly beautiful man, but fear of rejection caused anger at his acute perception of her children. She sprang from the bed, feeling dirty and gringy at having slept in her breeches and shirt.

"The one you find so much like his mother is Lynx," she said shortly, quitting the room, the closeness between father and sons causing her deep pain.

Cameron rushed from the cabin without noticing that her brother sat alert and awake, calmly eating an enormous breakfast. He stared in amazement as she rushed by. His mouth too full to talk; he could only wave his laden fork in greeting, but the cabin door slammed behind her. Goliath frowned and scratched his head. The sounds of Cameron's merry laughter had caused them all to grin happily at each other, but the girl who had just blindly charged through had been frantic and panic-stricken. Angus stood as though to follow, but Méron was halfway to the door in pursuit.

Alex felt a sudden depression. The bright, golden morning full of laughter and happy children was now flat and gray. He lay back on the bed deep in thought as the two boys minutely examined his face, arms, and chest. He realized that Cameron probably felt the same fear and awkwardness as he did but was less able to cover it up and cope with herself than he. But where had his iron self-control got him? he raged savagely. Little fingers pulled at his lips and examined his strong white teeth as part of him wanted to follow Cameron and force a private confrontation. Yet he was forced to realize that they both needed time and patience. Knowing of old her need for solitude, he decided to bide his time. Where or when would they ever find a space in the crowded menagerie? he thought hopelessly, hearing the low voices and clatter of pots and pans in the kitchen.

The two little boys wrapped trusting arms around Alex's neck as he strode into the kitchen carrying them. Jemmy grinned shyly, and he noted that her child's body had grown and rounded in the year and a half since he had last seen her at the Boston inn.

"Good morning. How do you feel?" asked Goliath conventionally.

"Confused," returned Alex frankly, staring at the large man who owed him many explanations.

"This is my brother, Angus MacLeod."

Alex tried to free one of his hands to shake the proffered one, but was hampered by the clinging twins.

"Let me take them?" offered Jemmy shyly, but the boys clung possessively to their new friend.

"I'm sure they'll hunger in a minute and forsake me for their breakfast," laughed Alex, enjoying the affection of their little hugging arms. "How is Méron?" he added sharply, seeing the empty pallet.

"Fine, nothing can keep that lad down for long," answered Angus proudly, reminding Alex of Mackie.

"He went achasing after his sister," offered Goliath dryly, as he thought it should be the husband doing the chasing and not the brother.

Alex felt his censure, and his amber eyes sharpened. The giant returned his gaze, tension prickling between them.

"I think you and I should talk, Goliath," he said grimly, and the other man nodded in agreement.

"Later, when the routine of our day is established and the horses and these young-uns are fed and groomed," he replied.

The antics of the two boys at the breakfast table soon

dispelled the tension, and Alex joined in the laughter, feeling a sense of belonging to the strange assortment of people in the warm, timbered room. He looked around with appreciation at the comforting blend of fur and wood, his eyes stopping at the carving on the wall that heralded the twin's birth, December 31, 1762. His face tightened with speculation and he turned to the two mucky boys, who gleefully splashed in their food, their green eyes twinkling merrily and their thick ebony hair liberally dabbed with oatmeal. Raven returned his intense stare, and Goliath leaned back in his chair, watching the tall man and the small boy, who, despite their difference in coloring, could be nothing short of father and son. Alex saw much of his own father in Raven's expression, and a fierce joy burned, which quickly turned to rage at Cameron and Méron's deception. He shook his mane of russet hair to clear his head and, cupping each small face between his large brown hands, examined each minute feature while his own face remained stern and unyielding. Lynx protested, wiggling and fighting against the firm clasp, but Raven solemnly stared back, as though committing the golden man to memory. Alex stood abruptly and shrugged into his hooded fur parka, needing to be alone with his tumultuous emotions.

Cameron stripped off her clothes in the cold, bright sunlight and plunged into the water, breaking the thin, crinkly icing that had formed. She reveled in the cruel shock and swam briskly to rid herself of the stale, uncomfortable feeling. Méron sat on her pile of clothes watching her from the bank, knowing that soon the temperature of the water would drive her back. Cameron swam strongly to shore. At seeing her brother she felt a combination of joy and the resurgence of her anger at his traitorous action in bringing Alex back with him.

Méron grinned, knowing only too well what to expect as his naked, stormy sister approached. He threw up his hands in mock alarm and backed away from the furious splashing. Cameron stood still, eyeing him, her brown skin getting goose bumps in the frigid air, before climbing into her clothes. Méron's happy expression faded, and puzzlement wrinkled his young brow. He had awakened that morning to see Alex's empty bed and to hear the laughter from behind Cameron's bedroom door. He had experienced a surge of joy and relief. The long, grueling weeks with Alex had served to dispel his anger and suspicion. They had learned to trust and rely on each other, putting their very lives in each other's hands as they forged their way on foot through the howling, inhospitable elements, both fighting to reach the person who now stood with fury and disdain emanating from every pore. Silently Méron turned on his heels and walked back to the cabin. He paused just outside the stockade wall as he saw Alex striding into the forest away from the lake. He debated following, but the set of the man's shoulders deterred him, so he shrugged and walked toward the happy, gurgling sounds of his nephews.

Cameron stood watching her brother's silent retreat. She had hoped for a furious exchange of words so she could release some of her raging pressure. His wordless departure left her afraid and infinitely lonely. She ran after him, wanting to embrace him but he had disappeared into the cabin, where there was no chance of talking privately. She felt a reluctance to enter, not wanting to be in Alex's presence, and with relief saw him in the distance.

Goliath looked up in surprise as Cameron entered and locked the door decisively with the heavy wooden bar. He and Angus exchanged worried looks.

"What are you about?" shouted Méron.

Cameron leaned against the barred door breathing heavily. Now she could be free, she had locked him out, blocked him from her sight. She felt a triumph at so easily accomplishing the deed as she stared into four set faces that seemed to glare accusingly at her. Jemmy sat on the floor with the twins, her small, freckled face expressing the shock she felt, Goliath's and Angus's good-natured features were molded in harsh lines, and Méron's fury blazed from his bright green eyes.

"Take the bairns to another room, Jemmy," growled Goliath, knowing there was to be a violent clash of wills between the older twins. Angus helped the girl scoop up the boys, and as the door shut behind Jemmy's anxious face, Méron approached his sister. Goliath sat heavily, feeling that his presence was justified as an arbitrator or referee, waiting for the storm that was definitely brewing.

"Take the bar from the door," ordered Méron, his aquiline nose whitening around his flaring nostrils. Cameron did not answer but remained leaning against the door blocking his way, her face mutinous.

"Either take the bar from the door or move aside," repeated Méron, his voice low and dangerous. Cameron shook her head fiercely from side to side. Méron grasped her shoulders, and Cameron tensed to attack, but instead collapsed sobbing in his arms.

"You dinna ken . . . you dinna ken," she cried helplessly.

"More than you know," replied Méron huskily, his heart aching for his twin. He took a deep breath and put her from him as he purposefully unbarred the door. Cameron's tear-filled eyes widened with the shock of his rejection. She wrapped her arms around herself, swaying in the middle of the room.

"You've all taken his side agin me," she mouthed slowly.

"Nay, lass, there are no sides," growled Goliath, wanting desperately to enfold the girl, who looked like as much of a small, lost child as one of her own bairns. He understood Méron's action and knew how hard it had been for the youth as their eyes met, communicating silently. Cameron needed comfort but not from them, that would only serve to keep her from the truth she fought so desperately to keep herself from admitting. The girl looked from her brother to Goliath, pain and bewilderment expressed openly on her face, before she hardened, threw back her shoulders, and stalked coldly to her room and slammed the door.

Alex questioned his sanity. What made him think he saw any likeness to his family in the round faces of the two infants? He had walked his blinding anger off, and now the cold light of reason dawned. Maybe he was seeing just what he wanted to see, for, despite the green eyes and black hair that made Cameron so clearly their mother, baby features could rarely be distinguished one from another. The carving on the wall nagged at him as by simple arithmetic he deduced their conception to be late March, when he and Cameron had arrived back at Glen Aucht. He frowned trying to remember the sequence of events. So much had happened in the intervening year and a half since leaving Scotland, that the past seemed to have a vague, night-marish quality to it. Was it possible that the children had been conceived at the mountain lodge where they had first come together? If so, they could only be his sons, as he was the first man to possess her

At the thought of her being possessed by anyone other than himself he felt his rage return. Over and over again he recalculated the months, forcing himself to remember Beddington's sickening attack. Could the twins be the product of that horrendous rape? He dismissed it hurriedly from his mind; after all, he was not certain that the de-bauched colonel had been successful, as Cameron had not seen fit to answer the question. The injustice and torture of not knowing either way boiled his blood, and his labored breath misted the cold air in angry spurts. Those beautiful children could not possibly have been formed from Bed-dington's seed. Not only was the idea ludicrous, but the attack had occurred in late April. Might the children have been premature? Alex stopped in his tracks. The children were his sons, and both Méron and Cameron thought to keep him from the knowledge, he decided. His rage ignited again, and although his natural cautiousness tried to rein him in, he threw patience and self-control to the wind as he purposefully strode back to the cabin, grim determina-tion etched across his face.

Goliath nodded his approval as he watched Méron care-fully carve the surname Sinclair on the wall after the given names of Lynx and Raven. The small cabin was quiet and peaceful. No sounds issued from Cameron's room, and Jemmy sat cross-legged sewing beside the sleeping children, who sprawled entwined on a large bearskin on the floor. The kitchen was fragrant with the smell of baking bread, and the sounds of Angus's whistling could faintly be heard as he tended to the animals in the stable.

Alex's feet firmly crunched the snow, and he thrust the

door open upon the tranquil scene. The blast of warm, homey air filled his senses for a moment, weakening his purpose. He steeled himself and, quickly ascertaining that Cameron was not present, stalked to her room, his stern look noted by the silent group. The children did not stir, but the tranquillity of the comfortable room was shattered as all tensed for the explosive confrontation they knew had to occur.

Alex shut the door firmly behind him and leaned on it, willing the still figure on the bed to look at him. The minutes ticked by, both of them aware of each other's presence. Noises from the other room as the children were awakened and dressed to be taken outside penetrated Alex's steely anger, and he held himself in check, knowing that soon he would be given the privacy he so sorely needed. Hushed voices and the crunching of feet in the snow were muffled by the decisive closing of the front door.

Cameron heard the sounds of departure with dismay, knowing that she was left alone to deal with him. She tried to detach herself, but her heart beat wildly as she felt the amber eyes rake her tense body. She closed her eyes, her fists clenched at her side, refusing to acknowledge him. A small cry of fear burst from her mouth as her shoulders were gripped painfully in his hard, brown hands. Her eyes flew open, and she gasped at the fury that smoldered.

"Are those my sons?" hissed his voice, low and distorted with intense rage. Cameron was paralyzed with terror. Never had she seen him quite so crazed. Unable to speak, she could do nothing but stare into the amber eyes that seemed to burn her to the very core. She felt herself plucked from the bed and set on her feet. She was propelled roughly into the main room and placed before Méron's carving. She stared blindly, not seeing the new addition giving the boys the surname Sinclair. Alex's eyes did not leave the back of Cameron's head.

"Are those my sons?" he repeated harshly.

Cameron blinked, trying to focus her eyes as the whiter letters of the newly carved wood gleamed from the dark, rich wood. Infuriated by no answer, Alex smacked the wood with his broad hand.

"December 31, 1762," he roared and stopped abruptly,

staring at the word that answered his question. "Lynx and Raven Sinclair," he added softly in a dazed voice. He stared mesmerized for a moment before turning Cameron to face him. "You would keep my own sons from me? And me from them?" he asked, shaken by the quivering hostility in her green eyes.

"I was taught well," spat Cameron, furious with Méron for taking away her last weapon, her only defense.

"To rob a father of his sons?" shouted Alex. "To rob sons of a father?"

"You did that to me!" screamed Cameron, pulling away from him as her words shocked him and his brow furrowed in astonishment. "You kept knowledge of my own father from me. They are my sons from my belly, fat from my milk, and you'll not take them from me!"

"They are our sons from my seed and your belly. Ours!" he stated firmly. "I was wrong in choosing not to tell you of your father, but I did it to protect you, not to wound you. You would keep me from my children just to hurt me, not caring that our sons would also be hurt, as you and Méron were, not knowing who you were or where you came from."

"You knew of their existence. You saw them that day you returned my horse, Torquod!" cried Cameron defensively, stung by his words and fired by the memory of her humiliation when she had opened herself to Alex, only to be taken and brutally rejected. Alex's face tightened as he also remembered. He reached out and gently ran his broad hands down her slim arms as he fought to find words to undo the terrible action.

"I was jealous and hurt, Cameron. I thought you had found solace in another man's arms," he said eventually, his voice husky with emotion. His fingers tenderly traced the long, arrow-shaped scar that ran from her shoulder to her elbow. "I want you just for myself."

Cameron quivered at his touch and the fierce possessiveness of his words. Fear streaked through her, mingling with the hungry desire his strong hands and close proximity evoked. It would be so easy to relax and lean on his rangy, golden strength. To be enfolded and clasped close to his heart. Not to fight but to give in to the safety of those strong arms and submerge herself into the nonthinking ecstasy his body could provide.

"And what if I have found solace, as you call it, in another man's arms?" she challenged, trying to push him away. Alex looked down at her silently, his face not betraying the pain he felt. "Is it any different from you and Fiona Hurst?" At the hated name on her lips, a flood of anger and pain was released. Cameron felt she had to drive him away from her for her own survival. Alex stepped back, dazed as the onslaught of accusations poured out.

"Aye, women and little lassies being raped, and you did nothing but be the perfect, polite soldier, letting Beddington spit on you. Even when your own wife was attacked and used . . . still you did nothing. . . . Och, but when the whore Fiona crooked her little finger, oh, then you could disobey orders and run to her in Edinburgh!" ranted Cameron.

"Did Beddington use you?" asked Alex quietly as she stopped for breath.

"What if he did? What difference does it make?" she challenged. "Does it change me?" she added when he didn't answer.

"No," replied Alex softly. "It just makes me wish I could kill him again."

"Again?" gasped Cameron. "You killed him?"

Alex nodded before turning away, his mind awhirl at all the hurts and misconceptions in Cameron's mind. No wonder she had fought him and taken the reins of her own life.

"When did you kill him?" demanded Cameron, breaking through the tangle in Alex's head as he tried to sort out where to start explaining.

"Does it matter?" responded Alex wearily. "He's dead."

"What of all those at Glen Aucht? Mackie? Fergus? Ian? Daft-Dougal?"

"All well. I've letters somewhere for you to read," he answered, staring at her sadly. "Cameron, I have lain wie other women since we've been parted, but I dinna go to Fiona in Edinburgh."

Cameron felt a streak of pain slice through her at the mention of other women.

"Then go back to them and let me be," she shouted,

trying to stop the tears that gathered and the trembling that shook her limbs. "I want to be free of you!"

"No," stated Alex. "For the past year and a half I've tried to be free of you. There's no way. You are in my head, my heart, my blood . . . and there we both are joined irreversibly in our twin sons," he said, pointing to Méron's carving.

"I don't want you!" screamed Cameron, trying to convince herself. "You hurt me . . . and hurt me."

"And you hurt me," confessed Alex, taking her by the shoulders. "Do you know why we are able to hurt each other so much?"

"I don't want to know," spat Cameron, trying to twist out of his strong grasp. His close proximity, the heat of him, the male scent of him, the strength of him causing a conflict of emotions.

"Why do we spend so much time fighting against the need we have for each other?" growled Alex with exasperation.

"If you have needs, go find one of your other women to rut with!"

Alex stared into the spitting green eyes that brimmed with unspilt tears. She is as jealous of me as I am of her, he thought. I could stand here explaining and defending myself for days, but no words are going to break through.

"I will have you, Cameron," he stated in a low, menacing voice as he threw caution to the wind and picked her up in his arms. She fought him and herself as he stalked purposefully to the bedroom, where he kicked the door shut behind him and deposited her roughly on the bed. Before she could scramble away, he covered her struggling body with his own.

Cameron was afraid. She longed to let go and give herself up, every part of her to him. His large, brown hands cupped her face, and he stared into her eyes before kissing her possessively. Tears streamed down her cheeks as she warred with her traitorous body, which longed to merge with his, feeling that if she surrendered, she would be vulnerable and defenseless, with no hope. Her passion flared, consuming her, and she returned his kisses, channeling her fury so that it fused with her aching need as she planned to return his hurtful insult of their last coupling. She would use him as he had abused her, she resolved, fanning her raging emotions as she remembered Fiona and the other women and justifying and absolving herself of any weakness as she writhed against him. The long months of hurt and frustration culminated in a savage, grim mating as both Alex and Cameron used their bodies to express the extent of their hurt and anger. They lay panting, hearts racing, still locked together.

Cameron glowed with triumph, feeling no tenderness as she tried to pull away from him. Thwarted, she stared up rebelliously at the golden face above her, the amber eyes twinkling humorously.

"Now that we've made war, can we have a truce and make love?" he said softly, tenderly sweeping her hair from her face. Cameron closed her eyes tightly, not wanting to see the warm gentleness that radiated from him. She could cope with fury, battle with passion, but felt defenseless against loving tenderness. She was confused and spent and wished she could sleep. They lay still joined, and Cameron felt regret as he gently slipped from her, although his arms still held her tightly.

"Sleep, my love," she heard from a great distance before, giving a shuddering sigh, she floated to an exhausted sleep. Alex smiled contentedly and softly kissed the ebony head nestled on his chest. The half undressed desperate mating wasn't the romantic reunion he had envisioned, but how else could two proud, willfully stubborn people come together? he mused, wondering what the next installment would be when she awoke refreshed and ready to do battle again. He grinned mischievously, remembering how trusting her sleeping mind and body were, and decided he would use the knowledge to his own advantage. He watched the patterns of the sun's reflections on the warm wooden rafters overhead, her soft breathing like music in his ears as he held her tightly to him, wishing he could feel her bared silky skin against his own. Carefully he unwrapped his arms, determined to divest himself of his clothes, and Cameron mewed a protest, trying to burrow back into his warmth. He laughed softly at the change in her. One moment a spitting, furious wildcat, the next a soft, nestling kitten. He quickly stripped off his clothes and turned to Cameron, who was curled in a fetal position hugging a pillow. Gently he undressed her, ignoring her sleepy grumbles as he examined every inch of her. He marveled at the firm, flat belly that had held his two sons, amazed that there was no sign of it. Tenderly he kissed and caressed the whole of her, mischief glinting his gold eyes as he saw her nipples harden like tight rosebuds.

Cameron was suspended in a golden haze. Sensations rippled through her body, and she arched hungrily. A warm, sweet mouth captured hers, and she drank thirstily, drowning in excitement. She opened, feeling like a flower embracing the sun, reveling and absorbing warmth and healing. Her hands slid across smooth hardness, and she delighted in the firm contours as slowly and inexorably sensations built and she reached for the object of her desire.

Alex lay back watching her explore his body. Although her eyes were tightly closed, her hands traveled as though committing each ridge of muscle, each inch of skin, each hair to memory. An exquisite pang of aching tenderness shot through him as he watched Cameron's small hand encircle his straining manhood.

"Is that the only part of me you'll accept?" he asked softly, emotion rasping his throat, and the green eyes flew open, confused and disoriented. She stared into his face, and Alex gave a groan at the undisguised pain and fear he saw. He enfolded her in his arms, wishing he had kept silent.

"I love you, Cameron," he whispered, feeling her heart beating frantically like a frightened bird as her tears streaked down his chest.

Cameron lay hearing his heart beat firm and true. She felt safe and warm but terrified that it all might be a cruel dream. She lifted her head and stared into his face, seeing infinite tenderness glowing from his amber eyes. She loved him so much that she felt she would burst from the extent of it, but even as she acknowledged it, there came a stabbing fear. He didn't want her, just his sons.

Alex saw the fleet change of expression. "What is it, Cameron?" he asked, but she shook her head and rolled off him. "No!" he protested, pulling her back. "We aren't children any longer. We canna run away from each other leaving fears unsaid. Think of our wee sons and their future."

"That's all you want. Them, not me," cried Cameron, struggling to get free of him. Her frantic movements were stilled by his response. She lay rigid on his chest, hearing the deep chuckle that reverberated through him.

"What's so funny?" she demanded hotly.

"You, my jealous darling," laughed Alex, knowing without a doubt that his love was returned. "And me," he hastily amended as he recognized the battle lights in her eyes. He knew that Cameron was confused and afraid, fighting against her love for him, but her fierce jealousy filled him with wild elation. His joyous laughter rumbled, fed by the flashing, mutinous face above him. He lifted his tawny head from the pillow, intent on kissing her rebellious mouth, but fell back shaking with mirth. Cameron shook his shaggy mane with exasperation. His laughter was infectious, sending wonderful shivers of happiness through her, and yet she held back. Alex rolled over, clasping her in his arms.

"Kiss me, my sweet little wildcat," he ordered roguishly. Cameron pouted thoughtfully, seduced by his carefree, joyous humor. This was a side of Alex she had not really experienced before. There had been glimpses, solitary, sunny moments that had not been sustained. An image of Alex on the boat dancing boyishly, his face alive and open, flashed into her mind. For a moment she was once again high up in the rigging with the thunder of the rising wind in her ears, the roar of the flapping sails deafening her. He had looked up and seen her, and all joy had faded. She now stared into the chiseled face that had been alight with infectious elation, and to her horror once more happiness had fled.

"What is it? Share with me, Cameron," said Alex softly, seeing her eyes dilate with terror.

"I rob you of your happiness," she intoned as though far away.

"We've robbed each other," comforted Alex.

"You dinna understand. There's something wrong wie

me . . . has always been. Maybe I am a changeling or a witch as people say. I canna help myself. I seem to hurt everyone wie out meaning to. I canna love you because of it—"

"Oh, Cameron," interrupted Alex. " 'Tis not true . . . 'tis just ignorance. There's people who'll always blame, usually picking on someone different."

"Why am I different? What makes me different?" challenged Cameron. "How am I different from the rest?" she demanded as Alex tried to think of an acceptable answer. "What is it that makes even the Indians afraid of me? See, you'll not tell me. Even you yourself told me all the terrible things I had done to you. Robbing you of your lands, friends, freedom, country!"

"I was angry. I was blaming. It wasna true. I wanted to hurt you because I was hurt and frustrated and feeling helpless," explained Alex.

"But you were right."

"Nay!" protested Alex, wishing he could have cut out his tongue that day on board ship when he vented his fury. "I was wrong. Cameron, you are different because you have nay been molded as most people. You were allowed to grow from childhood free from the restrictions of society and so do things a mite differently from others, who wish they had that freedom also," he added, trying desperately to undo the damage. "I am jealous of that freedom, too. I tried to harness you and make you conform," he went on, very conscious of the silence as Cameron stared at him sadly, her face mirroring her disbelief in his words.

"You're very kind," she said distantly.

"No! Goddamn it, I'm not kind, Cameron, and neither are you. I'm not saying you're a paragon of virtue . . . an angel or the like. You can be as infuriating, willful, and stupid as the rest of us. You can also be as cruel and unthinking as I can be. What I'm trying to tell you is that I said things in anger that I shouldna have said . . . and you believed them . . . and that breaks my heart. Should I believe everything you said to me in anger?"

" 'Tis different. Your words were echoed."

"By whom?" asked Alex, knowing the answer as he remembered the warrant for her arrest for witchcraft.

"The people at Durness on Cape Wrath when I was a child."

"Cameron, you were raised with a freedom to run wild and unfettered with the birds and the beasts . . . which made you different and threatening to those reined in by the rules of the church and society. But you were robbed of something else that stops your freedom now and makes you afraid."

"What?"

"Love," said Alex softly, undeterred by her stormy, closed expression. "What if Lynx and Raven had no one to love them? No mother like you? No Méron or Jemmy or Goliath or Angus?" Cameron's eyes filled with tears at the thought of her babies so deprived.

"And no father like you," she whispered.

"When my father, mother, and little sisters died, it hurt so much, some part of me decided that loving was too dangerous . . . and then I met you. I fought against loving you, as you well remember, but I couldna help myself. I loved you, and it was even more hurtful and dangerous, so I fought against love again. Now are we both going to fight against loving our sons because we might get hurt?"

Cameron shook her head slowly, mesmerized by the depth of pain she saw in Alex's eyes, and she realized he was as vulnerable and defenseless to her as she was to him. It shocked her. A shudder coursed through her as she recognized the naked, undisguised love that shone from him, making him as helpless as her babies. Once more waves of pure terror washed over her. Why was she so frightened? she questioned, fighting the urge to run and hide. It was like looking into her own heart.

Alex watched the change of expressions on Cameron's face and made no move to hold her. Instinctively he knew something was being resolved inside her. Something that could possibly affect their futures together. She sat motionless, staring at him, her naked body stiff and tense. Fear, terror, sadness, and many other emotions filled her eyes. Imperceptibly she started to relax. The tautness eased from her muscles, and the lines of her face softened, and she smiled tremulously at him. He caught his breath at the transformation. Cameron had in some indefinable way let

all her defenses drop, allowing him to see a lonely, frightened, unloved child . . . totally helpless, with no trace of
rebellion, defiance, anger, or hate. He couldn't move or
say a word, even though he ached to scoop her into his
arms. Her eyes were pinned to his, somehow telling him
to be still and patient. Alex watched the woman emerge.
It was almost as though under his eyes she shed her skin,
stepped out of the remnants of childhood to be trans-
formed into a confident woman whose love for him radiated unwaveringly with nothing held back. For several
minutes the silence and space between them was charged
as they took stock of each other. Alex opened his arms,
and Cameron entered.

Loud noises from the main room announced the return
of the rest of the household. Little feet scampered toward
the bedroom door, and piping voices protested as they were
restrained and hushed. Cameron was loath to move and
yet felt pangs of guilt at the desertion of her children. She
moved restlessly, but Alex held her tightly.

"Where are you going?"

"I should see to our sons," she said tenderly and then
tickled him so he'd release her.

"They have lots of loving arms out there, and I've only
yours," he pleaded mischievously, then sighed contentedly
as Cameron relaxed trustingly against him.

"Which is the elder?" he asked lazily after a lengthy
pause.

"Which what?" puzzled Cameron.

"Which of our sons?" replied Alex, tracing a pattern
on her breasts.

"Does it matter?"

"I suppose not, but usually the eldest is named for the
father," remarked Alex idly, aware that her body had
tensed.

"Why?" asked Cameron rolling over and leaning on his
chest.

"Tradition," he shrugged, thankfully seeing from her expression that it was genuine curiosity and not a challenge.
"The eldest usually inherits."

"Inherits what?"

"Title and lands."

"Are they so important?" asked Cameron sadly, remembering all the heartache and humiliation they had gone through in order for Alex to keep Glen Aucht.

"One day they may be important to our sons," Alex responded carefully, not wishing to shatter the languid contentment between them.

"Title and lands are very important to you," stated Cameron with no judgment in her voice.

"I don't know if they are," he answered honestly. "All I know is you are the most important to me," he added, kissing her hungrily.

"Again?" whispered Cameron in mock alarm. "I dinna think it possible."

"You've many many months to make up for, it seems," he said wickedly.

"But we should talk," protested Cameron halfheartedly. "In truth I dinna ken which babe came first."

"We've a lifetime to talk," he answered, smothering any words she might have had on the subject by covering her mouth with his.

Cameron's mind was alive with questions and fears. Glen Aucht and all it signified. She tore her mouth from Alex's.

"But we don't know which one to name for you," she worried.

"Neither and both. They are named Sinclair," he answered, nuzzling her neck and then propping himself onto one elbow and frowning at her furrowed brow. "Why the pained expression? 'Tis not very flattering when I'm making love to you."

"I was thinking of Glen Aucht and Mackie and Fergus—"

"And Daft-Dougal and Old-Petey and Ian Drummond," continued Alex, interrupting. "Not flattering at all to think of all those men when you're naked in my bed."

Cameron giggled roguishly, all her worries dissipating as she looked into his warm, whiskey eyes.

"I wouldna have you think there's only one part of you I want," she said impishly, licking her lips speculatively with a tantalizing pink tongue and peering suggestively down his long, rangy body.

"I dinna ken to what you refer, my lady," he said innocently, following her gaze to his unruly member.

"No?" teased Cameron, straddling his thighs and stretching her arms as though to yawn.

Alex looked at her lithe figure silhouetted against the sunset and marveled. " 'Tis impossible to imagine you fat and full of child," he murmured, running his broad hands down her taut belly. "I'm sad that I missed it." His hands caressed her lower down, at the joining of her straddled legs. "And to think that from this wee, precious part of you our children entered the world."

Cameron watched him caress her most intimate spot, and together with the rising passion she felt his loving tenderness.

"Must have been sorely stretched," he whispered, awed that the heads of his two husky sons had fit through such a small orifice and left no sign. He examined her gently, as though he were unfolding the velvet petals of a flower, until Cameron thought she would burst with the flood of emotions that filled her. Wanting finally to claim him she fitted herself to him and they moved as one.

Sated and glowing with happiness, Cameron lay in a rosy dreamlike trance. She turned and regarded Alex's sleeping face, which was relaxed, with no lines of cynical tension to disturb the inner harmony that seemed to radiate from each pore. She smiled, her eyes filling with tears as she remembered the incredible joy they had just shared. There had been a reverence to their loving that had not existed before. They had been totally aware of each other, their rhythms smooth and harmonious, as if they had been of one body, mind, and heart. No oblivion, no losing of oneself in a multitude of sensations, but a true mating, thought Cameron, trying to find the words to explain it to herself. It had been a reaffirmation, a pledging, a promise, a commitment, and at that knowledge she realized that together they were free. She could no longer run away from him and her feelings. It was as though a heavy burden had been lifted. She was tied irrevocably to this rangy, golden man and their two ebony-haired sons and yet she felt free, unshackled, and very, very young despite the responsibilities. Mischief glinted her green eyes, and she quietly wriggled free of his encircling arms, struggled into a fur robe and tiptoed out to the main room, where Angus, Goliath, Méron, and Jemmy squatted on the floor around the tub containing two contented baby boys. They crowed with delight at seeing her and splashed, reaching out chubby arms. Cameron held their wriggling, wet softness to her as she tiptoed back to the bedroom.

The damp quartet still squatting about the bathtub beamed at each other. Cameron's whole being glowed with a happiness that seemed to surround her like a golden aura in the steamy room. Like four conspirators they remained squatting, holding their breaths, waiting for the surprised chuckles and squeals of merriment when Cameron would deposit the wet babies on their peacefully sleeping father. They were rewarded with the expected musical sounds. Goliath and Angus stood stiffly, self-satisfied grins crinkling their burly face, as they set about preparing a celebration supper.

"Have to keep up young Sinclair's energy and strength," quipped Goliath. " 'Tis going to be a long winter . . . and none too boring, I'm thinking," he added, nodding his shaggy head toward Méron and Jemmy, who knelt by the tub sailing a little wooden boat back and forth to each other.

"She's but a child!" hissed Angus.

"Aye, they both are, and 'tis good for our lad," growled Goliath, looking lovingly at Méron and rejoicing in the relaxed boyish face. "He has his childhood back."

"But not for long, I wager," clucked Angus, watching Jemmy's animated freckled face haloed by a profusion of damp red curls and her newly budded breasts visible against her cotton shirt.

Alex and Cameron entered hand in hand, each holding a sleepy child. They stopped, gazing fondly at Jemmy and Méron, who were playing like two carefree bairns. The youth stood, sheepishly wiping his wet hands on his fringed buckskins. He felt awkward and embarrassed at being caught playing with his nephew's toys and very conscious of his sister's radiant glow caused by many hours of love-making. Alex laughed, dispelling Méron's discomfort, and the boy smiled.

"I was just entertaining the child Jemmy," he chuckled.

"Child Jemmy!" the red-haired girl protested, splashing him thoroughly. "I am nearly a woman. See, I have titties!" she stated, proudly pulling her shirt tighter and puffing out her chest.

Alex roared with laughter. "Oh, Cameron," he gasped. "You are a bad influence!"

Cameron grinned, delighting in the happiness that surrounded her as Méron splashed and chased the squealing Jemmy and her sons clapped their hands, wanting to join in the boisterous game.

"Not in my kitchen!" fussed Angus, waving a spurtle as Mackie had done many times at Glen Aucht and joining in the chase. Goliath put his head back, and his deep rumbling laugh chorused with Alex's as the little boys toddled on chubby legs, squealing with merriment and excitement as they tried to help Jemmy catch Méron and splash him. Cameron was overwhelmed with the loud happiness that surrounded her. She watched her brother, rejoicing in his open, young face. She squeezed Alex's hand as sadness welled, mingling with her elation. What did the future hold for them? she wondered as a pang of homesickness for Scotland ran through her. The thought of Cape Wrath no longer appealed to her. It seemed gray and desolate compared with the warmth and vitality of the little house in the woods. But this is not our country, she told herself, and for a few minutes she withdrew into herself, not daring to trust her newfound happiness.

Alex, sensing her bittersweet mood, returned the pressure of the small hand he held. He also felt conflicting emotions as he thought of Glen Aucht and the loyal friends so very far away. We are all fugitives, displaced people uprooted from our native soil. Would there ever be a way back? Will my small sons ever see their homeland? he wondered.

"To our home and family," toasted Goliath, handing out cups of rum.

"To this home and this family," echoed Alex, throwing off his gloomy thoughts and grinning lovingly down at Cameron, who basked in his warmth that melted her own sadness.

* * *

Much later Alex lay awake with Cameron nestled trustingly on his chest. He watched her sleeping face, marveling in the flushed tranquillity. They had been given another chance together, and their future lay ahead of them. He was too realistic to imagine it would be a peaceful existence, not with his wild, unpredictable bride nor with the painful turbulence of the New World, where the rightful inhabitants fought against the reins of another civilization, much like the small female who lay so deceptively docile within his arms. The future had bleak pain in store, he realized, knowing that he chose Cameron before his estate of Glen Aucht. For her to set foot again in Scotland could mean her life. He sighed deeply, feeling the loss, but as Cameron lifted an inquiring head and he stared into her questioning eyes, he knew that the sacrifice was infinitely worth it.

"What's the matter?" worried Cameron. "You made such a sad sound."

"It was a groan of contentment," smiled Alex, stroking her soft cheek.

"You were thinking of our other home, weren't you?" said Cameron softly, and Alex nodded. From now on there would be no more evasion and lies to protect her. Good and bad, happiness and pain—all would be shared.

THE TAMING

Aleen Malcolm

Cameron—daring, impetuous girl/woman who has never known a life beyond the windswept wilds of the Scottish countryside.

Alex Sinclair—high-born and quick-tempered, finds more than passion in the heart of his headstrong ward Cameron.

Torn between her passion for freedom and her long-denied love for Alex, Cameron is thrust into the dazzling social whirl of 18th century Edinburgh and comes to know the fulfillment of deep and dauntless love.

A Dell Book $3.25

At your local bookstore or use this handy coupon for ordering:

Dell	**DELL BOOKS** THE TAMING $3.25 (18510-6) **P.O. BOX 1000, PINEBROOK, N.J. 07058**

Please send me the above title. I am enclosing $_____
(please add 75¢ per copy to cover postage and handling). Send check or money order—no cash or C.O.D.'s. Please allow up to 8 weeks for shipment.

Mr/Mrs/Miss_____

Address_____

City_____ State/Zip_____

AN OCCULT NOVEL OF UNSURPASSED TERROR

EFFIGIES

BY **William K. Wells**

Holland County was an oasis of peace and beauty . . .

until beautiful Nicole Bannister got a horrible package that triggered a nightmare,

until little Leslie Bannister's invisible playmate vanished and Elvida took her place,

until Estelle Dixon's Ouija board spelled out the message: I AM COMING—SOON.

A menacing pall settled over the gracious houses and rank decay took hold of the lush woodlands. Hell had come to Holland County —to stay.

A Dell Book $2.95 (12245-7)

At your local bookstore or use this handy coupon for ordering:

| **Dell** | **DELL BOOKS** P.O. BOX 1000, PINEBROOK, N.J. 07058 | EFFIGIES $2.95 (12245-7) |

Please send me the above title. I am enclosing $ _____
(please add 75¢ per copy to cover postage and handling). Send check or money order—no cash or C.O.D.'s. Please allow up to 8 weeks for shipment.

Mr/Mrs/Miss _____

Address _____

City _____ State/Zip _____

Introducing Dell's New Mystery Series

Selected by Ruth Windfeldt, owner of the Scene Of The Crime Book Shop in Sherman Oaks, California.

SCENE OF THE CRIME™

☐ **A MEDIUM FOR MURDER**
   by Mignon Warner $2.25 (16245-3)
☐ **DEATH OF A MYSTERY WRITER**
   by Robert Barnard $2.25 (12168-X)
☐ **DEATH AFTER BREAKFAST**
   by Hugh Pentecost $2.25 (11687-2)
☐ **THE POISONED CHOCOLATES CASE**
   by Anthony Berkeley $2.25 (16844-9)
☐ **A SPRIG OF SEA LAVENDER**
   by J.R.L. Anderson $2.25 (18321-9)
☐ **WATSON'S CHOICE** by Gladys Mitchell $2.25 (19501-2)
☐ **SPENCE AND THE HOLIDAY MURDERS**
   by Michael Allen $2.25 (18364-2)
☐ **THE TAROT MURDERS** by Mignon Warner $2.25 (16162-2)
☐ **DEATH ON THE HIGH C'S**
   by Robert Barnard $2.25 (11900-6)
☐ **WINKING AT THE BRIM**
   by Gladys Mitchell $2.25 (19326-5)

At your local bookstore or use this handy coupon for ordering:

Dell   DELL BOOKS
P.O. BOX 1000, PINE BROOK, N.J. 07058

Please send me the books I have checked above. I am enclosing $_____
including 75¢ for the first book, 25¢ for each additional book up to $1.50 maximum
postage and handling charge.
Please send check or money order—no cash or C.O.D.s *Please allow up to 8 weeks for
delivery.*

Mr./Mrs._____

Address_____

City_____ State/Zip_____

Introducing Dell's New Mystery Series

Murder Ink.

Selected by Carol Brener,
owner of the Murder Ink.
bookstore in New York City.

☐ **DEATH IN THE MORNING**
  by Sheila Radley $2.25 (11785-2)
☐ **THE BRANDENBURG HOTEL**
  by Pauline Glen Winslow $2.25 (10875-6)
☐ **McGARR AND THE SIENESE**
  CONSPIRACY by Bartholomew Gill $2.25 (15784-6)
☐ **THE RED HOUSE MYSTERY** by A.A. Milne $2.25 (17376-0)
☐ **THE MINUTEMAN MURDERS**
  by Jane Langton $2.25 (18994-2)
☐ **MY FOE OUTSTRETCH'D BENEATH**
  THE TREE by V.C. Clinton-Baddeley $2.25 (15685-8)
☐ **GUILT EDGED** by W.J. Burley $2.25 (13082-4)
☐ **COPPER GOLD** by Pauline Glen Winslow ..$2.25 (11130-7)
☐ **MANY DEADLY RETURNS**
  by Patricia Moyes $2.25 (16172-X)
☐ **McGARR AT THE DUBLIN HORSE SHOW**
  by Bartholomew Gill $2.25 (15379-4)

At your local bookstore or use this handy coupon for ordering:

Dell | **DELL BOOKS**
P.O. BOX 1000, PINE BROOK, N.J. 07058

Please send me the books I have checked above. I am enclosing $_____
including 75¢ for the first book, 25¢ for each additional book up to $1.50 maximum
postage and handling charge.
Please send check or money order—no cash or C.O.D.s. *Please allow up to 8 weeks for
delivery.*

Mr./Mrs._____

Address_____

City_____ State/Zip_____

AMERICAN CAESAR

★★★★

Douglas MacArthur 1880-1964

#1 NATIONAL BESTSELLER!
BY WILLIAM MANCHESTER

The author of *The Glory and the Dream* and *The Death of a President* brilliantly portrays the most controversial, most complex, and most hated or loved American general since Robert E. Lee: Douglas MacArthur! "William Manchester has written a masterful biography. Anybody who has ever wondered whether General MacArthur was a military genius or a political demagogue will find here evidence of both."—John Bartlow Martin. "Fascinating. Dramatic."—*Time*. "A thrilling and profoundly ponderable piece of work."—*Newsweek*. "Electric. Splendid reading. Like MacArthur himself—larger than life."—*The New York Times*.

A Dell Book $3.50

At your local bookstore or use this handy coupon for ordering:

| Dell | **DELL BOOKS** | AMERICAN CAESAR | $3.50 | (10413-0) |

DELL BOOKS
P.O. BOX 1000, PINEBROOK, N.J. 07058

Please send me the above title. I am enclosing $_____
(please add 75¢ per copy to cover postage and handling). Send check or money order—no cash or C.O.D.'s. Please allow up to 8 weeks for shipment.

Mr/Mrs/Miss _____

Address _____

City _____ State/Zip _____

Dell Bestsellers

- [ ] **RANDOM WINDS** by Belva Plain $3.50 (17158-X)
- [ ] **MEN IN LOVE** by Nancy Friday $3.50 (15404-9)
- [ ] **JAILBIRD** by Kurt Vonnegut $3.25 (15447-2)
- [ ] **LOVE: Poems** by Danielle Steel $2.50 (15377-8)
- [ ] **SHOGUN** by James Clavell $3.50 (17800-2)
- [ ] **WILL** by G. Gordon Liddy $3.50 (09666-9)
- [ ] **THE ESTABLISHMENT** by Howard Fast........$3.25 (12296-1)
- [ ] **LIGHT OF LOVE** by Barbara Cartland $2.50 (15402-2)
- [ ] **SERPENTINE** by Thomas Thompson $3.50 (17611-5)
- [ ] **MY MOTHER/MY SELF** by Nancy Friday $3.25 (15663-7)
- [ ] **EVERGREEN** by Belva Plain $3.50 (13278-9)
- [ ] **THE WINDSOR STORY**
  by J. Bryan III & Charles J.V. Murphy $3.75 (19346-X)
- [ ] **THE PROUD HUNTER** by Marianne Harvey ..$3.25 (17098-2)
- [ ] **HIT ME WITH A RAINBOW**
  by James Kirkwood $3.25 (13622-9)
- [ ] **MIDNIGHT MOVIES** by David Kaufelt $2.75 (15728-5)
- [ ] **THE DEBRIEFING** by Robert Litell $2.75 (01873-5)
- [ ] **SHAMAN'S DAUGHTER** by Nan Salerno
  & Rosamond Vanderburgh $3.25 (17863-0)
- [ ] **WOMAN OF TEXAS** by R.T. Stevens $2.95 (19555-1)
- [ ] **DEVIL'S LOVE** by Lane Harris $2.95 (11915-4)

At your local bookstore or use this handy coupon for ordering:

Dell **DELL BOOKS**
P.O. BOX 1000, PINEBROOK, N.J. 07058

Please send me the books I have checked above. I am enclosing $ _____
(please add 75¢ per copy to cover postage and handling). Send check or money
order—no cash or C.O.D.'s. Please allow up to 8 weeks for shipment.

Mr/Mrs/Miss _____

Address _____

City _____ State/Zip _____